THE ‹SPECIALISTS›
ANTHOLOGY

THE ⟨SPECIALISTS⟩ ANTHOLOGY

BOOKS ONE-FIVE

Shannon Greenland

CONTENTS

‹MODEL SPY›
THE SPECIALISTS

BOOK ONE

NOWHERE TO RUN. NOWHERE TO HIDE

The entire greenhouse brightened with white light, and a shrill siren went off.

David grabbed my hand, and we took off down the path.

A mile later, we burst through the trees on the outskirts of an Ushbanian town, a different one from where the modeling school and hotel were located.

A police siren pierced the air. David grabbed my hand and yanked me down an alley. We ran past a Dumpster and skidded to a halt when a police car pulled in the opposite end. David backed me up against the side of a building and plastered his body to mine. Our chests heaved against each other with winded breaths.

He buried his mouth against my ear. "Wrap. Your. Arms. Around. Me."

I did as he instructed, my heart hammering, keeping the police car in my peripheral vision. It slowly rolled toward us. "It's coming," I hissed, desperately trying to think of what to do next.

"Sorry," he mumbled right before crushing his mouth to mine.

Oh my God, I'm sixteen, and I've never been kissed. Please let me be doing this right.

‹ONE›

<!ENTITY % phrase "em"[ ]>
 <!Element (%styfon;~%phse;)- -(%line:)>
 <(&#xOOOC;)-(&#x0009)-(𠀋)>
 "No, no, no," I muttered to myself.
 <!Attst (%leyst;)\%esa>

"There, that'll do." Pushing my glasses up the bridge of my nose, I shut down my computer and grabbed my books. I hurried out of my dorm room, heading toward the science building.

Late for class. Again. Why was my brain always three gigabytes behind where it should be?

At 8:30 in the morning, vehicles jammed the parking lot. Fast-forward fourteen hours and the spaces would be empty; everybody would be out partying, having fun. Except me.

I made my way across campus, cutting through the university's parking lot. I noticed a black four-door car pulling into the lot. Despite the tinted windows, I could see four shadowy figures inside. The car circled around the loop, slowing to a crawl. There were no parking spaces available.

What are they doing? Sightseeing?

Cutting across a row, I peeked over my shoulder. The dark car rounded the corner into my lane. I picked up my walking pace, my ears tuned to the engine behind me.

Why don't they pass me?

I zigzagged across another row, and the car sped up and followed. I swallowed, my heart ping-ponging irregularly, and started to run. The driver gassed the engine and came to a stop beside me, blocking my way.

All four doors opened, and I froze in place. Dressed in suits, three men and a woman stepped out.

"Miss Kelly James?" the woman asked.

Hugging my books to my chest, I gave a jerky nod, unable to do much else.

The woman pulled out a gold badge. "You're under arrest for threatening homeland security and suspected terrorism."

One of the men spun me around and pushed me up against the car. My books scattered on the pavement as he grabbed my arms and pulled them back.

The woman patted her hands down my body. "You have the right to remain silent . . ."

Her voice trailed to a faraway mute.

I can't believe this is happening. This must be a mistake!

***

I stared at my clasped hands on the table in front of me. I'd chewed my thumbnails down to the quick. I hadn't bitten my fingernails in years, not since I took up lollipops. Speaking of which, I would gladly give a few of my 191 IQ points for a watermelon-flavored one right now.

I peered up at the blurry clock and realized I still wore my reading glasses. Never could remember to take them off. Shoving them on top of my head, I read the time.

9:34.

I'd been in this overly warm, white-walled interrogation room with its stale coffee odor for exactly thirty-one minutes. It seemed more like hours.

Only a metal desk and three noncushioned chairs occupied the center of the room. I'd seen enough TV to know the wall-length mirror in front of me was two-way.

How could I have been so stupid?

Stupid. Stupid. Stupid.

And all for a guy. David. A hot guy. But still.

Lifting my head, I stared at my reflection. I looked tired. Worn out. Stressed. All those words popped into my mind as I studied my limp blond ponytail, pale face, and the dark shadows under my eyes.

Were people staring back at me? Talking? Discussing what I'd done?

I would tell them what they wanted to know. But no one had asked me any questions. They drove me in silence to the police station, escorted me in, sat me down in this room, and told me they'd be back. That had been thirty-one minutes ago.

9:36.

Correction, thirty-three minutes ago.

My mind shifted to David.

David. David. David. Until moving into the dorm two months ago, I hadn't realized guys existed. Well, I realized, just not *realized*.

He was popular at East Iowa University: He played baseball, was in a fraternity, and worked in the admissions office.

Not popular enough for me to go to jail for him, though.

His words came back to me as I closed my eyes. *I'm adopted and my parents are hiding it from me.* The way he'd said it, his urgency, made me go all mushy and decide to help. It's just . . . well, he'd been so nice to me. Before him, no one had ever taken the time to get to know me.

I found some papers. Letters from a man named Mike Share, saying if anything ever happened to him, the man I know as my father would raise his baby boy. I found an adoption document with a government seal and Top Secret *stamped on it. It had my name, my father's name, and Mike Share's name. When I turned eighteen I did some research, but the State Department told me I wasn't adopted. Something's going on, and I need to figure it out.*

Two men. David's adoptive father. David's real father, Mike Share. They corresponded. Were they friends? Associates? Mike Share must have known something would happen to him. Why else would he ask another man to raise his son? Government agency. Top Secret. Could Mike Share have been a spy? A double agent? Maybe he's still alive and deep undercover. Maybe he's dead, and the government was responsible, therefore they're hiding his records. Lots of questions. No answers.

I thought I could get the answers by using my computer skills and hacking into the government's computer system.

How wrong I'd been.

Forcing my dry lids open, I checked the time.

10:14.

How long would they leave me here? Hours? Days? Wait. They couldn't leave me here for days. That was illegal. Right?

What would happen to me? Juvenile detention? Prison? Would I be tried as an adult? Oh God, they hung traitors, didn't they?

7

I covered my face with my hands. *I don't want to die.* Not now. I still had to finish my latest invention, the proto laser tracker, for physics class. And my final in BioChem 440. And . . . and . . . and my keystroke memorization program.

I was about to die, and my geeky experiments were all that worried me.

Jeez.

10:53.

What had upset the government the most—my hacking their system or the information I'd been after? Did I leave a trail?

No. Not possible. I knew how to cover my tracks when entering systems.

11:02.

I shouldn't tell them about David. That would get me, not to mention David, into worse trouble. I should tell them I'd hacked just to hack, to see if I could break their system.

No. That made me sound like a juvenile delinquent.

I blew out a long, confused breath, wanting to get the whole thing over with. If someone would walk in, my mind would stop spinning, and I'd say whatever felt right to say.

12:21.

Oh God, I have to pee.

Someone? Hello?

I'm not a bad kid. I promise. I'm a good kid. I've never done anything wrong. I've never hacked into a system before.

Well, except that one time. My Calculus professor gave me a one hundred for the semester. I changed it to a ninety-eight. After all, it's what I deserved. That was the problem with having such a high IQ. Teachers assumed I was perfect and almost never graded my work.

Did the government know about that? Were they going to charge me for that, too?

12:45.

Please! Someone. Anyone?

Finally, I heard the jangle of keys outside the room. The door opened as if the government had read my mind, and the woman who'd arrested me walked in. She silently took a seat across from me. Then a man entered. I recognized him from the dark car, too. He stayed near the door, standing guard, arms folded over his beefy chest. As if I could escape and run away.

"Where were you last night?" the agent lady asked, placing a notepad and pen on the table.

"The town fair that our university was sponsoring. Celebrating my sixteenth birthday with my friend David."

Agent lady scribbled some words on the pad. "And after that?"

"My dorm room."

"What time did you get to your dorm room?"

Mentally, I calculated when David and I had left the fair. "Ten o'clock."

"What did you do when you got to your dorm room?"

Went to bed, I wanted to say. But I knew they knew I hadn't. Why else would I be here? "Played on my computer."

"How long did you 'play on your computer'?"

"Until six in the morning."

The agent lady looked up from her notepad. "All night long?"

"Yes, ma'am."

"What did you do on your computer?"

I swallowed. "Homework."

"I thought you said you played."

Shoot. "Um, that's what I meant. Homework is playing for me." *Homework is playing for me? Who's gonna believe that?*

The agent lady leveled intense blue eyes on me. "It's going to be a lot easier on you if you cooperate. Now let me ask you again. What did you do on your computer?"

My heart thumped my chest wall. "Hacked into the government's computer system." *Oh God, I'm going to prison for this.*

"What were you looking for?"

Something inside me told me not to tell. David might get brought in, questioned, put in prison. His secret was too important. Something in his past needed to stay there.

"What were you looking for?" the agent lady repeated.

"Nothing. I was just playing around."

"Liar," the agent man spoke quietly.

I jerked my attention to the door where he still stood. "No, sir. I'm not lying."

He strode toward me, keeping his glare pinned on me. I slid down in my chair as he got closer.

He stuck his pockmarked, snarly face right in mine. "Last thing I need this afternoon is to deal with some snot-nosed kid. Now let *me* ask you. What were you looking for?"

My thumping heart pounded so loud it deafened my ears. "N-n-nothing."

Agent man's jaw tightened, then he grabbed my arm and pulled me out of the chair. "I've had enough."

***

1:43.

I now sat in a holding cell with cement walls and no windows. The bars to my right looked out onto an empty hallway.

Leaning back, I closed my eyes. How stupid of me to think David was being nice because he liked me. I'd heard the gossip around the dorm.

Kelly's so goofy with those thick glasses, always scurrying around campus in her own little world, bumping into stuff. What a mess.

Well, she's from foster care. They don't really teach those kids good hygiene. David's smart to suck up to her, though. She can do his homework.

Nobody liked me. I was awkward and strange. I knew that about myself.

But why did David pretend to like me? I'd known him two months, and never once had he asked me for help on anything. Had he been cozying up to me, waiting for the right time to drop the government stuff? Knowing I'd hack in for him?

Oooh. What a fool I'd been. That's exactly what he'd done. What an idiot. How could I have fallen for that? He probably didn't even have a government secret. He probably wanted me to show him how to hack, so he could go back later and do illegal stuff.

And to think I had a crush on him. How sad. He thought of me as a sister. At least that's what he said.

Of course that's how he thought of me. He was eighteen; I was sixteen. No eighteen-year-old would actually be interested in someone my age. I was smart enough to understand that.

2:56.

Bouncing my leg, I opened my eyes and glanced at the stainless steel toilet in the corner. No way I'd pee out in the open.

Please! Somebody. Can I go to the bathroom? I promise I won't try to escape.

I had to calm down. Think computer code. That always helped.

<%attrs;--%corears, %oil8n, %events>

<Cite<hatru>/Q land="en"-us>

<;IQ ;stng 1-234-5 5</strng>

Okay. Not working. Because my bladder's about to explode!

Blowing out a breath, I ran my gaze over the other occupants in the freezing, dimly lit cell. Four adults.

Straight across from me sat a red-haired woman, her legs crossed, top one swinging, staring at a spot above my head. She wore lots of makeup, a tight tiger-print shirt, and a leather miniskirt. Maybe a prostitute?

A bony, dark-haired woman lay beside her, curled up, sleeping. Bruises dotted her arms, legs, and face. An abuse victim? A drug addict?

In the middle of the stained floor sat an old, gray-haired woman, rocking and crying. She wore a housecoat and slippers and had bed head. She looked like somebody's grandmother. Thirty minutes ago they put her in here, and I wondered nearly every minute since then what she'd done. At first I felt sorry for her with the crying, but now I wished she'd stop. And get off the floor. That's just gross.

A blond woman with a slick, chic bun and wearing an executive suit occupied the same bench as me. She appeared as if she should be working in a high-rise office building. Maybe she'd been arrested for corporate espionage.

Except for the bony, dark-haired, possible drug addict, I'd been here longer than anyone else.

Hours.

Hours had passed since the agent dragged me from the interrogation room and tossed me in here. And my growling stomach confirmed that it was late afternoon.

What was it with these government people? Why did they keep leaving me alone for hours on end? Were they hoping to break down my defenses?

Well, if that was the case, it worked. I never felt so scared in my whole life.

"Hello."

I jumped.

The blond executive woman stuck out her hand. "If I don't talk to somebody, the crying will drive me insane. I'm Connie."

Relief washed over me at the chance for friendly conversation, and I shook her hand. "Kelly."

"Don't you love the smell in here? Nothing like urine and cheap perfume."

I'd been in here for so long, I'd blocked it out. But now that she brought it to my attention again, it overpowered my senses. "You're awful young to be in here."

"They didn't have a juvenile holding cell."

Connie nodded. "Shall we ask the question on everybody's mind? What are you in here for?"

"Um . . ." I scratched my head, debating if I should tell . . . why not. "I hacked into a computer system." I purposefully left out the government part.

"No kidding?" Connie laughed.

I smiled. "How 'bout you?"

"Prostitution."

I blinked. "Really?" I took in her perfect hair, gray business suit, and expensive spiked heels. "You don't look like a prostitute."

"You don't look like a computer genius."

No, I didn't, and I'd wished my whole life I did. Five-foot-ten. Blond. Blue eyes. C-size boobs. Skinny. *You should model, honey.* How many times had I heard *that* suggestion over the years?

"WOULD YOU SHUT UP?!" the red-haired woman screamed.

Connie and I both jerked to attention.

Red Hair shoved off her bench, stomped over to the old woman, and started shaking her. "SHHHUUUT UUUP!"

The lady let out a wail.

"Leave her alone," Connie warned. "She's just an old crazy woman."

Red Hair turned toward us. She actually bared her teeth like a rabid dog. "You wanna go around with me, fancy?"

Connie shrugged, all nonchalant. "If I have to."

I watched wide-eyed as Red Hair approached us.

"Knock it off." A police lady rapped the bars with a black stick. "Visitor here."

All of us, except for the bony, dark-haired woman who was still sleeping, turned our attention to the hallway outside the cell. A tall, *really* gorgeous man stood staring right at . . .

Me?

Swallowing, I stared back into his light green eyes.

Why's he looking at me?

The police officer unlocked the door. "Back up," she ordered Red Hair.

Red Hair took a few steps back, fists clenched, shooting dirty scowls at everybody.

Police lady motioned for me. "Let's go, little girl. He's here for you."

‹TWO›

The tall, light-eyed man gave me two minutes to use the bathroom and then took me to an office. No interrogation room this time. No two-way mirror. No big acne-scarred agent standing guard at the door.

Ugly beige carpet covered the floor. It reminded me of the carpeting at my first foster home. A dark wood desk sat centered along the back of the room with two red, cushiony chairs in front of it. Pictures of the beach and the ocean hung from the yellow walls. Vanilla air freshener overpowered the small place.

A few portraits decorated the desk's shiny surface. The man wasn't in any of them.

This office must belong to someone else.

He motioned me to sit in one of the two chairs. He took the other one, right beside me, instead of sitting behind the desk. Like we were equal instead of him being the one in charge.

"Did they feed you?" he asked.

"No, sir."

Lifting the phone, he punched a button. "Miss James hasn't eaten."

Whoever picked up on the other end must have known this man because he didn't identify himself.

"Thank you." He ended the call.

I eyed him carefully. Who was he? What did he want with me? I'd never seen anyone quite like him. Light green eyes, dark skin, and brown curly hair. I'd guess he was around thirty years old.

Hands down, he was the most gorgeous guy I'd ever seen.

He didn't seem to notice me staring as he flipped through a folder. Good thing, because I'd never been so rudely curious in my life.

Should I introduce myself or wait for him to speak? Usually silence didn't bother me, but right now it did. Maybe he was waiting for the food to come.

I focused on the folder he held, curious what kept his interest. As I read the label, I sucked in a surprised breath.

Me?

He didn't try to hide the information. In fact, he held it out as if to give me a better look.

Pictures of me at different ages. School reports. Test scores. Psychological evaluations. Photos of my parents. Seeing them calmed my nervousness. I had a quick flash of my mom pushing me on a swing. It made me smile.

My whole life in one folder. Big deal. I didn't have any deep dark secrets. My parents died in a plane crash when I was six, and I'd been bounced around between foster homes and orphanages ever since.

I continued studying the papers as he sifted through them, and when he finished, I switched my gaze to his. I saw warmth there, and a sense of familiarity. The first time since early this morning I didn't feel like a criminal. I almost felt safe.

He extended his hand. "Thomas Liba."

"Kelly James." I introduced myself, then realized he already knew my name.

The door opened, and an old police officer limped in. He didn't glance at either of us as he put a plastic wrapped sandwich on the desk.

Feeling like a burden, I muttered "thank you" as he limped back out.

Mr. Liba pushed back his chair and crossed the office to a small refrigerator in the corner. He opened it, grabbed a soda, and brought it to me.

"Thanks."

He nodded once.

I unwrapped the sandwich labeled *turkey* and popped the top on the soda can. While he went back to analyzing my file, I ate faster than I'd ever eaten in my whole life. If it wasn't for my hunger, I would've been embarrassed at the chomping and gulping noises I made.

To my horror, I burped when I finished. "Excuse me," I whispered.

"Garbage can's by the door," he said, without looking at me.

Taking that as a hint, I pushed up out of the chair, rounded the armrest, caught my toe on the wooden leg, and toppled into Mr. Liba's lap.

"Oh my God, I'm so sorry." I scrambled off him.

"It's fine," he said calmly, and grasped my arm to help me regain my balance. "Go throw away your garbage."

Quickly, I did, then resumed my seat. *Idiot. I'm such an idiot.* Of all my imperfections, and I have a lot of them, I'd swap my klutziness for pretty much anything.

"I was like you once," he commented as he flipped through my file. "A system kid. Got in a lot of trouble."

Not knowing what to say, I remained quiet.

"Difference is, you haven't gotten into any trouble. Until now."

My throat suddenly went dry.

"You hacked nine levels of the government's main computer system. Know how many there are?"

"No, sir."

"Eighteen. You got halfway there. Farthest anyone's ever gone." He paused and looked at me. "Ever."

No one had hacked farther than me? That couldn't be right. It had been too easy. Their passwords were cleverly coded in the numbers of Pascal's triangle, a basic theory. Such a simple pattern, yet it'd taken me an hour to figure it out. I would've made it through all eighteen given more time.

Mr. Liba closed my folder, but kept it in his lap. "Quite impressive, young lady."

"Thanks," I mumbled, not sure if he'd really given me a compliment.

"I'd like you to tell me what information you were after."

I hesitated, and he patiently waited.

Then I told him everything involving David, the adoption paper, the letter he found, and the government seal.

Mr. Liba listened carefully, his focus glued to me. When I finished, we sat in silence a few minutes as he continued to study me.

"I appreciate you trusting me with the information," he finally responded.

He was right. I did trust him, and I had only just met him. I didn't even know if he worked for the government or not. For all I knew he might be a bad guy, and I'd given away information to the wrong person. But there was something about him that had made me want to talk.

"What I'm about to discuss with you is top secret. You must never repeat any of it to anyone. Never. If you do, there will be repercussions."

There will be repercussions? What the heck did that mean? I wanted to ask, but my heart raced so fast I didn't think I could speak without stuttering.

"I work for the IPNC, Information Protection National Concern. It's a special-operations division of the United States government. I'm in charge of recruiting and training what we at IPNC affectionately term the Specialists."

"The Specialists?" Sounded like the name of an exclusive club.

"The Specialists are a group of young adults. They each excel in one certain area. For you, that would be computers. We take them, house them, train them, give them new identities, and teach them how to one day go deep undercover."

"But wh-what about their parents?"

Mr. Liba tapped my file. "They're all like you. System kids that screwed up somehow. Nobody even knows they're gone."

Somebody would know, I wanted to say, but who was I kidding? Nobody would even miss me. David, maybe, but he'd probably be relieved he didn't have to be nice to me anymore.

"But is this . . . legal?" It couldn't be. Could it? Taking kids, giving them new identities, making them into some sort of secret agents.

"This is all on the up-and-up. I assure you."

"I can't do this. What about my education? I'm supposed to graduate from college this year. I can't go undercover. I'm a total klutz. I get nervous way too easy. I don't work well with others. People don't like me. They think I'm weird. I really won't fit in with th-this group of Specialists. I think you're making a really big mistake here. Wrong person you the picked." I shook my head. "I mean, you've picked the wrong person. See? I can't even talk right."

I stopped my tirade, realizing I'd gotten up from my chair and was pacing around the room.

"Miss James, I understand this is a lot to take in. Let me tell you a few things. First off, your education is at the top of my list. For all my Specialists. It's a requirement, as a matter of fact. No dropouts allowed.

"Second," he continued, "you'll be working from our home base. It's highly unlikely you'll be in the field. That's the beauty of computers. You can tap into them from anywhere. So your klutziness won't be an issue."

He stood, walked behind the desk, and brought out a banged-up blue suitcase. I gave it a quick glance and then another one. It belonged to me.

"And lastly, this is your chance for a family. A place to belong." He walked toward me. "You can either take me up on this offer or go to juvenile detention for your crime. If you choose the latter, you'll never see me again. This offer will never be repeated."

Mr. Liba placed the suitcase on the floor next to me. "I got everything in your dorm room, including your laptop, the drive containing the keystroke memorization program, and the proto laser tracker. Which, by the way, is a very impressive invention."

How did he know the name of my tracker? Stupid question. This man knew everything about me. Probably more than I knew about myself. Wait. He got everything in my room? That meant he grabbed the bras and undies I'd thrown on my bed. I held back a groan. At least they were freshly washed.

"What's it going to be, Miss James? You must make your decision now."

***

I decided to go with Mr. Thomas Liba. Within a day, all the arrangements had been made. In exchange for my new life, my crime disappeared, as did Kelly James. He gave me a new name. Kelly Spree. I had to admit, I liked it better than James, even though it erased all ties I had with my parents.

And I would have to move. But I absolutely refused to get on a plane to California, which would be my new home. My parents lost their lives in a plane crash that I survived. Didn't take a genius to figure out the root of my fear of flying.

To my surprise, Mr. Liba didn't argue. Over the next five days via a bus and a train, I traveled to the city of San Belden in northern California. He didn't join me, said he had another Specialist to see to.

Erin, a girl a little older than me, picked me up at the train station on the morning of the fifth day. She was friendly and talkative on the drive out of the city and into the countryside.

Thirty minutes later, we pulled up to an iron gate. A wooden plaque engraved with SAN BELDEN RANCH FOR BOYS AND GIRLS hung from the entrance.

Erin pointed to it. "That's our cover in the community. Everybody thinks this a foster home. Nobody knows what really goes on behind our gates and below our grounds."

"Below the grounds?"

"You'll find out soon enough." She smiled mysteriously.

"Are you a Specialist, too?" I should've thought to ask her that sooner.

She punched a code on the visor's remote. "I am. I've been a Specialist for two years."

The gate swung open and we made our way up a long gravel driveway. On both sides of us stretched neatly mowed fields. A standard wooden privacy fence lined the property. Off to the left sat a huge barn with a corral beside it. Beyond it spanned a garden.

Erin circled around the driveway and parked in front of a one-story, sprawling ranch house made of wood and stone. A four-car garage was attached to the side.

"How big is this place?" I asked.

"Hundred acres." She cut the engine. "We're running a little late. Let's go."

Late for what?

Grabbing my suitcase from the backseat, I followed her into the house. A large stone entryway gave way to a wide corridor. A dining hall opened to the left. It looked like a miniature version of a school cafeteria. Its aluminum table and chairs sat empty. Across the hall there was a common area with a big-screen TV, comfy chairs, a pool table, air hockey, and a card table. It sat empty, too.

She led me past a pretty, mountainous mural and down the long hallway. Closed doors, spaced about twenty feet apart, lined both sides. We stopped at the second one on the right.

"There're four dormitory rooms, two for the guys and two for the girls. The adult agents stay in private rooms." Erin took the suitcase from me and opened the door. "This is your room. You'll share it with Sissy and Molly. You'll meet them in a few minutes."

I caught a quick glimpse of twin beds as Erin put down my suitcase and closed the door. I followed her back down the hall to the mountainous mural. She placed her hand on a wall-mounted globe light, and the mural slid to the right, revealing an open elevator.

"Cool," I said.

Erin looked at me and smiled.

19

We stepped inside and the door slid closed. She punched a series of numbers on the control panel, and the elevator descended. I glanced up at the display. We passed floor one, two, three, and stopped at four.

Erin punched a series of numbers again. "This is Subfloor Four. It's where the conference room is located."

"What's on the other floors?"

"You'll find out when you're supposed to."

The elevator opened into a modern, high-tech workroom. Glass panels boxed in and separated a dozen small offices. Each space had matching black desks, sleek leather chairs, and flat-screen computers. I counted only three people dispersed throughout the workroom. One guy and two girls. The guy talked on a phone. The girls typed on their computers. None of them looked up.

Erin led me around the perimeter of the room and came to a stop at a closed door. She opened it and motioned me inside.

"Have a seat."

I walked into the large windowless room, and she closed the door behind me. A huge flat screen took up the whole back wall, but nothing played on it. Five other teenagers sat around a long, silver, metal table. They all stared at me as I rolled out a leather chair and took a seat. No one said a word as we waited, cautiously checking out one another. I felt sure their brains spun with the same questions as mine.

What's her story?

What's his name?

What illegal thing did she do?

What happened to his parents?

The girl sitting across from me would not stop staring at me. She was one of those Goth girls dressed in all black, with pale skin and a nose ring. Her short, purple hair stood out in all directions. She wore bold black eyeliner and bright red lipstick. The gum in her mouth had to be worn out with the furious way she'd been chomping it.

Made me want a cherry lollipop, actually, to help calm me down.

After a few more minutes, the door opened and Mr. Liba walked in. I expelled a silent, relieved breath at finally seeing a familiar face.

"Good morning. As you all already know, my name is Thomas Liba. My friends and associates call me TL. You may do so if you wish. I am your team leader."

"Does TL stand for Thomas Liba or team leader?" asked Goth Girl.

"Both, I suppose," Mr. Liba answered without skipping a beat. "I'd like to start off by going around the table and having everyone stand and introduce themselves. Molly, please start."

"Hello, my name is Molly Pullman."

She looked like Little Orphan Annie with her red hair and freckles. Small, too, maybe five feet tall and a hundred pounds. Her T-shirt read "YOU LOOKIN' AT ME?" She sounded so sweet and innocent. What in the world did she do that was so bad?

"Molly," TL continued, "please tell everyone your specialty and why you're here."

She smiled, showing two deep dimples. "Martial arts. I got busted for operating an underground fight club in Chicago."

Goth Girl snorted. "You?"

Molly continued smiling sweetly. "Yes, me."

"Darren," TL interrupted, "go next, please."

"I'm Darren Lightfoot. My specialty is linguistics. I speak sixteen languages. I was taken in for flying in a restricted airspace."

Sixteen languages? Wow. I barely kept English straight in my head. Darren was a Native American with strong features. I'd say he stood a little taller than me, maybe six feet, with a runner's build. Cute guy.

TL motioned with his head to the next.

"Joe Vornes. My specialty is clairvoyance. I can see objects or actions beyond the range of natural vision."

Goth Girl snorted again. "Puh-leeze."

What was it with this girl?

Joe merely gazed at her. Peacefully, as if he was in touch with the moon, the planets, and the stars. "I operated an illegal 1-900 psychic phone line."

To me, Joe seemed better suited as a linebacker. He was big and muscular, and had short blond hair.

TL pointed at Goth Girl to go next.

"Priscilla Ross. Friends call me Sissy."

I held back a laugh. For someone with such a tough attitude and look, she sure had a girlie-girl name.

"I'm a chemist," she went on. "Busted for mixing some chemicals I shouldn't have been mixing."

Hmm, sounded pretty vague, like there might be more to it.

"Frankie Board." The guy beside me introduced himself. "I excel in electronics. I was arrested for breaking into museums and banks and dismantling their security systems." He shrugged. "Did it for fun. Never stole anything."

I liked Frankie immediately. With his goatee and arm tattoos, he seemed more suited for riding a Harley than being an electronics specialist. Cute, too.

"Your turn, Kelly," TL prompted.

Everybody's eyes focused on me, and my stomach flopped over.

"Hi, my name's Kelly Ja—Spree, and I'm here because of my computer skills. I system government hacked." *Jeez, I hate when I do that.* I shook my head. "I mean, I hacked into the government's main computer system."

Sissy-the-Goth-chemist snorted. *Again.* "You? You look like you should be a Victoria's Secret model." She turned to TL. "Sure you got the right person here?"

Molly cracked her knuckles, still wearing her sweet smile. "Ya know, *Sissy,* if you don't shut your pie hole, I'll shut it for ya."

And these girls are going to he roommates? Sheesh.

TL calmly put his hand in the air. "Enough. Let me remind you, this is your life now. There is no going back. These people are your family now. Whether you like it or not, you're going to have to learn to live with each other. I am your guardian. I am legally responsible for each of you until you turn eighteen. For some of you, that's two years away. Don't mess with me. Because if you do, you will regret it."

I swallowed hard as he delivered the threat and glanced around the table. Everybody appeared to be as shell-shocked as I felt. Even Sissy, amazingly enough.

"We're going to take a few minutes," TL continued, "and get to know each other, then we'll begin today's lesson."

Frankie turned to me. "So, genius girl, you hacked into the government?"

I smiled. David had called me genius girl, too.

Molly leaned around Frankie. "Genius girl? Hey, we should call you GiGi for short."

Frankie nodded. "I like it."

GiGi? I liked it, too. I already had a nickname and two people who seemed to genuinely like me. Maybe this hadn't been such a bad decision I'd made, giving up my identity and joining these Specialists.

Conversation around me buzzed. I didn't say anything. Didn't trust myself to not sound like a dork. As I listened, my thoughts wandered back to David. Where was he right now? In class? I peeked up at TL and found him staring right at me. His expression softened almost to a slight smile, as if to say, *See, you're fitting in.*

Did TL know the secret in David's past? Would he tell me if he did?

Frankie nudged my arm. "So, do you miss your friends?"

Friends? I almost laughed. I didn't have friends. I had my books, my laptop, my inventions . . . my solitude. I had never fit in. I tested out of eighth grade at age nine, graduated high school at thirteen, and was supposed to graduate college this year. I knew guys my age couldn't relate, but I didn't begrudge them. Adults couldn't relate, either. Most of them treated me like a rare specimen, giving me polite respect.

"So do ya?"

"Sure," I lied.

TL stood up. "Today is Friday. On Monday, all of you, except Kelly—GiGi—will begin attending San Belden High."

I smiled at his use of my new nickname. Funny how it made me feel at home.

"Why doesn't she have to go?" Sissy asked.

"Because GiGi has already completed high school and will be graduating college soon. She'll be attending the University of San Belden."

Not sure how they transferred me midsemester. But they're the IPNC, they could do anything. Right?

TL began walking around the room, placing folders in front of each of us. "Understand that your public education is part of your training. It's socializing; learning to, quite frankly, lie to others about your past, current situation, and future. Each of you will wear a detection device for monitoring. The device resembles a small bandage, but it's woven with a series of wires. Some of the wires serve as GPS—a global positioning system—keeping track of your coordinates. Others serve as audio monitors. Everything you say and do will be recorded."

"You mean even when we take a, um, go to the bathroom, you'll know?" This came from Frankie.

"Correct."

They'll know I'm on the toilet?

TL placed a red file in front of me. "Inside these folders you will find your backstory. Memorize the information. Know it. You will be tested on this two days from now. You'll also see instructions for using the elevator to this level, Sub Four. And your code names. Each of you has been issued one based on your specialty. You will use these anytime we are communicating while in mission mode. If you choose to use them around the ranch, that is up to you. I encourage you to do so to get used to calling each other by these names. Do *not* use them while in public. Molly, our martial artist, will be Bruiser. Joe, our clairvoyant, is Mystic. Darren, our linguist, will be Parrot. Sissy, our chemist, is Beaker. Frankie, our electrician, will be Wirenut. And Kelly, our computer whiz, was code named Data. But we're going to change that to GiGi."

I smiled. I liked GiGi much better.

Joe/Mystic raised his hand. "TL, how long will we be expected to wear the detection devices?"

Good question, because I really did not want them knowing when I was using the bathroom.

"Until I feel confident you'll do fine without it." A knock on the door interrupted him. He opened it and turned back to us. "Now, I'd like to introduce you to your mentors. They are the original Specialists. Things have gone so well with them that the IPNC decided to do another program. You are the Specialists Team Two."

Erin walked in and smiled at the group. Then a girl strolled in. Nineteen, twenty, maybe twenty-one. A guy followed her, looking like the same age, then another girl. They filed in one by one, all sizes and shapes, much like my own team. Six in all.

The last guy walked in, his dark hair and face partially hidden by the girl in front of him. For some reason, I got this odd queasy feeling. He stepped to the side into plain view and looked straight at me. My stomach did one huge swirl.

David?

‹THREE›

TL nodded to team one. "This is Erin, Piper, Adam, Tina, Curtis, and David. Their code names are in your folders. They are here to get you acclimated to the ranch and answer any questions. Now on to . . ."

I sat through the meeting with the Specialists and TL, but didn't hear a word that was said. With a stoic look on his face, David stood against the wall behind Sissy/Beaker, listening to TL. I wished he had chosen a spot behind me so I wouldn't be distracted by all the staring I was doing. He didn't once glance in my direction and seemed to hang on TL's every word.

My thoughts tumbled forward, backward, and from side to side as I replayed the last two months in my head. David's friendliness, interest, and acceptance. The trust he had placed in me with his adoption secret, if he really even had a secret.

He'd said smart chicks were cool.

What if he really *did* use me for my brains? Manipulating me into hacking the government's system.

And how did TL factor into all this? Making me feel comfortable, warm, and at ease. Appealing to my sense of family and belonging with the Specialists offer. I'd trusted him.

Recalling everything left me even more confused. If David worked with the Specialists, what had been his assignment at East Iowa University? TL must have known David and I attended the same college. Why hadn't TL told me? What about Mike Share, David's father? True story or not? Was David even his real name? How long had he been a Specialist? What illegal thing had he done to be recruited?

I wanted to groan at the confusion going on in my brain. I felt betrayed and alone again. I *needed* answers.

"That's it for this morning," TL said as he closed his file.

I brought my wandering thoughts back to attention.

"Lunch is in fifteen minutes in the dining hall," he continued. "At one o'clock, we will meet in the barn for our afternoon session. Wear something you don't mind sweating in. We're adjourned. I'll let you all get acquainted."

TL strode from the room, and conversation immediately buzzed around me.

Molly/Bruiser threw her pencil into her folder. "Hey, Erin, what do they usually feed you guys in here?"

Darren/Parrot knocked on the table to get Frankie/Wirenut's attention. "Think we're meeting in the stables to ride horses?"

Mystic raised his hand. "Excuse me, anybody know where the highest point is on the ranch? I need to meditate, and I can only do that on a full moon. And there is a full moon tonight."

Beaker folded her arms. "I'm a vegetarian. If they feed us meat for lunch, I won't eat it."

I chanced one last peek at David. He was deep in conversation with Tina. Jealousy twinged inside me at seeing him speak to another girl. My reaction irritated me. I had no reason to be jealous, and I didn't want to be.

I pushed back from the table and quietly left the room. Not a single person followed me. They were all too busy talking and getting to know one another. I didn't want to seem rude or anything, but I'd never been the socializing type, and I wasn't in the mood to start now.

I made my way around the high-tech workroom, now sitting empty. Down a corridor to the left sat a series of closed doors. I imagined as the days and weeks rolled by I would learn what lay behind them.

Coming to a stop at the elevator, I referenced the instructions in my folder. I punched in my personal code, placed my hand on the fingerprint identification panel, then rode the car four floors up to the ground level.

The elevator opened, and I stepped out. The door disappeared back into the wall, revealing the mountainous mural.

I headed right toward my room. Thank God Bruiser would be one of my roommates. I'd lose a few brain cells if it were only me and the Goth chick, Beaker.

Opening the second door on the right, I walked in. My suitcase sat exactly where Erin had left it. Three twin-size, beige blanketed beds lined the peach-colored walls. A corkboard hung above each bed. I supposed our personal decorations would go there. The one in the middle had a piece of paper tacked to it with my name printed on it. That must be my bed. A four-drawer, white dresser separated each bed from the next. A closet stretched along the back wall. There was plenty of extra space in the long room for at least ten more beds.

In the back corner, another door hung open. I crossed the room and peeked inside. A bathroom with three sinks, three toilet stalls, and three curtained-off showers. It had peach-colored walls like the bedroom, but white tile flooring instead of beige carpet. It reminded me of a smaller version of my college dorm facilities.

Clean and sparse. Just the necessities. It disappointed me a little. I'd hoped it would be homier.

After rummaging through my bag and popping a cherry lollipop into my mouth, I sat on the edge of my bed, pulled my laptop from its case, and cranked it up.

"Not hungry?"

My stomach spun at the sound of David's voice, but I didn't look toward the door. "No," I answered flatly.

"You need to eat. It'll be six o'clock before they serve dinner."

I pulled the lollipop from my mouth and placed it on its wrapper on my dresser. "I'm not hungry."

An awkward moment of silence passed as I pretended to work on my laptop. What did he want?

He cleared his throat. "Feel free to put your clothes away. I'm only saying so because I noticed you never unpacked back at East Iowa."

"I'll get around to it," I fibbed.

I learned a long time ago that unpacking was a waste of time. Things inevitably changed. I averaged a new foster home about every six months, for a variety of reasons: I got too old and didn't match the Klines' "cute little angel" profile; Mrs. Von Harv turned up pregnant and didn't need a foster kid anymore; the Julians thought my blond hair and long legs distracted their precious little Alberto. The list went on and on and on.

David entered my room and sat on the bed beside mine. His cologne floated over me, and I resisted the urge to inhale deeply.

He blew out a long breath. "I know you're mad at me."

27

No, not really. Confused, yes, and definitely feeling deceived.

"GiGi—"

"Don't call me that," I immediately snapped. Okay, maybe I was a little mad. I'd never been so direct about my feelings until this moment. It felt surprisingly good.

"You were my first solo mission," he blurted out.

I looked away from my laptop and into his brown eyes. I saw compassion there, and sorrow, even though I didn't want to. "What are you talking about?" I couldn't help the edgy tone in my voice.

"TL sent me to East Iowa University for you. I was supposed to befriend you, gain your trust, and get you to hack the government's main computer system."

My heart clanged so hard I couldn't think straight. "I—I—I don't understand."

"I lied to you about my dad. I had to convince you to hack the system so TL could recruit you for the Specialists. It was a test to see if you had the computer skills he thought you did."

A test? "Why didn't he just ask me?"

"To hack the system?"

I nodded.

"Would you have?"

I paused. "No."

"There's the answer to your question."

I stared at David as questions spiraled through my brain, making me even more confused than before. "You said he sent you for me. How did he know about me?"

"That's a question you need to ask him."

"Did he do the same to all the others? Test them?"

David shook his head. "Only you. The others more than proved their specialties on their own. Got arrested in the process. But you? You wouldn't mess up. You never did anything wrong. TL needed a chance to see your level of expertise, and he needed you to do something wrong because he knew he wanted you on the team."

"So then this assignment to the Specialists in exchange for juvenile detention is a fake. I was set up. I can walk out of here right now and TL can't stop me." Anger boiled inside me as I recalled my arrest.

The way I'd been treated by the agents. Sitting in the freezing jail cell. Deprived of food, water, and a bathroom. For no other reason than that TL wanted me for the Specialists. I'd been manipulated and used.

And David had only pretended to like me.

He reached across the short distance and touched my shoulder, instantly putting warmth there. "I need you to understand you were an assignment for me. At first. But as I got to know you, our friendship became real. I hated lying to you, but I knew it would all come out eventually."

I shrugged off his hand, ignoring the hurt I saw in his reaction. "True friends don't lie to each other. I can't trust you. For all I know, you're lying to me right now."

He nodded, his expression flattening to blankness as he dropped his gaze to his lap. "I understand you're angry." He brought his eyes up to mine. "Please don't leave, though. We truly are a family here. And TL's great. You'll see that if you stick around."

Disregarding the twinge of desire *to* stay, I forged ahead with the questions. "What about you? What's your specialty? Why are you here with the Specialists?"

"I'm sort of a jack of all trades. Know the eighteen levels of the government's system, nine of which you hacked through?"

I nodded.

"My dad created those."

Too stunned to do much of anything, I simply stared at him.

"He was abducted ten years ago. One week before my eighth birthday. He's the only person in the world who knows all eighteen levels. He programmed a computer chip with the information shortly before his abduction."

"Where's the chip?"

"Nobody knows. My dad hid it."

"Who kidnapped him?"

David shrugged. "Another unanswered question."

"Is he still alive?"

"I hope so," David whispered.

I wanted to reach out and comfort him, to tell him I understood how it felt to lose a parent, but I stopped myself. For all I knew this might be another lie.

"I grew up here on this ranch. Originally it was a home for boys and girls whose parents worked for the government. A safe house to protect the children of the nation's highest agents. Now it's home base for the Specialists. Local people think it's a foster home."

"What about your mother?"

"Never knew her. She left when I was a baby."

Again, I tapped down the desire to comfort. I didn't know what to believe, who to trust.

"We're all a bunch of homeless kids here," David continued, "everybody for a different reason. We all have unique backgrounds, some with juvie records, some not. The one thing we have in common, though, is our need for a family. We are each other's family." He touched my shoulder again. "Please stay."

I glanced down at my laptop as his heartfelt request echoed through my ears. Seconds later he quietly got up and left the room. He'd come across just as sincere back at East Iowa University. Always attentive. Checking in on me. Seeming hurt and lost as he lied to my face so I'd hack the government's system.

I'd been lied to before, many times. By social workers appearing to be concerned.

Sweetie, you'll love this house.

Little one, no more moving around.

Darling, this is the last place for you.

I couldn't stay here surrounded by lies and false identities. This wasn't me. I couldn't hurt people on purpose, manipulate them, deceive them.

I pushed off my bed and hurried from the room. I needed to find TL.

***

With my heart racing, **I** walked across the dining hall straight toward TL. Beside him sat David, but I ignored him and kept my focus steady, concentrating on not tripping. In my peripheral vision, I saw the other Specialists and some adults I assumed were agents glance at me as I passed in front of them. It might have been my imagination, but I swore a hush fell over the room.

TL looked up from his tuna sandwich when I stopped in front of him. "Now's not the time," he responded before I even opened my mouth. "Meet me in my room in five minutes. I'm the first door on the right."

He must have known what I wanted; otherwise he wouldn't have greeted me in that manner. "Yes, sir."

"Why don't you grab a sandwich," suggested David. "Sit and eat with us."

You really expect me to sit here and eat like nothing's happened, I wanted to say, but it wasn't my nature to be so outspoken. "No, thank you. I'm not hungry."

I strode from the dining hall, my heart still racing, and went back to my room. I paced from one end to the next and back again, going over everything in my brain. I checked the clock hanging on the wall at least four times before I made my way to TL's door. I took a quick I-can-do-this breath and knocked.

"Enter."

He sat behind a light wood desk with a computer to his right. Through a cracked door behind him I saw his bedroom. Same colors as mine, except with a blue comforter.

TL indicated I should sit in one of the metal chairs in front of his desk.

He leveled his odd, light gaze on me. "I know why you're here, so I'm not going to waste time pretending otherwise. The IPNC has been keeping tabs on you for years. Anybody with an IQ of a hundred and ninety-one naturally draws attention. Not to mention the compendium computer program you wrote when you were seven years old. It won the National New Mind Award."

I blinked. I'd forgotten all about that program, and the award.

"You're brilliant and incredibly talented with computers. I wanted you for the Specialists Team One, but you were only thirteen. Way too young emotionally to handle your new life. Yes, I sent David for you. Told him to convince you to hack the government's system. I needed it for leverage in bringing you to the Specialists. Based on your psychological profile . . ."

Psychological profile? They had a profile on me? Of course they had a profile on me. This was the IPNC.

" . . . it was evident you would never come to work for me on your own. You're not a risk taker."

"What do you mean you've been keeping tabs on me?" Had they been watching me, following me, filming me?

"Let me assure you we never invaded your personal privacy. We only researched what was public record already. We know your school records, your accomplishments, your test scores. Your family history."

31

"I can walk out right now, can't I?"

TL nodded. "Yes, you can. It was my hope that once you got here, you would feel at home, find a purpose in life, want to stay." He folded his hands atop his desk and leaned in. "Before you make a decision, I want you to think about these questions: What's waiting for you back in Iowa? Where were you headed? Did you ever feel like you belonged? When was the last time you had a real home, a family? Have you ever done something new, exciting, risky?"

Jeez, he knew the right questions to ask.

He stood. "I'll give you until tomorrow morning to make your decision. It's a big one. Take your time. It will affect the rest of your life."

***

"What's going on?" Bruiser asked as I entered our room. "I know something's going on. Everybody knows something's going on. Are you leaving? You're leaving, aren't you?"

I lay down on my bed. She and Beaker had both changed clothes, wearing something they didn't mind sweating in, just like TL instructed. I stared at Bruiser a second, amazed at her body. She wore a tight, blue "Wanna Piece of This?" tank top and snug, red shorts. Every muscle stood out in lean definition.

Beaker, on the other hand, still wore her black combat boots, loose black T-shirt, and spiky dog collar. Her long, baggy, black shorts marked the only change in her apparel. All I had was my jeans, T-shirts, and two nightshirts. I owned nothing to get sweaty in.

"Helllooo?" Bruiser waved her hand.

I smiled at her impatient persistence and then told them everything. Why? I wasn't sure. I'd never blabbed to anyone about my thoughts, problems, or issues. I always figured stuff out on my own. But somehow it felt right sharing my circumstances with them. Maybe because they were sort of in the same boat. Except they hadn't been tricked into being here.

Bruiser whistled when I finished. "Yowza. That's some story. TL must want you really bad. He doesn't strike me as the type to do something underhanded. I bet he had a hard time lying to you. David, too. He and TL seem a lot alike. I think I'd be flattered if someone wanted me so bad."

Flattered? Hmm, I hadn't thought of it from that angle.

She pushed up from her bed. "I've only known you for half a day, but this place wouldn't be the same if you left. Right, Beaker?"

I glanced over at her. She sat on the carpet with her back to her bed. She'd had her nose in a book the entire time, chomping on yet another piece of gum. The title read *The Atomic Beta Particle*.

Bruiser nudged her with her tennis shoe. "Hey, I'm talking to you. Answer me."

I almost laughed at Bruiser's boldness.

Beaker shrugged as a response.

Bruiser rolled her eyes. "Pay no attention to her. She has issues. Listen, GiGi, I really want you to stay. And so does everybody else. We were all talking about it at lunch."

They'd discussed me at lunch? In a good way? Usually, people only gossiped about me. Hearing Bruiser say otherwise brought a warm fuzziness to my heart.

She peeked at her watch. "We're supposed to be out at the barn in a few minutes. Coming?"

I nodded. "But I need to use the bathroom first."

"Want me to wait?"

Again, the warm fuzziness. I never had a girl offer such a simple, friendly thing. "No. Go on ahead."

"Yo, Beaker head, coming?"

Beaker lifted her attention from her book. "Beaker head?"

"Yeah, ya know, Beaker. Your chemistry code name."

Beaker's lips twitched in amusement, but it was probably an optical illusion. She didn't strike me as the type to smile at anything.

"I need to finish this chapter."

Bruiser waved as she headed out, leaving me alone with Beaker.

I started for the bathroom, and Beaker closed the book and tossed it onto her bed. I thought she said she needed to finish a chapter.

She stood up, hands on her hips. "So," she asked through gum chews. "You staying or what?"

"I haven't made up my mind yet."

"How long"—*chew, snap, chew*—"TL give you?"

"Until tomorrow morning."

She grunted as a response. "Well, uh, ya know . . ." Then she sort of smirked and shrugged her shoulders, like she was trying to look indifferent but didn't really mean it.

Somewhere between the "well, uh, ya know" and her smirk, I made up my mind.

‹FOUR›

I decided to stay. Mainly because the Specialists were such a unique group. I felt compelled to see what types of people they would become, and maybe I was curious to see how I would change, too. And if this place would really turn out to be a home, my new family, like TL and David had said.

When I told TL I was staying, he simply nodded, shook my hand, and said, "Welcome aboard." Not what I'd expected. No smile, no song and dance, no exuberant anything.

So here I stood in the barn with my other teammates. TL, David, and a *gigantic* bald man stood off to the left, talking. The bald man wore a black eye patch. The three of them wore matching camouflage shorts and shirts, resembling a recruitment poster for the military. I tried really hard to ignore their muscles and focus on my surroundings.

Horses were corralled in the back half of the barn, while the front looked like an old-fashioned gym. Three knotted ropes dangled from the ceiling, a bunch of mats were piled in one corner, racks of weights lined the walls, and two punching bags hung from a wooden plank. Huge windows allowed the sun to warm and light the area. Hay and musty horse smells clung to the air.

"Okay, people." TL broke the silence. "It's already after one. GiGi, you were three minutes late. Be prompt next time."

I swallowed. "Yes, sir." Three minutes late? Sheesh.

TL flipped over a white dry eraser board, revealing a list of fighting terms and their definitions. "Welcome to your first PT. We'll do a warm-up, followed by an introduction to martial arts."

I whipped the spiral pad from my back pocket and began taking notes. Wirenut stuck his hand in the air. "PT?"

Exactly what I wanted to know. Thanks, Wirenut.

"Physical training." TL nodded over his shoulder. "As you can see, this barn doubles as a fitness facility."

Parrot sneezed.

Seeing as how I stood the closest to him, I mumbled, "Bless you."

He sniffed. "Thanks. It's the hay. I'm allergic."

I gave him a "that sucks" face, and he smiled.

"Bruiser," rasped the *gigantic* bald man, squinting in her direction. He beckoned her with a jerk of his head.

I was sure the others thought the same thing as me. *Phew, glad I'm not Bruiser.*

Bruiser stepped out of line and crossed the cement floor to where TL, David, and the bald man stood.

He extended his hand with a big smile. "Jonathan. Nice to meet you."

His oversize grin did not match his appearance or voice, nor did his name. Someone like him should be called Snake or Viper.

Wearing her "Wanna Piece of This?" tank top, Bruiser returned his handshake with a dimpled, toothy smile. Their size difference reminded me of the David and Goliath story.

Jonathan released her hand and immediately karate-chopped her head.

We all caught a collective breath.

She dropped to a split to dodge the chop, spun around, and kicked the back of his knee. Jonathan landed with a thud on his butt.

Bruiser rolled away and back onto her feet before I had a chance to blink.

Jonathan and TL exchanged knowing nods.

TL motioned with his chin toward us. "That's it for now, Bruiser."

She rejoined our line, all nonchalant, like she hadn't just kicked Goliath's butt.

As we stood in awe of Bruiser's talents, the members of the Specialists Team One filed in through the barn door. They all wore matching black T-shirts with SPECIALISTS printed in white.

Cool shirts. Wonder if we'll get them, too.

The differences between the two teams struck me then. Team One appeared focused, unified, controlled. Team Two stood in a hodgepodge line, each person with his or her own unique style.

Beaker with her nose ring, purple hair, thick eyeliner, and gum chomping. Bruiser with her innocent wide eyes, freckles, and red pigtails. Parrot sniffing and sneezing from his hay allergy. Mystic with his thick neck, blond crew cut, and peaceful aura. Wirenut with his Harley-Davidson T-shirt cut off at the shoulders, tattoos, and goatee.

And me with my little spiral notepad.

Jeez, sometimes I'm a real nerd.

TL cleared his throat, snapping us to attention. "Now that Team One's here, we'll begin with stretching. Afterward I'll pair you off for your first PT. Understand that although you're each here for your own specialty, fitness is a must. If you're not healthy and able to physically handle the extreme situations you may find yourself in, you'll let your team members down."

Extreme situations? Physical fitness? TL told me I would operate from home base. I was the most uncoordinated, unathletic, klutzy person in the world. Anybody could see that. Otherwise, I wouldn't be standing here in jeans. I'd own athletic wear and have muscle tone.

Okay, I can do this.

Although I really wanted to stick my hand in the air and say, *TL, sir, I'm the geeky computer person. May I please be excused from physical training? I have code to key.*

But somehow I knew that wouldn't fly.

If this was part of the training, then I would certainly participate.

"Spread out," Jonathan rasped. "Arm's length between you."

Specialists Team One immediately went into position while Team Two sort of shuffled around before we figured it out.

"Arms up." Jonathan raised his. "Stretch. Feel it through your sides and spine."

I'd never been one for stretching and considered myself about as limber as my laptop. But this felt good. I could do this.

"Down. Spread your legs. Work it side to side."

Ooowww . . . my legs weren't meant to be spread this wide. I gritted my teeth and held my breath and hoped for the best.

"Up," Jonathan grunted.

Oh, thank God. I managed to get up and noticed nobody else seemed to be having problems.

Oh, wait . . . a bead of sweat trickled down Beaker's cheek. She glanced over at me and smirked. Somehow it comforted me. I was beginning to like and expect her smirks.

"Roll your neck back." Jonathan demonstrated. "Stop at your shoulders. Up and forward."

David's neck rolling caught my attention, and even though there were twenty feet of cement floor between us, I zeroed in on his muscles as he rolled. Though my brain told me to stop, I couldn't stop my gaze from traveling down his body. How come I never noticed he had so many defined muscles?

"Feet together . . ."

I blinked back to focus and found David staring right at me. I'd never been a blusher, but my face caught on fire. And to make matters worse, a look of sexy intuitiveness creased his eyes.

"Palms to the floor." Jonathan performed the contortionist act.

Feet together and touch my palms to the floor? Is he kidding?

Beside me, Bruiser effortlessly did it, and so I tried. My palms made it to my knees. I gritted my teeth and held my breath and reached for the floor. Gravity or my weight or pure lack of coordination sent me swaying forward, and I landed on my head.

"GiGi, you okay?" Bruiser reached for me.

"I'm fine," I muttered, pushing to my feet.

I did not peek at David because I knew he'd seen the whole thing and was probably shaking his head in disgust. I did look at Beaker and caught her lips twitching. Well, at least I'd amused someone.

We finished stretching, then TL paired each member of Team One with a person from Team Two. As he partnered us up one by one, I slowly realized who I would end up with.

"And, David, you're with GiGi."

I stared at TL a moment wondering why he'd done that. David was the absolute last person I wanted to be around right now. TL had to know that. Was this some kind of test? Part of my overall training? Something along the lines of quickly overcoming and dealing with emotional stress.

With a slight curve to his lips that made my stomach swirl, David crossed the cement floor to where I stood. "Looks like it's gonna be you and me."

"Working with you I'm not." I shook my head, dazed from the smell of his cologne. "I mean, I'm not working with you."

He shrugged. "It's not an option." He picked my notepad off the floor and tossed it a few feet into the corner. "Always taking notes, aren't you?"

Looking over to where it landed, I tightened my jaw. *How dare he throw my notepad like an insignificant piece of trash?*

"You." I pointed at it. "Go. Pick. That. Up. Right. Now."

"No." He smiled. "I. Won't. Go. Pick. That. Up. Right. Now."

Was he making fun of me? I reared and shoved him hard in the chest, sending him stumbling backward. His jaw dropped in disbelief, and my heart kicked into overdrive.

I can't believe I just did that.

"Hey," TL barked from across the barn. "Save it for the mats."

I peered around the training area and found all eyes on me. Parrot's brows shot up in surprise, as if to say, *Whoa, didn't know you had it in you.* Beaker stopped chomping her gum and stood studying me, like she couldn't quite figure me out.

There was nothing worse than people staring at me. Resisting the urge to run away in embarrassment, I wiped my damp palms on my jeans and made myself stay.

TL began giving instructions, and slowly everyone's focus turned to him. My mortification slipped away. But I didn't hear a word he said as I replayed everything in my mind, over and over and over again. What had I been thinking?

Moments later, everyone grabbed mats and slid them to separate areas in the barn. I followed David's lead because I didn't know what we were supposed to be doing.

David situated our mats in the far corner away from everyone else. He picked up my notepad and handed it to me. "Sorry," he said. "I guess I shouldn't have done that."

I took my spiral pad. "I'm sorry, too, for shoving you."

He nodded, accepting the small truce. "Feel better now?"

"A little." Not really. Because every time I set eyes on him I recalled how nice he'd been to me back at East Iowa University. Under it all he'd been fabricating lie after lie after lie.

"Bet you didn't hear a word TL said."

David knew me too well. "You're right." I extracted my mechanical pencil from the spiral and flipped the cardboard cover over. "Shoot."

"We're practicing basic self-defense today using mixed martial arts. And how to keep yourself calm during stressful situations." He continued outlining everything while I scribbled notes. Different holds and twists of the body. Breathing. Which body parts you can get to the easiest.

When he finished, I slipped the pad into my back pocket. "Okay, where do we start?"

"Well, first of all," David looked me up and down, "where're your workout clothes?"

"Don't have any. I don't work out."

"We're going to have to buy you some. PT's four times a week. For everyone. You need something other than jeans."

Four times a week?!

"You need shorts."

I shrugged. "Or yoga pants."

If he thought he was getting me in shorts, he had another think coming. I looked *horrible* in shorts. All long, gangly legs like a giraffe or something. Pale, too. Whiter than Beaker, the Goth. Now if I had Bruiser's muscles, I would wear workout clothes anytime.

David circled behind me. "Basic self-defense. You never know what types of situations you'll find yourself in."

He grabbed me around the neck and stomach and yanked me back against him. I sucked in a startled breath.

"What would you do," he whispered against my ear, "if an attacker had you in this hold?"

This was all pretend, make-believe, but the position scared me out of my mind. His tight, constraining grip paralyzed me. I couldn't have moved if I wanted to.

I felt powerless. Helpless. I had no control. And I wanted more than anything to never be in this position again.

"GiGi." TL came up beside us. "Calm your breathing."

I realized I was panting to the point of hyperventilation.

He placed his warm fingers over my face. "Close your eyes . . . concentrate . . . relax . . . center yourself . . . even your breaths."

I did as he quietly instructed. As the moments passed, the sounds of the horses at the back of the barn and the other Specialists muted. I felt only the soft thud of my heart, heard my quiet exhalations. A sense of oneness with myself strengthened me. As if I, too, could take on Goliath and win.

His fingers slid from my face. "Now slowly become aware of your surroundings."

David's arms around my neck and stomach came to me first. In my meditative state, I'd forgotten them. Then his body along the length of mine. His warm breath on my cheek. His pulsing heart against my back.

"Estimate the height and weight of your attacker." I heard TL shift to stand in front of me. "What part of his body can you get to the quickest? What part of your body can you move?"

I opened my eyes, as focused as I was when keying code. "My head. I can move it back. We're around the same height. Head butting is an option."

Head butting? Never thought I'd ever say that, let alone do it. "My left arm. It's pinned, but I can move my hand back and grab his groin. My legs. Both are free. I can slip one between the two of his and knock him off balance."

"Good." TL stepped to the left. "Which option is guaranteed to cause the most pain?"

"His groin, of course."

David quickly released me. "You're right, and TL's sadistic enough to tell you to do it."

TL chuckled. "Nicely done." He slapped David on the back. "Take it easy on her," he said, then wandered over to another team.

"That was really cool." I turned to David. "I might like this PT stuff after all."

He patted me on the head, making me feel five years old. "We gotta make sure you can take care of yourself. I told you I feel protective. You're like my little sister."

Maybe it was the little-sister comment, the same one he'd made right before tricking me into hacking the government's system. Or maybe the pat on the head. But both gestures infuriated me.

Grabbing his wrist, I twisted his arm behind his back and jammed my foot into the rear of his knee.

He buckled to the floor and rolled to his back. "What the . . . where did you learn that move?"

I stared down at him, amazed I'd done such a Jackie Chan maneuver. *Guess watching movies pays off after all.* I made a dramatic show of dusting my hands, enjoying my momentary superiority as David sat stunned on the floor.

41

"Excuse me. I need a bathroom break." I strolled away, head up, hoping my rear end looked good. Because maybe then he'd realize I wasn't five years old or his little sister.

‹FIVE›

I hurried across the University of San Belden's library plaza and into the computer science building. I'd been attending classes for only a month, but already I liked the professors and students better than Iowa. Everyone seemed more laid-back. Maybe it was the California sun and the surfer attitude.

In the past month, I'd had the same schedule. Classes every day. Homework. PT after that. Dinner. Chores. Bed. Pretty mundane actually. Except I'd always managed to be late to one or more of the various things.

I unlocked the lab reserved for computer science majors and found my usual station in the back empty. There were only two other students, a girl next to my station and a guy in the front. But they were so into their work, they didn't even notice me. With a quick glance at the clock, I put my book bag down. I had two hours until David got out of classes. We were supposed to meet in the parking lot to go pick up my team from the high school.

I cranked up my laptop, laid out a couple of lollipops, and began keying code.

‹CTE› [IS0-0000] ‹ICTE›
‹P›=ABR TLE='wowdeb'›ABR‹›
‹SCE & FER› ‹003004001› I=~%›

"Hey, there's a *really* cute guy out there who wants you."

I nodded, having heard the student beside me. A few more keystrokes, and this code segment would be complete. . . .

"Um, it looks like it's important. He's pointing to his watch and jabbing his finger in your direction."

I nodded, having heard the girl *again*. Didn't people know it was rude to bother someone when they were working?

The student shook my arm. "He's knocking on the glass now. Who is that? Does he go to school here? Omigod if you don't want him, I'll take him."

Remember to never sit by this idiot again.

Across the computer lab, a blurry image of a tall, dark haired guy occupied the window. I shoved my glasses on top of my head and got a clear shot of David impatiently tapping his watch.

Shoot. I jumped to my feet as my gaze darted to the clock that hung on the wall. *TL's gonna kill me.* Thirty minutes late! How had so much time gone by already?

Tossing my lemon lollipop in the garbage, I signaled David to go on, knowing he'd wait by the ranch's van. Rapidly, I shut down the laptop and raced from the lab, through the computer science building, and out into the parking lot. David stood propped against the van talking to a dark-haired girl.

He's not in such a hurry now.

He glanced up as I approached. "Ah, here she is."

The dark-haired girl gave me a barely discernible once-over, like comparing herself to me. Like she had some sort of territorial right over David.

I wanted to tell her to save her immaturity for someone it actually intimidated.

"Is this where you work?" She pointed to the decal on the van. SAN BELDEN RANCH FOR BOYS AND GIRLS.

"Yes. It's part of my work-study program at school here." He surreptitiously checked his watch.

Dark-haired Girl turned to me. "Aren't you that genius kid that enrolled a few weeks ago? Everyone's been talking about you."

"That's her." David reached toward me, and I got the impression he was going to ruffle my hair or pat me on the head again.

I narrowed my eyes in warning, and he slid my backpack off my shoulder instead.

"Nice meeting you." He opened the passenger side, and I climbed in.

"Can I, um, give you my number?" the girl asked David.

Jealousy tingled inside me, but I busied myself putting on my seat belt, pretending everything was cool.

David turned to the dark-haired girl, and I imagined his mind clicking out of task mode into normal eighteen-year-old mode.

"Oh, sure. Sorry. My mind's on something else."

The girl scribbled her number on a scrap of paper and tucked it down his front jeans pocket. "Call me."

I stared out my open window at his front pocket, unable to comprehend such a bold move. I could never do that.

David cleared his throat and circled around to the driver's side. He returned her wave through the window as we pulled out of the parking lot.

"TL's going to be really pissed," David snapped, after we turned onto the main street.

It took me a second to register how upset he sounded. "I'm sorry. I wa—"

He sliced the air with his hand, and I blinked in astonishment. "Your life's no longer just about you. There're other people involved. Do you realize your teammates have been waiting at the high school for nearly forty-five minutes to be picked up? How do you think they feel standing out there doing nothing?"

I swallowed a lump of guilt.

"They probably think we're not showing. They probably already called TL."

"I'm sor—"

"You can't get lost in your own computer world anymore. There are people who depend on you."

My guilt morphed to anger. How dare he accuse me of not being dependable. Anybody, *anybody*, could depend on me. "Well, you didn't seem to mind my being late. What were you doing with that girl? Tricking another unsuspecting teenager into committing a crime?"

He shot a lethal glare in my direction, and I turned away. Silence filled the air between us as we drove through the city.

Warm air flowed in my open window. Outside, kids played in shaded parks, people bustled in and out of air-conditioned buildings, joggers and Roller Bladers spotted the sunny sidewalks. Everyone enjoying a normal afternoon. A normal life. I caught sight of a family picnicking and immediately recalled a picnic I'd gone on with my parents. The unexpected memory brought a slight smile to my lips. I missed them so much.

I sighed. I had to admit, I had "tardy" issues. Never could be anywhere on time. Not even alarm clocks kept me on track. Most of the time I tuned them out when they went off. It wasn't as if I didn't comprehend my flaws. I found it very hard to pull myself from my concentrated state. That's all. Something I needed to work on, but I didn't need David barking at me about it.

"Here," he murmured, and handed me an apple. "I know you forgot to eat."

Food. Right. I knew something had slipped my mind today. I took the fruit, and my fingers brushed his. The contact brought our eyes together for a brief second, then he switched his attention back to the road.

I looked at the apple and thought, *How can I stay mad at him?* Mere minutes ago we'd been in a fiery debate and yet he'd still worried about my welfare.

"Ohhh," he groaned, pulling into the high school parking lot. "I don't need this right now."

In front of the school, every one of my teammates was slinging punches in a street brawl. Beaker was rolling around on the pavement with another girl. Wirenut punched a guy in the face. Parrot charged a different guy. Bruiser leaped into the air, delivering a split kick to a girl and a guy. And Mystic, always at one with the universe, stood in the middle of it all trying to keep the peace.

***

TL folded his arms across his chest and stared hard at each of us. "I am extremely disappointed. I don't think this is amusing in the least."

Sitting around the conference table four levels beneath the ranch, my teammates and I guiltily dropped our heads. No one had said a word since coming home from San Belden High, so I didn't know what had caused the fight. My curiosity was about to burst one of my brain cells, though. Especially with the bumps and scrapes everyone was sporting.

"You've been here only a month and already I've been contacted by the principal three times. First, because of Beaker's explosion in the chemistry lab. Second, because of Mystic's palm reading in between classes, and now this. I didn't bring you here to resume your juvenile antics. I recruited you because you're the best and I saw potential. But let me say something: as easily as I brought you here, I can transport you right back out. So if you're thinking you're too talented for me to get rid of, then think again. I don't have the time or inclination to deal with behavioral issues. There is a whole list of other candidates on my desk as we speak."

TL circled the table and stopped behind Wirenut. "Tell me, what was the fight about?"

Why would TL ask that question? We all wore monitoring devices. TL knew the answer. Maybe it was a test to see if Wirenut would lie or tell the truth. Maybe TL thought Wirenut had forgotten about the monitoring device. They were easy to forget, being almost invisible. The only time I remembered mine was when I undressed.

"I will not repeat my question."

Swollen-eyed, Wirenut cast a quick glance toward Parrot as if silently asking if he should tell.

"Sir." Parrot raised his hand, displaying an oozing scrape on his forearm. "May I answer the question?"

TL raised one brow.

"The fight was about me."

"Go on."

Parrot straightened in his chair and inhaled a deep breath, like he dreaded giving his explanation. "This guy was making fun of my Native American heritage. I threw the first punch, sir. I'm sorry. I let my temper get the best of me."

"And your teammates? How did they get involved?"

"They jumped in when too many students ganged up on me."

"I see." TL circled the table, returning to his original spot. He looked at Mystic. "Your principal said you were the only one not involved. Why is that?"

"I don't believe in violence." Mystic gently patted his heart. "Peace."

Beside me, Beaker snorted.

TL slammed his fist on the table, and we all jumped. "Let me repeat. I don't find this amusing. Or"—he glanced at Mystic—"peaceful. This situation is just the type of thing that would make the IPNC pull our funding. And then where would you all be?" He paused for a second. "You've lost all free-time privileges for two weeks. Every one of you. This is a team, so the whole team suffers. You will go to school, come back, do chores, PT, eat, homework, and go to bed. Weekends are mine, too. Don't even *think* about violating these restrictions. Because if you do, I will, *guaranteed,* put you in juvie hall where you belong."

He pinned each of us with a light-eyed, icy stare. "Dismissed."

I followed my teammates from the conference room, around the high-tech work area, past all the locked doors, and then into the elevator. No one said a word as we rode it four floors up to the ranch level. We exited, the guys went to their room, and we girls went to ours.

Bruiser gingerly lowered herself to her bed. She raised her REDHEADS ROCK! T-shirt and carefully examined the bruises on her side. "Sucks having TL mad at us."

"Who cares?" Beaker flopped across her mattress.

"When exactly did you develop such a bad attitude?" Bruiser smoothed down her shirt. "Have you always been this way? Or did you wake up one morning and decide, 'Hey, I think I'll be the world's biggest crab.'"

Beaker flipped Bruiser off with a black-tipped finger. I held my breath, sure Bruiser would physically retaliate, and I'd be the one to have to break it up.

"Ya know," Bruiser pressed on, apparently unfazed by Beaker's middle finger, "just because your life sucks doesn't mean you can be nasty to the rest of us. Not like any of us have had rosy ones ourselves. You don't see us all sour moody. Get over yourself."

Beaker rolled onto her side, giving us her back. Runs and holes, remnants of the fight, zigzagged her black fishnet leggings. She'd bleached her choppy hair white in the past week. Very different from the purple it had originally been. I experienced a pang of sorrow for her. She seemed so . . . lost.

We all did, but she seemed helpless.

I glanced over to my bed. On my pillow sat a small, red plastic bag. I crossed the room and peeked inside. Clothes? I reached in and pulled out two pairs of shorts, one yellow and one gray. I held them up and eyeballed their extreme shortness. *We're going to have to buy you some shorts.* David's comment came back to me. Had he bought me these? My stomach swirled at the image of me poured into them. Had David conjured a similar one?

Bruiser went to her dresser and pulled open the top drawer. She took off her T-shirt, grabbed an Ace bandage, and began wrapping it around her ribs. "Should've bought a bigger size. Those'll crawl up your crack. They're a little teeny."

They *were* teeny. *Very* teeny. She assumed I'd bought them for myself. Fine by me. Last thing I needed was my teammates teasing me about David or thinking I got special treatment.

"Need any help?" I offered, purposefully changing the subject.

"Nah. I've done this plenty over the years."

I shoved the shorts back in the bag and made myself comfortable against my headboard. "Anything broken?"

"Only bruised."

"How do you know?"

"Ever had a broken rib?"

I shook my head.

"Believe me, there's a huge difference between a broken rib and a bruised one."

Parrot, Wirenut, and Mystic opened our door and strode into our room without knocking. "Can we come in?"

"Sure." Bruiser nodded them in, obviously not caring that she was wearing only her white cotton sports bra and jeans.

Out of all the space in the room, the guys crowded onto our beds like a big, comfortable family.

Parrot plopped across the foot of my bed. He'd bandaged his oozing forearm.

Mystic settled on the carpet cross-legged, like he was about to meditate. How did he get his big burly body in that limber position?

Wirenut pushed Beaker's feet aside and made himself comfortable next to her. She didn't move, and in fact kept her back to us all. He peeled a banana and took a bite.

We were like brothers and sisters hanging out. A real family. With a smile, I snuggled down into my freshly washed pillow.

Bruiser secured the Ace bandage with two metal clasps, then slid her shirt back on. She sprawled on her stomach across her mattress. "I was telling them how much it sucks having TL mad at us. And you"—she bopped Mystic in the back of the head—"are an idiot. I can't believe you said, 'I don't believe in violence.'"

Mystic rubbed the back of his head. "I don't. Besides, if Parrot here would learn to deal with his stress quietly, none of this would've happened. 'Sticks and stones will break my bones, but names can never harm me.' All of you could take a lesson from that. You can't go throwing punches when somebody mouths off."

Wirenut threw his banana peel at Mystic. "Shut up, man. You got it backward. You need to learn to get physical. Parrot did the right thing defending himself. Nothing wrong with standing up for yourself. If you weren't so busy becoming one with the stars, you'd see that."

Mystic steepled his fingers and pressed them to his lips. "If that's the way you feel, then I thank you for verbalizing it and not violently expressing it." Silently, he contemplated Wirenut. "Harmony lives in my soul. It should live in yours, too."

Bruiser shoved his head again. "Mystic, you're about to snap my last nerve. You look like you could hold your own in a brawl. You should've dug in."

Beaker snorted, and we all turned to look at her back. A second later short bursts of air jerked her shoulders. I smiled at her obvious ploy to control her giggles. The more she tried to hold it in the bigger I grinned.

My teammates began chuckling and slowly Beaker gave in to laughter that shook her whole body. She didn't stop and instead got louder and louder. She rolled onto her back, holding her stomach. Tears sent black eyeliner streaking down her cheeks. I glanced around at my teammates, who were getting as loud as Beaker. Their infectious laughter made me join in.

A clearing throat drew our attention to the door, and we all stopped goofing around. David shook his head. "Such children. You're having too much fun for guys who just got grounded." Bruiser snatched her pillow and flung it across the room toward the door.

David dodged it and charged. He tackled her onto my bed. "You little squirt."

I moved to get out of the way, but they rolled right into me and pinned me against the headboard.

"Uncle," Bruiser squealed. "Uncle. You win."

Laughing, David pushed up and held his hand out to me. "Come on. TL wants to see you at eighteen hundred hours."

Huh?

Mentally, I converted to real time. Six p.m. I glanced at my bedside clock. "That's in five minutes."

"I know. Let's go."

Ignoring David's hand, I rolled off the bed.

"Oooh," my teammates teased. "GiGi's in trouble. GiGi's in trouble."

I waved them off, enjoying the warmth their attention brought me.

David and I left my bedroom. I knocked on TL's door, and David stopped me. "TL's in the conference room."

"Oh. Am I in trouble or something?"

"Or something."

What the heck did that mean? I rewound my brain through the past month, searching for anything I'd done wrong. I'd been late to PT numerous times, and to dinner, and for chores, and I was late today meeting David. If there was anything TL wanted to discuss with me, it'd have to be that. Or maybe he wanted to tell me I needed to wear shorts during PT. Inwardly, I groaned.

David led the way down the hall toward the mountainous mural and hidden elevator. I tried really hard not to stare at his butt, but didn't succeed. He placed his left hand over the wall-mounted globe light, and the door slid open. According to the introduction folder TL had given all of us, a red laser housed within the globe scanned for prints.

Come to think of it, that signal would be much more effective if it were transparent. The red tone gave it away anyway. I whipped out my spiral pad and made a note to experiment with particle beams and quark energy, then stepped inside.

The door closed and down we went. Suddenly I realized I was alone with David. In an elevator. *Alone*. Going four levels beneath the earth's surface. *Alone*. With David. Okay, I'd been alone with him earlier, but that had been in the van, and we'd been driving through town.

This was different. Enclosed. Private.

I swallowed, and the gurgle echoed through my ears. Had he heard it, too? Shouldn't there be music in an elevator to mask all the other noises?

I moved only my eyes to the right. He stood a fraction of a foot behind me. He exhaled a breath and it ricocheted through my brain. The air-conditioning kicked on, sending his cologne shooting up my nostrils. They flared in immediate response. My heart kicked into light speed, and my head whirred on a dizzying wave. I squeezed my eyes shut and concentrated on breathing, like TL had taught me. Slow, even breaths. Block out my surroundings. Inhale through the nose. Exhale through the mouth. Inhale through nose. Exhale through mouth.

The air around me stirred, and my eyes flew open. David reached past me to my right. I caught my breath as I studied his tan muscles. The soft, dark hair. The veins trailing his arm. I followed the length of it to his fingers and watched him key in the code to exit to Sub Four.

I realized then that the elevator had stopped, and because I hadn't moved, David had no other choice *but* to key in the code. How long had I been standing here not moving? Had David said anything to me? Ooohhh, I must look like a complete idiot.

"Sorry, I was proton spread analyzing the." I shook my head. "I mean, I was analyzing the spread of a proton." I chanced a quick peek over my shoulder to see if he'd bought it and nearly ran straight into his face. My gaze focused on a small cut dissecting his lower lip.

He shifted so my eyes met dark ones, and they crinkled sexily as if to say he knew something he wasn't supposed to know. "Right. Did you get those shorts?"

I stumbled from the elevator. "Uh, yeah. Thanks."

"You going to wear them for tomorrow's PT?"

"They're a little . . . teeny."

"Teeny?"

"Yeah, they're teeny."

"Receipt's in the bag if you want to exchange them. You need shorts, though. So don't think you're getting out of this."

"Fine," I muttered, and strode toward the conference room with David close behind me.

"Tell TL I'll be there in a sec." He motioned me on.

David would be joining us? Why?

He headed down the hall with all the locked doors, stopping at the first one on the left. He keyed in a code and stepped through. I swayed to the right, trying to get a look in the room, but the door automatically shut too quickly.

Shoot.

"GiGi?"

I spun to see TL standing outside the conference room. Had he seen me being nosy?

"Let's go. You'll know what's behind those doors soon enough."

Okay, so he *had* seen me being nosy. "David said to tell you he'd be a second. Sir, am I in trouble?"

"Did you do something to warrant being in trouble?"

I hated when people answered questions with questions. "Um, I don't think so."

"You either know or you don't know. So which is it? Be decisive, GiGi. Yes or no?"

"Yes, sir."

He opened the conference-room door and we both entered and took seats.

"Tell me why you answered yes."

"I know I've been having a problem being on time."

TL nodded. "If you'd been prompt today, your teammates wouldn't have gotten into a fight."

Wait a minute. This was my fault? Uh-uh. I didn't agree with that at all. "Sir, I don't want to be disrespectful, but you can't blame me for the fight. My running late doesn't give my teammates an excuse to get into trouble."

TL smiled. "Quite right. And I applaud you for standing up for yourself. The old GiGi would've silently accepted the blame. You've grown in the month you've been here."

Jeez, he was right. The old me *would* have quietly accepted the blame. I sat up straighter, feeling a surge of pride.

"However, it doesn't excuse your lack of time concept. Let me make it very clear: you'd better figure it out. Wear some sort of watch with an alarm if need be. Brilliance is no excuse to be scatterbrained."

"Yes, sir."

TL pulled a small, brown cardboard box from his front pants pocket and opened it. "Place your monitoring device in here." My stomach swooped to my feet. "Sir?" Everyone else still wore theirs. Why take mine?

"Take off your monitoring device and place it in this box." Panic slammed my heart into my chest wall. Did this mean he was kicking me out of the Specialists? Because I couldn't keep track of time? But I didn't want to leave. Not anymore. I was really starting to feel like I belonged here. Like I was finally part of a family. I almost even unpacked my things last night.

"GiGi, everything's fine," he assured me, as if reading my thoughts. "Take it off and then I'll explain."

I pushed back from the table and rotated away. Lifting my shirt, I undid my jeans and peeled the flesh-toned device from my lower stomach. I didn't know who had created these, but they were ingenious.

If anybody outside the ranch had seen it, I was supposed to tell them it was a wart-remover strip. All of us Specialists had different explanations. Bandage. Nicotine patch. Scar treatment. Of course, no one except my roommates had seen my lower stomach in the past month, so it hadn't been an issue.

After putting my clothes back together, I dropped the device in the box.

TL put the lid on it. "You are the first in your team to remove the device. I suggest you keep this to yourself. If the others find out, it might spark some jealousy or resentment. As you know, I monitor each of you closely. From the start, you proved to be adept at your cover. You went about your day-to-day activities smoothly, naturally, and without a second thought. It's almost as if you've been here months instead of a few weeks. I'm impressed with how seamlessly you merged into this world. This tells me you are ready to move on to the next stage of your training." He stood. "Follow me."

I trailed behind TL, hardly breathing, thinking, or blinking. The things he'd told me—I couldn't wrap my brain around them. I was the first to prove adeptness? That couldn't be right. I hadn't done anything different from usual. At least I didn't think I had. Most days consisted of a jumbled haze, just like always, full of computer code, with my brain clicking away at the latest challenge.

TL stopped at a silver metal door with a control panel attached to the wall. "You're granted access to this room now. Starting tonight, you'll spend one hour each evening in here with Chapling. He's our computer specialist. Your code is the formula for the nth term of a geometric sequence. You may change it if you like, but please inform me if you do. Never give your code to anyone. Not even Chapling."

TL stepped to the side. He nodded to the keypad. Not a typical numbered keypad. This one contained coefficients, variables, powers, geometric shapes, and inequality symbols. Like a scientific calculator.

Quickly recalling the formula, I keyed it in. The door opened to reveal a computer lab I estimated at thirty by thirty. The coppery scent of solder hung on the warm air. Computers trailed along one wall, various components and tools were scattered on a worktable in the center, shelves lined another wall packed full of cables and assorted hardware.

The urge to touch and explore nearly overwhelmed me. I swallowed the excitement bubbling inside me and wished for a lollipop so I could get down to work. Then I caught sight of a TZ-60 system and sucked in a breath.

TL chuckled. "You'll have plenty of time to explore this room tonight."

I pointed across the room. "A TZ-60. Do you have *any* idea how rare those are?"

"Unfortunately, no. That's your and Chapling's area of expertise."

Mine and Chapling's. I liked the sound of that. Not Chapling's. But *mine* and Chapling's.

"Yo. Did I hear voices?"

TL and I glanced to the right. A red-haired man crawled from behind a patch panel. With the number of cables it contained, I assumed it must control the ranch's entire computer system. He stood and cracked his neck, rolled his shoulders, and shook out his hands. He looked up at me and smiled. I'd never seen such a small adult in my whole life. He stood maybe four feet tall. And I'd never seen such fire-red, Brillo-pad hair.

He waddled toward us, shook TL's hand, then reached for mine. "You're the computer genius, huh? Boyohboyohboy. You and I will make quite the team. Beauty and the shorty."

Laughing, I shook his small, dry, rough hand. He was right. We *were* exact opposites.

Chapling teetered over to a high metal stool—a stool I could have simply slid my hip onto—and climbed up. "What time you gonna be here tonight? 'Round eight?"

I had no idea. I looked to TL, and he nodded. "Eight sounds good."

"All right." Chapling clapped his hands. "See you then. Bring the caffeine. It'll be a late one."

TL shook his finger. "Not too late. She's got a morning class."

"Bring the caffeine anyway." Chapling snapped his pudgy fingers. "I'm gonna need it."

TL steered me toward the door. "Chapling never sleeps. He runs on caffeine. If not for me or David, he'd never leave his cave."

We made our way back to the conference room. David had come in sometime during our absence and sat studying a folder.

He glanced up as we entered. "What'd you think of Chapling?"

David knew I met Chapling? Of course he knew. In the time I'd been here, I'd quickly learned how much a part of things David was. At times it seemed that he and TL shared the leadership role.

I rolled my chair out and sat down. "I like him." I more than liked him. In the few seconds I'd met him, he seemed fun and interesting. I couldn't wait for eight o'clock, as a matter of fact.

TL closed the door and took his seat. "I wanted to introduce you to Chapling, but I called you two down here for another reason." He folded his hands on top of the table, looked at David and then me. "GiGi, in one month, I am sending you on your first mission. And, David, you will accompany her."

‹SIX›

My whole body went numb as TL's words slowly settled in. Sending David and me on a mission? Wait, had I heard TL right? I couldn't have heard him right. I switched my gaze to David, and his expression mirrored the shock I felt.

"B-b-but y-you"—I took a breath, and then another—"said you would I home base work." I shook my head. "I mean, you said I would work from home base."

TL calmly nodded. "My exact words were you would most *likely* work from home base."

"What?" Oh my God. *What?* He was playing word games with me?

I was suddenly hot and unable to breathe. I couldn't go on a mission. Was he crazy?

I'm going to be sick. I'm going to throw up all over this conference table.

Pushing away from the table, I swallowed again. "S-sick. I'm going to be sick."

David jumped up and TL motioned him back down. "No, you're not. Calm yourself. Close your eyes. Concentrate on breathing."

I gripped the arms of my chair and stared wide-eyed at him.

TL slowly stood, slid around the table's corner, and placed his hand on my face. Just like he'd done during my first PT. I closed my eyes and concentrated on the warmth and weight of his fingers. Their soapy scent. The white noise of the air conditioner. One second slipped into another. Gradually my sickness faded and my breathing slowed to normal.

He took my left hand between both of his. "I wouldn't be sending you if I didn't have complete confidence in your ability. Always remember that."

Complete confidence in my ability? What *exactly* had I done over the past month to warrant such high praise? Maybe this was some sort of reverse psychology. Maybe he'd said the exact same things to the other Specialists.

Memories of the deceit and manipulation from when I first got here came rushing back. I pulled my hand from between his. "Did you know about this mission when you recruited me?"

"No."

"Your exact words were I would most *likely* work from home base. Did you know I would most *likely* go on a mission?"

TL folded his arms across his chest. "No."

"You really believed I would work from home base?"

"Yes."

He wasn't lying. Somewhere deep inside me, I knew that for sure. Then again David had lied right to my face and I never suspected a thing.

"There's no way I would send you on a mission if it weren't absolutely necessary." TL slid back into his seat. "As you pointed out, I didn't recruit you to be a field operative. I recruited you to work right here with Chapling."

"Then why are you sending her?"

David's unexpected outburst made me jump. I glanced across the conference table. I'd never seen him so panicked. He always came across as controlled and easy going. Well, except when I was running late.

"Last night Chapling decoded intel from Ushbania, a small country in Eastern Europe." TL leveled a passive stare on David. "Your father is on the market, to be sold to the highest bidder."

Silence.

Seconds stretched to eternity and no one made a sound. I couldn't even hear anyone breathing. TL and David maintained eye contact, but not a single expression passed across their faces. I shouldn't be here. This was too private. But this meant David's dad was alive. Why wasn't David happy? Or crying? Or something? And what did I have to do with any of this?

David moved finally, dropping his head into his hands. He rubbed his face, then peered across the table at me. The emotion flowing from his brown eyes made me catch my breath. And in that moment I knew I'd do anything to reunite him with his dad. I'd do anything to reunite *any* person with their parent.

"Mr. Share"—TL spoke, bringing my and David's attention to him—"is owned by Romanov Schalmosky. Apparently, your father was sold ten years ago to this man. Whoever kidnapped him put a twenty-million-dollar price tag on his head, and Romanov happily paid the money. Mr. Share's intellect is world renowned. The government has been actively looking for him since his disappearance. But Romanov has kept him hidden well. We've had an agent working for Romanov for two years, and not even this agent knew Romanov had Mr. Share."

TL slipped a small, thin remote from his shirt pocket. He pointed it at the screen that stretched along the back wall. A picture of a man appeared. He had white hair and a yellowish tint to his skin. An oxygen tube ran up his nose. "This is a picture of Romanov, taken last year."

"Why have you had an agent working for Romanov?" David asked.

"Because Romanov's got his fingers in a lot of nasty business. He's a known terrorist. We've been keeping tabs on him."

"Why now?" David shrugged. "Why's Romanov selling him?"

"Romanov is dying, and he's going out in a fiery blaze of glory. Both of his sons are dead, so he has no one to leave his empire to. He's selling everything, including Mr. Share, to the highest bidder. And he's giving all his money to an Ushbanian terrorist cell. As I mentioned a second ago, your father's intellect is world renowned. He's created some of the most complex systems in the world, including numerous ones for the United States government. I don't think I have to tell you what it would do to our national security if Mr. Share is sold to the wrong person."

"The wrong person owns him now."

TL held up his hand. "I know. Preliminary reports show that your father has spent the last ten years hacking systems for Romanov and Ushbania, stealing money, making them more rich and powerful. Whatever he's done, we have a chance to stop it now, and we're taking it. We want Mr. Share back."

David nodded his head in my direction. "What's GiGi's part in this?"

Good question. I couldn't wait to hear the answer.

"Romanov owns numerous businesses around the world. Based on the intel Chapling decoded, Romanov has encoded the whereabouts of your father on a microsnipet located in a statue in one of his modeling schools.

The microsnipet cannot be removed from the statue. It has to be decoded from its embedded spot. Unfortunately we don't know which statue. Intel is cryptic with that part. Obviously, Chapling would never be allowed in a modeling school, but GiGi? Yes."

I swallowed the bile rising in my throat. Modeling? I couldn't even walk right. I was the *biggest* klutz in the world.

"What do you mean, modeling school?" David shook his head. "What does Romanov have to do with modeling?"

"One of his many businesses. He owns a string of schools across Europe through which he launders money."

"T—T—TL?" Both guys looked at me. "I can't do this. Have you seen me around the ranch? I can't even walk right. I stumble into everything. You've got to pick somebody else. There has to be an agent out there somewhere who can do this job."

David nodded. "She's right. She has no coordination. She tripped on her way out of the elevator not more than thirty minutes ago."

I pointed to David. "See, he agrees."

"Seriously, TL, pick somebody else. How 'bout that agent out of Texas? What's her name . . . ?" David snapped his fingers. "Jani. She's hot. She can pass for a model in a heartbeat."

Wait a minute. Jani's hot? What did he mean *Jani's hot?*

"Pick anybody but GiGi. *Anybody.*"

I narrowed my eyes. Really, I wasn't *that* bad.

"Plus"—David railroaded on—"there's not enough time. A month to get her ready? It would take *a lot* longer than four weeks."

Who did he think he was? I threw my arms across my stomach. How dare he say it would take *a lot* longer. And . . . I could be hot. Even Beaker said I looked like a Victoria's Secret model.

"I'll do it." *Oh, jeez, did I just say that?* Too late now. I showed TL all the determination I could. "I know I can do it."

TL nodded. "David's right. There are numerous agents who could do this. The modeling side, that is. But none of them have the computer skills you do. This isn't something Chapling can hack into. This is a stand-alone device. You must be right there to break the code and retrieve the data."

David leaned forward. "But, T—"

"The decision is final. I've enrolled GiGi in Romanov's Ushbanian modeling school. She starts in thirty days."

David sighed. "Well, why me? You said you were sending both of us in. Don't get me wrong. I want to go. He's my dad. But the logical side of me says I'm too close to the situation. I may not be objective."

Hadn't thought about that. But he had a good point. How admirable to put his dad and this mission ahead of his own desires.

"Before your dad's abduction, he created the eighteen levels of the government's system. GiGi is familiar with nine of those."

I flushed at TL's reference to my hacking crime.

"Mr. Share encoded the eighteen levels on a chip. The location of the chip is unknown. According to the intel Chapling received last night, whoever buys your father gets the chip. I don't have to tell you what could happen if someone gets their hands on the chip and infiltrates our system."

"I understand, but it still doesn't explain why you want to send me."

"Intel revealed that Mr. Share's son is the key to owning the chip." TL leaned forward. "To my knowledge you are his only son. Am I right?"

David barely nodded.

"Whether you know it or not, you're the key."

"My dad never told me anything. If he had I would've divulged it to the government a long time ago."

"Ah, and therein lies the mystery. And that is why you are going. As soon as GiGi decodes the microsnipet and finds his whereabouts, we'll extract him. You'll be right there to unlock the mystery of the chip he hid over a decade ago."

My stomach clenched with worry for David's safety. "Sir, what about David? What's to stop someone from kidnapping him now that word's out he's the key?"

"Very few people know his true identity. Only people with access to top secret IPNC documents know who David is. His secret is safe for now." TL shuffled his papers, quickly perusing them. "We're not sure where this statue and microsnipet are located. GiGi will be the only one with access to the entire school. David, you will travel with her as her photographer. I'll go as her bodyguard, and Jonathan will be her modeling agent. I've arranged for an IPNC agent out of Washington to fly in and run things here at the ranch while I'm gone."

Maybe it was the stress, or the whole mind-blowing situation; was this new life of mine actually real? I didn't know why, but I started laughing and wouldn't stop. Images flashed through my brain. Of giant, eye-patch Jonathan, our PT instructor, acting like a modeling agent. Of me walking down a runway all pouty-lipped, tripping over a piece of dust. Of David studying me through a viewfinder, clicking pictures.

Of David studying me through a viewfinder, clicking pictures.

Gulp.

My laughter died abruptly. *Shoot.* He *would* be taking pictures of me, wouldn't he? I closed my eyes on a silent groan. I was going to look like a *total* idiot.

TL stood. "Now that GiGi's done releasing her tension, you're both dismissed for dinner."

I opened my eyes, but didn't move. I needed to digest things for a while.

TL left, and David got up. "I don't think any of this is funny." He gathered his things without looking at me. "I don't think it's funny at all."

My stomach sank with his point-blank rebuke. I watched him stride from the room, feeling worse and worse with each step he took. He was right. None of this was funny. His dad had been kidnapped ten years ago, sold to Romanov Schalmosky, and was back up for sale to the highest bidder.

And out of everyone in the IPNC, they'd picked me to decode his whereabouts.

Me.

If I failed, David might never see his dad again.

***

Anticipating my meeting with Chapling had helped redirect my mind from obsessing over my upcoming mission.

A little before eight, I keyed in my code to the computer lab. This meeting with Chapling had been in the front of my brain all afternoon and evening long. I actually checked the clock dozens of times to make sure I wasn't running late.

I opened the lab door and stepped inside. Chapling stood off to the right, making a fresh pot of coffee.

I walked toward him. "Hey."

He jumped, and coffee grounds flew into the air. "Oh boy. Oh-boyohboyohboy." He slammed his hand over his heart. "Warn a guy next time."

I laughed, not bothering to point out that I'd been pretty loud coming in.

Chapling brushed coffee grounds from his red, Brillo-pad hair. He finished loading up the filter and pressed the on button.

I caught sight of the stained coffeemaker and cringed. "When was the last time you cleaned that thing?"

He shrugged and waddled off.

I never claimed to be neat and tidy, but that coffeemaker looked disgusting. A sink sat beside it with paper towels hanging above. I turned off the coffeemaker, tore off a wad of paper towels, wet them in the sink, and cleaned it up. I turned the coffeemaker back on, and while the coffee brewed, I wiped the spilled grounds from the table and floor.

Suddenly I felt like his mother.

"Hey, where are you?" Chapling called from across the lab.

"Cleaning up your mess," I called back.

"Oh, thanks. Thanksthanksthanks. Get over here. I can't wait to show you this."

I threw away the paper towels and found him sitting on the floor in the corner, behind a server, surrounded by wires and tools.

I sat down across from him. "Why are you in the corner?"

"It's comfortable. Here." He gave me a wire. "Wrap this around your finger."

I did. He touched the other end of the wire to a tiny, flat microsnipet. The contact sent a hot zing through my finger, and I jumped.

Chapling scrunched up his bushy red brows. "That hurt?"

"No. It startled me. What are we doing? What is this?"

"It's for your mission. The microsnipet's hidden in a statue. We need to develop a device that'll tell you which statue. Something that'll pick up the specific magnetic field that only microsnipets emit."

I unwrapped the wire from my finger. "But I can't go around with this on my finger touching wires to statues. That'll be a bit obvious."

"Quite right. I was thinking something silicone-based, nearly invisible."

My heart kicked in. "With a remote sensor?"

"Yeahyeahyeah, that's good." Chapling handed me a well-used spiral notebook. "Take a look at my notes. Tell me what you think."

I flipped over the cover. "So how long have you worked for the IPNC?"

"Fifteen years. They recruited me right after I patched into Miami's mainframe and blacked out the whole city."

"Um . . ." I blinked. "Okay. Want to tell me why?"

He waved his hand. "For the fun of it."

I smiled. Somehow I couldn't picture him being so devious. "Ya know, if you would've used a nesrent bug in the software, the city would've strobed like a nightclub."

Chapling looked up from the soldering iron he held. "Oh, thatsgoodthatsgoodthatsgood. Where were you fifteen years ago? Too bad I'm not a social deviant anymore. We'd totally have to do that to San Belden."

We both laughed, and I began skimming through his notes. . . . I was amazed. His computations were out of this world.

I studied his diagrams, and it hit me. "Silicone-based? How about something mirroring a fingerprint?"

He snapped his fingers. "You got it. Smartgirlsmartgirl." He took his spiral pad, jotted a few notes, and we got down to work.

‹SEVEN›

‹rbba/ a;×%#@›
  ‹: "'/ ‹eltit› "es"›
  ‹gnal ‹dOc̄nedlit› /ekup/›

"GiGi, watch out!"

I snapped out of my computer zone a split second before I ran straight into a wall. I'd been into my modeling training for two weeks and knew I wasn't doing too hot at it.

Bruiser burst out laughing, and Beaker snorted.

"GiGi," my modeling instructor, Audrey, said with a sigh. "You've *got* to concentrate. We have only two weeks left to get you ready. And frankly, you've shown little improvement."

"I know. I'm sorry." *I'm tired,* I wanted to whine. This mission had taken over my life. Between college classes and training after school each day at the ranch, I barely had time to eat, let alone enjoy a lollipop.

Perfect, beautiful, *coordinated* Audrey pointed at me. "One more time. Remember, you're a lady. Not a bull rider. Stand up straight, shoulders back, suck in your stomach, dangle your arms. One foot in front of the other, toe first. Pop your hip. And smile." She demonstrated down the length of our long room and back.

I paid very close attention, *I promise I did,* and successfully made it all the way down our makeshift runway. With a proud, relieved breath I paused for show, pivoted, and my spike heel buckled beneath me.

Beaker snorted. *Again.*

"If you're so perfect," I snapped at her from my sprawled position, "why don't you get up and do it yourself!"

She shrugged, ran her hand through her newly dyed pink hair, and went back to her homework.

Bruiser rolled off her bed, struck a pose, then exaggeratedly did the model stroll in her FRECKLES FREAKING RULE! T-shirt.

Her goofiness made me smile. Leave it to her to relieve a tense situation.

The instructor held her hand out to me. "Come on. Let's take a break and practice wearing clothes."

How pathetic was it that I had to *practice wearing clothes?*

She'd laid a variety of outfits on my bed. Sequined gowns, slinky dresses, spaghetti-strapped shirts, extremely *teeny* minis. Just as teeny as my shorts (that I still hadn't worn, or taken back. Sweatpants and PT went together *just* fine in my mind.)

I eyeballed the clothes on my bed. Did models actually wear this stuff?

"It's not enough to look good. You have to know you look good. Confidence is the key."

Comfort is the key, I wanted to say, but wisely kept my thoughts to myself. Didn't do me any good to fight the process. I had a mission to get ready for.

The instructor picked up a silver, teeny mini and a tight, pink tank top. "This argentine and salmon are great together."

Argentine and salmon? Why couldn't she just say silver and pink?

She handed me the clothes, and I turned toward the bathroom.

"No. Change here. You'll have no privacy among the other models. You'll be poked and prodded and nipped and tucked. Between the stylists, makeup artists, and designers, you won't be left alone. Start getting used to it. Lose your modesty. Strip."

Even though I'd spent plenty of time in orphanages, foster homes, and college dormitories, I still managed to find privacy.

I looked at Bruiser, then Beaker, and then Audrey. *I don't have anything they don't,* I reassured myself, but mine was mine and theirs was theirs. Know what I mean?

Quickly, I made a mental inventory of my underwear.

Bra: beige, one month old, slightly padded, clean, no holes, no frays.

Underwear: burgundy, bought same time as bra, bikini, clean, no holes, no frays.

Okay, now hair: shaved my pits, legs, and bikini line last night.

Things aren't as bad as they could be.

I stripped from my jeans and T-shirt and reached for my new clothes.

"Where's your patch?" asked Beaker.

Shoot. Forgot about that. I continued dressing as if she'd asked a normal question, like What time is it? "What patch?"

"What patch? The annoying tracking patch we're all ordered to wear. TL told you to wear yours on your stomach."

I zipped up my skirt while my brain formulated a dozen different responses and my heart raced with the lie I was about to tell. "It gave me a rash. So TL told me to take it off while I'm here at the ranch."

Staring Beaker straight in her bold eyeliner eyes, I showed her a hint of concern mixed with solid honesty. "And yours? It hasn't irritated your skin, has it?"

She shook her pink head but continued to study me like she wasn't quite sure whether or not I'd told her the truth.

I glanced beyond her to Bruiser, who quickly looked away. I got the distinct impression TL had removed her patch as well.

Someone knocked on our door, and I checked my bedside clock in immediate reaction. Ten minutes until my next session. Good. Not running late. I'd developed quite a bit of paranoia over that issue.

"Enter," Bruiser commanded in an obvious attempt at copying TL's voice.

David opened the door, and my whole body immediately warmed. "Not bad, Bruiser."

She grinned. "Thanks."

He switched his attention to me, making my heart kick my ribs. Slowly, he did a once-over, from the top of my head to the toes of my silver heels and back up again. I fought the urge not to cover my gangly legs. At least the tanning bed in town that Audrey made me lie in had taken the ghostly glow from my body.

"Isn't she hot?" Bruiser bounced her brows.

David cleared his throat. "Change of plans. We're all meeting in the barn in ten. Not Chapling's lab." David looked me over once more and then quickly left and closed the door.

"Well, I think you're hot," Bruiser said.

I curved my lips upward, although I really didn't feel like a smile. "Thanks, Bruiser."

She hugged me. "You're going to do fine on this mission. Don't sweat it. Isn't that right, Beaker?"

Beaker sniffed as a response.

Oh, well, at least I had Bruiser's support.

"We're all done here." Audrey began folding my model clothes. "Go ahead and get ready for your next meeting."

I unzipped my skirt, thinking back to David. He could've at least said I looked nice. Then again David hadn't said a whole lot to me in the past two weeks. Not since I broke into laughter at the news that his dad was up for sale. And my gut still guiltily clenched every time I recalled the whole thing.

David had to understand that was a nervous reaction. Did he actually think I'd find something so tragic funny?

Being the social reject I was, I hadn't ventured into the topic with him. And I'd had plenty of opportunities to do so over the past weeks. Maybe the whole thing would magically resolve itself.

Right.

Grow up, GiGi. You need to apologize.

But it felt strange, *me* apologizing to *him*. Ever since I came here he'd been the one in the wrong. Lying to me, tricking me. I hated to admit it but I liked having the upper hand.

And how immature was that?

Ashamed at my shallow thoughts, I changed back into my jeans and T-shirt. If I left right now, I could catch David alone before our next training. Apologize, clear my conscience.

I ran for the door and zipped down the hall to David's room.

Adam, one of his roommates, answered my knock. "Sorry, not here. Check below."

"Thanks." I bolted to the elevator, rode four levels down, and ran to the conference room. Empty. I spun around and sprinted to the hall with all the locked doors. My gaze fell on the one I had seen David go through two weeks ago. No use knocking. No one would answer if I did.

I darted to the computer lab, keyed my code, and stuck my head in. "Chapling?"

Crash. Bang. "Ow! What?"

"Seen David?"

"No."

I peeked at my watch. *Shoot.* Only five minutes until my next training. It wasn't enough time to check the common area. I'd have to apologize to David later.

Chapling waddled out from behind the patch panel rubbing his head. "Come in a little quieter next time. I'm an old man. My heart can't handle your youth."

"You're not that old. You're only thirty-five."

"Old enough to be your father. Fifteen years away from half a century. Factor in pollution, hormones in meat, artificial sweeteners, preservatives, fertilizer, and thermal pulsations emitted from this equipment." He swept his pudgy arm around the room. "And I might die tomorrow."

"How much caffeine have you had?"

"A pot of coffee and some soda."

I narrowed my eyes. "How many sodas?"

He coughed a mumbled answer.

"How many?"

Guilty as ever, he lowered his gaze to the floor. "Six."

"Chaaapliiing . . ." Much like TL and David, I had taken on a guardian role with Chapling. Go figure, me a parent. But he just *couldn't* take care of himself. If it weren't for TL, David, and me, Chapling would probably never eat anything remotely healthy or see the outdoors.

I tapped my watch. "Don't be late." The only person with a worse time problem than me was Chapling. Funny how I, queen of forgetfulness, reminded somebody else to watch the clock.

He waved me off. "Yeahyeahyeah. See ya there."

I strode toward the barn with two minutes to spare, sure I'd be the first one. Or at least the second. Maybe I'd have a chance to talk to David after all. I slid open the metal door, and everyone turned to stare. I double-checked my watch, then cast a quick glance to the clock hanging on the wall. Same time.

TL shaded his eyes from the late-afternoon sun shining in behind me. "Come on in, GiGi."

Gathered around a tall, wooden table stood Jonathan, TL, David, and Wirenut.

TL tapped his finger to the blueprints spread across the table. "These are the plans for the modeling school. Chapling hacked into Romanov's computer system and retrieved them. Wirenut has analyzed them, comparing them to similar buildings and security systems throughout Europe. He's come up with various scenarios GiGi may encounter while inside."

I slipped on my glasses and stepped up next to Wirenut.

He scooted over. "Want me to wait for Chapling?"

"I just saw him. He should be on his way."

Shaking his head, TL unclipped his cell phone from his belt. "I'll text him."

Text him? Oooh, Chapling's in trouble now.

Wirenut swept his hand over the plans. "Okay, here goes. Romanov's modeling school is three stories. Bottom's for shows, middle's where the girls get prepped, top's the offices."

"How 'bout rooms?" I readjusted my glasses. "Where do the models stay?"

TL replaced his cell phone. "It isn't a school in the literal sense. It's for finishing. Where models make their debut. You, Jonathan, David, and I will have a suite at a nearby hotel."

A *suite at a nearby hotel?* With TL and Jonathan? And David? I'd be the only girl on this trip. I glanced at each of them. They were studying the blueprints, obviously unfazed by the revelation that we would all be living together in very close quarters.

Wirenut drew penciled Xs on various spots over the plans. "My preliminary projections show standard video monitoring throughout. These will include optical sensors, so don't look directly into the cameras. You'll be scanned, ID'd, and entered in their computer system."

"I can extract the info if that mistakenly happens," I said. Probably the easiest thing I *would* do on this mission.

"Two weeks from now you'll be so well trained it won't"—TL accentuated the *t* in *won't*—"mistakenly happen."

O-kay. Nothing like the pressure of perfection to make me feel comfortable.

"Sorrysorrysorry." Chapling suddenly appeared, shuffling in from the back where the horses were corralled. "I'm here. Only a few minutes late. Only a few."

I peered around the barn wondering where he'd come from. Not through the main door like me. Maybe a secret passage? Hidden tunnel? Concealed cave? Or maybe a plain old simple back door. All this spy stuff made my imagination run wild.

David reached under the table and pulled out a stool. Chapling climbed up with a grunt.

TL cupped him on the shoulder. "Don't worry about it. Let's get down to business." He quickly repeated all the earlier information.

Wirenut penciled tick marks on the third floor of the plans. "Let's focus on the offices first. They have the most advanced security. Each door has one of three locking devices—either a kemot semiconductor, spoar OAK, or Bearn pamp. They'll work off various configurations of optonet modes, integrated wireless, and IC sock tubes."

Excitement kicked my heart a beat. I'd never actually seen this stuff, only heard about it. "In addition to optonet modes, doesn't the spoar OAK have a series of automated levilon strobes? They're nonspecified nel fuses working in conjunction with a row of thermal ferrit coders."

"Oooh, oooh." Chapling bounced on his stool. "What if instead of the ferrit coders they had unction sizers and oscilloscope meters? Then we'd get a sort of ENAM closure with ruptible del pipes and voltage suppression istors."

I laughed. "Yeah, but if they had micro murotos, it'd be a xican with vashiy fuses."

Chapling laughed so hard that he snorted. "Oh . . ." He grabbed a handkerchief from his back pocket and wiped his eyes behind his glasses. "That is . . ." Snort, snort, laugh, laugh. "So funny." He slapped his knee. "You kill me. You come up with the funniest stuff."

Until meeting Chapling, I'd never considered myself humorous. But in the weeks I'd known him, I cracked more jokes than I had in probably my whole life. We understood each other on a geeky level.

He took a deep breath. "Oh, goodness. Okay. I'm done now."

We smiled at each other, and I realized TL, David, Jonathan, and Wirenut were all wide-eyed, staring at us.

Welcome to Geek 101.

TL cleared his throat. "Wirenut, please continue."

Ignoring my nerdy embarrassment, I pushed my glasses up and refocused on the modeling school's blueprints.

Wirenut expertly outlined the entire school, including every room, hallway, bathroom, and office. He detailed the latest technology and the different scenarios I might encounter in each room. Everything from motion detectors and infrared video to microphoto recorders and gallium probes.

As I listened to him, it became clear why he'd been recruited by the IPNC. Wirenut, literally, was an electronic genius.

He paused to spread a transparent film over the blueprints. "Now bombs."

Bombs? No one had said anything about bombs.

"It's my opinion," Wirenut forged on, apparently unfazed by my sudden jerk-to-attention, "the microsnipet GiGi will extract will be rigged with explosives."

He went on to describe diode arrays and spectro components. But I barely heard a word, as focused on *bombs* and *explosives* as I was.

"That'll do it." Wirenut unwrapped a candy bar and took a bite. "Whaddaya think?"

TL nodded. "Very well done."

"Thanks."

TL looked across the table at me, and I got this nauseating feeling he was going to put me on the spot. "Repeat back everything Wirenut said."

I swallowed. Why me? Why not David or Jonathan? They were going on the trip, too. And oh, jeez, I totally missed the whole last part.

Taking off my glasses, I cleaned them as my brain clicked everything into order. If I blew my nose, it'd buy me some time, but I didn't have a tissue. I replaced my glasses and looked at everyone. They were all silently watching me. Beside me, Wirenut shifted, putting his shoulder right against mine.

It's silly, but the slight, warm contact brought me such comfort. I took a deep breath, opened my mouth, and spoke. Successfully. I reiterated everything, even the part I thought I'd missed. I only forgot one thing and considered throwing in a DTG module to cover my gap in memory, but chose honesty instead. "I'm sorry. I can't remember the type of discharge tubes used in the last bomb."

"Wow." Chapling rapid-fire clapped. "Is she smart or what?" Smart? I didn't feel so smart. I should've remembered the discharge tubes.

One corner of TL's mouth lifted in a sort of half smile. "Nice job. You're the first person I've ever worked with who has recalled their technology briefing in such detail."

"Oh." And to think I'd been sweating over the identity of a couple of tubes.

"That's a wrap." TL rolled the plans and tucked them beneath his arm. "Dinner in ten."

He strode from the barn, leaving me alone with the rest of the guys.

"I'm impressed," Jonathan rasped, "with you two teenagers. It's comforting to know you're on my side of the law."

Wirenut and I looked at each other with matching cheesy grins. "Thanks," we answered in unison.

Chapling hopped down from his stool. "Gotta get back to work. Gotta get back." He and Jonathan headed toward the door, and right before they exited, Chapling turned back. "You go, girl."

I laughed at his use of slang.

Wirenut put his arm around my shoulder. "Don't worry about anything. You've got this mission in the bag." He gave me a quick squeeze. "Coming to dinner?"

"Be there in a few. And Wirenut?"

"Hmm?"

"I'm really wowed by your knowledge. I wanted you to know."

He waved me off. "It's no big deal."

I doubted that. His shy, evasive expression said my compliment made him proud. My heart got all fuzzy. I suddenly wanted to praise someone else.

Another quick squeeze and he was gone, leaving David and me alone.

"You've made quite an impression on everyone."

His words were flattering, but the tone of his voice didn't match. I missed his warm smile and easy bantering.

"I'm sorry, David, for laughing about your father's situation. I don't know why I laughed. I know you probably think I'm inconsiderate and insensitive, but I don't find anything funny about his kidnapping. And I can't begin to understand what you're going through right now. I have a few wonderful memories of my parents, but that's it. At least I know they're dead." I should. I was right beside them when the plane crashed.

I took off my reading glasses to clear his image. "I've always had closure. But you? You've been in limbo for years. Not knowing if your dad is dead or alive, being tortured or treated nicely. And now you know he's alive, but there's no guarantee we'll bring him home. I'm so sorry you've gone through those emotions. I promise you I *will* decode his whereabouts from the microsnipet. I won't fail you or the IPNC. And I am so, so sorry I laughed at the situation."

I fell silent. I'd never spoken so much in my life.

David stared at me, expressionless. The more he stared, the slower and deeper my heart thudded. It never occurred to me that he *wouldn't* forgive me. Now I wondered.

He cleared his throat, then swallowed. "Apology accepted." He crossed the cement floor and kept right on going out the open barn door, leaving me standing there alone.

Time heals all wounds. A social worker told me that once. I sure hoped it held true in all situations. Because I couldn't picture my life without David's friendship.

***

One week later I strode into the barn wearing my brand-new gray yoga pants and white sport tank top. I felt a little like Bruiser all decked out in my athletic wear.

The teeny shorts still sat in their bag right where I'd left them almost a month ago.

Adam and Erin from Team One sat on the mats with Beaker and Wirenut, stretching and talking. I went over and joined them.

Jonathan, TL, and David were busy hanging punching bags from the roof beams.

Mystic, Parrot, and Bruiser wandered in a minute or so later. I caught their eyes and tapped my watch. *Ha ha, I'm here before you.* They all made faces at me.

The three of them joined us on the mats, and we continued stretching. I had to admit, this stretching thing felt pretty darn good. It was my favorite part of PT.

"Okay," Jonathan rasped. "Everyone up and over here."

We all filed across the barn to where six punching bags now hung.

"We're going to pair you up two to a bag. We're practicing punches today." Jonathan lined up with a bag and delivered a slow-motion punch. "Notice my left foot is slightly in front of my right. Notice my thumb is tucked down. Watch how my arm rotates slowly halfway there so my fist makes contact with the bag straight on."

In slow motion, he demonstrated a few more times and then sped up as he side-shuffled around the bag.

Okay, I could probably do the slow-motion punch thing. But the lightning-quick, side-shuffle thing? No way.

Jonathan paired me with Erin from Team One.

"You first," I insisted.

She did three slow-motion punches and immediately went into the speedy side-shuffle maneuver, making her way around the bag.

I enviously watched her, hoping, *hoping,* I would do half as well. Of course, she'd been doing this a lot longer than me.

"Switch," Jonathan shouted.

With a sigh, I lined up with the bag. *Here went nothing.* I positioned my left foot slightly in front of the right. Concentrating on my thumb position, I made a fist. In extra-extra-slow motion, I brought it back and then moved it forward, rotating halfway as Jonathan had demonstrated.

My fist barely grazed the bag.

I inched forward a little bit and did the whole thing again, attentive to my form, focusing on the instructions Jonathan had given.

In my peripheral vision, the others were already shuffling around their bags, throwing punches.

I blocked out the fact they were all ahead of me and refocused on my technique.

TL came up beside me. "You're thinking too hard. Just try one. Let your body take over."

Purposefully blanking my brain, I threw a punch. It was a little awkward, but I had to admit, it felt better than the slow-motion ones.

I tried again. Better.

And again. Better.

With each one, my confidence was boosted.

"Good," TL encouraged. "Now shuffle. Don't think. Shuffle."

I side-shuffled around the bag, throwing uncoordinated punches. As the minutes ticked by, my feet and arms developed an in-sync rhythm.

My vision zeroed in on the bag as I continued throwing punches. Sweat trickled down my neck. Adrenaline surged through my veins. I had the unnerving urge to growl or grunt or something equally aggressive.

"Stop," Jonathan commanded.

Breathing heavily, I stepped back and glanced over to David. He gave me a nod of approval, and I smiled.

I felt tougher right now than I had in my whole life. I was ready to kick some bad-guy booty!

***

Four days later, I stepped up onto an actual runway.

My modeling instructor, Audrey, handed up an umbrella to me. "One of the designers you'll be working with always accessorizes with umbrellas. There're only three days left before you leave. You can do this. I *know* you can."

Down the center of the barn ran a long, gleaming wood runway, about four feet off the ground. On both sides sat all the members of Teams One and Two, including TL, Jonathan, and Chapling. Everyone held a camera.

Audrey tapped beside my high heels. "This is an exact replica of the runways you'll be walking down. And they"—she nodded at everyone—"are here to mimic the reporters and photographers. It's important that you don't get distracted by all the flashes that will be going off."

I glanced down the length of the runway. It seemed to stretch for eternity. I ran my gaze over everyone sitting on both sides. They all silently stared back.

Swallowing, I fixed my focus on the barn doors and nodded. "Ready."

Audrey squeezed my ankle. "Smile. Suck in stomach. Shoulders back. And don't forget to pop your hip." She stepped away. "Lights."

The overhead lights went out, sending the barn into darkness. The runway was lit down both sides with a soft yellow glow. Everyone began flashing cameras.

Fighting the urge to squint against the flashes, I took my first step, and then the next, falling into the strut Audrey had taught me. *Smile. Suck in stomach. Shoulders back. Pop hip. Smile. Suck in stomach. Shoulders back. Pop hip.* My slinky blue dress swished against my upper thighs. I felt . . . sexy.

I got to the end and twirled my umbrella (Audrey didn't even tell me to do that). I pivoted and strutted back down the runway. I got to the end, and everyone broke into applause.

And I leaped, literally, for joy. I did it!

***

"GIGI? GIGI, are you okay?"

Feeling as miserable as a worn-out hard drive, I shuffled past Bruiser and, with a groan, flopped face-first onto my comfy bed.

"What is it? Are you sick? Dude, this is like the worst time ever for you to be sick. You guys leave for Ushbania tomorrow." Bruiser picked up the phone between our beds and punched some numbers. "I'm calling TL. He needs to know you're sick."

I slid my right arm from beneath me and plopped it over the phone, knocking it to the floor. "I don't want TL knowing I got my period."

"Oh." Bruiser picked it up. "That sucks."

Miserably I nodded. I was leaving tomorrow for the most important event in my life, and Mother Nature had decided to give me a farewell party. Perfect. I *loved* being a girl. Beside me I heard Bruiser opening and closing drawers.

She touched my shoulder a few seconds later. "Here. Some muscle relaxers from when I sprained my neck."

Bruiser always had some sort of injury going on.

Gritting against the cramps, I rolled onto my side. Her KICK SOME BOOTY T-shirt greeted me. In her small, outstretched hand lay two horse pills.

"Those prescription?"

She nodded.

"You're not supposed to take other people's prescriptions." Jeez, did I sound like a nerd or what?

Bruiser rolled her green eyes. "You're such a goody-goody. Take 'em already. Not like it's gonna kill you."

I did feel like a goody-goody, always following the rules. Even *I* sometimes annoyed myself. That couldn't be good. "What's the brand name?" I had to at least show some caution.

Bringing them close to her freckled face, she inspected them. "Huh. Whaddaya know? Motrin."

Motrin? A recognizable over-the-counter name. Not canpifretrin, asmopowprin, tyquilnoleny, or some other crazy long word no one ever heard of. "I'll take one. If I need the other, I'll ask you for it." Better to be on the safe side.

"You're so cautious," she teased.

I stuck out my tongue, and we both laughed.

"Hey." David peeked into our open doorway, and my stomach whoopdy-whooped. I saw him every day, but the unexpected sightings did it to me every time. "TL wants to see everyone in the common area."

Tossing the pill in my mouth, I washed it down with hours-old, warm soda.

David walked in. "What are you taking? What's wrong? Is that a pill? Are you sick?"

His concern turned my insides all mushy. It'd been two weeks since my apology to him, and we'd managed to return to a stable friendship. Nothing like before, though. His emotions surrounding his dad made him more serious and focused.

Bruiser held out her hand. "Calm down. No big deal. She got her p—"

"Points taken off my last exam and it, um, gave me a headache. That's right, I have a headache, and Bruiser gave me some pills." I smiled, even though my heart thundered, and I silently prayed that David would *immediately* drop the subject.

His lips curved up knowingly. *Oooh.*

"Be quick about it. TL doesn't like waiting."

As soon as David left, I slung my pillow at Bruiser. "I'm going to kill you," I hissed. "I can't believe you almost told him I'm on the big P."

She laughed. "So what? Not like it's a national secret that women have them."

"Well, no, but—"

"Come on."

I followed Bruiser down the carpeted hall to the common area, where the double doors sat closed. Strange, these doors were never shut. Bruiser and I exchanged curious looks, then she raised her fist and knocked.

"Enter," TL commanded.

She grasped the knob on the right, I took the one on the left, and we both pushed . . .

"Surprise!"

Balloons. Everywhere. Red, white, blue, pink, purple. With multicolored ribbons streaming in curls from each one. And people. Standing and grinning, holding glasses of champagne. Staring at me. All the members of Team One. Jonathan, TL, Chapling, and David. Wirenut, Mystic, Parrot, and the newly dyed, yellow-haired Beaker, who wore her usual smirk.

Bruiser smiled at me as she went to join the crowd. Twerp. She knew about this.

TL brought me a glass. "It's your send-off party. We do one for all first missions."

No one had ever, *ever,* thrown me a party. With a grin I knew split my face in two, I took the glass.

"To GiGi's first mission." TL lifted his champagne. "May her flight over and back and everything in between be successful."

I joined everyone in taking a sip. Wow. Real champagne. Not some sparkling white grape juice. Of course all of us minors had the equivalent of one sip. Hey, one sip's better than nothing.

Wait a minute. Did he say flight over? Of course he said flight over. How *did you think you would get there?* Sail across the ocean? But I didn't fly. TL knew that. I couldn't fly. I absolutely couldn't get on a plane.

I glanced around the room to see if anyone else had noticed the mistake. But they were all talking. Someone cranked on the stereo. Mystic and Wirenut walked toward me, smiling. Wirenut's lips moved, but I didn't hear a word.

The walls narrowed in, and I swallowed the sickness in my mouth. Champagne, even a sip, on an empty stomach with a muscle relaxer. Not a good combination with *FLYING*.

Heat flashed through my body, then icy dampness. I swayed.

"Somesome thingthing's wrongwrong withwith GiGiGiGi." Parrot's voice echoed through my ears.

Mystic doubled into twin thick-necked clairvoyants. They both grabbed me. I squeezed my eyes shut, and it made the dizziness worse.

"Lay her down on the carpet," TL instructed.

My whole world tilted. I pried my eyelids open. Fuzzy doubles of everyone's faces crowded my space. I tried to push back.

TL and his duplicate put their hands on my shoulder. "Lie still."

I swallowed another wave of nausea.

"She's gonna hurl," both Beakers announced a little too enthusiastically.

The TLs unsnapped my jeans and pulled my T-shirt out. "Give her some breathing room." The blurry doubles took a step back. "Has she eaten today?"

"I saw her sucking on a lollipop earlier." Bruiser and her twin placed a wet rag on my forehead. The coolness made me moan.

The TLs fanned me with a magazine. "Champagne on an empty stomach."

Bruiser put all four hands over her two mouths. "With a prescription muscle relaxer."

The TLs continued to fan me. "What's she taking muscle relaxers for?"

Nooo. I shook my head, and all the fuzzy doubles bounced around.

"Her period."

‹EIGHT›

Closing my eyes, I gingerly reclined my first-class seat. The sedative TL gave me hours ago was long gone. Gone before it had had a chance to kick in. I'd never thrown up so much in my life. Two times at the ranch, once in the limo on the way to the airport, two times in the terminal, and once just now in the plane's bathroom. And we hadn't even taken off yet.

If I hadn't been so nervously sick, I might have enjoyed my first time in a limo. If I didn't need to dry-heave again, I might be embarrassed that TL, Jonathan, *and* David saw me *hurling,* as Beaker so enthusiastically put it yesterday.

And Bruiser had announced to everyone that I got the big P. Oooh. She definitely had it coming when I returned from Ushbania.

If I got back. Bad guys, national security, bombs, a kidnapping. Big-time stuff. Things might not go right. I could really screw up.

Not to worry, Audrey, my modeling instructor, had reassured me when she came by the ranch to see me off. Hives had been her main concern. *Hives.* I was facing the biggest fear of my life, and she was worried about some little red rashy dots.

"Miss January, are you sure I can't get you something?"

Miss January? Oh, yeah, that's me. My modeling name. I forced my eyelids open. The flight attendant looked more nervous than I felt. Probably thought I'd throw up all over her first-class area, and she'd have to clean it up. At least in the fancy seats they call you by your name. Even if it was a fake one.

"Miss January?"

"Ginger ale after we take off," David answered for me.

With a nod, the attendant headed toward the back of the plane.

"How's she doing?" Jonathan whispered from across the aisle.

"She'll make it." David retrieved a blanket from the overhead bin. He tucked it in around me, then sat back down.

Funny how a tucked-in blanket can make a person feel better. Like armor protecting against the bad stuff. The bogeyman in a dark orphanage, shadows in an unknown foster home, or plain emptiness in my first dormitory . . .

Shaking off my momentary walk into the past, I concentrated on the here and now.

Jonathan, David, TL, and I were dressed and acting our roles for the mission. TL gave us fake passports with matching false IDs. We each had memorized our made-up backgrounds. That made twice for me in the past few months. Once when the IPNC recruited me and I became Kelly Spree/GiGi, and again for this mission.

My new modeling name? Jade January. Ridiculous or what? The IPNC actually employed a person who made up false IDs. What a job. Guess there're a lot of secret agents on missions if someone works all day creating their fake backgrounds.

In between worrying over hives and posture, Audrey picked out clothes and packed for me. She dressed me in knee-length, brown suede boots and a thigh-length, crème sweater dress. At the last second, a stylist snipped layers into my shoulder-length blond hair and made me promise not to pull it back in a ponytail. What he didn't know wouldn't kill him.

They'd also worked on David, TL, and Jonathan. David, my personal photographer, wore faded jeans, a white T-shirt, black leather jacket, and boots. He'd grown stubble and carried his camera equipment on the plane. His yum factor hit twenty on a scale of one to ten.

TL, my bodyguard, wore a black suit and matching shades. He hadn't taken the sunglasses off once. Very mysterious, serious demeanor. Other than in the limo, he hadn't spoken or showed any emotion.

Jonathan, my modeling agent, wore a white suit. A purple eye patch replaced his usual black one and matched his purple silk shirt and shoes. His bald head gleamed from where the hair stylist had buffed it. As soon as we stepped from the limo into public view, Jonathan and his cell phone had been inseparable. Part of his modeling-agent role.

"Ladies and gentlemen, this is Captain Steve Brusher speaking. Welcome aboard Air Transport commercial flight ten-eleven. Flying nonstop from San Belden, California, to Prost, Ushbania . . ."

Beneath the blanket, I dug my fingernails into my palms. I could do this. I knew I could. Just because my parents died in a plane crash didn't mean I would die in one.

" . . . It's going to be a beautiful flight today. Clear skies. Current temperatures in Prost are five above zero. We'll be reaching an altitude of thirty thousand feet . . ."

Thirty thousand feet. Really high up. Over the ocean. Something goes wrong. No place to land. Only the water. I squeezed my eyes shut and concentrated on calming breaths. *In. Then out. In. Then out.* Like TL had taught me.

" . . . flotation device beneath the seat. Should the cabin lose pressure, an oxygen mask will fall from the overhead bin. Reach up and pull the mask taut and put it over your nose and mouth. Oxygen will be flowing even though the bag does not inflate. Please place your own mask on before attending to children . . ."

I caught my breath as the memory flooded back. Six years old. Dangling oxygen masks. My dad had put his over me first. Because of him, I survived the crash. He pushed me free. I swam to the surface knowing he and Mom would be right behind.

Gripping my seat flotation. Dark. Wet. Debris popping up around me. Curling my legs up as tight as I could in the water. Searching . . . searching . . . everyone surfaced but them. *Daaaddddyyy! Mooommmmyyy!* Why didn't they surface?

"Shhh," David said softly. He smoothed a tissue over my cheeks, and I realized I was crying. He slipped his arm beneath the blanket and covered my clenched fist with his hand.

In. Then out. In. Then out. I paced my breathing, blocking everything else.

The plane slowly moved, backing away from the terminal. David ran his thumb across my fist, back and forth, in a soft caress. I gradually stopped concentrating on my breaths and focused all my energy on his tender touch. His thumb worked its way inside my fist, circling my palm and stroking the underside of my fingers.

I sighed with the release of tension and stress. He linked fingers with me and brought our hands palm to palm.

The engines roared and the plane sped down the runway. I opened my eyes and gazed out the window as the jet lifted off. The buildings and trees got smaller and smaller. Sometime later, clouds filled my view . . . and I smiled. I made it. I actually made it.

"Here's your ginger ale."

I turned my attention to the flight attendant, who placed the glass in the armrest's cup holder.

"Thank you."

David squeezed my hand as she strode off. "Better?

I nodded.

"Good." He slipped a rolled-up magazine from his jacket pocket with his free hand, spread it across his lap, flipped a few pages, then began reading.

Idly I studied the clouds outside my window, and one by one my brain cells zeroed in on our clasped hands. The warm, slightly roughened texture of his. Our linked fingers. His thumb skimming back and forth in a subconscious action. Normal. Like we had held hands hundreds of times before. Amazing how his touch provided the comfort I needed.

Was he thinking about my hand in his? He seemed preoccupied with his magazine. Maybe it was an act. Maybe he was just as focused on our hands as I was.

Then again, probably not. David was eighteen. He'd probably held hands with plenty of girls. He'd probably kissed lots, too. He'd probably even done more than that . . .

With the last thought, my palm immediately went clammy. I didn't want to stop holding hands, but I didn't want to gross him out, either.

Stupidstupidstupid.

He saw me as a little sister. He'd said so before. He held my hand like a big brother would hold a little sister's. Although his caressing thumb didn't feel very brotherly-sisterly.

Pulling his hand free from mine, he unclipped his seat belt. "Bathroom break." He took a lollipop from his jacket pocket and handed it to me. "It's grape."

How unbelievably sweet. "Thanks."

Jonathan stepped across the aisle and took David's seat. "You're looking better. Let's talk about . . ."

Grudgingly, I focused on his words, but my mind screamed, *YOU'RE IN DAVID'S SEAT, YOU BIG EYE-PATCH GALOOT!*

***

Turned out I spent most of the sixteen-hour flight beside everyone *but* David. Jonathan had carried on a brief agent/model conversation with me, more for show than anything. When he got done, TL and David were engaged in a deep conversation. It went on for so long, Jonathan fell asleep. Hours later he woke up, but David had fallen asleep. Hours after that I woke up, didn't realize I'd fallen asleep, and noticed that TL was sitting beside me. Apparently Jonathan had challenged David to a rousing game of tic-tac-toe.

Then a late-night dinner came and a movie, and everyone stayed in their shuffled-around spots. By the time the flight ended, David was back beside me, but so engrossed in his magazine that every chance of holding hands fizzled away.

Now, as we stood outside our hotel suite, I rolled my eyes at my immaturity. We were on a top secret national mission, and my biggest worry was holding hands. Jeez.

Our bellboy swiped a key card through the electronic lock, and we all filed into the suite. Romanov owned this hotel. All the models were staying at it.

Jonathan gave the young bellboy some money, and he left. TL rubbed his chin, then brushed imaginary lint from his shoulder. Our signal to get into character.

"I swear that boy stank." I flounced over to the blue velvet couch and plopped down. The perfect, spoiled-rotten model. "Haven't they heard of soap in this country?"

TL and David unsnapped the buckles from their belts, leaving two black leather straps dangling in place. Starting at the door, they worked in opposite directions, scanning every lamp, door frame, decoration, piece of furniture, light switch, and whatever else they could find. The tips of the belt buckles glowed steady green. It would blink red if it detected a bug. A brilliant device that Chapling had created years ago.

Jonathan meandered over to the marble bar. "Now, honey, you're just tired from the long trip." He took a crystal glass from a silver tray, some ice from the freezer, and poured in seltzer water. "Little bit of this, a good nap, and you'll be all better."

His light still glowing steady green, David disappeared into one of the bedrooms.

"Yuck." I plunked my high-heeled boots onto the dark wood coffee table. "If you don't have lime, I'm not drinking it. I'd rather have a regular soda."

"Regular soda?" Jonathan gasped, and I almost laughed. "Wash your mouth out. Do you know how many calories that has?"

David came out of a bedroom at the same time as TL stepped from a bathroom, both their buckle tips still glowing green. David strode across the red-carpeted living room toward me, focused intently on his buckle detection device.

"But all I've eaten today is yogurt," I whined. "One little soda won't hurt me." Amazing that people worried about stuff like calories. What a waste of valuable brain time.

"Tsk, tsk." Jonathan shook his finger at me. "Every calorie becomes a cheese dimple on your thigh."

David ran the detection device over, around, and beneath the coffee table where my feet sat propped. He scanned the couch, leaning around me and stepping over me. He squatted and inspected the underside. With every movement his cologne drifted around me, hazing my focus. Then he stopped and glanced up at me with his cheek mere inches from my thigh. He raised his dark brows in question. I furrowed mine in response. He widened his eyes and tightened his lips.

What . . . ?

Oh! Quickly I recalled the last thing Jonathan had said. "Cheese dimple," I replied. "Don't be so gross."

David went back to scanning, and I focused all 191 IQ points on Jonathan. I wouldn't have gotten distracted in the first place if David hadn't been kneeling and crawling around me.

"Let's not forget Mary Libby." Jonathan brought me my glass. "She lost her contract with Lovelace Lingerie for a dimple in her right butt cheek."

I held back a grin. Jonathan came up with the craziest lines. Who would've guessed a big, tough, mean-looking guy would play such a great modeling agent. "Oh, puh-lease. Mary Libby lost the contract because she farted on the runway."

Jonathan coughed to cover his laugh. It pleased me I'd finally caught him off guard with one of my lines.

84

"All clear." TL fastened his buckle back to his belt. "You two are almost *too* good at that."

Jonathan and I exchanged smiles. Did he like stepping out of his old self as much as I did?

TL grabbed the duffel bag that contained all our equipment for the mission. He'd had an Ushbanian IPNC contact deliver it to the hotel's front desk. "Three bedrooms. David and I will bunk in the one next to the door. Jonathan by the balcony. GiGi in the middle."

The guys each grabbed one of my beige leather suitcases, and I retrieved my matching carry-on. Why anyone needed so much luggage stretched beyond my comprehension. Apparently, models did, though.

Odd how I'd lived my whole life out of one knocked-around, dinged, Goodwill hard case.

They deposited my things in the middle bedroom, and it occurred to me that TL had put me in the center on purpose. Probably so they could protect me if anything happened. Another reality check. Bad guys might break in.

I wandered into my private bathroom with its whirlpool tub, white marble sink, blue tiles, and shiny gold fixtures. It was pretty darn fancy for a restroom.

Oooh, expensive body wash and shampoo. Imported from France.

Snatching them off the counter, I unscrewed the caps, inhaled . . . freesia. My favorite. And a loofah to go with it!

"Hey." David tapped on the open bathroom door. "Want me to help you unpack?"

Quickly, I fumbled everything back, my stomach fluttering with embarrassment. He'd caught me excited over shampoo and a loofah. I could be such a dork. "Urn, that's okay. I can handle it."

"You sure? I didn't think you knew how. You're still living out of that ratty suitcase at the ranch."

Who was he? The suitcase police? "I got it. I'm fine." How hard could it be to hang up some clothes and put stuff in drawers?

He held up his hands. "All right."

The doorbell buzzed, and everyone broke into action. David and I sprinted to the living room. He grabbed his camera from his bag and trucked it over to the balcony windows. I snatched a fashion magazine from the coffee table and plopped down on the couch. Jonathan whipped out his cell phone and slipped onto a wrought-iron bar stool. We were all in our preassigned positions, ready for any possibility.

TL peered through the peephole. He turned back to us and blinked his left eye twice. Our signal that one of Romanov Schalmosky's men stood outside. My heart raced with the knowledge that a real, live bad guy loomed only a few feet away.

TL rubbed his chin, then brushed imaginary lint from his shoulder. *Get into character.* David lifted his camera and began clicking off pictures. I quickly popped gum in my mouth and proceeded to flip through the magazine, as bored and spoiled as ever. Jonathan struck up a fake conversation on his cell phone. TL slipped on his shades and opened the door.

The bad guy stepped into our suite. I tried to seem indifferent to the intrusion, but jeez, the guy was huge. Like an evil-power-lifter kind of huge.

"Mizz Jade January?"

Cool Count Dracula accent. I blew a bubble and snapped it.

"Yeah?"

"Joo are cordially invited to Mizter Schalmosky's home." He cut his gaze to David, Jonathan, TL, then back to me. "Alone."

‹NINE›

‹%bLk.co;/Tpircs+!›
  ‹=*ptth *= l!attstli!/ %ocsorrtetat%›
  ‹#n8li# :Ius en/: g‹bsu›3‹bsu›g›

Ow! I scowled down at TL's hand squeezing my forearm, then over at him. He gave me a barely discernible shake of the head. How had he done that? How'd he know I zoned out?

I glanced at my watch. Exactly thirty-seven minutes and two seconds had passed since we left our hotel room.

The elevator in Romanov's castle dinged, and his goon motioned us to step out. I clicked my brain cells into focus and promised myself I wouldn't let my thoughts veer again. I really did need to work on that. Getting sidetracked was one of my biggest weaknesses. Especially at some of the most inopportune moments, like this one. When I was about to meet the ultimate bad guy, Romanov Schalmosky.

Thank God TL had insisted on coming. Thank God Romanov's goon let him. As my bodyguard, it actually made a lot of sense for TL to escort me. David and Jonathan, however, stayed at the hotel. Having our team split up made me edgy. Maybe that's why my mind had wandered to code. TL had trained me for just this sort of thing, but reality sure differed from simulation. A lot.

We strode down a long tiled-floor hallway lined with gleaming wood walls. I concentrated on holding my head high and shoulders back like the modeling instructor had taught me. At the very end of the hallway stood a door. It slowly opened as we approached.

I fought the urge to scope out the cameras. How else would they have known to open the door? Unless they'd installed potentio detectors in the floor or maybe laser sensors in the walls. *Neat.* My pulse raced with geeky tech excitement. I started to reach for my notepad and pencil at the exact same second I remembered I wasn't GiGi. I was Jade January, model. And models didn't carry notepads and pencils.

Another one of Romanov's goons, as huge as the first one, appeared in the open doorway holding a machine gun. My eyes and mouth popped open in sync. TL stepped in front, shielding me, and I grabbed onto the back of his suit jacket and scooted in close. Exactly what GiGi *or* Jade January would've done.

Goon number one, standing behind us, spoke to Goon number two with the machine gun. Their Ushbanian sounded deep and guttural, like they had a bad cold. Whatever Goon number one said made Goon number two move aside.

"Joo may enter," said Goon number one. "Mizter Schalmosky iz waiting."

TL slid his hand around and dislodged my fingers from his jacket. Reluctantly I released him, but wanted more than anything to stay pressed up securely against him.

As we entered a tiny waiting room, another door automatically opened, and a woman appeared. She was small, business-sophisticated, with Hawaiian features and shiny dark hair slicked back into a low bun.

"Good afternoon, Miss January." The beautiful woman extended her hand, and I shook it. "My name is Nalani Kai. I'm Mr. Schalmosky's personal assistant. Please don't be frightened by the formalities." She indicated Goon number one and Goon number two with a nod.

I couldn't help but smile at her. Her friendly demeanor eased my nerves. "Thank you for inviting me."

She nodded again graciously, and focused beyond my shoulder to where TL stood. Although her expression didn't change, I got the distinct impression she thought my bodyguard had it going on. *Hey, he's a hottie,* I wanted to tell her, *go for it.* They seemed about the same age. Why not?

Oh, yeah, she worked for the bad guys. Bummer. Maybe she didn't know they were bad. She seemed too nice to be working for the other side.

Nalani led us down another gleaming wood hallway and around a corner. She motioned us to proceed through an archway into an office as big as our living room back at the ranch. Straight ahead at a desk sat a gray-haired man dressed in a dark suit.

Behind him a bank of windows looked out over an indoor garden. Beyond that, snow drifted against the greenhouse walls. A stone fireplace to the right warmed the room to the point of too hot.

The gray-haired man peered up from his paperwork as we entered. Yellow tinted his skin. Beside him sat an oxygen tank. A tube ran from it into his nose.

He nodded at Nalani. "Zank you. Zat'll be all." Cool Count Dracula accent, like his goons. "Joo, sir"—he nodded to TL—"may stand against zee back wall."

As TL moved to the rear of the room, I wondered how he liked being given an order when he was always the one in command.

The gray-haired man came around the front of the desk, rolling his oxygen tank with him. It clicked, sending out an audible burst of oxygen.

He stood eye level with me as he extended his hand. "Welcome to my home. I am Romanov Schalmosky." His spooky, pitch-black eyes sent a chill dancing down my spine.

I accepted his hand. *Omigod, I'm shaking hands with THE bad guy.* "Thank you for inviting me, Mr. Schalmosky. I'm Jade January. So nice to meet you."

"Please, call me Romanov."

"Thank you, Romanov. Feel free to call me Jade."

He shook his head. "I vill call you Mizz January."

Okay. "As you wish."

He indicated the two brown leather chairs in front of his desk. I sat in one and he took the other. He held out his hand, and I stared at it a second . . . *oh!*

Ick. I have to hold hands with him?

Trying my best to act flattered that he wanted to hold hands with me, I reached out. He placed my palm on his knee and with a pat, settled his cool, dry hand on top. I fought the urge to glare at TL.

"Mizz January, I like to meet with all my models before their debut at my school. I enjoy a superior reputation for producing zee best of zee best. You vill maintain zee upmost ladylike demeanor. If any of my associates tell me differently, you vill be returned to zee States without any questions asked. Do vee understand each other?"

I swallowed the enormous nervous lump in my throat. "Yes, sir."

"It iz your place to look pretty and be a lady. If you have a tendency to snoop, correct zee imperfection now. If I catch you somewhere you are not supposed to be, you vill suffer zee consequences."

Consequences? What consequences?

He patted my hand. "Zere. Enough said. You vill be famous. I guarantee it. All my models are."

I didn't want to be famous. I wanted to get the H-E-double-L out of here. This guy scared the crap out of me.

"Get some rest. Take zee day off. Tomorrow night I am hozting a party for all my models. I know your agent and photographer traveled vith you. They are more than velcome to attend." He lifted my hand from his knee and pressed wet lips to the back of it.

Yuk.

"And you, my love, vill be my date."

What?!

***

David approached TL and me as we entered our hotel suite. "We downloaded new intel from Chapling," David said as we closed the door. "The statue and microsnipet may be at Romanov's home."

Numbly, I shuffled to my room.

"What's wrong with her?" I heard David ask. "What happened?"

I sank down on my bed, staring at the red carpet. Machine guns. Big, scary goons. A creepy old guy with a not-so-cool Count Dracula accent and spooky, pitch-black eyes. Consequences if I snooped. *And you, my love, vill be my date.*

With a nauseated stomach, I closed my eyes and lay back. What had I been thinking, accepting this mission? I was in way over my head. Calm, cool, and collected were not in my vocabulary. I was scared out of my genius mind. Seriously, TL had to find someone else. He had to. I couldn't do this.

As I rolled over and curled up on the bed, TL's words echoed through my head. *From the start, you proved to be adept at your cover. You went about your day-to-day activities smoothly, naturally, and without second thoughts. It's almost as if you've been here for months instead of a few weeks. I'm impressed with how seamlessly you merged into this world.*

I wouldn't be sending you if I didn't have complete confidence in your ability. Always remember that.

Whether I wanted it or not, our nation's security depended on this mission. TL had put all his faith in me. David needed my skills to find his dad.

"Hey."

I opened my eyes. David stood alongside the bed, staring down at me.

"TL told me what happened. You're going to be fine, GiGi. None of us will let anything happen to you. I promise. I know seeing all this stuff in real life is scary as hell. Especially for someone like you. I grew up in this world. You've been a part of it for only a couple of months. No one I know has ever been thrown into a mission in such a short time. We all recognize that. But let me tell you something. The IPNC would never have sent you, no matter the time crunch of the mission, if they weren't completely confident you would do it. Okay? You *can* do this. I know you can."

If Mr. Share weren't involved, would David still be saying all this? Immediately I pushed the negative question from my mind. Of course, he would still be saying it. Last thing I needed was to question my own teammates.

"Thanks." I sat up. Okay. I could do this. I could.

David smiled. "You're welcome. We have nothing to do but wait for this party. Romanov has left strict orders that none of the models leave the hotel until tomorrow night."

"Must be nice to order people around like that."

David chuckled. "Yeah, really. If you feel like cards, come on out."

I took a long bath instead and then tried to get some sleep. The next day, I gave myself a manicure and pedicure. I practiced my modeling walk. I practiced putting on makeup. I keyed code. I watched a little TV. I tried to sleep, but didn't. When room service arrived, I ate a little bit. I went back over everything in my mind. I'd never been so wound up in my life. I just wanted everything to be over with.

All three guys tried talking to me. I couldn't focus on a conversation. I managed to sleep some. And finally, *finally,* it was time to get ready for the party.

I dug in my purse for a lollipop and the "cheat sheet." *Here,* Audrey had said, handing me the paper. *This will help you know what to wear when.*

I had never used a cheat sheet before in my life. How ridiculous was it that I needed one for clothing?

After slipping the banana lollipop in my mouth, I scanned the typed paper. Two columns. The left column listed all the possible functions, situations, or outings I would encounter as a model. The right column detailed which outfit and accessories I should wear.

Party at Romanov's home I found on the left, looked across to the right . . . *One-piece silver jumpsuit.*

I groaned. I *hated* the silver jumpsuit. It was so hard to get on and off.

Forty-five minutes later I emerged from my room in the skin tight one-piece, complete with silver stilettos and dangling diamond earrings. Too bad the front of the jumpsuit V-necked down between my boobs. It was like zero degrees outside. What I really needed to be wearing was a turtleneck and a pair of flannel-lined pants.

"I'm ready."

TL, Jonathan, and David all glanced up from the living room, where they sat discussing a map. No one uttered a word. They just stared at me.

Automatically, my brain clicked through a checklist, making sure I hadn't forgotten something.

Hair not in ponytail. *Check.*

Makeup. *Check.*

Earrings. *Check.*

Underwear. *Check.*

Jumpsuit zipped. *Che—*

Jonathan let out a low, slow whistle. "Zowee, girl. If I were twenty years younger, you'd have to beat me off with a stick."

"Oh." My face heated with his compliment. I immediately looked at David, but he diverted his gaze.

TL rose from the couch. "I need to throw on a tie. Give her the devices."

He headed to his room and disappeared inside.

Jonathan followed. "TL, one last thing . . ." he was saying as he left David and me alone.

David grabbed two black boxes from the end table, one square and one rectangular, and crossed the room to me. "You'll wear two pieces of equipment tonight. A tracking device and the microsnipet detector."

David flipped the top on the square box. Inside lay a tiny brown flake. He pressed his index finger to it. "It's a freckle. As long as this stays on your body, I'll—I mean, we'll know where you are."

He took a step closer, and his cologne zinged my synapses. In my stilettos, we stood eye to eye. He searched my face, neck, and chest. "So . . . so where do you want it?"

Was it possible I affected him more than he let on? My heart danced a happy pitter-patter.

"It should be on your neck or chest. Unlike cotton fabrics, some, like this with metallic threads, tend to interrupt the signal, and you were in a cotton turtleneck yesterday. Romanov has seen your face. He'll know if there's something different. So neck or chest?"

I didn't answer. I couldn't. His nearness made me mute. I shook my head.

"Saliva adheres it." He touched his tongue to it and then pressed the brown flake to my collarbone. As he held it there, his dark gaze traveled slowly up my neck and face and locked onto my eyes. We stared at each other with only inches of space between us. I became hyperaware of his moist finger, his breath skittering across my cheek, and my heart pounding so hard it reached my ears.

"Ready." TL emerged from his room, followed by Jonathan. "Got the finger pads?"

"Uh . . ." David took a quick step back, and I grabbed onto a bar stool to steady myself. "Yeah. Right here."

He opened the rectangular box. Side by side lay the four transparent pads that I had assisted Chapling in developing. One for each of us, specially designed for our middle fingers. Thin, silicone-based, invisible once in place. Activated by magnetics. They were programmed to send a quick, hot jolt if one of us touched the statue containing the microsnipet.

David passed the box around. I pressed my middle finger to the remaining pad, and it suctioned on like it had a life of its own.

TL checked his watch. "Let's go."

Our black limo drove through town out into the country. For miles around nothing existed but fields and woods, everything white from a fresh winter snow. We pulled up to Romanov's castle exactly twenty-seven minutes and thirteen seconds later. I knew this because timekeeping was part of David's job, and he'd just told us.

We cleared the guards and entered the iron gates. Where it had been empty yesterday, shiny cars now lined the cobblestone driveway. Even in the nighttime, the vibrant colors stood out. Red Rolls-Royce. White Ferrari. Yellow Porsche. Orange Mercedes. And the variety went on and on.

Pretty impressive, if I said so myself.

Tiny, white lights twinkled in the trees and shrubs lining Romanov's castle and property. Like a fairy tale, only my prince was a creepy, old guy.

One big goon opened our limo's door, and we all piled out. I squinted against the icy-cold air and pulled my white, faux fur coat around me. The goon escorted us up the castle's front steps. Not the same entrance TL and I had used yesterday. We'd entered through the side.

Two large wooden doors I estimated at twenty feet tall opened, gushing out warmth, light, and music. We stepped in and the doors closed behind us. Standing on a marble landing, we gazed down at the festivities in the enormous ballroom. Gorgeous women, hot guys, and old men. Dressed in gowns, tuxedos, suits, and even jeans. Drinking, dancing, and talking.

We were right on time, but the number of partygoers already here implied our tardiness. Guess people didn't mess with fashionably late when Romanov was involved.

"Mizz January. Velcome."

I didn't have to look to know who that voice belonged to. Inwardly I groaned, but outwardly I plastered on a smile and turned. "Romanov!"

He held his hands out and I took them. He wasn't wearing his oxygen tube, but his yellow skin looked even more jaundiced under these lights.

With wet lips, he kissed both my cheeks in greeting and then introduced himself to David and Jonathan.

Romanov turned me around and slipped my coat off, skimming his chilly fingers down my arms as he went. I fought the urge to gag. "You are very enticing this evening." He held his arm out. "Shall vee?"

I chanced a quick glance at David. He quickly snapped his attention to the party. With a slap on the back to TL and a quick nod to Jonathan, he made his way down the steps. I shouldn't have peeked at him. I could blow my cover doing something so stupid.

Romanov silently indicated a spot against the back wall where other bodyguards were standing. TL nodded and headed off in that direction. Jonathan trailed behind him. I experienced a flash of panic at being left alone, but immediately squashed it down. My teammates knew exactly where I was.

Sliding my hand into the crook of Romanov's arm, I followed him down the marble stairs and along the perimeter of the ballroom. More than one set of eyes turned curiously in our direction.

Smile. Suck in stomach. Shoulders back. Smile. Suck in stomach. Shoulders back.

I chanted Audrey's commands so my brain wouldn't focus on my flip-flopping stomach. Being escorted by Romanov was a privilege. I met the other models' jealous stares with a Jade January, he-likes-me-better-than-you preen, when all I really wanted to do was hand him over with a *here, take him.*

We stopped at one of the many bars positioned around the room. "What would you like?"

"Seltzer with a twist of lime, please."

"Good girl. Alcohol haz too many calories."

Good girl? What was I, his pet?

A young, bald guy approached from the right. He gave me a cursory glance as he spoke to Romanov in Ushbanian. At least I assumed it was Ushbanian. The bartender set my glass down, and I took a tiny sip.

Romanov lifted my hand and placed a damp kiss on my knuckles. "Pleaze excuse me. I'll only be a few minutes."

He and the bald guy rounded the bar and disappeared through a door. Hmm, wonder where they're going? To do some bad-guy thing for sure. I'd seen enough movies: bad-guy leader excuses himself from joyful get-together. Shows up in basement where other bad guys are waiting. Good guy is chained to chair, bloody and beaten. Won't give bad guys information. Bad-guy leader orders torture until good guy gives in.

I focused on the pink marble floor beneath my stilettos. If only I possessed laser vision and could see the basement and tell whether or not a good guy was chained there.

A pair of shiny black shoes stepped into my line of sight. I looked up at a gorgeous guy. Blond. Green eyes. Impeccably dressed in a light gray suit. He bowed. "Mizter Schalmosky asked me to dance vith you. He vill be longer than expected."

I nodded, said thank you, and slipped my arm through his. "I'm Jade January. What's your name?"

"Mizz January, you may call me Petrov."

"Petrov." I tried his name, staring at his scrumptious face. Too bad he was a bad guy.

We made our way onto the packed dance floor and through the gyrating bodies. He stopped somewhere in the middle and began dancing. Quickly, I recalled my lessons from last week and moved my shoulders and feet to the beat. I scanned the ballroom for my teammates (being tall has its advantages), turned a slow-hipped circle, and stopped.

There danced David with one, two, three, *four* beautiful, perfect, exotic, seductive, gorgeous models. They sandwiched him, two in front, two in back, doing a grind move straight off a music video. He lifted his arms, laughing, getting quite the groove on.

He winked at me. I snapped out of my momentary trance and kept right on dancing. *Okay, David's role is to be a flirtatious, single photographer,* logic reminded me. But he acted the role a little *too* well, if you asked me.

"You should see the statue in the ladies' room," I heard a woman yell over the music.

Statue. I signaled Petrov, and he leaned in. "I need to go to the restroom. I'll be back."

He shook his head. "I vill valk vith you."

Pouting flirtatiously, I touched his arm. "I'd like privacy, please. I'll meet you at the bar in ten minutes." I pivoted and strode off, not giving him a chance to argue.

Please don't follow me. Pleasepleaseplease don't follow me.

Passing David and his models, I scratched the back of my head with my left hand. Our statue signal.

I did the same as I crossed in front of TL, who stood with the other bodyguards along the back wall. Like soldiers, lined up, a few feet of space between them. All without expressions.

Jonathan sat on a stool at one of the bars. He sipped an umbrella drink while carrying on a loud conversation with another beautiful model.

Statue-signaling him, I meandered past the bar. Good. All my teammates knew now. I pushed open the bathroom door and found myself bringing up the rear of a long line. Figured.

Taking my place, I surreptitiously peered around the lounge area that preceded the sinks. Straight-backed couches, fancy wood end tables, delicate wrought-iron stools, makeup mirrors, but no statue.

One woman came out, and another went in. The line inched forward.

A wall divided the lounge area from the sinks. From where I stood, a mirror gave me a clear shot. No statue in there, either.

Maybe this wasn't the only bathroom. A big place like this had to offer more than one, especially with all the females. "Excuse me."

The short, elderly lady beside me arched a penciled-in eyebrow as a response.

"Is this the only bathroom?"

"No. Zere is one across zee ballroom."

"Thanks." Probably the one with the statue.

One woman came out, and another went in. The line inched forward. A couple more models came in and took their place behind me.

Jeez, how many toilets were there? One? Never understood why it took girls so long in the bathroom. You got in, did your business, and got out. What's the big deal?

Clearly, this had to be the wrong bathroom. Okay, I'd make some spoiled, rich model comment about the wait and hoof it across the ballroom.

A tall redhead passed me on the way out. "I have to take a picture of that statue."

Statue? I perked up.

"I know," her tall blond friend agreed. "It's the funniest thing. Wonder who made it?"

One woman came out, and another went in. The line inched forward.

Just the short old lady now and then I could get in. The statue must be in the toilet area. I tapped my stiletto and peeked at my silver watch. Eighteen minutes. Petrov expected me in ten. Ugh.

One woman came out, and the old lady went in. I inched forward, glanced across the sink room to the toilets. Sure enough, one door. What had Romanov been thinking? You can't have one toilet in a ballroom bathroom.

The old lady came out. "Toilet's clogged."

The models behind me sighed and strode from the bathroom.

I crossed the tile floor, went in, and closed the door. I stood, taking in all the art decorating the huge room. Portraits and landscapes hung from the pink walls. Figurines stood on dozens of small wood shelves. In the corner sat the clogged toilet and beside it the statue.

It stood at least six feet tall and depicted a naked Romanov surrounded by four of his models, each wearing a robe. Luckily, one of the models' legs covered his privates. Funny, I would have expected the opposite. Romanov in the robe and the models naked.

Quickly, I put my middle finger on the statue. No heat. Both relief and disappointment hit me. Relief that I'd have more time to prepare for the microsnipet extraction. Disappointment that I'd have to go through all this again.

I opened the door, raced across the tile, rounded the wall into the lounge area, and ran smack into David.

"What are you doing?" I hissed.

"You've been in here forever," he hissed back. "We got worried."

"Petrov, what is it?" I heard a woman ask from outside the bathroom.

David and I both froze.

"Mizz January has been in zere far too long. Mizter Schalmosky iz waiting for her."

"Well, I heard the bathroom's out of order, but I'll check and see." The door creaked open.

Before I could panic, David quickly spun me around and yanked down my jumpsuit zipper.

‹TEN›

Nalani pushed into the bathroom and came to an abrupt stop. Her eyes widened as the door swung shut behind her. "Oh." She let out a nervous laugh. "I didn't realize . . ."

"Looks like what this isn't." I shook my head. "I mean, this isn't what it looks like."

"Of course, this isn't what it looks like." David maintained a solid grip on the unzipped, very open back of my jumpsuit, prohibiting me from stepping away. "Stupid thing," he mumbled, and I realized he was pretending my zipper was stuck.

"As you can see"—I elaborated on his ruse, avoiding eye contact with Nalani—"the clogged toilet ran everybody off. I, um, accidentally dropped something down my jumpsuit. And then I, uh, came in here to get it out, and now I can't seem to get this darn—"

David's fingers and warm breath brushed my lower back. My brain went blank. I stood there, aware I should be saying something, but for the life of me couldn't recall what. He gave my fastener a firm tug, and I snapped back to the moment.

"I can't get this darn zipper up. I stuck my head out the door, and he"—I jabbed my thumb over my shoulder—"was the only person within yelling distance." I sighed, all bothered and impatient.

"There." David dragged the zipper up the length of my spine, under my hair to my neck, leaving a shiver prickling my skin. He turned to Nalani. "You're Mr. Schalmosky's assistant, right?"

She inclined her head. "Yes."

"I heard there's a garden of statues. I'd like to take pictures of Jade out there. It'll round out her portfolio."

"Certainly. I'll escort you and then let Mr. Schalmosky know where you'll be." Nalani peeked at her slim diamond watch and motioned for us to follow.

With legs I hoped appeared steadier than they felt, I crossed to the door and followed her out. We'd almost gotten busted. If not for David's quick thinking, there was no telling what might have happened. Clearly, I was not cut out to go on missions. I did much better behind closed doors, safely sitting at a computer. Lots of time to think and formulate plans.

But coming up with a story like his stuck-zipper idea had been pretty darn ingenious. Gave me a little excited rev once I got focused. Once I ignored the fact that he'd seen my entire bare, braless back.

Fifteen minutes later, I leaned against the black iron rail as David snapped pictures.

Clickclick. Clickclick.

Behind me spread a conservatory with statues nestled among the greenery. Above, the transparent ceiling of the greenhouse showed the night sky, stars, and snow floating down. To my right, French doors led back into the ballroom. Petrov stood there, watching us. Obviously, Romanov didn't trust David and me out here alone. Smart man. Bad guys didn't become bad guys by trusting people.

"Good." *Clickclick. Clickclick.* "Now arch your back."

Arch my back? I wanted to narrow my eyes at David, but refrained. After all, Petrov loomed nearby. I arched my back, or in other words stuck out my boobs, and smiled for the camera.

"No smile. I need pout. Sexy. Full lips." *Clickclick. Clickclick.*

Pout? Sexy? Okay, David was taking it too far.

"Pout for me, baby." *Clickclick. Clickclick.*

Baby?

"Perfect!" *Clickclick. Clickclick.* "Break." David slipped the camera strap over his head and crossed the brick patio to where I stood.

He rearranged a few pieces of my hair while I quietly inhaled his cologne. "You've got to relax," he mumbled. "You don't seem like you know what you're doing. Petrov's going to pick up on your inexperience if you don't focus. Think Jade January, the sexy, spoiled model. Not GiGi, the gorgeous, shy genius."

Gorgeous? My stomach flip-flopped.

David brushed an imaginary something from my shoulder. "Remember, I'm focusing on the statues behind you. I've taken six of the eleven. Move to the left so I can get the remaining five."

With his index finger, he smoothed my eyebrows up, keeping his gaze level with mine. "Think Jade January, not GiGi." He winked, then turned and strolled back to his spot, his backside looking as yummy as ever.

Clickclick. Clickclick.

David waved me to the left, and I moved. He only said the gorgeous thing to keep my mind occupied.

"Right hand on rail. Arch. Left hand in hair." *Clickclick. Clickclick.*

I maneuvered my body into place. And the fiddling with my hair, brushing shoulder, smoothing eyebrows. All meant to keep me sidetracked.

"Chin up. Moisten lips." *Clickclick. Clickclick.*

Chin. Moisten. And the meaningful gaze-deeply-into-my-eyes. Again, meant to keep my thoughts from veering. Oh, he was good. He was real good. Manipulating my brain . . . *and my body, too,* I slowly realized. Standing here all arched with my hand in my hair and moistened lips.

Clickclick. Clickclick.

Time to reverse things. Show *him* a little manipulation game. Played my way.

I spread my legs in a power, Wonder Woman stance. The silver stilettos made me tower over six feet tall. Leveling sultry eyes on the camera, I stared straight into the lens. Straight into his dark brown eyes.

I ran my tongue slowly from one corner of my top lip to the other. Closing my eyes, I tilted my head and arched my back. I skimmed both hands up the front of my skintight jumpsuit, over my cheeks, and into my hair.

Then all my senses returned in a pop, and my heart skipped a beat as my eyes snapped open. No *clickclick, clickclick.* Only silence.

I looked at Petrov first, who stared, eyes wide, mouth hanging open. He obviously didn't think I was an amateur model now. And then to David, standing frozen, camera poised in the air.

"Uh . . ." He fumbled with the protective lens cap. "Th-that's a wrap."

Inwardly, I smiled. Clearly, I'd won the manipulation game. I refrained from doing a victory dance, clapping my hands, chanting, *I won! I won!* I set him off balance more than he set me.

Girl power, schmirl power. I possessed full-blown woman power.

David closed the distance between us, stopping at my side, putting his back to Petrov. "You . . . wow. Not bad."

Curving my lips sensually—at least I hoped it appeared sensual—I arched a brow. "Get all the pictures you needed?" I could not *believe* myself, all confident and self-assured. And enjoying it.

David studied me for long seconds. He shook his head with a chuckle. "Yeah, I got the pics. Now we need to figure out how to touch the statues."

We stared at each other, puzzling, and then it hit me. "Petrov, my night wouldn't be complete without a stroll in the garden. Will you escort me, please?"

"Certainly Mizz January."

I gave David a little pinch on his bristly cheek, which by the spark in his eyes, infuriated him. After I'd accepted Petrov's arm, he unlatched the wrought-iron gate, and we stepped onto a cobblestone walkway.

"I vill do the honors, Petrov." Romanov emerged from the shadows.

Immediately I smiled to cover my frantic thoughts. Oh, dear God, how long had he been standing there? I should've known. TL had trained me better than that. David should've known. He'd been in this business longer than me. Maybe he'd known and it was all part of the act.

I glanced his way. He tapped his collarbone in the same location as my tracking freckle. *I'll—I mean, we'll know where you are.* Breathing easier with the silent reminder, I followed Romanov into the garden as David and Petrov disappeared into the ballroom.

Had Romanov heard David's and my mumblings from his hidden spot? No, not possible, too far away. He'd seen the photography session, though. How could he have missed it? Maybe he missed it. Please, God, make him have missed it.

"I saw your session just now."

Inwardly, I groaned. "I got off to a rough start. Couldn't get my mind focused." Didn't want him to question my modeling ability.

"Yes. But you ended, how do you Americans say, vith a bang?"

"Yes, yes, I ended with a bang." Great, he'd seen me in my woman-power sexy mode. Just what I needed. To get an old man excited.

Okay. Strategy: keep him talking while strolling the garden and touching every statue.

Problem: I wore the microsnipet detector on my right middle finger, which was currently linked with Romanov's jacketed left arm.

102

"Oh, I must smell that flower." I stepped in front of him and buried my nose in some red plant, which, by the way, smelled like nothing. I then linked my left arm through his right, and we continued down the path.

Romanov gave a detailed explanation of the plant's origin, root system, drainage, blah blah blah. I made little "oh" and "Is that right?" sounds mixed in with occasional nods. All while watching him through wide, I'm-so-interested eyes.

Men, I just began to realize, were so easy to manipulate.

The first of eleven granite statues stood off to the right, approximately three feet tall. A little shepherd boy with a lamb. Surrounded by pink and yellow flowers. Why girls always wanted to smell flowers, I didn't know. They all smelled the same to me. But hey, it had worked to get me close to the statues, so I said, "What beautiful colors. Oh, Romanov, tell me about these."

Slipping from his side, I wandered over and stuck my nose in those, too. Kind of a fruity scent. I pretended to balance myself with my right hand on the lamb's head while sniffing the flowers.

No hot zing in my middle finger. Dang. One down, ten to go.

We continued down the path to the next statue. A teenage guy holding a bow and arrow. This one roughly five feet tall. I ran my fingers over it. No hot zing. "Is this marble?"

Romanov launched into another blah-blah explanation. Imported stones and aging techniques, to which I did the wide-eyed, interested thing.

Third statue stood among purple flowers. Six feet tall. Man holding a book. Bent, sniffed, touched. No hot zing.

"Zis one vill complement your complexion." He snapped off a flower and tucked it behind my ear, trailing his cool finger over my cheek. "You are very beautiful."

Swallowing, I glanced around, unable to see the French doors or the ballroom lights. We'd lost ourselves in the conservatory. Romanov stepped closer. "Do I make you nervous?"

"Yes," I responded before I stopped to think. So much for woman power.

"Good." He chuckled, humorlessly, slow and deep.

Ug. I didn't know how much more of him I could take.

"Shall vee?" He held out his arm, and I carefully took it.

Reality check. Me? Not in charge. He owned complete control of this situation. Stiffly, I matched his casual, confident stride. I needed to get my mind off my sudden nervousness and onto something else. *Relax, GiGi, relax.*

I spied his watch nearly covered by long, black arm hair. Yuck. Never seen one like it before, though. "What kind of watch is that?" I was honestly interested.

"Cuztoom-made. It keeps time."

Yeah, no kidding, Einstein. "What are those other dials and spindles on the inside?"

"Ah, yes. It's complicated for all but zee sharpest of minds."

I resisted the urge to roll my eyes. I could handle it, buddy, believe me. "Will you tell me anyway, please?"

"Why zee interest?"

"I'm shopping for a present. A friend of mine collects watches." Good, quick lie. Not bad.

"Not only are you lovely, but generous, too."

Whatever. But I smiled sweetly anyway. Just tell me the frigging mechanics. Chapling would devour this.

We stopped walking, and he pointed to the spindles. "Zee four inner circles display time in countries of your choice. Press zis button"—he pushed a dial on the side—"and zee four circles switch to other countries."

Hmm. Easy enough to do. Little lead probe soldered to a frequency duct, satellite-controlled.

"Iz good for people who travel."

"What about the infrared glow?"

"How do you know zee term *infrared?*"

Crap. "Video games." I leaned in. "My secret obsession."

"Ah, zee infrared glow is a weapon."

My jaw dropped.

"Vatch." He pointed the watch at a plant, pushed a button, and a red laser shot out, frying the tip of a leaf.

"Cool. A mini infrared beam signaled by a tilt scope." Oh, I wished Chapling were here. I reached for my notepad and pencil, then immediately realized the *huge* mistake I'd made.

Romanov tapped the center of my forehead with his index finger. "I zink you are more intelligent zan you let on."

Oh, crud. I shrugged innocently and decided on honesty. This man would see through anything else. "You're right. I am smart. But models aren't supposed to be. They get further if they pretend to be a little dumb."

"Who told you that?"

"My mother." People tended to pity someone who'd been berated by a parent. And right then I could have used a little pity from Romanov so he would forget about my smarts.

He nodded. "Ah."

I turned away and noticed a statue behind us. Small. One foot tall. Of a puppy Doberman. "Do you have a Doberman?" I asked, walking toward it. "Is that why you had one sculpted?"

"I own ten Dobermans. All trained to attack on command."

Attack on command? My stiletto caught on a cobblestone, and I tripped forward, smashing face-first into the statue. "Ow!"

Romanov rushed toward me. "Mizz January!"

Tasting coppery blood in my mouth, I reached up, grabbing ahold of the Doberman, and a hot zing shot up my arm.

The microsnipet!

‹ELEVEN›

Apparently Romanov's doctor only treated Romanov. So here I sat in our hotel suite roughly thirty minutes later. David applied stinging antiseptic to the corner of my mouth while I held a small bag of ice to my eye. TL sat on the bar stool beside me, studying his iPad. It held digital blueprints of Romanov's home, modeling school, and whatever other buildings we downloaded from the satellite.

With a quiet sigh, I closed my good eye. I knew I would screw up. I just knew it. If it weren't for my klutziness, we'd still be at Romanov's party. I might have been able to tap into the microsnipet and extract the information. We could be rescuing David's dad right now instead of sitting in our suite tending to my stupid cut lip and bruised face.

David shifted, and I opened my eye. He threw the cotton ball away and searched through the first-aid kit. He hadn't uttered a single word to me. No one had. Not in the limo on the way here, nor in the ten minutes we'd been back.

Well, that wasn't exactly true. TL had said *here* right after fixing me a bag of ice in the limo. David had said *sit,* pointing to a bar stool, when we got back to the suite. *Here* and *sit.* Two one-syllable words. Not the silent treatment, but it might as well be.

I tried not to take the quiet personally. They needed time to think, reformulate plans.

Mistakes happen. No one's perfect.

That's what I kept telling myself, but I wanted to be perfect. I didn't want to mess up. I wanted to be a genius in this area of my life, too. Perfect, gifted GiGi saved the day. I wanted TL and everyone to be proud of me. Awed by my talent. I wanted to shine, to be the star. Just once I wanted to be someone I wasn't. And succeed at it.

David peeled the backing off a butterfly bandage, then smoothed it over my lip. My bottom lip quivered, and I immediately stilled it. I would not cry. I absolutely would not cry.

He took the ice bag, set it on the bar behind me, and leaning close, tried to study my eye. I focused on my lap. I would not cry. I absolutely would not cry.

David put his finger under my chin, gently pushing up until our gazes met. His eyes crinkled, and he presented me with a lollipop.

My bottom lip trembled, and I inhaled a choppy breath.

"I'm sorry," I mumbled, a couple of tears streaming down my cheeks.

Playfully, David poked me in the shoulder. "Are you kidding? Everyone screws up. Even our fearless leader. Tell her, TL."

His joking poke caught me off guard. I'd expected a hug. Pat on the back at least.

TL glanced up from his digital maps, saw my blubbery face, but didn't react to it. "Oh, yeah. On my second mission, I knocked out the vice president of the Jalys Island Nation. Thought he was the head of the opposing force."

"Really?" I sniffed.

He smiled. "Turned out the VP and the head of the bad guys were twins."

I smiled, too, and it dried my tears. Amazing how humor turned a situation around. I'd be having a full-blown, snot-nosed, crying jag right now if they had tried to console me. But then, they probably knew that.

Six quick knocks sounded on the door. Our code that one of us was with one of them.

Snatching the ice bag from the counter, I sprinted across the room and lay down on the couch.

David grabbed the remote, plopped in the chair beside me, and began flipping channels. Quickly, he leaned over, slipped the lollipop into my mouth—hmm, sour apple—and resumed his position.

TL hid the digital maps beneath the bar and went to the door.

"Hey." Jonathan patted TL's cheek. "Forgot my key. Look who I brought."

Nalani stepped inside. "Good evening. I apologize for the late hour." She acknowledged each person, her stare lingering briefly on TL. "I wanted to hand-deliver something to Jade."

Closing the door, TL went back to his bodyguard stance, his face hard and blank. If we hadn't been on a mission and were back living our normal lives, would TL have responded to Nalani's interest? Hmm, or had the love of his life dumped him, emotionally scarring him for all others?

Inside, I grinned. What a little soap-opera writer I'd become.

"How are you?" Nalani crossed to the couch.

I lifted the ice bag from my eye and pulled the lollipop from my mouth. "Never better."

Smiling at my sarcasm, she sat down next to my hips. "I brought a few things." She dug in her purse and pulled out a small white jar. "For your black eye. Apply only at night. It'll be gone in three days. It's a mixture of ary root and dent stem."

How sweet. "Thanks."

"Unfortunately, I don't have anything for your lip. But"—again, she reached inside her purse, this time bringing out a small black velvet box— "I brought a gift from Romanov."

"Oh." Didn't expect that. I opened the lid. Diamond earrings sparkled back at me. "Ohhh, they're beautiful." No one had ever given me jewelry before.

She took my hand. "I'm sorry, but I have to deliver bad news."

Bad news? What bad news?

"I'm sure you understand your injuries prohibit your making your debut from Romanov's school. But he's willing to offer you an invitation to have your debut six months from now."

"Oh, well . . ." How was I supposed to respond? Good thing I already located the microsnipet. Otherwise we'd really be screwed.

"Not to worry, honey." Jonathan strolled over. "You've already got a contract with Lasjet Sportswear."

Nalani kissed my cheek. "You'll enjoy the greatest of success. I'll see you in six months." She made her way to the door, turned with a wave. "Safe journey back to the States."

TL closed the door behind her. He rubbed his nose, then brushed his shoulder. *Stay in character.* He unclipped his belt-buckle bug detector.

"I like her. She's really sweet. And I like Romanov even more. Check out these rocks."

TL examined the earrings from Romanov. His belt buckle glowed a steady, bug-free green.

"Mmm . . ." Jonathan pursed his lips. "My expert eye says they're only half carats. You should've kissed him. You would've gotten full carats then."

"Gross!"

"All clear." TL clipped his belt buckle back into place. "Get a good night's sleep. We'll infiltrate Romanov's castle tomorrow evening." He strode off to his bedroom.

Get a good night's sleep? Was he kidding? He had to be kidding. Jet lag or not, there was no *way* I'd get a good night's sleep until we were safely back at the ranch.

***

After staring at my bedroom ceiling for an hour, I wandered into the kitchen, found a soda, and settled on the couch with the laptop.

For an hour I worked on my keystroke memorization program and then connected the foldable satellite dish and scrambler. I instant messaged Chapling. Sure enough, he answered.

"Hey."

I jumped, and the computer bounced off my lap onto the cushion beside me.

"Sorry," David whispered.

Heart pounding at the scare, and stomach fluttering because of him, I put the computer back on my lap. I peered across the living room. Blurrily, he lounged against the kitchen counter, his arms and ankles casually crossed. I shoved my glasses on top of my head. "That's okay. How long standing there you been?" I shook my head. "I mean, how long have you been standing there?"

He held his smile for a couple of long seconds, studying me. "Not long."

"Oh, um . . . oh." He'd been watching me? *Please, God, promise me I didn't look stupid.*

"Can't sleep?"

Shaking my head, I finger-combed my hair, suddenly conscious of the way I looked: huge sweatshirt, baggy pajama bottoms, white athletic socks, black glasses, and a greasy eye from the ointment Nalani had given me.

Dressed the same as me, minus the greasy eye and big glasses, David's yum factor was off the scale. Covering the short distance between us, he sat down on the couch cushion beside me. Off the coffee table, he picked up my proto laser tracker, which I'd brought with me. I'd been working on it for a physics professor back in Iowa. Back in my old life. Seemed like eons ago now. David turned it over. "What exactly *is* this?"

"Something I've been working on."

"What does it do?"

I tried to ignore his knee brushing mine, but failed miserably. "Tracks objects."

"Hmm." David rotated it, studying it. "Looks like a digital camera."

Inside, I did a happy dance. It's exactly what I'd been going for.

"How does it work?"

"Well, uh . . ." This was the part where people tuned me out. My explanations were always too scientific. "A proto neuro chip, when embedded, emits a KED code that disintegrates to CONUSE capable of traveling light speed parallel to its plane of origin based on x, y coordinates—"

"Stop." He held his hand up with a laugh. "Think first, then speak. Make it simple. I'm bright, but not that bright. Start again." No one ever asked me to explain stuff again. Usually they got a glassed-over look, nodded politely, and went on their way.

I focused on the proto tracker in his hands, really wanting to do this right. "Point the tracker at an object and click the button. A laser beam sends out a microscopic tracking device that embeds itself in the object. Use the LCD screen to follow the object." I switched my gaze from the tracker to his eyes. "How was that?"

David nodded once. "Very nicely done."

My face heated with his compliment.

"Is there anything like this on the market right now?"

"Don't think so."

He tapped the object to my forehead. "Impressive."

"Thanks."

"What about your computer? What's all that code you were typing in?"

"Oh." I shrugged. "Just a program."

"A program that does . . ." He motioned with his hands, encouraging me to elaborate.

It felt so . . . *good* when someone showed genuine interest in me. I took a moment to simplify the explanation in my brain. "It's a program that memorizes keystrokes and mouse clicks. Kinda like those cars that remember the seating and steering position of the driver. This program remembers usage, so if your PC crashes, a separate computer chip holds everything for easy retrieval."

"Sort of like a constant backup of your hard drive but without specifically backing anything up?"

"Right."

"Cool. Does it go with the proto laser tracker?"

"No. They're separate projects." I nodded to the laptop. "I've got Chapling on the line right now."

"Yeah?" David scooted closer, leaning over to type a message. I stared at the side of his face, lit by the glowing blue of the laptop. He laughed and typed something else. I inhaled deeply his soapy David scent mixed with lingering cologne and nearly passed out from his deliciousness.

He glanced over at me, smiling, and his grin slowly faded as he took in every detail of my face.

I didn't breathe.

David focused on my bruised eye. "Hurt?"

I shook my head.

He dropped to my mouth. "How 'bout there?"

Shook my head again. Still not breathing.

"Beautiful," he mumbled.

The laptop dinged, and we both jumped. David slid over a cushion, and I focused on the screen, heart racing, everything a blur.

"What does he say?"

Blinking a few times, I cleared the fog from my brain and concentrated on the words Chapling had typed. "He downloaded intel. Romanov will be gone from his house at eight tomorrow night. He takes half his guards with him when he travels. Chapling advises we wait until then to make our move."

"Good." David pushed up from the couch. "We'll tell TL and Jonathan in the morning." He studied me for a second, like he wanted to say something.

Holding my breath, I waited for his words. Seconds ticked by. He closed his eyes and shook his head, blowing out a breath. "G'night." He made his way across the dimly lit living room, through the kitchen, and into his and TL's room.

I sat on the couch frozen, my mind racing. What was all that? A you're-so-beautiful-I-don't-know-what-to-do-with-you shake of the head? Or a you're-only-sixteen-I'm-eighteen-are-you-an-idiot blowing out of the breath? But then, why had he called me beautiful?

I dropped my head back with a groan. Life had gone a lot easier when only computers rocked my world.

***

The following evening, I found myself with TL, crouching in the icy dark woods surrounding Romanov's home, watching the castle.

Minutes later, David and Jonathan came up beside us. They'd secured the perimeter, to use TL's lingo, by scouting the property, assuring themselves that none of Romanov's goons lurked about.

TL two-finger-waved David toward the gate. With a nod, David silently slipped from the woods, crossed the road, and came up beneath the guards' building. David's black clothes and face paint, same as we all wore, merged him with the shadows. So much so I had a hard time keeping him in sight.

Inside the small, brick structure, the guard picked up the phone. Right on time.

Beside me Jonathan spoke into his satellite phone, pretending to be Vitro, Romanov's commander, alerting the guard of a disturbance along the east wing. With half the security gone, procedure dictated that the gate goon respond to emergencies.

The guard hung up the phone and, after slipping on his coat, pushed a few buttons on the security panel. He opened the door, rounded the corner, and David jabbed him with a numbing dart. It happened lightning quick. All I caught was David dragging him behind the surrounding bushes.

The guard would be out for about an hour. Jonathan would impersonate him, reporting in every fifteen minutes. All in all, plenty of time to extract the information and get out before anyone even discovered we'd broken in.

David entered the building. Although I couldn't really see him, I knew what he was doing. We'd gone over it right before leaving the hotel suite.

He popped open the security panel, cut a wire, and patched it over. Fusing the video feed. All monitors throughout the castle would display a normal scene. No one, hopefully, would know we were here.

He spliced three wires together, disengaging the electric wrought-iron fence circling Romanov's property.

"Clear," David whispered into the mike he wore as a capped tooth. The same device we all wore. It was connected to a transceiver bracketed inside our ears, much like a hearing aid, and activated by a button we wore on our collars. All wireless.

TL two-finger-waved Jonathan and me, and we soundlessly preceded him across to David. The four of us scaled the ten-foot wrought-iron fence. David first, followed by Jonathan; TL boosted me up and over, then brought up the rear.

With quiet feet, we jogged around the property, following the fence until we stood even with the greenhouse and statue garden. Remnants of yesterday's snowfall iced the ground. Thanks to the shoe-sole warmers Chapling had created, our boots melted the ice instead of crunching it.

TL pointed at Jonathan and then the ground. *Stay.* TL sprinted across the open lawn to the bushes bordering the greenhouse.

Seconds ticked by. "Clear," we heard him whisper.

David and I followed suit, bolting over open ground to TL and the bushes. Jonathan stayed behind to keep watch. David pulled a two-inch-long laser burner from his pocket. Starting at the bottom, he cut a circle in the glass, big enough for a person to crawl through. I watched him, feeling a surge of pride. Thanks to me, the laser glowed green to match the greenhouse lights. It used to be red, definitely a color someone would spot at night.

Using suction cups, he quietly lowered the clean-cut glass and then crawled through the hole. I followed, with TL staying put in the bushes as lookout. The four of us worked like bug-free software, everything in perfect rehearsed sync. A beautiful thing.

Inside the enormous, warm greenhouse, David and I scurried through perfumey flowers and more bushes until we stood on the cobblestone path. We checked our watches: 21:08:20. Ten seconds until one of the goons did his hourly stroll.

David touched one finger to his cheek, then pointed to a row of trees. *Hide.* Quickly I did as he directed while he took cover across the path.

Amazingly enough, my heartbeat steadied, my breath flowed evenly, and my stomach just existed. No erratic pulse. No choppy breath. No churning intestines. No wandering thoughts. I felt more sure, confident, and focused than I had ever felt in my whole life. Go figure. Maybe TL did know what he was doing when he put so much faith in me.

"Ah, my little bird. You make me vish my shift vas over." A guard rounded the path, a cell phone to his ear. Smirking like a stupid fool, he crossed in front of my tree. "Oh, you better stop—"

David slipped from his hiding spot, poked the guard with a numbing dart, and while soundlessly lowering him to the ground, caught the phone before it clattered across the path.

"Ah, my lovely little bird," David mimicked the goon, "zomething has come up. I vill call you back later."

It was amazing how his voice perfectly matched the bad guy's.

He dragged him the few feet to me, and together, we hid him behind the trees. Like the first guard, this one would be out for an hour.

David and I took off in a sprint down the path, past flowers, bushes, and statues, until we came to the granite Doberman statue.

Unzipping my black fanny pack, I pulled out the microsnipet locator and put on my glasses. Slowly, I ran the square device over the Doberman's legs, across its body, around its head, keeping my eyes peeled to the light indicator. It glowed a steady yellow. The light would black out when I ran it over the microsnipet. I trailed it under its belly. The light went out as I passed over the tip of its tail.

"Status," TL's voice whispered into my earpiece.

David turned from watching the path and raised his brows. I pressed the button on my collar and activated my tooth mike. "Microsnipet located. Beginning extraction now."

Tucking the locator back inside the fanny pack, I pulled out a folding, miniature keyboard and snapped it open. It came complete with a satellite feed and one-by-four-inch monitor. Too cool.

Crouching, I studied the tiny, flat, square microsnipet. Lucky for me, it had been plastered to the surface, which meant I didn't have to break open the dog's tail to get to it. Just connect the linking wire, break the code, and download the information.

No problem. We'd know the whereabouts of Mr. Share in mere seconds.

I snapped one end of the copper linking cable to the keyboard, squeezed a dab of bonding agent to the other, then stuck it on the microsnipet. My fingers raced over the keys as I dialed the scrambler code and connected to satellite.

GOTCHA! You're in, I read on the screen. Chapling. Made me smile to think he was right here with me.

I began entering a series of standard codes, but came up against a firewall each time. I paused, focused my thoughts. Tried keying subscripts. More blocks. Worked in the opposite direction, typing synthesized indexers. Again, security barriers. Punched a list of idiosyncratic elements. Another block. What the . . .

"Status."

Jumping at TL's quiet request, I peeked at my watch. *Fifteen minutes!* I'd been at this fifteen minutes? I pressed the button on my collar. "Any second," I lied.

Okay, think, GiGi, think. Romanov owned David's dad, the most brilliant man in the world. Wouldn't it make sense that Romanov would have him create the castle's security codes? Yes, it would. Mr. Share had designed the government's security using Pascal's triangle. If he maintained the same mathematical theme, he might use quadrilateral or polynomial factoring.

My heart danced an excited little rhythm in tune to my fingers racing over the keyboard. This had to be it.

I hit the return key and—

Bingo! "I got it!"

"Shhh." David hushed me through a chuckle.

Sorry, I mouthed, grinning like a goof, watching the microsnipet info scroll onto the gray screen.

YOU GO GIRL! Chapling typed.

I stayed connected a few more minutes while he downloaded the information on the whereabouts of David's dad to our server. I disconnected from the satellite and stowed everything back in my fanny pack.

Suddenly the entire greenhouse brightened with white light, and a shrill siren went off.

I must have set off an alarm when I disconnected.

David grabbed my hand, and we took off down the path. Metal grids began unrolling from the ceiling, securing the greenhouse's glass panes and prohibiting anyone from exiting. I pumped my legs, keeping up with him. We cut through hedges and greenery, ignoring the thorny scratches, leaped over flower bushes, and slid through a spiny shrub to our entrance hole.

TL was right there, waiting for us. I glanced up to see a metal grid grinding toward us. David grabbed the back of my shirt and pants and shoved me through, then dove after me. A split second later, the grid slammed over our hole, shutting us out.

We bolted across the open frosty lawn to where Jonathan waited. In the distance we heard the pack of Dobermans as they rounded the castle and headed straight for us. TL let out a stream of curses and reached back for me. He didn't have to reach far. My fear propelled me to light speed.

Snapping and snarling, the dogs ate up the ground. Jonathan dropped to his hands and knees at the base of the wrought-iron fence. Using him as a step, David bounced onto his back and over the ten-foot-tall barrier. I went next, with TL giving me a helpful push up and over. David caught me, TL landed beside us, and Jonathan quickly scaled the fence.

The Dobermans slid to a stop, half of them barking and biting at Jonathan as he wiggled over the fence, and the other half trying to attack us through the wrought-iron spaces. With Jonathan safely on our side, we took off across the road and into the woods.

A mile later, we burst through the trees on the outskirts of an Ushbanian town, a different one from where the modeling school and hotel were located. I'd hated physical training back at the ranch, but now I was thankful for it. There was no way I'd be keeping up right now without it. I knew from our preoperations session that we would split up if something like this happened. David and I in one direction, TL in another, and Jonathan in yet another. We each wore tracking devices connected via satellite with our watches. I'd know where they were at any time, and vice versa.

TL unclipped my fanny pack, leaving me with no evidence of the mission we'd just completed, and he and Jonathan took off. Quickly, David and I removed our black face paint with wet wipes, then sprinted straight through the center of the town.

Music pounded from a nightclub four blocks up, our planned destination. Our dark clothes served two purposes, allowing us to hide in shadows, yet stylish enough for clubbing.

A police siren pierced the air. David grabbed my hand and yanked me down an alley. We ran past a dumpster and skidded to a halt when a police car pulled in the opposite end. David backed me up against the side of a building and plastered his body to mine. Our chests heaved against each other with winded breaths.

He buried his mouth against my ear. "Wrap. Your. Arms. Around. Me."

I did as he instructed, my heart hammering, keeping the police car in my peripheral vision. It slowly rolled toward us. "It's coming," I hissed, desperately trying to think of what to do next.

"Sorry," he mumbled right before crushing his mouth to mine.

‹TWELVE›

David held his lips firmly to mine.

Oh my God, I'm sixteen, and I've never been kissed. Please let me be doing this right.

But . . . this was it? This was about as exciting as having my hand kissed.

The police car rolled down the alley, getting closer, keeping their spotlight pinned to us. I just hoped they were convinced we were two lovers stealing a moment alone.

Closing my eyes, I tightened my arms around David as the car slowly drove past. I concentrated on his warmth, his scent. And suddenly David was the only thing that occupied my mind. I tilted my head and opened my mouth a little bit.

"Status," TL's voice boomed in our ears.

We jumped apart. David spun away, quickly pressing the talk button on his collar. "Four blocks from club," he answered TL's interruption, all calm, as if he'd just been relaxing and reading a book.

Me? To save my life coherent thought I couldn't form. I mean, I couldn't form a coherent thought to save my life.

Squeezing my eyes shut, I half listened to them talk, replaying the kiss in my mind.

"Cop's gone."

I opened my eyes. David was looking down the dark, slushy alley. Good thing, because I had no clue what to say to him.

"I—" He stopped. "I . . ."

Oh, good God. I what? *I do believe that's the best kiss I've ever had, GiGi. Or, I think we made a huge mistake, you little sixteen-year-old stupid genius.*

Please don't let it be the last one.

Stepping away from the wall, I pulled my shoulders back. By God *I* would be the one to declare it a mistake, not him.

"Listen, that was a mistake. You know it, and I know it. So let's chalk it up to hormones or getting caught up in the moment or whatever." I lifted my chin and strode off down the alley like I'd seen people do in the movies.

"GiGi."

So much for my grand exit. I stopped, but didn't turn around.

"I wanted to say I was sorry because we've never talked about kissing, and I don't kiss girls unless I know for sure they want to be kissed."

But I did want to be kissed. Since the first day I saw him, I'd wanted it. I spun around. "B—"

"Like you said." He shrugged. "It was a mistake. So . . . okay. Let's get going." He breezed past me.

I turned and stared as he walked away brusquely. *Wait!*

Please! I want to change my mind. Can I change my mind? It isn't a mistake.

***

We spent three headachy, earsplitting hours in the club dancing on the packed floor with a strobe pulsing. The club closed at two, and we exited with the sea of bodies. Perfect cover as everyone wore black clothes like us.

Now, as we trudged into our hotel suite, TL greeted us. "Good, you're back. Let's go."

Go? What about a shower and bed? I peeked at my watch. These guys never stopped.

"Chapling decoded the info you downloaded. We know where Mr. Share is. With the alarm having been triggered, it's highly likely Romanov knows someone tapped into the microsnipet. We have to move now before Romanov relocates David's father."

David didn't blink an eye. "Let's do it."

Pivoting, I followed the guys out. David seemed amazingly calm. If I were about to rescue my dad, whom I hadn't seen in years and thought dead, I'd be a nervous wreck. "So where is he?"

"Modeling school," Jonathan answered from beside me.

Huh, I would've guessed an abandoned warehouse or the dungeons in Romanov's castle. That's where the bad guys hid good guys in the movies.

Bypassing the elevator, TL opened the stairwell door, and we each passed through. "According to the blueprints, there's a steel-walled room off Romanov's office on the third floor. I assumed it was a weapons room. Makes sense that's where Mr. Share is."

"So it's still a weapons room." I took a couple of steps down. "Because David's dad is the ultimate weapon."

Jonathan stopped, and I ran straight into his hard back. In the cramped stairwell, all three guys turned to stare at me. *What?*

"You're right." TL spoke first. "Never thought about it that way. He *is* the ultimate weapon."

Okay. Nothing like saying something profound to get everyone's attention. Although it only made sense. Mr. Share could hack his way into anything. He could squirm through the military's system and set off nuclear bombs.

Wait a minute. So could I.

A chill raced through my body at the evil I was capable of doing. No wonder the good guys recruited me. But was I at risk of being kidnapped like David's dad? For my brain? TL said the IPNC had kept tabs on me since I was a child. Had all the bad guys out there in the world done so, too?

Gulp.

We continued descending the hotel's stairs, rounding the second floor to the first. "Why am I with you? You don't need me to rescue Mr. Share."

Jonathan opened the exit door, sending in the icy night. "We're not leaving you alone in the suite. Plus we need a lookout."

"Oh." I tucked my gloved hands into my jacket pockets.

On foot we trekked four cobblestoned blocks and then cut through the woods to the modeling school. At this early-morning hour, Prost, Ushbania, sat dark and empty. Yellow streetlights provided the only illumination. It was a cute little town. Like if a shepherd and his flock wandered across the street, it wouldn't surprise me a bit.

The modeling school stood three stories high between two other brick buildings. A street ran in front and a small stream along the back.

The four of us lay belly down on the other side of the stream, staring across at the buildings. Behind us stretched miles of wooded hills that eventually led to Romanov's castle.

TL spread leaves over my back and legs. He pointed at me, then the ground. *Stay.* He waved Jonathan to the right, David to the left, and TL slipped back into the woods. My job in all this? To lie on the cold, damp ground, camouflaged by leaves, watching the back side of the modeling school. Of course if I saw someone, I would press my collar talk button, activating my tooth mike, and notify my team.

Jonathan and David appeared moments later on the other side of the stream, creeping down opposite ends of the back alley. TL popped up on the roof. I did a double take. Jeez, the man moved quick.

He disappeared into the shadows, but I knew what he was doing. "Clear," he whispered seconds later. He'd disabled the security system.

David and Jonathan sprinted to the back door. Kneeling, David picked the lock and the two of them slid inside. TL signaled me from the roof. *Five minutes.*

They'd be five minutes. Shielding my watch, I pressed the indiglo button, confirming the time: 3:20:03. I knew TL well enough to know that at precisely 3:25:03 they would reappear at my side.

With a quiet sigh, I ran my gaze over the dark modeling school, studying the windows, hoping to see a flicker of light, a movement of shadows. They were too good, though. They'd be in and out before anyone was the wiser.

3:21:15.

Little under four minutes to go. A frosty breeze blew past, sending leaves rolling across the ground. I fought the urge to shiver and pull my coat tighter around me, concentrating instead on keeping very still. I thought about a nice cup of hot chocolate when we got back. Followed by a cinnamon lollipop. Oooh, gonna be good.

3:22:31.

TL would want to leave for the States as soon as possible, though. Hot chocolate or not. It made sense. Who'd want to hang out in Ushbania after stealing back a man worth millions of dollars? Not I.

3:23:17.

Did they have him yet? Had David been reunited with his dad? They were probably hugging at this very second, sharing a moment. Wished I could be there to see it.

3:24:05.

Oh, yeah. In under a minute they'd be back. We'd be off through the woods and on a plane to the States. Any second now I'd be meeting Mr. Share.

A twig snapped behind me, and I let out a relieved breath, then immediately caught it. Wait a minute, they wouldn't be coming up from behind.

"Don't do anyzing stupid."

I froze.

"Get up."

Carefully I pushed to my hands and knees, my heart banging so hard it'd probably break a rib. With my hands raised above my head, I slowly turned around. Two giant goons stood with feet braced apart, aiming matching guns at my head.

One grabbed my arm and yanked me toward him. He pressed a gun to my side, and we charged off into the woods.

I yanked back. "Helllp!"

The goon behind me shoved me forward. "Quiet."

They dragged me around trees and over downed limbs.

This isn't supposed to be happening! I dug my heels in. "Helllp!"

He jabbed the gun into my ribs. "Ooowww!"

"Shut up."

I hit a pile of muddy leaves and slid to my butt.

He jerked me up. "Stupid girl."

Wait, I should scream. Surely by now my team was outside the modeling school and would hear me. I took a breath, ready to let loose with a loud one.

"Don't"—the goon ground the gun into my ribs—"even zink about it."

I chanced a quick glance over my shoulder, couldn't even see the dim lights of the buildings. What if my team was still inside the modeling school? They wouldn't even know I'd been kidnapped. Of all the time for them to be running late, this was not it.

"GiGi," TL whispered through my earpiece.

My earpiece! I'd forgotten I was wearing it. I tried not to react to TL's voice so as not to tip off the goons.

"Don't fight them," he continued. "You're wearing a tracking device. We know exactly where you are."

That's right. Under my cotton shirt I still wore the freckle on my neck from Romanov's party, and my watch linked via satellite. The whole IPNC knew my GPS coordinates.

"We'll get you back safely." David. His voice made my breath hitch. "I promise."

The goon jerked me from the woods and across the street to a waiting black sedan. He opened the car door. I tugged at his grip. "Nooo."

He shoved me inside, pushing in behind me. The other goon took the front seat, and the car peeled out.

I scooted over as far as I could. Where were they taking me? When would my team find me?

The goon grabbed my wrist and tore off the watch.

Ow! "Hey . . ." That hurt.

He rolled down the window and hurled out the watch. I watched in shock as it sailed into the night. How'd he know to take it off of me? Were these GPS watches standard for both good guys and bad?

Leaning across, the goon briskly frisked me, running his hands clumsily along my legs, arms, front, and back.

Shoving me over, he secured my wrists behind my back with industrial tape. He pulled a black hood from his pocket and fit it over my head.

He and the other goon exchanged words in Ushbanian. The car cut a corner, and I slid off the leather seat onto the floor. He yanked me back up. A few seconds later, he began a one-sided conversation, presumably on a cell phone. Probably talking to Romanov about what to do with me. I heard him say Jade January. Well, they knew who I was.

Underneath the hood, I closed my eyes. Somehow the darkness of my lids didn't bother me as much as the blackness of the cloth.

Calm down, GiGi. Calm down. Think code. That always settles you.

<ILNI= 1 S:%-11-:00=ISLI>

<1/foo.hlt: 15-30#@// lmt>

Unfortunately it didn't work this time. I sniffed. *I won't cry,* I promised myself as a tear slid down my cheek.

In, then out. In, then out. I concentrated on my breathing, trying to stay as calm as possible. Trying not to imagine all the things they might do to me before my team rescued me.

I still wore my tracking freckle and ear transceiver. With my hands tied, I couldn't access my collar talk button, but at least I would hear my team if they spoke. At least they knew my coordinates.

It could be a whole lot worse.

That's what I told myself. Convinced myself of, really.

The car slowed to a stop. Based on the time we'd driven, I'd say we were probably in the country at Romanov's castle.

Gripping my arm, the goon pulled me from the car into the frozen night. He led me along a path, and we entered a warm, musty building. We descended 102 steps. I counted them like TL taught me. *Be aware of everything,* he'd said.

Something metal creaked in front of me, like a door being opened. The goon ripped the hood from my head and shoved me forward, slamming the door behind me.

I gritted my teeth in anger, pleased to feel that emotion over fear. They didn't have to be so rough. I'd go on my own if they'd ask.

Dimly lit, the square room was approximately twenty by twenty feet. One single metal chair sat dead center on the cement floor. No way I'd sit in it. That's where the bad guys tied the good guys while torturing information from them. The drain under the chair probably made for ease in washing away blood. Although no red remnants stained the sterile room.

Where was this place? The dungeons of Romanov's castle? A deserted building? Maybe they'd driven me around to make me think we were going someplace else, and we were actually still at the modeling school.

Starting in the corner, I paced the perimeter. With my hands still tied, I could only visually inspect the cinder-block, windowless walls. I didn't see any cameras. Not to say they weren't hidden somewhere. Surely they wouldn't put me in here without monitoring me.

Minutes rolled by and I continued pacing.

The door unbolted, and I spun around right as a goon tore a hood off someone and shoved him inside. David!

Relief hit me hard, and tears burst free. The bravery I'd talked myself into, the irritation at being roughly handled, gushed free. Only euphoria at not being alone and comfort at seeing someone familiar flooded my senses.

The goon slammed the door, closing David and me up. With his hands tied behind his back, he covered the short distance between us. No one had ever looked so welcoming as he did at this very moment.

He pressed his cheek to mine. "Shhh . . ."

I sniffed, but more tears fell. All the fear at being kidnapped and not knowing what would happen flowed from my soul. All the warm support of his cheek against mine made me want to sob. Yet sobbing was the absolute last thing either of us needed.

Questions ping-ponged through my brain as I slowly regained composure. What's he doing here? Did the bad guys get TL and Jonathan, too? Where's David's dad?

Sniffing, I wiped my cheek on my shoulder. David leaned back with a slight curve to his lips, which made me smile. "What happen—"

David placed his lips against my ear. "Stay in character," he murmured. "Not sure how much they know. They're watching and listening. Remember that. Got caught on purpose. Didn't want you alone. Help's on the way."

Got caught on purpose. Didn't want you alone.

My stomach fluttered at his meaningful words. Shifting, I pressed my lips to his jaw. *This might be the last kiss of my life,* I thought, taking in his warmth, enjoying his stubble brushing my face.

The door unbolted, and we reluctantly moved away from each other.

Petrov, the GQ guy from the party, came into the room. He'd been so nice. I couldn't imagine him harming anyone.

Romanov followed, and dread settled in. He didn't strike me as the type to play nice. Quietly, he approached us, coming to a stop right in front of me. He studied me through black, soulless eyes.

Keeping my back against the wall, I fought the urge to fidget, to swallow, to hide my eyes from his evil gaze. The longer he scrutinized me, the more aware I became of my thundering heart and irregular breaths.

He lifted his hand, and David took a step forward. "Leave her alone."

"I vill"—Romanov didn't take his eyes off me—"not hurt her."

He caressed a finger down my cheek. His creepy softness scared me more than his goons' brute force. "I do not vant her touched. Such beauty should be vorshipped."

The do-not-touch order gave me a flicker of faith.

Romanov brushed a thumb over my black eye. "Seems like my statue did great damage to your delicateness."

He pressed my black eye just enough to make me cringe, killing off the flicker of faith. He knew exactly what he was doing.

"A model who knows how to extract information from a microsnipet. Hmm . . ." Romanov patted my cheek. "So tell me, how long have you been a spy?"

"I don't know what you're talking about."

His lips curved into a creepy smile. "Ah, you vill tell me in time."

In time? How long did he plan on keeping me?

He turned and strolled from the room, Petrov following. They closed and bolted the door, and I blew out a long, shaky breath.

David came to me. "You okay?"

Okay? I was far from okay. Kidnapped, locked in a dungeon, shoved around by goons. No telling what came next. I nodded, though. "You?"

"Fine."

Roughly ten minutes later, the door unbolted again, sending nausea straight to my mouth. Nalani stepped in. Not her, too. I really liked her.

"Come quick," she whispered.

‹THIRTEEN›

I glanced at David.

What if this was a trap? What if Nalani worked for a different bad group and was leading us straight to them? What if she was only pretending to help us as part of some twisted game Romanov was playing?

David nodded. "It's all right. She's one of us."

She's one of us? Why hadn't he told me?

"I'll tell you later," he said, reading my mind.

With a pocketknife, Nalani sliced the duct tape binding our hands. We followed her silently from the dungeon through a maze of narrow, dark tunnels. Jogging soundlessly, barely breathing, making as little noise as possible.

We came to a slim, steel door. She dug a key from her pants pocket and quickly unlocked it. Frosty air gushed in as we rushed out. The three of us bolted over frozen leaves and dirt toward bordering woods.

I peeked over my shoulder but didn't recognize the house. Small, neat, and tidy. Who would ever guess it contained a dungeon? Behind the house, in the distance, loomed the castle. We were on Romanov's property.

We sprinted into the dark woods. TL and Jonathan emerged from the shadows, and I nearly leaped for joy.

Nalani gave David and me quick hugs. "Be safe. I'll see you in a while." She dashed off in the opposite direction.

Leading the way, TL ran through the woods, and we followed, with Jonathan in the rear. A gazillion questions zinged my brain. Where were we going? Where was David's dad? Who was Nalani? What about Romanov and his goons? Had David known Nalani would rescue us?

We emerged from the woods and came to a skidding stop.

There stood Romanov, seven goons looming alongside him.

Uh-oh.

They must have heard us because they all turned at once. TL, Jonathan, and David moved lightning quick before I blinked or Romanov's men registered what was going on. Fists and feet shot out in calculated, high-flying kicks and swings. Bones cracked. Blood flew. Men grunted. Within seconds, three goons lay passed out on the road, or maybe dead, and my team moved on to the next set.

Snapping from my shocked trance, I quickly recalled self-defense training and ran toward the mob. Bruiser popped into my mind. For the first time in my life, I wished I was a small, redheaded, freckled girl with killer fighting capabilities.

In my peripheral vision, I caught Romanov slinking back into the woods. *Wimp*.

Petrov charged me. I spun and roundhoused him in the stomach. His face registered disbelief as he stumbled backward.

That's right, buddy, disbelieve this.

I stalked his stumbling body, gaining ground, and uppercut him in the nose. Blood and curses gushed from him. His shocked expression transformed to squinty eyes and hard jaw. Like he was thinking, *Zere's no way zis female vill vin.*

Yeah? Well, he'd never fought a possessed genius until now.

I chopped him in the Adam's apple, ignoring the popping sound, then whipped around and smashed my heel into his kneecap. Gagging, he grabbed hold of his throat and fell to his knees.

Scowling at his hunched form, I circled behind him. I put him in a headlock, my right arm around his throat and left pressing the back of his neck. He jerked against my hold, clawing at my jacketed arm, wheezing for breath. Seconds later, he went limp.

I released him and stepped back, resisting the urge to dust my hands in victory. Ready to take on my next opponent, I glanced up. TL, Jonathan, and David stood with their feet braced apart and arms folded, watching me. On the ground around them sprawled Ushbanian goons in various passed-out positions.

My team broke into matching grins and applauded.

Smiling in return, I gave in to the urge to dust my hands, and they burst out laughing.

Just then a windowless, black van came barreling down the dirt road. Great, more bad guys.

TL started toward it. "Ride's here."

My shoulders drooped in relief. That meant an airplane back to the States was mere hours away. I was actually excited about getting on a plane. Go figure.

Stepping around Petrov, I followed the guys toward the van. Fatigue hit me hard, and my boots dragged in the dirt. I'd had little or no sleep since leaving California. Hard to believe so much had happened in the span of four days.

From the driver's seat, Nalani nodded as I passed by. I tripped as I did a double take, which made her smile. I bet she was the insider TL had told us about.

TL opened the back door. "Let's go."

I climbed in ahead of the guys, expecting to see Mr. Share, but empty cargo space met me instead. I took a seat on the hard floor, as did the guys, and Nalani drove off. A thick screen separated her from us, and I barely saw her profile.

No one spoke, so I kept quiet, too, but jeez, I wanted answers.

David sat across from me, his eyes closed, head lolling in pre-sleep. Beside me, Jonathan did the same. Next to David, TL dialed the satellite phone. A few seconds later, he began speaking in hushed tones. I made out the words *plane, four people, twenty minutes,* and *coffin.*

Coffin? Oh, no, did that mean Mr. Share was dead? I shot a quick glance across the van, but David hadn't moved a muscle. He would've told me by now, wouldn't he? Yeah, right, not like we'd had any time to talk.

How awful for him. To have just been reunited with his dad only to discover he was now dead.

I looked at TL, hoping to learn something, anything, but he'd already ended the call and closed his eyes as well. How anyone could sleep in the back of a noisy, bumpy cargo van was beyond me. But I shut my eyes anyway . . .

"GiGi." Someone nudged my leg. "We gotta move."

My lids popped open in dead-asleep-to-wide-awake alertness. "How long—"

"An hour." David knelt beside me. The van shifted as TL and Jonathan jumped out.

I gripped David's forearm. "Is your dad okay? I heard TL say 'coffin.'"

David shook his head. "That's how we're smuggling him out of the country."

"Oh." I smiled. "I'm glad. Wait, can he survive in a coffin that long?"

"In our coffin he can. Plenty of oxygen, snacks, and water. He'll be fine. Come on, we gotta move."

We hopped from the van into a dawning, icy morning. A forest surrounded us. We were, literally, out in the middle of nowhere. A small, wooden shack stood off to the right, hidden among towering pines. A limo and a hearse sat alongside the shack, looking so out of place I almost laughed.

We crossed the short distance to the shack. David opened the creaky door, and the van cranked its engine. I whipped around.

Nalani. She waved as she drove off through a rough-cut path.

"Who is she?"

"Tell you later." He ushered me inside. "We've got only five minutes."

Already dressed, TL passed us on the way out. Jonathan followed, tucking in his shirt. They'd changed back into their bodyguard and modeling agent clothes.

Except for our suitcases heaped in the middle, a camping stove in the corner, and a small window above it, the dark, wood shack stood dusty and empty. "What is this place?"

"Safe house."

Safe house. Hmm. There was probably more to it than there appeared to be. Maybe a hidden hatch leading to an underground passage. Or a secret panel that opened onto a cache of tucked-away weapons. The whole structure was probably wired with microfilters and thermal thirystors. My pulse kicked in at the techie possibilities.

A man emerged from the shadows, and I jumped.

He smiled and held out his hand. "Mike Share."

My jaw dropped. "Oh, my goodness." I took his hand. "It's so great to meet you. I'm GiGi."

He pumped my hand. "I know."

David threw open my biggest suitcase, snatched the first thing he put his hands on, and threw it to me. "Hurry. You can use the bathroom."

Bathroom? I gazed in the direction he indicated. Sure enough, a door sat seamlessly in the wall. I hurried over and inside and came to an abrupt stop.

Yuck.

A filthy toilet, minus the seat, occupied one corner. Dirty water filled the bowl. A grimy sink stood beside it. Above that hung a mirror layered so thick in dust it prohibited me from seeing myself. No tub. And it smelled like . . . well, you can guess what it smelled like.

"Hurry," David shouted.

I jumped into action, quickly changing, touching as little of the bathroom as possible.

With my old clothes in hand, I opened the door. David had already put on his photographer's clothes. He took one look at my low-rise jeans and blue turtleneck and dug in the suitcase. He tossed me a pair of black, chunky-heeled boots and a black leather jacket.

I threw him my old clothes. "Why are we changing? The mission's over."

"Missions are never over until we return home." He shoved everything back inside the suitcases. "When you assume a new identity, you maintain that identity until you're back at home base. In case some last-second thing goes wrong."

"Makes sense."

While he zipped the suitcases closed, I rapidly finished off my outfit.

We grabbed the luggage and bolted out the door toward the limo and hearse.

David and his dad exchanged a long, hard hug. Then Mr. Share climbed into the back of the hearse.

After throwing the baggage in the trunk of the limo, we joined TL and Jonathan in the back. The limo pulled off, and I closed my eyes with a sigh.

Almost over. Nearly home. So many unanswered questions.

A soft buzzing made me open my eyes. Across from me, TL and Jonathan were shaving with electric razors. Beside me, David brushed his teeth.

TL handed me a small gray bag. "Get in modeling role. Wear sunglasses to hide your eye."

I unzipped it. A butterscotch lollipop lay right on top. My heart warmed with love. How sweet—they packed my candy.

Makeup and toiletries filled the pouch. I rifled through, found a mirror, and took a peek. Sheesh, what a mess. I pulled out a wet wipe and began washing my face.

Whoever thought I'd be riding in a limo with three guys, getting ready, like sharing a bathroom or something?

We pulled up to the international airport, stepped from the cozy, warm limo, and it was like nothing had ever happened. Jonathan whipped out his cell phone, TL stuck stoically to my side, and David strutted cockily behind. I led the way, strolling through the terminal, head up and shoulders back.

"Your autograph?"

Smiling down at the young boy, I took his pad of paper and pen and scrawled *Jade January*. He had no idea who I was. But with my entourage, I sure seemed like someone famous.

The airport announced our flight. With a good-bye wave to the boy, we made our way onto the plane.

"Who's Nalani?" I whispered to David after we took our first-class seats. "And what about Romanov? What happened to him?"

David shook his head with a yawn, closed his eyes, and lay back. "Later."

I peered across the aisle to where Jonathan and TL sat. They'd already reclined their seat backs. With a resigned sigh, I shut my eyes.

David shifted in his seat. He slid his arm over the top of mine and we linked fingers. "Breeeeaaathe," he muttered sleepily.

Breeeaaathe. He was worried about my fear of flying. How sweet. I lowered my head to his shoulder, cradling our intertwined arms between us, and cuddled into his warmth.

Seconds later, he rested his cheek on my head. "Mmmm . . ."

Mmmm, indeed.

***

Sixteen hours later, our limo pulled up in front of the ranch with Mr. Share's hearse behind us.

David leaped from the limo before it came to a full stop and sprinted to the hearse.

I stepped out with Jonathan and TL following. We all still wore our mission clothes.

David flung open the back of the hearse and disappeared inside. Seconds later, he emerged with his father. Mr. Share squeezed David's shoulder and said something. David laughed. The sound brought a smile to my face. I hadn't seen him so genuinely happy in a while.

His hand still on David's shoulder, Mr. Share approached us. He and David didn't look anything alike. Exact opposites really. Mr. Share stood a little shorter than David and had blond hair instead of brown. David must favor his mother.

TL popped the trunk on the limo. "How was the coffin?"

"Soft jazz, Cheetos, sweet tea, a down pillow, full night's rest." Mr. Share smiled. "All my favorite things. It's been ten years since I've had them. I can't complain."

His coffin ride sounded more comfortable than our first-class seats.

I was dying to ask him about the last ten years of his life. But TL had told me Mr. Share was not allowed to say anything or access a computer until IPNC officials had debriefed and cleared him.

Mr. Share closed his eyes and lifted his face to the sun. He drew in a slow, deep breath.

I watched him, wondering what it would be like to be locked away for ten years without fresh air, the sun, the rain. To sit at a computer year in and year out and steal money for a terrorist. It was amazing that he hadn't gone insane from the isolation. Thoughts of David must have kept him going.

TL grabbed two suitcases from the limo's trunk. "We'll pile the luggage in the hall and head straight to the computer lab."

My teammates would be home from school in a little while. The thought excited me. I realized that I'd missed them.

Jonathan and David each took a duffel bag. I reached for a suitcase at the same time as Mr. Share.

"Sorry." I laughed.

He smiled at me. "ST and BIR," he whispered, as he quickly picked up another piece of luggage and strode toward the front door.

ST and BIR?

Scrunching my brows, I studied his back, slowly following everyone inside. I tried to catch Mr. Share's eyes to silently ask him what he meant, but he wouldn't look at me.

Minutes later, we entered Chapling's and my lab. Chapling's and *my* lab. I loved saying that.

Chapling stood at the coffeepot, pouring himself what I felt sure was his billionth cup of the day.

He glanced up as we strode in. "Hey!" He caught sight of Mr. Share. "Mike!" Chapling put the pot down and hurried over. "Wow!"

Chuckling, Mr. Share leaned down and hugged him. "Hey, Chap, been a long time. You look just the same."

"Oh, yeah. Yeahyeahyeahyeahyeah. Still short and redheaded."

Everyone laughed.

Chapling gave me a quick hug. "Missed you."

I squeezed him back. "I missed you, too."

He waved everyone in. "Come in. Welcomewelcomewelcome."

We all scooted in.

Chapling wiggled up onto his stool. "So where's this famous chip you programmed with all the government's information?"

Mr. Share leaned against the table bisecting the lab. "It's in David's butt."

David and I exchanged confused glances.

Chapling burst out laughing. "It's in his what?"

"You heard me right." Mr. Share nodded.

TL shook his head. "I don't understand."

Mr. Share turned to David. "Know that tiny scar on your backside?"

David nodded.

"That's where I had it surgically inserted over a decade ago."

Nobody uttered a sound. Probably because they were thinking the exact same thing as me. What the . . . ?

"You mean"—David laughed—"I've been carrying around the key to our nation's security in my rump?"

"Yep."

"Man, Dad, you're a loon."

Mr. Share shrugged. "I have my moments. So, if GiGi will excuse us, the doctor should be here any second. We can finally get it out, transfer the information, and then lock it away for good."

"Well," I glanced at David, dropping my gaze to his backside. "Good luck."

He shook his head with a chuckle. "Thanks."

TL followed me from the lab. We made our way through the ranch's underground hallways, past the locked doors that still remained a mystery to me.

At the elevator, TL stopped me. "I'm proud to say I've been on a mission with you. You not only met my expectations but far exceeded them. You've proven time and time again how valuable you are to this team. Don't ever question or forget that."

Pride swelled inside me. TL rarely gave accolades unless he really meant them. So when he did, it made it even that much more special. "Thank you."

He nodded.

My brain replayed his praise over and over again as I rode the elevator to the main floor. We parted ways in the hallway, he to his office and me to the girls' bedroom. Amazing how many changes I'd been through over the past couple of months. Emotionally and physically.

I never imagined I'd turn out this way.

I entered the girls' bedroom, heading straight for my old dinged-up suitcase. Time to unpack. Time to make this place my real home.

Beaker sat cross-legged in the corner with Wirenut. She'd dyed her hair blue while I was gone. They were unpacking their book bags. They must have just gotten home.

I smiled at them both. "Hi." Boy, it felt good to see them.

Wirenut glanced up and returned my smile. "Welcome home, GiGi. Everyone missed you."

"Thanks."

"Nice shiner." Beaker smirked.

Okay, apparently everyone missed me *but* her. I didn't take offense, though. Her smirk was her way of saying she'd missed me.

I wanted to tell them everything about my mission, but I wasn't allowed. They knew that and didn't ask for details. TL would tell them what he wanted them to know.

Wirenut nodded to my dresser. "Your new glasses came in. They look *a lot* better than those weird wire ones you've been wearing."

I made a face at him and he laughed.

Bruiser rushed into the room, closing the door behind her. Her T-shirt read JUST TRY ME. She gave me a quick hug. "Glad you're back." She held out her hands. "You're not going to believe what I just overheard. TL's on the phone with somebody, and I heard him say, 'What do you mean the Specialists lost funding?'"

135

‹FOURTEEN›

I stayed rooted to my spot, one hand hovering over my suitcase, staring at Bruiser.

The Specialists lost funding? What the . . . ? It didn't make any sense. "I don't understand."

Bruiser shrugged. "I don't know. He's arguing with someone right now. I heard him say, 'Where are the kids supposed to go? We're family.'"

Wirenut pushed to his feet, knocking over his and Beaker's chemistry experiment. "Darn right we're family. First one I've had, and I'm not losing it." He strode to the door. "I'm finding out what's going on."

Beaker jumped up. "Wait for me."

"Me, too." Bruiser hurried after them.

I followed behind at a numb, slower shuffle, too stunned to do much of anything else. Where would I go? What would I do? I could go back to East Iowa University and finish up my studies. But somehow I couldn't picture myself back in that old lifestyle.

My future was different now. *I* was different now. For the first time in my life, I belonged somewhere. People here relied on me and needed me. I needed each and every one of them, too.

Even Beaker and her sour moods.

Tears welled up in my eyes as their faces flashed across my brain. Chapling's fuzzy red head and caffeine-induced hyperactivity. Bruiser's innocent freckles and kick-butt moves. Wirenut's goatee and electronics brilliance. Mystic's football neck and peaceful aura. Beaker's Goth clothes and chemistry tubes. Parrot's Native American heritage and multilinguistic tongue. Jonathan's eye patch and physical training. TL's unending patience.

And David . . .

I caught my breath on an overwhelming feeling of loss. This hodgepodge of a group was my family. I couldn't say good-bye. I *wouldn't* say good-bye.

Wirenut tapped on TL's door.

"Enter."

"What's happening?" Mystic whispered from down the hall.

Bruiser put her finger to her lips and motioned him and Parrot to join us where we stood.

Wirenut pushed TL's door open and stepped inside. We crowded in behind him. "We would like to know what's going on."

Sitting behind his desk, TL leaned back in his chair and crossed his arms. He made eye contact with each of us, slowly moving from one to another. "I take it one of you overheard me on the phone."

"Me, sir." Bruiser raised her hand.

TL nodded, accepting. "We lost our funding as a result of the government's budget cuts." He closed his eyes briefly, then reopened them. Sorrow and devastation contorted his face.

I stared in stunned amazement, unable to grasp the emotion he displayed. This from a man who was always in control.

"I'm sorry." He lowered his chair to the floor. "I'm truly sorry. I'll call an official meeting in one hour after I know more." He picked up the phone. "Close the door on your way out."

We shuffled into the hall and just stood there. Silently. Our shoulders weighted with worry. I felt sure the same question replayed in everyone's brain.

What's going to happen to us?

With a sigh, Wirenut turned away first. The rest of us trudged behind, back down the hall to the girls' bedroom. Nobody uttered a sound as we sprawled across the beds, fixing our gazes on the carpet, walls, ceilings, or furniture.

Silent moments ticked by, broken only by someone's sigh.

"This sucks." Bruiser interrupted the quiet.

Parrot flopped from his stomach to his back. "You got that right."

"Not like TL doesn't want us." Beaker heaved a frustrated breath. "It's money, right? If we could find money, we'd be set."

Mystic shoved a pillow under his head. "Hey, Wirenut, feel like going back to your old ways? Break into a bank or two."

Wirenut chuckled halfheartedly. "No, I'm not going back to my old ways."

If we could find money, we'd be set. Beaker's words echoed through my brain as I lay beside Wirenut, staring at the ceiling.

ST and BIR.

I jackknifed up, realization slapping me in the face.

Shooting off the bed, I raced from the room and down the hall to the elevator. Faintly, I heard the others call after me.

Shaking with anticipation, I placed my hand on the globe-light print scan. While the laser skimmed my fingers and palm, dizziness waved through me.

Oh, no, not now.

The door opened, and I staggered inside. *Hold on, GiGi, you're almost there.*

As I plastered my body to the wall, the elevator tilted, and I squeezed my eyes shut. *Don't pass out.*

Three years ago I did. From my rapid-fore processes. The doctor said my brain worked too fast for my body. I felt that familiar trance coming on now.

The elevator opened, and I stumbled out. Right into David's arms.

"GiGi, you okay?"

With a jerky nod, I pushed away. "C'puter."

"Wha—"

Shaking my head, I stumbled a few feet toward Chapling's and my lab. The hallway morphed to a stretched blur. *Don't black out. Hold on.*

David slipped his arm under my knees and swooshed me off the ground. He sprinted down the hall with me bouncing lightly in his arms.

At the lab's door, he lowered me and, holding me tight, punched in the code. I dropped my forehead to his shoulder, my brain triple-timing, fighting the urge to give in and pass out.

He carried me across the lab to my computer, slid me into the seat, and placed my hands on the keyboard.

My fingers took on a life of their own, racing over the keys, translating my cerebrum's processes.

I sat hypnotized by the scrolling screen, letting my body and brain lead the way.

Seconds passed, or maybe minutes. David slipped a lollipop in my mouth—yum, mango—then glasses on my nose. The screen cleared, and immediately my fatigue lifted. Like I'd gotten a shot of caffeine.

"Oh, smartgirlsmartgirl," Chapling mumbled from behind me.

"What's she doing?"

"Ohyeahohyeahohyeah. Gogogogogo."

"Chapling?"

"Oh, sorry." Chapling giggled. "She's worming her way through ST and BIR."

"ST and BIR?"

"Security Trust and Banking International Records."

"That's not legal."

"Shhh."

David cursed. "She's not stealing, is she?"

"Nonononono. Nothing like that. She's looking for Romanov's money. Shhh, let her work."

"Exactly what I was hoping she would do," Mr. Share whispered. I hadn't even realized he'd come in.

They stopped talking as I wound through one account to the next. Spiraling through special-interest funds, jumping from government finances to private. With each successful hop, my crowded brain cleared a little, popping focus and energy back into place.

Aaahhh. Excitement jolted through my veins. *There you are, you sneaky little weasel.*

Couple more keystrokes and I clicked print. "Let's go."

***

TL closed the conference-room door. With a contented curve to his lips, he swept his gaze around the packed room. The Specialists Teams One and Two, Jonathan, Chapling, and Mr. Share all crowded in. I stood along the sidewall between Parrot and Mystic.

"By now, all of you know the government pulled our funding in recent budget cuts. I don't think I have to say how much this place means to me. To all of us." TL cleared his throat. "Unbeknownst to me, GiGi took it upon herself to find the needed monies."

Everyone turned and looked at me, and my stomach turned one huge flip.

"Romanov Schalmosky made a career of stealing. Not only from the United States, but from other countries as well. He took technology, money." TL glanced at Mr. Share. "People, too. GiGi found Romanov's money and deposited it back in the accounts of the rightful owners."

The entire room broke into cheers, and I grinned, literally, from ear to ear. I glanced across the room to where Mr. Share stood, and he winked at me.

TL held his hands up for silence. "We've notified everyone that she's found and returned their money. And they, in turn, gave us a generous percentage. The Specialists are back in action. We're private now, though. No more government funding. We work for whoever hires us. So let's call it a day and celebrate. Everyone meet up top in the common area in ten. We got a party going on."

Everyone cheered again, catcalling and whooping.

Mystic poked me in the ribs. "Go, GiGi."

Parrot bumped my shoulder with his. "That's our genius girl."

Smiling, I bumped him back.

Specialist Team Two passed me on their way out, punching my shoulder and thanking me.

Jonathan bear-hugged me. "I'm so proud of you."

Chapling did some sort of jig. "Smartgirl, smartgirl."

TL took my hand and clasped it warmly between both of his. Like he'd done so many times over the months to calm, comfort, and reassure me. "I knew you'd fit in."

He was right. I did fit in. More than I ever thought possible.

Mr. Share kissed my cheek. "Young lady, I don't know what to say to you. Thank you is too small to express my gratitude. If it weren't for you, there's no telling who would own me now. I owe you my life. If you ever need anything, you just ask. I'll do everything in my power to make your every wish come true."

The meaningfulness in his voice and words left me humbly mute. I *had* saved his life, hadn't I? "And thank you. ST and BIR?" I whispered.

He winked. "I knew where Romanov's money was. And I thought that a computer whiz with access to a keyboard could use that information."

"Will I see you again?"

"Perhaps. I have a series of debriefings to go through. I've been gone a long time. A known terrorist has kept me prisoner for the past ten years.

The United States government has a lot of questions for me. I'll be relocated soon with a new identity."

"What about David?"

"We'll see each other occasionally." Mr. Share kissed my cheek again, and then he leaned back and studied my face. "Gosh," he said, chuckling. "You look just like your mother."

I looked just like my . . . ? What . . . ? My mother . . . ? H-how . . . how did he know what my mother looked like?

With a quick pinch to my chin, he headed from the room.

My file. He'd probably seen my file.

My team shuffled in, surrounding me. I stood in the center, looking at each of their silly smiles. What were they up to now?

"GROUP HUUUG!" they yelled, and collided together, smooshing me in the middle.

We laughed and giggled and jabbed one another.

"Okay, okay, break it up." David wedged us apart. "Scat. I want a moment alone with the woman who saved the day."

"Ooohhh," my team teased. "He wants a moment alooone."

David chuckled and waved them off. "Get outta here."

We watched them file out and close the door.

I smiled. "I really missed them."

"Ya know, it's neat that you all have chosen to go by your code names all the time."

Yeah, it was. "Why doesn't Team One?"

David shrugged. "Don't know. We just don't."

They had their matching Specialists T-shirts, and we had our nicknames.

Slowly, David moved in, backing me up against the wall, until we stood toe-to-toe, our faces only inches from each other. My normal, happy, pitter-patter pulse revved to hyperdrive mode, and my stomach nose-dived to the floor.

"Smell good you." I shook my head. "I mean, you smell good." I groaned. "Did I actually say that out loud?"

His dark eyes crinkled with amusement. "You're nervous right now. Do you know how I know you're nervous right now?"

Swallowing, I shook my head.

"Because you always mix up your words when you get nervous."

"Oh."

David tapped my forehead. "I think smart chicks are cool."

141

He'd said the exact same thing back at East Iowa University.

"So, smart chick, I just wanted you to know you did a great job."

"Thanks," I croaked.

Smiling, he pressed a kiss to my cheek, linked fingers with me, and led me from the conference room. "Come on. TL's waiting."

My coherence slowly returned as we made our way through the underground corridors, past the mysterious locked doors. "What's behind all those?"

"You know I can't tell you. Everyone finds out when TL wants them to."

"Well, that's a bummer."

David laughed.

"Hey, what about Nalani? And Romanov, too. What happened to him?"

We came to the elevator. David punched in his code and placed his hand on the fingerprint-identification panel. We stepped inside.

"Nalani apprehended Romanov. He's not expected to live long. He'll die in custody."

It took a moment for that to sink in. "Who is she?"

David folded his arms across his chest and leaned back against the elevator's wall. I enjoyed a delicious second of staring at his tanned biceps, curved out from his white T-shirt.

"Don't say a word about this to anyone, okay?"

I nodded, peeling my gaze away from his muscles.

"Nalani's TL's wife."

My jaw dropped. "Shut up. Are you serious?"

"Yep."

"Wow. That's huge."

"She works for the IPNC. She's what we call a preoperator. She goes in before the actual mission and gathers intelligence. Cements herself within the opposing organization."

"That's so dangerous."

"She worked for Romanov almost two years." David lifted off the wall when the elevator stopped.

"Unbelievable." What dedication she had to her job. "Why aren't she and TL living together?"

David shrugged. "Don't know the details. This mission was the first time I met her."

"Why didn't anyone tell me her identity?"

"TL and IPNC were concerned that she might have defected. But obviously she's still on our side."

"Will we see her again?"

"Probably."

We stepped into the hall. Laughter, music, and the scent of burgers floated from the common area.

He took my hand. "Let's go party."

"You go on. I'll be there in a minute."

"Everything okay?"

"Fine. I just need a minute. I want to change clothes and clean up a little."

"All right." He let go of my hand. "See ya in a few."

As he headed to the celebration, I made my way down the hall to my room. I dragged my suitcase from under my bed and opened it. As I pulled out a pair of jeans and a T-shirt, my gaze lingered on all my other clothes. I glanced over to my dresser and then back to my suitcase.

With a smile, I grabbed a wad of clothes, opened a dresser drawer, and tossed them inside. I snatched up another handful and threw them in, too. Then another, and another, and another.

Finishing up, I shoved the suitcase under my bed with a salute. "So long, suitcase. I'm home now. I'm here to stay."

BOOK TWO

ONE MISSTEP AND THE MANSION WILL EXPLODE. . . .

In our wet suits, we flutter-kicked our way through the dark ocean. Wirenut first, me second, and TL brought up the rear.

Water plugged my ears, permitting me to hear only my heartbeat and slow deep breaths.

Through my night goggles, I kept my vision focused on Wirenut's fins. *One misstep rigs the mansion to explode.*

Talk about pressure.

We made it through the fence and continued underwater around the island to the east side.

We exited the water and stripped our diving gear, then piled it on the sliver of rocky beach.

From his vest, Wirenut pulled four pressurized suction cups. Two he strapped to his knees and two he held in his hands. TL and I did the same. Air release controlled the suction, allowing for silent attachment and release. They worked on any surface.

Wirenut turned to us, touched his eye, and held up one finger. *Watch closely. One at a time.*

TL and I nodded. Wirenut suctioned onto the stone and began a spiderlike crawl. I scrutinized his form, memorizing his technique and rhythm.

He made it to the roof and signaled for me.

One misstep rigs the mansion to explode.

With a deep breath I suctioned onto the wall.

‹PROLOGUE›

Using his homemade, handheld computer, the HOMAS B28, Frankie flipped through prescanned floor plans.

Impenetrable. That's what all the suppliers, media, and tech journals were bragging about the Rayver Security System.

We'll just see about that.

He tucked the B28 in his zippered thigh pocket and pulled out a granola bar.

Unwrapping it, Frankie studied the dark New Mexico Museum of History from the sidewalk. Easy enough to get in the front door. Standard nixpho lock with a keypad. Any kindergartener with half an IQ could do it, too.

He folded the chewy bar in half and shoved the whole thing in his mouth. Apple cinnamon. Not his favorite, but it was all the corner store had.

The true challenge of this job lay in the triple-sealed, flexsteel vault. Protected by the oh-so-impressive Rayver Security System.

Frankie didn't know what was in the vault. Didn't care. He was here to crack the impenetrable Rayver System. No more, no less. Just to prove he could do it.

Tossing the wrapper in the already full garbage can, he crossed the shadowed street.

The two-story brick museum stood at the end of a long dead end road with woods along the back and sides.

It was deserted. Too good to be true.

Frankie pulled his hood down over his face as he neared the entrance.

Five-five-six-four-three-zero. He punched in the code he'd seen the museum manager use every night this week. Anybody with binoculars and enough patience could've retrieved it, too.

Click. The door unlocked, and he slipped inside.

Standing in the entranceway, he scanned the dimly lit interior, recalling the layout. Left. Two rooms. Stairwell down. One room to the right.

"Okay, Frankie," he whispered to himself. "Game's on. Don't get too confident. Never know what might happen."

He closed his eyes and blew out a long slow breath. Then, with quiet feet, he shuffled left into the African Bone Boom. A glass display case ran the center's length.

With his back to the west wall, he watched the corner camera. From his last visit to the museum, he recalled that it scanned in two-second intervals, moving a fraction of an inch to the right with each scan. He needed to make it across the room before it scanned back. No problem.

Staying in its blind spot, Frankie baby-stepped on each two-second interval and made it safely to the other side.

He entered the New Zealand Hat Boom. No display cases here.

No cameras either. Strange-looking hats hung on the walls, each rigged with an alarm should one be removed.

He squashed the mischievous urge to take one down just to prove it could be done and crossed the carpet to the stairwell on the other side.

Suddenly, he stopped in midstep. Cold prickles crawled across his skin. *Somebody's in here.*

Slowly, he pivoted, searching every corner, shadow, and inch of space.

Nothing.

A good solid minute ticked by as he listened closely. Soft air-conditioner hum. Nearly inaudible camera ticks. Quiet laser alarm buzz.

Nothing else. No shuffle of a person's feet. No breath.

Funky imagination. That's all. Although he really didn't believe himself.

From his vest pocket Frankie pulled out a wad of homemade gray putty and a six-inch length of bamboo that he used as a blowgun. Balling the putty, he fit it in the end of the bamboo.

The stairwell's camera hung catty-corner near the bottom. He rolled his black hood above his lips. Sighted down the length of the bamboo. Took a breath. Put it in his mouth. And blew.

The putty flew like a dart and plunked right on the lens.

Yeah, that's what I'm talking about.

He tiptoed down the stairs and hung a right, and his pulse jumped like it did every time a new security system challenged him.

The impenetrable Rayver System.

Impenetrable, his big toe.

He pulled down his fiber-lit goggles used for laser detection from on top of his head and fit them over his eyes.

Bingo.

Yellow lasers zigzagged the room preceding the vault. One-twothreefourfivesix . . . twenty ankle high. The same at the waist. Six on the ceiling.

Child's play. Except for the yellow, skin-sizzling color. Whatever happened to the reliable red set-off-the-alarm-but-don't-fry-the-burglar color?

Leaning to the left at a seventy-degree angle, he spied a tunnel-like opening void of lasers. *You'd think the tech geniuses would've figured this out by now.*

Frankie unbuttoned a pocket in his cargo pants and pulled out the remote-control expander. Pointing it toward the opening of the tunnel, he pressed the expander button.

A skinny metal wire snaked out, becoming stiff as it left the remote control.

Steady, Frankie, steady.

One slight movement and the wire would collapse into the lasers.

It made it through the small tunnel void of lasers, across the room, and straight into the tiny hole below the vault's lock.

The lasers flicked off, and he quickly set his watch. He had exactly one minute and seventeen seconds until they turned back on.

Reeling in the expandable wire, he ran over the open tile to the vault. He yanked a tool kit from his vest and laid the triple-folded leather pouch on the ground. He took nitrox, a metal adhesive release, and squirted the control panel.

It popped off, and Frankie caught it before it clanged to the ground. Anything over twenty-five decibels would set off the alarm.

Multicolored wires crisscrossed and tangled with one another.

A diversion.

He reached in, grabbed the clump, and ripped them right out. Red lasers immediately flicked on, filling the control panel opening.

Frankie took the extra-long needle-nose wire cutters from his tool pouch and, leaning to the left at a seventy-degree angle, found his opening.

Carefully, he inserted the wire cutters through the opening surrounded by lasers and snipped the one remaining white wire at the very back.

The vault clicked open. The control panel lasers flicked off. Frankie checked his watch.

Twenty seconds remaining.

Snatching up the tools, he flung the vault door open. A small wooden man, an artifact of some sort, sat on a stand in the middle of the vault.

A weight-sensitive stand.

Crud.

He hadn't expected that.

Frankie estimated the artifact at three pounds and took three one-pound pellets from his tool pouch. Holding his breath, he slipped the artifact off and the pellets on all in one smooth motion.

And froze.

Nothing. Only silence.

No alarms. No lasers.

He checked his watch.

Three seconds remaining.

Frankie sprinted back across the room. His watch alarm dinged. He dove the last few feet and whipped around to see the yellow lasers flick back on.

Whew.

Smiling, he did his victory shoulder-roll dance.

Oh, yeah. Frankie got it going on.

Go, Frankie. Go, Frankie. Go. Go.

He packed his stuff, slipped a yellow ribbon from his sock, and tied it around the artifact. It was his signature. He wished he could be here to see them discover it outside its *impenetrable* vault.

With a pat to its head, he stood.

"Cute," a voice spoke.

Frankie spun around. Another person stood behind him.

Pointing a gun.

His heart stopped. Then he saw the gun shake.

Why . . . he's nervous.

The other guy flicked it toward the artifact. "Give it to me." Something distorted his voice.

Frankie ran his gaze down the length of the other burglar and back up. He looked like a skinnier version of Frankie. Black cargo pants and vest. Black hood. Black martial arts slippers.

"I said, Give it to me."

Frankie shrugged. "Sure." Why did he care? He hadn't come for this silly thing anyway.

Behind the hood, the burglar narrowed his eyes, like he didn't believe it'd be that easy.

"It's all yours." Frankie stepped to the side.

The burglar paused. Shook his head. "Hand it to me."

Frankie sighed. "Oh, all right." He snatched it from the ground and tossed it to the burglar.

The burglar's eyes widened as he fumbled with the gun and caught the artifact.

Frankie watched him juggle the two things. He could totally take down this idiot. The burglar was *way* too amusing, though, and Frankie needed a good laugh.

Holding the artifact to his chest, the burglar scrambled to get the gun pointed back at Frankie. "You think you're funny, don't you?

He shrugged. Yeah, actually, he did.

The burglar backed his way up the stairs, still pointing the gun at Frankie.

"Can't fire that thing, ya know. You'll set off the alarms in this place."

The burglar paused in his backward ascent as if he hadn't thought about that. "You're the Ghost, aren't you?"

Frankie gave his best sixteenth-century bow. "The one and only."

"I . . . I've studied you."

The small admission pumped his ego. "Then you know I'm no threat. I did what I came here to do."

Seconds ticked by. The burglar slipped the gun inside his vest.

"Safety," Frankie reminded him.

"It's not loaded."

He laughed at having been tricked.

The burglar raced up the stairs toward the New Zealand Hat Room, and Frankie followed. With his back to the west wall, the burglar inched around the African Bone Room.

Frankie watched his fluid, timed movements as he kept pace with the camera that scanned in two-second intervals. Not such a novice. He'd been trained.

"Who are you?" Frankie whispered across both rooms.

The other burglar stopped and looked back.

"Keep moving!" Frankie hissed at the exact second the burglar missed his two-second step and set off the alarm.

Crud.

The burglar bolted from the room and up the steps to the second floor.

Frankie raced after him, through a narrow hallway and into a huge room. Then he disappeared behind the door to a janitor closet.

Staying right on his heels, Frankie flung open the closet door. The burglar snaked up a rope hanging fifteen feet from an open skylight.

Quick guy.

He'd rigged the skylight alarm with an eraser, a small piece of aluminum foil, and, although Frankie couldn't see it, he knew a dab of olive oil. That particular combination of three elements shorted out standard valumegal wiring. He'd introduced that five years ago, and criminals had copied it ever since.

Sirens filtered through the air, and his pulse jumped. Cops. About a quarter of a mile away.

Yeah, baby, thrill of the chase.

The burglar made it to the roof, and Frankie started his ascent. Halfway there he looked up to see the burglar holding a knife to the rope.

No.

"Sorry," the burglar mumbled, and sliced it clean.

Son of a—Frankie fell and landed on his back. "Umph."

Footsteps pounded outside the door. He jumped to his feet and leapt for the skylight.

The door flew open. "Hold it right there."

Frankie froze and squeezed his eyes shut.

Crud. Double crud.

"Put your hands up."

He stuck his hands in the air. *I'm going to prison for this.*

"Now turn around. *Real* slow."

Opening his eyes, Frankie pivoted.

Someone yanked off his hood and shined a light in his face. Frankie squinted.

"Well, look here. You're just a kid." The cop jerked Frankie's arms back and handcuffed him. "You have the right to remain silent. . . ." The cop hauled Frankie through the museum and out the door.

As the cop shoved Frankie in the squad car, Frankie glanced toward the woods. The burglar stood in the shadows, watching.

***

Frankie sat at a table in an interrogation room. He'd been there for hours.

"Where is it?" The red-faced, big-gut cop slammed his fist on the table. *For the trillionth time.*

It scared Frankie the first, say, two times he did it. Now it just annoyed him. "I don't have it," he repeated. "The other guy took it."

The cop clinched his jaw so hard it made his puffy cheeks vibrate.

Calm down, man. You're gonna have a heart attack.

"Nice *ballet slippers*, fancy boy."

For your information, these are handmade, double-layered martial arts slippers. The outer coating slick for sliding. Peel away to the rubber underneath for climbing.

Frankie's stomach growled loudly. "Can I please have something to eat?" They didn't understand. His metabolism ate calories fast. If he didn't get something soon, he'd get the shakes.

"Eat?" the cop growled. "Are you kidding me? Tell me where the artifact is, and I'll personally shove a burger down your throat."

"Thanks, *buddy*, but no. However inviting that burger sounds." Smart-ass remark. But the cop deserved it.

The cop's entire body shook in response.

I'm really pissing this guy off. "Listen, take some breaths. You're about to pop an artery." Although that'd be mildly satisfying to watch.

The cop reared back and shoved Frankie in the chest, and he flew out of the metal chair.

The interrogation room door clicked open and a guy in a brown suit walked in. He looked at the heavy-breathing, shaking, red-faced cop, then turned calm eyes on Frankie. "Come with me."

Flipping the cop off in his mind, Frankie pushed up from his sprawled position on the floor. He followed the guy through the police station and out the front doors into a hot, dry New Mexico morning. Not a single cop tried to stop them.

The guy led Frankie to a black SUV with tinted windows.

Opening the back door, the guy nodded Frankie inside.

What was going on? Something didn't feel right. Serial killers abducted people this way.

Frankie glanced back at the police station. No one had stopped them. This guy must be legit.

The guy reached inside his jacket and pulled out a wallet. He flipped it open. "Thomas Liba. IPNC."

IPNC?

Frankie studied the man's identification. Same light brown skin. Weird green eyes. Curly brown hair.

Frankie peeked inside the vehicle. It looked more like a cargo van than an SUV. Two benches faced each other, and locked cabinets lined the walls.

With one last look at Thomas, Frankie stepped up into the SUV and got the odd sensation his whole life was about to change.

Thomas closed the door. He opened a wall-mounted fuse box, pressed a button, and air- conditioning began to flow through the vents.

Taking the seat across from Frankie, Thomas pointed to a cooler under Frankie's bench. "Help yourself."

Food! He dove in. Sandwiches, sodas, cookies, chips, fruit, carrot sticks. Oh yeah, a starving man's paradise.

Thomas opened a folder. "Francisco Badaduchi."

Yep. That'd be me. He swallowed. *Love* ham and cheese. "I go by Frankie."

Thomas nodded. "Italian American. Five feet ten. One hundred and seventy pounds. Seventeen years old. One hundred fifty IQ. Black hair. Dark brown eyes. Goatee. Various arm tattoos." He tapped his folder. "You've got quite a record. Mostly five-finger discount. Seems a bit beneath your skills."

Beneath my skills? How would he know that?

Frankie popped a cookie in his mouth. "See something I want, I help myself to it." Anything to get arrested.

"Like juvy hall better than the boys' home, I take it."

Frankie stopped chewing. He stared across the SUV at Thomas, a hunk of cookie in his mouth. *How'd he know that?*

"I was like you once. A system kid. Hated the boys' home. Hated what they did to me there. Juvy hall's safer. Patrolled. I know."

Forcing the unchewed cookie down his throat, Frankie closed the cooler. Food didn't seem so interesting anymore.

Thomas consulted his file again. "Your uncle's on death row for—"

"What do you want with me?" Buried panic tightened Frankie's gut.

"You have a scar on your upper left shoulder where he—"

"What do you want with me?" Memories Frankie did *not* intend to relive.

"Okay. We don't have to talk about your past." Thomas closed the file. "According to court psychologists, you are highly intelligent and handle yourself with humor. You have the potential to be dangerous because of what you witnessed as a child. No one wanted to adopt you because they were afraid of your mental stability."

Idiots. All of them. What did they know anyway? "I said, what do you want with me?"

"I know you're the Ghost. I've followed your career since your first breaking and entering at ten years old."

"I don't know what you're talking about." Bluffer. No way he had evidence. Frankie was too good.

"No more juvy hall. You're going to prison. For a long time. No escape. Know what they do to guys like you in there?"

Frankie swallowed, trying not to be intimidated. "I've heard."

"Then you know it's a place you don't want to be." Thomas opened his file again and flipped through some pages. "You've got quite an online fan club. They buy your homemade electronic contraptions and keep you in business."

Crud. This guy did know a lot about him.

"Fictitious accounts. Rerouted IP addresses. Clever. You've cracked the most secure systems in the world. Systems the highest trained agents haven't even broken."

It came naturally for Frankie. What could he say? "Listen, it's obvious you have my whole life right there in that handy-dandy file. So why don't you tell me what you want?"

Thomas looked up from the folder. "I want you to come work for me."

\<ONE\>

In her skin-tight JUST TRY ME! T-shirt, Bruiser boinged onto her bed. Her red braids boinged with her. "I love a good soap opera. I think it's so cool you two are getting a groove on." She bounced off her bed.

"Shhh." I glanced from my bed toward the open door. Now that I'd managed to convince David I wasn't his "little sister," I didn't want him to know I'd told Bruiser that I liked him. "And we're not getting a groove on." As a matter of fact, it seemed like we rarely had a moment alone.

Laughing, David entered our room, and my stomach swooshed to my feet. Please tell me he didn't just hear us.

He pointed at Bruiser. "I heard that."

Groan.

"You're more trouble than you're worth." He lifted her up in a fireman's hold and tossed her back onto her bed.

She rolled over, grinning. "But don't you all just looove me?"

Over the four and a half months I'd been with the Specialists, Bruiser's silliness hadn't changed at all. It was hard to believe that tiny freckled Molly, or Bruiser, as she'd been code-named, was our resident martial artist. At fifteen, she was a year or two younger than the rest of us. Except David—he was eighteen. But she could outlast all of us. She was a real-life version of the Energizer Bunny.

David threw a pillow at her. "We tolerate you, squirt."

He stretched out beside me on my twin-size bed, and my heart skipped a beat. His cologne swirled up my nose, and I resisted the urge to roll over and bury my face in his neck. Whatever kind he wore, I planned to buy him a whole case of it.

Wirenut strolled in. "Oh, GiGi. Brilliant, klutzy, drop-dead gorgeous GiGi. Ya know, David, you're killing all chances I could've had with this tall blondie. But that's all right. It's all good."

My face warmed at his flirting. I didn't like Frankie, aka Wirenut, our resident electronics expert, in *that* way. He was like a brother or a really cool cousin.

I glanced at him, and he winked, and I knew he was purposefully messing with me.

Wait a minute. Did he just say David killed all his chances? So Wirenut knew I liked David, too?

David stacked his hands beneath his head, and his hip brushed mine, sending a warm wave through my body. Of course Wirenut knew I liked David. Everybody probably knew. How could they not with the fumbling fool I made of myself every time I was around him?

Beaker came out of the bathroom. She snagged her chemistry book off her bed and slid down in her corner of the girls' dormitory room. She stuck her nose in her book and started reading.

Beaker, whose real name was Sissy, didn't seem to like anybody. Me especially. I didn't know what the problem was. I tried not to take her moods personally, but I wished she'd snap out of it. She seemed to get more and more distant as the months went by, when all the rest of us were becoming a family.

Wirenut jumped over Beaker's bed and came down next to her. He put her in a headlock and knuckle-rubbed her choppy blue hair. She pushed him away, grumbling to hide her giggle.

He pushed her back, smiling. Wirenut was the only one who could make her halfway laugh.

Who would've guessed Beaker, the Goth girl with a nose ring and dog collar, would be one of the most brilliant chemists in the world? Looks were *definitely* deceiving, as this group had proven.

"Now, now. Let's all be at peace." Mystic walked in with Parrot and parked it right in the center of the carpeted floor. He folded up his legs and touched his thumbs to his middle fingers, assuming his in-touch-with-the-world position.

Mystic, or Joe, as his real name was, had a NFL player's body, but he possessed the unique gift of clairvoyance. For some reason I never imagined a psychic would be so muscular.

Parrot sprawled across the foot of Bruiser's bed. Darren, aka Parrot, was our linguist. Sixteen languages to be exact. "Almost time for our weekly conference."

Wirenut pointed to a banana on top of my dresser. "Gonna eat that?"

"We just had burgers. You're seriously hungry?"

"Serious."

Wirenut was always eating. He should be like three hundred pounds with all the food he put away. But he just burned it all off like it was nothing. I reached over and tossed him the banana.

David's watch alarm went off. "It's time. Let's go."

We all made our way from our room, past the guys' room and TL's office, and down the long hallway to the elevator.

David placed his hand on the globe light fixture. The hidden laser scanned his print pattern, then the mountainous wall mural slid open to reveal the secret elevator. We all crammed into the small space. David punched in his personal code, and the elevator descended four floors beneath the California ranch where we lived.

We filed out and down the underground hallway, past all the locked doors, including mine and Chapling's computer lab, and came to a stop at the conference room. Thomas Liba, TL, our team leader, sat at the head of a long metal table studying a file. Erin and Adam from Specialists Team One sat to TL's left.

Rolling out the black leather chairs, we took our seats around the table, with David sitting in his usual spot to TL's right.

TL leaned over and whispered something in David's ear, and he nodded. David was TL's right-hand guy. David had lived here his whole life, longer than anybody else. The ranch used to be a safe house for the children of the nation's top agents. With his father being an agent, David grew up here. Now he was being trained to be a strategist, just like TL.

TL stood. "Afternoon, everybody."

We all greeted him.

He closed the file in front of him. "This'll be a quick meeting, as I have a prospective client to meet with. I want to begin by saying that this has been a productive week. We've been a private organization for a month now, and it has opened all sorts of avenues."

With a contained grin, Bruiser nudged me. "Go, GiGi," she mumbled.

I smiled. I'd found the funding that allowed the Specialists to break away from the government and become private.

"As you can tell"—TL motioned around the room—"Piper, Tina, and Curtis from Team One are not here. The girls are in Australia, and Curtis is in Japan. The money we'll make from those two missions alone should sustain us for the next three years. So"—he nodded—"as I said, this had been a productive week."

Everyone applauded.

TL held up his hand for quiet. "Everyone met Mr. Share, David's father, after the last mission to Ushbania. The mission that GiGi went on, and a successful one at that. We were all very proud of her performance on her first mission."

Bruiser nudged me again.

"After being kidnapped by a terrorist cell and held hostage for the past ten years," TL continued, "there was a lot up in the air about Mr. Share. I'm happy to say he's been cleared and is settled in his new life with his new identity."

I glanced at David, wondering when he'd be able to see his father again. I'd have to remember to ask him later on.

"Erin," TL motioned across the table, "give us a quick update on what you and Adam are doing."

Erin rolled her eyes. "That guy who hired us to track his son is wasting his money. All the kid does is go to classes, the library, and the cafeteria."

Adam laughed. "It's too easy a job. I keep waiting for the real fun to kick in."

David smiled. "We're getting paid good money, though, to play private eye. So grin and bear it."

"Easy for you to say," Erin grumbled. "You're not the one yawning on the job."

David chuckled at that. "Speaking of job. How are you tracking him right now?"

Adam held up his watch. "Good ole GPS. We planted a bug on him."

"All right, moving on." TL propped his fingers on the table. "Everyone's report cards came in from the university and San Belden High. With the exception of Mystic's D in gym, we have all As and Bs."

Everyone looked at Mystic, and he shrugged.

"That's it for me. As I said, this would be quick." TL picked up his folder. "Questions?"

We all shook our heads.

"Dismissed." TL motioned to David, and the two of them filed out.

***

The next day I stood with Chapling in our computer lab, staring at his computer.

He rubbed his hands together, looking like a little boy with a really cool toy. "Ready?"

I nodded.

"Computer," he commanded.

HELLO, MR. CHAPLING, the computer typed back.

He giggled. "Coolcoolcool. It worked."

I looked down at him. "Mr. Chapling?"

He shrugged, all innocent. "What? I deserve some respect." Chapling elbowed me. "Now you try."

"Computer," I commanded.

HELLO, GIGI.

"It said my nickname." I laughed. "That is cool."

"*It's* a she," Chapling informed me.

I held back a smile. "Of course."

"I'm so smart." He clapped. "Smartsmartsmart."

Chapling had been working on this new voice-activated system for months. And obviously, he was thrilled with the fact that it worked. But of course it would work; Chapling was a genius.

"Watch this." His eyes brightened. "Computer, give me everything on . . ." He glanced at me, and I shrugged. "Costa Rica," he said.

ONE MOMENT, PLEASE.

Chapling bounced. "I always wanted to go to Costa Rica. Thought I might try surfing."

"Surfing? You?"

He looked offended for about a second. "What? You can't see me surfing?"

I thought about that—his little, chubby, redheaded self riding a wave-— and shook my head. "Nope. Can't see you surfing."

Chapling shrugged. "Yeah, well, me neither. But it's fun to think about."

Information scrolled across the computer screen, and we watched. Pictures, newspaper articles, history . . . anything a person could ever want on Costa Rica.

He did a jig. "Is she awesome or what?"

Smiling, I checked my watch. "Shoot. I'm going to be late for PT. Gotta go."

I raced from the lab, through the underground corridors, up the elevator, and down the hall into our bedroom. Quickly, I changed clothes for physical training, slipping on a sweatshirt and a pair of exercise shorts. David had bought them for me during my first few weeks on the ranch. I'd shoved them into the depths of my dresser, planning on returning them. *Guess I changed my mind.*

I zipped into the adjoining bathroom and gave my body a quick once-over in the mirror. I checked my front and sides and triple-checked my butt. You wouldn't have caught me anywhere near these shorts a few months ago. With PT, though, I'd developed some tone and felt more confident now. I used to think these shorts were too short. They weren't. Girls wore them all the time around campus.

Pulling my hair into a ponytail, I rushed across the room and out the door, straight into Bruiser.

"Hey." She grabbed my arm. "I was wondering where you were."

How sweet.

"Yowza, babe." She whistled. "You're hot."

Let's hope David thinks so, too.

She pointed to her snug long-sleeve T-shirt, YO! I'M MEAN, DO I LOOK IT? "Got it yesterday. Like?"

"Yeah, I like." Bruiser always had on a different custom-made T-shirt. "I swear, with the money you spend, you probably keep whatever online store you buy these from in business."

"Probably." She skipped down the hall. "Come on."

She'd drawn martial arts symbols on an ace bandage that was wrapped around her knee. Bruiser *always* had an injury.

"What'd you do this time?"

"I tried a triple back flip from the ranch's roof." She shrugged. "Ended up a double."

We exited the building, and I glanced up at the roof. That had to be at least twenty feet. No way I'd try anything off that, unless lots of ropes and harnesses were involved.

Bruiser had no fear.

We passed our brand-new in-ground pool, which sat beside the house. "Wanna go for a swim later?" Bruiser asked.

"Sure."

"Let's go." She raced across the yard to the barn, where our physical training was always held, and I followed. We opened the door and made our way toward Mystic, Parrot, and Beaker, who were standing off to the right near the dumbbells.

Beaker wore her usual combat boots, dog collar, and black clothes. She'd chosen green lipstick over black and changed out her nose jewelry. Instead of her ring, a chain connected her nostril to her ear.

Let's hope it doesn't get yanked out during PT.

They all glanced down at my shorts as we approached. They weren't used to seeing me in them since I usually wore yoga pants.

"Well." This from Mystic.

"Huh." That from Parrot.

"Nice chicken legs," snided Beaker.

Bruiser was always kidding with me about my chicken legs, too. From her it came out totally amusing and fun. One friend teasing another.

From Beaker? Lighthearted camaraderie wasn't part of her personality.

Nice nose chain, I wanted to snide back, but didn't.

Bruiser looped her arm through mine and turned me around. She rolled her eyes to the right. "What do you think of Adam?" she whispered.

Adam from Team One stood across the barn talking to David and Erin. David had his back to me. He didn't know I'd come in yet.

"Well?" Bruiser prompted.

I surveyed Adam's messy blond hair and tall, lean body. I'd say he stood at least six feet five. Definitely the tallest person here at the ranch. "He's all right, if you like blonds."

Bruiser elbowed me. "You're a blond."

I elbowed her back.

"He's been talking to me a lot more lately. I used to not think he was cute. But now I do. Weird, huh?"

"Nah, it's not weird. He's got a great personality, and he's cute."

"I'd need a ladder to kiss him. I'm like five feet, and he's like, what, a giant?"

I busted out laughing. Leave it to Bruiser to say something like that.

David turned from his conversation. His gaze dropped to my legs and then came up to meet my eyes. My entire body shot to boiling point, and I knew my face had to be flaming red.

He didn't look away, *wouldn't* look away.

164

I wished I was one of those girls who could boldly hold a guy's heated stare. Honestly, I was about to be sick.

Smiling, David bounced his brows, breaking the sexually tense moment, and I released a shaky breath.

Jonathan clapped his hands, and my attention shifted from David to our PT instructor. "Everyone over here."

As we followed Jonathan's instructions, my first PT came back to me with clarity. Falling on my head. Praying I *wouldn't* be paired with David.

I'd come a long way.

We all came in closer, and I found myself standing next to Erin.

"Remember that PT a few years ago when we bumped heads and I broke my nose?" Erin said to David, nudging him with a smile.

He grimaced. "Don't remind me," he said, and playfully nudged her back.

I didn't know why, but their cuteness bothered me.

"Spread out," Jonathan graveled, knocking me from my thoughts. "Arm's length between you. Feet together. Palms to the floor."

I followed Jonathan's orders, gritting my teeth, missing the ground by more than a foot.

Okay, so maybe I *hadn't* come such a long way.

Five minutes later he split us into partners. *Please give me David. Pleasepleaseplease give me David.*

"Know what I heard?" whispered Beaker, who was standing on the other side of me.

I shook my head, listening to Jonathan pair us up.

"David and Erin used to date."

What?

"Parrot's with Adam." Jonathan pointed to Bruiser. "Bruiser and Mystic. Beaker's with GiGi. And David's with Erin."

David's with Erin?

Wait a minute. I'm with Beaker?

I glanced over at her. She narrowed her eyes ever so slightly. *What* exactly was her problem?

We each grabbed a mat and dragged them over to the corner. I glanced at Erin, sizing her up. Average height. Shoulder-length dark hair. Athletic build. She'd always been nice to me. She was the first person I met, actually, when I arrived here in San Belden.

She and David used to date? Why hadn't David told me? Did they feel anything for each other now? Did David want to get back with her? Did she want to get back with him? Was Erin jealous? Was I? I glanced at Beaker—maybe she was just messing with me. But by the look on her face, I didn't think so.

"We're practicing floor restraint today." Jonathan stepped onto a mat, interrupting my rambling thoughts. "When you're on the bottom, how to gain control of the guy on top."

Suddenly, David shot across the room, and I jumped.

He tackled Jonathan, plastering him to the floor. Wrapping both legs around David's waist, Jonathan looped their arms together and bent David's back.

Shifting, Jonathan straightened one leg and crossed the other over David's back. "Notice the position of my legs. This prevents my opponent from rolling out of the shoulder lock."

Jonathan rotated David's wrist toward his head. "Continuous pressure in this direction will dislocate my opponent's shoulder."

David and Jonathan released each other and jumped to their feet, our signal to begin the maneuver.

Beaker and I looked at each other. Her frown said she dreaded this as much as I did.

Behind me someone grunted. A body smacked to a mat. Someone else growled.

Everyone was already at it while Beaker and I continued eyeing each other.

A girl giggled. A guy laughed. Wait a minute. I knew that laugh. *David.*

I whipped around. David had his legs wrapped around Erin's waist and her arm bent back. She giggled again.

I narrowed my eyes. They were having *way* too much fun all intertwined like that.

"Aren't they cute," Beaker sneered.

I whipped back around and lunged, tackling her. She landed so hard her nose chain rattled. I couldn't quite believe I just did that.

TL stepped into the barn. "David, GiGi, Wirenut."

Beaker shoved me off her. I gave her my best don't-mess-with-me glare before turning to TL.

"Conference room." TL headed off. "Five minutes."

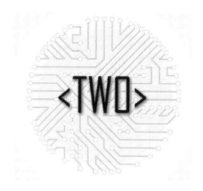

‹TWO›

David, Wirenut, and I stepped onto the elevator.

"Why do you think TL wants to see me?" Wirenut smoothed his fingers down his trim goatee. "Food, school, physical training, homework, chores, sleep. That's been my week. I haven't done anything wrong. Did anything go wrong on the Ushbania mission? Did my schematics provide faulty information?"

Simultaneously, David and I shook our heads, hiding our amusement. Poor Wirenut. I was just as nervous the first time TL had wanted to see me away from the rest of the group. Right before he sent me on my first mission.

Which meant that Wirenut might be going on his first mission, too. But why would I be meeting with TL? It made sense David would; TL involved him in everything. But why me?

Unless he was sending me on another mission. I groaned inwardly. Whatever happened to working from home base?

"Last week I swapped chores with Mystic," Wirenut continued worriedly. "We didn't tell TL. Do you think he's pissed about that? Ya know, overriding his authority or something."

David shook his head, all calm. "No. But I wouldn't do that again."

Wirenut expelled a short burst of air. "Crud. What have I done? Since joining the Specialists, I've been living cleaner than ever before."

I linked arms with him. "Everything's going to be okay." And I truly believed that. It was one of the most important things I'd learned since being with the Specialists. TL had only our best interest in mind. He really cared about each one of us.

The elevator stopped on Subfloor Four, and we made our way past a few locked doors to the conference room where TL waited.

Wirenut rapped on the open door. "You ever gonna tell me what's behind those locked doors?"

He made stupid attempts at humor when he was nervous.

Without looking up, TL motioned us in. "When you're ready." He pointed to me and Wirenut. "You two have a seat." TL rolled his leather chair out and stood. "David, come with me."

"When I'm ready?" Wirenut asked after TL and David left. "What does that mean?" He looked at me. "You've got access to one of the doors. Apparently, *you're* ready."

TL had given me access to the government's highest-level computer lab. Although we had split from the government, we were still able to access their resources. My team knew that it was a computer lab and that Chapling worked in there, but I wasn't allowed to give them the details of what went on inside. The secretiveness of the lab was both a curse and a privilege. Right now, with Wirenut's remark, it felt more like a curse.

"When I'm ready," Wirenut mocked. "I could break into those stupid locked doors if I wanted to."

"Wirenut—"

"TL should be rewarding me for having such self-control," he railroaded on. "That in and of itself proves I'm ready. Maybe I should tell him that."

He was right. With his electronics expertise, Wirenut *could* break into anything. It was the whole reason TL recruited him. Right now, though, his stress was making him act tough and ridiculous.

"Should I speak first?" Wirenut shifted in his chair. "Ya know, break the ice. Conversation comes easy for me. Light. Fun. Nothing serious. Who wants serious? Serious sucks. Silence comes easy, too. Hey, I'm not called the Ghost for nothing." Wirenut expelled another short burst of frustrated air. "Okay, this is officially driving me insane. Why did TL tell us five minutes if he didn't really want us here in five? I mean, it's been seven minutes. Where is he? What, he wanted to see how long it took us to get down here? What'd he think, we'd drag our feet or something? What the hell, man, I don't drag my feet around this place. If anything, I'm faster than the others on my team. Well, except for Bruiser. But come on, she's like a freak of nature."

He was rambling to himself now. This wasn't good. "How about we talk about something else," I suggested. Wirenut needed to get his brain on another topic.

He looked across the table at me, clearly expecting me to come up with something to talk about. Oh, okay. Um . . .

Suddenly the first day we all met popped into my mind. "Do you remember the first day we all met? The six of us sat around this same table."

Wirenut smiled. "We were all scoping out one another. Curious. Wondering what our new lives would be like."

I grinned as TL and David returned. Closing the door, TL took his seat at the head of the table. He opened a file and studied it. The header, QUID PLUOLIUM, ran across each page of small typed paragraphs. "Top Secret" had been stamped in red at the bottom.

Squinting my eyes, I studied the upside-down paragraphs. But the small print and my lack of glasses kept me from making out the details. I glanced up at TL. He didn't acknowledge any of us.

Beside me, David waited patiently, his gaze calmly fixed on the windowless wall behind Wirenut.

Across from me, Wirenut tapped his finger on the table, obviously as anxious as me.

We waited in silence for what felt like hours. Nothing from TL.

"So," Wirenut finally interrupted the silence.

Without looking up, TL shook his head in response.

Wirenut tightened his jaw, and I sent him an it's-going-to-be-okay, I-know-exactly-how-you-feel look.

My impatience brought on a teeny bit of nerves, and just when I decided to run code sequences through my brain, TL closed the file.

"Take off your monitoring patch," he said to Wirenut.

I smiled. I bet he *was* going on a mission. TL had taken my patch right before sending me to Ushbania.

With some hesitation and a reassuring nod from David, Wirenut reached beneath his T-shirt sleeve and peeled off what looked like a nicotine patch. That's what he told anybody outside the ranch who asked about it.

He gave TL the skin-colored device. "Why do you want my tracker? Did it malfunction?"

"No. You don't need it anymore."

Wirenut grinned. "Does this mean that I'm a full-fledged Specialist?"

TL chuckled. "Yes, you're a full-fledged Specialist."

I loved when TL smiled and laughed. It made me all cozy inside. He didn't do it enough. He seemed too focused and serious most of the time.

He held up the device. "Do you remember what I told you when you first put this on?"

Wirenut nodded. "Yep. You said, 'Understand that your public education is part of your training. It's socializing; learning to lie to others regarding your past, current situation, and future. Each of you will wear a detection device for monitoring. Everything you say and do will be recorded. You will wear this until I feel confident you'll do fine without it.'"

Wow. How unbelievable that he remembered every single word.

Wirenut leaned back and folded his arms, looking very full of himself. "How was that?"

TL shook his head, like he did every time he had no clue what to do with Wirenut. "Nicely done."

"Thank you very much. Feel free to applaud."

TL's lips twitched. "All right, all kidding aside. I took GiGi's device before she left on her mission to Ushbania."

Wirenut sat up. "Does this mean I'm going somewhere?"

TL held his hand up. "I'll tell you what I told her. You've proven to be adept at your cover. You've gone about your day-to-day activities smoothly, naturally, and without a second thought. You've seamlessly merged into this world. But what I'm most impressed with is that you've had a lot of temptation. Not only around here, but at school. And not once have you given in to the mischievous urges that drove the Ghost."

Wirenut grinned, obviously pleased TL recognized that.

"The old Frankie would've been sneaking around the ranch at night, trying to break into restricted areas. I know you wouldn't have stolen anything. You would've just tied a yellow ribbon and gone on your way. But the fact that you haven't tells me you're ready to move on to the next stage of your training."

Wirenut grinned again, and I could just visualize the happy dance going on inside of him.

TL stood. "Follow me."

We left the conference room and headed down the underground hallway.

As we passed Chapling's and my computer lab, TL nodded to it. "Later on this evening, GiGi will show you around her lab."

Wirenut and I exchanged surprised glances (more on my end than his). In a few hours, Chapling's and my computer lab would no longer be a secret. It sort of bummed me out. I liked having something just mine and Chapling's.

We stopped at a door ten feet from my lab. "This will be your studio," TL said to Wirenut, stepping to the side. "Do your thing."

Oooh, neat. I was about to see inside another one of the mysterious locked doors. Wirenut must be ecstatic. Okay, now I couldn't *wait* to show him the lab.

He scrutinized the steel door and then tapped it with his finger. "Four-decibel, hollow echo. Double-reinforced. Lined with . . ." He tapped it again. "Glass. Interesting. Counter-sunk hinges."

Leaning down, he studied the lock. "Triple-plated. Imbedded." He sniffed. "Copper wax. Rigged with a laser crawler."

He got down on his knees and put his ear against the door. "Bottom left quadrant. Tsss. *Tsss. Tsss. Tsss.* One-second electrical surges. A dom sensor." He held out his hand. "I need my tools."

David extended a triple-folded leather pouch.

Wirenut took it from him. He closed his eyes and rubbed it between his hands. He brought it to his face and inhaled. "Old leather, oil, and metal. It's been a long time since I've held this. I never imagined I'd miss an old pouch so much."

He spread it open on the tile floor beside him. He slipped out three wrenches, some silver wire, a lighter, a stopwatch, and some electrical tape. He inserted one wrench in the lock and wedged one in the door's upper-right corner. "This last one will be taped at a sixty-two-degree angle in the lower-left quadrant." Sixty-two-degree angle? Jeez, that's precise.

With the lighter, he soldered silver wire to each wrench, connecting the three. He touched his knuckle to the wire. "Laser crawler rhythm is *cchhh. Chch. Cchhh. Chch.*"

He pressed the stopwatch. "On the eleventh second, the door will open."

It clicked open, and my jaw dropped. Wow. Wirenut knew his stuff.

He did what he called his victory shoulder-roll dance. "Go, Wirenut. Go, Wirenut. Go. Go."

David shook his head. "We've had the best of the best test out our security."

TL slapped Wirenut on the back. "You're the first to successfully break in. Congratulations."

Wirenut's face beamed with pride. "Thanks."

I knew the feeling. Nothing felt better than pleasing TL. David pushed open the door and turned on the light. "Get your tools and go on in."

Wirenut packed up, and we followed him in. He skidded to a stop, and I nearly ran right into him. "That's my stuff. That's everything I've ever sold online."

All kinds of electronic contraptions lined the tables and shelves.

Wirenut shook his head. "How di—Where di—What's going on?"

TL picked up a remote control from a shelf. "You may have had ghost accounts and rerouted IPs, but I rigged it so that I was always the highest bidder when you auctioned things off."

"You mean you've been buying my contraptions for years?" TL and David nodded.

"Man." Wirenut laughed. "That's too funny. I guess I'm not as clever as I thought."

TL pointed the remote control at the back wall, pressed a button, and the wall slid open. Wirenut sucked in a breath.

Thousands of the latest electronic devices jammed the shelves of a hidden mini-warehouse.

I laughed at his amazed face. I was sure I'd looked the same way when TL had first shown me the computer lab.

Wirenut stepped through the secret wall. "Optotronics, micromodules, semiconductors, circuit protection, passive components, audio devices, sensors, enclosures, transformers, protoprods—Do you have any idea"— he picked up a cable—"how much this xial costs?"

TL folded his arms. "Yes, I do. I sign the bills around here." Wirenut stood there a few seconds, holding the cable, staring at everything. Then, slowly, he paced down the center of the warehouse and back, scanning the metal racks. "It's everything I've ever wished for. Like Santa dropped the mother lode."

We all laughed.

"You'll have time to look through everything later. Anything else you need, let me or David know, and we'll get it for you. But for now, put down the cable and come on out."

Wirenut put it down, stepped out from the mini-warehouse, and TL showed him how to use the remote control to close the door. We left Wirenut's room and made our way back to the conference room, where we resumed our seats around the table.

TL tilted back in his chair. "I want to express a concern I have."

Wirenut nodded. "Okay."

"You're confident with your abilities. That's good. That's important. But sometimes your confidence comes across as a little too cocky."

Wirenut's brows drew together. Nobody wanted to disappoint TL. "Sir—"

TL held up his hand. "Let me finish."

Wirenut wisely closed his lips.

"I've watched you. I know that when something is requested of you, you become a different person. You become focused. Attentive. Ready."

"You know how to prioritize important things," David added.

Wirenut's face relaxed a bit with their compliments.

"I want you aware of the fact that cockiness and overconfidence can get *any* person into trouble. Fast. Do we understand each other?"

Wirenut nodded. "Yes, sir."

TL was right. Wirenut did come across as cocky sometimes. But it was a funny conceited, not a serious one. It was mostly for show.

"Before a job I always say to myself, 'Game's on. Don't get too confident. Never know what might happen.'" Wirenut shook his head. "Don't know why I just told you that. I guess so you know *I* know that flaw about myself."

"Good. That's good." TL opened the file. "As long as you're aware of your talents and your shortcomings."

"I am."

TL tapped his finger to the open file. "Do any of you know what quid pluolium is?"

We all shook our heads.

"Quid pluolium is a neurotoxin. One drop kills thousands of people."

I blinked. Thousands of people?

"Quid pluolium," TL continued, "is currently under development in a private lab in Rissala. Yesterday, someone broke into that lab and stole half a dozen vials of the toxin."

"Rissala? Where's Rissala?" I asked. Geography had never been my strong point.

"It's a small country located near Greece," David answered me. "It's bordered by the Mediterranean Sea."

TL pulled a piece of paper from his folder and slid it across the table to us. "Whoever stole the toxin left this."

We all leaned in.

"What language is that?" I asked. "What does it say?"

"It's written in Rissalan. Parrot translated it for us. It says that there are three data-encrypted messages hidden throughout the country of Rissala. These messages are some type of computer code. The first message leads to the next, and that one points to the final. The final message reveals where the stolen neurotoxin has been hidden."

Wirenut scoffed. "Sounds like someone's playing a twisted game of cat and mouse."

"Yes, it does," TL agreed.

I raised my hand, my stomach clenching with nerves. "Um, computer code?" I didn't feel good about this.

"You'll be working from home base on this one," TL answered my unspoken question.

I blew out a quiet breath. Home base. Sounded good. Sounded *more* than good.

"Octavias Zorba," TL continued, "is a very wealthy entrepreneur in Rissala. He funded the quid pluolium research and development. He has hired us to find these messages and recover the toxin." TL tapped the paper written in Rissalan. "This says the first encrypted message is hidden in a small ceramic egg in the Museum of Modern Art. Chapling has done some preliminary work and discovered this ceramic egg is protected by the Rayver Security System. As Wirenut knows, he is the only person to have ever broken through the Rayver System."

Wirenut straightened in his chair. "Does this mean I'm going to Rissala?"

TL didn't answer him and instead got really quiet. Seconds passed, and then TL took a breath. "That piece of paper also says that one of the encrypted messages is hidden in the hilt of a seventeenth-century, double-bladed, lion-engraved sword."

Wirenut went very still. I'd never seen him look so paralyzed with fear.

I glanced at David, and he shook his head.

What was going on?

174

Wirenut shoved back from the table, and I jumped. "Forget it. This is insane. You have to be an *idiot* if you think I'll do this." He jabbed his finger across the table at David and me. "And this is *none* of their business. None of *anyone's* business. Find someone else. I'm not going to Rissala."

‹THREE›

The following afternoon, I pulled the ranch's van into the high school's lot and parked in the first available spot. I'd had my license for only a week and *loved* being able to drive. It made me feel . . . well, grown up, for lack of a better description. And free.

David, Erin, Adam, myself, and the rest of Team One attended the University of San Belden. Generally, we left there around three and picked up my team from San Belden High. Today, though, David had left classes early because TL had paged him, Erin and Adam didn't have afternoon classes, and the rest of Team One was away on missions. Which left me going to San Belden High alone.

Pocketing the van's keys, I checked my watch. Minutes to spare. I was getting good at this time-management thing. And to think it had once been one of my biggest flaws.

As I climbed out, I caught sight of Wirenut sitting on a bench under a tree. I'd been thinking about him nonstop since yesterday's meeting. He'd been distant last night when I showed him around my lab. I'd seen him this morning at breakfast and wanted to talk to him, but I didn't know what to say. He'd seemed so lost in thought that I figured he needed space. And from his comment at the meeting, he obviously didn't want David and me knowing about his business.

But now, as I approached Wirenut, all my hesitation disappeared. I wanted to be whatever I could for him. A friend, a sounding board, someone he could yell at if need be.

"Hey." I took the wooden bench across from his. "Did your last class get out early?"

"I'm skipping."

"Oh."

I'd never skipped a class in my whole life. I was probably the only person on the planet who actually looked forward to class. Well, except for gym. But then, what nerd *did* look forward to gym?

"You're sitting right outside the school. Aren't you worried about getting caught? TL will be really upset if you get in trouble for skipping. Maybe you should go back in."

"There's only one like it in the whole world," Wirenut mumbled, apparently unfazed by the fact he might get caught cutting. "My dad told me that right before he allowed me to touch the double-bladed, lion-engraved sword. It was one of many unusual weapons he collected."

Unsure of how to respond, I simply sat and listened.

"The cops never found that sword. My testimony put my uncle on death row. I never saw him again. Case closed."

"Testimony?"

Wirenut squeezed his eyes shut, and my heart clinched at the pain evident on his face. "Twelve years ago," he whispered, "I watched my uncle use that same sword to kill my entire family."

My mouth fell open as his words ricocheted through my brain. Twelve years ago he would've been five years old. I'd been nearly the same age when I lost my parents. "Oh, Wirenut." I reached across the bench and gripped his forearm.

He sat frozen, his eyes tightly shut. I could only imagine the horrible, gory scenes flashing through his mind. Images no person, let alone a five-year-old, should ever experience.

Wirenut shook his head, fighting the emotion. I moved beside him and wrapped my arms tightly around him. We stayed that way for a few long minutes, our heads touching as I held him. With all my mental energy, I willed away his horrible memories.

Sometime later he stirred, and I sat back, giving him space.

"I was too young. I couldn't help. How could I have helped? It was impossible." He wasn't talking to me. He was talking to himself, staring at the grass beneath our feet. I didn't know what to say anyway.

Wirenut brought his gaze over to mine. "Don't you think it's weird that my first mission has something to do with my past? Do you think TL knew that when he recruited me?"

Shrugging, I moved back over to my bench. "I doubt it. The neurotoxin was just stolen. But I don't know. It's possible. TL seems to know everything about everybody. I've learned, though, that there's a purpose for the things he does. He wouldn't keep information private unless he had a good reason to do so."

"Maybe there's no stolen neurotoxin. Maybe this is a test to see how I perform under emotional stress. More of my training." Wirenut was talking to himself again, and so I quietly listened.

"No," he said, answering himself. "TL wouldn't stoop to that level. There're other ways to prove my mental stability. Or are there? Challenging someone with their worst fear *is* the ultimate test." He blew out a breath. "A test I'm not ready for."

The bell rang, and students piled out from the high school. Idly, I watched them load into buses, get into cars, and file off down the sidewalks.

Two girls in miniskirts passed by our benches. "Oh, *my* God," one sneered to the other. "Did you see what she was wearing? Puh-lease. Where'd she buy her clothes anyway?"

I sneered right back. They weren't talking about me, but they reminded me of the horrible girls I used to live with in the dorm. They'd made fun of me and it used to intimidate me. Now it just made me angry.

Sensing movement to my right, I glanced up and squinted against the sun.

"Hi!" A brown-haired girl plopped down beside Wirenut.

He flinched from his contemplative state.

"Sixty-four degrees on this beautiful day. Forty percent chance for evening showers. Another gorgeous San Belden, California, day." She stretched her arms over her head.

This must be Nancy. I'd heard my roommates talk a lot about her. She wanted to be a meteorologist and a journalist. They said she started every annoying conversation with a weather report.

Her big yap would make her a better gossip columnist, Wirenut had commented.

I looked over at him. Poor guy. He came out here for a little thinking room, and look who invaded his privacy.

She straightened her shirt. "Did you know one degree Celsius equals Fahrenheit minus thirty-two divided by one point eight?" Wirenut and I just looked at each other.

"Can you believe we'll graduate high school soon?" She crossed her right leg over her left. "Time just flies, doesn't it? Before you know it we'll be graduating college." Bouncing her crossed leg, she smiled at me. "Are you a new student here?"

"No, I go to the university."

"University? What are you, a freshman?"

"Actually, I'm graduating this year."

She perked up. "You're that whiz kid, aren't you? I've heard all about you. My brother's a junior at the U. He said you're hot."

I felt my face grow warm.

"I bet you didn't have a childhood, did you? How sad." Nancy shook her head, all dramatically concerned. "Kids shouldn't be promoted until they're emotionally ready."

I wasn't sure how to respond, so I glanced at Wirenut. He rolled his eyes.

Nancy inched closer to him, apparently done making small talk with me. With his arms sprawled along the bench's back, they looked more like a couple than tolerant acquaintances.

He dropped his arms and put his book bag between them. If she didn't get the hint from that, I didn't know what to tell her.

"So"—she pushed her sunglasses up her nose—"how do you like it out there at the San Belden Ranch for Boys and Girls?"

A foster home for boys and girls was our cover in the community. If only people knew what *really* went on behind our gates.

"It's all right," Wirenut answered.

"I was thinking about doing an article on all of you for the school paper. Ya know, about how those less fortunate can, if given the proper guidance, turn into fine, upstanding American citizens."

Wirenut rolled his eyes again. "Maybe your ride's waiting for you in the other parking lot."

I almost laughed at the second blatant hint he just dropped.

"Nope. This is the exact spot I'm supposed to be." Nancy sighed. "What is the world coming to? The crime rate these days. You heard about that missing artifact out of New Mexico? What a shame. Happened months and months ago."

Wirenut cleared his throat. "Artifact?"

His slouched posture straightened a little bit. His bored eyes became alert. Small changes that I noticed, but anybody else would say he appeared the same. He was interested in this artifact thing and doing an excellent job of hiding it. TL would be proud.

Nancy finger-fluffed her short hair. "Oh, yeah. But something *really* juicy just came across my desk."

Came across her desk? Who was she, Katie Couric?

Nancy brushed a fallen leaf from her jeans. "It was the Ghost who stole it. You know, the New Mexico thing."

Oh. She was referring to the event that led TL to recruit Wirenut.

"You've heard of him," she whispered, "haven't you? The Ghost?"

Wirenut and I exchanged a quick glance.

Yeah, we've heard of him. He's sitting right beside you.

"No," he responded.

She sucked in a surprised breath. "Well, he's only the most notorious criminal of this century. Some even say he's the most notorious ever."

Wirenut rubbed a hand down his face, hiding his smile. Apparently, his reputation amused him.

"But as I was saying, something really juicy just came across my desk. He just broke into a museum in China and stole another artifact. Apparently this museum in China was supposed to be burglar proof." Nancy glanced around as if the Ghost was going to jump out at her or something. "He's the first to have gotten in."

Wirenut stiffened a little. "How do you know it was the Ghost?"

She wiggled back on the bench, getting comfortable, obviously wallowing in the fact that she was delivering hot-off-the-press news. "His signature."

Wirenut lifted his brows, all nonchalant. "Signature?"

Nancy leaned in. "A yellow ribbon."

Wirenut's jaw tightened.

So, the burglar guy who screwed Wirenut was now impersonating him. Interesting. I wondered if TL knew this. "And how did you get all this information?"

"I told you." She fluffed her hair again. "It came across my desk."

I just looked at her.

"Oh, all right." Nancy waved her hand. "It's in the papers."

"Weeell," drawled Beaker, "isn't this sweet."

Nancy jerked to her side of the bench, straightening her clothes, like she and Wirenut had been messing around or something.

Get a life.

Beaker hitched her chin. "Whaz up?"

Behind her purple-tinted lenses, Nancy narrowed her eyes. Mystic, Parrot, and Bruiser came out the gym door. Everyone present and accounted for. I stood and fished the ranch's van keys from my jeans pocket.

"Let's go."

"Oh," Nancy extended her hand, "I forgot."

Groan.

She smiled at Wirenut. "Have a good trip."

He frowned. "Trip?"

"Yeah. I'm an assistant in the admin office. I saw your excuse note come over the fax. I figured since you were going to be out of school for a while you were going on a trip." She blinked. "Where are you going?"

Wirenut's face went blank. "Nowhere." He spun and charged off across the parking lot.

We all rushed after him.

"What's going on?" Bruiser asked.

I shook my head. I had the sick feeling TL was sending him to Rissala anyway.

In silence, I drove everyone home. My teammates sat, staring out the windows. I suspected they all knew something major was up. I glanced at Wirenut in the rearview mirror. He hadn't moved from his hard-jawed, arms-crossed, angry position.

I pulled up in front of the ranch's gate. A wooden plaque engraved with SAN BELDEN RANCH FOR BOYS AND GIRLS hung from the entrance.

Keying in my access code, I drove through. A standard privacy fence lined the hundred-acre ranch. Invisible static sensors wound through it, detecting the smallest of movements. No human, animal, or plant could touch it without Chapling knowing. If the electricity went out, generators and solar panels kept the whole ranch active.

To any ordinary visitor the place resembled a nice homey environment for us system kids. Little did anyone know a top-secret, intricate series of sublevels zigzagged the earth below us.

I drove up the driveway and parked in front. Wirenut slung open the door and jumped out. He stormed across the gravel and into the house.

"Wirenut, stop." I raced to catch up. He ignored me and charged down the hall straight toward TL's office.

"Stop." I cringed, following him. "You're going to get in trouble."

Wirenut slammed through TL's door without knocking. "*What* is going on?"

TL motioned me in, and, silently, I stepped into his office. David stood in the corner, a map in his hands. It'd been only a few hours since I'd seen him, but my stomach still whoop-dee-whooped.

TL leveled unreadable eyes on Wirenut. "Close the door. You three have a seat."

David closed the door, and we each took a metal chair in front of TL's desk.

He pressed a keyboard button and then turned his attention to Wirenut. "I'm assuming you're referring to the Ghost impersonator?" TL shook his head. "Not much I can say about that. Your alter ego is being copycatted."

"I told you," Wirenut forced out through clenched teeth. "I'm not going to Rissala."

TL didn't blink. "I know."

His calm acceptance seemed to zap the rage from Wirenut. He slumped back in his chair. "Then why would Nancy say that?"

"Nancy?" TL asked.

Wirenut shook his head. "A girl at school. She said she saw an excuse note on the fax."

TL nodded. "Yes."

Beside me, Wirenut tensed. "Well? I told you I'm not going."

"I know. David and I are. You have forty-eight hours to train him how to be you. The Ghost."

***

That evening I stood in Wirenut's electronics room, idly watching him prepare.

I tried not to be bummed that David would be leaving. I tried to focus on the mission and my part of things. But it just wasn't fair. Other teenagers didn't have to deal with this. They could do what they wanted. They could date and get to know each other without "save the world" pressure. They could go out and have fun. Hang out. Laugh. Just exist. Heck, they could lie around all day and watch TV if they wanted.

"All right," Wirenut interrupted my pouting. "I've turned my room into David's training grounds." He checked his watch. "It's already eight o'clock, and we've got a lot to do. So let's get started" He motioned to the equipment he'd set up in the open area. "TL and I spent the last few hours putting all this together. It's a replica of the Rayver System, complete with lasers and a vault."

David nodded. "Tell me what to do."

Taking a seat in the corner out of their way, I pulled a notepad and pencil from my back pocket. TL told me to take notes. He wanted me aware of all aspects of this mission. I wasn't sure why. After all, I'd be operating from home base, decoding the messages. But I figured TL had his reasons.

"Everything I do is based on degrees. Anybody can jury-rig something, but if done at a different angle, a different degree, you get a completely different result. I'll teach you the Rayver System first, then we'll go over all the possible scenarios you may encounter other than the Rayver System." Wirenut handed David a pair of goggles and tossed a pair to me. "These are fiber-lit. Put 'em on."

All three of us did. Red lasers became visible, zigzagging the area in front of the guys. Cool.

Wirenut nodded toward the lasers. "These will be yellow, not red. But yellow fries your skin. Figured you'd want to train on the nonfrying color."

David chuckled. "Gee, thanks."

Wirenut pulled David over. "Always begin in line with the object you're after. In this case, the vault. Now lean to the left at a seventy-degree angle. Do you see an opening tunnel in the lasers?"

Seventy-degree angle? There's no way I could guess that and get it exactly right.

David leaned. "No."

Wirenut studied David's form. "Your body's twisted. Move your right shoulder back."

David did. "Still don't see it."

Wirenut got in position behind David. "I can see the tunnel just fine. Your feet are closer together. Slide your left foot to the left seven inches."

"Seven inches?" David glanced over his shoulder at Wirenut. "Do you have a ruler? How do you know this?"

Wirenut shrugged. "I just know."

David slid his foot over. "Okay. I see it."

Wirenut gave David a remote control. "This is the expander. Extend your left arm down the tunnel. Don't touch the lasers." *DingDingDingDingDing.*

"That'd be the alarm." Wirenut slapped David on the back. "Let's try again.

***

Wirenut gave David the remote control. "Now extend your left arm down the tunnel, pointing the expander."

I held my breath. They'd been at this more than two hours. Please let him get it right this time.

David inserted his arm into the tunnel surrounded by lasers. Quiet.

Peace and quiet.

No alarm.

I nearly cried with excitement.

"Keep it steady," Wirenut whispered. "On the expander there is a blue button. When you press it, a metal wire will snake out. The wire cannot touch the lasers. Your destination is that tiny hole below the vault's lock. Do you think you're ready?"

David barely nodded.

"Press the expanding button now."

David pressed the button. The wire snaked out, becoming firm and straight as it left the remote control. One inch. Two. Three. Four. My heart banged with each inch interval. Steady, David, steady.

His hand shook ever so slightly.

DingDingDingDingDing.

Wirenut ran his hand down his goatee. "Let's do it again." With a huge sigh, David cracked his neck. "Give me a sec." He walked to the other side of the room and stood with his back to us, staring at the wall. I heard him sigh again.

I felt bad for him. He was trying so hard and barely succeeding at anything.

David turned back around. "Okay, let's do this thing."

***

"Got drinks and sandwiches. Anyone interested?"

184

David whipped around. "I didn't even hear you leave."

I carried the tray over. The guys had taken only one break since beginning ten hours ago. Both of them looked as exhausted as I felt. And I was just observing and taking notes.

They each grabbed a bologna and cheese sandwich.

"Nothing like bologna for breakfast." David took a huge bite of his. "So, who taught you all this stuff?"

Wirenut popped open a soda. "Nobody. Taught myself. It's my life. Security, electronics. All I've ever done is study it, tinker with it. It fascinates me." He smiled a little. "And I'm good at it."

"Impressive. Really impressive. We've been at this for hours, and I can't get it. And I'm a real quick study. It's not just about breaking a system. It's about your body's position. The angle at which you do things. It really is incredible, Wirenut. I knew you were skilled, but I didn't understand the scope of it until now."

Wirenut shoved a hunk of sandwich in his mouth, obviously embarrassed, but loving the admiration. His shy avoidance made me grin.

We finished off our sandwiches and downed the sodas.

David and Wirenut got back into position as I gathered up the garbage and headed out the door, dreading what I knew would come next.

DingDingDingDingDing.

***

Wirenut and I watched, holding our breaths, as the wire snaked through the tunnel, across the room, and straight into the tiny hole below the vault's lock.

The lasers flicked off, and the three of us just stayed in our spots. Them standing, me sitting. Nobody moving. Unable to wrap our tired brains around the fact that David had done it. He'd actually done it. Finally. After sixteen hours.

Slowly, the guys turned and looked at each other.

"Crud!" Wirenut jerked the stopwatch from his pocket and pressed the button. "Go!"

They raced across the floor, reeling in the expandable wire. Wirenut yanked a tool kit from his back pocket and spread it on the ground in front of the vault.

"Nitrox." He shoved the can at David. "Quick. Got to make up for lost time. Squirt it on the control panel."

David did. The panel popped off and clanged to the floor. *DingDingDingDingDing.*

I dropped my head.

Wirenut sighed. "My bad. You have to catch it *before* it hits the floor. Anything over twenty-five decibels sets off the alarm. I'm so tired I forgot that detail."

The door opened and TL stepped into the room. "Chapling downloaded intel. Someone tried to release quid pluolium in an office building."

My stomach tightened. "What? Why?"

"To prove that whoever has the toxin will use it." TL's face hardened. "Thirty-three people almost died. Luckily the toxin was found in time. Give me a status on how David's doing."

We all exchanged defeated gazes. Thirty-three people almost died. If we didn't find the quid pluolium, hundreds, thousands, possibly millions could die.

"I said status. Now."

David took a step forward. "Sir, I haven't been able to penetrate the Rayver System."

And according to Wirenut, the Rayver System was only the beginning. There was so much more to go over. All the different scenarios. There was no way to accomplish it with only hours left of training. Clearly, no one could do this but him.

As if reading my thoughts, Wirenut stepped up beside David. "I'll do it. I'll go to Rissala."

TL nodded, then turned to me. "I asked you to be in here, taking notes, for a reason. You're going with us."

What the . . . ?

186

<FOUR>

Maybe I'd heard TL wrong. I pushed up from my spot in the corner. "What do you mean I'm going with you all?"

"The data-encrypted messages, the computer code, is on a timer. We're not sure what kind of timer. Possibly the message disappears? Some sort of chemical reaction to the paper the encryption is on? I've asked Beaker to look into that side of things." TL's cell phone rang. "We need you onsite to immediately decode the data Wirenut obtains."

I *had* heard him right. *Crap.* "But—"

"GiGi," TL checked the caller, but didn't answer, "you'll be fine. You work best under pressure. That's why I waited until now to tell you. You get nervous if you have too much time to think about something."

But you said I would work from home base, I wanted to whine. "What about Chapling?"

"He's working on a couple of other things right now."

Wait a minute. *That's why I waited until now to tell you.* So he'd known days ago that I was going?

Immediately, I recalled all the lies that had originally brought me to the Specialists. Lies that had eventually been justified, sure, but still.

I've learned there's a purpose for the things TL does. He wouldn't keep information private unless he had a good reason.

That's what I'd told Wirenut a few days ago. Remembering that rational statement deflated my building irritation.

And TL was right. I *did* work well under pressure. If I had known days ago I would've been obsessing over the trip instead of focusing on the mission.

TL reached out and cupped Wirenut's shoulder. He didn't utter a word as he stared deep into Wirenut's eyes. "I'm proud of you. You put aside your own needs to help others. Only an honorable man would do that. This will be an emotionally difficult mission for you. I realize that. You have my utmost respect for the decision you just made."

Wow. What an awesome compliment.

TL squeezed Wirenut's shoulder and released it. "Get some rest. Our plane for Rissala leaves tomorrow morning."

With that, TL strode from the electronics room. I turned and looked at Wirenut. He stood there, staring at nothing in particular, probably trying to comprehend the mind-numbing words he'd just heard. It's exactly how I felt the first time TL said he was proud of me.

David packed up Wirenut's tool pouch. "It's humbling when he tells you he admires you, isn't it?"

"Man," Wirenut half laughed. "You can say that again."

"Respect goes two ways. He gives it and expects it in return." David flicked off the Rayver System lasers. "You lose it, and it takes forever to get it back."

"Thanks for the warning." Wirenut snatched up his tools. "Catch ya later."

He disappeared through the door, leaving David and me alone.

"Looks like things are reversed now. You're going, and I'm staying." David took my hand. "Don't be nervous."

"Not I'm." I shook my head. "I mean, I'm not." I closed my eyes. I *hated* when nerves made me jumble my words.

I felt him move closer, and I opened my eyes. "What am I going to do? I'll have to get on another plane." And he wouldn't be there like last time.

"You'll be fine. Wirenut will be there. And TL, too."

"They're not you," I whispered.

David's eyes crinkled. "No, they're not. But I'll be there in spirit. Just close your eyes, and I'll be there."

I smiled through a sigh. Months ago I never would've gotten on a plane. I never would've made it over to Ushbania if not for David sitting beside me, holding my hand.

The door opened again, and Erin stepped in. "TL's sending me to town. You two need anything?"

We both shook our heads.

With a nod, she shut the door, leaving us alone again.

David exhaled a heavy breath. "We're always getting interrupted, aren't we?"

I nodded. It did seem like every time we had a moment alone, someone ruined it.

"So, umm, did you two used to date?" It probably wasn't the best time to ask him such a thing.

"We did. For about a month."

"What happened?"

He shook his head. "I've known her a long time. We're friends. We weren't meant to date. There wasn't any chemistry."

Chemistry was the one problem David and I didn't have.

"I was thinking . . ." David ran his thumb over the top of my hand and looked down at my lips.

My stomach did a jig as I recalled the horribly embarrassing kiss I'd given him in Ushbania. "You were thinking?" I croaked.

He closed the small distance between us, putting his face a mere inch from mine.

I shook my head. Hold on. We couldn't kiss yet. I needed to brush my teeth. Our first real kiss had to involve fresh breath. But maybe it doesn't matter—we're finally getting our kiss.

I held my breath and looked into his eyes . . . and then the door opened again and TL stuck his head in. "David, I need you."

My heart paused a beat with disappointment. Yet again I'd have to wait for a kiss.

TL turned to me. "GiGi, the briefing will be back here in thirty minutes."

"Yes, sir."

"When you get back?" David whispered.

I nodded.

He smiled and dropped a quick kiss to my cheek. "Good." Then strode across the room to join TL.

My paused heart kicked to light speed. A kiss. When I got back. Oh boy. How was I supposed to concentrate on the mission with *that* waiting for me?

***

Thirty minutes later, I walked back into Wirenut's electronics room. TL, David, and Wirenut were already there standing on opposite sides of a tall wooden table.

I stepped up beside Wirenut.

David slid a yellow folder across to me. "In there you'll find your new identity, information on Rissala, and details about the mission."

Opening the folder, I quickly perused the inserted sheets. My name for this assignment would be Dana. Wirenut was Stan, and TL's new name would be Tim. Our cover? Vacationers. Simple enough.

TL opened his file. "To recap. There are three encrypted messages. We know the first one is in the Museum of Modern Art. That message will lead to the next, and that one points to the final. Finding these messages will uncover where the neurotoxin has been hidden."

"We know the first message is protected by the Rayver Security System. We also know the messages are on some sort of timed computer code, which is where GiGi comes in. This code might have to be deciphered right there on the spot. It might not. There could be a delay in satellite transmission, so with everything being on a timer, we don't want to take any chances sending the code back to here." TL clicked his pencil and slid it into the folder's pocket.

Wirenut raised his hand. "Sir, are you saying that GiGi has to go in with me while I break the Rayver System and retrieve the messages?"

"With the timed computer code, we don't know what to expect." TL looked at Wirenut and then me. "So, yes, GiGi will be going in with you."

Wirenut cut me a sideways glance, and I swore he looked a little sick to his stomach.

Come on. I wasn't that bad.

***

Early the next morning, the plane's engines vibrated beneath me, and I shut my eyes.

"You want a sedative?" TL asked from my right.

Shaking my head, I curled my fingers into my thighs.

You can do this. You can.

"It's going to be okay," Wirenut whispered from my left. "Think about computers or something."

Not a bad idea.

190

I forced my brain to run code.

[%TENLEME sartt:! Q—]

[<& nqouitat - - >tsroh]

[#<#> IUR gsm 118(*)]

The plane picked up speed as it rolled down the runway, and I squeezed my eyes tighter. David's words came back to me. *I'll be there in spirit. Just close your eyes, and I'll be there.*

I conjured his image. Tall, dark, great brown eyes. Wearing his faded jeans and that pale blue T-shirt that hugged his biceps. I saw him laughing, eyes crinkling, flirting with me. His jaw had dark stubble and he smelled . . . heavenly. We'd had a lot of stolen little moments since the Ushbanian mission. Holding hands, talking, a kiss on the cheek. I couldn't wait for the real thing.

The muscles in my body relaxed, and I rested my head back. I opened my eyes and immediately felt both TL and Wirenut looking at me.

"I'm fine," I reassured them.

"Oh, good." Wirenut blew out a dramatic breath. "Didn't want to contend with a puke bag."

I elbowed him.

Wirenut glanced around me to TL. "Thanks for the send-off party."

TL smiled a little. "You're welcome."

I recalled the send-off party they'd given me for my first mission, and how I'd passed out.

TL lowered the window shade, shutting out the sun and clouds. "Long flight to Rissala. Try to sleep."

Hours and hours and *hours* later, our plane began its descent into the capital city. With the time change it was early morning again.

Glancing past TL, I gazed out the window, taking in the scenery. The capital city sprawled across a large cliff, looking out over the sparkling Mediterranean Sea. One-, two-, and three-story stone buildings crammed the cliff, trickling off as the city stretched west from the water. Green hillsides rolled from there with an occasional house or farm.

We took a cab from the airport, zigzagging through a tight maze of the town. The only vehicles I saw were cabs. The few people out and about this early either drove mopeds, rode bicycles, or walked.

Narrow dirt roads led to cobblestone, back into dirt, and then rock. No pavement. The pastel-colored stone buildings sat close to the road with no sidewalks. Our driver honked as we neared a woman, and she plastered herself to the wall.

Roughly fifteen minutes later, we bumped to a stop in front of a two-story tan stone building.

The driver climbed out. "Hotel."

We grabbed our luggage and trucked it through the arched, open doorway. The inside mirrored the stone outside. To the left, a dark-haired woman stood behind a wood counter. She smiled as we approached.

As TL checked us in, I wandered the rustic lobby decorated with bamboo furniture. Paintings with flashes of color in no particular pattern hung on the walls.

"Let's go." TL led the way through the lobby and past an elevator to the stairwell. We climbed a flight of stairs up to our floor.

"This place has only twelve rooms. Six on bottom, six on top." TL handed me a key. "You're in room ten. We're eleven."

The guys let themselves in their room, and I went into mine. There was nothing unique about it. Tan stone walls and tile floors just like the hallways and lobby. Two double beds with a painting like the ones in the lobby hung above each. A small desk sat between the two beds. A door connected my room to the guys' room.

I peeked in the bathroom. Standard porcelain toilet and sink with a shower stall and no tub.

Crossing the room, I gazed out the small window down to the red-tile roof of a house. A tiny alley separated the two buildings. So tiny I could probably climb out of my window and easily jump down to the roof.

I cranked the knob on the window and let in the fresh cool air. I wished David were here.

A knock on the connecting door brought me out of my thoughts, and I opened it.

TL stepped in. "Upload intel."

Fishing my laptop from my backpack, I quickly connected to the satellite and keyed in the scrambler code. "Nothing new."

TL nodded. "The Museum of Modern Art is a ten-minute walk west of here. There's a café right across from it. Get some breakfast. I have calls to make. I'll meet you two there."

Wirenut stuck his head in. "Did someone say café? Food?"

I laughed. "Let's go."

We left the hotel and walked around the corner to the shadowed side alley. We headed west, away from the sparkling sea. Minutes passed as we strolled, and I trailed my fingers along the stone buildings bordering the street. The texture ranged from gritty to chalky to smooth. The narrowness of the cobblestone path prohibited cars. Only bicycles and the occasional moped zipped past. The city seemed to be waking up, with people opening windows, sweeping their small doorsteps, shaking out blankets.

Pipe music drifted from a couple of the windows. Must be a popular type of music from this area.

Ten minutes later, we neared the café. A green canvas awning billowed out, covering a dozen or so empty wrought-iron tables. Wirenut and I chose one in the center and made ourselves comfortable. Yawning, I closed my eyes, enjoying the early-morning breeze. The scent of fresh baked bread and strong coffee floated through the air.

Wirenut inhaled long and loud, bringing me from my sleepy haze. "Nothing compares to traveling. Seeing cool places. Meeting different people. Trying new foods. Speaking of which..." Wirenut signaled the Rissalan waitress.

Before joining the Specialists, adventure was absolute last on my list of things to do. I had to admit, though, being somewhere different *did* excite me. It made me feel like a completely different person.

Smiling, the waitress wound through the outdoor seating area, her long flowery skirt blowing in the dry, cool air.

She stopped at our table. "*Naz o jimo zua?*" May I help you?

"Oh, yes." I slipped an English/Rissalan dictionary from my back pocket and flipped through it. "O." I. Flipflipflip. "*Xuamf* Would. Flipflipflip. *"Moli."* Like. Flipflipflip. *"E."* A. Flipflipflip. *"Hmett."* Glass. Flipflipflip. *"Ug."* Of. Flipflipflip. *"Odif."* Iced. Flipflipflip. *"Duggii."* Coffee.

I beamed a grin up at the waitress, proud of my bilingual abilities.

"You could've just said *'odif duggii'* and she would've gotten it." Wirenut pointed to the chalkboard menu sitting on the cobblestone walkway. It displayed a breakfast special. *"Qmieti."* He held up two fingers.

With a nod, she made a note on her order pad and headed past us. Wirenut discreetly glanced over his shoulder, looking the waitress up and down as she swerved around a table and entered the restaurant. I smiled to myself and thought again of how much I missed David.

"Mmm-hmm." Wirenut approvingly mumbled of the waitress.

"Hey," I laughed, throwing my napkin at him. "You're here for a reason, remember?"

Grinning, he settled back in his chair. Behind his shades, he surveyed the two-story white stone building that stood across the cobblestone walkway. The Museum of Modern Art.

It wasn't a coincidence TL sent us here. Plenty of time to eat, drink, and get the museum's layout.

A bank stood to the left of the museum and a jewelry store to the right. A sliver of space separated each stone building from the next. Just like both sides of the whole street. Building after building after building. Houses, offices, businesses. It wasn't really beautiful, but more interesting, unique. I'd never been in such a crammed space before.

Sounds of laughter drifted with the wind. I blinked out of mission mode and glanced around. We'd been alone when we first sat down. Now an elderly woman sat to the right and a businessman occupied the table straight ahead.

"Hot chick to the left," Wirenut mumbled.

I glanced over. A sunbeam lit the wrought-iron table where "hot chick" sat alone. She wore a long, gauzy, white skirt, and her straight black hair hung halfway down her back. It blew with the wind, and she held it out of her way while talking with the waitress.

Wirenut was right. "Hot chick" *was* beautiful. With her dark skin and gorgeous smile, she and the waitress could be sisters. Or maybe mother and daughter.

"Hot chick" laughed again. She and the waitress exchanged a few more words in Rissalan, then, carrying her tray, the waitress meandered back over to us. She put our plates and coffees down then pointed to our water glasses. *"Nusi?"* More?

"Pu vjepl vua," Wirenut replied. No, thank you.

We both dove in, forking up big bites of the food Wirenut had ordered us. Fried pork, eggs, and spicy rice. Why didn't they feed us stuff like this at the ranch?

I paused in stuffing my face to take a sip of my iced coffee.

"Please tell me I didn't look like a starving hyena just now."

"Huh?" I glanced over at Wirenut. He was staring at the girl as she stared back at him.

She smiled. *"Jimmu."* Hello.

Wirenut cleared his throat and took a sip. "Don't screw this up," he mumbled to himself. "Play it cool." He sent her a small wave. *"Jimmu."*

"Enisodep?" American?

"Zit." Yes.

"I speak English," she said.

Wirenut smiled, obviously relieved. I mean, how much would that suck? Trying to communicate in Rissalan with somebody you liked. *Hello. Yes. Please. Where's the bathroom?* That conversation would last all of one minute.

"My name is Katarina."

I loved her melodic accent.

"Stan," he introduced, using our fake names. "And this is my *friend*, Dana."

I caught his emphasis on the word *friend*, making sure "hot chick" knew I wasn't his *girl*friend. "Hi."

Wirenut took another bite, chewed. "Ask her a question," he mumbled to me without moving his lips.

Ask her a question? Was he kidding? Conversation was not my strong point. I dug around in my head. *How old are you? Where do you go to school? Come here often?* I nearly laughed at the last one. It sounded like a corny pickup line. And Wirenut was the one picking her up, not me.

"Live around here?" he asked before I had a chance to open my mouth. He shot me a forget-it look.

I shrugged and went back to my food.

She nodded. "On a boat on the canal."

A boat? Neat.

The waitress crossed in front of us. She placed a bowl of fruit on Katarina's table. While they talked, we finished our breakfast.

They shared a laugh, and the waitress looked over her shoulder at us.

"Great. They're talking about us." Wirenut wiped his mouth.

"Hush," I whispered. "They're not talking about us." I thought I was the only one who obsessed about stuff like that.

He propped his feet on the chair beside me. The waitress left Katarina's table, and Wirenut did not hesitate to continue the conversation. "Do you go to school around here?"

"I'm taught at home."

"You mean on the boat?"

She nodded.

"How old are you?"

Katarina cut a chunk of melon in half. "Sixteen. How old are you?

"Seventeen."

In my peripheral vision a man stopped in front of the museum. Sipping my iced coffee, I studied him. He was the first to show. Must be the manager. I peeked at my watch. 7:05 A.M. Museum opened at 8:00 A.M.

"How long are you here for?" She bit into her melon.

"About a week." Wirenut touched the screw on the right side of his sunglasses, holding his finger there for a count of three. It activated the built-in cameras.

Smooth. I wasn't even sure he'd seen the man. I clicked my watch head twice counterclockwise, engaging the microchip recorder. His glasses contained the same recorder. Mine served as a backup in case something went wrong. The glasses were a nifty little electronic device he had created.

"Are you here with family?" Katarina drank a bit of her hot tea.

"No. Vacation with friends." Wirenut put the glasses on the table and pointed them directly at the museum.

There were two cameras. One filmed the building's exterior, and one, according to Chapling, X-rayed through the stone walls to tape what went on inside.

Katarina pushed back from her table and stood, grabbing her bowl of fruit. She put some bills down and crossed the short distance between us.

Wirenut's jaw twitched as he watched her come toward us. I could only imagine what thoughts spiraled through his head. *Don't go, hot chick. Don't go.*

She extended her hand. "Nice to meet both of you. I wish I had more time to visit."

He shook her hand, looking so bummed I wanted to hug him. "Nice to meet you, too."

Her light brown eyes twinkled. Exotic eyes, kinda catlike. But it was the friendliness of them, the intelligence behind them that caught my attention more than anything, like they invited true, soul-bonding conversation.

She shook my hand. "I'm here every morning for breakfast, if you want to join me sometime. I'd be happy to show you around."

Wirenut's bumminess immediately lifted. "Sounds good."

With another smile, she caught the waitress's eye and held up the bowl. The waitress nodded.

"I'm a regular. They let me take stuff because they know I'll bring it back. Until later." Katarina turned and strolled off down the cobblestone walkway.

Wirenut watched her until she turned the corner and disappeared from sight.

TL passed her coming toward us. He wound around a table, stopping at ours. "Let's go."

Wirenut and I looked at each other. Something wasn't right.

TL put some bills on the table, and we strode off down the cobblestone walkway.

When we got far enough away, TL stopped walking. "Chapling decoded the name of the person who stole the quid pluolium."

Wirenut nodded. "Who is it?"

TL's jaw hardened. "Octavias Zorba. The same man who hired us to find it."

"Oh, my God."

TL turned to Wirenut. "Chapling also uncovered Zorba's real name. It's Antonio Badaduchi. Your uncle."

‹FIVE›

Wirenut clenched his jaw. "That's impossible. My uncle's on death row."

TL glanced down the sunlit cobblestone walkway back to the outdoor cafe, where more people had gathered. "Come on." He led us down a narrow alley bordered by the back side of a row of stone buildings. From his pants pocket, he pulled out a key chain with a small blue pyramid on it.

Wirenut glanced at it and then did a double take. "That's my white-noise audio-feedback blocker."

I blinked. "Your what?"

TL turned the pyramid's top counterclockwise. "Although no one can detect it, the pyramid emits a static pulse that blocks others from hearing our conversation. Instead of hearing us, they hear white noise."

"You made this?" I leaned in, curious as all get-out.

Wirenut nodded. "Two years ago. I was bored and decided to see if I could do it." He shrugged. "I succeeded."

TL stopped halfway down the alley. He turned and looked at Wirenut.

Seconds ticked by, and, with each one, my heart clanged harder. When TL stared at you like that, it always preceded life-altering words.

"Your uncle," TL finally spoke, "was never on death row."

It took a pause for Wirenut to comprehend TL's words. "B-but I put him there. I testified against him."

"He was sentenced to death row. But he never made it."

"What do you mean he never made it? He's been on death row for twelve years."

"En route to prison, he was taken by his own men."

"Men? What men? My uncle didn't have men. He managed an antiques store and collected junk."

"That was his cover. He's had his fingers in a lot of illegal stuff."

"That's impossible. I would've known. I was only five, but I would've known. My dad would've known."

TL cupped his shoulder. "I know this is a lot to take in."

Wirenut shrugged away. "Don't talk to me like I'm stupid." He paced a couple of steps. "Let me get this straight. You're telling me that maniac slaughtered my family and has been roaming free every since?"

"Yes."

"Son of a bitch!" Wirenut spun and crashed his fist into the stone building.

I took a step back. I'd never seen him so angry.

"Look at me," TL requested.

Wirenut hit the building again. "Why didn't I know? Somebody should have told me."

TL grabbed his arm. "Look at me," he commanded.

Wirenut opened his eyes.

"We'll get him. You hear me? I promise."

Anger visibly vibrated through Wirenut's body. He stared at TL, shaking, clenching his jaw, his fists, seeming barely to control his fury. "You knew, didn't you? That he never made it to death row."

TL nodded once. "Obviously, though, I had no idea Antonio and Octavias Zorba were one and the same. His identity was hidden deep. I've never even met him. He sent a representative to hire us. And believe me"—TL narrowed his eyes—"I'm *extremely* irritated that I've been duped."

"But you knew," Wirenut gritted, "that he never made it to death row. You should have told me!" Wirenut reared back and rammed his fist into TL's jaw.

I sucked in a breath.

TL barely moved with the impact.

I glanced from TL to Wirenut, and then back to TL. My heart broke with the hurt and sorrow I saw in their eyes.

A split second later, Wirenut bolted down the alley.

I looked at TL and started to go after Wirenut.

"GiGi," TL murmured, "let him go."

Wirenut Stayed gone the whole day. TL didn't seem to be as worried as I was. As evening approached, I wondered what we would do. According to intel, we had to break into the Museum of Modern Art that night to retrieve the first encrypted message. Even with all my notes, I knew I couldn't penetrate the Rayver System. We needed Wirenut.

I disconnected the scrambler from the laptop as TL stared at the screen. He'd said barely a word to me since the episode this morning in the alley. Normally, I didn't mind silence, but this was driving me mildly insane.

"What are we going to do if Wirenut doesn't show up?"

TL shook his head. "He'll come back."

"What about Octavias Zorba?"

"He doesn't know that we know he stole the toxin. He doesn't know that we know he's Wirenut's uncle." TL rubbed his hand across his jaw. "We're going to do the only thing we can do. Decipher these encrypted messages, find the neurotoxin, and bring Octavias down."

"But what if it's all a trap?"

TL sighed. "It probably is. That's why we've got the best people on our side. We'll stay one step ahead of Octavias."

Someone rapped on the hotel door six quick times (our secret knock). Wirenut. Thank God.

Sliding my glasses to the top of my head, I looked away from the laptop as he let himself in. Poor guy. He looked so worn-out. Being on an emotional roller coaster does that to a person. I just wanted to hug him.

TL didn't move from his spot next to me, just kept studying the screen. "We move out in one hour."

"What if I hadn't come back?"

TL still didn't look at him. "I knew you would."

All of us, actually, had been on an emotional roller coaster since joining the Specialists: being recruited by TL, settling into our new lives, forming trusting friendships and family-type bonds. But Wirenut . . . this first mission connected to the single most horrible event of his life. How huge. Was there anything else TL was hiding from him?

Wirenut trudged across the room and settled right behind us on the edge of the bed. He studied his lap.

TL finally turned.

Wirenut brought his eyes up. "I'm sorry."

"Apology accepted." TL tapped his jaw where Wirenut had hit him. "That was your free one. Punch me again, and I *will* punch back."

"Yes, sir."

"It takes a real man to apologize."

Tears filled Wirenut's eyes, and he lowered his head.

I sniffed back my own tears, glad they were making up.

TL smiled a little. "It's okay to cry."

Wirenut laughed humorlessly. "Jeez, man, don't you stop?" He scrubbed his eyes. "I'm fine."

"Is there anything you want to ask me?"

Nodding, Wirenut lifted his head. "Why didn't you tell me my uncle never made it to death row?"

"Part of my job involves secrets and knowing when to tell those secrets. Oftentimes it hurts people I care for, and I am sorry for that. Believe me when I say I tell you things when it's the right time for you to know. I wanted you to be mature enough to handle it. After the conversation we just had, I have no doubt you are."

Wirenut pressed his fingers to his eyes. "I'm acting like such a girl."

"Hey," I said jokingly, defending all girls.

Chuckling, TL sat down beside Wirenut. He looped his arms around both of our necks and pulled us in for a quick hug. "The good news is that we know your uncle's identity now. That man has been at large for twelve years. He's finally going to pay for what he did to your family."

***

One hour later, I lay belly down on the museum's browntile roof. Getting up here had been much easier than I thought. Stairs led up from the back.

I watched as Wirenut chiseled a notch six inches northeast of the roof's one and only window.

He looked over at me and grinned.

Bingo.

Double-coated EDF wire.

With a lighter, he melted two drops of copper onto the wire. The combination of the two short-circuited, and the window popped open.

He shook his head. "Accu Security. Come on, people, update your technology. This hit the market three years ago."

He packed up his tools while I secured the small foldable satellite dish to the roof. We pulled our hoods down over our faces. He tossed a rope through the roof window, and we dropped eight feet to the floor of a cleaning closet.

"Okay, game's on. Don't get too confident. Never know what might happen."

Pressing the talk button on my vest, I activated my tooth mike. "We're in." I checked my watch. "Twenty-three oh-three hours."

"Copy that," TL answered into my ear transceiver, from his lookout spot outside the museum.

Quickly, I recalled the blueprints I'd memorized. The upstairs of the 3,000 square-foot building served as offices and storage, and downstairs was the museum. We needed to go down one flight and hang a right.

On silent, slippered feet, we shuffled out of the closet and down the marble hall to the stairs. In the dimly lit hallway, I studied the descending treads. Probably rigged with weight sensors. Wirenut had said buildings that still used the Accu system on the roof window would have weight sensors on the stairs. They came in the same security package.

Which meant the wooden banister was our only way down.

Wirenut hopped up, struck a surfer pose, and slid all the way down. He sailed off the end and quietly landed on his feet.

He turned and bowed, all full of himself, then motioned me on. If he thought I was surfing the banister, he was sadly mistaken. *Need I remind him I'm a total klutz?*

I climbed on, straddling the banister very grannylike, and slid down to where he stood.

We crossed the marble foyer and came to a stop in the pottery room's doorway. The ceramic egg that held the first encrypted message sat on a stand in the room's center. A glass box encased it.

That's worth millions? You've got to be kidding me.

Taking a moment, I ran my gaze around the room, passing over wall-mounted, ceramic figurines. It didn't seem like there was anything unusual, except the egg wasn't in a vault, which was supposed to be part of the Rayver Security System.

But I wasn't the expert here. Wirenut was.

This was as far as I went. It's up to him now. I reached inside my vest for the mini-laptop.

A shadow flickered, and my gaze jumped to the other side of the room. I froze.

Another person. Dressed just like us.

I looked at Wirenut and he tensed up. "It's him," he whispered.

Oh, my God, this must be the other burglar. The one who got Wirenut busted. The same one who impersonated him in China.

"I knew you'd be here." Some sort of voice box warbled his actual speech.

He knew we'd be here?

The burglar took the fiber-lit goggles from the top of his hood-covered head and fit them over his eyes.

We did the same with ours. Yellow lasers spanned the distance between us and where he stood on the other side of the room. The ceramic egg sat smack dab between us. Through the lasers' crisp, zigzagging pattern, I watched the burglar pull a remote control expander from a pocket on the calf of his pants.

Not only did he dress the same as Wirenut, but he kept his tools in the same locations. Complete, sneaky copycat.

"Can he disengage the Rayver System from that side, too?" I whispered.

Wirenut nodded. "There're two locks. One on each side. Some Rayver System setups have that option."

The burglar pointed to the egg, then to his chest. *Mine.*

My jaw dropped. The nerve.

Wirenut got his remote-control expander, and they both moved at once.

My pulse jumped.

Leaning to the left at a seventy-degree angle, Wirenut spied his opening tunnel. He pointed the control down the tunnel and pressed the expanding button. The skinny, metal wire snaked out.

Steady, Wirenut, steady.

I switched my gaze across the room to the burglar. Through the field of lasers, I watched him perform the mirror image of Wirenut's actions. I looked at his wire snaking out and then at Wirenut's, which appeared to be a fraction ahead of the burglar's.

Wirenut's wire connected with the hole below the stand's lock, and the lasers flicked off.

The yellow sizzlers on the burglar's half of the room stayed on. *Yep, we're definitely ahead of him.*

His lasers flicked off.

Crap, not as far ahead as I'd hoped.

Wirenut set his watch, and so did I. One minute and seventeen seconds until everything turned back on. Reeling in the expandable wire, he sprinted to the middle of the room. He yanked the tool kit from his vest and spread it out on the stone floor.

A mere foot of space separated him from the burglar. Wirenut crouched on one side of the stand and the burglar on the other. Wirenut could reach out and strangle him they were so close.

Taking the nitrox first, Wirenut squirted the control panel below the lock. It popped off, and he caught it. Multicolored wires crisscrossed one another. He grabbed the diversion and ripped them out.

The burglar's clump landed right beside Wirenut's.

Jeez, the other guy's quick.

Wirenut took his extra-long, needle-nose wire cutters and, leaning to the left, found his tunnel through the red lasers. He inserted the cutters and snipped the white wire at the very back.

ClickClick. Their locks opened simultaneously.

Come on, Wirenut. Come on.

Grrrgrrr.

Wait. There shouldn't be a *grrrgrrr*. That wasn't the right sound.

The burglar reached for the protective glass. Wirenut stretched around the stand and quickly seized the burglar's wrist.

"It's a trap," Wirenut whispered.

He held his hand up to the burglar. *Don't move.*

I barely breathed as I watched Wirenut dig in his vest. This was what he meant when he said there were all kinds of scenarios that could happen. As good as David was, there was no way he could've learned everything in such a short time.

Wirenut slipped mini—jumper cables from his vest. He clipped one end to the control panel, leaned around the stand, and clipped the other end to the burglar's control panel. I knew from our hours of training that the two connections would cancel each other out and disconnect the alarm.

Lifting the glass, Wirenut snatched the ceramic egg. He unclipped the cables and swept up his tools. He dashed across the open floor back to me, with the burglar right on his heels. They both dove, and the yellow lasers flicked on behind them.

The burglar tackled Wirenut, and I tackled the burglar. The three of us rolled across the marble foyer. The ceramic egg flew through the air. The burglar kidney-punched Wirenut and then head-butted me, stunning me for a quick second. Just enough time for him to scramble out between us and across the floor.

"You broke it," he hissed, holding up half the egg.

Wirenut pushed to his knees, grasping the other half. "Give me what's inside, and you can have this half."

It took the burglar a second to understand. He looked into his half, reached in, and pulled out a small piece of paper. He held it up. "What is it?"

"None of your business," Wirenut snapped.

People's lives depended on that message. We had to get it.

"Listen, you would've set off the alarm back there if it wasn't for my partner. Now give us that paper."

The burglar studied the scrap as if he thought he had some negotiating power here.

Give us that paper or you're going down.

Putting his half of the egg in his vest, he held out the paper. "Count of three, you give me your half, I'll give you this paper."

Wirenut nodded. "One, two, three."

They quickly exchanged, and the burglar jumped on the banister and climbed it to the top floor. Obviously, he knew about the stairs' weight sensors.

Wirenut handed me the paper. "Hurry."

I pulled out my mini-laptop and quickly punched in the encrypted computer code. A series of numbers. As I keyed, the numbers began to slowly fade. "Oh, no." I typed faster, staring at the paper, memorizing the strands near the end that were almost gone.

"What is it?" Wirenut leaned over me. "Oh, crud. Already?"

I shook my head, keying faster, finishing up from memory.

Wirenut pressed the talk button on his vest. "Message secured. Taking alternate route out." He released the talk button.

"We're not going out the roof window. That dude screwed me the last time I followed him. Not again. Let's go."

I followed Wirenut past the stairwell, through a room with modern steel sculptures, and out into a back hall. He clipped a white wire in the corner of a window frame and slid the glass up.

I climbed through first, and Wirenut followed. TL met us in the dark alley outside. Quickly, we filled him in on the burglar and the disappearing message. Then we slipped our street clothes on over our black outfits and, in the midnight moonlight, made our way back through town.

I ran the encrypted numbers through my head, analyzing the strands, the sequences. I itched to get to the hotel, contact Chapling, and crank up my laptop.

Ten minutes later, we walked into TL's and Wirenut's hotel room. TL activated the blue pyramid audio-blocker so no one could hear what we were doing.

Slipping on my glasses, I powered up my laptop and got down to work. I sent Chapling the encrypted message. GOT IT, he typed back, THOUGHTS?

THE DE NUOWSI'T THEOREM, I answered. It had hit me during our walk through town. The De Nuowsi't theorem was a mathematical code that translated to letters. There were lots of theorems like this used for computer language, but the De Nuowsi't one was created by a man who lived right here in the Mediterranean.

SMARTGIRLSMARTGIRL, Chapling typed.

A few seconds passed while I waited for his comments.

TRIWALL, he typed.

Huh. I didn't expect the theorem to be protected, GIVE ME A SEC, I responded, running code through my brain.

More seconds passed, or maybe minutes.

And then it hit me. TRY <Ide>4</Ide><sni>6/sni>, < . . . =yoj-liki+[#@jum%^]>

OH YEAH, YOU'RE GOOD. GOODGOOD.

I smiled.

"David," TL spoke into his cell phone, and my ears perked up. "Get me anything you can on this Ghost impersonator and why he would be after the same thing we are. And how he knew we were going to be there. See if Beaker has anything on this disappearing message. What kinds of chemicals would cause it and what can we do to stop it? Also, contact Octavias Zorba and arrange a meeting. He has no idea we know who he really is." TL clicked off. "Now we wait for our guys back home to come through."

At this point there really wasn't much I could do but wait for Chapling to run the encrypted message through the De Nuowsi't theorem. So I logged onto e-mail and smiled when I saw David's name. I clicked on the message:

"Hi. Just wanted to make sure you made it safe and sound. How'd your flight go? Miss you. D."

I glanced over my shoulder to make sure TL and Wirenut weren't watching and typed back:

"Hi! Flight went good. I did exactly what you said. I thought of you. It worked. I miss you, too. A lot. GiGi."

I read what I'd typed, deleted the "A lot," and hit send. "A lot" seemed too much.

HERE YOU GO. Chapling IMed me and sent the decoded encryption.

"I got it," I told TL. "Chapling's sending it right now."

TL and Wirenut leaned in to look at the laptop.

RISSALA MUSEUM OF HISTORY. KING'S CROWN.

USE ELEMENTS TO RETRIEVE DATA.

"Elements?" I asked.

TL rubbed his chin, thinking. "Chemicals. It's telling us we'll have to chemically treat the crown to retrieve the encrypted data." He touched my shoulder. "Give me everything you can on that crown. I'll get Beaker busy on chemical analysis."

***

TL had an early-morning meeting with a local agent. He sent Wirenut and me to check out the Rissala Museum of History.

So here we sat on the hilltop above the capital city, watching the early sun peek out over the Mediterranean Sea. It was the most beautiful clear blue water I'd ever seen. From our high vantage point I scanned the canals, idly watching the boats sway in the gentle breeze. Below us the city crammed the cliffs. Our hotel was smooshed in there somewhere. It'd been quite a climb getting up here.

Beside me, Wirenut zipped up his windbreaker halfway. "A little chillier this morning than yesterday. In an hour it'll be just as warm. No rain expected."

"You sound like Nancy."

He laughed at that and pointed in the distance to the boats that lined the canals. "You suppose that's where Katarina lives?"

"What are you doing thinking about her?"

Playfully, he shoved my head. "Nothing. Shut up. I shouldn't have said anything."

I shoved him back. "Oooh, Wirenut's got a crush on a girl." He rolled his eyes and made a face.

Laughing, I shaded my face from the brightening sun and squinted down the hill at a one-room, pastel green stone building. The Museum of History.

I took a swig of the now-cold coffee I'd gotten from the hotel. Beside me Wirenut popped a chocolate-covered espresso bean in his mouth. "I've crossed the tired zone into punchy exhaustion."

I eyed his espresso beans. "Where'd you get those?"

"I brought them with me." He held out his hand. "Want some?"

"Sure." I grabbed a handful.

Wirenut popped another espresso bean. "Maybe I should just hook up to a caffeine IV."

I smiled a little. "Chapling's rubbing off on you."

Wirenut slipped the paper cup from my hand and sipped. "Uck. Cold."

I checked my watch. 7:30 A.M. "You got everything you need?" We'd been here on the hilltop above the city since predawn getting the layout for tonight's break-in into the Museum of History.

Wirenut nodded. "Let's hit that cafe again. I'm starving."

We pushed up from the ground and made our way down the winding dirt road. Tiny white stone cottages dotted the hillside. The buildings' doors signified the only colors. Bright blues and reds.

Other than the little houses, the museum, and a cemetery, nothing existed on the hillside.

A movement off to the left drew my attention. I looked and saw . . . *Katarina?* Wirenut must have seen her, too, because he stopped walking.

"Let's go say hi." He crossed the dirt road.

"She's praying," I whispered, but followed him anyway.

We stepped through the cemetery's arched gate and stopped about ten feet away at a mausoleum.

In the sparse brown grass, Katarina knelt next to a grave with her head bowed. She glanced over her shoulder at us.

Her eyes smiled, and she softly waved at us. We stayed at the mausoleum until Katarina was finished.

"Hi," she whispered as she approached. "I was just visiting my mother. She died when I was a little girl."

"M-my mother died, too," Wirenut murmured.

She looked up at him, surprise obvious in her eyes. I decided to stay silent. It seemed as if they were having a private conversation. I felt like I should leave and give them time alone, but I couldn't make myself walk away.

I missed David.

"What'd you do?" Katarina changed the subject, pointing to the red, scabby marks on Wirenut's right hand.

"I got mad and hit the side of a building."

"Hmmm . . . well, remind me never to make you mad."

"I've never gotten that way before. Really. I hope it doesn't scare you."

She shook her head, smiling. "I'm not scared." She slid her straw purse onto her shoulder and looked at me. "Café?"

I returned her contagious smile. No wonder Wirenut was so drawn to her. "That's where we were heading."

We exited the cemetery and strolled past the Museum of History.

Katarina rubbed her chin. "I like this on you, Stan. This . . . this . . . Oh, how do you say it in English?"

"Goatee."

"Goatee, right. It's sexy."

He glanced away, and I pressed my lips together to hold my smile. Sometimes I wished I could be that direct.

She bumped his shoulder with hers. "Did I embarrass you?"

He laughed. "Yeah, actually, you did."

Katarina laughed, too. "I'm sorry." She repositioned her purse on her shoulder. "I'm going to the marketplace later, if you want to join me. It's along the cliffs. I'll be there around lunchtime."

Wirenut nodded. "Sounds good."

In content companionship we continued strolling down the hillside road to the outskirts of the city. We rounded the corner onto a street.

"Qeqis!" Paper! shouted a kid, waving today's edition.

"Just a second." Katarina dug a coin from her purse and gave it to the boy. "My father wanted me to buy one." She opened the folded newspaper, perused it.

I peered over her shoulder at the Rissalan headlines. "What does it say?"

"Yellow ribbon says the Ghost strikes again."

Wirenut and I exchanged a quick look. He hadn't left a yellow ribbon last night. The burglar must have.

Crap.

‹SIX›

Thirty minutes later, after a quick breakfast at the café, we strode into Wirenut's and TL's hotel room.

Wirenut tossed the newspaper onto the bed. "Have you seen the headlines?"

TL didn't turn from staring out the small window. "Yes."

"We didn't leave a yellow ribbon."

"Of course you didn't." TL lifted a hotel mug to his mouth and took a sip. From the square of paper dangling off the edge, I assumed it contained hot tea. "I've decided we're going to catch the burglar."

Wirenut perked up. "Really?"

TL moved from the window. "My gut tells me he's going to be at the Museum of History tonight. After the king's crown, just like us. He's involved with Octavias Zorba. Has to be. Catching the burglar, the Ghost impersonator, will lead us to Zorba."

I sat down on the bed. "Did David get the meeting scheduled with Zorba?"

TL dunked his tea bag a couple of times. "No. Zorba is conveniently out of town on business. He won't be back for weeks. I've got David working on where exactly this business is."

"What about the burglar?" I crossed my legs. "Anything on him?"

"Just that he's been impersonating the Ghost all over the place. He did a job in Australia a few weeks ago. Left a yellow ribbon and all." TL shook his head. "Whoever he is, his identity has been hidden well."

"Want me to get cranking on it?" I asked.

"No. Chapling's got it under control. What about the crown?"

I nodded. "I've got all the information."

"Good. We'll put it all together later in a conference call."

Wirenut folded his arms across his chest. "How are we going to catch the guy?"

"We're going to get the king's crown with the encrypted message. Then we'll sit back and wait for the burglar to show."

Wirenut plopped down beside me on the bed. "What do we do for the day? Sit around here?"

TL put his mug down on the windowsill. "I've got another meeting with a local agent. You two enjoy a little scenery. There's nothing to do until tonight."

"There's a marketplace along the cliffs," Wirenut suggested. "Mind if we go there?"

I held in a knowing smile. The marketplace where Katarina would be.

"That's fine." TL tucked his wallet down his back pocket. "Make sure you have your cell phones with you at all times."

***

Wirenut and I left the hotel and walked east through town toward the sea. About ten minutes later, we reached an outdoor market that stretched for almost a mile along one of the cliffs. According to the lady at the hotel, everybody made a stop at the marketplace for daily goods.

We wove through the crowded walkways, wandering the cobblestone paths, taking in all the interesting stalls. Clothes, handmade toys, fresh fruits and vegetables, purses, hats. I bought some figs, wishing I could find a stand that sold lollipops.

Soft music trickled somewhere in the distance. "Do you hear that?"

Wirenut strained to listen over the crowd. "Yeah."

"Oooh," a tourist behind me cooed in English. "That's Gio. I saw him perform yesterday. He's really good." She pushed between me and Wirenut, pulling her friend with her. "Excuse us."

"Gio." Wirenut grumbled. "Probably some sexy musician. Why do girls always think musicians are hot? I need to learn an instrument. Something manly. Saxophone, drums, guitar. Whadaya think?"

True. Musicians *were* hot. "Saxophone."

Through the crowd we followed the two girls as the music got louder and louder. In the center of the street a small group had gathered. On a stool in the middle sat the oldest man I'd ever seen. He held a small weird-looking guitar.

I glanced at Wirenut. "Sexy."

He smiled sarcastically.

A dark-haired girl knelt beside the old man. I studied her a second, realizing, "That's Katarina."

Wirenut perked up.

The old man handed her tiny silver cymbals that she slipped onto her middle fingers and thumbs.

Neat. She was about to perform.

She kissed him on both cheeks, and his face brightened into a wrinkly grin.

Gio began strumming the odd guitar, using all his fingers to go up and down the strings. A mellow, hypnotic beat emerged. I watched him for a second or two, then switched my full attention to Katarina.

She stood with her eyes closed, head back, one hand extended above her head and the other down by her side. Her sandaled feet were tight against each other, and her knees bent slightly. She was beautiful.

Gio began singing in Rissalan. A sad song in a tenor's voice.

Katarina's hips slowly rotated. Gently, she tapped the cymbals together. *Taptap taptap.* With her eyes still closed, she brought the hand extended in the air down in front of her face, trailed it between her breasts, over her stomach, and across her hips.

Her eyes snapped open at the exact second Gio upped the rhythm.

She whirled away, tapping the cymbals to Gio's beat. Her long black hair and loose burgundy skirt flowed with every movement.

Katarina circled Gio and then came straight toward us.

Leveling her eyes on Wirenut, she crooked her finger. He stepped from the small group.

She trailed her hand down his bare arm and clasped the tips of his fingers, pulling him into the center of the group.

She circled around him, *taptap taptap*, crossed her arms, *taptap taptap*, moved them at different angles, *taptap taptap*. He followed her movement with his eyes.

Her skirt swept his legs. Her hair brushed his arms. She closed her eyes, *taptap taptap*, then opened them and gazed straight into his.

SHANNON GREENLAND

Strangely enough, he didn't look nervous. More hypnotized than anything else. Totally blocked to anything but her. I couldn't fathom performing that dance, alone or in a crowd.

The music came to an end, and I applauded along with the small gathering. We all tossed coins into Gio's guitar case.

I walked up to Wirenut, who hadn't moved since the music stopped.

"Hi." I greeted Katarina.

She kissed my right cheek and then my left. She did the same to Wirenut, and he grinned. He had it bad for this girl.

Katarina slipped the tiny cymbals from her fingers. "That was the Sotrys. It's the oldest Rissalan dance. I perform it almost every week with Gio. What'd you think?"

"It's gorgeous," I answered.

"Wow." Wirenut shook his head. "That was . . . wow."

Katarina and I laughed.

"Do the girls dance like that in America?"

Wirenut blew out a breath. "None that I know."

"Come. I want you to meet Gio." She handed the old man the cymbals. "*Vjiti esi na gsoipft, Stan epf Dana.* These are my friends, Stan and Dana," she translated.

He extended his weathered hand, and we shook it.

"Gio *mowit up vji cuev piyv vu uast.* Gio lives on the boat next to ours."

The old man nodded. "*Jux na gevjis ot?*"

"He asked how my father is." Sadness replaced her carefree mood. "*Vufez't e huuffez.* Today's a good day."

Gio began strumming his guitar as another small group formed around him. "*Vimm jon vjeplt gus vji muctvis.*"

"Tell him thanks for the lobster," she interpreted, then kissed the old man good-bye. "*O xomm.* I will."

"Is your father okay?" I asked Katarina after we left the small group, although I knew something wasn't right.

She lowered her gaze to the cobblestone beneath our feet. "He has a brain tumor. Doctors have given him six months."

Whoa. "Are you okay?" Stupid question. Of course she wasn't okay. Her mother's dead, and her father's about to die.

Katarina gave us a somber smile. "Actually, I am okay. I've known for a while and have had time to adjust."

213

Wirenut put a comforting arm around her. "Who are you gonna live with?"

She wrapped her arm around his waist. "My uncle and aunt." We crossed through a tent filled with hats and clothes.

"You mentioned lobster. Is that what your dad does?" It made sense. People who lived on boats probably fished for a living.

"No. My father's a businessman. Investments, real estate, and more, but I don't keep up with it."

Businessman and boat living didn't go together in my mind. Katarina smiled. "Anyway, what happened this morning? You took off so quick."

"We," I fibbed, "remembered something we were supposed to do."

"Oh." She waved around the marketplace. "Mind if I join you?"

Wirenut stepped to the side. "Lead the way."

We followed her off the sunlit sidewalk and ducked into a shaded tent filled with bright silks. She raised her hand in greeting. *"Jimmu."*

From the other side of a table, a small girl grinned. *"Jimmu, Katarina. Jux esi zua?"*

Katarina nodded. *"Gopi. Vjepl zua. Fu zua piif epzvjoph?"*

The girl shook her head. *"Pu."*

From my back pocket, I pulled out my English/Rissalan dictionary and began flipping through it.

Katarina tapped the dictionary. "She asked me how I was and I told her fine. Then I asked her if she needed anything, and she said no."

I laughed. "Thanks."

The girl nodded to another customer, and they began discussing the fabrics. Or at least I assumed they were discussing fabrics.

Katarina trailed a finger down a bundle of white silk. "Her name's Rashon. She runs her family's business."

I glanced over at the shiny-faced, happy girl. "She runs the business? She's just a kid."

"Twelve."

Wow. That's a lot of responsibility for a twelve-year-old. Then again, at twelve I was being watched by the government for recruitment. Who would've figured?

Katarina waved good-bye to the little girl and led the way from the shaded tent back onto the sunlit cobblestone walkway. "I just wanted to check in on her. Oh, look." She stopped at a tattoo booth.

Behind the small table sat a . . . well, I suppose "a warrior" described him best. Large, muscular, no shirt, long dreadlocks, Polynesian. Ancient tribal tattoos decorated his face. He worked on a woman's back, designing a snake.

"I *love* tattoos. I'd never get one. I'm too much of a wimp for the needles. But I *love* them. I think they're so sexy." Katarina whipped around as if just realizing what she said, and her gaze dropped to Wirenut's arms. I remembered the first time I met him, I thought it was the coolest thing.

Reaching out, she traced her finger all the way down one of his pieces all the while staring him in the eyes.

Okay, time for me to make my exit. These two needed to be alone. "I'm, um, going to check out the jewelry."

Without taking her eyes off Wirenut, Katarina nodded. "The jewelry lady hand makes each item."

I crossed the cobblestone path. An old, sun-charred lady sat on the ground twining gold wire. Necklaces and earrings decorated the blanket surrounding her, each one unique in its own way. Kneeling, I fingered a row of silver earrings.

I glanced over my shoulder back to the tattoo booth. Wirenut and Katarina had gone. With a smile to the jewelry lady, I got to my feet and headed from the marketplace.

Outside the market I spotted Wirenut and Katarina sitting beneath an olive tree on a cliff. The ocean stretched in front of them, sparkling in the sun. A constant dry, warm breeze blew the water's salty scent past. Neither of them spoke as they watched dolphins lazily peak the blue horizon. Muted sounds from the marketplace flowed past.

Comfortable. Content. Cozy. Words that streamed through my mind as I watched the two of them. They couldn't have asked for a better romantic afternoon.

God, I missed David.

They glanced at each other, lips curved slightly. Lifting his hand, he tucked her dark hair behind her ear and asked her something. With a smile, she nodded.

Bbbzzzbbbzzzbbbzzz.

They jumped apart, and I snapped from my trance.

Our phones. With a quick glance at the *** readout, TL's code, I strode down the hill to where Wirenut and Katarina sat.

Clenching his jaw, Wirenut snapped his cell off his pants and checked the display. He turned to Katarina. "I'm really sorry."

"It's all right." She pushed up off the ground. "I have to go anyway."

He helped her up. "Café? Tomorrow morning?"

She smiled. "Sure."

I didn't want to remind him that we might not even be here tomorrow morning. Somehow, though, I knew that wouldn't matter to him.

As she strolled away from us along the cliff, Wirenut put his hand over his heart. "That smile shot straight through me."

"Bummer she's here and you live in California."

Ignoring my comment, Wirenut and I took off in the opposite direction back into the outdoor market toward our hotel. "She's so perfect. I've never clicked with anyone like I have with her. And I've had only three conversations with her." He half laughed. "Go figure. I asked her if I could kiss her. I've never asked any girl that question before."

I smiled. It reminded me of David. He told me he never kissed a girl unless he knew she wanted to be kissed.

Our phones buzzed again with urgency, and we took off running.

‹SEVEN›

Wirenut and I rushed into the hotel room.

TL sat at the desk between the two beds. "Conference call. Now." He activated the pyramid-shaped audio-feedback blocker in case someone passed by in the hall.

Wirenut and I situated ourselves on either side of him on the beds. TL ran his finger across the laptop's touch pad, and the screen flickered on.

Chapling's, Beaker's, and David's faces appeared, transmitted via satellite.

David looked right at me, and his eyes crinkled. I smiled as my stomach jingle-jangled.

Chapling waved. Next to him, Beaker remained blank-faced.

She'd dyed her green hair black, and I wondered, as I had many times before, what her natural color was.

A five-pointed crown popped up on the bottom left corner of the screen.

"Here's the crown you're after tonight," Chapling began. "This belonged to the first king of Rissala. It's currently located in the Museum of History and holds the next encrypted message. GiGi, tell us what you found out."

I slipped on my glasses. "I input the crown's dimensions into the SNI system and coded the chemical makeup I found on file. I interpreted the history and prohibited rendering of visual framework. Attributes of the ID class were discouraged, but I forced a break by controlling the elements. Traditionally, intrinsic scripts render subsequences. But after only a few moments, I addressed the stylistic treatment of pontdu. So that's no longer an issue. However, with quote blocks marching ores, we secured a designated source document. Abbreviated text shows—"

"Uh," David stuck his finger in the air, "you lost me way back at the crown's dimensions." He patted his T-shirt pocket. "And I forgot my secret decoder ring. Can you make it simple for me? For us?"

This happened all the time with me. "Oh, right. Sorry."

Chomping her gum, Beaker snorted.

Chapling perked up. "I understood you."

I gave him a thank-you-but-of-course-you-understood-me-you're-a-nerd-too smile.

He bounced his bushy red brows, and I silently laughed. I adored Chapling.

TL shifted. "You're doing fine, GiGi. Finish up."

I took a second to ungeek all the mumble jumble in my brain. "After digging through various online archives, I discovered crowns have been used for centuries to hide objects. The encrypted message should be located in one of the jewels decorating the crown's five points. We don't have time to remove the jewels and break them all open. Beaker, this is where you come in."

With a nod, Beaker took the gum out of her mouth. "Each crown point has a ruby and an emerald. One drop of barium gentrea will expose any imperfection in a ruby. Two drops of carmine nitrate will take care of the emeralds. I suggest you try the rubies first. My research revealed that more people embed messages in those than in emeralds because rubies are easier to manipulate. Once they're transparent you can see which one hides the message. Voilà. Nothing fancy about it." She tossed her gum back in her mouth.

"What about the encrypted message?" I asked. "The fading. Anything on that yet?"

"Oxygen activates it." She shook her head. "That's all I know. I don't know how to stop it. Sorry. You'll just have to work quickly."

"That's all right," TL said. "GiGi did it last time. She can do it again."

Nothing like pressure.

"Where do we get these chemicals for the gems?" asked Wirenut.

"We have a local contact. I'll take care of it." TL reached for the laptop. "Still nothing on the burglar's identity?"

Chapling shook his head.

"Okay. Signing off." TL pressed the escape key, and the screen went black.

I didn't even have a chance to look at David one last time.

***

That evening, Wirenut and I knelt behind a gravestone, scoping out the back side of the Museum of History. Three entrance possibilities: front door, side window, rear door. No other entry points existed on the one-room stone structure.

To the untrained, the building had the lure of an easy job. The old *looks can be deceiving* held true in this instance. I'd learned a lot from Wirenut during this morning's surveillance.

A camera mounted on the building's upper-left corner pointed straight at the back door. A novice would avoid the back door and break in the side window because of that camera. Wrong decision. Everything's about illusion in this business. A mere breath, change in temperature, or slight touch on that window would immediately set off the alarm.

"Any other night I'd go in that window," Wirenut whispered. "For the sheer challenge of it."

"Don't get sidetracked," I warned. But I totally understood. Nothing felt more satisfying than cracking a system no one had ever broken. The only difference was I had to have a reason. Wirenut would do it just to do it.

He shook his head. "Not tonight."

Twenty feet of warm night air separated us from the mounted camera. Wirenut pulled out a piece of bamboo. He rolled some putty, pushed it into the end of the bamboo, then peered down the length. He sucked in a breath, held it to his lips, and blew.

The putty whistled through the air and splatted right on the camera lens.

My jaw dropped. Wow. "You need to teach me that."

He grinned.

Pulling our hoods down over our faces, we sprinted from the cemetery through the museum's backyard and halted at the rear door.

Wirenut peeled down the right-index-finger portion of his leather glove. Placing the tip of his finger on the steel door, he closed his eyes and counted.

His eyes shot open. "Water pulse," he whispered.

I blinked. *Water pulse?*

"I didn't expect that. Nobody's *ever* penetrated a water-rigged security system. I've studied all about it. It came out after I joined the Specialists. Otherwise, I would've already tackled it and proven it faulty."

Of course.

"Can you do it?" I had no doubt he could.

He rolled his eyes. "Please. Give me a second."

Slowly, he rubbed his hands together. His gaze focused on nothing in particular as he drifted into deep thought.

"One wrong move, and the entire museum locks down. The building will flood with water stored in oversize pipes in the walls, trapping us and the display pieces. But the display items are protected. We'll drown."

We'll drown? Wait a minute . . .

"Pretty nifty security idea."

I don't think it's too nifty we're going to drown.

"Too bad I'll have to be the first to prove it faulty."

He'd better prove it faulty.

Wirenut reached for his tool pouch. "Okay, think. A building rigged with water will have 1009 proc-gauge wiring. Plastic-coated. It'll be charged by aluminum cantver currents. The water and electricity will flow together, not against each other. Any sort of contact between the two will spark the release. So as long as there's continuous motion of the two, the system will be fooled."

He sounds like he knows what he's doing.

"Let's see." He touched the tip of his finger to the door again and held it steady while he counted. He moved it up a fraction, held, counted. He slid it down, held, counted. "A five-second lead interrupts the inch intervals. Which means five-inch segments of black electrical tape, separated by five inches of space, connected by five thicknesses proc-gauge wire will do the trick."

He winked at me. "No problem. What is it with the number five? The crown has five points, too."

"They got a little theme going here."

He took a roll of wire and electrical tape from his vest. He tore off segments of tape, stretched the wire across the door, and then secured the wire at exactly spaced intervals. As he smoothed down the last piece of tape, he gave me a confident nod.

A few seconds later, the door clicked, and Wirenut smiled.

Boy, he's good.

He opened the door, we quickly scooted inside, and it closed behind us with a *click*.

He glanced back. "Wasn't expecting that. Five seconds to get in before everything locks down."

"Good thing we're quick."

He did his victory shoulder-roll dance, and I shook my head at his silliness.

"Okay, don't get too confident. Never know what might happen." Wirenut pressed the talk button on his vest. "We're in."

"Lookout copy," answered TL.

Wirenut took his fiber-lit goggles from his vest. "Let's do this."

In the southwest corner of the one-room museum sat a small wood table. A vault underneath stored the crown at night. According to our research, the crown was pretty much the only thing the museum had. People came from all over the country of Rissala to see it.

We fitted the goggles over our eyes, illuminating the skin-sizzling, yellow lasers.

From my vest I got out the small bottles of chemicals, then flipped open my mini-laptop and keyed the scrambler sequence.

YOU'RE IN, typed Chapling.

HI, I typed back.

From my spot at the back door, I watched Wirenut complete the steps to breaking the Rayver System: leaned at seventy-degree angle, spied tunnel, engaged remote-control expander, wire snaked out and into vault's lock, lasers flicked off, squirted control panel with nitrox, ripped out diversionary wires, red lasers flicked on, found opening tunnel, snipped remaining white one, vault popped open.

Wow, he's quick.

He squatted down, reached inside the vault, and brought out—

A yellow ribbon? What the . . . ?

A ribbon tied around a ruby and a piece of paper. No crown. The burglar had already been here.

Fisting the ruby and paper, Wirenut reared back to slam the vault shut.

"Shhh," I reminded him.

He paused, closed it softly instead, grabbed his tools, and raced back across the tile. The yellow lasers flicked on behind him.

I threw the yellow ribbon aside and took the ruby. "See what the paper says."

Quickly, Wirenut unfolded it. "My boss said to leave this gem behind."

"Is it typed or handwritten?"

"Typed."

"We'll worry about it later." Opening the bottle of barium gentrea, I squeezed out one drop. It glided over the gem. Holding it close, I scrutinized it, studying the chemically bonded numbers as they became visible. Five sets, separated by five spaces with raised edges on every fifth number. Different than the last encrypted message.

"It might disappear on you," Wirenut reminded me.

Like I would forget such a thing. I quickly began keying in the numbers.

"Hurry."

My fingers raced over the keys as I noticed the numbers beginning to disappear.

"Hurry."

My fingers dashed lightning quick to keep up.

"Hurry."

"Got it." I pressed save and made sure Chapling had everything.

The gem went back to normal, appearing as if it hadn't even been touched.

I closed my laptop. "Please don't ever tell me to hurry again. It makes me nervous."

"Sorry."

"That's all right. Let's get out of here."

He did the tape/wire thing to the door, deactivated it, and we slipped out.

***

Wirenut flung the yellow ribbon and note on the hotel bed. "I can't *believe* he got there before me. I can't *believe* he penetrated the water pulse system." He jabbed his chest.

"*I'm* the one who cracks new systems. Not other people. *I'm* the Ghost."

I didn't think it'd be wise to remind him that technically he was no longer the Ghost. He'd left that behind with his old life when he joined the Specialists.

222

TL picked up the ribbon. "Sounds like your ego's talking."

Wirenut flopped down on the bed and slung his arm over his eyes. "Leave me alone."

In the months I'd known Wirenut, he'd always maintained a calm, cool demeanor with a spice of humor. I'd seen him irritated and upset more in the past week than I had since first meeting him. It worried me.

This mission was pushing at him from all angles: horrid memories resurfacing about his family, the burglar impersonating him, his meeting Katarina.

All I could do was be a friend, be there for him.

TL picked up the paper. "His boss? He has to be working for Zorba. How else would he know to leave that gem?" TL motioned me to the desk. "Let's see what Chapling's got."

I opened up the laptop. WELL? I typed.

NO GO ON THE DE NUOWSI'T THEOREM, he responded.

"Huh." Slipping on my glasses, I studied the sets of numbers on my screen. "The number five is the theme for this encrypted message. Give me a sec." I took the numbers and rearranged them. Ran them through text identifiers. Cut through user markings. Tagged them defined. Changed the ELD spacing. Wrapped the preformatted fragment. Deleted fixed processing. Soft-charactered the numerical breaks.

Bingo. "It's code for an image." I ran the code through my vortex imaging program.

OH YEAH. YEAHYEAHYEAH, Chapling typed. SO GOOD.

A 3D image of a small island appeared. An old mansion occupied pretty much the entire area. The image rotated, and a room appeared. I plugged the coordinates of the island into GPS. "The island is located five towns north of here, five kilometers off shore. I wonder what it is about the number five."

"I was the youngest of five children," Wirenut mumbled from the bed.

I glanced back at him. He still had his arm over his eyes. *Was.* He *was* the youngest of five. How awful to have to say that in the past tense.

TL tapped my knee, and I looked at him. He shook his head slightly, indicating I shouldn't respond to Wirenut.

Pushing my glasses up, I focused back on the laptop. TL was probably right. Wirenut needed to be with his own thoughts right now.

"Cue up the satellite, and let's see what's inside this mansion," TL said.

I pressed a few keys. "According to the original note when the toxin was first stolen, there are three data-encrypted messages. We've retrieved two, so this is the last one. It has to be the sword."

I keyed in the access code to the government's satellite, and through the darkness of midnight, it zeroed in on the mansion. A few more key strokes and it switched to infrared. A couple of clicks and it X-rayed the roof. I zoomed in on the room. "The room is located on the fifth floor, behind the fifth door on the right." I saw an object hanging on the wall and isolated it.

Wirenut sat up and scooted to the edge of the bed.

Beyond the various shades of infrared, a long object became visible.

Wirenut looked over my and TL's shoulders. "Yeah. That's the double-bladed, lion-engraved sword."

The sword his uncle had used.

The laptop bleeped, and Chapling appeared in the lower-left corner. I waved, but he didn't wave back. My stomach clenched with the devastation I saw in his eyes.

Something was wrong. Something was *really* wrong.

TL nodded. "Go ahead."

"New intel. A message came over the line that whoever is looking for the stolen toxin isn't working quickly enough. In two days the toxin will be released. You *have* to get that sword. You *have* to retrieve the last encrypted message. You *have* to find the stolen neurotoxin."

I'd never heard Chapling so adamant.

"We leave at oh eight hundred hours." TL reached for the laptop. "Signing off."

No one said a word as we sat, digesting everything. People were going to die if we didn't retrieve the last encrypted message. And Wirenut's uncle was behind it all. "How can someone be so sinister?"

"I can't believe I'm related to this man," Wirenut whispered. "Someone told me once that evil is genetic. . . ." His voice trailed off.

The pain in it cracked my heart.

TL gripped the back of Wirenut's neck. "You look at me, and you listen very closely. You wouldn't be a part of the Specialists if you had that kind of blackness in your blood, in your heart. People like your uncle are driven by money and sickness. They get off on watching others suffer. They live to manipulate."

TL let go of Wirenut's neck and grabbed his shoulder. "You are a good man with kindness in your heart that one day will make you a great man." TL released Wirenut. "Now, did you hear everything I said?"

Wirenut closed his eyes. "Yes, sir. Thank you. Excuse me." He crossed the hotel room and walked out the door.

‹EIGHT›

Early the next morning, TL counted Rissalan currency into my hand. "I've reserved a car to take us north of here, then we'll catch a boat over to the island and mansion. The reservation place knows you two are picking it up. Be back here in one hour. I'll meet you out front."

"Yes, sir." I folded the bills and stuffed them in my pants pocket.

Wirenut and I slung our backpacks on and left TL.

As we strolled down the hotel's tile hallway, I cut a quick glance in Wirenut's direction. From the puffiness of his eyes, I'd say he'd had no sleep.

I hadn't seen him since he left his and TL's room last night. I'd gone to mine and crashed. I had no idea what time Wirenut returned or if TL had gone out looking for him.

Looping my arm through Wirenut's, I laid my head on his shoulder. "I love you." I knew he knew I meant sister to brother.

The last time I'd told anyone that, I was six years old, and I'd said it to my parents.

With a sad smile, he kissed my temple. "It's been a long time since I've heard those words."

He was probably afraid to care again. Everyone he'd ever loved had died.

We took the stairs down a flight, crossed the lobby, and exited the hotel. We slipped on sunglasses to cut the early-morning glare and headed up the cobblestone street.

Unzipping my front pocket, I rifled around for my ChapStick and pulled out a lollipop. "I didn't put this in here, did you?"

Wirenut shook his head.

Thinking of you was printed on the stem. *David.* I grinned. "It's from David."

"I see that. And I know you two have been e-mailing each other, so you can stop trying to hide it."

I poked him in the ribs. "You're not supposed to know that."

Smiling, Wirenut looped his arm around my neck. "Come on."

I unwrapped the blueberry lollipop and popped it in my mouth. *Mmmm.*

"Do you mind if we make a quick stop at the café? I told Katarina I'd meet her there. We have time. I want to tell her good-bye. Maybe get her number or something."

I smiled, glad to see his mood lifted. "Sure."

We cut down an alley in the direction of the cafe and walked in silence. Ahead of us, a red-haired woman opened bright blue shutters. As we passed, I peeked inside. Her children sat around a wood table eating breakfast. A warm, sweet scent floated from their kitchen. The old-world, homey scene brought a contented curve to my lips.

"Let me stop here for a second." He pointed up the alley to where it opened onto a dirt street.

The old, sun-charred jewelry lady, the same one from the marketplace, had spread out her things on a doorstep. She sat on a blanket behind them, creating a new piece.

Wirenut perused her handmade items. He pointed to a gold necklace with an amber stone. "That one. It matches Katarina's eyes."

Aw. I hugged him. He was the best guy ever. Except for David, of course.

Wirenut laughed. "What's that for?"

"Nothing. You're a great guy. That's all."

Ducking his head, he pulled out his wallet. His embarrassed, shy avoidance made me want to hug him again. He paid the lady, took the wrapped necklace, and we continued on our way.

I stuck my lollipop back in my mouth, but I couldn't stop grinning.

He shoved my shoulder. "Stop it. You're ruining my bad-guy image."

We shared a laugh as we rounded the corner to the cafe.

Katarina stood under the green canvas awning. Behind her, the waitress set the outdoor tables, getting ready for breakfast. No customers had arrived yet.

Katarina watched us approach. She didn't smile or wave or anything. In fact, she didn't seem happy to see us at all.

We stopped beside her and Wirenut slipped off his sunglasses. *"Jimmu,"* he greeted her softly, as if sensing something wasn't right.

She smoothed her long hair behind her ear. "Hello."

And then nobody said a word. We all just stood in silence, Katarina looking at Wirenut and me and him looking back at her.

Biting her lip, she dropped her gaze to the ground.

Wirenut switched what's-going-on eyes to me.

I shrugged. I had no idea.

He cleared his throat. "Um . . . here." He held out the wrapped necklace. "I bought you something."

She took the small package. "Thank you."

Wirenut clasped her hand. "Katarina, what's going on?"

She swallowed. "My father . . . my father . . ."

Oh, God, no. Had her father died?

"My father saw us together at the marketplace yesterday and got really mad. I'm sorry." A tear slid down her cheek. "He doesn't want me to see you again."

***

In silence, we continued on to pick up the rental car, then TL, and now here I sat, idly staring out the open passenger window as TL drove up the coast to our destination. Warm, salty air flowed through the car, through my body, relaxing me a little. Clear aqua water spanned to eternity on my right, and jagged cliffs boxed us in on the left. I'd never been one to sit and "smell the roses," as they say, but this part of Rissala was definitely the most beautiful place I'd ever seen.

Wirenut sat in the backseat studying the mansion's schematics and the private island the mansion occupied.

He hadn't said a word about Katarina. He had to be thinking about her, though. I'd asked him a few hours ago if he was okay. He'd simply nodded and continued analyzing the blueprints. I supposed it was good he had something to occupy his brain.

"Okay," Wirenut called over the wind. "I'm ready."

We rolled up our windows, and TL cranked on the air. I turned in my seat to listen.

Wirenut tapped his legal pad. "This mansion's locked down tight. But I've figured it out. There's an invisible fence surrounding the private island. The fence is located in the water. The only way in is to swim under it."

TL adjusted the rearview mirror. "How far down?"

"Hundred feet."

A hundred feet? I'd had only a couple of diving lessons back at the ranch as part of our PT. But that'd been in a twenty-five-foot-deep pool. A *hundred feet?* That was *really* far down.

"You'll do fine," TL reassured me, as if sensing my wandering, I'm-starting-to-freak-out thoughts.

"There's only one location we can swim under," Wirenut continued. "The opening is located on the west side, fifty feet off the island's shore. Once we're through the invisible fence, we have to scale the east wall of the mansion. There're only five windows on the east side. We'll have to climb between the fourth and fifth windows. Once we're on the roof, we'll rappel down through the fifth chimney into the mansion. According to the X-rayed image GiGi pulled up last night, we'll be in the room where the sword is located."

Wow. As always, very thorough.

TL turned off the coastal highway onto a dirt road. "Good work."

"One last thing." Wirenut pressed the off button on his handheld, electronic schematics. "With this particular security setup, one misstep rigs the mansion to explode."

Explode?

***

Hours later, TL pulled into a marina parking lot. "Whatever I say or do, you two play along with it."

Wirenut and I nodded.

I held up my finger. "Can we talk about the exploding thing again?"

Both guys sighed. "GiGi, you'll do fine."

They'd said that about a zillion times since Wirenut mentioned it. Their not-this-again, chorused answer made me smile. They knew me too well.

TL slid the keys from the ignition. "Give GiGi and me a second."

With a nod, Wirenut exited the car.

TL turned to me. "Under no circumstances do you show any recognition of the person we're about to see. Understand?"

"Who are we about to see?"

"Do you understand?"

I *hated* when he didn't answer my questions. "Yes, sir."

TL opened his door and climbed out. "Get your stuff, kids. It's going to be a *fuuun* day."

Kids?

Beside us a couple with twin boys pulled towels, fishing rods, duffel bags, and other vacationy things from their car. Other than them and us, the marina parking lot sat empty.

TL popped the trunk. He handed a cooler to Wirenut. "Carry that. We got some yummy munchies in there."

When had we gotten a cooler? And "yummy munchies"? TL would never in a million years say "yummy munchies."

Wirenut must have thought so, too, because he laughed.

TL ruffled Wirenut's hair. "Whatcha laughing at, sport? It's going to be a *beee-uuu-ti-ful* day." He tossed a couple of backpacks at me. "Carry those for me, girlie girl."

Sport? Girlie girl? I tried not to laugh.

Slinging diving bags over his shoulder, TL slammed the trunk. "Glory *be*, it's magnificent here. Maybe we'll see some of those *enooormous* stingrays."

He led the way across the marina parking lot and onto a wooden path. Trees bordered both sides and opened to a rocky beach. The path led to a dock that stretched out over the water.

TL pointed off to the right. "Look at that water. Have you *ever* seen *anything* so gorgeous in your life?"

Wirenut cut a quick glance in my direction, and we shared a smile. TL was never this talkative or happy.

"Well, have you?"

"No," Wirenut quickly responded. "Never have."

We came to the end of the dock, where a rickety wooden boat floated, tied off. Behind us, the parking-lot family boarded a safer-looking one.

TL sat his dive bags down. "Here we go. Doesn't look like much. But we're going to have *tooons* of fun."

Shielding my eyes from the early-afternoon sun, I surveyed the twenty-five-foot weather-beaten boat. It didn't appear as if it could float, much less take us safely five kilometers to the private island and mansion.

A crash-bang echoed from the small pilothouse, followed by a string of curses. Dressed in filthy overalls, a woman stumbled out, rubbing her ball-cap-covered head.

She snorted, hacked her throat, and spit.

Nasty.

She took off her cap. Long, greasy, black hair fell down her back. Scratching her scalp, she looked up at the three of us and stretched her lips into a toothless grin.

I froze. *Nalani?*

What was TL's wife doing here? The last time I'd seen her, we'd been in Ushbania running for our lives. She hadn't looked anything like she did now. She'd had teeth. And manners. And clean hair. She'd been beautiful.

Nalani put her cap back on. "Welcome aboard, maties. *Mi casa es su casa.*" She snorted a laugh. "That's Spanish, not Rissalan."

TL tossed her the dive bags. "We're *sooo* excited. My name's Tim. That's Stan holding the cooler and Dana with the backpacks."

Wirenut and I waved. Well, I waved. Wirenut nodded because of the cooler. I tried to catch Nalani's eye, but she was completely in role. A stranger to us. Someone we'd hired for the day.

Nalani saluted. "Call me captain. Now get on board. Times a wastin'. We're shoving off in one minute."

She disappeared into the pilothouse. The engine sputtered to life a second later. We loaded our things, untied the boat, and motored away from the dock.

I stood beside Wirenut, watching the rocky beach disappear until only water surrounded us. An unsettled feeling weighed down my stomach, and I thought back all those years to the plane crash I'd been in with my parents. All the water. Swimming. Crying for them . . .

Sighing at the memory, I glanced over my shoulder to the pilothouse. TL stood just inside the door, staring at Nalani's back as she drove the boat. My heart ached for him. For both of them. It had in Ushbania, too. Their covers prohibited them from interacting like a couple.

He took a step into the pilothouse, peering over her shoulder. His fingers trailed across her lower back as he pretended interest in the boat's control panel. He shifted a little closer, and, although I couldn't see real well, I thought he kissed her on the neck.

I wondered, as I had before, why they weren't together. Why didn't she live at the ranch with us? Why did they even get married?

For hours we zigzagged the coast, pretending to sightsee, each time getting a little closer to the private island. Anyone who might be watching, listening, or have us on radar would assume we were just another group of tourists.

Sitting in the distance, the small island stretched about a half mile long and a quarter mile wide. The centuries-old stone mansion occupied roughly half the island. It stood dark and spooky on the horizon. According to my research, no one lived in the mansion. It was owned by the country of Rissala and rented out for special occasions.

Not that stolen neurotoxin was considered a special occasion.

The sun slipped into darkness. Nalani cut the engine and dropped the anchor.

Wirenut handed me an apple and a cheese sandwich. "Eat this. We've got a long night ahead of us." He sat down beside me, dangling his feet over the side of the boat. "The captain works for us, doesn't she?"

Biting into my apple, I shrugged. In Ushbania I'd been the only one who didn't know Nalani was on our side. I hadn't suspected anything and didn't find out until the very end that she was one of us.

Silly to admit, but I liked being in the know this time around.

Clearly, though, Wirenut was more perceptive than me.

We finished our food and continued sitting, patiently waiting, staring at the dark water until TL touched our backs.

He tapped two fingers to his left shoulder. *Time to go.*

Behind him, Nalani opened the cooler, revealing equipment piled inside. She handed Wirenut and me black Velcro belts. "Tool belt. Strap these to your thighs so they're hidden."

Leaning in, Wirenut smiled. "I knew she worked for us," he whispered.

***

In our wet suits, we flutter-kicked our way through the dark ocean. Wirenut first, me second, and TL brought up the rear.

With our rebreathers, no bubbles trailed upward. Water plugged my ears, permitting me to hear only my heartbeat and slow deep breaths.

Wirenut extended his arms out to his sides, indicating in ten seconds we would pass through the opening in the invisible fence.

Through my night goggles, I kept my vision focused on Wirenut's fins. *One misstep rigs the mansion to explode.*

Talk about pressure.

We made it through the fence and continued underwater around the island to the east side. The sandy ocean floor rose gradually until we swam in only ten feet of depth. Our slow ascent decompressed our bodies.

We exited the water and stripped our diving gear, then piled it on the sliver of rocky beach.

Still in our wet suits, we jogged over the flat rocks to the mansion's east wall. Between the fourth and fifth windows, Wirenut gazed up five stories to the roof. He leaned to the right a little and tilted his head.

He placed his ear against the wall, moved a few feet to the left and listened there, then went back to his original spot. From his vest he pulled four pressurized suction cups. Two he strapped to his knees and two he held in his hands. TL and I did the same. Air release controlled the suction, allowing for silent attachment and release. They worked on any surface.

Wirenut turned to us, touched his eye, and held up one finger. *Watch closely. One at a time.*

TL and I nodded. Wirenut suctioned onto the stone and began a spiderlike crawl. Left arm, left leg. Right arm, right leg. I scrutinized his form, memorizing his technique and rhythm. At the third story he scooted to the right and continued crawling. At the fifth story he moved back to his original spot.

He made it to the roof and signaled for me.

One misstep rigs the mansion to explode.

With a deep breath I suctioned onto the wall.

‹NINE›

Trying to be a spider crawling up five stories of stone was *not* as easy as Wirenut made it look.

A week after my Ushbanian mission, I'd seen him using these suction cups at the ranch. I'd played around with them on the side of our two-story, wooden barn, more for fun than anything. But that time wasn't anything like right now.

Wood versus stone. Big difference.

Two stories versus five. Another big difference.

You'd think I'd have learned by now to expect the unexpected. Maybe years into this secret-agent thing, I'd be so experienced nothing would faze me.

Like TL.

At the third story I stopped to catch my breath. Shutting my eyes, I inhaled the musty scent of stone and blew out slowly through my mouth. Again in deeply through my nose and out my mouth. Like TL had taught me.

Gradually, my thumping heart stilled to a normal putter. Only two more stories to go.

Bruiser would have no problem scaling this wall. She'd already be on the roof doing back flips or some such thing.

I opened my eyes to moldy, moist stone. Ignoring my shaky, fatigued muscles, I used my thumb to depress the button on my right suction cup. A tiny puff of air indicated that the seal was broken. I moved my hand farther up the wall and reattached.

I scooted to the right like I'd seen Wirenut do and then back to the left at the fifth story. Mere feet from the roof, I stopped, my breath rushing in and out, and tilted my head back. My entire body screamed with exertion as I met Wirenut's eyes.

He lay belly down on the mansion's roof, his hand stretching out toward me. I inched a little farther up, and he latched onto my forearm.

Oh, thank God. I'd thought I was in better shape.

With a stifled grunt, he tugged me onto the roof, and I rolled onto my back, gasping for air.

"Shhh," he reminded me.

Staring at the night sky, I focused on the half moon and concentrated on steadying my breath and heart.

Exhale.

Inhale.

Exhale.

Inhale.

TL quietly stepped up beside me, breathing normally. As if he'd gone for a leisurely stroll in the park.

I definitely needed more physical training.

Never thought I'd actually think those words.

Swallowing to moisten my dehydrated mouth, I got to my feet and looked around.

Fat brick chimneys dotted the roof. A dozen of them. This mansion must have a lot of fireplaces.

Wirenut stood beside one about three feet tall, looping rappelling wire around a protruding brick. I scanned the haphazardly placed chimneys, wondering how he knew that was the fifth one.

He signaled us, and we wove through the maze to him. Wirenut climbed up and disappeared over the edge. I peeked past the bricks and watched him slip into the darkness.

Well, this is something new. I'd never rappelled. TL had gone over the procedures in the car on the drive up the coast. But as I mentioned earlier, real life *never* mirrored simulation.

It was impossible to prepare completely for every single situation. I was such a novice, thrown into these missions quite unexpectedly. Eventually, I'd have the skills needed.

TL touched my shoulder and then tapped his watch. *Go.*

He had faith in me, so that had to count for something. I did do all right on the Ushbanian mission. Well, aside from a few mishaps.

I slipped on night-vision goggles, climbed up the chimney, and attached hand grips to the rappelling wire like TL had told me to. Folding my legs around it, I slowly slid down the passage. The cushioned hand grips did most of the work. I just had to hold on. For once, something physical came easy for me.

Through my goggles, I made out gray shades of bricks and cobwebs. No spiders. This passage had to be at least six feet wide. I hadn't imagined chimneys would be so roomy.

About twenty feet later I landed with a soft thud on the fire grate. No ashes. No coals. No wood. No signs that a fire had ever been built.

Squatting down, I stepped from the oversized opening into an empty room. No furniture. No decorations. Nothing.

Wirenut stood in the center of the room staring at a spot above me. I turned. The double-bladed lion-engraved sword hung right above the fireplace, a few feet from my head.

The sword Wirenut's uncle had used to kill his entire family.

The sword holding the final message that would lead to the stolen neurotoxin.

TL stepped from the fireplace and immediately looked up to see what Wirenut and I stared at.

"Don't," Wirenut mumbled, "touch it."

TL and I turned back to Wirenut.

He pointed to the row of marble tile leading straight toward him. "Come to me. Do not step off the tile."

One misstep rigs the mansion to explode.

I went first down the row of foot-wide tile, and TL followed. We met Wirenut in the middle.

Wirenut tapped his fiber-lit goggles. "I can tell that this," he indicated the circular change in marble pattern about five feet in diameter, "is the safe zone. Do not step from it. As soon as I start working, that tile you walked down won't be available. It'll be covered with lasers."

TL replaced his night-vision goggles with fiber-lit ones. "Put yours on."

I followed his instructions. Yellow lasers flicked into view, completely filling the room, zigzagging inches from our circular safe zone and the path we'd come down.

Jeez, and to think if I'd lost my step I would've been fried.

236

A blue glow enveloped the sword. As Wirenut contemplated it, I took the mini-laptop from my vest.

"Son of a—" he breathed. "We activated that when we came down the fireplace."

"What is it?" TL asked.

"It's a pulse bomb. Incinerates anything with a heartbeat." My whole body jerked to attention. "That means . . . that means . . ." I swallowed. I knew about pulse bombs. They were the most lethal ones on the market. "That means every human and animal within two hundred miles will be a pile of ashes if we trigger it."

Wirenut nodded.

TL cupped Wirenut's shoulder. "You can do this. Don't focus on the pulse bomb. Concentrate on doing what you do best, and we'll make it out alive."

TL turned to me. "Don't you think about it either. Get the laptop ready. Focus."

I barely heard him over my hammering heart.

"Both of you, we've made it this far knowing the mansion could explode. This pulse bomb is just another obstacle. Let's do it."

Yeah, but everyone within two hundred miles? That meant people back in the capital city, Katarina, Nalani—

Suddenly, the door to the room opened. We whipped our heads around to the right. The burglar, the imposter Ghost, stood in the threshold. One step inside and the lasers would fry him.

"You don't want to do this. Not now." Wirenut indicated the sword. "That's a pulse bomb."

"I know." The burglar pointed a tiny silver disc at the sword. He pressed the top of the disc, and the blue glow went out. "Pulse bomb's not a problem anymore. I'm here for the sword."

Something digitized his voice, masking its real sound, just like before.

"What is that?" Wirenut asked. "Where did you get that?"

The burglar slipped the disc inside his vest. "You're not the only one gifted in the homemade-electronic-contraption department."

"B-but . . ."

"What? Don't like being shown up?"

"Ignore him," TL whispered. "Focus on the sword. We'll get him later."

"Oh, and one last thing." The burglar slipped another object from his vest. A slim black square.

He pointed it at each corner of the room. On the last corner, the yellow lasers flicked out. Pink ones immediately took their place, zigzagging everywhere but the circular safe zone, the area in front of the fireplace, and the entrance to the room.

The burglar stepped inside and closed the door behind him.

Wirenut sighed. "Great."

I shifted. "What is it?"

"Contortion lasers. Named that because you have to be a freakin' gymnast to get through them." Wirenut took off his vest, leaving him dressed in only his wet suit, hood, and goggles. "No equipment needed. Just like the others, they'll definitely fry you."

The burglar took off his vest, too. He slid to a split, grasped his left calf, and flattened his upper body along the length of his leg. He rolled under a laser not more than eight inches from the floor.

I cringed. *That* had to hurt.

Extending his arms above his head, Wirenut leapt up and dove through a laser opening about six feet off the ground. He landed on the other side.

I caught my breath. *Wow.*

Still in a split, the burglar tilted his body a tiny bit. He curved his left leg forward, his right leg back, and lifted up with his hands. Hovering a few inches from the tile, he rotated like a slow-motion windmill through the crisscrossed lasers.

I blinked. *This guy's good.*

From his handstand position, Wirenut lowered himself inch by inch, bowing backward, slinking beneath a laser. Halfway under he paused, tucked in his left arm, and balanced his entire body on his right hand. Carefully, he crept the rest of the way, using only his fingers to crawl forward.

My jaw dropped. I had no idea Wirenut was that strong.

The burglar stood pencil straight. Lasers zigzagged all around him, literally a millimeter's width from frying him. I scrutinized him and the lasers and couldn't see an opening anywhere.

In a flash, he moved. Jumping, spinning, flipping. Landing in a tight little ball. He flinched and hissed in a breath. His black bodysuit spread open on his lower back. A thin stream of blood trickled out. One of the lasers had gotten him.

I gritted my teeth. *Ow.*

Squatted down, Wirenut swept his left leg around. He pushed up, spun, and caught air on a scissors kick, then corkscrewed through a diamond-shaped opening.

I smiled. *Bruiser would be so proud.*

The burglar shot forward at an angle, shoved off the wall with his boots, and back-flipped to the fireplace. Right in front of the sword.

I snapped my focus to Wirenut.

One single wall of interwoven lasers separated him from the other guy and the sword. The burglar straightened; he pulled his shoulders back in a lazy stretch, obviously showing off the fact he'd made it to the fireplace first.

Wirenut thrust his arm through an opening, gripped the burglar's throat, and yanked him forward. The burglar went very still, barely breathing.

With dozens of skin-sizzling lasers between them, Wirenut held the burglar inches from his face. "Who are you? What do you want?"

The burglar didn't respond.

"Why are you imitating me?"

No response.

"Do you work for Zorba?"

No response.

Wirenut pulled him a threatening fraction closer, and my stomach contracted.

"No," TL commanded. "Do not harm him."

Wirenut reached through with his other hand and ripped away the burglar's hood.

I gasped. *Katarina?*

All the zigzagging lasers flicked off. Immediately, a green glow encompassed the two of them, trapping them together.

A door hidden in the wall slid open, and a tall, olive-skinned man dressed in a white suit stepped out.

He bowed, all proper. "Good evening. I am Octavias Zorba. So nice of everyone to come."

Oh, my God. Wirenut's uncle.

I shot a quick glance at Wirenut. He stood frozen, staring through the green glow at his uncle.

Octavias tapped his black cane to the floor, pleasantly stern. "Now, let's see who everyone is. Remove your hoods."

I looked at TL. He didn't acknowledge me, just kept his focus level on Mr. Zorba.

Seconds rolled by, and nobody moved.

Octavias sighed, dramatically put out. "All right then. If you insist." He pointed his cane at TL. "This button right here," he tapped the silver handle, "will activate the paralysis cathode."

Oh, crap. A paralysis cathode could be dialed to severity, either rendering someone unconscious or paralyzed for seconds or putting him in a coma for days.

Octavias pressed the button.

TL dropped to the ground.

I sucked in a breath. "T-TL."

I scrambled the few feet to him, fumbled with his wet suit and hood, searching for his neck and a pulse.

TL's eyes flew open, and I jumped back.

With obvious discomfort, he sat up. "Do what he says," he rasped.

He took his hood off, and we followed his lead.

"Stan?" Katarina whispered.

They stared into each other's eyes, not moving, confusion and betrayal evident in both their faces. My heart broke for the two of them.

Wirenut looked at her. "You . . ."

She didn't answer, just dropped her head in shame.

Octavias tapped his cane. "Do it." His tone wasn't so pleasant now.

Katarina shook her head.

"I said," he barely moved his lips, "do it."

She lifted a distressed gaze to Octavias. "I can't, Papa. I know him."

Papa?

What the . . . ?

That meant Wirenut and Katarina were cousins?

Octavias pointed his cane at me, and my heart nearly stopped. "Do it."

Do what? Somebody do something. I don't want that thing pointed at me.

With a worried, indecisive glance my way, Katarina tenderly cradled Wirenut's face in her hands.

"I'm so sorry," she murmured, a tear slipping down her cheek.

She went up on her tiptoes and softly pressed her lips to his.

The green glow dissipated, and Katarina stepped away.

240

Groaning through a grimace, Wirenut hunched forward, gripping his stomach. Seconds later he slumped to his knees. TL and I moved, and Octavias shook his cane, emphasizing he still had it pointed at us.

Helplessly, we watched Wirenut. Quivers began to spasm his body, little jerks, as though somebody were shocking him.

Or had poisoned him.

The kiss.

I glared at Katarina. "What did you do?"

She peeled a clear film from her lips. "Arsenic mouth tape."

My stomach dropped.

Katarina avoided my gaze. "It won't kill him."

"How could you?" I said, staring at her.

She raced across the room and disappeared through the door Octavias had come from.

Wirenut fell to his side. Foamy spit seeped out of his mouth as his spasming body morphed into an all-out seizure.

"Stop it!" I screamed at Octavias.

He sneered.

Lifting his cane, he pressed a button, and the tile opened beneath me.

I sailed into darkness.

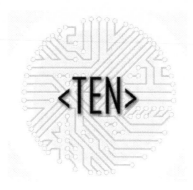

\<TEN\>

Slowly, carefully, I opened my eyes, cringing from the invasion of a little light into my skull.

My entire head throbbed, like someone had crawled inside it and banged my brain with a sledgehammer.

Shutting my eyes, I didn't move, allowing myself to regain consciousness naturally. Like TL had taught me to.

Hone in on your senses, he'd told me.

I focused on taste first, moving my tongue around my mouth. Dry. A little puffy. Other than an obvious need for water, nothing out of the ordinary.

I moved to my nose next, inhaling. My nostrils flared at the subtle scent of incense burning somewhere.

I switched to my ears. Silence. No, wait . . . breathing. Someone else was breathing.

My head lifted . . . then fell.

Lifted . . . then fell.

I'm lying on someone's stomach, I realized, as my head lifted again with the sound of the breath.

I opened my eyes again, relieved the sledgehammer in my brain had eased.

Above me stretched a wood ceiling. Shadows played across it in the dimly lit room, as though a candle flickered nearby. Maybe the incense was really scented wax.

My arms were beneath me. My legs stretched out and crossed at the ankles. I tried a tiny movement and failed.

Tied. Just as I expected.

I wiggled my numb, cool fingers and twisted my wrists. It felt like metal ties bound me, not rope or tape. A chain maybe? Or steel band?

"Stay still," a voice spoke.

TL. I breathed a sigh of contentment. Amazing how much a familiar, trusted voice can calm you.

"You took a hard hit to the head when you fell."

"Guess that explains the sledgehammer in my brain."

He chuckled, and my head bounced (*ow*) with his stomach's movement. At least I knew whose belly I was on now.

I moved my tongue around, trying to work up saliva. "Where are we?"

"Somewhere in the mansion."

"Are you tied up?"

"Yes. Different than you, though. I'm shackled to the floor. I haven't figured it out yet, but I'm certain we're booby-trapped."

I rolled my head and eyes just enough to the left to see his face. "Can I get up?"

"Try. Carefully."

Slowly rotating toward him, I smooshed my face into his side, using it for leverage to push myself to my knees.

Suddenly, the chains began to crank. TL groaned.

"Oh, my God. Did I do that?" The release of my weight must have triggered the booby trap.

They clanked to a stop.

"It's okay," he breathed.

Still dressed in his wet suit, TL lay spread-eagled on the cement. Chains coming from holes in the floor restrained each arm and leg separately, pulling them tight, like a medieval torturing device.

I looked up then, straight into Wirenut's eyes, and sucked in a breath.

Like TL, Wirenut was shackled spread-eagle. But to the wall instead of the floor. He stared wide-eyed, unblinking, into space. His relaxed mouth and unfocused gaze told me he lacked consciousness. His expanding and contracting chest proved he was breathing.

Thank God.

I looked down at TL. "What happened?"

"Right after you dropped through the floor, Zorba hit me with the paralysis cathode again. I woke up here, chained, Wirenut on the wall, you on my stomach."

"How long have we been here?"

Lifting his head, TL nodded across the room. "Clock on the wall."

It read five. We'd entered the mansion at one in the morning.

We'd been here four hours. And the two people I counted on the most were locked up with me. The only chance of rescue was . . . "Nalani?"

"GiGi," TL sighed. "There's nothing she can do. This mansion is locked down tight. You know that. You saw what we went through to get in. If it weren't for Wirenut, we *wouldn't* have gotten in. She's not coming. She's waiting for us on the boat where she dropped us."

I squeezed my eyes closed as the realization of our situation hit me hard. Wirenut chained. TL chained. Me bound.

No one's coming. *No one's coming.*

Fear rocked my body, and my muscles tensed.

We're going to die.

"GiGi," TL snapped, and my eyes shot open.

He pierced me with one of his lethal glares. "We do not have time for you to get scared. You have to focus. You're the only one mobile. Do you understand?"

I jerked my head into a nod.

"Now shift your legs, flex your muscles, see if your tool belt is still strapped to your thigh."

Blowing out a shaky breath, I did as TL said. "Yes."

"Good." TL nodded. "Now that you're awake, you've got a better view than me. Describe the room."

I glanced around, consciously forcing my fear aside. "About a forty-by-twenty rectangle. Brick walls. Cement floor. Wood-beam ceiling. Two-foot-tall candle lit in each corner, encased by an urn." I nodded to my right. "That wall is covered with photos and newspaper clippings."

TL rolled his head back to see. "Photos of what?"

I squinted. "Can't tell."

"Move closer. Cautiously. Stop as soon as you can make it out."

With my eyes glued to the wall, I scooted my knees over the cement. Right, then left. Right, then left. Inch by inch I shuffled away from TL and across the room.

I stopped and sucked in a breath. My eyes bounced from one picture to the next. "They're all of Wirenut. At different ages. Everything from a baby to a boy to now." *How weird.*

"Are they posed?"

"No. They're candid snapshots of everyday life. Walking into a home, playing on a swing, coming out of school. Pictures of houses, buildings, and other people, too."

"Looks like Zorba's been keeping up with his nephew."

"Yeah, this place is like a shrine."

"What are the newspaper clippings?"

I squinted, studied each one. "They're about the Ghost. I'd say there's three dozen. From all over the world." Wirenut had international fame. "Guess Zorba knows Wirenut and the Ghost are one and the same."

Wirenut moaned, and I jerked around. His eyelids dropped. Groggily, he tried to move.

"Stay still," TL instructed. "You're alive. GiGi and I are right here with you. You're chained up. Don't fight it. Focus on your surroundings. Block the . . ."

While TL continued calmly coaching Wirenut to consciousness, I knee-shuffled back across the room.

Wirenut opened his eyes and looked straight at me.

I smiled a little. I didn't think I'd ever been so relieved to see another person awake in my entire life.

He tried to smile back, but it came out as more of a lip twitch. He looked so exhausted I wanted to hug him.

He licked his lips. "Where are we?" he slurred.

TL relayed everything he had said to me.

I pointed with my head toward the picture wall. "Your uncle's been keeping up with you."

While Wirenut studied the wall, I described to him what I had seen.

When I was done, he sighed. "What does he want with me?"

"We'll find out soon enough." TL lifted his head. "Look around the room. Tell me what you think."

Wirenut took a minute, studying the walls, corners, ceiling, floor, chains. It seemed as though he didn't leave a single inch unscrutinized.

"Turn around, GiGi. Let me see what Zorba put on you."

I did.

Wirenut nodded. "These chains make it look old world. But it's not. At all. Motion sensors in each corner. When triggered the chains crank tighter. The room's divided into small zones.

Certain spots will activate my restraints. Other spots TL's. And yet others, both of ours."

"What's the trigger?" asked TL.

"The steel bands around GiGi's wrists."

What? "Me? I'm the trigger?"

Wirenut nodded.

TL tugged on his holds. "So my movement's okay?"

"Yes." Wirenut moved. "Mine, too."

I twisted my wrists. "Then all we have to do is get my bands off?"

"That's right."

I glanced around. "And a door? How do we get out of this place?"

Wirenut indicated the picture wall. "Hidden door's there. The release of all of our bonds will trigger it to open."

Before TL or I could respond, a portion of the picture wall soundlessly slid open. Octavias Zorba stepped through the opening. Before the doorway glided closed, I saw that a dark tunnel stretched behind him.

I scooted closer to TL. Not that he could protect me or anything. But being near him made me feel safe.

"I see that everyone's awake. Good." Zorba lifted his cane and pointed it at Wirenut.

"No!" I screamed. Hadn't he been through enough?

Zorba shot me a condescending, amused glance. "Dear, your concern touches me."

I clenched my jaw. I wanted to rip off his face.

He pressed a button on the cane, and a panel next to Wirenut's head slid open.

Whistling, twirling his cane, Zorba strolled across the room.

If we could get that cane, we'd be home free. It seemed to control everything in this mansion.

Unmoving, Wirenut watched as his uncle got closer and closer. I could only imagine what horrid scenes raced through Wirenut's brain, staring into the eyes of the man who slaughtered his entire family.

Zorba stopped only an inch away. Wirenut didn't look away and, in fact, lifted his chin a notch.

I was so proud of him for not being intimidated. Or at least not showing it if he felt it.

Zorba reached into the panel and pulled out the double-bladed, lion-engraved sword. Two shiny, silver blades extended from a black handle. A red lion had been etched into each long, sharp edge. A small space separated the twin blades. If a person was stabbed, they'd have two puncture wounds instead of one.

The fierce reality of the weapon stunned me.

Slowly, Zorba brought it down, trailing it across Wirenut's chest. Taunting him.

Wirenut swallowed, but made no other movement.

Zorba twirled away, wielding the sword and the cane, slashing them through the air.

I stared at Wirenut, hoping he'd look at me, willing him all the emotional support I could. He wouldn't take his eyes off his uncle, though.

Zorba tapped the picture wall with the sword. "As you can see, I've kept tabs on you. I knew you'd turn out to be great. I saw the possibilities in you even when you were a baby. That's why I saved you, you know? Because you were gifted. The rest of your family"—Zorba flicked his wrist—"useless. All of them. Especially your father, my *big* brother. I hated him. I always hated him. And your mother? We were engaged. Did you know that? She used to be mine, until my *big* brother met her."

His venomous words spoken in a nonchalant, whatever tone brought tears to my eyes. *He'd massacred Wirenut's family because they were useless?*

"And actually, I told your father I'd kill his family if he went to the police about all my business dealings. Guess he didn't believe me." Zorba sauntered over to one of the urns. "I'm a man of my word." He stroked the blade through the flame of the candle that sat in the corner. "I lost track of you after the New Mexico arrest. Where you first met my precious Katarina."

He slid the cane into a side holster on his hip. "I set all this up, you know? Katarina impersonating the Ghost. The neurotoxin. It was all to test you. To flush you out. Turns out I flushed out a few people with you. But don't worry, I'll take care of them when I'm ready."

He turned from the candle. "So look at me. I'm brilliant. Because here you are."

"What do you want with me?" Wirenut asked.

"Why, nephew, I'm surprised by your query. I want you to come work for me, of course."

"Never."

Zorba slid his finger over one of the sword's tips, bringing blood. "You're probably wondering why I didn't just keep you. Raise you myself." His cordial tone turned menacing. "Kind of hard to do with being arrested, getting a new identity. And you got lost in the system there for a while, too. Turns out it worked better to watch you from a distance. To see where your gifts lie. Unfortunately, I think I should've taken you sooner. Seems this organization you work for has brought out too much goodness in you. Time to get you back." Zorba stroked his bloody finger down one cheek and then the other.

Wirenut's chains rattled, jerking my attention away from Zorba. Wide-eyed, shaking, Wirenut stared at his uncle, seeming hypnotized by him.

The bone-deep fear sent a chill through my body.

Zorba trailed blood across his forehead. "Look familiar?"

Wirenut gasped for a breath. And then another.

This was probably what Zorba had done right before butchering Wirenut's family. Some sort of ritual.

Which meant Zorba planned on doing the same . . . to us.

TL rotated his wrist in a steady, repetitive pattern. *Clickclack. Clickclack. Clickclack.*

The soft clinking of his chains drew my frantic thoughts. I focused hard on his bound wrist and seconds later looked into his eyes. The assured calmness in their depths brought me peace and confidence. I knew what TL was doing. He'd told me once that making a repetitive noise would calm a nervous teammate.

"Good, GiGi. Now Wirenut," TL whispered. "Let's get him focused and under control."

In unison we *clickclacked*. TL with his chains and me tapping my nail to the steel band around my wrists. Little by little, Wirenut's body stopped shaking. He dragged his eyes from his uncle and focused on us.

Mentally, I transmitted all the confidence I felt.

We're going to be okay.

Seconds later his expression softened, and I knew he felt it, too.

Zorba turned and pointed the sword at me. "Tell me, dear, where do your talents lie?"

I glanced down at TL, and he nodded.

"Computers," I answered. "Code."

"Oh, yes. Can't have a team without a computer genius." Leisurely, he crossed the short distance between us, stopping at TL's head.

Zorba loved being in control, toying with a person's psyche. He reveled in it. It was written all over his face.

He put the sword tip down next to TL's ear. "I'll assume you're the man in charge. Tell me, man in charge, how did you go about getting such talented kids? I'll bet you have a whole group of them somewhere."

TL shrugged. "Not that I know of."

Zorba teetered the sword back and forth. "Don't suppose you'd be in the mood to do a little swap. Your life for the location of your special kids?"

TL didn't take his eyes off Zorba. "No deal."

"I'll pay."

"No thanks."

"All right then." Zorba flicked his wrist, and TL stiffened. Blood flew across the room.

"You bastard!" I screamed.

Zorba snickered at my outburst.

I glanced down at TL. I couldn't see exactly where he'd been cut, but it looked like his ear.

Zorba whistled his way over to Wirenut. "Let's see if my little nephew still has his scars. He tried to save his family, you know? He jumped on my back and tried to choke me." Zorba clucked his tongue. "Silly five-year-old boy."

Zorba trailed the sword from Wirenut's shoulder across his chest down to his hip. Then did the other side, tracing a giant X on Wirenut's body.

Wirenut kept his attention fastened on TL. Good thing, because he wouldn't see calmness in my eyes. He'd see downright pissed-offness.

"Leave him alone," I warned, anger boiling in my veins.

Zorba cut me another one of those condescending, amused glances. "Or what?"

I tightened my jaw.

He peeled Wirenut's wet suit away, revealing his entire upper body. Wirenut flinched. A long, jagged scar bisected his shoulder.

The gruesomeness of it morphed my boiling anger into full-on rage.

Way back in the crevices of my subconscious, I felt TL's eyes on me. But my fury made me ignore him.

Zorba tapped Wirenut's scar with the sword. "Scars make great conversation pieces. I think it healed quite nicely."

Wirenut's breath quickened. His stomach contracted. And I went over the edge.

With my bound ankles and wrists, I propelled my body weight headfirst over TL, dropped to a roll, and swung my feet out.

Zorba tripped to the ground.

Chains clanked. I'd triggered my teammates' torturous restraints.

One of them groaned.

I blocked my need to help them and focused on Zorba instead.

I tumbled toward him just as he pushed up, brought my feet back, and rammed them into his crotch.

He dropped to his knees with a grunt.

I swung around to my back and crammed my heels into his throat.

He gagged.

I swerved to my knees, grabbed the cane with my mouth, and ripped it from his side holster.

Immediately, I tasted blood.

Chains cranked. TL and Wirenut groaned.

With the cane clenched between my teeth, I slid away. I put it on the ground pointing toward Zorba, and, with my nose, I mashed the button I'd seen him press.

The paralysis cathode.

Zorba thunked to the floor.

"The red button!" Wirenut shouted over his pain.

I ground my nose into the red button. The chains halted. My heart stopped.

I looked at TL, stretched to the limit, gritting his teeth against the pain. Blood from his injury pooled under his head.

"What do I do?"

"Get your tool belt," Wirenut hissed.

Get my tool belt? It was still strapped to my thigh.

I hobbled up beside Zorba and lay down next to the sword. I slid my thigh along one of the blades to cut it from my leg. Instead, the blade nicked my skin, and I cringed. My wet suit split open.

"Hurry!" Wirenut yelled. "He's waking up."

I glanced up, right into Zorba's eyes.

<ELEVEN>

Zorba's black eyes narrowed to two tiny slits.

Not giving him a chance to think, move, or even breathe, I used my knees to ram the sword in his direction.

He roared in pain as blood squirted my face.

"The cane!" Wirenut yelled.

I rolled away from Zorba over to the cane, squirmed my body toward the handle, and crammed my nose into the button controlling the paralysis cathode.

Zorba passed out.

I looked at him to see where I'd stabbed him. Both blades stuck clean through his knee, visible on both sides. Any other time I would've gotten queasy at the sight.

Retribution settled my stomach though.

"Come to me." TL sounded as though he'd adjusted to the pain of being stretched.

"You have three minutes," Wirenut informed us, "before he wakes back up."

I pushed to my knees. "How do you know?"

"I watched the clock when you knocked him out the first time. The cathode's only good for two shots. Then the fuse has to be switched out. So when he wakes up, he wakes up."

Glancing at the wall-mounted clock, I made a mental note of the time and shuffled toward TL.

He wiggled his fingers. "Put your tool belt next to my right hand."

Lying down next to his hand, I scooted my thigh as close as I could.

"What do I need?" TL asked Wirenut.

"Get the number three giclo wrench," he answered. "Should be right in front."

TL's fingers slipped past one tool to the next, and he tugged it from its slot. "Got it."

There was no way I could identify a tool by touch. Hammer, sure. But a number three whatever wrench? No way.

He positioned the wrench between his thumb and forefinger. "Put your wrists next to my hand."

I checked the clock as I sat up. "One minute, fifty-eight seconds." I positioned my steel bands next to his fingers.

TL inserted the tool. "Wirenut?"

"Right ninety degrees. Left forty-five."

Two tiny *tings* and my hands were free. I grabbed the wrench from TL. "Same for my feet?"

Wirenut nodded. "Yes."

I took a couple of steady breaths and then slipped the tool into my feet bonds.

Right ninety degrees. Left forty-five. Two tiny *tings*, and I was free.

I jumped to my feet and glanced at the clock. One minute, one second.

"Wirenut first," TL instructed.

"Different locks. You need a four-point-one tes wrench."

"Four-point-one tes wrench? What the hell's a four-point-one tes wrench?" I reached down and yanked the belt off my thigh. I ran to Wirenut. "Show me."

Quickly, he scanned the tools. "Third from the left."

Pulling it out, I dropped the belt. "What do I do?"

"My right foot first. Insert the wrench into the foot bond one centimeter, click it left thirty degrees."

"One centimeter? Thirty degrees? Are you serious?" *I can't do this.*

"GiGi," TL barked. "Focus."

Oddly enough, his harsh tone didn't intimidate me. It zapped me full of confidence.

Ignoring the ticking time, I squatted at Wirenut's right foot. I inserted the wrench and clicked it left. *Ting.*

"Now my left foot. This time click it right, though."

I did.

Ting.

"Right wrist, clicking left again."

Ting.

I moved to his left hand. "Click it right. I got the pattern."

Ting.

As his iron bonds fell free, Wirenut dropped from the wall, and Zorba shot straight up.

Wirenut shoved me out of the way. "Get TL. Same pattern. I got Zorba."

I scrambled across the cement to TL. In my peripheral vision, Zorba jerked the sword from his knee right as Wirenut leapt.

My heart banging, I zeroed in on TL's restraints.

Right foot. Insert one centimeter. Click left thirty degrees. *Ting.*

Out of the corner of my eye, Wirenut kicked Zorba's hand. The sword sailed across the room and landed, handle down, in one of the candle urns.

I focused on TL's left foot. Clicked right. *Ting.*

Zorba punched Wirenut, snapping his head to the left.

I scooted over TL's body to his right hand, inserted the wrench, clicked left. *Ting.*

Wirenut whipped around and delivered a flying roundhouse to Zorba's stomach.

Left hand. Clicked right. *Ting.*

Zorba stumbled back a few feet and then came roaring forward, striking Wirenut's sternum and jaw at the same time.

TL's bonds fell away.

Grabbing his chest, Wirenut sucked in a breath, and Zorba sneered.

TL sprung to his feet, and Wirenut held up his hand. "Don't. He's mine."

Wirenut dropped to his knees, spun, and swept Zorba off his feet. The older man landed hard on the floor, his head thudding against the cement. Wirenut scrambled on top of him and rammed his elbow into Zorba's throat.

Gagging, Zorba reached up, seized Wirenut's hair, and yanked.

Gritting his jaw, Wirenut grabbed Zorba's head and slammed it into the cement again.

Sounds of bones crunching echoed through the chamber.

With my heart stampeding in my chest, I glanced over at TL. *Aren't we going to do something?*

He shook his head.

Zorba twisted his body and threw Wirenut off. He rolled across the floor.

Zorba staggered to his feet at the same time Wirenut jumped to his.

He rushed Zorba, pushing him across the room, right toward the sword and the urn. Wirenut shoved, and Zorba flew backward, straight onto the double-bladed, lion-engraved sword.

Both blades sliced clean through his back and straight out his stomach.

His body twitched and then slumped lifeless over the urn.

I turned away from the gory scene and covered my face with my hands.

Zorba's tool for sick, twisted pleasure had brought him to his end.

***

Twenty minutes later, Nalani cut through calm water, motoring us away from the private island back toward mainland Rissala.

Dark red lit the horizon where the sun would rise in the next thirty minutes or so. A thin layer of fog hovered on the water's surface. Under other circumstances, this would've been a beautiful, peaceful morning.

TL stood on the other side of the boat, talking on his cell phone. Wirenut sat beside me, arms folded, staring at the boat's floorboards.

He hadn't said one single word since exiting the mansion. I knew if I asked him if he was okay, he'd just nod his head. So I kept quiet and left him to his thoughts. He'd talk when he felt ready.

TL clicked off his cell phone. "Clean-up crew's on their way."

I furrowed my brow. "Clean-up crew?"

"They'll take care of the mansion, evidence, Zorba's body." TL connected the satellite and punched in the scrambler code.

Balancing the laptop in his lap, he took a seat between Wirenut and me. Chapling, David, and Beaker appeared on the screen. All three sets of eyes widened in matching shock.

In that second, I realized what we must look like. Wirenut shirtless, tiny nicks on his chest, bruised eye, scar on display. TL with a makeshift ear bandage, soaked through with blood.

And me with dried blood on my face and mouth, sporting a (I moved my tongue around) yep, missing tooth. I touched my forehead, grimacing at the knot.

"Um." Chapling cleared his throat. "Need I ask what happened?"

David frowned as he studied me, but didn't say anything.

I sent him a small smile to let him know I was okay. His frown softened to a slight curve of the lips.

TL punched a few keys. "I'm sending you a digital image of the sword. We have it here on board if you need a live shot."

"Okay, give me a sec." Chomping her gum, Beaker did some key strokes on her end. She zoomed in on the image TL had sent. "Code is in the handle. Million to one says it's engraved. That's thirty-three-hundred-strength sterling. Mix one part citeca acid to two parts riumba enzyme. Heat to one fifty Celsius. Coat handle with mixture using a rubber rod. It'll take three seconds, and you'll see the final message."

TL nodded. "Fantastic work, Beaker. Anything else?"

They all shook their heads.

"Signing off." TL closed the laptop and dialed his cell phone. He began a conversation in Rissalan.

I heard citeca acid and riumba enzyme. He was probably arranging to have those chemicals waiting when we got to our destination.

Nalani stuck her head out of the pilothouse. "Six minutes to dock." She tossed a duffel bag at us. "Clean up. You guys definitely need it."

I unzipped the duffel. Three sets of clean clothes lined the top; first-aid supplies scattered the bottom. I handed the guys their stuff and then stepped inside the pilothouse to change.

Nalani glanced at my thigh as I peeled my wet suit down. "You'll need a couple stitches and some antibiotics. Tape it together for now. Bandage it up good. Let me see your mouth."

I opened wide.

She whistled. "Tore the root out and everything. It's a molar. Don't worry about it. We'll get you a replacement."

I wiped my face with a wet nap. "What about TL?" That slice had been bloody.

Nalani idled down. "You'd be surprised what plastic surgeons can do. Everyone'll be good as new in no time. Hurry and put on your clothes. We're almost there."

Over my bathing suit I slipped on an island dress. Similar to the flowy, gauzy ones the locals wore.

Nalani pulled the boat alongside a rocky slope.

Wirenut and I followed TL over the rocks, up to a dirt road where a car waited. Behind us Nalani motored off in the opposite direction. She'd done the same thing in Ushbania. Just disappeared.

255

This time I knew I'd see her again.

We climbed into the car, TL cranked the engine, and we were off. He cut across a field and into the woods. Twenty minutes later we parked behind a stone shack hidden in thick overgrowth.

"Safe house. Katarina's here. She turned herself in. We had a local agent bring her here." TL opened his door. "Let's go."

We helped TL cover the car with bushy tree branches and then followed him inside.

Katarina sat in the corner of the shadowed shack, handcuffed to a pipe coming from the floor. Still dressed in her black burglar suit, she glanced up and quickly looked away.

What an awful girl.

A short man handed TL a canvas bag, said something in Rissalan, and exited through a hidden panel in the floor.

TL unwrapped the sword and laid it on the only table in the shack. He emptied the canvas bag, too. Chemicals, burners, stir sticks, and tubes fell out. All the things Beaker had said we'd need.

I sat on the floor and cranked up the laptop, ready to decipher the last encrypted message.

Wirenut and TL worked in silence. Mixing chemicals, heating them. Wirenut stuck a thermometer in the liquid, and they waited, watching the temperature.

"One fifty." He nodded.

TL spread the smoking mixture on the sword's handle. Three seconds ticked by. I placed my fingers on the laptop's keys.

He held a magnifying glass to the handle. "Five one two. Three spaces. One zero one two. Two spaces. One five one two. One space. Two zero . . ."

TL continued reading off the number patterns, and I typed. One hundred sequences in all. A lot of data crammed onto the handle of a sword.

I went to work. My fingers raced over the keypad. I wove in and out of security barriers, tunneled through safeguards, zoomed around blocked systems. I designated principles, specified components, wrapped codexes. I stranded screeds, followed copeperis, formatted algorithms.

"Got it." *Clickclickclick.* "The neurotoxin is on the other side of the world. It's located on a sailboat in the Pacific five miles from Myralap Island."

"Great job, GiGi." TL dialed his phone and gave the information to the government's retrieval team he'd hired.

I put down my laptop and stood, stretching my fatigued muscles. Another successful mission gone by.

Clicking his phone off, TL turned to Katarina. "Who are you?"

She didn't look up. "Katarina Leosi."

"Why did you turn yourself in? Why did you disengage the mansion's explosives?"

Katarina's shoulders slumped. Her patheticness didn't faze me.

"I thought my father was collecting rare art pieces. I didn't know about Stan or the stolen neurotoxin or Papa's deceit."

TL put his phone on the table. "Who, exactly, did you think your father was?"

"A businessman. An art collector. A descendant of a long line of famous burglars. He was training me to follow in his footsteps."

"And you're okay with being trained into a life of crime?"

She closed her eyes. "It was his dying wish. I lost my real parents when I was a baby. He took me in. He's the only father I've ever known."

"He wasn't dying. He lied to you."

Long pause. "I know that now," she murmured.

I glanced across the shack at Wirenut. He stood with his back to us, staring out the dirty window. He and Katarina weren't cousins after all. Interesting.

So Zorba killed Wirenut's family, moved to Rissala, and took in a baby girl? It didn't make sense.

I stepped forward. "Can I ask a question?"

TL nodded.

"Why did Zorba raise you?"

Katarina finally looked up. Sorrow and bewilderment weighed heavy in her eyes. It softened my heart a little.

"He told me my real father worked for him. He said he was responsible for my parents' deaths." She lifted a shoulder. "That's all I know."

TL stepped up next to me. "Who did you think Stan was?"

"Who he said he was, a guy here on vacation."

"And the Ghost?"

"Another burglar after the same pieces we were. I copycatted him, trying to keep the trail off me. I had no idea Stan and the Ghost were one and the same."

TL crossed his arms over his chest. "And you considered poisoning him fair play?"

"No! Of course not." She looked over at Wirenut. "I'm so sorry. I never meant to hurt you."

He turned from the window. An unreadable expression blanked his face. "Then why poison me?"

Katarina quietly sighed. "Papa told me the Ghost was selling the artifacts and funding terrorism."

"What about the last time I saw you? You said your father saw us in the marketplace? Zorba was there?"

"He was. I had no idea. He saw us talking and got really mad. I've never seen him so angry. It scared me. But . . . what was I supposed to tell you? That I was a burglar?" Her voice cracked. "That I really like you?" She ducked her head, sniffed.

Wirenut didn't say anything in response, just stood staring at her.

"And the messages?" I asked. "Didn't you wonder about the paper hidden in the egg and the jewel?"

"When I found the paper in the egg, I asked Papa about it. He said the paper meant nothing to the Ghost without the artifact. And then before I went in to get the crown, Papa told me there was a replica of the ruby from the crown I needed to leave behind. I didn't ask any questions; I figured he knew what he was talking about."

Seemed to me Katarina was a manipulated pawn like the rest of us. Only more so. She'd been lied to her whole life.

That is, if she's actually telling the truth now.

The shack's door opened. An old, gray-haired woman appeared. Something about her seemed familiar. I studied her as she closed the door and crossed the short distance to where we stood.

TL acknowledged her with a nod.

"You're the jewelry lady from the market," I realized aloud. *How funny.* I'd had no idea.

She winked at me and then leveled Katarina with a hard glare. "I'm Special Agent Pierson. You're in my care now. *Don't* underestimate me based on my age."

I was glad that lethal glare wasn't aimed in my direction.

"Let's go." TL grabbed his cell phone and headed from the stone shack.

Wirenut and I followed. He didn't take a last look at Katarina, but I did. She still sat with her head dropped, shoulders slumped.

I felt sorry for her. How lost she must feel.

After I helped the guys uncover the car, we climbed in and drove off.

I rolled down my window. Cool morning air flowed in. "What's going to happen to Katarina?"

TL shifted gears. "If her story checks out, she'll go free."

"Free where? She doesn't have any family."

TL turned onto the coastal highway. "She'll become part of the system."

Part of the system? That sucked. Not a lifestyle I'd wish on anybody. "And if her story doesn't check out?"

"She'll be tried as an adult. Depending on what she's involved in of Zorba's, she could face the death penalty."

I blinked. *The death penalty? Whoa.*

In the backseat, Wirenut lay down. He put his arm over his eyes and turned his head away. The sunlight brought out his facial bruises, where Zorba had punched him.

I wanted so badly for Wirenut to be okay. I wanted to see him smile, hear his smart-aleck remarks, watch him do his victory shoulder-roll dance.

"We got in a car accident," TL informed us, "in case anyone asks."

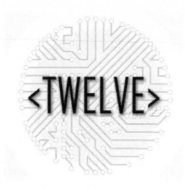

‹TWELVE›

The next morning, we caught a flight back to America and unfortunately got grounded in Chicago because of bad weather. We got a hotel for the night and grabbed a plane to California early the next day. As we were pulling up to the ranch's iron gate, I breathed a sigh of relief.

Home.

TL slipped a remote from his jacket pocket and punched in his personal code. The gate slowly swept open, and we pulled through.

It swung closed behind us as we made our way up the long driveway.

Off to the left Bruiser bounced along on a riding mower, doing her afternoon chores. The machine dwarfed her tiny body, making her look like a little girl. She caught sight of us and enthusiastically waved. I waved back.

Hard to believe we'd been gone only about a week. Seemed like a month at least.

Beyond her in the corral, Parrot washed one of the thoroughbreds. Funny that a guy with horrible hay allergies loved horses so much.

Beside the corral the barn sat wide open. Jonathan was inside, punching a hanging bag. I checked my watch. 4:00 P.M. It'd be time for PT in another thirty minutes. Wonder what kind of muscle-screaming torture he had in mind for everyone today?

I squinted but didn't see David. He usually warmed up with Jonathan before PT.

TL circled around the driveway and parked in front of the sprawling, one-story ranch house.

Mystic came around the side, garden tools in hand. He'd been tending his herb garden.

I smiled, realizing I'd missed everyone.

Beaker stepped out the front door, chomping gum, sporting a black-and-white-striped Mohawk.

Okay, I'd missed *almost* everyone.

TL opened the driver's door and got out.

Wirenut leaned up from the backseat. He put his hand on my shoulder. "Don't tell anybody about what happened. About me, Zorba, Katarina. Anything. I don't want anybody to know."

I nodded. "You don't have to worry about that with me."

I didn't bother reminding him that we weren't *allowed* to speak of the details.

We climbed from the car as TL popped the trunk. "You two are excused from PT. Get some rest." He handed us each our oversized backpacks.

Wirenut shouldered his. "I'll be in my room." He brushed past Beaker with barely a hello.

She frowned. "What's up with him?"

Where's my knuckle rub? I knew she was thinking. Wirenut always knuckle-rubbed Beaker's head. And she loved it, even though she pretended not to.

"He's tired. That's all." I zipped up my windbreaker.

"I'd still say hi to him," Beaker grumbled, shuffling off, "even if *I* were tired."

Carting my pack through the door, I surreptitiously glanced around. I didn't want David to catch me looking for him. I wanted to "accidentally" run into him.

I peeked into the dining hall, a miniature version of a school cafeteria. Its aluminum table and chairs sat empty. Two hours from now the place would come alive with people eating, talking, laughing.

I slipped across the hall into the common area. Empty, too. No one watching TV, shooting pool, or playing cards. Later this evening Parrot and Bruiser would definitely be here, continuing their ongoing air-hockey match.

I passed by the mountainous mural that hid our elevator to the below-ground levels. Maybe David was down there with Chapling.

Okay, game plan: drop my things in the girls' room and then go to the computer lab where I'd "accidentally" run into David.

Rolling my eyes, I strode down the hall to the girls' room. David's room sat two doors down on the left. From my vantage point the door stood open. What could be my reason for *having* to go down there?

I lingered, studying his open door, coming up blank. There really was no reason for me to go down there. What would be my excuse?

Except to say hi, of course.

But I wanted *him* to find *me*. Not the other way around.

Stupid. *I know.*

And childish.

But . . . here went nothing.

I coughed.

He didn't come out.

I sneezed.

Nothing.

I cleared my throat.

Nada.

"GiGi?"

I jerked around. *David.* My stomach leap-frogged to my throat. If it weren't for my lips being closed, it probably would have boinged right out of my mouth.

I swallowed. "Hi."

Okay, that came across good. Calm. Casual. Not too excited. Not too nervous. It sounded I-missed-you-but-not-desperately. The tone was definitely I'm-my-own-woman.

Mentally, I gave myself one firm, agreeable nod.

His lips were moving. *Crap.* He was talking, and I missed it. David's lips stopped moving.

He waited.

He wanted me to respond. *Double crap.*

I cleared my throat. "Sorry, what'd you say?"

David quirked a smile. "I said, what are you doing?"

"Urn . . ." I shrugged. "Getting home just." I shook my head. "I mean, just getting home."

Inwardly, I sighed. *Guess I'm not my own woman.*

His dark eyes dropped to my lips. "Heard you're missing a tooth."

I gave a jerky nod.

262

He took a step toward me, staring at my lips, and my heart revved to light speed. *Please let my lips look good right now.*

"Can I see?"

I blinked. "What . . . no!" *Gross.*

He laughed. "Are you relaxed now?"

I laughed, too. I couldn't help it. He knew me too well.

Taking my pack, he gave me a quick hug and a kiss on my head. "Missed you."

His cologne swirled into my senses, and I wanted to hold on longer. "I missed you, too."

David had no *idea* how much I'd missed him. It'd probably scare him if he knew. Like, my-girlfriend's-freakishly-obsessed-with-me kind of scare.

Then again I wasn't his girlfriend. Not officially.

Yet.

He led the way into the girls' room. "Did you get my little surprise?"

The hidden lollipop. Thinking of you. "Yes." I smiled. "Thank you so much. That was very sweet."

David put my stuff on the floor. "So did you?"

"Did I what?"

He sat down on my bed. "Think of me?"

Only every second of every moment of every day. "Yes."

"A lot?"

I laughed. "Yes. *Sheesh*, what do you want from me? Yes, I thought of you. A lot. Happy?"

"I'm getting there."

I'm getting there. What did that mean?

I put my hands on my hips. "Did you think of me?" *I can't believe I asked him that question.*

It felt good. Bold. Sexy of me.

"Yeah." He held out his hand. "Come 'ere."

My stomach cycloned as I crossed the room and took his hand.

He tugged me down beside him, reached under my bed, and brought out—

A lollipop bouquet! Full of dozens of suckers. Raspberry, cherry, watermelon, lemon, mango, passion fruit, apple, banana, and I don't know how many more.

"For you." He put it in my lap.

"I can't believe you did this." I threw my arms around his neck. "Thank you."

He squeezed me tight. "You're very welcome."

Someone rapped on the open door, and we pulled apart.

Bruiser grinned. "I see you got your surprise."

David shot her a playful glare. "Your roommate's a real pest. She's been in my face all week long, like an annoying gnat."

Bruiser batted her lashes. "I'm really glad you're back. Coming to PT?"

"Definitely." I put my lollipops on my nightstand. "Let me change."

David stood. "You don't have to."

"I know. Never thought I'd actually say this, but I *want* to."

Bruiser and David gave me matching are-you-kidding-me looks.

I laughed. "Really. I *do.*"

Suddenly, David's cell buzzed. At the same time, so did mine. We checked the displays.

TL's stat code.

‹THIRTEEN›

David and I rushed off the elevator and to the conference room. We opened the door just as TL came out.

"Have a seat. Chapling and I will be right in."

David and I sat on the right side of the table. Neither of us mumbled a sound as we waited.

What's going on? Another mission? Already?

It couldn't be. We hadn't even been home a couple of hours yet.

Wirenut appeared in the door. "Got the stat code. What's up?"

We shrugged.

Wirenut took a seat across from us.

A couple of weeks ago David, Wirenut, and I had been in this conference room finding out about the neurotoxin for the very first time. Wirenut had been fidgety, restless, nervous. Looking at him now you'd never guess he had been any other way but calm and collected.

TL entered the conference room with Chapling hobbling behind him.

He climbed up into the chair beside me and leaned in. "Welcome home," he whispered.

Thanks, I mouthed back. Gosh, I'd missed his little, frizzy-headed self.

TL pressed a button on the remote-control panel housed within the table. The back wall slid open, revealing a wide flat screen.

Katarina appeared.

I glanced at Wirenut. His brow twitched. Other than that he showed no emotion.

"Specialists," TL began, "Katarina Leosi has been found innocent of all charges related to Antonio Badaduchi, aka Octavias Zorba."

I sent her a small smile to let her know I was glad for her. Way down deep inside I knew she was a good person. And I'd been right.

"Katarina," TL continued, "has found three documents in her bedroom that have prompted her to contact us." TL nodded to the screen. "Go ahead."

She cleared her throat. "Approximately forty-five minutes ago while packing my belongings, I found documents hidden in a secret compartment of my dresser. I wasn't aware my fath—Octavias knew I had a secret compartment. Perhaps he hid these papers there because he knew his office contents would be confiscated if anything went wrong."

Katarina's image slid to the screen's upper-left corner. Three images of handwritten paper appeared in the center of the screen. "This is Octavias's writing. I'm sure he handwrote them to avoid a computer trail. They're in code. From my limited knowledge of cryptography, I pieced together they're about Stan, or Frankie as I now know is his real name. That's when I contacted you."

"Thank you, Katarina," TL said.

With a slight nod, she disappeared from the screen.

Chapling raised a finger. "That's where I come in. I've deciphered only page one. What I found, though, stopped me in my tracks."

TL propped his fingers on the table. "Zorba admitted he devised the neurotoxin plan in order to flush out Wirenut. What has had us perplexed and Chapling working extra hard is how Zorba initially located Wirenut. How Zorba knew Wirenut was here in San Belden, California."

Chapling pushed away from the table. He waddled over to the screen. From his pocket he slipped a metal retractor and expanded it.

He touched document one, enlarging it to full screen. Then he tapped it again, zooming in on one single line. "This is line five."

Again with the number five. Quickly, I read the code, isolating the prime numbers, matching them to letters of the alphabet. I yanked my notepad and pencil from my sweatshirt pocket, scribbled the letters. And sucked in a breath.

Everyone looked at me.

Chapling retracted his pointer. "GiGi, tell your team what you just figured out."

No. *It couldn't be.* I glanced at TL for confirmation, and he nodded his go ahead.

"Th-there's an insider." *Oh. My. God.*

Wirenut straightened in his chair. "An insider? What are you talking about?"

TL leaned forward. "Someone on this ranch leaked information that the Ghost is here in San Belden. When Zorba heard, he composed his twisted charade."

Wirenut shot to his feet. "Who?"

"We don't know." TL's face hardened. "Yet."

"But why? Why would someone do that to me?"

"I seriously doubt this was personal. Whoever released your whereabouts did it for money." TL's phone beeped. He checked the LCD. "I think you forget how famous the Ghost was. *Is* still. People, the media, would pay big money to know who you are. My only hope is that your true identity hasn't been leaked as well."

Minutes later, Chapling and I stood in front of the wide screen studying pages two and three of the handwritten documents. Strange letters and numbers I'd never seen before. Not English, nor Rissalan.

"What other language would Zorba write in?"

Chapling sniffed. "He was an international terrorist. There's no telling how many languages he knew."

"Why would he compose document one in English and the other two in a different language?" I scrunched my brow. "Doesn't make sense. Unless they're in different languages because they're about different things. Could Parrot help translate these?"

"Why, when we have our computer," Chapling said, smiling. In the screen's upper-right corner, the computer continued scrolling through international records, searching for an identifiable language.

"My guess is that Zorba *wanted* us to easily decipher page one. He wanted us to know he had an insider." Chapling took out a tissue and blew his nose. "Zorba liked games. He planned on pages two and three being a puzzle. My gut says that whatever's encrypted there is very important. Life or death."

"Got it." I spun around. "Wiren—"

The conference room sat empty. I'd forgotten everybody had left Chapling and me to our work.

I took my phone and punched a series of buttons. "I'm texting Wirenut to get down here."

We continued scrutinizing the documents while we waited on Wirenut.

I looked down at Chapling. "You got a cold?"

267

He rubbed his nose. "Little one."

"Taking medication?"

"Over the counter."

"Laying off the caffeine? Getting rest?" Chapling was twice my age. *Look who's taking care of whom?*

"What's going on?" Wirenut stepped into the room.

I waved him over. "Come look at these."

He approached and Chapling quickly explained the situation while Wirenut examined the documents.

"The language is vaguely familiar." Wirenut moved a step closer and perused the screen. "I'll be right back." He raced from the room.

In the upper-right-hand corner, the computer continued scrolling. Whatever Zorba had used was buried deep. Could be some old-world dialect of an ancient culture. "Wonder how many different languages and dialects there are in the world?"

Chapling sneezed. "Including biblical times? Thousands. Easily."

Wow.

Wirenut zipped back into the room and over to the screen. He held up a small silver bracelet next to the documents. "I wore this home from the hospital when I was a baby. It's from my mom."

I squinted. Tiny letters engraved the back of the nameplate. "What's it say?"

"It's a prayer. '*Lex fic nisabs dosoqua.*' May God protect your future."

Chapling pulled a tissue wad from his pocket. "Looks a lot older than you."

"It is. It's been passed down from generation to generation. Every time a boy is born it passes on."

I shifted closer to get a better look. "You're the youngest of five boys. All of them wore this, too?"

Wirenut nodded.

A chill shivered my body. *May God protect your future.* Ironic that Wirenut was the last to receive it and the only survivor of his uncle's wrath.

Wirenut rotated it, catching the light. "Someday my son will wear it, too."

His sentiment brought a smile to my face. "What's the language?"

"Kusem. I don't think it's spoken anymore."

I extended my hand. "May I?"

With a nod, Wirenut gave it to me.

Holding the lightweight bracelet to the screen, I compared the letters and symbols. "It's a match."

"Oh good. Goodgoodgoodgoodgood." From his shirt pocket, Chapling slipped a silver mike resembling a mechanical pencil. "Daisy," he spoke into the eraser end. "Halt."

The computer stopped scrolling.

Daisy? I mouthed.

"Dukes of Hazzard. It's the only show I watched as a kid." He shrugged sheepishly. "Always had a thing for the female Duke cousin."

Wirenut and I exchanged amused glances. I had no idea Chapling had named our ranch computer.

"Do the other guys call it Daisy, too?"

Chapling waggled his brows. "What guy doesn't have a thing for Daisy Duke?"

"Well, I don't want to be the odd one out." I took the microphone. "Hello, Daisy. Sorry I didn't know your name before."

THAT'S OKAY, the computer typed. HOW CAN I HELP YOU?

"Search language Kusem. K-u-s-e-m." I glanced at Wirenut for spelling confirmation, and he nodded.

Daisy scrolled. KUSEM LOCATED.

"Good work. Translate documents two and three. Print to computer lab."

Daisy's screen strobed. PRINTING NOW.

Chapling rapid-fire clapped. "Oh, she's fast. Fastfastfast."

I handed him the mike. "Imagine the world before computers."

He shrieked, "Perish the thought."

I laughed. "Let me change and I'll meet you in the lab." I needed to get out of the clothes I'd worn home from Chicago.

We crossed the conference room to the door. At the elevator, Chapling went back to the lab and I punched in my personal code, placed my hand on the fingerprint-identification panel, and rode it up four floors with Wirenut. We stepped off and halted in our tracks.

In total silence, every member of Specialist Teams One and Two lined the hallway. No one had changed from their PT clothes.

David stood at the very end near his room. He caught sight of Wirenut and me and came down the hall toward us.

"What's going on?" I whispered.

"Lock down. TL's searching our belongings."

What? "You mean . . . like everything?" *Underwear, bras, tampons?*

"Yep, everything."

I closed my eyes on a silent groan. I had *so* many dirty clothes. "Even your stuff?"

David lifted his brows. "Can't trust anyone when there's been a breach in security."

Yeah. But David? He's TL's right-hand guy. "You're okay with that? Not being trusted?"

"GiGi, it's part of this life. Even Jonathan and Chapling get searched, and they have the same clearance level as TL."

"What about TL? Him, too?"

"Yes. Someone higher up will search him. This is serious business. And it won't stop here. The barn, the house, the property, the rooms below us. The entire place will be thoroughly investigated."

Wow.

TL stepped from one of the guy's room. He looked down the hall right at me. "What are you both doing up here?"

All eyes turned to me.

I swallowed. "I change clothes wanted to." I shook my head. "I mean, I wanted to change clothes." Seemed like a good idea at the time.

"You and Chapling are supposed to be working on the documents. You were given a job." TL crossed the hall and unlocked the door to the room I shared with Bruiser and Beaker. "Get to it, and Wirenut get in line."

"Yes, sir," we both mumbled, completely humiliated.

As Wirenut shuffled over to get in line, David turned his back to everyone, blocking me from their view. He linked pinkies with me and gave my little finger a quick squeeze. Somehow that gesture made me want to smile and cry at the same time.

"Don't take it personally," he whispered. "TL's extremely irritated right now."

I nodded. But all I really wanted to do was bury my head in code for like a million years. Or maybe bury my head in David's chest for the same amount of time.

Minutes later, I shuffled into the lab Chapling and I used. He sat hunched over his workstation, his fingers racing across the keyboard. I imagined that's what I looked like when I existed in my zone.

Except for the whole he's-a-red-headed-little-person-and-I'm-not thing.

I rolled my chair out. "Hey."

He jerked straight up. "Ow!" And grabbed his neck. "Whiplash."

Jeez, you'd think I'd screamed the greeting.

"Genius at work here. Heeelllooo? Give a warning next time." He scratched his head, making his Brillo-pad hair poof out.

"You need a haircut."

He waved me off. "Yeahyeahyeah." He tapped his screen. "I'm working on the documents. You get cranking with phone records, postal, e-mail. Any communication between San Belden, California, and Rissala. We got an insider to nail."

I slipped on my glasses and dove into cyberspace.

I visited the San Belden Phone Company first. Tried a couple of commonly used passwords to enter their system. Broke through on the fourth try.

Their IT guys needed a lesson in password protection.

Zipping through the past twelve months of phone calls, I isolated the ones to and from Rissala, tracing each one. Standard stuff. Family, friends, a few business calls.

I skimmed the numbers and matched them to the Rissalan police department, newspaper, radio, and TV. I hacked into police records . . . and silently laughed. Reporters from all over the world were bugging them for news on the break-ins and the Ghost.

Leaving the police records, I wove my way in and out of ISP servers. Lots and lots of e-mails to and from Rissala. Again, standard stuff. Family communication. Friends. And, of course, reporters looking for breaking news.

"Wait. What's this? A pellucid image?"

I clicked a couple keys. Someone sent an alias e-mail and then wiped the image from the server. *Idiot.* Didn't they know that nothing was ever truly wiped clean?

My heart revved as my fingers clicked away. *I'm onto something. I'm* definitely *onto something.* The e-mail was sent from a coffeehouse in town.

Sequestering the message, I ran it through a clarity program. At the same time I brought up the coffeehouse security cameras and scrolled the archives until I located the time matching the e-mail's time/date stamp.

The clarity program dinged. I scanned the message. Definitely about the Ghost. I selected the camera archive link. A picture popped up on my screen.

I sucked in a breath. *Oh no.*

"The documents." Chapling looked up from his screen, his eyes wide with numb shock. "We've got to get TL. Now."

"I'm right here."

Chapling and I jerked around. TL stood inside the door. How long had he been there? I hadn't even heard him come in. I glanced at my watch. Hours had gone by.

He came toward me, staring at my screen. "Is that the insider?"

"Yes, sir."

With a hard jaw, TL turned to Chapling. "And the documents?"

"There's neurotoxin. Here on the ranch. Set to be released at thirteen hundred hours tomorrow. According to the document, Katarina and Wirenut have to be together when it's found."

‹FOURTEEN›

Minutes later, we stood in the conference room waiting in silence.

The door opened, and David escorted Erin in. Jonathan took her and pushed her down into the chair at the head of the table.

Along the back wall I stood beside Wirenut, silently observing. Immediately, I recalled my arrest months ago before the Specialists had recruited me. How roughly the cops had treated me. How frightened I'd been. Erin must be petrified right now. The only difference was that she deserved it.

Disgust and anger rolled through me at that thought. How could she have done it? *Why* would she have done it? No amount of money, *no* amount, was worth it. We were family. Didn't she care? I would *never* intentionally harm anyone at this ranch.

TL took the seat to her right. "You *know* why you're here. Don't even *think* about playing games with me." He leveled lethal eyes on her. "What is your connection with Octavias Zorba?"

Silence. Erin didn't blink. Twitch. Speak. Nothing.

A minute passed as she kept her expressionless gaze on TL.

He switched his focus beyond her shoulder to Jonathan and gave a barely discernible nod.

Jonathan placed his finger on the back of her neck, and she screamed.

Every muscle in my body contracted at the painful wail. She's a traitor, I reminded myself, concentrating on keeping my face reactionless.

He stepped away, and Erin slumped forward.

"Sit up," TL snapped.

Pulling her shoulders back, she tossed her dark hair, like she'd just finished blowing it dry or something. A smirk replaced her expressionless face.

I watched her, unable to wrap my brain completely around her new facade. This was an Erin I'd never seen. She seemed . . . demented.

TL propped his hands on the table, appearing unfazed by her dramatics. "What is your connection with Octavias Zorba?"

Silence. Again. Other than her smirk, she made no response.

TL shot from his chair, grabbed her hair, and pulled her head back.

I caught my breath. I'd never seen him get violent with one of us. If Erin's momentary shock held any indication, neither had she.

He stuck his hard face an inch from hers. "Zorba's dead. You're not going to get whatever it is he promised you."

She sneered. "How do you know I haven't already got it?"

"You're a fool to admit it if you did. You're an even bigger fool if you think I believe it. Zorba wasn't stupid. He wouldn't pay up until a job was done." TL leaned a fraction closer. "What you don't seem to comprehend is that his *pay up* wouldn't be what you're expecting. He'd think nothing of slicing his sword through your pretty little body."

I cringed at the mention of the sword. More than anything I wanted to turn to Wirenut and make sure he was okay. But I kept myself still, wishing any gory flashbacks from his brain.

Erin swallowed, and TL tracked the movement with his eyes. "Scared? Good. What'd you think? You wouldn't get caught? Zorba'd rescue you? You wouldn't go to prison? You wouldn't die?"

"You can't harm me," she snipped.

With a humorless chuckle, TL released her and stepped back. "Erin, you're not new to this. You know my powers. I can make you disappear. Forever."

She glanced over her shoulder at David. I couldn't see her face, but he held her glance with a flat stare. It was all part of a facade, knowing how to put your emotions aside in a tense situation. TL was the master of it. I knew David's expressions, though, and saw the hurt and confusion deep in his eyes.

What was he thinking? I mean, here sat one of his teammates, a former girlfriend at that. A girl he'd trained with and lived with for years, and she'd crossed to the other side.

It'd be like Wirenut or Parrot, Bruiser, Mystic, or even Beaker going bad. I'd be crushed. Betrayed. Confused. And I'd known them for only a few months. David and Erin had known each other a lot longer.

TL folded his arms across his chest. "We know you sent an anonymous e-mail to the press about the Ghost. We know hundreds of reporters contacted you offering money for Wirenut's true identity. We know you started a bidding war. We know Zorba heard of this and devised his plan to flush out Wirenut. We know Zorba contacted you while we were over in Rissala. We know he offered you two million dollars to hide the neurotoxin on the ranch."

TL cocked his head. "Would you like to know how we know all this?"

Erin lifted her brows.

"Because you're STUPID!"

Everyone but Jonathan jerked at TL's sudden temper. I'd *never* heard him yell like this.

He clamped his hand around her neck. "Every one of your e-mails left a pellucid image. GiGi found them all." He got right in Erin's face. "You disgust me. I can't believe I even *considered* you for the Specialists."

I would die if TL ever said something like that to me.

He squeezed her neck. "Where's the toxin?"

She shook her head.

TL applied more pressure. "Where's the toxin?"

Erin gasped.

He squeezed harder. "Where's the toxin?"

Red splotches crept up her cheeks and across her forehead.

Still standing along the back wall, I concentrated on keeping my body and face stoic. As if none of this fazed me. Inside, though, my heart raced, nearly deafening me with its uncontrollable banging.

How far would TL take things? And . . . did I really want to watch? It'd been different with Zorba and in Ushbania with Romanov Schalmosky. I really hadn't cared about their welfare. They were horrible, horrible men.

This, though? I *knew* Erin. Even if she *was* bad now. It'd be like Bruiser sitting there being strangled by TL. I'd find it extremely hard just to stand here and watch.

TL knows what he's doing, I reminded myself. *You have to trust his tactics. He knows Erin. He knows what will work. Thousands of lives are at stake.*

His bicep contracted. Veins popped on his hand and forearm. Erin's eyes glazed over with an eerie, unfocused gaze.

He's squeezing the life out of her.

I tried to swallow, but my throat had swelled with dryness. Dragging my eyes off TL and Erin, I focused behind them on David.

With a stiff jaw and clenched fists, he stared unblinking at a spot above my head. Clearly, this bothered him as much as me.

"Okay," she wheezed.

David's eyes snapped down to her and so did mine.

"I won't stop next time." TL eased the pressure. "What do you have to say?"

Erin gagged. "I . . . c-can't . . . breathe."

"I don't care." He retightened his grip. "What do you have to say?"

She gurgled. "To-xin . . . buried . . ."

After she choked out the coordinates, TL released her. "Get her out of my sight."

Erin grabbed her neck, wheezing for air.

Wrenching her out of the chair, Jonathan led her from the room.

What's going to happen to her? I wanted to ask, but I kept quiet, waiting for TL's instructions.

He checked his watch. "Let's go."

***

Standing in the Southwest corner of the ranch's property, I stared at the coordinates Erin had given: 122.04.70 north, 38.18.70 west. A patch of moonlit grass.

TL flipped on a flashlight. "There's no evidence the dirt has been disturbed."

David tucked his hands in his jacket. "You think Erin lied? That nothing's buried here?"

"What about injection?" Wirenut squatted down. "A small toxin vial could be inserted, leaving the area virtually untouched."

"Let's X-ray." TL pressed the talk button on his two-way radio. "Chapling, cue satellite. You've got the coordinates. Let's see what's below us."

"Satellite cued," Chapling answered through the radio.

Opening my mini-laptop, I watched the dark screen. Seconds later a black-and-white picture flicked into view. "Upload complete."

The guys moved in around me to see. David, TL, Wirenut, and I appeared as phantom images. I had a weird urge to wave, just to see myself move.

Rows of piping and wiring tunneled the earth beneath us, everything the ranch needed for security.

"There it is." Wirenut pointed over my shoulder at the screen.

Slipping on my glasses, I leaned in. Sure enough, a tube of liquid lay about a foot beneath us. Scary to think that small amount could infect and kill everyone here at the ranch. As well as the city of San Belden and beyond.

"Huh." Wirenut tapped the screen. "See those two wires? One coming out the top of the vial and the other the bottom."

I nodded.

"Those are hematosis detectors."

Hematosis detectors?

"They're still under development. No one's actually used them yet."

"Um, not to be ignorant here, but what are hematosis detectors?" I seemed to be the only one who *didn't* know.

"Hematosis detectors," TL explained, "are a security measure, programmed to unlock with certain blood, certain DNA. They can be used on anything: explosives, government documents, safety deposit boxes."

I propped my glasses on top of my head. "According to Zorba's documents both Katarina and Wirenut have to be present to disarm the toxin. So obviously we're going to need both their blood." It all made sense now.

Wirenut moved away. "Couple of issues we're looking at here. Number one: hematosis detectors are *still under development*, meaning they've never been documented successful. Basically, we're doing a trial here. There's no proof they'll work. Number two: these detectors are rigged to read a certain number of drops."

"Five." The number popped into my head and out my mouth.

Everyone looked at me.

"Zorba's theme has been five." I closed the laptop. "How much you wanna bet it's five here, too? Five drops of blood." *Oooh, I'm good.*

Wirenut smoothed his fingers down his goatee. "Okay, so going with that, there're two detectors. Each has to get the same number of drops. Five of me, five of Katarina."

Sounds easy enough.

He blew out a quick breath. "Only problem is—"

Why does there always have to be a problem?

"My blood and Katarina's have to hit the detectors in sync. Neither of us can be off by one tiny millisecond. The documents said thirteen hundred hours. That means the first drops have to touch at that exact second and then every five seconds, staying with the theme, after that."

"B-but what if something goes wrong? What if I'm not right about the number five? What if the vial's timer chip isn't calibrated to our clocks? What if your blood doesn't drop in sync? An-and you said this thing's still under development. What if it shorts out?" *Do they not see all this?*

TL flipped off the flashlight. "Then we all die."

***

Hours later, Katarina's helicopter from the airport crossed over the ranch's border. Squinting against the whirling dust and grass, I held my hair back and checked my watch. 12:30 P.M.

Only thirty minutes until the toxin releases.

The helicopter touched down on a cleared area behind the house. The passenger door opened, and Katarina jumped down. Gripping her leather jacket together, she ran toward TL, David, Wirenut, and me.

"Hello," she yelled over the loud whipping.

I gave her a welcoming hug.

It surprised her, and for a second she didn't return the gesture. "Thank you," she mumbled, squeezing me quick.

Behind her, the copter lifted off.

"Hey." Wirenut smiled a little.

She smiled back. "Hey."

TL and Katarina exchanged handshakes, and he introduced David.

TL pointed to his truck. "Our protective gear is in the back. Get it on, and let's move out."

We all zipped into thick white suits with clear facial hoods and put on gloves. We hopped in the back of the truck and barreled over the ranch's property to the southwest corner. As we bounced along, Wirenut briefed Katarina on the hematosis detectors.

TL pulled to a stop, and we all piled out.

"Get your laptop, GiGi." TL pressed his two-way radio. "Chapling, give us our X-ray."

I opened my computer. The image flicked into view. "Got it."

TL handed Wirenut a garden shovel. "You're up."

Wirenut knelt at the patch of grass. He inserted the shovel a tiny bit and then quickly removed it. Rotating to the right, he inserted the shovel again and removed it. Quickly, he moved around and around the vial, keeping the same rhythm, each time the shovel going in a little farther.

On the laptop I watched his phantom image and the sharpness of the shovel as he got closer and closer to the vial. Almost a little *too* close.

What if he accidentally nicks it?

The dangerous thought jumped into my head, and I immediately shoved it right back out. He knows what he's doing, I reminded myself, although my pounding heart didn't quite believe my rationale. Accidents *did* happen, after all.

Wirenut inserted the shovel and left it there. "Let me see."

I knelt beside him, showing him the X-ray.

Sweat trickled down his forehead. "We're good."

I glanced at the laptop's digital time and caught my breath. "It's twelve fifty-one." I hadn't realized that so much time had gone by.

Wirenut nodded. "I know."

"B-but that's only nine minutes." *Nine minutes.* To remove all this dirt, patch into the time chip, drop the blood. And the time chip might be seconds or even minutes off. So we could really only have like five minutes to go. *Hello?*

Wirenut gripped my knee through the protective suit. "GiGi."

I jerked my focus from the shovel to his eyes.

"Listen to me and hear me good when I say this."

I swallowed.

"I lost one family. I *won't* lose another." He squeezed my knee. "Now let's get this done."

The conviction in his tone washed over me in a settling wave. *We're going to be okay.*

He took the shovel from the ground and laid it aside. TL handed Wirenut a metal rod. He twisted the end, twirling it open into a clawlike shape. "Let me see the screen."

I held it out for him.

Studying the image, Wirenut carefully inserted the claw, stopping right at the vial. He twisted the end, and the prongs closed together. "Ready."

David and TL squatted across from each other, gripping a wide plastic tray.

"Not a single speck of dirt can fall on the vial," Wirenut instructed. "If it's disturbed in any way, it'll trigger the toxin."

David and TL nodded their understanding.

"Three. Two. One. Now." Wirenut yanked the claw straight up. TL and David slid the tray beneath it.

I kept my eyes locked on the screen, holding my breath, searching for falling debris.

Nothing.

They moved the tray and claw aside. Down about twelve inches sat the tiny vial with a thin wire sticking out of either end.

Wirenut pulled a slim, red rectangle from his protective suit's pocket. "Something I've been working on. It'll read the timer chip without patching into it. I won't even have to touch the vial."

Good thinking, seeing as how the toxin would release with the slightest disturbance.

"Now's not the time to test a new gadget."

"I know that, sir. I've completed the standard trials."

TL nodded. "Go ahead then."

Wirenut pointed the chip reader at the vial. "Time check."

Everyone looked at their watches.

"Twelve fifty-eight thirty-one."

Little over a minute to go. We all set our watches.

TL stripped sterile plastic off two needles and handed Katarina and Wirenut each one. They each took off a glove and lay belly-down on the grass on opposite sides of the vial. Holding their hands to the side, they pricked their middle fingers and squeezed until blood dripped onto the ground.

Wirenut lifted his eyes to Katarina. "Hey."

Across the small distance, she met his steady gaze.

"We've got this. No problem."

She nodded.

"Twelve fifty-nine fifty," David reported.

Only ten seconds to go.

"Clean." Wirenut and Katarina wiped the blood from their middle fingers.

"Here we go." David tapped his watch. "Five. Four . . ."

280

Bringing their fingers over, Wirenut and Katarina held them steady over the opening in the ground and applied pressure with their thumbs.

"Three. Two. Drop."

One single drop welled, hovered, and then fell, landing precisely on the detectors. *Wow.*

Only four more times to go.

"Five. Four . . ."

They cleaned their fingers, held them over the opening, applied pressure.

"Three. Two. Drop."

The blood welled, hovered, fell.

Three more times . . .

Two more times . . .

"Five, four . . ."

Cleaned fingers, held them over opening, applied pressure. "Last. Time. Drop."

Welled, hovered, and then Katarina sneezed.

‹FIFTEEN›

Everyone froze.

No one breathed.

No one moved.

My eyes stayed pasted to the laptop's X-ray image.

As if in slow motion, I recalled it all. . . .

Katarina's breath hitched twice, and I knew, I *knew* she was about to sneeze. Before I had time to digest that thought, she did. A big one. Possibly the loudest I'd ever heard. No matter how beautiful she was, nothing pretty existed about this sneeze.

But the incredible part? No portion of her body moved. Not even a tiny bit. She kept herself frozen in place as the blood on her middle finger welled and then fell, landing precisely on the vial in sync with Wirenut.

The hematosis detectors fell off and the vial disengaged. Numbly, I watched, suddenly swamped with everything that had transpired. All of it. Not just the sneeze.

Zorba, Rissala, Wirenut, Katarina, Erin, documents, the sword, neurotoxin, Nalani, chains . . .

The past week of my life smothered my brain in a blur.

The Rayver Security System, jewelry lady, boat, plane, Museum of History, Museum of Modern Art, ceramic egg . . .

I squeezed my eyes shut against the onslaught.

Yellow ribbon, cemetery, marketplace, Gio's guitar, tattoos, water-rigged system, crown, mansion, chimney . . .

"GiGi?"

Rental car, necklace, island, diving, marina, pulse bomb, contortion lasers, paralysis cathode . . .

"GiGi?"

Cane, green glow, arsenic mouth tape, seizure, blood, TL's blood, my tooth, tool belt, Wirenut's scar . . .

"GIGI!"

I jerked alert. "What?"

Everyone stared at me.

David put his hand on my shoulder. "You okay?"

"Umm, yeah."

He smiled. "Good. You spaced out on us there."

"Sorry." I pressed my fingers to the plastic covering my forehead. "My brain's on overdrive. A lot's happened."

Taking my laptop, he clicked it closed. "We all need to relax a little. And to breathe." He unzipped my protective gear. "Get out of that thing."

We all did, greedily taking in the cool night air.

Wirenut swooped Katarina up in a huge hug. "This might be bad timing, but I think we make a great team."

Katarina smiled. "I *know* we do."

Laughing, he twirled her around and around. Their happiness made my heart dance.

He released her and went into his victory shoulder-roll dance. "Go, Wirenut. Go, Wirenut. Go. Go."

I smiled. It seemed like *forever* since I'd seen him do that.

Wirenut pulled Katarina back into his arms. He lowered his head and closed his eyes. She lifted up on tiptoes and their lips met.

And held . . .

And held . . .

They stood wrapped in each other's arms, holding their closed lips together.

The most beautiful, loving, simple, sensuous kiss I'd ever seen. Breathing each other in. Cherishing the other.

Warmth washed over me as I watched them. I should look away, give them privacy. But I couldn't. Their special moment hypnotized me. Mesmerized me.

I wanted that intimacy. That *exact* kiss.

"You all walk back." TL tossed the shovel in the truck. "I'll dispose of the vial."

David picked up our suits and threw them in the truck. "Want me to help?"

"No. Jonathan'll be here soon. I want him to assist me with this."

Wirenut and Katarina pulled back, smiling at each other. He took her hand. "You all ready?"

David placed the tray and claw in the truck. "We're ready."

Wirenut and Katarina strolled off ahead of us, hand in hand, talking. David and I followed.

I stared at their clasped hands, wishing David would take my hand. Why wouldn't he?

Maybe because they're in my pockets?

Oh, yeah.

I took my hands out and stretched my fingers. Sure enough, he wrapped his hand around mine.

A contented smile crept onto my face.

He caressed his thumb along my skin. "You did good."

My entire body hummed in response. "Me? Oh, I didn't do anything. They"—I nodded at the lovebirds—"did it all. Did you see how steady and confident they were? I would've been shaking and rattling like a . . . like a . . . oh, I don't know. Like a something."

"You underestimate yourself. I've seen you in action. You're good."

That comment rolled around in my head for a few seconds. TL had said the same thing. Under pressure, when I *knew* something needed to be done, I did it. Competently. My brain took control of my body's hesitancy. *Well, except for that time in Ushbania when I tripped and split my lip open. And then that time—*

"Stop." David laughed. "You *are* good. Stop trying to disprove it."

"How'd you know what I was thinking?"

He squeezed my hand. "Because I *know* you. I know how that incredible brain of yours works."

Incredible brain. Those two silly words made me all warm and fuzzy on the inside.

I squeezed back. "It's nice to be known." So *nice.*

Wirenut glanced over his shoulder. "What's gonna happen to Erin?"

"Prison."

I moved a little closer to David. "You all right?" I would feel *horrible* if one of my teammates went to jail.

"Yeah, I'm okay." He spared me a brief smile. "TL gave me a letter from my dad. It's the first communication I've had with him since the Ushbanian mission."

"Oh, David, that's wonderful. Is he doing okay?"

"He is. Hopefully, we'll get to see each other soon."

In front of us Wirenut said something to Katarina in Rissalan.

"When'd you learn Rissalan?" I asked.

Wirenut lifted their clasped hands and pressed his lips to Katarina's knuckles. "I picked up a few words while we were on the mission. I don't know much, but I figured I'd better start studying it."

So sweet. I had the best teammate in the whole world. "What'd you just say to her?"

They *both* glanced over their shoulders this time. Katarina's amber eyes held privacy, secrecy, and a hint of mischievousness. Wirenut's? Downright, ornery, none-of-your-business. Neither of them answered my question.

It made me want to know even more.

"What did they say?" I whispered to David. "You know a little Rissalan, don't you?"

"Why are you whispering?" he whispered back.

I narrowed my eyes. He knew why I was whispering.

As we neared the ranch house Wirenut led Katarina off toward the barn. "Catch you all later."

Where ya going? I wanted to tease. *Whatcha gonna do?*

When they were far enough away, I turned to David. "Well? What'd they say?"

He laughed. "When did you become so nosy?"

Gosh, he's right. When *had* I become so nosy? But . . . boy, I wanted to know.

Parrot and Bruiser came out the back door.

Bruiser tossed a football in the air and caught it. "Lookee here. You're alive. Guess everything went okay."

Leave it to Bruiser to be nonchalant about almost dying.

Parrot! I grabbed his arm. "You're the exact person I need to see. Will you translate Rissalan for me?"

David shook his head. "GiGi, GiGi, GiGi."

"What?" I turned back to Parrot. "Well?"

"Now?"

"Yes. Now."

Parrot waved me on. "Okay. Shoot."

"Um . . ." I relayed everything I could remember to the best of my nonlingual ability.

Parrot blinked. "You kidding me? That's not Rissalan. What'd you do, form your own language?"

I punched his arm. "I never claimed to be you."

David opened the back door and gave me a little push inside. "Ignore her. You all have fun."

He grabbed my hand and tugged me down the back hall.

"Where we going?" Suddenly I didn't care anymore what Wirenut said to Katarina.

We crossed through the kitchen, rounded the refrigerator, and David opened the pantry door. He pulled me inside, turned on the dim light, and locked the door behind us.

Gulp.

I'd never been in the pantry before. Small room. Three by five. Lots of shelves and food. What a pantry should look like, I supposed.

What does it matter? I rolled my eyes. *You're locked in here with David, remember?*

I looked at him then, propped against the shelves, arms crossed, staring back at me. His intense dark eyes made my stomach flip.

"Somebody know won't we're in here?" I shook my head. "I mean, won't somebody know we're in here?"

"Maybe. Doesn't matter."

"Oh." *Think of something to say, you idiot.* "Um—"

David pushed off the shelves.

Suddenly, it's very warm in here.

He took a step toward me, and I backed up. Not sure why I backed up. I wasn't afraid or anything.

Well, a little. But scared in a good way. Like excitedly fearful, if that made sense.

David took another step, leaving barely any space between us.

I swallowed.

He ran his hand down my jacketed arm. "Hey."

"Hey," I breathed.

David trailed his finger over the top of my hand. "Nervous?"

"N-no." *Okay, it's not warm in here. It's hot. Very hot.*

286

I reached for my zipper. Wait. *You can't take your jacket off, you imbecile. He'll think you're undressing*

"No?" He smoothed my hair behind my ear. "I am."

"You are?"

Nodding, David shifted closer, and I swayed back, finding the door solid behind me. Good thing, because his nearness shot my balance.

He stretched his arm above my head, and my heart skipped a beat. "I've been thinking about this a lot."

"This?"

David toyed with the hair on top of my head. "This."

"K-kissing?"

He pressed his body against mine, and I stopped breathing. "Speaking of which."

"I haven't brushed my teeth," I blurted, then realized what an extremely stupid thing that was to say.

His eyes crinkled. "Hmmm, did you brush them this morning?"

"Yes," I croaked.

"Good." He tilted his head.

"Bu—"

David's lips touched mine, and all rambling thoughts poofed from my brain. His cologne flowed through my senses, buzzing every skin particle on my body.

Soft. Warm. Yum.

If not for his weight holding me up against the door, I would've slid down to my butt.

Cupping my cheek, he slid away from my mouth and over to my neck, nuzzling it. "Better this time?"

Oh, yes. Much better.

Tilting my head, I gave his talented lips and bristly cheek better access. Goose bumps pricked my skin. My breath drained out in a moan.

"GiGi?"

"Hmmm?"

"Is that a yes?"

"Mmm-hmmm." I didn't open my eyes. "Can I have another one?" If not for the turned-on haze fogging my brain, I would've died from asking a question like that.

"Definitely," he murmured.

A week later, Specialists Teams One and Two, along with Jonathan and Chapling, packed the conference room.

David and I stood side by side along the wall. I tried to focus on what TL was saying, but my brain wouldn't cooperate.

David.

David. David. David.

Even though inches separated us, his warmth permeated my clothes. I closed my eyes and inhaled.

His scent. *Oh, his scent.*

Nothing like it in the whole world. If I were blindfolded and had to sniff a hundred guys, I'd pick out David in a second.

I opened my eyes. TL was still speaking. I'd find out from Bruiser later what he said.

David shifted, and his shoulder touched mine. On purpose? Accidental? He left it there, barely skimming.

On purpose. I smiled, and warmth crept into my face. I remembered all the kisses we'd shared over the past week.

Did I distract him as much as he distracted me?

He folded his arms, drawing my attention (not that I had any anyway) away from TL. David's muscles stretched the fabric of his long-sleeve T-shirt, molding it to the contours and lines of his arms.

Everyone in the room applauded, and I snapped to attention. Quickly I brought my hands together, clapping, glancing around.

I tried to read expressions, but couldn't figure out what we were celebrating.

"TL recapped the Rissala mission." David nudged me. "You better pay attention. You might get in trouble. I'll have to lock you in the pantry again."

"Shhh," I hushed, although I loved the teasing.

TL lifted his hand for silence. "And now onto the next thing. With Erin gone, we have an opening in the Specialists. I've asked Katarina Leosi to fill the slot, and she's accepted. She'll be our special-entry operative. Her code name is Cat."

Oh, wow!

TL opened the door, and Katarina stepped inside. She wore a yellow ribbon, the Ghost's signature, around her ponytail. The necklace Wirenut had bought her back in Rissala hung from her neck.

It made my heart all mushy.

Everyone applauded, and I joined in (this time for real). Across the room I caught her eye and waved. Grinning, she waved back. Sitting at the table, Wirenut grinned, too.

So great to see him happy again.

The noise died down, and TL dismissed us. "David and GiGi, I need you to stay."

Huh. Wonder what's up?

Please, not another mission. Pleasepleaseplease, not another mission. I needed time to be me. I wanted to get back to classes. I had to kiss David some more. *Had* to. I wanted to hang out with Bruiser and Katarina and the rest of my friends, my team.

Wait. Maybe TL's going to get onto us for making out in the pantry.

Groan.

TL closed the door, giving the three of us privacy. "Have a seat. There's something you two need to know."

David and I sat beside each other with TL at the head. He slipped a tiny envelope from his back pocket and laid it on the table.

"I thought it was time to show you this. Open it." He slid it toward us.

David flipped open the unglued envelope and pulled out an old picture. A tiny blond girl stood beside a dark-haired boy a little older. They appeared to be around four to six. Dressed in shorts and T-shirts, they held hands, cheesing it for the camera.

I studied the girl's long hair and blue eyes and then zeroed in on her missing-tooth smile. *Wait a minute . . . what the . . . ?*

I glanced up at David.

Frowning, he stared down at the picture.

I looked back at the boy in the picture and over to David. It couldn't be, could it? "Is this . . ."

TL folded his hands on top of the table. "Yes. That's a picture of the two of you."

"What?" I gasped. "How?"

"You both lived here and knew each other when you were children. I thought it was time you knew."

I looked up at David and saw his confusion.

I was too numb to understand.

What does this mean exactly?

Somehow, I think I'll find out when TL is ready to tell us the whole story.

BOOK THREE

ON THE TRAIL . . .

Twenty minutes later, I made it to the other side of the island. I stopped and checked my cell phone. The blue dot was beginning to fade, indicating the thirty-minute tracker was dissolving, but from what I could tell, Eduardo was to my right.

I rode into a deserted parking lot of the state park. Behind me stretched a half mile of beach highway leading back into town. In front of me spanned the dark ocean lit only by the half moon. To the left stood a small concrete visitor's station.

With the DNA glasses still on, I scanned the area. A red trail led from the parking lot, where the car must have dropped him and drove off, and onto the beach.

Leaving the bike, I followed the red trail across the beach and down the length of a long pier. The red trail stopped at the end of the pier, where a boat had probably picked him up.

There was no telling how far out he'd gone.

I unsnapped my pocket and pulled out the cell phone. I activated the audio recording/eavesdropping software Chapling had coded in.

Here went nothing.

‹PROLOGUE›

Sisissy. Sisissy. Di-did yooouuu hear wh-what I aaassskkked yo-you?

Sissy pried open her heavy eyelids and focused on the fuzzy image of Ms. Gabrier. The teacher's lips were moving, but Sissy couldn't make out her words.

Ms. Gabrier stopped talking and stood still.

From across the classroom Sissy squinted, bringing her teacher into focus. She was looking right at Sissy.

Ms. Gabrier's lips started moving again. Her words filtered into Sissy's ears, slowly swirling through her head, echoing off her skull in distorted vowels and syllables.

Sissy dragged her dry tongue around her mouth, trying to moisten it, and smacked her lips. She needed a soda.

Faintly, she heard some giggles, and in her blurry peripheral she saw other students laughing at her.

So what? She could care less. Let them and their perfect little selves laugh.

"*Sisissy?*"

Dragging her head from the top of her desk, Sissy slouched, sliding her butt down in her chair. She propped her boots on the desk in front of her and let her eyelids fall back down. Sleep. Beautiful, much needed sleep.

"*Sisissy?*"

"What," she grumbled. Couldn't they see she wanted to sleep?

"Priscilla," Ms. Gabrier snapped.

Sissy's eyes shot open. "What?" she snapped back. *Nobody* called her Priscilla.

Her teacher's eyes narrowed. "Do you realize you're failing this class?"

Sissy shrugged. Of course she realized she was failing. She never turned in any homework or studied for tests. Her mom didn't care. No one cared. Sissy's life wasn't going anywhere, anyway. And why did teachers always ask stupid questions that they knew you knew the answer to?

"All right." Ms. Gabrier jabbed the off button on the overhead projector. "You know what?" She pointed her pen at Sissy. "I've had enough of you. I don't care if you *do* have the highest test scores in the school. I don't want you in here. If you don't care, I don't care. Look around you. Look!" her teacher shouted.

Sissy jumped, took her feet off of the desk, and sat up straight. She'd never heard her teacher raise her voice.

Ms. Gabrier's jaw tightened. "I said *look.*"

Suddenly very awake, Sissy dragged her gaze over the thirty or so other students in Advanced Chemistry. Mostly preps and nerds. Everyone was college bound. Some with scholarships, others with Daddy's and Mommy's money. All of them were staring back at her with mixed expressions. Haughty, disgusted, amused, pitying, scared.

Scared of what? Scared of her?

Ms. Gabrier tapped her nail to the podium. "Do you see any of them sleeping through this class?"

Sissy swallowed.

"Do you?"

She barely shook her head.

"That's right. Because they know what an honor, what a *privilege,* it is to be in here." Ms. Gabrier placed her pen on the podium. "There are exactly seventy-one students on the waiting list to be in this junior class. Do you know how many students are on the waiting list to be in this high school?"

Sissy shook her head.

"One thousand eight hundred and twenty-three."

Silence.

She'd had no idea that many kids were on the waiting list.

"You were placed in the Jacksonville Academic Magnet School because of your brilliance. This school made the top ten list in the nation. Do you know how incredible that is for a public school?" Ms. Gabrier closed the teacher's edition lying on her podium. "What a waste. I'm tired of trying. This is what it's like day in and day out with you . . . when you're here."

Ms. Gabrier pressed her fingertips to her temple. "I'm done. You're out of here." She closed her eyes. "Go fry your brain on drugs in someone else's classroom."

The blond girl beside Sissy snickered.

She turned and snarled back at her. Why did everyone assume Sissy did drugs? She was just tired. Exhausted. Working the night shift at the Laundromat to make enough money so she wouldn't have to rely on her mom would do that to you.

Her teacher punched the projector back on. "Jami, please escort Sissy to the office. And Sissy, take all your stuff. You're not coming back."

***

Thirty minutes later, sissy climbed in her friend Courtney's open window. She snatched a piece of gum from the pack on the dresser and caught sight of her reflection in the dingy mirror.

She looked wasted. No wonder everybody always thought she was.

Heavy black eyeliner smeared her puffy bottom lids. Day-old black lipstick crusted her dry lips. Her dyed black hair stuck out in short, gelled clumps. And the bruise from last week's fight with her mom still colored her chin.

Ms. Gabrier was the only teacher who had asked about the bruise. Sissy had told her she got in a fight with a friend. It was a better excuse than "I ran into a wall." Who actually believed that anyway?

The other teachers had seen the bruise. How could they not? But none had asked. If you asked, then you had to follow up. Paperwork, reporting to authorities, blah, blah, blah. Who had time for all that junk? None of the teachers cared. Or at least none cared when it came to Sissy. Now if it had been cute little Kirstie or peppy, athletic Lisa . . .

Whatever. Everyone expected this from Sissy. Bruises, drugs, zeros.

Outside, a train bumped by, rattling the apartment walls. Sissy plopped down across the unmade bed and popped the gum in her mouth.

She should've botched the stupid state test that put her in the academic magnet. That way she'd still be in her old school with Courtney. At least there Sissy hadn't stuck out like a freak.

But she hadn't been able to resist the temptation to see, just to *see,* how she would do on the test.

Sissy knew she was smart, even though she'd made D's and F's her whole life. No one else had thought she was smart. In fact, she'd been recommended to attend a "special" school once.

She snorted. "Puh-lease." A "special" school?

Showed how much they knew.

Sissy blew everyone away when she aced the state test. Thinking back on it brought a smirk to her face.

She toasted the air with her middle finger. *Here's to everyone who ever thought I was a loser.*

The bedroom door creaked open. Pam, Courtney's mom, peeked in. "Oh, hey, Sissy. Thought you were Courtney."

Sissy didn't bother reminding Pam that it was eleven in the morning and Courtney was in school. Pam wouldn't care one way or the other anyway.

Dressed in a long T-shirt and boxers, Pam shuffled across the worn carpet to the dresser. She opened the top drawer, pulled out a pair of socks, and slipped them on. "Aren't you supposed to be in school?"

Sissy shrugged. "Got kicked out." Story of her life.

Tucking her wet brown hair behind her ear, Pam leaned back against the dresser. "Me and Courtney are moving back in with her daddy."

Sissy got really still, knowing what came next.

Pam took a deep breath and then blew it out slow. "You can't come with us. I know your momma booted you out again, and I'm sorry. But me and Courtney's daddy, we got enough to work on without you tagging along."

Why me? What did I ever do to anybody to deserve this reject of a life? Sissy pushed the irritating voice in her head aside. It did no good to give in to the depression. "When do you want me out?"

"End of the day." Pam glanced over to the black garbage bag that held Sissy's clothes. "I got an old suitcase if you want."

"It's all right," Sissy mumbled, rolling onto her side to face the window. She'd lived with Courtney and Pam on and off over the years. A week here, a month there. They let Sissy come and go as she needed, whenever her mom brought another guy home, whenever they fought, whenever her mom drank, whenever she got violent . . .

Behind her, Pam left the room.

Outside, another train approached, sounding its horn.

Sissy chomped down on her gum. *What am I supposed to do now?*

That evening sissy squatted under the bleachers of Jacksonville Magnet, surveying the school's gym. The night janitor locked up, crossed the parking lot to her truck, and drove off.

Sissy waited in the grass, smacking at Florida's enormous mosquitoes, watching the school for any more activity. Humid air hung heavy around her, making her baggy clothes stick to her skin. She spit her gum into a wrapper, put a new piece in her mouth, and continued to wait.

Thirty minutes passed, and the coast stayed clear. Sissy picked up her bag of clothes and jogged across the football field to the gym. She rounded the side to the boy's locker room, popped open the vent leading into the showers, and crawled through.

The smell of bleach overpowered her senses, and Sissy murmured a quick thank-you to the janitor gods. Two nights ago when she'd come, the janitor had been sick and the place had been a disgusting mess.

She tiptoed through the dark locker room, out the door, and down the hall to the windowless boiler room. She didn't know why it was called the boiler room when all it held was old classroom junk. Tons of it. Broken copy machines; old wood desks; books, books, and more books; rolling chalkboards; bulletin-board paper; storage bins; old gym mats.

And chemistry supplies.

Sissy walked in and flicked on the desk lamp.

She'd come across the place by accident. At the end of last school year she'd seen the janitor unloading desks off a cart. Sissy had stopped to help. After all, the janitor *was* old.

But the janitor had left without securing the door, so Sissy was able to rig it not to lock—easy to do with a gum wrapper—and went back that night.

And again the next night.

And the next.

All summer long she'd gone, slowly making it into her space and escaping life. Many nights when she didn't work, she slept over, using the girl's locker room to shower.

She'd be here tonight. No way she was crawling back to her mom.

Sissy wound her way through the dusty desks to the big wood chemistry cabinet. Hidden beneath it, she pulled out her notebook.

Her spirit lightened as it did every time she lost herself in her experiments, her solutions, her chemicals. Years ago she'd found a kid's chemistry set in the garbage and pulled it out. She'd cleaned it up and followed the instruction manual carefully as she'd composed her first basic experiments. And her life had never been the same since.

She smiled at the memory. Being here in this makeshift lab was the only time she was in a good mood. The only time things felt right. *She* felt right. Her life didn't suck.

Flipping through the notebook, she scanned the handwritten pages, searching for the metcium formula . . . ah, there it was. Something about it wasn't right, and she'd puzzled over it for a week straight. Then it hit her last night as she was folding clothes at the Laundromat.

Beside the chemistry cabinet stood a stack of poster boards propped up against the wall. Hidden behind them was her box of supplies.

Sissy moved the poster boards aside and slid out her box. Any spare money she had she spent on chemistry supplies. Some legal, some not. A good majority of her powders and liquids were her own derivatives of marine life. Easy enough to obtain when you lived in Jacksonville, Florida.

She opened the box and carefully pulled out flasks of ciumdroxide, coloride, and trosesineo—all highly flammable liquids. From the cabinet she got two rubber mats, a burner, two beakers, and some stirring rods.

Sissy carried all the supplies over to the desk. She unrolled a rubber mat, spread it across the desktop, and then placed a smaller one on the floor for her to stand on. Both would absorb any electricity created from her work.

She put on her goggles and rubber gloves and got down to business. . . .

As she poured the trosesineo into the beaker that held the coloride, her experiment consumed her. Her concentration mixing the two liquids held her total focus. Any other time she would've noticed the flame getting too high. She would've paid attention to the ciumdroxide she'd already put to heat bubbling too close to the edge.

In her peripheral vision through her goggles, she caught sight of the ciumdroxide a split second before it boiled and foamed over the edge.

She jerked her head up, accidentally bumping the flask of trosesineo. It toppled over, flowed straight into the boiled-over ciumdroxide, and both liquids immediately caught on fire. Sissy's heart lurched as she reached for a fire extinguisher at the same time pink smoke preceded a bright flash. Then an explosion sent her flying backward.

An hour later, sissy sat handcuffed beside some cop's desk. How stupid could she have been? She'd *never* lost track of her experiments. If it weren't for the gym mats she'd landed on, the explosion could've caused some broken bones.

With a sigh, she glanced over to the left where a coffeemaker sat on a small table. Some old guy had just made a fresh pot, and it smelled heavenly. In front of her sprawled the station's open workroom with desks placed here and there. Each desk had a phone and a computer. No walls separated them. Only three other cops were present this late in the evening.

The cop beside her hung up the phone. "Your mom doesn't want you."

Sissy could've told the cop that and saved him a phone call.

His chair squeaked as he leaned back. His red hair and baby face made him look about the same age as Sissy. Sixteen. He probably had just got out of cop school.

He folded his hands over his skinny stomach. "What about your dad?"

"I don't have one."

"What do you mean you don't have one? Everyone has a dad."

Where'd this guy grow up? "Well, I don't."

The cop frowned. "What do you mean?"

Sissy ground her teeth together and wished for a piece of gum. Why'd they take her gum anyway? It wasn't like she could break out of jail with it. "I mean, I don't know. I don't know his name. I don't know where he lives. I don't know anything. Zilcho. My mom doesn't even know." How much more did Sissy have to spell it out?

Sissy's father could be any number of men. Of course she'd always fantasized that he was some famous chemist, that she'd inherited her talent from him.

Whatever. Not like her mom would ever be with some famous chemist.

The cop's chair squeaked as he brought it back down. "What were you doing with those chemicals?"

Sissy shrugged. "Nothing. Just playing around." Little did he know, little did *anyone* know, the discoveries she'd made.

The cop shook his finger at her. "If you were making a bomb, you better come clean right now, young lady."

She nearly snorted at his sudden authoritative tone.

And a bomb? Puh-lease. She had better things to do with her time than make bombs. "When do I get my notebook back?"

His desk phone rang, and he picked it up. "Officer Roman." A few seconds passed as he listened to whoever spoke on the other end. "All right." He hung up the phone and rolled his chair back. "Let's go."

The cop escorted Sissy through the workroom and out into the empty lobby. He uncuffed her and nodded to the chairs. "Sit. Someone will be out."

"When do I get my notebook back?"

"Sit." He left and closed the door in her face.

Way to ignore my one and only question, idiot. Sissy stomped across the tile floor and sat in the metal chair farthest away. *Someone will be out.* What did that mean?

She looked across the lobby to where the front desk clerk sat. "Did someone make my bail?"

"Yes," he answered without glancing up.

Who? Who would make her bail?

Suddenly, the same door Sissy had come through opened. A chubby red-haired woman stepped out.

Ms. Gabrier?

***

A few minutes later, Sissy climbed into her teacher's car. "Why'd you make my bail?"

Ms. Gabrier cranked the engine. "You're welcome."

Sissy rolled her eyes. "Thanks. Do you have my notebook?"

Ms. Gabrier pulled from the police station's parking lot. "Let's wait until we get to my house." She turned on a jazz station, and with that, they rode in silence.

Sissy stared out her window, idly watching the buildings and houses they passed, everything dimly lit by streetlights. Since it was already after midnight, there was little to no activity.

Why did her teacher bail her out? And why were they headed to her house? It didn't make any sense. Ms. Gabrier didn't even like Sissy.

Fifteen minutes later, they pulled into a neighborhood with small one-story houses, each with a tidy yard. A cookie-cutter place with nothing unique about the brick homes.

Ms. Gabrier parked in her driveway and led the way up a mulch path to the front door. She unlocked it, stepped inside, and flipped on an interior light.

She pointed to the right into the living room. "Have a seat. I'll make coffee."

She strode down a hallway into a kitchen that lay straight ahead, and Sissy turned into the living room. A blue leather sectional sofa framed the back and side walls in an L shape. A circular wood coffee table sat in front of it. A bookcase ran the length of the other wall, with a stereo in the center and CDs lining both sides. There was no TV. And the whole place smelled . . . clean.

It was just the sort of cozy living room she'd always fantasized about. She had the weird urge to ask Ms. Gabrier if she could stay. Forever.

Sissy crossed the soft carpet to the bookshelves and began browsing. Some fiction, but mostly science manuals and chemistry journals lined the shelves.

"It's instant. But it'll do," Ms. Gabrier said, coming up behind Sissy and handing her a mug. "Have a seat."

Sissy followed her over to the couch. They settled on opposite sides of the L.

"I have your notebook. The police released it to me." Ms. Gabrier scooted back on the sofa, making herself comfortable. "It's in some sort of cryptic writing. Will you tell me about it?"

Only Sissy could decipher her personalized shorthand. "Can I have it back?"

"Yes, of course. I'd like you to tell me about it first, though."

Sissy hesitated, sipping her coffee slowly, deciding how much to say. "Experiments. I like tinkering with chemicals."

"You're doing more than tinkering. Tell me about coloride and trosesineo."

Sissy narrowed her eyes. "How do you know about coloride and trosesineo?" She'd personally created those chemicals.

Ms. Gabrier's lips curved. "I saw the terms in your notebook."

Sissy studied her teacher's mischievous smile. "Who are you?

Slowly, Ms Gabrier rotated the mug in her hands, studying the dark liquid. A few seconds passed, and then she glanced over to the doorway, making Sissy turn to see.

A tall, dark man stood silently in the dimly lit entryway. His glacier eyes seemed to glow green in the shadows. He stepped into the room, holding Sissy's notebook. "Hello, Priscilla. My name is Thomas Liba. Ms. Gabrier and I work for the IPNC, Information Protection National Concern, which is a special-operations division of the government."

Sissy jerked her eyes over to her teacher.

Ms. Gabrier put her mug on the coffee table as Thomas Liba came into the room. He sat down on her side of the couch's L.

"I've worked for the IPNC for thirty years," Ms. Gabrier said. "I've done a variety of jobs for them, including training." She nodded toward Mr. Liba. "In fact, Thomas was one of my trainees. Ten years ago, the IPNC placed me undercover as a teacher in the Jacksonville Academic Magnet School so I could monitor gifted kids like yourself."

Gifted kids like myself?

"The government," Mr. Liba picked up, "has had their eyes on you since last year. Since you aced the Florida state science test."

"You came out of nowhere with that one," Ms. Gabrier put in. "I did some research and discovered you'd taken plenty of state tests over the years. You didn't even try, though. Anybody could tell that if they'd taken a few minutes to actually review them."

"So what does this have to do with me?" Sissy asked.

"In the IPNC," Mr. Liba continued, "we have a group called the Specialists. They're made up of young adults your age and a little older. They're all system kids. No family. Or in your case, no family who wants to keep you close. No ties. Nobody wants them. Each Specialist is gifted in one particular area. Clearly, for you that would be chemistry. As a Specialist you are given a new identity and trained to one day go undercover."

Sissy didn't respond. She couldn't. Her shock left her mute. She sat on the sofa staring back at both Mr. Liba and Ms. Gabrier.

What is going on?

Shifting, Ms. Gabrier crossed her ankles. "Mr. Liba is here for you, Sissy. He wants you for the Specialists."

<ONE>

I stared at the picture on the conference room table as TL's words replayed in my head. *That's a picture of you and David. You lived here and knew each other when you were children.*

There stood four-year-old me with six-year-old David beside me, our arms wrapped around each other as we grinned for the camera. We were both dressed in shorts and T-shirts.

We looked happy. Truly happy.

I recognized a sequoia tree that towered behind us. It stood along the back fence close to where we were a week ago with Wirenut and Cat diffusing the hematosis detector.

David moved closer to me and leaned in. I slid the picture between us so we could both get a better look.

I was the same back then as I am now. Tall, lanky, blond. David looked different. His boyhood chubbiness had transformed into athletic hotness, and his light brown hair had darkened to almost black.

I glanced over at him. "Did you know about this?"

David shook his head.

We'd had numerous trust issues when we first met. In fact, he'd outright lied to me. But it had all been worked out, and there'd been no dishonesty since then. Still, sometimes I found myself questioning things.

Like right now.

Obviously, when TL recruited me for the Specialists, he'd known I'd once lived here at the San Belden Ranch for Boys and Girls. And obviously, he hadn't told me; otherwise, I wouldn't be so shocked right now.

However, I'd learned over the months that TL always had a good reason for his actions. His job required a keen sense of timing, knowing when to do certain things, when to say other things. He was highly trained. Everyone knew they could trust and rely on him.

He would die for any one of us Specialists.

But still . . . why hadn't he told me? Why hadn't he told David?

"David's right," TL commented as if reading my rambling thoughts.

He did that a lot. Sometimes I wondered if he didn't have a touch of Mystic, the Specialists' clairvoyant, in him.

"David was raised here. He's always known that. This is the first he's heard that you lived here, too." TL folded his hands on top of the table. "The ranch used to be a safe house for the children of our nation's top agents. Now, of course, the Specialists train and live here."

I knew the ranch used to be a safe house. David had told me that months ago when I first moved in. I paused and slowly brought my eyes up to TL's. "So . . . are you saying my parents were government agents?"

"Yes."

I stared at him, dumbfounded, unable to comprehend fully what he just acknowledged. My parents used to be agents? It didn't make any sense. My mom had been a kindergarten teacher and my dad an insurance salesman. I had very few memories of them, but I definitely remembered visiting my mom's kindergarten classroom. I'd ridden a seesaw with a little freckle-faced boy and practiced tying shoes on a big stuffed blue boot.

How could I have such vivid memories if they weren't true? "Did my parents live here with me?"

TL shook his head. "No. They visited you here. You have to understand, GiGi, it wasn't safe for you to be with them. They traveled constantly, sometimes together, sometimes separately."

"B-but I remember visiting my mom in her classroom. I remember going on a picnic. I remember . . ." Wait, did I *really* remember all that stuff, or had someone told me that had happened to me?

"Your memories are true." TL nodded toward the picture. "That was taken the day your parents picked you up from the ranch after they resigned from the agency. They wanted a normal life for you, a real family, which was why they moved you to Iowa. They loved you very much."

I closed my eyes as memories of my parents flooded my brain. My beautiful mother laughing. My father smiling. My parents kissing. My dad swinging me around. My mom brushing my hair.

305

My lips curved with the tender memory of my dad teaching me to ride a bike. My mom had been there, too, clapping and cheering me on. They *had* loved me. Very much. Sometimes it was easy to forget that simple, wonderful fact.

Suddenly, I recalled something Mike Share, David's dad, had said to me months ago. *You look just like your mother.* I'd thought he'd seen my file. Now I knew differently.

I opened my eyes. "Mr. Share knew my parents."

TL smiled and nodded. "Mike Share and your father were best friends. Like brothers."

David and I exchanged a small grin. How neat to know our parents had been best friends.

Under the table, David put his hand on my knee, and my stomach swirled. One week ago we'd been making out in the pantry, and his warm touch now gave me a quick flashback of the encounter.

He squeezed my knee. "How come GiGi didn't come here to the ranch when her parents died?"

TL sat back in his chair. "Legally, that wasn't possible. Her parents had resigned. If they'd still been IPNC employees, GiGi would've come here. As it was, she became a ward of the state of Iowa."

And I bounced around between orphanages and foster homes for the next ten years of my life.

I wanted to ask why TL kept all this from me, but I knew the answer. It wasn't the right time to tell you, he'd say.

He propped his elbows on the chair's arms. "Your parents died in a plane crash."

I nodded and looked down, a wave of sadness passing over me at the memory of the crash.

TL linked his fingers across his stomach and took a breath. "But that crash wasn't an accident."

Slowly, I looked at him. "Wh-what do you mean?"

He leveled serious eyes on me. "Your parents were murdered."

What? My whole body went numb. My mind blanked. The faint sound of the air-conditioning muted to a faraway hum. I couldn't move, talk, blink. I felt paralyzed. No thoughts formed in my brain.

Only the word *murdered* echoed through my mind.

Faintly, I registered the spike in my body temperature and then the immediate chill.

TL's cell phone buzzed, and I blinked.

He checked the display. "I'm sorry. This is the head of the IPNC. I have to take this."

I felt myself nod, slowly, unconsciously.

Murdered.

David took my hand. "Come on."

I blindly followed him out of the conference room, shuffling behind him, letting him lead the way.

Murdered.

We walked around the underground, high-tech workroom and came to a stop at the elevator. David punched in his personal code and then placed his hand on the fingerprint identification panel. The elevator slid open and he led me inside.

Murdered.

I swallowed and shook my head, trying to clear the fog.

The elevator door slid closed.

David took my left hand and rubbed it between both of his. "You're freezing." He took my right hand and did the same.

As he continued rubbing my hands, I slowly regained my equilibrium. "Murdered?" I finally spoke.

He pulled me to him. "I'm so sorry. I had no idea."

I wrapped my arms around his waist and held on tight. Burying my face in his neck, I breathed deeply his wonderful, comforting scent.

We stayed in that position for what seemed like forever as David stroked his hand over my back. I replayed TL's words over and over and over again. I tried to connect with how I felt about this new information, but I couldn't quite register it all yet.

My parents had been dead a long time. I'd already dealt with that loss. But murdered? I needed to know more. How? Why?

I needed my computer.

Kissing my head, David pulled away. He punched his code on the elevator panel, and it began its ascent.

Linking fingers with me, he stared at my face, his gaze casually roaming over my features.

Usually, I got nervous when he did this, but right now, all I could think of was, "What do you see when you look at me that closely?" I hadn't meant actually to voice the question out loud.

But I had, and now it hung in the air between us.

The elevator stopped four floors up at the ranch level. Neither of us moved to punch in our code that would open the door.

With his brows drawn slightly together, he continued staring at me. And the more he stared, the more I wished I could take the question back.

He was probably trying to come up with a nice way of saying he saw the biggest, most uncoordinated geek in the world when he looked at me.

"Never mind," I mumbled, reaching for the control panel.

David sighed. "Well, I was going to ask you to go to dinner. But if I know you, you're anxious to get on your computer and research your parents."

One hour ago I would've leapt at the offer. *Our* first date. *My* first date ever. But there was no way I'd have fun. I'd be preoccupied the whole night with my parents. "Let me figure all this out. And then yes, *yes,* I want to go to dinner with you."

Leaning in, he kissed me softly on the lips. "All right, I'll hold you to it." He punched in his code and stepped off the elevator into the hallway of the ranch house, leaving his cologne lingering behind. Before the door closed, he turned and said, "If you want to talk after your research, I'll be in my room."

"Thanks," I said.

He turned again and walked away, and I stood there a minute, not even realizing that I came upstairs for no reason. Shaking my head to clear my brain, I pressed my code and the elevator descended back to Subfloor Four. Quickly, I made my way around the workroom with a wave to Adam, David's roommate, who sat at one of the black desks typing on a computer.

I walked back into the conference room, expecting to see TL and wanting to talk to him to find out more, but found Jonathan, our PT instructor, instead.

"Hi."

He glanced up, and his bald head picked up the gleam of the overhead lights. "Hey back to you," he rasped. Jonathan had a perpetual smoker's voice even though he didn't smoke.

"Seen TL?"

Jonathan readjusted his eye patch. "He's been called to Washington. He'll be back late tomorrow." He opened a folder on the table and pulled out a picture. "He said to give you this."

The picture of David and me. I took it from Jonathan. "Thanks."

I left the conference room and walked back around the workroom and down the hallway to the computer lab. I punched in my personal code and stepped inside the warm, coffee-scented room.

Chapling, my mentor, sat hunched over his station with an oversize coffee mug beside the mouse. His red-haired head bobbed as his stubby fingers raced over the keys. He didn't acknowledge me, and I didn't expect him to. Like me, he was lost in his own world pretty much most of the time.

I rolled out my chair and took a seat. I propped up the picture of David and me on the keyboard and got down to work researching my parents' plane crash.

***

For two solid days, I hid out in the computer lab, investigating my parents' deaths, comparing all the newspaper articles to the TV and radio manuscripts. All the reporters said the same thing:

Our plane went down over Lake Michigan because of air in the fuel line. Out of one hundred and twenty passengers on board, only thirty-one survived. All bodies had surfaced but my parents.

We'd been on our way to Canada for a family vacation.

Some vacation.

Not one reporter mentioned anything about it not being an accident. No one thought it was strange my parents were the only bodies that did not surface.

So I moved on to investigative documents from local and state offices. Take out all the technical jargon and their reports mirrored the media's. The crash was an accident.

I went to the national level next, the IPNC, and came up against a firewall. I could've hacked through it within seconds, but chose to follow proper procedure instead—permission and a password from TL.

I knocked on TL's office door.

"Enter."

Turning the knob, I stepped inside. From behind his desk, TL glanced up and then went back to typing on his computer.

"Sir, I'd like you to give me access to the IPNC files regarding my parents' death."

He stopped typing, sat back in his chair, and brought his gaze up to meet mine.

Pulling my shoulders back, I straightened my posture. Not only did it make me feel confident, it showed my seriousness.

"When was the last time you ate?" he responded instead of addressing my request.

I thought for a second. "David brought me a sandwich at one o'clock this afternoon."

TL glanced at his watch. "It's twenty-two hundred hours right now. You haven't eaten in nine. Looking at your bloodshot eyes and the dark circles beneath them, I'd say you haven't slept much either. And I won't mention the fact that you've skipped out on every single meal, chore, training session, and your university studies."

I just looked at him. I didn't need a lecture right now.

"What exactly are you looking for?" he asked.

Although I hadn't told him what I'd been researching over the past couple days, I knew he knew.

TL knew everything.

"Answers. Discrepancies. New knowledge. Old knowledge. An understanding of what exactly happened." I had been six when that plane crashed. Until this week I'd never bothered reading the reports.

The social workers, cops, and psychologists had explained to me what had happened. I'd simply accepted it, never questioned it. Frankly, I hadn't wanted any reminders of that day.

TL pointed to the metal chair in front of his desk. "Sit."

He hadn't agreed to my request about the file access, but I closed his door and took a seat anyway. I'd take what I could get. "How do you know my parents were murdered?"

"The IPNC found your dad's body."

I sat very still, absorbing what he said. "What do you mean you 'found my dad's body'? All the reports say neither one of my parents surfaced."

"They didn't. The IPNC took your dad." He paused. "But we couldn't find your mom."

I sighed, exhausted, confused, and rubbed my dry eyes. "Will you please just explain to me what's going on? I'm too tired to figure it out."

After a long pause, he shifted in his seat. "For almost a decade, your parents followed a chemical smuggling ring. The people involved would import illegal substances into the States and resell them to overseas terrorists for manufacturing bombs."

In the time I'd been with the Specialists, I'd learned how horrible people could be, and how some would do anything for the right price. I experienced a quick flash of pride that I was a member of an organization that fought those people, the bad guys.

"The leader of this chemical ring," TL continued, "was, and still is, Eduardo Villanueva. Your father infiltrated the ring and became a member of Eduardo's team. He lived and worked with Eduardo for two years, secretly feeding information back to your mother. Eduardo wasn't just involved in the bomb business. His money filtered into all kinds of other things: drugs, guns, prostitution, gambling, murder."

I leaned forward. "So what happened?"

"Someone on the inside—we're not sure who and how—discovered your father's true identity. They found out about your mother, too."

My stomach clenched.

"Eduardo put a price tag on both their heads. Immediately following, your father and mother resigned from the IPNC and ran. They picked you up, got new identities, and moved to a small town in Iowa. They lived there for two years without a single problem."

My heart picked up pace.

"Then the IPNC intercepted a message that Eduardo knew where your parents were. We notified them immediately, and they hopped on a plane to Canada. There was a contact there waiting for the three of you with yet another set of new identities."

"I thought we were going on vacation," I mumbled.

TL scooted forward in his chair. "Eduardo rigged that plane to go down. He had divers ready. He wanted to make sure your parents died."

TL's expression softened. "The IPNC responded to the crash before local and state authorities. When we pulled your dad's body from the water, he had been shot once in the head."

I flinched, not expecting those words.

"We couldn't find your mother. We don't know if Eduardo took her body, or if it floated away with the current. But the IPNC couldn't take the chance that the authorities would discover your dad's body and the bullet hole. Then the media would've known he'd been murdered, and that would've started a domino effect the IPNC couldn't risk. So he was cremated, and, officially, your parents died in a plane crash, their bodies were never found, and they left one surviving daughter, Kelly."

Kelly. It seemed like forever since I'd heard my real name. "And Eduardo Villanueva?"

"Still being pursued by the IPNC. Every time they think they have him, he outsmarts them. He manages to slip through their fingers every time."

I sat for a good solid minute, digesting everything. "No one ever found my mom's body? So . . . she might still be alive?"

"GiGi," TL sighed. "Eduardo wanted her dead. She's dead. You need to accept that."

But if no one ever found her body . . . bull crap, I didn't need to accept anything. "Why didn't you tell me all this two days ago when you first showed me that picture?"

"I wanted to see what you'd do with the information you had. Yet another one of the many tests you will go through in your training." He paused. "Plus, knowing your personality, I knew you'd do your own research and try to find out the answers yourself."

Sometimes I didn't understand TL's reasoning. Why put me through all this? For two days I'd been down in my lab, barely eating and sleeping. All for what took him ten minutes to tell me. I closed my eyes, irritated, aggravated, and raw with the truth about my parents. My dad had been *murdered.* My mom might, *might,* still be alive.

I opened my eyes, purposefully showing him all the frustration weighing me down. "Would you have told me this two days ago if I'd asked?"

"No."

My frustration morphed into anger, and I snapped. "I don't understand you. I know you have a reason behind everything you do. And I'm sure in this instance it was something about me maturing or gaining independence or whatever. But these are my parents, and you had no right to keep that information from me."

Without giving him a chance to respond, I shot to my feet, pumped with adrenaline. "You said Eduardo Villanueva is still out there, still at large. Well, I want to go after him." I jabbed my finger in TL's direction. "And since I can't do it alone, you're going to have to help me."

‹TWO›

TL maintained a dead-pan expression as I stood defiantly in front of him, staring unblinking into his icy eyes.

Silence stretched between us.

Long seconds ticked by, and my heartbeat pulsed in my neck, my veins, my temple. In the quiet room I heard only its thumping and my raspy, quick breaths.

I didn't resist the anger and sadness fueling me. I allowed it in. It felt *good*.

"I want to go after Eduardo Villanueva," I repeated. "And I want you to help me."

"I realize you're upset, but make no mistake, I give the commands around here. Not you."

His intimidating comment made my jaw tighten.

"I suggest," he continued in a measured tone, "that you leave my office to cool down and collect your thoughts before you say something you're going to regret."

"How do you expect me to sit back and ignore the fact my parents' murderer is still out there. What if it were Nalani?" I blurted out. "What if someone murdered your wife? You wouldn't stand by and calmly accept it. You'd go after them."

Every muscle in TL's face hardened. Slowly, he got to his feet. No one else but David knew TL and Nalani, our pre-op agent, were married. And until this second, TL hadn't known that I knew.

Not giving him a chance to answer, I railroaded on. "You have no hold on me. Remember, I'm the only Specialist who didn't do anything illegal on my own. You tricked me into coming here."

Somewhere in the back of my mind, I knew I was taking things too far. But I couldn't seem to stop myself. "I can walk out right now, and you can't stop me."

"So walk out then."

Suddenly, my boiling anger faded to a concentrated focus. He'd once given me an ultimatum; now it was my turn. I knew exactly what I wanted to do, without a doubt in my mind. "You have until tomorrow morning. If you're not prepared to help me find my parents' murderer, then I'm leaving."

I quickly turned and opened his door.

"Don't drop a threat," he said, his voice steady and stern, "unless you're ready to go through with it."

I turned around and looked him in the eye. "Oh, I'm ready. More ready than I've ever been in my life." And I was. I'd never been more sure of anything.

I walked out, clicked his door closed, and, with measured steps, made my way down the long hallway to my bedroom. The usual scene greeted me when I walked in.

Mystic sat cross-legged on the floor studying some sort of Tarot cards.

On her bed, Bruiser and Parrot faced each other, engaged in a rip-roaring game of thumb wrestling.

Chomping her gum, Beaker lay stretched out on the carpet, scribbling in her chemistry notebook. I wondered, not for the first time, what mad-scientist formulas she had in there.

Cat, the newest addition to our team, and Wirenut reclined across Cat's bed, sharing a set of earphones and a bag of cashews.

I experienced a quick pang of loss. Come tomorrow morning, I might never see any of them again.

I'd put it all—my whole new life—on the line.

Bruiser glanced up and grinned. "Yo! Where you been? I've barely seen you in the past two days."

Giving her a small smile I really didn't feel, I shuffled over to my bed and sat down. My tennis shoe bumped my suitcase underneath. The same dinged-up blue suitcase that had carted my belongings around the last ten years of my life.

I'd been so excited finally to unpack it, so thrilled to settle permanently into a place I could call home.

In a few hours I might be repacking the same suitcase I swore I'd never use again.

My gaze fell on the lollipop bouquet David had given me when I returned from my mission with Wirenut. With a sigh, I chose a coffee-flavored one and slipped it in my mouth.

Wirenut took his earphone out. "What's going on? You don't look right."

With that question, everyone stopped what they were doing and focused on me.

I took a second to meet each of their curious gazes.

Calm, peaceful Mystic—the clairvoyant. With his thick neck, huge body, and short blond hair, he always made me think of a football player, not an in-touch-with-the-universe kind of guy.

Red-haired, freckled Bruiser. One hundred pounds of hyper-activity. Always sporting an innocent dimpled grin and tight, customized T-shirt. Today her shirt read, HEY! YOU GOT A PROBLEM? No one would ever guess she was one of the world's best fighters.

Shy Parrot, with his dark, Native American features and sweet heart. For a guy so quiet, it amazed me he spoke sixteen languages.

Our electronics specialist, Wirenut. His trim goatee and tattoos made him look like bad news. His silly humor said he was anything but.

Beside him lay his girlfriend, the beautiful, Mediterranean Katarina. Recently code-named Cat—our cat burglar.

And Beaker, the Goth chemist, always with different-colored hair— black-and-white-striped this week. She wore a perpetual smirk and never seemed to be in a good mood. And she *always* chewed gum ferociously, like if she didn't, she'd explode or something.

"Well?" prompted Wirenut.

Screw keeping everything a secret. I was tired of secrets. I took the lollipop out of my mouth, took a deep breath, and told them everything. About my parents. About Eduardo Villanueva. And that I'd given TL an ultimatum—help me go after my parents' killer or I'd leave the Specialists.

No one uttered a sound when I finished. Mystic, Parrot, and Beaker just stared at me while the others exchanged silent glances.

From their shell-shocked expressions, no one could really believe what I'd just told them.

More time went by, and still no one said anything. Only the faint sound of Wirenut and Cat's iPod filtered through the air.

Finally, Bruiser cleared her throat. "What can we do to make sure you stay?" Her soft tone, so unlike her, made tears press against my eyes.

"Nothing." I swallowed. "TL knows where I stand."

***

Bzzzbzzzbzzz.

My cell went off. I reached over to my dresser, picked it up, and checked the display: *** It was TL's stat code.

Wide awake, I quickly swung my legs over the side of my bed and tiptoed into the bathroom. Since it was five in the morning, Cat, Bruiser, and Beaker still slept.

I washed my face, swished mouthwash around in my mouth, and then tiptoed back across the girls' room. I tugged on jeans and a T-shirt and quietly made my way out.

The long, dark hallway seemed to stretch to eternity as I strode down it toward TL's room. My stomach flip-flopped in anticipation.

Coming to a stop at his door, I closed my eyes and took a couple of deep, fortifying breaths.

This was it. In a couple of minutes, I'd find out if I was staying or leaving. I'd gone over our conversation an endless number of times last night. I felt no regrets for giving TL an ultimatum.

I'd had to do it.

I hoped he understood and didn't make me leave. I loved my new life and wanted more than anything to stay.

Opening my eyes, I tapped on TL's door.

"Enter."

I turned the knob and stepped inside. David sat in one of the metal chairs in front of the desk. What was he doing here?

He didn't look at me as I took the seat beside him. I sensed he was upset about something. He was probably mad I hadn't told him about the ultimatum. I would have, but I hadn't seen him since my conversation with TL.

Behind TL, his bedroom door sat propped open. His covers and pillows didn't appear disturbed.

TL picked up his mug with a tea bag dangling over the side. "I'm going to say this only once, and there will be no more discussion on the subject." He made eye contact with first me and then David. "My marriage to Nalani Kai is no one's business but mine. Neither of you will tell anyone she is my wife. As far as you're concerned, she's a field agent. Nothing more. Do we understand each other?"

"Yes, sir," David immediately answered.

"Yes, sir," I echoed.

It occurred to me then that David had probably gotten in big trouble for telling me about TL and Nalani's marriage.

I chanced a quick look at David, but he still didn't make eye contact with me, I owed him a huge apology.

"GiGi," TL continued, "you've turned into someone I wasn't expecting. I'm not disappointed. Surprised is a better way to describe what I'm feeling. You proved your psychological profile wrong in stepping beyond your comfort zone of reclusiveness, of living inside your brain, of not taking chances unless forced to. I thought one day you might. I'd *hoped* one day you would. I just wasn't expecting it to happen this soon."

I didn't know if I should take his words as complimentary or not, but I remained quiet and kept listening.

"As I mentioned last night, the IPNC has been after Eduardo Villanueva for years. He's managed to squirm his way out of being captured every single time we came close." TL rubbed his fingers over his shaved chin. "As you two already know, the Specialists are now private. We're no longer run by the government, by the IPNC. Legally, we can't go after Eduardo Villanueva unless the IPNC hires us."

TL dunked his tea bag a few times. "I've spent most of the night on the phone with senior IPNC officials. They've agreed to give us the case."

My heart skipped a beat in anticipation. I hoped this conversation was leading to where I thought it was.

TL sat back in his office chair. "They've given us sixty days to find, apprehend, and bring down Eduardo Villanueva." TL picked up a folder and tossed it in my direction. It landed in front of me at the edge of the desk. "Since you're so interested in going after Eduardo, I'm giving you the case. You're in charge. You will be putting together the mission."

"E-excuse me?" He was kidding, right? I didn't know how to put together a mission.

TL's brows lifted. "You heard me. You want to bring down your parents' killer?" He looked at the folder. "There it is. It's all yours. It's this way or no way. This is a challenge, GiGi. It's part of your training. You've boldly stepped beyond yourself and requested my help. Well, I'm helping you by getting the case. Now let's see how you continue to handle that boldness and plan the mission."

I stared at the folder, itching to peek inside. This was what I'd wanted, to go after my parents' killer. But . . . I didn't know how to be in charge.

TL took a long, leisurely sip of his tea. "There are a couple of conditions."

"Conditions?" Why did there always have to be something else?

He put his mug down. "David will assist you in designing and planning the mission." TL looked at David. "Whatever you come up with, make sure you set yourself up as backup from a separate location."

David nodded. "Yes, sir."

I released an inaudible, relieved breath. Good, David was going.

"I will need to see and approve all plans, the budget, and the equipment lists."

I nodded my head.

"You will be monitored every step of the way." TL tapped his eye. "Never forget, I'll be watching you. Even when you don't think I'll be watching, I *will* be watching."

I nodded again. I didn't expect any less.

"And," TL continued, "Beaker and I will travel with you."

"Beaker?"

TL nodded once. "Beaker. She will be your partner on this mission."

Groooan. Anybody but her. She *hated* me. For that matter, I didn't much like her either.

"Make your decision now. Yes or no. What's it going to be? It's this way or no way."

Without hesitation, I slipped the folder from his desk. "Yes."

***

Minutes later, David and I stood in the hallway at the mountainous mural. He placed his hand on the globe light fixture. A hidden laser housed within scanned his prints, and the mural slid aside to reveal the ranch's secret elevator.

We stepped inside, David punched in his personal code, and the car descended.

Without looking at me, he pulled two energy bars from his back jeans pocket and handed one to me. "Breakfast." Still not making eye contact, he opened his energy bar and took a bite.

I studied his bent head as he chewed, swallowed, and took another bite. He was really upset. Either that or his flip-flops must be real interesting with the way he was staring at them.

"David?"

He didn't look up.

I sighed. It'd been so long since this kind of friction stood between us. It felt awful. And I was the reason why.

The elevator stopped on Sub Four. David reached for the control panel.

"Wait." If I didn't say something now, we wouldn't have privacy later. "I know you're upset."

He took his hand away from the control panel but still didn't make eye contact.

"I'm sorry. I'm really sorry that I told TL I knew about Nalani. You trusted me with that information, and I screwed up. I never intended on saying anything, but I was so mad that it came out before I had time to stop it."

David shrugged a shoulder, still studying his flip-flops. "My fault. I should've known better than to tell you. To tell anybody."

That made it worse. In other words, David couldn't trust me.

But . . . how fair was that? Everyone made mistakes. This one shouldn't mean David suddenly couldn't confide in me.

I reached out and took his hand, hoping he wouldn't pull away.

He didn't, thank God.

"I *am* really sorry. Please know you can trust me with anything. I made a mistake and it won't make it again. I promise." I squeezed David's hand. "Was TL really mad at you?"

"He wasn't happy."

Translation: Yes, TL's mad.

David respected and admired TL. Everyone did. But David had lived here for years and had known TL longer than anybody. They had a working relationship, sure, but their friendship was rooted in years of mutual loyalty.

And my uncharacteristically big mouth had come between them. Of all the times for me to get lippy, I had to do it with two people I cared for a lot.

Finally, David brought his eyes up to mine. I saw hurt in their dark depths. "Why didn't you tell me you'd threatened to leave?"

My heart paused. While I sensed he was upset about this when he didn't look at me in TL's office, I was hoping it was just my imagination. "I didn't tell anyone." I shook my head. "Well, I mean, I told my roommates and the guys last night after my meeting with TL."

"But why didn't you tell *me?*"

"B-because . . . because you weren't in our bedroom, I guess. Everyone else was, so I told them. If you would've been there, I would've told you, too." Even to my own ears, my reasoning sounded weak. I should've told David first.

He let go of my hand, and I immediately missed the warm contact. "Reverse the situation, GiGi. What if I'd threatened to leave? Wouldn't you be upset to find out through someone else?"

My shoulders drooped. "Yes." He had a point. I'd feel awful if someone else told me David was leaving. It'd make me feel like he didn't return the feelings I had for him, that he thought our relationship insignificant.

"How do you think I felt when TL told me? I didn't know what to say. I was shocked."

"I'm sorry."

David ran his fingers through his hair. "Do you understand that if any one of us leaves, we're not allowed to have contact with anyone here? If you would've left, none of us would've seen you or spoken to you again. *Ever.*"

I swallowed. "I didn't know. I'm sorry." I'd never thought to ask about such things. I'd never planned on leaving.

He shook his head. "Why didn't you come to me? We could've figured out a game plan. We could've sat down and talked things through. Come up with something other than you leaving. We could've gone to TL professionally. You're lucky he didn't kick you out last night."

"I'm sorry. I was so tired and frustrated and . . . sad." *God,* what had I done?

David punched in his personal code on the elevator panel. "That's no excuse for making rash decisions. If you've learned anything in the Specialists, it should've been that."

I threw my hands up. "I'm sorry again." What else could I say? I'd made mistakes, but everything turned out all right. I got to stay here at the ranch, and we were going after Eduardo Villanueva.

He stepped off the elevator. "Stop apologizing. It's getting on my nerves."

My jaw dropped.

David took off down the hall.

"Everyone makes mistakes," I called to his back. "You're not perfect either. I can't believe you're this mad at me."

He whipped around. "Yeah, I'm mad. I spent months telling myself I liked you only as a friend. And when I finally admit there's something more, you almost up and walk away without any thought to it."

"But I didn't walk away. I'm still here." *He'd spent months?*

"You know what I mean." He turned and stalked off down the hall again.

"David." I jogged to catch up. "This isn't about you. It's about my parents. It's about finding their killer." If anybody understood that, it should be him. It wasn't too long ago we were after his father's kidnappers.

"I know. Believe me, I know." He stopped at the computer lab door. "Listen, I need time to think. I need time to cool off. And you've got a lot to deal with. Let's just focus on the mission."

‹THREE›

I preceded David into the computer lab with a mix of emotions swirling in my heart. I'd hurt and disappointed him with the decisions I'd made. And even with that, he still admitted he liked me. He'd told me that before, but this time it seemed to come from his soul.

I just hoped things could go back to the way they'd been.

The computer lab door suctioned closed behind us, making a cool swooshing noise straight out of a sci-fi movie.

David headed to the coffeemaker in the far corner. In the sink beside it, he poured out Chapling's thick muck, cleaned the pot, replaced the filter, and started a fresh pot.

I crossed the tile floor to the four computer stations that formed a square. One was mine, one was Chapling's, and two sat vacant. I sat down at my station, taking in my setup. Wide, flat screen. Wireless keyboard and mouse. Made to order to my specifications, too good to be true. I loved my computer.

I placed the case file TL had given me next to the keyboard and touched the mouse. A dancing cartoon screen saver of a redheaded little person—courtesy of Chapling—flicked off. I keyed in my password.

HELLO, GIGI, Daisy, the ranch's system, greeted me.

"Hi, Daisy," I greeted her back.

"Shhh," David hushed me, and I glanced over at him.

Chapling, he mouthed, pointing behind the standing metal cabinets that bordered the right side of the lab.

Pushing back from my computer, I shuffled over and peeked around the end of the cabinets. Chapling lay on the floor in the corner, curled up in a chubby little ball. His tools and the guts of a computer were scattered all around him.

He inhaled a soft snore, and I smiled. I'd never seen him sleep before. Actually, I'd never seen him so quiet and still. Guess the caffeine finally drained out of his system.

David waved me over to the computer stations and, rolling out a chair, sat down at a vacant station next to mine. "Let's be as quiet as possible," he whispered, "so we don't wake him."

Nodding, I sat down behind my computer.

David pointed to the energy bar I'd shoved down my front jeans pocket. "Eat that, please, before you forget and hours go by and you still have nothing in your system."

"Sorry," I mumbled, taking out the energy bar. For some reason, eating was one of those things I rarely remembered to do. If it weren't for David and my friends, I'd probably eat once a day, if that.

I opened the package and took a nibble.

David pivoted his black leather chair toward me. "Before we get started on the mission planning, I need you to listen closely to what I'm about to tell you."

Swallowing my bite, I pulled my notepad from my back pocket and slipped the miniature pencil from the spiral. "Okay, shoot."

He gave the notepad a quick look.

I frowned. "What?"

David's lips twitched. "Nothing."

I narrowed my eyes. He better not have anything to say about my dorky notepad.

"Okay." David rolled his chair a little closer. "This is one of the best, yet most difficult things TL has ever taught me."

I nodded, focusing.

"You have to remove yourself emotionally from a mission. Personal feelings muddle rational thinking and effective decision making. Remember the Ushbanian mission? My father was being held hostage. Talk about emotional disruption." David tapped his head. "Find a place in here to keep your emotions separate. Otherwise, they'll mix and mingle and affect rational decisions."

I remembered the Ushbania mission. "When TL first presented the mission to us, you thought it was best you didn't go." That must have been so hard for David, knowing his dad was being held hostage.

323

David nodded. "That's right. When all I really wanted to do was storm over there and kick some butt."

And to think he'd been in such control. Calm. Focused. "You did great."

He smiled a little. "Thanks. Which brings us to you. *Your* parents are involved this time around. As hard as it is, you have to emotionally separate yourself. Look at the mission objectively, as though it's someone else's family, not yours."

I blew out a breath. "That's going to be *extremely* difficult."

"Yes, it is. But you can do it. You'll *have* to do it in order for the mission to succeed." He rolled his chair out and stood. "Coffee's done brewing." He pointed to my energy bar. "And you need to finish that."

While he poured the coffee, I quickly ate the rest of my energy bar. As I chewed, I slowly clicked my brain into mission mode, compartmentalizing my personal emotions away from logic, just as David had suggested. It didn't work so well, though. I couldn't get my mom's smile out of the forefront of my mind.

He placed a mug beside my notepad. I took a sip. Mmm, exactly the way I liked it. Lots of sugar and no cream.

It occurred to me then that I'd never told David how I liked my coffee. He must have watched me make a cup and remembered.

He put down his mug and took his seat. "First thing we have to do is scan through Eduardo Villanueva's history and then find out where he'll be next. Once we find out where he's going to be, we'll study the area and build our cover around that."

David took the folder from beside my keyboard. "Let's review the case file and familiarize ourselves with Eduardo and his affairs."

I watched as he scanned a page, then flipped it and perused another. "Looks like he was born into the business. His father and grandfather had their fingers in all sorts of things." David turned another page. "Eduardo's brothers, sons, and nephews are all involved. One branch of the family tree handles drugs, another guns, and our guy, of course, smuggles chemicals." He shook his head. "One big, dysfunctional, happy family."

"What about the women?"

David quickly read, shuffling through papers. "The women have the children and stay home, supporting their wealthy crime husbands. The entire family lives in South America."

"Interesting," I commented.

"I'm going to keep browsing through this. You see what you can find out about his next operation."

With a nod, I took a long, sugary sip of my coffee. Staring at the blinking cursor on my black screen, I let my brain click through its processes and organize a plan to trail Eduardo's transactions, which would lead me to his network and personal computer. From there I'd hack and be in.

I picked my glasses up off the table and slipped them on. I placed my fingers on the keys, and they suddenly flew. I cross-connected networks to cover my tracks. I wove in one grid and out the next, then leap-frogged through satellites. I ran an interpretation program to translate Spanish to English and located Eduardo's last bank transaction three days ago in Venezuela. I created an algorithm to sneak in.

A few more clicks and . . .

ACCESS DENIED.

Hmmm . . . *click, click, click* . . .

ACCESS DENIED.

Huh . . . *click, click, click* . . .

ACCESS DENIED.

Okay, think, GiGi. What's the most important thing to Eduardo? Chemicals? "Do you have a list of the chemicals he's smuggled in?"

David flipped some pages in the folder and pulled out one. He handed it to me. "Two sided."

I ran my gaze down the three columns of substances and flipped it over to see just as many. Randomly, I picked out a dozen and typed them in.

ACCESS DENIED. ACCESS DENIED. ACCESS DENIED.

On and on I typed chemicals as passwords. And one by one my access was denied.

With a sigh, I sat back and thought from a different angle. The most important thing to Eduardo obviously wasn't chemicals. David told me Eduardo has a big family and that they live in South America.

I did a quick search on South American countries and cities and tried a few of those.

ACCESS DENIED.

Okay, let's try family. "Give me the birthdates of Eduardo's children."

David flipped a paper, perused. "Six, seventeen, sixty-eight. Eight, five, seventy-one. And eleven, thirty, seventy-three."

I keyed them youngest to oldest first.

ACCESS DENIED.

Then oldest to youngest. ACCESS GRANTED. "Finally, I'm in." Stupid me. I should have tried family first. Most passwords were derived from relatives' names and dates. You'd think the bad guys would know this and choose something else.

His transactions scrolled across my screen. It came to a stop, and my gaze fell on the last figure. "H-holy cow."

David glanced up from the case file. "What?"

I blinked. "Whatever chemicals he sold in Venezuela made him seven million two hundred thousand dollars. And change." I shook my head. *Unbelievable.*

He tapped the open folder. "According to this, Eduardo lives in Potasi, Colombia. The only computers inside his mansion belong to his grandkids. All communication from him happens via remote access."

"I figured as much." I clicked some keys. "So let's see if we can find that computer of his."

Click, click, click . . .

ACCESS DENIED.

Staying with the family theme . . . "Give me his grandchildren's names."

David shuffled through the papers. "Wafiya, Arturo, Unice, Ciceron, Sophronia, Emilio, Quetcy, Caspar, Odette, Ivan, Kemen, Moises."

On my notepad, I jotted down all the names. Twelve in all. Jeez that's a lot of grandkids. "Now ages."

David read those off, too, while I scribbled.

On the Venezuelan transaction, he arranged his kids from oldest to youngest using their birthdates. So I needed to try the opposite order with his grandkids, using their names.

But passwords can't be more than twenty-one characters long. If he used the first letter of each of their names arranged youngest to oldest . . . quickly, I typed the letters, my blood zinging with the awesome energy that came with figuring out a puzzle.

Bingo. "Got it."

David glanced up. "You're kidding. It's been only," he checked his watch, "seventeen minutes and fourteen seconds since we sat down. I haven't even drunk half of my coffee. And I've thoroughly read through only page five in the case file."

I shrugged. Seemed like it'd been a lot longer. "I would've been quicker if I'd thought of the family angle first."

David smiled and shook his head.

Click, click, click . . . "I'm copying his hard drive." I watched the screen flick. "It's encrypted. I'll work on that in a minute."

David came to stand behind me. "Are we talking everything? As in decades ago?"

I pushed up my glasses, ignoring his cologne drifting around me. "It appears so." My screen continued scrolling. "I'll know for sure when I run this through some of Chapling's decryption software."

As my computer continued copying, I started processing batches of the data through various decryption programs. I tried a standard alpha-numerical package first, then a beta platform. I ran it through a transcendental process, and slowly the encrypted data became readable.

"Here we go." Suddenly, a thought hit me. "Wait. If this is everything, then we have him. We have evidence. He can be arrested as soon as right now."

The screen stopped scrolling. David reached to my right, and, using my mouse, he clicked through the decrypted files, opening random ones and quickly scanning them. "What we have, essentially, is a journal. Yes, it chronicles everything he's had his fingers in, but TL will tell you Eduardo has to be caught in the act."

David let go of my mouse. "So we need to figure out where he's going to be next."

While I continued to click away with the files, weaving through Eduardo's hard drive, David resumed his seat. He flipped a page in the case file and continued studying.

"Barracuda Key," I announced, looking at a satellite map of Florida that popped up on the screen. "It's one of many tiny islands trailing off the southern tip of Florida."

David rolled his eyes up from the file. "Do you realize I've read exactly one and a half paragraphs?"

I shrugged innocently. "Do you want me to work slower?"

He sighed through a smile. "No, of course not. Sometimes I forget what a genius you are." He closed the file. "Barracuda Key?"

I nodded.

"What's going on in Barracuda Key?"

I started searching his journal again. "Let me see"—*click, click, click*— "Huh"—*click, click, click*—"Oh my God"—*click, click, click* . . .

David rolled his chair over. "What?"

"He's not just smuggling in chemicals." A few more clicks. "According to this, people are actually going to Barracuda Key to get these chemicals and make their own bombs on site. Then they'll be shipped out from there." I rubbed a tight muscle in my neck. "So what's next?"

"Find out when he's going to be in Barracuda Key."

Click, click, click . . . "In four weeks."

"Where's he staying?"

"Give me a minute." I pulled up all the hotels in Barracuda Key and hacked into their systems, cross-referencing phrases in Eduardo's journal. "From what I've been able to gather, the Hotel Marquess."

David rolled his chair closer to see my screen. "Now bring up every tourist function and event going on in Barracuda Key, Florida. Preferably at the same hotel. We have to find your cover. You can't just show up as a vacationer. You have to blend in with a group. We need to have a reason for you being there."

"Makes sense. Let's see . . ." I went to the tourist Web site for Barracuda Key island and began searching. "Boy Scout Jamboree?"

David shook his head. "Won't work with Beaker. It'd work if TL wanted one of the guys to go."

"Why *is* Beaker"—I tried not to cringe as I said her name—"going?"

"I thought that was pretty obvious with the chemicals involved." David's eyes crinkled. "My other guess is because you two don't like each other, and everyone knows it. This is TL's way of making you two get along."

"Beaker doesn't like anyone," I defended myself. "It's not about me not liking her. I like her all right." Who was I kidding?

"Mmm-hmm. Right."

I narrowed my eyes.

"Back on track." David pointed to the screen. "What else?"

Click, click, click . . . "Elderly lawn bowling tournament?"

"No. Let me see." He took my mouse and scrolled through Barracuda Key's Web site and upcoming events.

"Heeeyyy," Chapling yawned, stumbling out from behind the metal cabinets.

I smiled, seeing his red, Brillo pad hair lying in clumps, some flat to his head, others sticking straight out. "Morning, Sleeping Beauty."

He yawned again on a stretch, reaching his stubby arms toward the ceiling. His T-shirt rode up over his pale, pudgy stomach. He blinked a few

328

times and yawned once more. "One of you two kids made coffee." He inhaled loudly. "I smell it."

While David continued clicking through the Web site, Chapling poured a cup and wandered over.

He took a sip. "Little weak."

I gave him a sympathetic look. "David made it."

"Ah, that explains it."

David shot him a playful glare.

Chapling took another sip. "TL says we'll be hacking into Eduardo Villanueva's computer today."

"I already did."

He rubbed his bloodshot eyes. "Let me get a little more java in me and we'll—Wait . . . what'd you say?"

I lifted my brows. "Already did it."

He sighed. "Why do I come to work anymore?"

I didn't bother reminding him he never left work.

He circled around me and climbed up onto his chair. "Smartgirlsmartgirl. Course, with a little bit of time," Chapling muttered, "I would've figured out how to hack in, too."

"Of course," I agreed. Chapling was, hands down, the most intelligent person I knew. I'd learned a lot from him.

"Got it." David stood up. He pointed to my computer. "I found yours and Beaker's cover."

I narrowed in on the screen, and my eyes widened. "Uh-uh. Forget it. There's no *way* I'm doing that. There's no way *Beaker* would do that. You've got to be crazy. No." I shook my head. "No. No. No. No. No."

<FOUR>

After an hour of David's trying to convince me this cover would work, reluctantly—let me repeat that—reluctantly, I went with his idea. But I was seriously dreading presenting it to Beaker tomorrow morning.

Putting that aside, David and I spent the rest of the day designing the Barracuda Key mission. He taught me how to view everything omnisciently and then step into the mission and go through the different scenarios we might encounter.

The entire process was incredibly involved, detailed, and organized. It amazed me that TL went through this every single time. But that was his job as the strategist, in charge of planning and implementing the missions, as well as keeping all of us Specialists in line. A lot of pressure came with designing a mission. If something went wrong, then all the blame fell on the strategist's shoulders. In this case, that would be me.

Frankly, the whole process wore me out. And made me admire TL even more.

It was late when we finally finished putting together the mission. Then I practiced presenting it over and over again while David watched and gave input.

Now it was early morning, and here I sat in the conference room. David was across from me, calmly waiting on TL's arrival.

Beside me, Beaker slumped in her chair, chomping on yet another piece of gum. "Don't know why you can't just tell me why I'm here."

I studied her ever-present sour profile while she scowled at the wall behind David. She was going to be *so* PO'ed when she found out our cover.

"What are you"—*chew, snap, chew*—"staring at?"

How beautiful you are, I wanted to snide, but instead asked, "Why do you chew so much gum? It's not good for your jaws, you know."

She slid me a sideways smirk. "Anything else, O Gifted One?"

My nostrils flared. I couldn't recall ever having that reaction to anyone before. Then again, Beaker brought out the worst in me.

The door opened, and we turned to see TL step in.

He nodded. "Good morning. Glad to see everyone's prompt." He took his seat at the head of the table and placed a small, thin box in front of him.

I recognized it. It held the monitoring patches we were each given months ago when we first arrived. The patches allowed TL to track us, to know where we were at all times, and to monitor our conversations. But when he felt confident we'd settled into our new lives, he took them away.

He'd taken mine right before the Ushbanian mission, and he'd taken Wirenut's before Rissala. Which meant TL was probably about to take Beaker's.

"Beaker, you have proved adept at your cover. You've learned how to go throughout your day-to-day activities smoothly, naturally, and without a second thought. You've seamlessly merged into this new world."

TL had said the same thing to Wirenut and me, too.

"It's time for you to take off your patch." TL removed the lid and slid the box toward Beaker. "Place it in here, please."

For a few seconds, Beaker stared at TL and didn't move. Didn't even chomp her gum.

She moved her eyes off TL to me and then over to David. I'd never seen her so vulnerable, so full of disbelief, so . . . stunned. I had the unnerving urge to hug her or something.

Gradually, she resumed her gum chomping and pushed away from the table. She leaned over, pulled her baggy pant leg up, and, from the underside of her knee, peeled away the bandage looking device.

She dropped it in the box and slid it back toward TL.

He nodded. "Congratulations."

Beaker lips curved. "Thanks."

He got up and opened the door. "You three come with me." Filing out behind him, we followed TL around the glass-paneled, high-tech workroom and down the hall with all the locked doors.

331

I'd bet my next lollipop TL was about to show Beaker her personalized workroom. He'd given me access to the computer lab after taking my patch, and he'd given Wirenut access to the electronics warehouse after taking his.

If history repeated itself, Beaker was about to get the surprise of her life.

At the end of the long hall, we stopped at a steel door that had a large hole in the center.

TL turned to Beaker. "This is your room. You can come and go anytime you want, unless you're expected to be somewhere else. No one has access to this room but myself, you, Chapling, and David."

"Why Chapling?" I asked.

"Chapling has access to everything. He monitors the whole ranch." TL pointed to the hole. "Beaker, insert your hand as a fist. When you're inside, spread your fingers as wide as they'll go. You'll feel a flash of ice and then immediate warmth. It will not hurt. Make sure you *don't* flinch."

"Ice and then warmth? That's blumeth and parabendichlor." Beaker put her fist in the hole. "You're chemically reading all five of my prints."

One side of TL's mouth lifted. "Very good. As soon as you remove your hand, immediately step back from the door."

Beaker slid her hand free, took a quick step back, and the door dropped straight down into the floor.

I jerked. Sheesh, that was quick.

TL stepped through the opening, and we all followed. He showed Beaker a flat, silver disk on the wall next to the opening. "This operates the door from the inside." He pressed it, and the door whooshed back up, making my hair fly sideways.

Turning, I surveyed the room. Of course, I knew next to nothing about chemistry, but this looked pretty darn cool. And if Beaker's wide-eyed expression held any indication, she thought so, too.

As she began slowly wandering around the room, I took in the details.

Tall, see-through glass-front wood cabinets bordered the right side, with all sorts of jars, bottles, tubes, and flasks. It seemed like hundreds of them lined the cabinet shelves. A variety of substances filled them: liquids, powders, roots, stems, moss, granules . . . so many different colors and things it was impossible to take it all in.

Matching see-through cabinets bordered the left side of the lab, with dozens of different tools: burners, scales, thermometers, scissors, bowls . . . again, so much it was impossible to take it all in.

A closed metal cabinet labeled SAFETY GEAR sat along the back wall with a few sinks and even a shower beside it. I supposed a chemist would need a shower in case something went wrong with all the dangerous chemicals.

A contemporary stainless steel refrigerator occupied each corner of the room. Four long, black, granite-topped tables lined the center, with tall stools underneath. Equipment dotted the back two tables. I recognized the microscopes, but I was clueless about the rest.

I'd never seen anything like this room. The labs in high school and college certainly didn't compare.

Across the space, Beaker leaned over a machine with spindles. Slowly, she turned a knob, studying it.

"What do you think?" asked TL.

Beaker looked up. "Are you kidding me?" She grinned. Actually grinned. "This place rocks!"

We all laughed.

She pointed to the cabinet with all the liquids. "This is like something straight out of my dreams. A fantasy come true. This is unbelievable."

My mind jumped back to the mission I'd done with Wirenut and Beaker's involvement in it. "How did you help out Wirenut and me without this lab?"

Beaker didn't respond. I doubted she even heard me, too involved in exploring her new room. I'd been the same way when TL first showed me the computer lab.

"She didn't need all this," he answered for her. "She already had a lot of the knowledge. Plus her notes and books and, of course, the Internet." Crossing his arms, TL turned to me. "Do you know what makes Beaker such an extraordinary chemist?"

I glanced across the room to where she stood bent over a microscope. I didn't.

Sad to say, I didn't know anything about her. And I hadn't really had a desire to find out. I'd made no effort with her. Nor had she with me. From the first moment we met, we'd clashed, and it had never gotten any better.

"What makes Beaker so unique." TL continued, "are her methods. She can walk outside and gather grass, rocks, and a bird feather, break them down, and combine them in an infinite number of ways." TL pressed the silver disk on the wall, and the lab door whooshed down. "You're privileged to have such a talented young woman on your team. As she is to have you."

I trailed behind everyone as we exited the lab and made our way back to the conference room.

Mulling over everything TL had said about Beaker, I began to see another side to her. A side that didn't surprise me. Every one of us was gifted in our own special way. But I'd been so caught up in disliking her, I hadn't taken the time to comprehend fully her intelligence.

I glanced at her as we entered the conference room and wondered what her life had been like before the Specialists. What had happened to make her the person she'd become?

TL closed the conference room door, and we resumed our spots around the table. He looked at me expectantly, and David handed me the remote control. "All yours."

Taking the remote, I rolled my chair back and stood. Not a single nerve danced in my belly. Only confidence flowed through me. "I'll begin by recapping Eduardo Villanueva's case file."

I detailed every single thing about him, tracing his life from childhood to adulthood. From what school he went to, to the women he married, to his children and grandchildren. I described every man and woman he'd ever worked with. I defined every drug, gun, and crime deal he'd been involved with, and, of course, the chemical smuggling ring.

You name it, I gave the information.

The entire time I spoke, I used the remote control to flash pictures up on the flat screen. I showed images of where he lived, of his kids, of his business partners.

I displayed images of all the men, women, and children he'd murdered. As my parents' picture flashed onto the screen, I tried to keep my emotions in check, but took pause for a second to breathe. Just to breathe.

When I felt ready, I continued, and for thirty minutes I dumped even more information. When I finished, I paused. "Questions?"

Everyone shook their heads.

"This brings us to the here and now. Mr. Villanueva will be in Barracuda Key, Florida, in four weeks. According to intel, this will be his largest chemical shipment yet." I pointed my remote at the screen. "These are the chemicals that we know are coming in. There are five or six unknown ones, too."

Slowly, I scrolled through the list of chemicals. "We're unsure of how they're being smuggled in, where they're being stored, and where his buyers are going to be making the bombs. But we do know where he's staying." I looked at Beaker. "How familiar are you with these chemicals?"

"I've studied them all. Some I've actually worked with. I'll tell you a combination of many of those can blow up a whole city. They can be tweaked, though, and some of those can be used to defuse the others." She scooted up in her chair. "Most of those substances are on timers. In other words, they have to be used in a certain amount of time to be effective. Or they have to be defused in a space of time or they will self-combust."

"Beaker," TL addressed her, "in case you haven't figured it out yet, you will be going on this mission."

She smiled a little. "Yeah, I sort of guessed that."

TL held up his hand. "Let's pause here for a second and go down a different avenue. I want to know who's on the team and what the cover is."

"The team will consist of myself, Beaker, David, Nalani, and you, TL. We'll be staying at the same hotel as Eduardo." I clicked the remote control. "Here at the Hotel Marquess. We'll be able to monitor his moves and track him through that venue. David will be staying at a different location as backup. Nalani will obtain a job at the Hotel Marquess and act as our insider. Here at home base, we'll have Chapling and Parrot on standby. We'll need Parrot on call for translations, because Eduardo operates his transactions in a variety of different languages. And our cover . . ." I swallowed, inwardly groaning over what I was about to say.

I took in Beaker's black-and-white-striped hair, her nose chain, green lipstick, dog collar, black baggy clothes, and black nail polish.

I cleared my throat. "Our cover will be cheerleading."

***

Thirty minutes later, I was back in my room, and Bruiser was laughing hysterically. "Beaker's going to be a cheerleader? You've got to be kidding me. That's so funny."

I sat on my bed with Cat, both of us trying not to laugh along with her.

"Wait." Bruiser sniffed and held out her hand. "Can't you just see it? Beaker's nose chain in exchange for a *pretty little daisy.*" Ha, ha, ha, ha.

"Oh *my* God," Bruiser made her voice airheady, pulling an imaginary piece of gum from her mouth. "This Bubba Jubba is *so* chewed."

This time I smiled. I couldn't help myself.

"And you"—Bruiser pointed to me—"a cheerleader, too?" She grabbed her stomach. "This is too good."

"Hi," Bruiser did the airhead thing again. "My name's GiGi. That stands for Girl Genius." She flipped a red braid over her shoulder. "I can factor, square, and quadruple any of your cheers."

I rolled my eyes. Bruiser could be such a dork.

She fell back onto her bed laughing and rolling around. "Ohhh . . . ohh . . . oh . . ." She wiped her eyes. "Okay." Sniff. "I'm done now."

Good thing Beaker was still down in the conference room with TL. Or rather, TL requested she stay when she started getting irate about the cheerleading thing. She'd probably have busted Bruiser's lip by now.

Cat chuckled. "Now that Bruiser's done being Bruiser, are you and Beaker joining a squad or what? And what's TL's role in this?"

"Beaker and I are going as a pair. Cheerleaders from all over the nation are meeting in Barracuda Key to try out for America's Cheer. It's a national team. TL's going to act the role of our coach, our choregographer."

Bruiser flopped over onto her back. "Beaker actually agreed to this?"

"Not exactly." I wasn't too thrilled with it either. "That's why she's still down there with TL."

Our bedroom door slammed open, and Beaker stomped in. She railroaded right past me, down the length of our bedroom, and stopped at the bathroom door.

She spun and jabbed her finger in my direction. "I'll *never* forgive you for this." She wrenched open the bathroom door and banged it closed behind her.

Cat and I exchanged a glance.

"Does this mean you're going?" Bruiser sweetly called after her.

The toilet flushed.

‹FIVE›

A couple of days later, Beaker and I shuffled into the ranch's barn, which would double as our cheer training facility.

"Okay, girls," a short blond woman shouted and clapped her hands. "Front and center."

We crossed the cement floor to where she and TL stood on a large square of mats.

Dressed in a tight warm-up suit, she spread her legs wide and planted her hands on her boyish hips. "My name is Coach Melanie Capri. My purpose here is to get you ready for cheer tryouts in Barracuda Key. You don't have to be experts, but you do have to look like you know what you're doing."

I knew all about this woman. TL had arranged for her to come and train us, and David had briefed me on her background. Melanie Capri. Five feet tall. Exactly 105 pounds. Thirty-five years old, although she looked a lot younger. Cheerleader all throughout middle school, high school, and college. After graduating, she coached high school cheerleading for two years and then joined the CIA. One year later, she transferred to the IPNC, where she'd been ever since.

But the best part? She'd actually traveled with America's Cheer, the same team Beaker and I would be trying out for. As far as the cheerleading part of this mission, it didn't get any better than Coach Melanie Capri.

She reminded me of Audrey, the modeling coach for my first mission. Not the way Coach Capri looked, but her no-nonsense demeanor. My mind flashed back to that training and all the awkwardness that came with it. If I hadn't had it, though, the thought of this cheerleading preparation would be more uncomfortable for me than it already was.

"America's Cheer," she began, "is a weeklong competition. Every year there are approximately one hundred competitors, fifty teams of two. Generally there are ninety percent girls and ten percent boys. The weeklong competition will be grueling. You'll get up at the crack of dawn and fall into bed late. You'll have team rehearsals, attitude-building activities, group instruction, and physical-fitness training. You'll be judged all week long not only on technique, but attendance, talent, personality, and beauty. No one gets eliminated until the final day, and at that time, they will pick the twenty-one new members of America's Cheer national team."

Crossing her arms over her stomach, Coach Capri surveyed first me and then Beaker. "When's this one getting a makeover?" she said to TL.

Beaker snarled. *"This* one's name is Beaker, and I'm not getting a makeover."

Coach Capri arched a blond brow. "Oh yes, you are, darling, attitude and all."

Beaker rolled an irritable glare toward TL.

He maintained a stony face. "Coach Capri is in charge. Whatever she says goes. I'm behind her all the way."

"Let's start with you taking out that nose thing."

"Excuse me?" Beaker ground out.

Coach Capri smiled humorlessly. "You heard me."

With her jaw clenched so tight I thought her teeth might crack, Beaker reached up, disconnected the chain from her ear, and then slid the hoop from her nose.

I grimaced as I watched the piercing slide through its hole. Slowly, twirling the chain in the air, she smirked at Coach Capri. "Better?"

Coach Capri grinned. "Yes, thank you. You can give that to TL. You won't be getting it back until after the mission."

Beaker narrowed her eyes.

TL held out his hand, and, after a defiant few seconds, Beaker tossed it to him, and it clanked to the floor in front of him.

Coach Capri cleared her throat. "Pick it up and hand it to him nicely."

Beaker glared at her but didn't move.

"Pick it up and hand it to him nicely."

Beaker stood her ground.

Coach Capri's lips curled up, and something about their sinister tilt said she was about to take Beaker down.

Beaker must have seen it to because she walked over—albeit slowly—retrieved the fallen chain, and placed it in TL's outstretched hand.

"Perfect!" Coach Capri complimented a little too brightly.

Pocketing the chain, TL walked to the corner of the room to observe our training.

Coach clapped her hands. "Now let's pop and lock."

Pop and lock?

Coach strode over to where TL stood next to a portable stereo sitting on the floor. "Luckily, we can skip the fitness conditioning, since you two get plenty of that in PT. We're going to go straight into skills. Popping and locking is the most important technique a cheerleader needs." She pressed the play button on the stereo, and techno music started.

"Listen for the thump in the background of the music," she shouted over the noise. She snapped her arms up to her chest and popped them straight out to her sides. "Notice my joints are locked. No spaghetti arms allowed."

She snapped her arms back in and popped them straight out, this time at a different angle. In and out she went, popping and locking, each time at a different angle. Right arm up, left arm down. Right arm sideways, left arm up. Right arm diagonal, left arm down. Some with her fists clinched, others with her fingers straight.

As I watched, I noticed she executed each snappy movement to the bass thumping of the music.

"Now you two," she instructed, still popping and locking.

Stepping away from Beaker, I tried my first pop and lock and winced.

Coach nodded. "Don't throw your arm so hard, GiGi. You don't want to bruise a joint."

I tried again, and in my peripheral noticed Beaker's halfhearted attempt as she slung her arms into place. Her purposeful difficultness annoyed me, although I fully expected her not to cooperate.

Coach Capri moved closer, and Beaker defiantly continued her slinging-arm routine.

"Beaker," Coach warned.

With a smile, Beaker popped and locked her arms, but once coach turned around, Beaker went back to scowling and being lazy. I was starting to get irritated. Why couldn't she take anything seriously? I glanced over at her again, and her defiant look put me over the edge.

I dropped my arms. "Would you stop being the way you're being and take things seriously? This mission is really important to me. I don't need you ruining it."

"Ugh. Everything's always about you," Beaker snapped back.

Pure angry frustration made me take an intimidating step toward her.

She echoed my step, puffing out her chest. "Problem?"

"Yeah, actually I *do* have a problem. With you."

"I don't know why *you* have a problem. I'm the one who has to make all the changes around here." She took another step toward me. "I'm the one who has to get a *makeover* for this mission."

"Oh, would you grow up? Training and getting made over isn't *that* difficult. Just deal with it."

"Oh, that's right. I forgot. This *is* your *third mission.*"

"Girls," TL interjected, walking toward us. "Enough. You are going to have to work with each other on this mission to make it successful. So I suggest you suck it up, get over yourselves, and focus on the task at hand."

Beaker and I eyed each other for a couple of long, threatening seconds. Then gradually, without turning our backs on each other, moved back to our spaces.

"Again," Coach Capri commanded, as TL returned to his viewing spot.

I brought my arms up, trying pop and lock, and noticed Beaker's arms took on a snappier technique.

Coach Capri backed away. "Now to the music."

Doing my best to ignore Beaker, I listened intently. I heard the thump, but I couldn't seem to pop my arms to the rhythm. I either snapped a second too early or a second too late.

Coach tapped her ear. "Listen to the beat." She went to the stereo and started the music over.

Tuning everything out, I listened and tried again. I popped too early. I tried again. I locked too late.

Pushing out a sigh, I shook my arms out and cut a sideways glance to Beaker. She didn't seem to be having a problem staying in rhythm, and her smirk said she knew she was better than me.

Coach Capri came toward me. "GiGi, concentrate."

"I am." I thought about telling her I had no coordination. Instead, I looked over to TL, and he gave me an encouraging nod.

I tried again. I popped too early. Again. I locked too late.

Dropping my arms, I closed my eyes and took a deep breath.

My brain zoned in, as focused as when I keyed code. I tuned into the music, absorbing it, feeling it pulse through my body. Letters, numbers, and symbols took form, merging together to the beat. GSLK computer code linked in my mind in the same steady rhythm of the techno's bass.

<6E 74 3E 20 78 66 72 6D> Pop.

<3B 0D 0A 69 6E 74 20 6A> Lock.

<3B 0D 0A 66 6F 72 28 6A> Pop.

<3D 30 3B 20 6A 3C 31 30> Lock.

"Good, GiGi," TL complimented.

Opening my eyes, I smiled and snapped my arms into their next position. I *would* get through this training . . . and deal with Beaker.

***

Every day for the next week, Beaker and I woke up early to do homework, went to school, came home, and immediately began cheer training. We were now masters at pop and lock as well as handstands, clapping, and shouting cheers at the top of our lungs. It never would have occurred to me that people needed to practice clapping and shouting.

At night, David and I would meet in the lab to review things for the mission, run budget numbers, and complete any of the dozens of minute details involved. He'd update me on the tasks he was doing to help the mission run smoothly, like completing the enormous America's Cheer registration pack.

And while Beaker still held no excitement about the upcoming mission, today she was downright pissed. Leaning back against the bathroom vanity, I eyed a very snarly-looking Beaker staring at a very eager Coach Capri. Today was makeover day and, clearly, Beaker was not happy about it. Then again, she was never really happy about anything.

Coach Capri dabbed a cotton ball with makeup remover and came toward her. "I don't know how you can see through all that black gunk on your eyes."

Beaker slapped her hand away. "I like my *black gunk.*"

"I take it you're not going to do this by yourself?"

Beaker smirked. "You take it right. If you want it done so badly, you do it."

Coach shrugged. "Very well." She grabbed Beaker's wrist, twisted it behind her back, and smooshed the cotton ball across her right eye.

Beaker jerked away, leaving a black mark smeared across her cheek. "Hey!"

"Well, if you'd hold still."

Beaker jerked away again. "Let me go."

"You going to do it yourself?"

"No," Beaker snapped.

Coach Capri backed her up against the bathroom wall. For such a little woman, she was very strong. And her drill sergeant personality made her seem six feet tall.

Holding firm to Beaker, Coach cleaned her eye while Beaker rolled her head, trying without success to dodge Coach's efforts.

"Get me another one," Coach said to me.

Quickly, I sopped another cotton ball with the remover and handed it to her. Beaker shot me a deadly look. I wanted so bad to laugh, but I held it in. She was purposefully being difficult, as usual. And a big, huge, giant baby.

Still holding Beaker, Coach cleaned off her other eye and then let her go. "See. Was that so bad?"

Beaker growled.

Coach Capri didn't even seemed fazed. "Now hair."

"What?!"

"You heard me." Coach picked up a bottle of color. "You can't look like a skunk if you want to fit in at America's Cheer."

Beaker dodged for the door.

Coach intercepted her. "GiGi, lock us in from the outside."

I rolled my eyes at the ridiculousness of the situation. "All right. You two have fun."

Beaker cursed.

I left, locking the door from the outside at the same time someone tapped softly on our bedroom door. Bruiser tiptoed over and peeked out.

"Shhh." She put her finger over lips, shushing whoever stood on the other side.

Cat and I exchanged a "what's up?" look.

Bruiser widened the door a little, and in crept Wirenut, Mystic, and Parrot. The guys spread out in the room: Mystic cross-legged on the floor, Wirenut next to Cat, and Parrot stretched out on Beaker's empty bed.

A muted crash came from the bathroom, followed by a stream of curses.

Bruiser suppressed a giggle.

Coach Capri was one little woman I did *not* want to mess with. I was scared of her, and I wasn't ashamed to admit it. If she snapped an order, I hopped to it. Beaker, on the other hand . . . They went head to head over everything. Literally. From Beaker's clothes, to her oh-so-pleasant demeanor, to her gum chomping, to the way she walked. Coach Capri got in her face about everything.

A bang rattled from the bathroom, shaking the door. Another stream of curses followed.

Everyone in the bedroom exchanged an "oh no" look.

Beaker was going to be so upset when she found all the guys in here. I almost felt sorry for her.

Almost.

More banging, rattling, and yelling came from the inside, while my teammates giggled on the outside. A half hour later, a blow dryer kicked on and minutes after that the bathroom door opened.

Coach Capri emerged. Clearing her throat, she smoothed her short hair into place. "Well, everyone's here. Good." She smiled a little *too* sinisterly. *"Real* good."

In the short time I'd known her, I'd gotten the impression she enjoyed her battles with Beaker.

"You can come out now," Coach Capri called.

Nothing.

"You can come out now," she called again, her voice a bit harder.

Nothing.

"Get your butt out here," she barked. "Now."

This time *I* held in a giggle.

The bathroom door slammed open, and Beaker stomped out.

My jaw dropped. Beaker had gone through a complete transformation. Like an I-wouldn't-recognize-her-if-she-walked-up-to-me-on-the-street kind of transformation. Her hair was colored dark chestnut brown, and it lay in short, layered, loose curls.

She wore very little makeup, and I noticed for the first time her clear blue eyes. With all the overpowering dark eyeliner she usually wore, I'd never seen beyond it to her natural color.

No nose or eyebrow jewelry existed. And even though I couldn't see, I was sure Coach Capri made Beaker take out her tongue stud.

I couldn't believe I was looking at the same person. Beaker looked . . . sweet—a word I never thought I'd associate with her.

Her red cheerleading vest, the same as mine, stopped right above her belly button. Her red-and-white miniskirt came to her upper thighs, revealing white legs, and red-and-white tennis shoes completed the outfit.

Other than her pale legs and the frown on her face, she looked beautiful—another word I never thought I'd associate with Beaker.

She scowled at each of the guys, and then her gaze immediately narrowed in on Bruiser.

Bruiser blinked innocently.

Coach Capri slapped Beaker on the back. "It's a good thing everyone's here. You've got to get used to being around people in your new identity."

"Hey, Beak." Wirenut popped a piece of candy in his mouth. "Chin up, babe. You're hot. Who would've thought you had all those goods under your Goth getup."

With a laugh, Cat poked him in the ribs.

Beaker blushed. Actually blushed. I'd never seen her embarrassed before.

"Sissy," Coach Capri addressed Beaker by her real name. "Cheerleaders never frown. Smile, please."

"What's Sissy short for?" Bruiser asked, getting off topic.

Beaker shot Bruiser another scowl. "Priscilla. My mom was an Elvis fan."

Elvis fan? Huh. I hadn't known. I was sure there was a lot about Beaker that I didn't know.

She pointed her finger at Bruiser. "But call me Priscilla, and I'll poke your eyes out."

Bruiser held up her hands.

"Cheerleaders never frown," Coach Capri repeated herself. "Smile, please."

Beaker's ever-present scowl became scowlier, if possible.

Coach Capri arched a blond brow.

Beaker huffed out a sigh. She stretched her lips away from her teeth, looking more like a dental patient then a smile.

Everyone in the room held in a laugh.

Coach Capri cleared her throat. "I said smile, please."

"I am smiling," Beaker hissed through her stretched lips.

Coach Capri bopped her in the back of the head, and Beaker's forced expression curved into an actual smile.

Wirenut tossed another chunk of candy in his mouth. "Now if you could just stay that way and not open your mouth . . ."

Cat bopped *him* in the back of the head this time.

Beaker flipped him a black-polish-free middle finger.

Wirenut rubbed the back of his head. "There's the mad chemist I know and love." He winked.

Bruiser jumped up on her bed. "Let me see you do a cheer." She lifted her left leg from behind, grabbed her foot, and brought it all the way above her head.

I grimaced. From all the cheerleading books I'd been studying, I knew that was called a scorpion—definitely a move I wouldn't be doing on this mission.

"Give me a B!" Bruiser shouted.

Coach Capri arched a brow at me. I knew that arch. I didn't mess with that arch.

Immediately, I pushed off my bed and snapped straight into a liberty, with my right foot on the inside of my left knee and my arms straight up. It should be called the stork the way it looked.

"Give me a B!" I shouted louder than Bruiser.

Coach Capri nodded her head once in a show of approval. Then she turned to Beaker and arched her do-it-now-or-else brow.

With slumped shoulders, Beaker slung her right leg into the same position as mine and flopped her arms up. "Give me a B," she said with all the enthusiasm of a slug.

Coach Capri bopped her in the back of the head again.

I sighed. Here we go again.

***

A week later, David and I stood in Beaker's lab. The large tables were filled with burners, beakers, and vials of various chemicals.

Beaker propped goggles on top her head. "I've been studying all the chemicals Eduardo has used in the past and what we currently know he will be smuggling in. I'm only one person, and I'm definitely going to need help diffusing things when we get to the final hour."

She handed David and me each a thin pack of stapled pages. "I've put together all the various combinations I think will be used in making chemical bombs. As you can see, I've detailed what to add to various solutions, what to take out, which to heat, ones to chill . . ."

As she continued describing her papers, I looked them over . . . and was suddenly intimidated. She'd used symbols I recognized from high school chemistry and thoroughly explained each one. She'd expertly noted how many millimeters of this, what temperature of that. She'd organized which stir rods, whisks, and other things to use. But the brilliant detail overwhelmed me. I knew she knew her stuff—after all, this was her specialty—but the sheer magnitude of her knowledge boggled my mind.

Beaker nodded to the table in front of David and me. "Slip on those lab coats and goggles. I'm going to walk you through how to read my notes and defuse a chemical bomb."

"Wh-what?" I blinked a few times. "D-did you say defuse a chemical bomb?"

She smirked a little. "Scared, GiGi?"

I narrowed my eyes. "No. I'm not scared." *Yes, I am scared.*

Beaker rolled her eyes. "Relax." She pointed to the flasks of chemicals lined up in front of her. "We're not actually going to make and defuse a bomb; we're just going to go through the motions. So you know how to read my directions during the real event."

David and I put on our gear while Beaker brought her goggles down to cover her eyes.

She turned on a flame under a flask of yellow liquid. "Refer to scenario one. We'll use that for the purpose of demonstration."

Beaker checked her watch, then turned the flame up a little higher. "Notice in scenario one you have a simple combination of creino and oteca."

"How will we know if its creino, oteca, or any other substance?" David asked.

"You won't know. That's my job. I'll perform some quick tests, tell you what's in the bomb, and you'll refer to the outlined scenarios to defuse it."

"What if there's no time to do the quick test?" I asked.

She shrugged. "It's no big deal, really. It won't take me long to figure out what's in the bombs. If you have any problems, I'll be right there. Don't freak out or anything."

"I'm not freaking out." *I am freaking out.* I mean, what happened if I didn't defuse it correctly? Oh, yeah, it's a bomb. It would *explode*!

Beaker checked her watch again and put two drops of a purple liquid into the now-boiling flask of yellow. "Okay, in scenario one, it says to do what to defuse this bomb of creino and oteca?"

My heart kicked a little. "I thought you said you weren't making a bomb."

With a sigh, David looked at me.

I returned his look. "What? I'm just asking."

"I'm *not* making a bomb." Beaker rolled her eyes again. "Do you not think I know what I'm doing? This would have to reach a *much* hotter temperature before it actually became bomb-worthy." She pointedly looked at the flame. "Of course if you don't tell me how to defuse this, it *will* be hot enough to become bomb-worthy."

I quickly referred to the papers. "It says to take it to at least negative five degrees Celsius within two minutes."

With a nod, Beaker slid over a capped bottle filled with tiny green crystals. "Six of these diumfite crystals will immediately drop its temp to negative five."

She extinguished the flame from the boiling soon-to-be bomb and inserted a thermometer. She dropped six tiny green crystals into the mixture. I watched the boiling liquid turn solid.

Beaker pointed to the thermometer. "Check it out."

David and I scooted in. Sure enough, the thermometer read negative five degrees Celsius.

David smiled. "You are too cool."

Beaker returned his smile, and it occurred to me that I couldn't recall ever having Beaker smile directly at me. "Any questions?"

We shook our heads. With the demonstration, her notes really were pretty simple to follow.

She scooted her frozen bomb to the side. "Now, I wanted to ask you two something. I've been working on a tracking dust that works with a person's DNA. It chemically reacts to their blood. I'm still doing tests, but if I have it ready by the time we leave for Barracuda Key, I'm confident it will be valuable in trailing Eduardo."

David nodded. "We'll have a mission briefing right before we leave. Be ready to show everybody how it works."

Beaker propped her goggles back on top of her head. "It'll be ready. Also, I've developed a powdered GPS compound. It'll last five days in a person's body. I'm calling it crystallized siumcy. I've already told TL about it and he said to talk to you two . . . ?"

David nodded again. "Sounds good. I'm proud of you for being proactive in your thinking and not waiting to be told what to do. That shows real initiative."

She beamed with pride.

He'd sounded just like TL, and David's words had elicited the same devotion that TL's words did. I glanced over at him, swelling a bit with respect and esteem for the guy I liked. If he kept this up, he would be a great strategist one day.

<SIX>

We were at week three of our cheerleading training, and things had gotten tough.

"That was pathetic. That's all you've got?" Coach Capri jabbed her finger toward the barn door. "Go out and do it again. Both of you. You're jogging in here like a computer genius and chemisty whiz undercover on a top-secret mission." Coach Capri widened her eyes. "You. Are. Cheer. Leaders. *Comprende?*"

With a sigh, Beaker and I both nodded our heads.

We're tired, I wanted to whine on behalf of us both. We'd been at this all day long. And a break seemed nowhere in our future.

Turning, we shuffled across the barn and out into a cold, sun-setting evening.

"My project for Excelled Physics is due tomorrow," I grumbled. "And I haven't even started." The story of my life these past weeks.

Beaker stopped to adjust her cheerleading shorts. "I hate these things. They barely cover my ass."

I commiserated. These shorts reminded me of the ones that David had bought me when I first came to the ranch—the ones I had initially refused to wear.

Rubbing her bare arms, Beaker jostled in place. "It's freezing."

"Okay, girls," Coach Capri yelled from inside the warm barn. "Let's see it."

Beaker and I rolled here-we-go-again eyes at each other. In the past few weeks, we'd established a small—let me repeat that—a *small* camaraderie.

We definitely hadn't had any heart-to-hearts. But as slight as it was (usually a look or a mumbled complaint), it made things better.

Beaker stepped back into the barn. "Let's do this."

We jogged in, side by side, our feet nearly touching our butts. In my opinion it was a ridiculous way to jog. With our elbows into our sides, we clapped. "H-E-Y. Hey! We're ready for today! P-U-M-P. Pump it up! H-E-Y. Hey! We're ready for today! P-U-M-P. Pump it up! H-E-Y. Hey! We're . . ."

We kept jogging around the barn, grinning, chanting the stupid cheer. According to Coach Capri, at America's Cheer, all cheerleaders would be expected to enter the morning meeting doing this chant.

I didn't see why we couldn't just go in and have a meeting. And why, exactly, did cheerleaders feel the need to spell everything?

"Perfect," Coach Capri yelled over our chanting. "Halt."

"All this peppiness wears me out," Beaker grumbled.

"Okay," Coach said. "TL got called away to a meeting. So David's here to assist with back handsprings." She nodded to the rear of the barn.

From the shadows stepped David.

Inwardly, I groaned. Please tell me he didn't see us.

He passed by us, smiling. "Nice *perky* cheerleading, girls."

Beaker narrowed her eyes.

"We're going to warm up for our back handsprings by doing twenty-second handstands." Coach Capri led the way to the blue mats that ran the length of the barn. "I'll spot Beaker, and David has GiGi."

I groaned. *Again.* Working with David normally thrilled me. But if he was my spotter, I knew where his position would be.

Right in line with my butt. And the shorty-shorts.

Great. *Juuust* great.

At least I'd shaved my legs.

Beaker and I stepped onto the mats. Coach Capri and David were a few feet in front of us.

"Feet together," Coach reminded us. "Point toes. Straight knees. Squeeze thighs. Butt tight. Back taut. Shoulders hollowed. Head neutral. Elbows locked. And arms . . ."

Pressed to your ears, I finished her directions in my head. Coach Capri had said it so many times over the past weeks, I wouldn't be surprised if I mumbled it in my sleep.

Amazingly enough, these handstands came easy for me. Probably because of all the PT conditioning I'd been through since joining the Specialists.

No wonder TL insisted on PT. It made the physical part of training for a mission go much easier.

Now back handsprings on the other hand—I'd yet to nail one.

Beaker and I brought our arms straight over our heads, slid our right toes out, came toward the floor with our hands, and lifted our legs straight up.

Behind me, David lightly grasped my hips.

"Perfect," Coach Capri complimented us. "In sync. Nice job. Now hold for twenty seconds."

I fixed my gaze to a spot on the other side of the barn, concentrating on keeping my body tight, locked, and steady. Trying not to focus on the fact that David's eyes were in line with my butt.

"GiGi, you're not squeezing a penny."

Closing my eyes, I pretended not to hear Coach Capri.

"GiGi, squeeze a penny."

Through my nose I exhaled a sharp breath. *Why me?*

"GiGi, you squeeze a penny now or you're going to hold that handstand for twenty minutes instead of twenty seconds."

Opening my eyes, I glared at that same spot across the barn . . . and then I squeezed my butt cheeks together as if I had a penny between them.

I tried hard to block out what David must be looking at right now. I tried hard . . . and failed.

"Okay, down for ten," Coach instructed.

Beaker and I lowered our right feet and came back to a standing position, our arms stretched above our heads.

I kept my eyes focused on the floor as I waited for the ten-second break. I knew if I looked at David, I'd die of embarrassment.

"And up," Coach Capri said.

We executed perfect handstands again, squeezed a penny, held for twenty, down for ten.

Again and again we repeated it until I didn't think I could hold a penny anywhere.

We brought our feet to the floor, and Coach Capri stood. "Let's take a short bathroom break, and then we're on to back handsprings." She jogged across the barn and out the door.

Beaker grabbed her towel and wiped her face. "I'd better have a good ass after all this is over with."

David laughed.

"I'm going to get some water." Beaker trotted across the barn and out into the night.

Still avoiding eye contact with David, I picked up my towel and folded it. Maybe I should go get some water, too. Or go to the bathroom. Anything to get out of here.

In my peripheral, I saw David.

"Nice pinched penny," he said, looking at my butt and chuckling as he walked past.

I smiled. I couldn't help it.

***

After three weeks of training and preparing, we were ready for the mission. David and I got to the conference room early for the team briefing. I placed a stack of folders neatly in front of my seat, waiting on Parrot, Beaker, TL, Chapling, and Nalani to arrive.

TL had requested that David conduct this meeting as part of his overall training in becoming a strategist. It felt good knowing David would be in charge. I felt like I was getting a little bit of a break. A lot of pressure came with being the leader. Put that together with training for the mission and going to school, and my life remained beyond busy.

Give me a computer and solitary research any day.

I sat down at my place and let out a long breath, my gaze drifting to the folders stacked in front of me. A folder for every person involved. Every individual who would help me bring my parents' killer to justice.

Slowly, I lifted my finger and trailed it along the spine of the top folder. What if things didn't work out? What if Eduardo got away again? What if, after my hard work, my team's hard work, things still didn't come to fruition? I'd let David down, TL. I'd let my team down. I'd dishonor the memory of my parents.

My parents . . . I closed my eyes as their faces drifted through my head. That time my dad caught a green garden snake and teased my mom with it. She'd giggled and ran around the yard like a crazy woman. And that time they found me hidden behind the couch, waiting for Santa. The tent my dad made out of a sheet. We'd all slept under it in their bedroom. And that ridiculous hat my mom always wore when she cleaned house.

"Shhh." David massaged my shoulders. "It's okay."

Sniffing, I wiped the wetness from my cheek. I hadn't even realized I'd been crying.

I took a couple of deep breaths to clear my head just as the door opened. Beaker and Parrot came in first, taking seats on the other side of the table. Beaker carried a black satchel and set it on the floor at her feet.

"You okay?" Parrot asked me, and I nodded.

Minutes later, TL entered with Nalani right behind him.

Nalani was one of the most beautiful women I'd ever seen. Polynesian, sleek black hair, olive skin, dark eyes. The last time I'd seen her had been during the Rissala mission with Wirenut. She'd driven our getaway boat. In her disguise, she'd had no teeth, greasy hair, and stained overalls.

Now she looked much like she had when I first met her in Ushbania. Very put together and professional. If she and TL ever decided to have children, they would be gorgeous.

Smiling, I got up and gave her a huge hug. "How are you?"

She squeezed me back. "I'm fine."

"How's your job at the Hotel Marquess?" She'd obtained employment weeks ago after David and I had put together the mission.

Nalani nodded. "So far so good."

Chapling waddled in behind her. "I'mhereI'mhere." He glanced up. "Nalani!"

She smiled and leaned down to give him a hug and kiss.

His pale, freckly face turned red. "Oh my. Ohmyohmy."

David closed the door. "Okay, let's get started."

Everyone took seats around the table, and I started handing out folders.

"Beaker, Parrot," David began, "I'd like you to meet Nalani. She's working pre-op on this mission. She's been at the hotel getting things set up."

Beaker, Parrot, and Nalani smiled and nodded to each other.

David began walking around the room. "In two days, myself, TL, Beaker, and GiGi will leave for Barracuda Key, Florida. Eduardo Villanueva, our focus on this mission, will be arriving shortly after us. He's staying in the presidential suite, which is located directly above the room Nalani has reserved for GiGi and Beaker to stay in."

Pointing a remote at the wall-mounted screen, David brought up the hotel's schematics. "These are the blueprints for the Marquess." He zoomed in on a portion. "This is the presidential suite, with GiGi and Beaker's room below. The first objective is to inject his room with DNA dust, which Beaker will describe in a few minutes. This will be done by drilling a small hole into the floor of his room with a silencer."

David zoomed back out. "The second objective is to get an electronic tracker on him. We're taking six different types of trackers, so we'll be ready in any situation. Whether we manage to get close enough in person or are only able to get at him from afar, one way or another we'll get an electronic tracker on him."

He clicked the remote, and different schematics popped up on the screen. "Third objective is to get his room on video surveillance. Notice the presidential suite and the room below share the same ductwork. We'll be using a device Wirenut created called The Fly. It's a mobile camera that can move through the ductwork and into Eduardo's suite through a vent. GiGi will program The Fly to land in an inconspicuous location. And from there, we wait and see where he goes."

David brought up an aerial view of the island. "Barracuda Key is surrounded by the ocean and bordered on the north and south sides by other smaller islands. We don't know how Eduardo is smuggling in the chemicals or how he's shipping out the bombs that will be made. Chapling hasn't been able to decipher that through intel."

Chapling nodded in agreement, as David continued his lecture. "Once we know where and how Eduardo is smuggling the chemicals in, we'll better understand the scope of this operation. He could have three people with him or twenty. Again, something else we've been unable to decipher with our intel. We'll notify IPNC officials once we've organized concrete details, and they'll work in conjunction with us for the takedown. By the time Eduardo has been apprehended, there could be only one chemical bomb to defuse or there may be multiple ones."

David paused and looked around the table. "Are there any questions so far?"

Everyone, including TL, shook their heads no.

David indicated the folders. "Inside you will find complete details of this operation. New identities for me, Beaker, GiGi, and TL; an equipment list; chemical details; miscellaneous logistics; the island layout; travel documents; hotel blueprints and technology; the Marquess' security design .

. . ." On and on he went, listing things. He pulled the equipment list from his folder and looked at Nalani. "Do you think there'll be any problems getting these things put in place?"

She shook her head. "Not at all. I've already acquired the audio/video monitoring devices. TCVC cable for manually transmitting video from any camera in-house. Socarmi recorders, bugs to plant where we want. Lome cameras to install where we feel necessary, et cetera . . . And I've arranged for a hidden compartment under one of the beds in the girls' room."

She pulled a picture from her jacket pocket and handed it to me. "This is a picture of the bed and headboard. I've had an opening device installed in the headboard's design. You'll notice that there's a shark etched into the headboard. When you bang on its fin, it opens the hidden compartment within the bed."

I studied the picture of the bed. It seemed easy enough.

David turned to Parrot. "You'll need to be on call twenty-four/seven. Intel reports Eduardo operates most often in Spanish and Portuguese, so we may be sending you e-mails or digital recordings of conversations."

Parrot nodded. "I know both those languages very well."

"We won't know the exact combination of substances Eduardo is using until we're there and begin to track him." David pulled a chemical list from his folder. "Beaker has put together a list of all the possible scenarios and how to defuse them. Any changes to this list, Beaker?"

She shook her head. "It's comprehensive."

David switched his attention to Chapling. "Okay. You're up."

Chapling's eyes brightened as he wiggled up a little straighter in his chair. I recognized that look. He couldn't wait to tell everybody about his new software.

"Okay. Okayokayokay. This is way cool." He unclipped his cell phone from his pants. "Now this hasn't been field-tested yet, but I'll get that done before you all leave." Chapling held up his phone. "I've coded in audio software on each of your cell phones that can record anything within a five-mile radius." He giggled. "You can eavesdrop to your devious heart's content as long as you have open air. In other words, you can't record through a wall."

"Tell everybody what you used," I encouraged him.

Chapling bounced his bushy red brows. "A little syntactical code mixed with high-level source data. Then I sprinkled in SPLI mnemonics for good measure." He wiggled his chubby fingers. "Of course, it all has my personal spin on it."

I looked around the table. "Isn't he brilliant?"

Everybody nodded with one of those confused, yep-sure-I-understood-him smiles.

Chapling pulled on the collar of his shirt, all playfully full of himself. "Well, you know, I do get paid the big bucks."

David nodded to Beaker, indicating it was her turn.

She placed the satchel on top of the table. "I've been working on this for a couple of weeks now. I've run the standard trials and proved it successful." She opened the satchel and pulled out a sealed bottle of red powder. "It's a tracking device that works off a person's DNA. It only lasts for seven days, though." She unscrewed the bottle, took an empty syringe from her satchel, and extracted a full vial of the red substance.

Holding the syringe up, she slowly depressed it. I watched as the red dust turned invisible immediately upon meeting air.

"You don't realize it, but right now this is absorbing through everyone's skin and into their bloodstream." She pulled rose-tinted glasses from her satchel and passed them down the table to TL. "Put those on and tell me what you see."

While he put on the glasses, Beaker pushed back from her chair and began walking around the room.

"Everywhere you move you're leaving a trail of red." TL said, pulling down the glasses. "It's invisible to the naked eye."

Beaker nodded. "No matter where I go over the next seven days, you can track me as long as you're wearing those glasses."

"But if everybody leaves a red trail," I asked, "how do you know who is who?"

From her satchel, she pulled out a small yellow envelope. From the envelope she took what looked like a black toothpick. "Swipe this through the red trail and it'll hold on to the DNA. You can run it through any standard DNA program to see who the trail belongs to. I'll have a DNA kit with us on the mission."

Wow. Neat.

"So what do you think?" she asked, resuming her seat.

David smiled. "Great work, Beaker."

Chapling bounced in his chair. "Oooh, oooh, I wanna try."

Everyone laughed as TL took the glasses off and passed them down the table.

***

Later that evening, with both hands, I grabbed the barn door and slid it open. Stepping inside, I flipped on the dimmer lights. In two days we would leave for Barracuda Key, Florida, and I still couldn't do a successful back handspring. Call me crazy, but I had an issue with blindly flipping backward and falling on my head.

Striding over to the blue mats, I recalled Coach Capri's repeated warning.

You absolutely have to do a back handspring. It's expected of you. You'll be kicked out of the tryouts if you can't. And then your cover will be blown.

Taking mats from the stack in the corner, I spread them down the length of the barn.

I warmed up with a few handstands and then executed perfect cartwheels and roundoffs. I did four front walkovers in a row and repeated going back. All things I couldn't do weeks ago when I'd started this cheerleading training. Not bad for a girl who repeatedly tripped over her own two feet.

Coach Capri should be applauding me for how far I'd come.

Taking off my sweatshirt, I tossed it aside, adjusted my tank top, and went to stand in the center of the mats. I locked my arms straight above my head and took a couple of deep breaths.

I can do this.

Bending my knees, I sprang up and dove backward. I caught a glimpse of ceiling braces, the stalls in the back of the barn, and then splatted face-first onto the mats.

I slammed my fist down. "Oh!"

I laid there, staring at the mat, frustrated beyond belief. Thoughts of my mom and dad began to flood my mind. Did they ever get frustrated at training or had they been naturally gifted at it? Were either of them as klutzy as me? Was klutziness genetic? I shook my head to clear my focus.

"Hey, you becoming one with that mat?" came Beaker's voice.

I glanced up to see her standing in the doorway.

"What do you want?" I pushed to my knees. "I'm not in the mood for sarcasm or jokes."

Beaker shrugged. "I suspect I want the same thing as you, to get some more practice in."

"It's midnight. You're breaking curfew." I stood.

"You're breaking curfew, too."

"True. I'm just surprised you're here. I thought you hated all this cheer training."

"I do." She came the rest of the way in. "Doesn't mean I don't want to be ready, though."

"You don't need to practice. You know how to do back handsprings."

"And you don't." She stepped onto the mats. "So . . . do you, um, want some help?"

I eyed her for a few suspicious seconds. "Why are you being nice to me?"

"I'm not being nice," she said unconvincingly. She took off her sweatshirt, revealing double-layered tank tops, and tossed it on top of mine. "I don't want you making me look bad at the competition, that's all."

"Mmm-hmm." Well, well, well, could it be that Beaker's actually being nice to me?

She rolled her eyes. "Whatever," she said, and turned to walk away.

"All right." I stopped her. "I'll take any help I can get."

Beaker nodded. "Let's do it," she yelled.

Wirenut stepped through the door, followed by Parrot, Bruiser, Mystic, and Cat.

I sent Beaker a confused look. "What's going on?"

"I rounded up everyone." She shrugged, as if that wasn't the sweetest thing ever. "We're here to help." Playfully, she smirked. "Don't go thinking I like you or anything, though."

I smiled a little. "Of course not."

Wirneut unzipped his windbreaker and threw it aside. "Watch us do handsprings first. Notice we all have different styles. You need to find and do what feels right to you."

Stepping off the mats, I watched first Wirenut, then Bruiser, followed by Cat, and finally Beaker.

Sheesh, was there anyone who *couldn't* do one?

I looked at Parrot and Mystic. They both shrugged.

"We're here for moral support," Mystic offered with a smile.

His smile made *me* smile. What great friends I had.

Wirenut dusted his hands. "Okay, tell me," he instructed, "what did you notice different about all of us?"

"Speed," I answered. "Height. Hand placement."

"It took me five days to learn how to do one," Beaker reminded me.

"You don't have to brag about it," I grumbled.

"My point is," she continued, ignoring my snarkiness, "I would've learned in three if I could've figured out my hand placement. Coach Capri kept telling us to keep our thumbs touching. But when I separated mine by a few inches, I nailed it."

Cat pulled three, long black strips of material from her sweatpants pocket. "Mind giving something a try?"

Eyeballing the black cloths, I shook my head. I'd try anything at this point.

Cat stepped onto the mats and motioned me to follow. She wrapped one of the cloths around my eyes, blinding me. "This is so you won't get distracted by anything." She tightened it. "Don't worry. We're all here to spot you if anything goes wrong."

"Now lift your arms," Cat instructed. She tied my arms tight against my head. "This will keep your arms in place. You'll still be able to flex your shoulders and elbows for the push."

She wrapped the last cloth around my thighs. "There. Now all your body parts will stay where they're supposed to be."

"Remember," Bruiser added. "Reach for the floor with your hands, not your nose."

Someone grabbed my hips and turned me around.

"We're all here," Wirenut spoke from my left. "You can do this."

"Visualize exactly what you want your body to do," Mystic suggested, "and it'll work. I promise you."

Behind the black cloth, I closed my eyes and visualized my body going through the motions of a successful back handspring.

I took a deep breath, bent my knees, and sprang back, diving onto my hands. My palms connected with the floor, and I pushed off, flipping back onto my feet.

I stood for a moment in disbelief. I'd actually done it!

Everyone cheered, and I grinned, literally, from ear to ear.

‹SEVEN›

Two days later, dressed in matching red-and-white warm-ups, TL, Beaker, and I boarded the plane. David had already boarded and sat midway in the cabin. As of this moment, none of us knew him. He was traveling to Barracuda Key to do some diving. That was the cover we'd decided on for him. He'd rented a cottage on the other side of the island from our hotel. Once we arrived and went our separate ways, I probably wouldn't see him until the end of the mission.

At least we'd be able to communicate via phone, texting, and e-mail.

As I passed his aisle seat, I slowed, hoping for a slight contact. He surreptitiously reached over and tucked a piece of paper into my palm. My whole body buzzed at the contact.

TL, Beaker, and I found our seats in the back of coach, and after storing our red-and-white backpacks in the overhead bins, we sat down and buckled in. I took a few deep breaths to calm myself—flying was not my favorite thing to do. But I had gotten used to it a little, having had to fly on my first two missions.

Beside me, Beaker raised the window shade. She calmly flipped open a cheer magazine that she'd brought with her and began perusing. I knew she'd rather be reading one of her chemistry books, but we had officially taken on our cheerleading covers when we stepped into the airport.

"Hey," I whispered.

She glanced over.

"Thanks for doing this. It means a lot." I hadn't had a chance to say those simple words to her. "This mission is important to me. And I know you didn't want to go. And well . . . I appreciate all your hard work getting ready for it."

Beaker kept her blue eyes leveled on mine. I got the distinct impression she wanted to say *you're welcome.*

Instead, she shrugged and went back to her magazine. "Yeah, well, I had no choice. TL made me."

I'd like to think it was her way of saying *you're welcome.*

She glanced around me to TL. "Thanks for my send-off party," she whispered.

He smiled a little. "You're welcome."

Beaker went back to her magazine and TL closed his eyes. After a few seconds, I peeked at the note David had slipped me. "I'm right here" was penciled on the inside.

I smiled to myself. He wanted me to know it would be okay. I'd make it through this flight and this mission okay. The loving gesture warmed me.

***

It took eight hours to fly nonstop from California to the island of Barracuda Key in Florida.

We made our way from the plane through the airport to baggage claim and retrieved our matching red-and-white suitcases.

In the shuttle bus zone, a burgundy Hotel Marquess van waited. Beyond it, I saw David climb into a taxi. Although the windows were tinted, I felt his eyes on me as the cab pulled away.

The elderly bus driver climbed out as we approached. "I take it from your outfits you're here for America's Cheer."

"Yes, sir," Beaker and I answered in unison.

"You guys are the last flight of the day." He took my suitcase first, groaning as he slowly hefted it up into the back of the van. I grimaced at the sound. This little old man was too old to be doing this. He reached for Beaker's suitcase next.

"I got it." She quickly hoisted it into the back before the old man could argue.

TL followed her lead.

I felt horrible. I should've done that, too.

The old man straightened his white uniform jacket. "There was a time when I could've lifted all three without creaking and moaning."

TL slapped him on the back. "No worries. How far is it to the hotel?"

The old driver opened the side door for us. "Straight across the island. Five miles."

With our backpacks, we stepped up into the shuttle van. The driver shut the door, climbed into his side, and pulled out.

Mild, early evening air flowed through the windows as we zigzagged across the neat and tidy island. I knew from my research that Barracuda Key was five miles wide and only two miles long.

A variety of colorful shrubs and trees filled the landscape, planted at exactly the same distance apart. I didn't know any of the names except for the palms.

We passed shopping centers and grocery stores, all of which stood one-story tall and were painted either beige or white. Brown block lettering on each building indicated the names of the stores or shops. It surprised me not to see any fast-food restaurants.

A black wrought-iron fence surrounded each individual neighborhood subdivision. Inside, the houses had the same one-story, two-car-garage design, and were painted pastel green or pink.

People strolled the sidewalks in perfect, preppy, island outfits.

I supposed Barracuda Key was pretty if you liked the organized, clean, nonunique look.

"Makes me want to pull up a shrub or something," Beaker mumbled under her breath.

"Does the whole island look like this?" I asked.

"Pretty much," the driver answered. "Some of the beach areas are a little deserted, and there's a state park for camping." The driver pointed out the front window. "There it is."

Off in the distance, on what had to be the only hill on the island, stood the Hotel Marquess. Its towering presence came off like an island king looking down over his tropical village.

With huge columns out front, the white-washed hotel stood only three stories tall. The hotel's front and sides covered the entire grassy hillside, and the back extended out on stilts over the ocean.

I knew from my planning sessions with David that the 32,000-square-foot structure housed 449 rooms, nineteen conference rooms, three ballrooms, an underground shopping mall, four restaurants, a spa, indoor and outdoor tennis courts, two pools, an eighteen-hole golf course, and one presidential suite. Where Eduardo Villanueva would be staying.

A person could move into this hotel and never leave. The place had everything.

We pulled up under the portico. Bellmen in matching white-and-burgundy suits emerged, opening the doors, helping us out, getting our luggage.

I couldn't help but feel like a movie star with all the first-class treatment.

A bellman stood on each side of the hotel's entranceway. As we approached, they opened the glass-and-gold doors. "Welcome," they greeted in unison, bowing.

I couldn't recall ever having been bowed to before.

"Thanks," I mumbled, a bit uncomfortable with this royal treatment.

Odd, but this whole place seemed like a foreign country, not a little island off the coast of south Florida right here in good old America.

A slight nudge from TL made me move forward. We crossed through a marbled-floor waiting area. Two more bellmen opened two more glass-and-gold doors. Beaker and I stepped through them and came to an abrupt stop.

In stunned amazement, we stared at hundreds of girls.

Everywhere.

Boinging and bouncing.

Squealing and giggling.

Cheering and chanting.

Tall, short. Skinny, muscular. Blondes, redheads, brunettes. Ponytails, braids.

Wearing a variety of shorts and T-shirts with matching ribbons in their hair.

I'd never seen so many happy, excited, color-coordinated girls in my life.

"Hey!" A dark-haired girl jumped right into our faces.

Beaker and I flinched.

"Isn't this just great?!" she squeaked.

I blinked. Was that voice for real?

"Well, isn't it?!" Her long, brown ponytail swung with her bubbly jostling.

TL put a hand on Beaker's and my shoulders and came up between us. "Yes, it is." He grinned. "You're having way too much fun without us."

The girl giggled.

TL hugged us to him. "Where do we check in?"

The girl snapped her arm straight, pointing across the lobby to the front desk. "Give me an R! Right! Give me T! There!" She spun around and skipped off.

"She could've just said 'right there,'" Beaker grumbled.

"Stay in character," TL whispered and headed toward the front desk through the mass of exuberant girls.

I looked at Beaker, she looked at me, and we both plastered the biggest, fakest smiles on our faces.

With a light spring to our steps, we followed TL across the lobby.

"Hi!" A girl as tall as me bopped up in my face. I stepped back a bit.

"Hi!" Beaker and I greeted her simultaneously. I almost laughed.

The girl's brown eyes widened as she took in Beaker. "Oh my *God*! I *love* your ribbon!"

Beaker's smile became even smilier, if possible. "Thanks!"

The tall girl slammed her hand over her heart. "I *love* how you tied it around your neck. And I *love* how it has little tiny red and white stripes."

Beaker kept cheesing it up, but I knew that underneath lurked her trademark smirk. I could only imagine what was going through her mind right now.

Someone kill this girl and put her out of her misery. No, someone kill me and put me out of my misery.

"Hi!" Another girl danced up.

"Hi!" Beaker and I greeted her.

I wondered how many times I'd have to say 'Hi!' over the next few days.

I purposefully dropped my jaw. "I *love* your T-shirts."

"Thanks!" They answered in unison.

They pointed to their boobs and the green-on-pink lettering stretched across them. "Cheerleaders *are* better athletes!" they agreed with their shirts.

Beaker and I nodded, and I racked my brain for what else I could say.

I love your matching green-and-pink shorts.

I love your matching green shoes with pink socks.

I love your sparkly pink eye shadow.

"Girls," TL called, rescuing me from the dilemma.

"That's our coach. Gotta go. 'Bye!" I gave a quick wave.

"'Bye!" They waved back.

With our huge smiles still in place, we wove through the other joyful girls to the front desk and TL.

He grinned. "Here they are. The next two members of America's Cheer."

"We' re glad to have you," the woman on the other side of the counter welcomed us.

Nalani.

Showing no recognition of us, she handed Beaker and me each a big white envelope and card key. "Inside you'll find everything you need. Event schedule, mealtimes, workouts . . . If you need anything while staying here at Hotel Marquess, please don't hesitate to ask."

I glanced at TL to see if I could recognize a hint of love, pain, sorrow, or longing. But I saw nothing except the same fake I'm-so-happy-to-be-here face.

"Unfortunately," Nalani continued, "the room you had been preassigned to is still occupied by yesterday's visitors."

My face dropped a little.

"They decided to stay an additional day. But they've scheduled an early checkout for tomorrow, so we'll have things ironed out in no time."

I glanced at TL, but he was still smiling as if this bit of information was no big deal.

"We'll put you in another room for tonight and then relocate you to your preassigned room in the morning." Nalani pointed down a marble-floored hallway. "Elevators are there. You're in room three-zero-three. I'll let the bellman know where to take your luggage."

TL knuckle-tapped the counter. "Let's go, girls."

Sounds from the lobby faded as we strode down the hall to the elevators. TL pressed the button, and we stood waiting. I was dying to ask him what was going on.

Seconds later, the elevator dinged open and out poured a pack of bubbly girls.

"Hi!" A few of them chirped.

"Hi!" A few more echoed.

"Hi!" Beaker and I returned, our grins in place.

They shuffled by, and we three stepped inside. The door slid closed, and Beaker's smile fell away.

"Ack." She grabbed her throat. "I think I'm going to hurl. This is my worst nightmare come true. Hi!" she sarcastically imitated them. "My name's Pixy, and I don't have a cell in my brain. But I know how to do a toe touch. Woo."

I turned to TL. "What's going on? If we don't get in our room tonight, that means we'll have to wait until tomorrow morning to access the equip—"

TL cleared his throat and shook his head. He brushed imaginary lint from his shoulder. *Stay in character.*

I sighed.

Beaker slumped back against the elevator wall. "I need gum," she grumbled.

TL cleared his throat again, and Beaker rolled her eyes up to his.

He brushed imaginary lint from his shoulder. *Stay in character.* He narrowed his gaze ever so slightly. *Or else.* He rubbed his eye. *Camera watching.*

Smoothing my fingers down my ponytail, I surreptitiously glanced up. Sure enough, in the upper-left corner sat a mini-camera hidden in a speaker. From David's hotel specs, I should've known that, but in my momentary frustration, I'd forgotten.

Reluctantly, Beaker pushed away from the elevator wall. Her scowl inched upward into her rendition of a pleasant face.

The elevator dinged open, and we stepped out. We read the number sign and took a left. Room three-zero-three sat halfway down the hallway.

TL followed us in and shut the door. "Don't worry about the room."

"I know, but I wanted to get a start on figuring out the equipment and reviewing the plans," I said.

"Well, things happen, and plans need to change. We can't control what others do. We'll get you moved into the correct room tomorrow. We'll be a little behind schedule, but not too bad. There's nothing on the cheerleading schedule until tomorrow, so feel free to order room service if you want." He opened our door. "I'm in room three-twelve. See you tomorrow."

"B-Y-E. Bye," Beaker mumbled.

"I heard that," TL called.

He closed the door, and I set my laptop down. "This sucks."

"Yeah, but, oh well. Nothing we can do about it."

Logic told me she was right. But it still sucked.

Tossing down the rest of my stuff, I looked around. A bathroom lay immediately to the left of the door and was decorated with the same gold-

and-marble design of the lobby. The shower and toilet each had its own separate little room. Pretty cool.

Farther inside, two king-size beds occupied the majority of the room, decorated with burgundy-and-white comforters and pillows. A long shark had been engraved on each headboard, and, as Nalani said, the fin would release the hidden compartment—in the correct room, of course.

A deluxe wood desk sat in the corner with a brown leather chair in front.

Gauzy curtains covered a medium-size window that looked out over the sun-sparkling ocean.

Matching the color scheme, standard hotel carpet covered the floor.

All in all, it was a great room.

Beaker flopped across the bed closest to the window. "I haven't even been here an hour and my jaw already hurts from smiling."

Mine did, too, actually.

Unzipping the front pocket of my backpack, I pulled out a pack of gum. "Here."

Beaker eyed it warily. "What is it?"

I lifted my brows. "Gum. What do you think it is? Poison?"

She gave me a skeptical look. "Why are you being nice to me?"

Rolling my eyes, I tossed it onto her bed. "Because I'm a nice person."

Beaker snorted, and I turned away, busying myself by reading the Barracuda Key pamphlets on the desk.

Behind me, a wrapper crinkled, and I smiled.

TL and David had done the same thing for me on my first mission, giving me lollipops when I least expected it. It'd always made me feel cozy, comforted, and, well . . . loved.

"Ya know"—*chew, snap, chew*—"you'd think with all the gum I chew, my jaw would be strong enough for the smiling."

It wasn't often Beaker made casual, nonhostile conversation with me. I turned around, hoping I wouldn't screw up the moment. "Different set of muscle groups."

Staring at the ceiling, she grunted her agreement.

So far so good. "Don't let anybody catch you chewing that."

Beaker blew a huge pink bubble, and it silently popped. "Don't worry. I won't."

I dug around in my backpack, searching for nothing in particular. "So why *do* you chew so much gum?"

Silence.

I dug a little deeper, keeping my hands busy.

More silence.

Great, GiGi. Good job. Way to screw up a rare, sort-of-friendly moment with Beaker.

She sniffed, and I glanced up.

"Urn . . ." she started, still staring at the ceiling. "It controls my anger."

Okay. Not what I'd expected her to say. But it made sense with the way she always furiously chomped it. "You must have a lot of anger."

She half laughed. "You have *no* idea."

I found a lollipop in the bottom of my pack. "So what happens if you don't get your gum? Do you explode or something?"

Beaker rolled her head over and looked at me. "Probably."

We both smiled.

She scrunched her face. "Gets pretty bad, actually. I've cussed people out. Hit things."

"Well, remind me to always have emergency gum on hand."

That comment earned a chuckle.

I peeled the wrapper from my lollipop and slipped the blackberry flavor into my mouth. "You should do yoga or something."

Beaker snorted. "Puh-lease." She scooted across the bed, grabbed the room service menu, and began browsing. A few seconds passed.

"Um . . ." she began and then her voice trailed away. "You doing okay? Ya know, with everything's that's going on? Your parents, this mission, blah, blah, blah."

Smiling a little, I sat down in the desk chair. I totally hadn't expected that. Blah, blah, and all. "Yeah, I'm doing okay. Thanks for asking."

She nodded a little and continued studying the menu. "What do you want to eat?" And that question effectively ended our tiny little heart-to-heart.

***

Early the next morning our room's phone rang. While I scrambled for the phone, Beaker pulled the covers over her head.

"Hullo," I mumbled into the receiver.

"Good morning," Nalani greeted me in her polite, hotel voice. "Your preassigned room will be ready in one hour. The Hotel Marquess is sorry

368

for any inconvenience this may have caused you. Please enjoy breakfast on us."

She hung up the phone, and I fumbled to return the handset to the base. While Beaker grabbed a few more minutes of sleep, I got showered and dressed and began packing what little I'd taken out for the night. Beaker finally got up and did the same.

We skipped the free breakfast, moved our things to our preassigned room, and began unpacking. I turned on my laptop and connected to the ranch's mainframe right as our door clicked. We both jerked around.

"Lord have mercy!" A petite Asian-American girl wandered in, talking to someone behind her. "Wait 'til you see this place!"

I looked at Beaker.

What's going on? She mouthed.

I shrugged.

The girl gasped. "Look! The toilet's got its own tiny room!"

"Hello?" I ventured.

The girl spun around. "Hi!"

The girl behind the first girl came up beside her. "Hi!"

I glanced from one small face to the other and then back to the first. Twins.

"We're twins!" They announced.

I smiled. "I see that!"

And I couldn't care less. All I wanted to know was what they were doing here in our prearranged private room, located directly below the one and only presidential suite where Eduardo Villanueva would be staying.

"I'm Lessy!" the first girl introduced, pointing to herself.

"I'm Jessy!" The second girl parroted.

"And we're your roommates!"

‹EIGHT›

Beaker and I stayed rooted to our spots, staring at the twin Asian-American girls with the southern accents.

Lessy and Jessy.

Or was it Jessy and Lessy?

"Did you say roommates?" Beaker asked.

The twins nodded enthusiastically.

I kept smiling while my brain scrambled to make sense of things.

"Sorry." Beaker laughed, covering my silence. "We thought our roommates were going to be someone else," she lied.

Lessy, or maybe Jessy, frowned. "Is there something wrong with us?"

"No." Beaker pushed up from her bed. "Not at all." She crossed the short distance to where the twins stood and stuck out her hand. "I'm Tiffany, and this is my partner Ana," she introduced, using our aliases for the mission.

Still smiling, I remained where I was. I needed to find TL and figure out what our next steps would be.

Beaker cleared her throat, drawing my attention over to her. Without moving her head, she rolled her eyes to the twins.

Oh! I sprung forward and shook each of their hands. "Hi, nice to meet you."

"Make yourselves comfortable," Beaker kept going with the niceties. "We were just on our way out to see our coach."

"Oh, okay!" The twins flopped down on one of the beds. "'Bye!"

"'Bye!" Beaker returned, ushering me out of the room. The door closed behind us. "What is wrong with you?" she hissed.

"I'm sorry. I froze. What are we going to do?"

She tugged me down the hall. "You're not supposed to freeze. You planned this whole mission, remember? If anybody would be allowed to freeze, it'd be me. This is *my* first mission, not yours. And 'What are we going to do?'" She scoffed. "Get it together. I thought you'd be better at this."

She was right. I needed to get it together. It was just . . . well . . . I'd been so thorough during my planning sessions with David, I really hadn't expected anything to go wrong.

Naive of me, I know.

We got to TL's room, and I rapped six quick times—our secret knock. He opened the door, and we slipped inside a room identical to ours.

"My roommate went to get ice," TL fired off. "Make it quick. What do you got?"

Rapidly, I told him the situation while he listened intently.

"What are you going to do," he asked when I finished.

The question caught me off guard. What was *I* going to do? But he always solved the problems. Not me.

"GiGi," TL prompted. "My roommate will be back any second. This is your operation. You asked for this. Now what are you going to do?"

"Text Nalani." I slipped my cell phone from my warm-ups pocket. "We need to meet and find out what's going on."

TL nodded. "Good."

I text messaged Nalani. All of our texts were coded for extra security. She responded within a second. "Third-floor utility closet," I read the display. "Five minutes."

Beaker popped a piece of gum in her mouth.

The door opened, and we all snapped back into role. In walked a guy I assumed to be TL's roommate. He stood a little shorter than me and had neat blond hair. I'd say he was in his early twenties.

"Well, hey!" He grinned. "You must be Ana and Tiffany. Your coach here has been telling me all about you two."

"Hi!" We greeted him in unison.

"Yep." TL squeezed the back of Beaker's neck. "These are my babies. Best girls I've ever had the privilege to choreograph."

Babies? TL would never call us his babies back at the ranch.

He turned to us. "This is my roomie, Coach Luke. He came with the pink-and-green team out of Portland."

The pink-and-green team? That'd be the Cheerleaders Are Better Athletes girls we met in the lobby.

Coach Luke shook his finger at Beaker. "Now, Tiffany. You know you're not supposed to have gum."

With a playful sigh, she rolled her eyes. "Sorry."

Beaker pulled the wrapper from her pocket, squished up the gum, and threw it away. "Won't happen again."

"Well," TL guided us out, "catch you later."

"'Bye!" Coach Luke waved.

"'Bye!" We waved back.

Beaker's smile faded as the door closed. "Do you think these people ever get tired of being in a good mood?"

"Shhh," TL hushed her.

We strode to the end of the carpeted hall and cut a left into the ice and vending machine alcove. The stairwell door sat right beside the utility closest. With a quick glance over our shoulders, we slid inside. The smell of bleach and soap overpowered the tiny space.

Nalani stood waiting, surrounded by bottles and boxes of cleaning supplies. She pulled a small blue pyramid from her uniform pocket and rotated the upper half. I recognized the device from the Rissala mission. Wirenut had developed it. It emitted an inaudible static pulse that blocked others from hearing our conversation.

He'd be so excited to find out Nalani had used it.

Beaker leaned in. "What is that?"

I quickly explained it to her.

"I've got only a few minutes," Nalani hurriedly said. "They think I'm in the restroom. The hotel is packed solid. No vacancy. Your unexpected roommates were last-minute America's Cheer contestants. I didn't check them in; another receptionist did. That's why they're in your room."

"And there's nothing you can do? There's nothing else available?" I asked, almost desperately, even though she'd just said there was no vacancy.

Nalani shook her head. "All the contestants are four to a room. Two to a bed. Your extra bed is the only available one. I'm sorry. If I had checked them in, I would've lied and told them there were no beds, but the other receptionist got to them first."

"What about the room we slept in last night?"

"It's reserved as well."

"And the coaches?" TL asked. "I've only got one roommate."

Nalani checked her watch. "You and your roommate are the only two male coaches. All the rest are women. And, yes, they're four to a room, too. There's no other way. You'll have to work around the situation."

Lightly, Nalani grasped my upper arm. "Eduardo Villanueva checked in a few moments ago."

My entire body chilled as the reality of why we were here hit me. Swallowing, I nodded my head.

With a quick squeeze, she released me. "The equipment is in the bed closest to the wall. Any questions?"

We all shook our heads.

"Wait ten seconds after I leave." Nalani rotated the top of the blue pyramid, turning it off. She handed it to TL. Scooting between us, she opened the door a sliver and peeked out. Then soundlessly, she slipped into the alcove and down the stairs.

Ten seconds later we followed, heading back down the hall to our rooms.

TL stopped at his. "It's ten o'clock. The opening meeting is in thirty minutes. I'll meet you in the lobby."

Beaker and I nodded, continuing on. We passed room after room, some with blaring loud TVs, others quiet. We got to ours and slipped the card key in the lock. No sounds muffled through the cracks. Maybe the twins had left.

"Hi!" Jessy and Lessy perked up when we opened our door.

Or maybe not.

"Hi." I noted the lack of enthusiasm in my return.

Beaker disappeared into the bathroom.

"So where ya'll from?!"

Vaguely, I registered the question as I glanced to the ceiling. *Eduardo Villanueva is up there right now.*

Slowly, I pulled my focus down to the bed closest to the wall—the same bed the twins currently sat on, propped against the headboard. I narrowed in on the shark behind their backs. What if one of them accidentally pressed the fin?

Both twins turned and looked at the shark, and I snapped to attention.

"Sorry." I laughed. "Brain fade."

They turned back around, and I plopped down on the other bed, recalling their last question. "Tiffany and I are from California. How about you two?"

"Giiive us an A!" They steepled their skinny arms above their heads. "Alabama!"

I grinned, while my mind hyperdrived. I wanted to get them out of here so I could get inside that bed. I wanted to look at the equipment and get set up. I wanted to tap into Eduardo's room.

Actually, I needed to get the twins off that bed permanently in case one of them pressed the fin.

Beaker came from the bathroom, pressing her fingertips to her forehead. "Can you all do something for me?"

The twins nodded. "Sure!"

"Can you please not talk in so many Ex! Cla! Ma! Tion! Points?!" Beaker slid her hands down her face. "You're giving me a headache."

I closed my eyes on a silent groan. *Beeeaaaker.*

"For real?" one twin asked, and I snapped open my eyes.

Beaker sat down in the desk chair. "For real."

The twins looked at each other, and, gradually, matching smiles lit their faces. Real, happy, genuine smiles. Not the fake ones they'd flashed before.

The twin on the left slid down on her pillow. "Oh, thank you."

Her voice sounded different now. Deeper. More relaxed.

"Yeah." The twin on the right toed her purple-and-white tennis shoes off. "We don't even want to be here."

Well, isn't this an interesting twist?

Twin on the left punched the pillow beneath her head. "Our momma makes us do all these stupid events. This is our twelfth year of competitive cheer."

"Your *twelfth* year?" Beaker asked. "How old are you?"

Twin on the right brought her outstretched legs up into a crossed position. "We're nineteen years old." She pointed between me and Beaker. "Thought we were twelve or something, didn't ya?"

Yeah, actually, I had.

"I know. I know." Twin on the left raised her hands in the air. "Why, you ask, are we nineteen and still letting our momma tell us what to do?" She dropped her arms over her eyes. "Weee dooon't knooowww."

Twin on the right patted her sister. "One more year. That's all we need. And then we'll have a record deal and our own money."

"Record deal?" I questioned.

"See." Twin on the right turned to us. "We're singers. Country music. Faith Hill's our favorite." She narrowed her eyes at me. "You kinda look like her, ya know?"

Twin on the left lifted her arms from her eyes. "No, she doesn't."

"Yes, she does." This came from the twin on the right.

Beaker and I looked at each other.

"Anyway," twin on the right continued, "any day now we'll have our record deal."

Cheerleading, twin, country music singers. Interesting.

Twin on the left rolled over, propping her head in her hand. "Enough about us. What about you two?"

I shrugged. "Nothing special. Average ordinary girls. Ana and Tiffany, at your service." If they only knew.

Twin on the right pouted her bottom lip. "Bummer. I was hoping you were spies or something. Then we could all be undercover together. Jessy and Lessy, the hidden country talent. Ana and Tiffany, out for cold blood."

Beaker and I gave our best, ha-ha-that's-so-funny-spies-snort-snort laugh.

"Since we're going to be together for the whole competition," I suggested, "I suppose we should be able to tell you apart." This twin-on-the-left, twin-on-the-right business was about to drive me nuts.

"Oh, sure. We get that all the time." They scrambled together, kneeling side by side on the bed.

"Look at our faces." Twin on the right lifted her left brow. "What do you see that's different?"

I studied one face, then the next, and back to the first. I glanced at Beaker. "Well?"

"Scar."

"That's what I got." I pointed to the twin on the right. "You've got a scar running through your left brow." A scar so slight I would have never noticed it if I hadn't really studied their faces.

Twin on the right bounced her scarred brow. "I'm Jessy. Jagged-scar Jessy."

Lessy bounced off the bed, rattling the headboard and drawing my attention to the shark.

I eyeballed the fin. I had to get them off that bed. "Do you, um, mind if we sleep in that bed instead of this one?"

Jessy wedged her foot back into one of her purple-and-white tennis shoes. "Why?"

Why? I hadn't expected her to ask why. "Because . . . because . . ." Because there's a secret panel in your bed.

"Because," Beaker stood, "Ana's got this thing about sleeping near windows. She's afraid the boogeyman's going to climb in and get her. She's got to be near the wall."

With my best, innocent face, I shrugged. "I'm a freak that way. You don't mind, do you?"

Jessy tightened her laces. "Nope. But if the boogeyman comes in the door, he'll get you first."

I laughed. "I'll take my chances."

Lessy checked herself in the mirror. "Let's go. We don't want to be late for the *opening ceremony*. Yeah!" She rolled her eyes.

Laughing at her mock enthusiasm, we filed out of the room and down the hall. Beaker pressed the elevator button, and we waited.

Lessy and Jessy began discussing lyrics to a song they were working on, and, slowly, the discussion turned into an argument. Then Lessy started singing to block out her sister, and I had to admit she had a pretty darn good voice.

The elevator door slid open. Four men stood against the back wall— three overly muscular and one average, ranging in height from five eight to six one. Dressed in black suits, with dark hair and tanned skin, their faces displayed no expression as they stared at us.

Realizing who these men were, my stomach dropped. I was about to get in the elevator with them. I took a silent, deep breath and ran my gaze over each of their faces. Scrutinizing their features, I stopped at the last one on the right. The average-built one, but the tallest. The only one with silver glinting in his dark hair.

Eduardo Villanueva. My parents' killer.

My jaw tightened as I took in his tight curly hair, sinister brown eyes, and dark shadowed cheeks.

Lessy and Jessy stepped onto the elevator, still arguing and singing, oblivious to the four men.

Beaker turned, purposefully bumping into me, silently telling me to snap out of it.

I forced myself to drag my focus away from Eduardo's awful face when all I wanted to do was fly into the elevator and gouge out his emotionless eyes. I wanted to scream at him for what he'd done to my parents, to my life.

Instead, I sniffed, cleared my throat, and then lightly coughed. *Cover for me.* "Oh, I forgot something in the room. I'll meet you guys down there."

Lessy and Jessy didn't even hear me. Beaker nodded. She'd gotten my code.

I flicked one last look to Eduardo before turning from the elevator. With his head bent toward the man beside him, he listened to whatever the man was whispering. Probably discussing what horrible thing they planned to do next.

The elevator door slid closed. I hurried back down the hall and into our room, locked the door, and ran over to the bed.

I studied the body of the wooden shark and the fin attached to the top. I didn't see how anything could serve as a release button.

I leaned over the pillows and pushed the fin.

Nothing.

I pushed again, harder.

Nothing.

Crawling onto the bed, I traced my fingers around the edge of the fin. A slight gap existed where it had been attached to the headboard. A gap so tiny, no one would even notice it unless they felt for it.

I balled up my hand and knocked it hard, once, quick, with the side of my fist. It rattled the headboard.

Click. The bed shifted a little.

Scrambling off the bed, I surveyed it from head to foot and back up again. Nothing appeared different.

I yanked off the pillows and covers and threw them onto the other bed. Lifting up the mattress, I peered beneath.

Nothing but a thin piece of plywood.

Huh.

I got down on my hands and knees and looked underneath the bed. Carpet, hair, dust, a suspicious stain, and one forgotten flip-flop. Nothing else.

With a sigh, I sat up and glanced over to the clock. I'd already been up here ten minutes. I needed to hurry up and figure this out and get down to the meeting.

Okay, think, GiGi, think. You've got 191 IQ points. Put them to work. One bed with a hidden panel, one without. I knew I released the panel because

I'd heard the click. And the bed shifted. So I had the correct bed. I hadn't misunderstood Nalani.

I glanced from the unmade, secret panel bed to the other one, and it hit me. Compare one with the other.

I lifted the mattress of the made bed and peeked underneath.

Bingo!

There was no plywood, just regular strips of wood supported its mattress.

Turning back to my bed, I wedged my fingers under the plywood and lifted to reveal a hidden compartment. Four trays set side by side as large as the king-size bed.

Audio and visual monitoring. TCVC cables, Socarmi recorders, Lome cameras, Wako lenses, Nociv monitors, and on and on and on.

Sweet. Top of the line. Every single thing from the equipment list.

Metal arms supported the plywood on both sides and held up the mattress. Locking the arms in the up position, I picked up a TCVC cable right as my phone vibrated. Yanking it from my pocket, I checked the encrypted display. Punching in my password, I decoded the message from TL.

TAKING ROLL. DOWN HERE. NOW.

I released the lock on the arms and brought the plywood back down. I banged the side of my fist into the fin and heard the click. I tried to lift the plywood just to make sure it was locked back in place. Sure enough, it didn't budge.

Quickly, I spread all the covers and pillows back in place and then hurried from the room.

I zipped down the hall, cut through the ice machine alcove, then the stairs, and raced across the lobby. I caught Nalani's eye with a where-do-I-go face. She discreetly pointed to a closed conference room door.

Quietly, I clicked it open and slipped inside. The coaches lined the back wall, and the cheer competitors sat in blue plastic chairs, filling the large room. The current America's Cheer team stood across the front dressed in matching red-white-and-blue shorts and T-shirts.

The one with the microphone pointed to someone in the crowd. She didn't look happy. "Get up."

Every head in the room silently turned in that direction.

I searched the crowd, curious what was going on.

"You." The microphone woman jabbed her finger. "In the red-and-white ribbon. Get up."

Red-and-white ribbon? Oh, no.

"Now," microphone lady echoed.

From the crowd, a dark-haired girl slowly stood.

Beaker.

‹NINE›

Narrowing her eyes, the America's Cheer team leader pointed across the crowd to Beaker. "Spit it out."

Beaker lifted her brows, all innocent. "Spit what out?"

The team leader buried her lips in the microphone. "The gum."

Throughout the crowd, cheerleaders gasped.

I rolled my eyes.

Beaker delicately cleared her throat. "I don't have any gum."

Team leader crooked her finger. "Come here."

Beaker inched her way past the other cheerleaders sitting in her row and out into the aisle. Whispers trickled through the crowd as she walked down to the front. In unison, the current America's Cheer team authoritatively shook their heads at her.

This was ridiculous.

The team leader pinched Beaker's chin. "Open up."

Beaker did.

Pursing her lips, the team leader inspected Beaker's mouth. "Tongue."

She lifted her tongue.

Letting go of Beaker's chin, the team leader turned toward the crowd. "Who in here saw this competitor with gum?"

Almost everyone's hand went up.

Come on, people.

The team leader turned back to Beaker. "Clearly, you have swallowed it. Give me three times around the room. The cheer is 'G-U-M. Gum makes me look like a bum.'" The team leader leaned in. "And make it look good, or you're going to do it again."

SHANNON GREENLAND

Beaker's jaw clenched, and I could almost visualize the steam shooting from her ears.

I glanced down the row of people with me along the back wall. Stoically, TL stood near the end, keeping his gaze glued on Beaker.

His concentrated expression reminded me of the Rissala mission. He'd taught me how to send supportive, mental energy to Wirenut.

I know. It sounds weird. But it really works.

I turned my attention back to Beaker at the front and focused all my brain cells on sending her you-can-do-this vibes.

Inch by inch her cheeks crept upward into a gigantic, face-splitting grin. She took off around the room, clapping and jogging. "G-U-M! Gum makes me look like a bum!"

She circled around the back, came right past me, and didn't even spare me a glance.

I bet she hated me right now. Thanks to me and my friendly gum, she was running laps.

Beaker went down the room's other side and back across the front. "G-U-M! Gum makes me look like a bum!"

Some of the girls sarcastically clapped with her; others snickered. A few started bee-bopping in their chairs.

How would they feel if they were the ones put on the spot? I bet they wouldn't find it so entertaining then.

Beaker circled three complete times, smiling as she jogged, clapped, and chanted. She didn't look at me once.

She trotted to a stop back at the front and went straight into a back handspring. She came out of it and into a liberty, with her right foot on the inside of her left knee and her arms straight up. "Go, America's Cheer!"

And make it look good, or you're going to do it again.

Beaker's handspring definitely made it look good.

The America's Cheer team did matching liberties. "Go, America's Cheer!"

Everyone in the crowd hopped to their feet. "Go, America's Cheer!"

And then the place broke into wild applause. They were like possessed, brain-washed cheerleaders.

You will be obnoxiously excited. You will snicker and make fun of others. You will spell everything you say.

I smiled. Sometimes I really amused myself.

The cheering died down, and everyone took their seats again.

The team leader brought the microphone back to her mouth. "Okay. Let's finish taking roll, then we'll briefly go over the schedule and break for lunch."

Quickly, she went through the list, hitting my name a fourth of the way down and Beaker's a little after.

After she finished, the team leader shuffled some papers. "Each of you has a schedule in your registration packets. That schedule could change, depending on various things. You will be notified immediately of any changes. You are expected to be prompt for meals. Breakfast at seven, lunch at noon, dinner at five. All mornings are reserved for physical fitness and learning new routines. Afternoons are for run-throughs, team practice, and meetings. Evenings will be group functions. All contestants are expected to attend everything. Any absences mean points deducted from your team's final score."

On and on she went, seeming to fill every minute of every day. I didn't know how we would find time to do the things we needed to do for our mission.

"Dismissed," the team leader announced without asking for questions.

Girls filed passed me as I hung back, waiting for Beaker and TL.

"I'll have some juice, but that's it. I weighed in two pounds too heavy this morning."

"This bra is driving me nuts."

"Oh my *God*! My ribbon broke!"

"Good thing nobody saw the gum in *my* mouth."

"Hi!" Jessy and Lessy waved as they passed me.

I waved back.

With Beaker behind him, TL grabbed my arm and kept right on going out the door. We cut off from the lunch line, down a hallway, and around a corner.

He glanced around to make sure we were alone and let go of my arm. He did not look happy. Pulling the blue pyramid from his pocket, he rotated it on. "Where were you?"

"I-I was in my room looking at the equipment."

"You are always, *always* to inform me of where you are and what you are doing." His jaw hardened. "Do we understand each other?"

"Y-yes, sir." But I thought this was *my* mission. I thought *I* was the one leading.

"You designed this mission," he continued, "but it doesn't mean you act on your own accord. I am the one who is ultimately in charge. I have to know where you are at all times. What if something had happened? What if something had gone wrong? What if someone from home base had contacted me and wanted to know your whereabouts? I can't say 'I don't know.' How do you think that would make me look? Us look?"

I hadn't thought about it like that. I swallowed. "I'm sorry. I should've texted you to let you know I was going back to the room."

TL took a step back. "I'm not saying you can't make your own decisions. I'm saying you *must* keep me informed of your locale."

TL turned to Beaker. "Or *you* should've told me. We're a team. We work as a unit."

Beaker and I nodded.

"Okay. Enough said." His cell phone buzzed, and, unclipping it from his waistband, he checked the display and answered his phone, "One second." He reached inside his pocket and pulled out two sugar packets. "It's the crystallized siumcy Beaker created. Nalani slipped me a couple packs. Make sure each of your roommates ingests this. The Tricsurv it goes with is in your equipment supplies. You'll know where your roommates are at all times."

Beaker turned to me. "What's a Tricsurv?"

I took a second to simplify the explanation in my brain. "The Tricsurv is a tracker. It looks like a computer chip and is usually inserted into a specialized watch. But since we're not allowed to wear watches, Chapling and I rigged everyone's cell phone to accept it. It'll give us our roommates coordinates at all times."

"When did you create that?" Beaker asked.

I shook my head. "I didn't. The Specialists already had it. When you told David and me about your powdered GPS compound, I knew it would work perfect with the Tricsurv. Tricsurv's been used for years in GPS situations. By the way, does the siumcy taste like anything?"

"Nothing," Beaker answered. "The twins won't even know."

I pocketed the sugar packets, excited to use them.

"Okay. I don't want either of you skipping meals on this trip. Keep your energy up." TL strode off down the hall, and we headed back the way we came.

"Let me give David a quick update." I got out my cell and punched UNEXPECTED ROOMATES. LOCATED EQUIPMENT . . . SAW EDUARDO.

He responded within seconds. FOCUS ON DNA DUST NEXT . . . YOU OKAY?

I knew he was referring to the "saw Eduardo" part. I WILL BE. BYE. BYE.

Beaker untied the ribbon from around her neck and crammed it in her pocket. "This thing's choking me."

"Sorry about the gum," I apologized.

She shrugged. "Whatever."

"That back handspring was pretty impressive."

She smiled a little.

We crossed through the hotel's lobby and walked into the large meeting area that would serve as America's Cheer's meal room for the week.

A buffet stretched along the side wall. Tables and chairs had been set up cafeteria style, already occupied by bubbly cheerleaders eating their food.

Lessy and Jessy sat right in the center. They waved to us. "We saved you seats," they yelled over the chattering noise.

We waved back.

The buffet line had died down to nothing. We grabbed plates and loaded up. Turkey sandwiches, potato salad, chips, apple wedges, ginger cookies, carrots with ranch dressing, and cheese cubes.

I took some of everything and extras of the cookies. I didn't realize how *hungry* I was.

Beaker and I wove around the tables, heading toward Lessy and Jessy. Whispers followed us.

"What cows."

"Oh my God. Did you see all their food?"

"And they think they're going to make the team?" Snort. "Not on that diet."

I glanced around at the other girls' plates. Carrot sticks on one. A piece of turkey on another. One lousy scoop of potato salad on another.

No wonder they were all so skinny.

Beside me, Beaker grabbed a cookie and shoved it in her mouth. "Mmm-mmm, good."

I rolled my lips in so I wouldn't laugh.

We sat our plates down at Lessy and Jessy's table.

"Hi!" I greeted them cheerily, then realized I didn't need to. This was Lessy and Jessy, aspiring country singers. They were acting a role just like us.

In fact—I glanced around—I'd bet there were more people who didn't want to be here either.

"Lord." Jessy blinked a few times. "You're really going to eat all that?"

"Yep, and I'll probably go back for seconds," I bragged.

Lessy put her hand over her heart. "My hero."

"Dangit." I got back up. "I forgot to get sweet tea. Ya'll want some?

They looked unexcitedly at their water, then across the room to the drinks table.

"Oh, come on," I teased. "Live a little. I dare you to have *extra* sugar in it." Nobody could refuse a dare.

They both narrowed their eyes. "Bring it on."

I put my hand over my heart. "My heroes."

They giggled.

Beaker and I crossed the room to the drinks table. She grabbed two teas and I did, too, dumping in real sugar combined with my tracking "sugar."

"That was almost *too* easy," Beaker mumbled as we made our way back to Lessy and Jessy.

Eagerly, they gulped down half of their tea. Jeez, these girls needed to live a little.

Jessy wiped her mouth. "Nice gum chanting, Tiffany."

Beaker playfully smirked.

The pink-and-green team out of Portland strolled past, slanting us a haughty look. What the heck? They'd been so friendly earlier.

Jessy leaned close to me. "Don't you hate that? To your face everyone's all smiley and friendly. But they're all a bunch of back stabbers. Especially if they think you're better than them."

Better than them? I almost snorted. I could barely do a back handspring.

"Don't look." Lessy surreptitiously pointed her carrot across the room. "But I heard the red-haired girl on the black-and-yellow team is a genius. She's got an IQ higher than like Einstein or something."

A *genius?* I turned and looked.

Jessy yanked me back around. "She said don't look."

Sorry.

A genius? Wow. For some reason I hadn't thought of cheerleaders as geniuses.

Lessy gulped down the rest of her tea. "We're going to walk down to the beach. Wanna come?"

I shook my head. "Nah. I'm going to watch some TV." Perfect time to check out the equipment and possibly rig Eduardo Villanueva's room for surveillance.

Beaker swallowed her turkey bite. "Me, too." She checked her watch. "There's only thirty minutes before our first practice."

Jessy grabbed all of her and Lessy's garbage. "Suit yourselves. Later, ya'll."

We waved as they strolled off, quickly shoved in a mouthful of food, and hightailed it out of there.

Up the elevator, down the hall, and into our room we went. Beaker texted TL to let him know where we were while I texted Nalani.

EV LOCATION? I typed.

ROOM. Nalani responded.

Perfect. "He's in his room. We can do the DNA dust."

Quickly, I showed Beaker how to open the bed's secret panel.

I took two Tricsurv chips and plugged them into my phone and into hers. A satellite image of our hotel and surrounding area flicked onto the display. Two red dots popped up.

"That'd be Lessy and Jessy." I tapped the dots. "And they're on the beach just like they said. The Tricsurv will beep when they get within twenty feet of us."

"That's barely enough time to put all this back together."

"I know." I put the phone on the nightstand. "We need to work quickly."

Beaker lifted a tray full of all sorts of powders, liquids, and chemistry stuff from the secret panel.

She grabbed a bag of clear crystals.

While she began mixing the DNA dust, I pulled the mini-laptop from my luggage, powered up, and connected to our satellite. I slipped on my glasses and keyed in the scrambler code and the coordinates to Eduardo Villanueva's room. The satellite zeroed in on the hotel and X-rayed through the roof and straight into the presidential suite.

Indeed, Eduardo was there along with all his men. And an easy chair sat right on top of where I needed to drill.

386

Good. No one would see a thing. "I'll use the silencer so they won't hear. It's a one-sixteenths bit for your syringe, right?"

"Yes."

From one of the hidden trays, I retrieved the drill, inserted a one-sixteenths bit, and screwed on the silencer.

I replaced my glasses with protective goggles and climbed onto our bed and over to the far edge, where it sat only a few inches from the room's corner. Standing on the edge, I silently drilled through the ceiling straight up into Eduardo's suite.

Plaster sprinkled me as I pulled the drill back out. "Ready?"

"Yeah." Beaker poured a fine red dust into a syringe and handed it to me. "Remember to go slow to give time for the dust to dissipate, turn invisible, and absorb into Eduardo and his men's skin."

Over the next few days, anywhere they went, we'd be able to see their DNA trailing behind them. Whatever they got into, we'd have proof.

I inserted the syringe into the hole and slowly admitted the dust. "Ya know," I whispered, "this DNA dust you created is incredibly brilliant."

Beaker shrugged. "Yeah, yeah. Whatever."

Whatever? There was no way I could've come up with something like this. But then, I was the computer specialist, not the chemist.

Finishing off with the dust, I handed Beaker the syringe and she gave me a tube of spackle.

I squeezed it into the hole, and the ceiling looked normal again. "Now all we gotta do is figure out how to track him electronically."

"Somehow I doubt we'll get close enough to put crystallized siumcy in his ice tea."

Suddenly, the Tricsurv in my cell phone beeped, and Beaker and I jolted into action.

We quickly tossed everything back in the trays, slammed the shark's fin, threw the covers and pillows back in place, cut the light, and jumped into bed.

Our door opened and in tiptoed Jessy and Lessy. Beneath the covers, my heart raced.

"You asleep?" One of them whispered. "Thought you said you were going to be watching TV."

Beaker yawned. "It's all right."

Lessy ripped open the curtains. "We met the *hottest* guy."

I squinted against the afternoon sunlight. "Yeah?"

Jessy jumped onto their king-size bed. "Oh, yeah. Major hot. His name's CJ, and he's eighteen."

Lessy hopped onto our bed. "Major hot. Major, major, *major* hot."

Scooting my legs out of the way, I laughed, trying to sound carefree, when all I could think was, *Oh my God, she's bouncing on our secret panel bed!*

Jessy dove between me and Beaker. "He's got blond hair and blue eyes, and did I tell you he's hot?"

I moved over, trying to protect the headboard.

Lessy body-slammed her sister, and, giggling, they rolled into me. I caught a quick glimpse of Beaker trying to come between the twins and the headboard a split second before one of them rammed into the fin release lever.

Click. The bed shifted.

They stilled. "What was that?"

‹TEN›

Someone rapped on our door.

"I'll get it." Silently thankful for the distraction, I leapt off the bed. I had no *clue* how to answer the twins' question.

I opened the door to see TL in the threshold.

"Ready for practice?" he asked.

"Sure."

We spent the entire rest of the day practicing cheers, doing routine run-throughs, and sitting in meetings. The next day was just the same, and when dinner finally came, I couldn't wait to eat and get back to our room. I just wished the twins would go to the beach or something so I could get some work done.

After dinner, my roommates and I filed into our room. The twins plopped across our bed. What was it with them and our bed?

As soon as we closed the door, someone knocked.

I opened it to an America's Cheer team member.

She flipped a paper over on her clipboard. "Hi! There's been a change in the schedule. The bonfire rally scheduled for tomorrow night will be tonight on the beach in thirty minutes."

Bonfire rally? The schedule said free time until tomorrow morning. I'd had things planned. Lots of things. Like ditching the twins and setting up more surveillance. Figuring out how to physically plant a tracking device in addition to the DNA tracker on Eduardo. And possibly following him if he went somewhere.

Using a red-white-and-blue pen, the America's Cheer team member checked us off on her pad. "This is a mandatory event, so everyone must be present."

I planted the fakest, Im-so-thrilled smile on my face. "Sounds super! I'll let my roommates know."

She two-finger waved me. "Too-da-loo. See you in thirty."

I waved back.

"This sucks," Lessy pouted when I closed the door.

"Yeah," Jessy joined her. "We were totally going to blow this joint and go into town for the night."

Beaker snorted. "And do what? Did you not see this place when you came in? There's nothing to do but exercise your neat and tidy skills."

Playfully, she shoved the twins off our bed and spread out on it. "And stay off my bed, would ya? I like my space. I don't play well with others."

Not bad, Beaker. Maybe that would keep them off our bed.

Lessy checked herself in the mirror. "I'm not going to sit around here for thirty minutes. I'm going to go on down." She turned to us. "Coming?"

"I need to use the bathroom," Beaker and I answered at the exact same time.

Jessy laughed. "Just don't do it together."

The twins bounded out the door. As soon as they left, I snatched up my cell phone from the nightstand and did a quick scan. Two red dots moved as they rode the elevator down.

I nodded to Beaker. "They're in the lobby."

I quickly texted David to let him know our progress. DNA DUST IN PLACE. TRACKERS ON ROOMMATES.

He responded right away. GOTCHA. GET ELECTRONIC TRACKER ON EDUARDO NOW.

Beaker hopped off our bed, lifted the mattress and plywood, and grabbed the rose-tinted, silver-framed glasses from one of the hidden trays, the same glasses she'd showed us in our pre-op meeting. "These are for the DNA dust. We'll be able to see anywhere Eduardo goes. It's all we've got until we figure out a way to put an electronic tracker on him."

I nodded. "Good. I'll let Nalani know to text us if he's on the move."

Beaker pulled out another one of the trays. "What do we have in the way of trackers?"

I hit send to text Nalani, then ran my gaze over everything in the trays. "Breath mints. Pepper. Stick-on freckles. Blow darts that simulate mosquito stings . . ." I snatched everything up, gave half to Beaker, and we loaded down our backpacks. "Let's take it all so we'll be ready in any situation. One way or another we're going to get a tracker on Eduardo."

Quickly, we put our bed back in order and headed from the room.

TL stood with Coach Luke at the elevator.

"Hi!" We joined them.

TL rubbed his hands together. "You girls ready for the bonfire?"

We enthusiastically nodded.

Coach Luke tapped the DNA glasses propped on my head. "Those sure are spiffy glasses."

"Thanks!" Who actually used the word *spiffy*? And by God, if he put a fingerprint on the lenses . . .

The elevator dinged, and as the doors slid open, four men in black suits came into view. I caught my breath. Eduardo stood in the back with his guys, in the exact same position they had been in earlier today. Their blank expressions dropped ever so slightly with annoyance at seeing us. I bet they *were* tired of us bubbly cheerleaders. And this was only the beginning.

Just then, my phone vibrated. I knew it was Nalani texting me back that Eduardo was on the move.

Okay, focus. Here's a chance to get a tracker on him. My eyes narrowed with orneriness. Maybe I should make it a little more annoying for them. I *am* a cheerleader, after all.

Yeah, why not?

As I bounded inside, I quickly rummaged in my backpack and pulled out the first small electronic tracker—the tracking bug—that I could get a grip on. "Hi!" I said cheerily, my ponytail boinging behind me. "Are you all with America's Cheer?"

Eduardo and his men made no move. They didn't even look at me.

Keeping my grin, I blinked a few times. "Are you all with America's Cheer?"

Slowly, all four sets of dark eyes moved over to me. Simultaneously, they shook their heads.

Still grinning, I blinked. "Oh! Are you with the hotel?"

They shook their heads.

Grin. Blink. "Oh! Are you here for vacation or business?"

They shook their heads.

I reached out and tugged on the suit jacket of the man beside Eduardo. "You look *spiffy* enough to be here for some business meeting."

"Miss."

Maintaining my grin, I turned to Eduardo. It was the first time I'd ever heard his deep voice. It caught me a little off guard, and I felt my stomach drop. I immediately thought of my parents and wondered if they had hated his voice as much as I did at this moment. "Yes?"

His lids fell slightly, hooding his menacing eyes. "Stop talking to us. And don't ever touch me or anyone with me again."

My grin faded as I nodded and forced myself to turn around. I wanted to ram my foot into his kneecap.

Beside me, Beaker cleared her throat. "I didn't get a chance to brush my teeth after dinner. Do you have those mints with you?"

I reached inside my backpack, pulled out the box of tracking mints, and handed them to her.

She opened the top, tapped one out, and tossed it into her mouth. "Mmm-mmm, good." She turned to Eduardo. "Want one?"

I laughed. I couldn't help myself.

The elevator dinged open, and we filed out.

TL waved on Coach Luke. "I'll be there in a sec. I want to talk to my girls."

Eduardo and his men filed past us, through the lobby with a dozen or so loudly gossiping cheerleaders, and straight out the door. I pulled the DNA detector glasses off my head and slipped them on. Sure enough, a red trail followed in their wake.

I lifted the glasses and checked out the difference. No trail existed. These things were cool.

Putting an arm around both of us, TL hugged us to his sides and companionably strolled with us down the hallway. We cut a corner and walked straight into a small meeting room.

He closed the door behind us, pulled the blue pyramid from his pocket, and rotated the top. He turned to me. "You know you stepped beyond boundaries in the elevator. What was the number one thing David taught you when you were designing this mission?"

I took off the glasses and looped them in my T-shirt. "Not to let personal emotions muddle effective decision making."

"Well, guess what? You just let your emotions make you stupid. Because that was the most ignorant thing I've ever seen you do."

His harsh words didn't make me feel guilty *or* apologetic. They made me downright mad. "So."

TL got right up in my face. "Young lady, you watch your tone with me *and* show some respect. This is the second time you've messed up. This mission is beginning to lack focus. You need to get back on track."

I clamped my teeth together so I wouldn't say anything I'd regret. This mission did *not* lack focus.

He held his steely eyes level with mine for a few long seconds, letting me see *he* was the one in charge.

I didn't tell him I'd transferred a tracking bug when I touched that man's suit. Being mad made me keep that information to myself. I'd track the guy myself and then go to TL with the information. He'd be proud of me then.

TL took a step back. "Beaker, give me a rundown."

She did, detailing everything we'd done on the mission so far. The whole time she talked, I stood beside her *itching* to get out of here and activate the tracking software on my cell phone. Eduardo and his men could be miles from here by now.

And the tracking bug I'd transferred to Eduardo's man could, at any time, be uncovered by a detector, if they had one. Then they would definitely know someone was here following them. So maybe transferring that bug hadn't been such a good idea.

Although, it was only a thirty-minute bug. It would dry up and fall off his jacket when that time had passed. And the DNA dust would only show where they'd been, not where they were going.

That was why I *had* to get a tracker into their bloodstream via the mints, or the sugar, or the simulated mosquito sting. Trackers in the blood were the only type that couldn't be detected and would definitely give us their coordinates.

"GiGi?"

I snapped to attention. "What?" I glanced around. TL had gone on ahead to the bonfire.

"I said, are you ready?"

I grabbed Beaker's arm. "Listen, you gotta cover for me. I transferred a thirty-minute bug to one of Eduardo's men. If I don't go now and follow them, I'll lose them"

"What am I supposed to say if someone asks where you are?"

"I'm in the bathroom with girl issues," I said, taking out my cell phone and activating the tracking software. "No one argues when someone has girl issues."

Two red dots popped up on my screen. The twins. And a blue dot. Eduardo's man. I raced for the door. "Be back before you know it."

With a glance down the hall toward the lobby, I headed in the opposite direction, past a few rooms, and out the side exit door. I trailed along the length of the hotel to the front and slipped the rose-colored glasses back on.

I checked out the portico where two bellmen lingered near their stand, reviewing a logbook. A red DNA trail led from the hotel's front doors across the portico, and then stopped where Eduardo and his men must have gotten into a car. This was why we definitely needed a tracker on them. Anytime they got in a car, we'd lose their DNA trail.

Looking again at my cell phone, I confirmed the blue dot was still there. I took off down the long driveway, staying behind the bushes and palms, praying no one would see my tall blond self or red-and-white cheerleading getup. I wasn't exactly dressed for espionage.

In the distance, cheerleaders hooted and hollered at the bonfire rally. Poor Beaker. At least she had Lessy and Jessy.

Streetlights kicked on along the hotel's driveway and down in town. To the right, the sun dipped into the ocean's horizon.

Perfect. It would be pitch-black in no time.

I reached the bottom of the driveway and checked the blue dot on my phone screen. Eduardo and his men had already made it across the five-mile wide island to the other side.

Shoving my phone into my warm-ups pocket, I snapped the flap and took off running through town.

I tried to make it look more like a healthy jog than a frantic chase. I didn't need anyone calling 911.

Hello, officer? There's this tall blond girl running for her life through town.

Wouldn't *that* be great?

I had said it before, but I would say it again. Thank God for PT back at the ranch. There was no *way* I could make this run without it.

One mile in, I passed a boy on a bike and cut a U-ie. "Hey, kid, let me borrow your bike. I'll give you twenty bucks."

The kid narrowed his eyes. "Let me see the money."

Smart kid. I reached into my back pocket and pulled out my zipper pouch, hoping I did indeed have twenty bucks.

Thirty in all. Phew. I gave him twenty and pointed to the grocery store across the road. "I'll leave it in the bike rack in front of that store on the right. Cool with you?"

"Cool." He pocketed the money.

I climbed on his mini—dirt bike and away I went, pumping down the sidewalk, my knees nearly hitting my chest.

Twenty minutes later, I made it to the other side of the island. I stopped and checked my cell phone. The blue dot was beginning to fade, indicating the thirty-minute tracker was dissolving, but from what I could tell, Eduardo was to my right.

I rode into a deserted parking lot of the state park. Behind me stretched a half mile of beach highway leading back into town. In front of me spanned the dark ocean lit only by the half moon. To the left stood a small concrete visitor's station.

With the DNA glasses still on, I scanned the area. A red trail led from the parking lot, where the car must have dropped him and drove off, and onto the beach.

Leaving the bike, I followed the red trail across the beach and down the length of a long pier. The red trail stopped at the end of the pier, where a boat had probably picked him up.

There was no telling how far out he'd gone.

I unsnapped my pocket and pulled out the cell phone. I activated the audio recording/eavesdropping software Chapling had coded in.

Here went nothing.

I programmed it to record everything within a mile in front of me. Slowly, I scanned the ocean, moving from left to right, degree by degree, listening closely.

Static. Birds. Wind. Bugs. Nothing else.

I reprogrammed it for two miles and started over, left to right, degree by degree.

Bingo!

A faint conversation in what sounded like Spanish. Definitely Eduardo's deep, ugly voice.

Holding the phone steady, I pressed the record button and listened for fifteen solid minutes, wishing Parrot was here with me to translate immediately.

Through the phone I heard the boat's motor crank. Depressing the record button again, I sprinted back down the pier across the beach to the bike.

Down the highway, headlights pierced the night.

Crap.

Praying, *praying,* no one would see my blond head and flashy cheerleading outfit, I picked up the bike and ran for the visitor's station.

Right as the car pulled into the lot, I ducked into the shadows behind the concrete structure.

I drew in deep breaths and blew them out slowly, repeating the process a couple of times. Gradually, my thumping heart and heavy breaths normalized.

Peeking around the building's corner, I watched as a black Cadillac with tinted windows rolled to a stop.

A dark-haired man dressed in a suit climbed from the driver's side. I recognized him as one of the guys who had been in the elevator with Eduardo back at the hotel. I switched my phone to infrared mode, killed the flash, and snapped a picture of him.

He shut his door and leaned up against the car.

Minutes later, Eduardo and two more men emerged from the beach's darkness. I zoomed in on each face and got a picture.

They began speaking. From the distance between us their voices came across muffled, but I could still make out the conversation.

"What are we going to do with him?" one of the men asked in perfect English.

"Kill him," Eduardo responded, as if he was answering a pleasant question.

"And the woman and children?" the man asked.

"Did any of them see you deliver the money?"

The man nodded. "Two of them did."

Eduardo shrugged. "Kill them, too."

"How do you want it done?"

Eduardo stepped toward the car. "The usual—bullets to the head. All of them."

My whole body froze as I listened to them discuss killing an entire family. That easy. Bullets to the head. Just like my parents.

You can't just kill a whole family, I wanted to scream. What had they done that was so wrong?

The driver opened the door for Eduardo, the other men climbed in, and the car drove away.

I made myself get up when all I wanted to do was stay cowered in the shadows, grieving for the family that was about to die. A family that, although I didn't know them, was just like mine.

Crossing behind the visitor's center, I got a picture of the license plate as they pulled from the lot.

Waiting until its rear lights disappeared, I climbed on the bike and pedaled my way back down the highway, through town, and to the grocery store with the bike rack. I walked the remaining mile to the hotel, my footsteps heavy to match my thoughts.

David had said not to let my emotions cloud the mission. But this time I couldn't help it. I thought about what my life would have been like if Eduardo hadn't ruined it. Hadn't taken the two most important things from me. Where would I be right now? Still in Iowa? I'd probably live in a really cool house with maybe a dog. We'd go on family vacations every year. I'd help my mom cook dinner at night and help my dad on the weekends do lawn work. My mom and I might have planted a flower garden. Our Christmas tree would have been medium-size, with white lights and blue decorations.

Someone pushed through the exit door of the hotel as I approached, bringing me from my reverie. I walked in the hotel and took the stairs up to our floor.

Sweaty from my bike ride and worn out from my thoughts, I entered our room. There sat TL and Beaker. Him on one bed, her on the other, and the blue pyramid on the nightstand between them.

I knew I was in trouble. It didn't take a genius to figure that out.

TL indicated the desk chair. "Sit."

I glanced at Beaker as I sat. She gave me a good-luck look. "Where're the twins?"

"Downstairs," Beaker answered, "practicing their routine for tomorrow."

Nodding, I turned my attention to TL, wanting to get the whole thing over with.

"Back at the ranch I told you that you were developing into a person I hadn't expected you to. At least, not this quickly." He shifted on the bed. "There's nothing wrong with being an independent thinker and making your own decisions. But there's a time and place for that sort of thing. This isn't it. There's something wrong when you're with a team and you're not using them."

He pointed across the room to me. "You are sixteen and a half. Letting you plan this mission was a test. You have not had enough training to be making some of the decisions you're making, like going after Eduardo by yourself. And you have enough intelligence in that head of yours to understand that."

Reluctantly, my brain agreed with him.

"GiGi, you are extremely gifted. In so many ways. I don't think you fully comprehend what you are capable of." TL shook his head. "But I'm really disappointed in you. And that's something I never thought I'd say to you."

I glanced down at the carpeting, my heart sinking, but all I could think about was the family. "There's a family that's about to die," I whispered.

"I know. I know where you've been. I know what you've done. And I know you have a recording and pictures."

‹ELEVEN›

"What?" I brought my eyes up to his.

"I told you I'd always be watching you."

TL reached inside his pocket and pulled out a cell phone. "Everything you did tonight is right here." TL held the phone up. "Courtesy of Chapling."

I sat up in the desk chair. "How?"

"I had monitoring devices installed everywhere. Your phone. The stitching in your clothes." He waved his hand around. "This hotel room."

Anger bubbled inside of me.

"You are sixteen and a half," TL reminded me again. "And this is the first mission you've designed. Of course I'm going to monitor you. If you would put aside your agitation, logic would point that out."

"But don't you trust me?"

His brows lifted. "What have you done here in Barracuda Key to earn my trust?"

That question bounced around in my head for a few seconds, and I came up with . . . nothing. And if I had done something, it was negated by the other. I'd purposefully deceived him.

I sighed.

"I see logic is trickling in." TL stood. "From this moment, this mission is officially mine. You do not say or do anything unless it's a direct order from me. And one more anything out of you and I'm sending you back to California. Beaker and I can finish this on our own."

"What about the family?"

"I'll do everything in my power to help them, but odds are we're not going to find out who they are. I'm sorry. Get the recording sent back to home base so Parrot can translate it." Grabbing the blue audio-blocker pyramid, he strode straight past me and out the door.

Beaker took in a breath like she wanted to say something, but I ignored her. I walked over and turned on my laptop, connected my phone, and punched in the scrambler code.

HI. Chapling typed.

HI. I typed back. Usually his online presence made me smile. Not this time, though. I really wasn't in the mood.

WHATCHA GOT FOR ME?

NEED PARROT TO TRANSLATE. I clicked some keys. SENDING NOW.

I watched as my screen flicked, transmitting the recording back to home base.

GOT IT, he typed. YOU OKAY, SMARTGIRL?

Amazing how he could pick up on my mood from across cyber space.

I'M FINE, I typed back. I didn't need him worried about me.

My cell phone beeped. I checked the display. "Lessy and Jessy are coming."

GOTTA GO, I quickly told Chapling.

BYE! BE SAFE.

I closed my laptop, and Beaker and I lapsed into silence, staring off into space, waiting for the twins to appear. All I could think of was how bad I'd screwed up and of the family that was going to die.

Blowing out a silent breath, I dropped my head into my hand.

"Um . . ." Beaker started.

"It's okay. You don't have to say anything."

"I'm sorry you know people are about to die."

I barely nodded. Sometimes this new life of mine really sucked. I didn't like having the inside information on bad stuff that was about to happen, especially when I was powerless to do anything.

My cell phone buzzed, and I punched in the password to decode the incoming message.

THINKING OF YOU.

I silently read the message from David and smiled inwardly at the comfort and peace it brought. I didn't tell him how I'd screwed up.

ME TOO, I typed back.

***

The next day came way too early and was way too packed. Breakfast, training, rehearsal, lunch, and break. More training, another rehearsal, dinner, then a team-building activity where we all sat around with linked arms, singing. And in between, in the few moments we got to ourselves, I had to switch gears and try to focus on the mission.

At the end of the day, Beaker and I trudged into our room after the annoying sing-along.

Frustrated, I plopped down into the desk chair. "We haven't done *anything* today regarding the real reason we're here."

"Tell me about it," Beaker grumbled. "I can't believe I'm about to say this, but I'm happy Coach Capri made me work as hard as she did. There's no way I would've been prepared for all this cheery stuff without all her barking." Beaker jabbed her finger in my direction. "But tell her I said any of that, and you're dead."

I laughed.

Our door clicked open, and Lessy and Jessy bounded in. "Hi!"

"Hi," Beaker and I returned.

Jessy flopped across their bed. "Looord, I hate cheer training."

Smiling at her whining, I slipped out of my chair and onto the floor, where my backpack sat under the desk. I unzipped it and dug around, searching for a lollipop.

On the bed, Beaker stretched out on her stomach. "Me, too."

Lessy plunked down next to her sister. "You've got the hottest coach."

Jessy grabbed a pillow. "Yeah, everybody's talking about it."

Beaker and I glanced at each other. Yeah, TL *was* hot. Actually, the first time I saw him I thought he was the best-looking guy I'd ever seen.

"Ooh!" Jessy threw her hands up. "Speaking of hot. You know CJ, that blond guy we met yesterday?" She cut Beaker a sideways glance. "Guess who I saw talking to him?"

Beaker diverted her attention to the bedspread and suddenly became very interested in the pattern.

I found a pineapple lollipop in my backpack and unwrapped it. "Who?"

"Apparently he's a delivery guy for the hotel. He was in the lobby after lunch, and I saw him talking to our own little Tiffany." Lessy pursed her lips as she surveyed Beaker.

I slipped the lollipop in my mouth. "Is that so?" I teased.

Beaker shot me a snarl. It cheered me up.

"He asked me if I was here with the cheerleading thing." Beaker rolled her eyes. "As if he couldn't figure that out by looking at my stupid getup." She rolled off her bed. "I need a soda. Anybody want one?"

Actually, a soda sounded good. "I'll go with you." I dug around in my backpack and fished out some money.

Jessy started undressing. "Get me diet orange."

Lessy hipped on the TV. "Me, too. You'll have to go to the lobby, though. The vending machines on the floors don't carry orange." She cringed. "Sorry."

I shrugged. "No big deal."

Beaker and I left the room and got halfway to the elevator.

"Just a sec." I jogged back down the hall to TL's room and knocked.

Seconds passed, and, just as I turned to leave, he cracked open the door. He didn't look happy. Behind him, Nalani sat on a bed, wiping her cheeks.

I looked at TL. "Is everything okay?"

He moved in front of me, blocking my view of her. "What do you need?"

"Where's Coach Luke?"

"He went into town. What do you need?"

Obviously, TL and Nalani were having a personal issue, and he didn't want me asking about it. And frankly, it was none of my business. But . . . what was *wrong* with them?

TL lifted his brows.

"Sorry." I pointed down the hall to where Beaker stood. "We're going to go get some sodas. Just wanted to see if you wanted anything."

"I'm fine."

With a nod, I turned.

"Ana?"

I turned back.

"Thank you for asking."

I smiled a little. "You're welcome."

TL shut the door, and I trotted back to Beaker. We rode the elevator and headed down the long hall toward the back of the hotel where the vending machines were.

Beaker pushed open the door that led into the vending area and came to an abrupt stop. A blond guy stood at the snack machine, eyeing the selections. He had sun-dried, straight hair to his shoulders and was dressed in board shorts, a T-shirt, and flip flops. 'Surfer dude' popped into my mind first.

He looked up, and surprise lit his blue eyes. "Hey."

Beaker didn't respond, and so I answered back. "Hey."

He stepped forward and extended his hand. "I'm CJ." He nodded to Beaker. "I met Tiffany earlier today."

I stepped into the small room and shook his hand. "Ana."

CJ stood shorter than me, but definitely taller than Beaker. I'd say five feet eight. One side of his mouth lifted in a half smile, and instantly I recognized what the twins saw in him.

He turned his attention to Beaker. "How's it going?"

With a little nod, she glanced away. How cute. Who would've thought she'd be so shy?

"Um . . ." He started and then stopped. "Urn, I was just heading to a beach party. My friends are already there. You wanna come?"

Beaker blushed. *Actually* blushed. "No, thanks."

CJ's brow twitched, and I could tell he was really bummed she'd turned him down. He cut his eyes to me. "You can come, too."

Poor guy. He was obviously hoping my agreement would persuade Beaker. "Thanks." I smiled to let him know I really meant it. "I'm tired. It's been a long day."

He shifted uncomfortably. "Well, okay then." He went back to the machine, quickly made his selection, and snatched up his chips. "See you all around."

"Nice to meet you," I said as he pushed through the door.

"You, too," he returned.

I moved over to the soda machine and fed in a dollar bill. "You could have gone with him if you wanted. You know that, right?"

Beaker shrugged.

I selected two diet orange drinks for the twins. "I mean, just because we're here on other business," I whispered in case anyone might be listening, "doesn't mean you can't go out."

She shrugged.

I fed another dollar in. "How do you think Wirenut met Cat?"

She shrugged.

I selected a regular cola for me. "Which do you want?"

She shrugged.

Sighing, I pressed regular for her, too. "You want to tell me what's going on?"

"Nothing," she grumbled. "I'm just not used to this, that's all."

"Used to what?"

Beaker flung her hand in the air. *"This."*

"This what?"

"Never mind." She reached past me, grabbed two of the drinks from the vending machine, and tucked them in her jacket pockets. "You wouldn't understand."

"Understand what?" Honestly, I had no idea what she was talking about.

Beaker shoved through the door and strode off.

Grabbing the two remaining drinks, I followed after her. "What's wrong with you?"

She shouldered open an exit door that led out near the hotel pool area and beach. "Just leave me alone. Go be . . . perfect or gorgeous or something."

Her gruff words didn't match her hunched shoulders. She needed some serious lightening up.

"Perfect? Are you serious?" I laughed, stepping through the exit door and into the night. "Did you just meet me? Come on. I trip over my own feet. I drop food on my clothes. I stumble over my words. I can barely carry on a conversation unless it deals with binary numbers and algorithms. And, oh yeah, I'm a social reject."

She marched off down a mulched path that led to the beach. "Whatever. You have the perfect looks and the perfect boyfriend. And no one's ever made fun of you."

"Oh, please. That's all anyone ever did back in Iowa. Everyone in the dorms thought I was weird." I glanced around the dimly lit path, assuring we were alone. "Being a Specialist is the first time I've ever felt somewhat normal."

Beaker turned around. "People thought you were weird?"

"How many girls do you know with a one-hundred-ninety-one IQ who spends her days buried in her own brain?"

"Just you."

"See?"

Beaker studied me for a couple of long seconds. "I guess we're both weird in our own weird way."

I smiled. "Seems like it."

Thoughtfully, she gazed through the night toward the beach.

I put my drinks down on a lounge chair and dried my hands on my shirt. "So are you going to tell me what's wrong?"

Beaker heaved a heavy sigh. "Don't laugh, okay?"

I held up my hands.

"I've never been on a date before. I've never had such a cute, normal guy like me. And I'm more than freaked about it because"—she motioned to her hair and clothes—"this isn't me."

I had the unnerving urge to hug her. Underneath all her gruffness, Beaker had a soft, sweet, insecure side. But I knew if I got gushy, touchy-feely, she'd push me away.

Instead, I shrugged. "I've never been on a date either."

She blinked. "David?"

I shook my head. "Nope. It's definitely on my list of things to do, though."

That earned a small laugh.

I took a step toward her. "Don't worry about CJ. And smile the next time you see him. It won't kill you." Listen to me giving relationship advice. "Something tells me he wouldn't care if you were Goth or not."

"Really?"

"Really. Come to think of it, I miss your Goth uniqueness. I don't like you looking like everyone else."

Beaker's lips twitched.

Playfully, I shoved her shoulder. "You're not so mean after all."

"Yeah, I am," she disagreed with a slight smile.

In that second it occurred to me her harshness was a wall to keep everyone at a distance. Put there because of the way she'd been treated over the years. In fact, I could've easily developed the same wall. Who would have thought Beaker and I were so emotionally similar?

I gave my head a quick shake, snapping out of my retrospective moment. Sometimes I could be quite the psychoanalyst.

My phone buzzed, and I checked the display. "It's David!"

Beaker snatched my drinks off the lounge chair and headed back up the path. "See ya back in the room."

"Okay." I pressed the Talk button on my phone.

"Hi," I greeted him with a huge grin, even though he couldn't see it.

"Hi, back."

His voice made my insides pure goosh.

"Where are you?" he asked.

I meandered down the path. "Heading toward the beach."

"What's at the beach? Another bonfire rally?"

"No. Beaker and I were having a private talk."

"Everything okay?"

"Yeah." I blew out a breath. "No. I mean, yeah, everything's okay with me and Beaker. But, no, not with me. Or, I don't know." All the mistakes I'd made on this mission came rushing at me, and I sighed in pure frustration. "David, I've really screwed up."

"What do you mean?"

"With you," I answered. "With this mission."

"Listen, as far as everything that happened back at the ranch between you and me? I don't want to think about it anymore. It's over with. We're fine. Can we do that? I know your emotions are running high over all this, and I understand that."

I made it to the beach and sat down in the sand. "My connection to this mission and my emotions are making me stupid."

"That's why I called. I know about everything that's happened. TL and I talk numerous times a day."

I stared up at the half moon. Great. Now I had to hear it from David, too. "And? Are you disappointed in me?"

"No. I wish I was there to hug you, though."

My heart paused. "Oh, David . . ." His quiet words sank deep into my soul, filling all the empty voids. I closed my eyes. "I needed to hear that so bad."

"GiGi, you should know TL's had me following you. I was right there watching you on that bike trailing Eduardo."

Silence. Long seconds ticked by as indignation hit me first, slowly followed by logical reasoning. Of course TL would have me followed. He'd be stupid not to.

"And," David continued, "back at the ranch, I secretly met with TL nearly every night to give him a rundown on our day's activities."

I didn't have a response to that one either. I didn't feel double crossed, really. Naive better explained my thoughts. It was naive of me to think I could do such a complex job without TL closely monitoring me.

"Don't take it personally. To my knowledge, he's never just handed over the reins to someone. He *is* in charge. Even when someone goes on a solo mission, like I did in Iowa, he's still on top of it all. That's his job. And that'll be his job until he one day steps down and turns his duties over to someone else."

"Over to you."

"Maybe. Being a strategist is not easy."

"Tell me about it." Suddenly, I missed David so badly I could barely stand it. "I really miss you."

"I miss you, too."

And then the line clicked off.

‹TWELVE›

Later that night I lay wide-eyed, staring at the dark ceiling of my hotel room. One A.M. I knew it was one A.M. because I'd been incessantly checking my watch since my return from the beach.

The air conditioner kicked on. Its rush of air and motored hum muted Jessy's (or maybe Lessy's) soft snore. Beside me, Beaker twitched in her sleep and then rolled to her side.

A hotel exterior light filtered through the curtains' crack, flickering shadows across the walls.

My mind was racing. I couldn't stop thinking about everything that had happened since we got here. I'd started thinking about other stuff in order to get my mind off David and why the line clicked off.

I knew *my* cell phone hadn't cut off. I'd had a full battery *and* all my bars. Believe me, I immediately checked as soon as we got disconnected.

So that meant *his* phone went dead. But did it go dead because of his battery or his bars?

Couldn't be his battery. David always had a charged battery.

Which left bars. That didn't make sense, though. Anywhere we went we had full bars. Even underground. It was one of the benefits of being members of a high-tech, secret organization.

Two-thirteen A.M.

He wouldn't have hung up on me, would he? Right after telling me he missed me? Was the "miss you" part getting too deep?

Gggrrr. Shut up, GiGi. You're driving yourself insane.

I squeezed my eyes shut and concentrated on not talking to myself. I needed to sleep. Think code. That always relaxed me.

<!Element (%styfon;~%phse;)- -(%line:)>
<Cite<hatru>/Q land="en"-us>
<=*ptth* = /!attstli!/ %csorrtetat%>

Three twenty-one A.M.

Why didn't he call me back? I'd tried calling him back and had gotten his voice mail. In fact—I lifted my cell phone from my stomach and checked the display—no missed calls. No voice mails. No nothing. Nada. Finito. And if I had Parrot's linguistic skills, I'd give it in sixteen other languages, too.

Four forty-two A.M.

Surely lying on my back this long would give me bed sores. Or a flat butt.

Rolling onto my side, I stared at the back of Beaker's head . . .

***

"Goood morning, Barracuda Key, Florida!"

I shot straight up in bed.

"It's six A.M. on this beee-u-ti-ful day!"

One of the twins slammed her hand over the alarm radio. "Shut up."

Six A.M.? I must have fallen asleep and gotten exactly—I quickly calculated—one hour and eighteen minutes of sleep.

With a groan, I dropped my head into my hands. This day hadn't started and it *already* sucked.

One of the twins opened the curtains, allowing the morning sun to pour in. Squinting, I held my hands up to block the glare shooting straight into my skull.

Beaker stretched. "What are you, a vampire?"

No, but I felt like one.

Beaker swung her legs over the side of the bed. "You look like somebody broke you into pieces and didn't quite get the puzzle when they put you back together."

With another groan, I fell back into bed and crammed the pillow over my head.

"Good morning, good morning, good morning, how are you? I'm fine. I'm fine, I hope you are, too. Good morning, good morn . . ." I didn't know which twin was singing (and dancing by the way her voice bounced

409

around the room), but I wanted to duct-tape her little mouth and shove her from the room.

One bathroom and four girls did not make good odds, but an hour later, we all managed to be ready. I'd always been a low-maintenance girl. It didn't take much to get me going. Fifteen minutes tops—showered, ribbons tied, and all. Watching the twins made me thankful of that.

I didn't know so much could be done to fingers and toes, eyebrows and hair, makeup and shaving, and whatever else in preparation for one single day. Heck, it took them fifteen minutes just to apply lotion. It wore me out watching them.

Then again, I was *already* worn out, so maybe that was my problem.

We left our room and joined the other color-coordinated girls trickling through the halls and down the elevator.

TL caught up with us in the lobby and motioned us to follow. He led us down a hall, around a corner, and into a vacant conference room.

That was the good thing about hotels. Lots of nooks and crannies to duck into.

TL pulled the tiny blue pyramid from his pocket and rotated the top. "Eduardo and his men were in their room all night. Parrot translated the Portuguese you recorded."

Portuguese? I'd thought it was Spanish. Guess that's why I wasn't the linguist of the group.

"Everything's definitely on," TL continued. "But they didn't talk times, dates, or locations."

Beaker held her finger up. "So basically we still have nothing."

"No," TL corrected. "We have the recording, pictures, the DNA dust. Some proof. It's a start. We need a location, though, where it's all going down. We need the smuggled chemicals. We need the location of where his buyers will be making the bombs. We need to know how he's shipping them back out. We need Eduardo Villanueva in the middle of it all. And we need to get a tracker on him so we know when he's on the move."

"The simulated mosquito sting," I suggested, "is going to be our best bet. That way we can plant the tracker from a distance."

TL nodded. "I agree. And I want a camera in his room today. No audio function on it, though. We don't want him to pick up our signal if he happens to scan his room for bugs. The IPNC has given us a lip reader." TL handed me a piece of paper. "This is his IP address. Make sure all film goes directly to his computer so he can analyze it and tell us what Eduardo and his men are saying."

I pocketed the paper. Great idea sending silent film to a lip reader. Why hadn't David and I thought of that while we were planning things?

"That's it for me. You two got anything?"

We shook our heads.

TL extended his hand. "Give me one of the simulated mosquito stings."

I slipped my backpack off my shoulder, unzipped the front pocket, and gave him what looked like a mechanical pencil. The stings were cool little devices, able to shoot up to twenty feet. They were a combination of Chapling's technology, my proto laser tracker invention that I'd brought with me from Iowa, and Wirenut's putty-blowing bamboo that he'd used on the Rissala mission. I'd thought Wirenut's homemade device was so neat that Chapling and I had immediately started tinkering with it after Rissala.

Once programmed, the simulated stings worked like those military missiles that swerve through the air until they find their target. The pencil's lead end held the tracking component, and the eraser served as the release lever. Line the lead up with the target (person), and press the eraser. A tiny chunk of lead would shoot through the air and straight into the person's body, feeling like a mosquito sting.

TL slipped the pencil in his T-shirt pocket. He rotated the pyramid counterclockwise to the off position. "You two go and eat breakfast. No skipping." With that, he strode from the room.

Beaker and I slowly made our way down the hallway back to the lobby.

"How'd your call with David go?"

"Fine. We got cut off." I didn't tell her I'd stayed up all night obsessing over it.

"Huh. That's weird."

"Tell me about it." I stopped at a water fountain and took a quick sip.

"I, uh . . . I saw CJ again last night after I left you at the pool area, as I was heading back to the room."

"You did?" I smiled. "How'd it go?"

Shrugging, she glanced away. "It went all right."

Her nonchalant tone did not match her shy avoidance.

I dropped the CJ subject. Something told me she wouldn't give me more even if I pressed. And pressing, I figured, might ruin our newfound bond.

Crossing the lobby, we entered the meal room. Like yesterday, everyone had already served themselves and been seated. And like yesterday, Beaker and I loaded up our plates: eggs, strawberries, muffins, bacon. *And* like yesterday, our hearty appetites drew snide attention.

After breakfast, we headed across the lobby into the practice hall. As we walked in, music throbbed from speakers positioned around the room. Contestants were already spread out, stretching, getting ready for rehearsal.

In hindsight I should've had a muffin and called it quits, because here I stood thirty minutes later feeling a bit queasy. Girls surrounded me on all sides, sweating, dancing, ponytails sagging.

With clipboards in hand, the current America's Cheer team meandered through us, stopping here and there, observing, checking things off.

Beaker stood diagonal to me, her jaw convulsively flexing. She needed gum. I'd keep an eye on her in case she blew one of her chemically talented gaskets.

Wearing a head mike, the team leader stood on a riser at the front of the room demonstrating the moves. "Five, six, seven, eight."

She spun, dipped, kicked, swirled, and did about a dozen more fancy things. All around me girls effectively followed her. I barely made it to the kick part.

An America's Cheer member wandered by, stopping a few feet from me. She watched me, her brows slightly puckered. Then she flipped a few papers on her clipboard and checked things off. I could only imagine:

Ana. Red-and-white team. Complete reject. Check.

The clipboard Nazi moved on, and all around me girls snickered.

I rolled my eyes. What losers. Get a life.

"Five, six, seven, eight." Team leader busted into a rapid-fire series of moves.

Yeah, right. Like that's going to happen.

All around me, girls gyrated. I didn't even try.

Wiping my hand across my forehead, I gazed longingly over everyone's heads to the mats stacked along the side wall. I'd give my last segment of code to flop across them for a few seconds.

"Take five," Team leader echoed through the speakers.

Oh, thank God.

I found the closest America's Cheer member and pulled her aside. "I'm going to need more than five. I'm not feeling well. I need to go to my room."

"That's going to cost you points on the competition."

So. "I know." I gave her my best disappointed look. "But I'm really not feeling well."

"All right." She made a note on her clipboard. "Take as long as you need."

"Thanks." For good measure, I put my hand over my mouth and puffed out my cheeks.

She jerked back. "Go!"

Nothing like the threat of impending vomit to make things real. I snatched my backpack from the pile of everyone else's purses and bags, gave Beaker an I'm-out-of-here look, and then bolted upstairs to our room. Finally, some time to work.

I walked into the room and turned on Lessy's and Jessy's signals on my cell phone. Two red dots popped up on my screen. Cranking up my laptop, I keyed in the access code to the satellite. I plugged in the coordinates to our hotel, X-rayed through the roof, and brought up a picture of Eduardo Villanueva's suite.

He and his men sat around the room as if they were having a pleasant afternoon. One read the paper. Another talked on the phone. Eduardo played chess with the last.

Too bad the lip reader couldn't watch them via satellite. It would make things a lot easier than planting a camera. But with cloud coverage and storms between here and Denmark (where the lip reader lived), the image would constantly flicker and go out.

Speaking of which. I froze the image to stabilize it and studied the room's layout. The wide angle camera would definitely have to be placed high in order to film the entire room and all the men.

I zeroed in on the ceiling fan and the globe light attached to it. If I could get the camera inside that globe, it would be the perfect location.

My heart jolted with excitement as a plan clicked into place.

I accessed the secret panel beneath the bed and found The Fly—a nifty little gadget Wirenut had developed way back before he even became a Specialist. It was a wide-angle camera that looked, big surprise, like a fly. Once programmed it would buzz to its destination, land, and begin filming. According to Wirenut, it had enough battery life to last a year.

Sticking my pencil under its tiny wing, I pressed the on button. It fluttered, and I smiled. Cute little thing.

I brought up the software that I had developed for The Fly and, through a wireless connection, programmed it to its final destination—the globe light.

I deactivated The Fly's audio function and then input the lip reader's IP address so all film would be copied to his hard drive.

In mere minutes, we would know what was being discussed in that room.

Climbing on top of the bed, I lifted The Fly to the vent and let it go.

From studying the hotel's blueprints, I knew the ventilation system from my floor connected to the presidential suite. One way or another, The Fly would find its way there.

Reactivating the live satellite, I kept my gaze glued to the ceiling vent in Eduardo Villanueva's living room. Minutes later, The Fly zoomed out, buzzed across the ceiling, and flew straight into the light fixture. None of the men even looked up.

I flipped from satellite to The Fly's software. Sure enough, it had already begun filming.

I wanted to hug both Wirenut and his bug for their awesomeness.

In the bottom corner of my screen a message popped up from the lip reader, acknowledging the transmission.

Good. Almost everything in place.

We had implemented DNA dust, and pictures of it along with swabs would give us documented proof of where Eduardo had been. The Fly provided film of them in their suite. And now I just had to get a tracking device on them longer than thirty minutes to electronically monitor where they were going.

One way or another, we'd know where everything was going down.

***

On our morning break the next day, David texted me. HEY. BEEN BUSY. A LOT OF UNEXPECTED THINGS ARE GOING ON. TELL YOU LATER. WANTED YOU TO KNOW I GOT YOUR MESSAGE.

What unexpected things? BE SAFE, I texted back.

"Ana?" TL approached me in the lobby.

I showed him David's text. "What's going on?" I whispered.

TL shook his head. "I'm not at liberty to say right now."

I *hated* when TL did that.

"Patience," he said.

Patience was usually a strong point for me, but not when it came to all this top-secret stuff. I didn't like not being in the know.

"The lip reader just texted me that Eduardo has a video conference call scheduled in five minutes." He started walking to the elevator. "Let's go. You're going to hack into it. Chapling already knows and has Parrot ready."

My heart gave one giant leap. A video call was exactly what we needed. Hopefully, we'd find out something worthwhile.

TL keyed a message into his cell. "I'll let Beaker know to cover for us."

We rode the elevator up and hurried into my room. I snatched the laptop from my case, powered up, and keyed in my scrambler code. In the bottom-left corner of the screen I brought up The Fly's software and watched as Eduardo opened his laptop. He plugged in an interpreter box and typed in a password. I watched closely, memorizing it.

I zoomed in on the interpreter box and read its model number. Then I zoomed in on the screen and saw which conferencing software he was using.

Chapling appeared in the bottom-right corner in a video feed. "What do you got?"

"He's using the micro parley software," I told Chapling.

"One second." Chapling's fingers raced over his keyboard. "Sending it to you now."

My screen flicked as my laptop accepted the software Chapling sent me.

"Got it," I told him, activating it.

Through the micro parley software, I hacked into the interpreter box on Eduardo's computer and entered his password. The upper-left corner of my screen mirrored Eduardo's computer exactly.

I signaled TL, and he sat down beside me on the bed.

Parrot appeared in the upper-right corner of my screen, wearing a headset.

I ran a quick stereophonic code patching Eduardo's audio to Parrot. At that exact second, a dark-haired man appeared on Eduardo's screen. He began speaking in another language. Parrot gave a nod to let us know the transmission was coming through.

Chapling's fingers raced across his keyboard again. "That's Eduardo's brother, Pedro."

Parrot began translating simultaneously with the movement of their mouths. He preceded each translation with the name of the person speaking.

"Pedro: Eduardo, how are you?"

"Eduardo: Fine brother, you?"

"Pedro: Fine. I'm missing my son's soccer game."

"Eduardo: I'm missing lunch."

I looked over at TL. "Is this for real? They're talking about stupid stuff."

He shook his head. "Could be code for something."

"Pedro: I ordered pizza for lunch and it came wrong. I had to send it back."

"Eduardo: Did you get your money back?"

"Pedro: No. They made me a new one for a discounted price."

"Eduardo: When's the new pizza getting delivered?"

"Pedro: At the time we previously discussed."

"Eduardo: Are you waiting on me then?"

"Pedro: Yes, I know you'll be hungry."

"Eduardo: And where is it being delivered?"

"Pedro: The emporium."

Eduardo nodded and signed off.

Parrot took off his headset with a shrug. "Sorry, guys."

With a disappointed smile, I waved at him. "Thanks, Parrot."

I clicked a few keys, and he disappeared from my screen.

Chapling lifted his bushy brows. "Obviously the pizza is the shipment."

Oh, I hadn't thought about that. Made sense, though.

TL nodded. "I agree. Get cranking on emporium," he told Chapling, "and see what you can come up with."

Chapling nodded and clicked off.

I powered down. "Now what?"

"Back to cheerleading rehearsal."

I trudged through the hotel beside TL, wishing that call would have gone better. I didn't feel like we'd gotten anything.

For the rest of the day, Beaker and I went about our rehearsal/dance/smiley annoying daily routine. Eduardo and his men didn't move from their suite. According to a text I received from Nalani, they'd even canceled maid service.

Same held true for the next day, too. I didn't want to say anything, but four guys in a room without maid service? Can anyone say yuck?

They did have food service. But the waiter had been instructed to leave the cart outside the presidential suite in the morning and pick it up at nine P.M.

I spent that night restless, thinking about David. I didn't try calling or texting him back. Something was going on, and he didn't need me crowding him. I wanted to ask TL again, but I knew it'd get me nowhere.

At this point, I felt that the mission had stalled. And I was beginning to wonder if it would even come to fruition.

I checked The Fly's film. The lip reader's report came back with nothing significant. Chapling had figured out emporium meant warehouse, but there were dozens of warehouses on Barracuda Key and the surrounding islands. So basically, we still had nothing.

I had morphed into Beaker, snarling at everything and everybody. If Eduardo didn't do something soon, this mission would be over. All my research and planning would go down the proverbial drain.

‹THIRTEEN›

Late the next morning, the last day of America's Cheer, I stood in the lobby with Beaker, Lessy, and Jessy, tuning out the twins as they prattled on and on about who had said what to whom. In just a few minutes we would go into our final America's Cheer meeting and find out who had made the national team. Our mission cover would be done—we'd have to leave and Eduardo would escape capture once again.

Suddenly, my cell phone vibrated in my pocket, and my whole body jolted. I yanked it free, checked the display, and my heart kicked into overdrive with what I read.

Beaker yanked her phone from her pocket, too.

Simultaneously, we punched in our passwords to decode the encryption, and I read the text message from TL: EV ON THE MOVE. HEADING TOWARD FRONT DOORS OF HOTEL. ETA: 3 MINUTES.

Both our phones vibrated again.

Nalani this time. EV GO.

Our phones vibrated again.

The lip reader. EV MOVING

Jessy and Lessy leaned in. "Lord, someone wants you two pretty bad."

Quickly, I pocketed my phone. "Just our coach."

"Yeah," Beaker agreed. "He can be a real pest."

I gave Lessy a little nudge toward the rehearsal hall. "You two go on in. We'll be there in a few minutes. Remember, today's the last day. We'll all find out if we're part of the new America's Cheer team."

"Yay," Jessy sarcastically enthused, linking arms with her sister. "Don't be late, you two. I don't feel like listening to you get yelled at."

"Or watching you run laps around the room." Lessy hopped in place. "L-A-T-E! Sorry we're late!"

Laughing, Beaker and I waved them on. They disappeared inside the room, and we bolted out the hotel's doors and across the portico to the palm trees lining the other side.

A bellman approached us. "Anything I can help you with, ladies?"

Beaker flashed him a smile. "No thanks. We're fine. We're just, um, waiting for someone."

The bellman bowed. "As you wish."

He backed away, and I slipped my backpack from my shoulder. I unzipped the front pocket and rifled around. Chapstick, pen, lollipop . . . where the heck were the simulated mosquito sting pencils?

Bouncing her leg, Beaker watched me. "Hurry," she murmured.

I stifled the urge *to* hurry. Jerky, quick movements would draw too much attention. This was supposed to be a casual conversation between Beaker and me as we stood here under the palms.

"I'm about to rip that from your hands," she gritted. "Eduardo's going to walk out those doors any second."

Purposefully ignoring her, I continued searching with a tiny bit of panic settling in. They were in here last night. I lifted a piece of paper and underneath lay two sting pencils. My heart gave a relieved beat. Oh, thank God.

I grabbed them and handed one to her. "Remember," I said through a smile, "we're supposed to be hanging out talking. Not about to shoot someone with one of these."

She plucked the pencil from my hand, narrowing her eyes, and I knew she was about to do something ornery. "Oh!" Loudly, she faked a laugh. "Is that what we're supposed to be doing?" Hahahahaha. "Oh, silly me. And to think, one would wonder." Hahahahaha.

Bellmen began to turn and look.

I kept my smile in place as I put my backpack on the ground. "You can shut up now."

"Ohhh," she breathed, dramatically wiping her eyes.

I narrowed mine. Smart a—

The hotel doors opened, and we immediately snapped into our planned positions.

I lifted the eraser end of the mechanical pencil to my mouth and pretended to chew on it. Beaker stepped slightly in front of me to give the appearance I was looking at her instead of over her shoulder.

"So, anyway," Beaker struck up a nonsense conversation, "I told the guy no way. I mean, what was he thinking asking me that? And then that girl . . ."

Pretending to hang on her every word, I watched Eduardo and his men stride through the hotel's doors. They were all dressed in suits, leaving only their hands, necks, and faces exposed. The only place I could shoot the tracker.

" . . . and I was like, no way." Beaker flipped her hand in the air. "I mean, who was she kidding, right? Saying all that. Oh, and then . . ."

Closing my right eye, I sighted down the length of the pencil. One of Eduardo's men stood in front of him. *Good thing I'm farsighted.* The needless thought popped into my brain as I lined up the lead end of the pencil with the man's forehead. With my tongue, I pressed the eraser. A tiny, nearly microscopic tracker sailed from the pencil twenty feet across the portico.

A couple seconds later, Eduardo's man brushed his forehead and glanced into the air. *One down, three to go.*

" . . . Mr. Scallione. You remember him? He totally made a pass at me. Did I ever tell you that?" Beaker shook her head. "I couldn't believe it. I was visiting my grand . . ."

Nodding at Beaker's babbling, I handed her my pencil, she handed me hers, and I resumed my eraser in the mouth position. In my peripheral vision, Beaker recalibrated the pencil I'd just handed her, getting it ready for the next usage. To an onlooker, it appeared as if she was merely twirling it as she continued talking.

" . . . all that ended, and she made me eat her famous egg casserole. I don't know what's so famous about it." Beaker gagged. "I almost threw . . ."

I bet this is the most brainless yapping Beaker has done in her whole life. Another needless thought, but it popped into my head as I sighted down the length of the pencil, narrowing in on another one of Eduardo's men. He shook hands with a bellman as they exchanged a key. Lining up the lead end of the pencil with the man's hand, I pressed the eraser.

A couple seconds later, he gave his hand a little shake and wiped it on his pants. *Two down; two to go.*

". . . later that night I climbed up on the roof." Beaker propped her hand on her hip. "Guess who was up there? Timmy, our next-door neighbor. Only he didn't look like the Timmy I remember from first gr . . ."

Exchanging pencils with Beaker again, I kept Eduardo and the one remaining man in my sight. Eduardo said something to the man, the man nodded, and then headed back into the hotel. TL was positioned in the lobby. He'd get that one.

". . . the horse's name was Bunny. Or maybe Sunny." Beaker shook her head. "Either way it was the most beautiful horse I'd ever seen. I can't believe my sister got it for gradu . . ."

Putting the pencil in my mouth, I sighted down the length and lined up the lead end with Eduardo's neck. I put my tongue on the eraser, and a bellman moved right in front of Eduardo.

"Crap," I mumbled around the eraser.

Beaker kept right on talking. " . . . do you know what he's probably going to get me? A set of encyclopedias or something equally boring and educat . . ."

The bellman shifted away. I resighted Eduardo, lined up the lead end, and clicked the eraser.

A couple seconds later, he smacked his neck and looked straight across the portico at me.

My heart lurched.

As carefully, smoothly, and naturally as I could, I opened my right eye and moved my gaze to the left a fraction. I kept chewing on the eraser, pretending to be enthralled with Beaker's prattling, and gave an understanding nod for good measure.

"Keep talking," I murmured. "He's looking right at us."

". . . it's been that way my whole life." Beaker threw her hands in the air. "Anyway. Hey, did I tell you I went to the zoo? It was the saddest thing that poor monkey . . ."

Taking the pencil from my mouth, I gave Beaker all my attention. "The monkey had been abused?" I grabbed her up in a huge hug. "That *is* sad."

She didn't hug me back.

I pulled away, and it occurred to me that I'd never hugged Beaker before. And from her sour face, I gathered she didn't much appreciate it.

Nodding down the driveway, I grabbed my backpack from the ground. "Let's go for a walk." We headed off away from the sun, giving every appearance we were out for a morning stroll.

Eduardo's car passed us about a minute later, and we kept right on strolling until it disappeared from sight.

Beaker and I nonchalantly turned and headed back up the driveway to the hotel. I wanted more than anything to sprint it, grab TL, and book it out of here. But the last thing I needed to do was to draw attention to us.

Reaching inside my pocket, I pulled out my cell phone and clicked over to tracking mode.

Four blue dots popped up—Eduardo and his men. Lessy and Jessy's red dots appeared in the bottom corner of the screen.

Smiling, I put my cell away. "Everything's in place." I turned to Beaker. "You're pretty good at carrying on a one-sided conversation. Mr. Scallione? Egg casserole? Timmy? Bunny? Sunny? Encyclopedias? A monkey?" I laughed. "How'd you come up with all that?"

Beaker shrugged. "I have my moments."

It made me remember all the fake conversations Jonathan and I had struck up on my first mission. I'd gotten such a kick out of saying stuff that took him off guard. It had surprised me more than anyone that I had come up with the things I had.

TL met us in the lobby when we entered. "Twenty-one hundred hours. Be ready." With that he strode off.

Twenty-one hundred hours. Nine o'clock tonight. In under ten hours I'd hopefully see the end to Eduardo Villanueva and finally stop this madman before he ruins another family.

That thought echoed in my mind as Beaker and I quietly opened the rehearsal hall door and slipped inside.

From her spot up front, the America's Cheer team leader pointed across the crowd.

In unison, all heads turned toward us.

"You're late," team leader echoed in her mike. "L-A-T-E! Sorry we're late!" She circled her finger in the air. "Three times around the room and make it look good."

Beaker and I exchanged annoyed looks while snickers filtered across the crowd.

We took off around the perimeter of the room, clapping, chanting, "L-A-T-E! Sorry we're late!"

As when Beaker had chanted her gum mantra, some girls began sarcastically clapping, others bopped in their chairs. I caught sight of the twins on our second time around. They shook their heads in amused pity.

We circled the third time, came to a stop at the front, and went into simultaneous back handsprings. "Go, America's Cheer!"

Everyone leapt to their feet. "Go, America's Cheer!"

Thank *God* this was the last meeting.

***

Seven P.M.

We were back in our room with the twins after getting cut from the team. In two hours Beaker and I had to be ready to go, and we still hadn't gotten rid of Jessy and Lessy. And I'd tried, *believe* me. We needed, more than anything, to access the secret headboard panel for supplies.

"You all should go down to the beach for one last stroll," I suggested. "Come tomorrow morning, you'll be heading back to Alabama. No more Barracuda Key, Florida, sand."

Lessy shrugged. "Don't feel like it."

"Come with us." Jessy perked up. "Yeah, let's all go."

Beaker and I exchanged a this-is-not-working glance.

"Nah." Beaker flopped back on our bed. "We don't feel like it either."

Seven thirty-one P.M.

"You two should go into town and gorge on pizza," I suggested. "You know your mom won't let you have any when you get home."

"Come with us." Lessy perked up.

Beaker and I exchanged a glance.

"Nah." Beaker rolled over. "We're not hungry."

Eight oh-four P.M.

"You two should go sit in the hot tub," I suggested. "Make use of the spa facilities before you head back home."

"Come with us." Jessy perked up. "Yeah, let's all go."

Beaker and I exchanged a glance.

"Nah." Beaker shoved a pillow under her head. "I don't feel like getting wet right now."

Eight forty-nine P.M.

I stared at the clock, my jaw getting tighter and tighter. We had to be outside in eleven minutes, and still no luck with the Jessy/Lessy issue. They'd changed into their pajamas and lay under the covers watching TV.

With the way they were settled in, I highly doubted we were getting rid of them.

"You two," I tried one last time, having no idea what to suggest, "should . . . hurry and get dressed and . . . go down to the, um, lounge, and start singing right there. Yeah, that's what you should do." I jabbed my finger in their direction. "If you were *really* serious about this singing thing, you would do it."

Even to my own ears, I sounded stupid.

The twins just looked at me.

I cleared my throat and glanced at Beaker, hoping to get some backup.

She rolled her eyes and fell back on the bed.

I sighed.

A knock sounded on our door. I trudged across the room and opened it.

TL grinned. "Thought I'd take my two favorite girls out for an ice cream to cheer you up for not making the team."

"Wow." This came from one of the twins. "Your coach is so nice. Ours yelled at us for an hour."

Beaker and I grabbed our back packs and followed TL out into the hall.

"Sorry," I whispered. "No supplies."

He shook his head. "Got it covered."

Of course he had it covered. TL had a backup for everything.

In, down, and out the elevator we went. Bypassing the lobby, we cut through a hall and out the back exit door. We jogged past the pool and down the path leading to the beach, followed the moonlit shoreline about a quarter of a mile, then jogged through the dunes and came out at the back side of a grocery store.

A black van sat idling, waiting. TL led us to it and opened the back door. Beaker and I climbed up and sat down. TL followed, shutting the door behind him, and the van pulled away.

I stared across the cargo space at Nalani and a woman sitting beside her. They both wore black jumpsuits and black knit caps.

"Hello, Sissy," the woman greeted Beaker.

Beaker looked up and blinked. "Ms. Gabrier?"

Ms. Gabrier focused on me. "I was Sissy's chemistry teacher back in her old life. I helped her find her way to the Specialists."

"Really?" I smiled. "That's cool."

Ms. Gabrier turned back to Beaker. "I'm here to assist you with defusing the chemicals."

"You're," Beaker pointed at her, "assisting *me*?"

Ms. Gabrier inclined her head. "Yes. I've been hearing good things about you."

Beaker furrowed her brow. "You have?"

Amusement played across Ms. Gabrier's lips. "Yes, I have. I always knew there was something special hidden in there."

Beaker stared at her for a few seconds and then glanced down to her lap. Shifting uncomfortably, she cleared her throat.

I looked over at Beaker. She seemed so . . . amazed and honored, maybe even a little humbled.

If Wirenut were here, he'd put her in a headlock and knuckle-rub her. I wasn't a knuckle rubber, so I found a piece of gum in my backpack and handed it to her. She took it and smiled.

TL opened a laptop and turned it toward all of us. A map of Barracuda Key and the surrounding areas filled the screen. He tapped on an island north of Barracuda Key, zooming in on it. "This is Mango Key. It's connected to Barracuda Key via a bridge."

He tapped again, giving us an aerial view of a warehouse. "This is where Eduardo and his men have been all day. A huge delivery was made earlier today. Mike has confirmed it's chemicals."

"Mike?" I asked.

"Mike Share."

"David's dad? What is he doing here? I thought he was in the protection program." I hadn't seen him since the Ushbanian mission and his rescue. He'd gone into hiding shortly afterward.

TL nodded over his shoulder. "He's driving the van."

My attention snapped to the solid wall separating us from the driver.

"He heard about the operation and put in a special request to come. Remember, he *was* best friends with your father. And aside from that, he has another personal reason for being here. You'll find out soon enough."

Personal reason? If I was going to find out soon enough, why couldn't TL tell me now?

Ignoring my confused expression, TL continued, "Tonight, at twenty-three hundred, Eduardo will commence auctioning off the smuggled chemicals. Buyers, most of whom are known terrorists, have flown in from all over the world. After all the chemicals are sold, they'll begin the bomb-making portion of the evening."

"Sounds like they've put together quite the entertaining night," Ms. Gabrier commented. "How many people are we talking about?"

"Mike has been there all day with surveillance. Eduardo and his men are now up to twenty. There're only thirty-one buyers."

"*Only* thirty-one buyers? That's fifty-one in all." I waved my hand around the van. "We can't take down fifty-one people."

"The IPNC hired us to find Eduardo and track his next moves, which we've done." TL checked his watch. "By now there are close to twenty IPNC agents in place, ready to raid the warehouse. I've brought in Specialists Team One: Piper, Tina, Adam, and Curtis. David met with them earlier and briefed them. They'll be assisting with diffusing the chemical bombs."

Twenty IPNC agents and Team One? Still not very good odds. But then, one highly skilled agent *was* like two or three people. TL, for example, could easily take on three or more regular people and win.

TL looked to Beaker. "How much time will you need?"

"It depends on how far along they are with the bomb. What chemicals they used. How they mixed or premixed the chemicals. There're a lot of factors that will tell me what defuse substances to administer." Beaker shrugged. "Could take me hours."

"As soon as IPNC moves in and the warehouse is cleared, you and Ms. Gabrier get to work. Nalani and GiGi will assist, along with Adam and Curtis." TL indicated a black suitcase next to Ms. Gabrier. "That's got all the supplies you requested. According to intel, the warehouse has been set up like a chem lab. You'll have a lot there to work with. Plenty of supplies."

He ran his gaze over each of us. "This mission has morphed into a size none of us expected. Beaker, stick close to Ms. Gabrier and GiGi to Nalani. Neither of you girls have the experience to be anywhere by yourself."

We nodded, completely agreeing with him. No wonder David had been too busy to text or call me.

Nalani slid a duffel bag from beneath her seat. She pulled out black clothes and handed them to us. "Put these on before we get there."

Beaker and I slipped the loose-fitting jumpsuits over our regular clothes and zipped up. TL did the same. We three put black knit hats over our heads.

TL handed me the laptop. "Cue into satellite. Let's take a look inside the warehouse."

I keyed in the scrambler code, connected to our satellite, and X-rayed through the warehouse's roof.

Sure enough, one half of the warehouse mirrored a chemistry lab with microscopes, tables, safety equipment . . . pretty much exactly what Beaker's lab looked like back at the ranch.

In the other half of the building, boxes and crates filled the center of the room. People dressed in expensive suits stood around, sipping drinks. Men in military fatigues and machine guns lined the walls. Women in skimpy outfits hung on the arms of some of the suited men. Eduardo stood off to the side talking to one of the suited men.

The van pulled to a stop, and the back door immediately opened. A team of gorgeous men stood there all big and muscular, decked out in dark clothes, Kevlar vests, and headsets.

Simultaneously, they all folded their bulging arms and looked into the van.

"Well, well," Ms. Gabrier commented.

I blinked a few times. Yep, definitely real.

‹FOURTEEN›

The gorgeous men helped us down from the van out into a dark, slightly chilly Florida night.

I took a second to survey the new location. Gigantic, grassy sand dunes spotted the landscape, and to my right, the ocean stretched to the horizon. Our van had pulled in between two dunes. Big oak trees bordered the area beyond the sand dunes.

Men and women dressed in matching black/Kevlar/headset outfits milled around. IPNC agents, for sure. A couple of Jeeps and one Humvee sat off in the distance. A satellite occupied the top of a particularly high dune. I saw Piper, Tina, Curtis, and Adam next to one of the Jeeps. Adam caught my eye and gave me a little wave. I waved back.

The whole scene seemed alien. All this high techiness out in the middle of a beach. We should have coolers and lounge chairs and bathing suits. And oddly, I wanted to remind everyone that it was illegal to walk on sand dunes.

"Hey."

I turned around. "David!"

He grinned and grabbed me up in a huge hug.

My heart jigged around in my chest as I squeezed him back. *God,* this felt good.

David let me go and took a step back. "How are you doing?"

"Fine. I just want to get this mission done already."

"I know." David turned a little. "You remember my dad."

Behind David stood Mike Share. He smiled.

"Of course I remember your dad!" I gave him a hug. "How are you, Mr. Share?"

"Fine. Doing great, actually." He pressed a kiss to my cheek. "And how are you, GiGi?"

"I'm good." I pulled away. "TL told me you were driving the van. I couldn't wait to see you. He said you're here for a personal reason." I waved that off. "But I know, it's none of my business."

He chuckled. "You'll know soon enough."

That's what TL had said.

Mr. Share glanced beyond me to Beaker and held out his hand. "I'm Mike, David's dad."

She smiled a little and shook his hand. "I know. I remember seeing you at the ranch after the Ushbanian mission. You can call me Beaker."

I moved closer to David. "Where's the warehouse? And what about the other agents? I see only a half dozen or so here."

"Warehouse," David answered, "is through the woods a half mile west of here. The other agents are already in place."

"Let's move out," TL shouted.

I grabbed my laptop from the back of the van, and Beaker got her small suitcase of supplies. When we turned around, all the IPNC agents had gone. Including Mr. Share and Team One.

Sheesh, they're quick.

TL and David took off at a medium-paced jog, and we followed in pairs—Ms. Gabrier and Beaker first—as Nalani and I brought up the rear.

TL and David led us across the beach, between two dunes, and into the trees. Spooky thoughts popped into my mind as I took things in. Like something out of a fairy tale gone bad.

Hundreds of live oaks towered around us, their knotted arms twisted together like gnarly, long, arthritic fingers. Their branches climbed out and up in a maze of thick coverage. Intermittent moonlight filtered through, casting weird shadows.

I kept my focus on the terrain as we jogged through the dense woods, ducking low branches and hopping downed limbs. These were woods I *definitely* wouldn't want to be alone in.

Minutes later we trotted to the top of another dune. Down a sandy hill about one hundred feet away stood the warehouse. Crouching in the dark tree line, we surveyed the back of it. Fancy cars in neat little rows lined the sides of the place.

A dirt road led out from the front, trailing away through dunes into the darkness. Four exterior lights, one on each corner, glowed softly, providing the only illumination. Night blanketed the rest of the isolated beachy area.

This warehouse was so out of place. Like Eduardo had plunked it down in the middle of nowhere. But then, I knew from the aerial view that TL had shown us that this island north of Barracuda Key sat basically deserted.

Men in military fatigues with machine guns patrolled the exterior. I counted ten in all, which meant ten more guarded the inside. Seemed like a lot. But then we were talking millions and *millions* of dollars here. Eduardo wanted to make sure his investment remained safe.

"I trained a couple of those men," Ms. Gabrier barely whispered. "Years and years ago. Don't underestimate them. They know what they're doing."

"Some of those guys used to be on our side?" I couldn't believe it.

She nodded gravely. "Bad pays better."

I didn't care. It didn't matter how much money someone paid me. I'd *never* turn bad.

TL signaled for me to turn on my laptop.

Stepping behind a tree, I activated the dimmer mode, assuring there'd be minimal glow. I cued into satellite and X-rayed through the warehouse's roof.

Boxes of chemicals sat open, some had already been transferred to the chem lab portion of the warehouse.

"Keep an eye on that screen," TL instructed me. "Tell Nalani as soon as they make their first bomb; then we'll have all the evidence we need and can move in." He turned to Beaker. "Don't forget, Adam and Curtis will be on your defuse team. They know to go straight to the lab."

Beaker nodded, and, signaling for us to stay, TL and David took off into the woods.

I felt bad for Nalani having to be my babysitter. I knew she'd probably prefer to be down in the action. "Sorry you have to stay here with me," I mumbled.

Nalani shook her head. "It's not like that." She pointed out different men on the screen. "Those are all known terrorists. We're raking in quite the bundle on this bust."

Taking my eyes off the screen, I studied the side of her face for a few seconds. "I know about you and TL." He would kill me for saying that.

She glanced over at me with a sad smile. "I know."

Why are you two so distant? I wanted to ask. "Is everything okay?" I questioned instead. "I saw you crying . . ."

Nalani switched her attention to my laptop screen, drawing mine as well. More chemicals had been sold and moved to the chem lab. But no bombs yet. As I watched, Eduardo carried a flask of green liquid to a table.

"Our life is . . . unusual. We, um . . ." she hesitated, like she was trying to decide how much to tell me. "We knew each other when we were kids. We spent time in the same foster home."

Nodding to the screen, she put her finger over her lips, signaling no more talking. I focused in on the laptop as the buyers moved into the lab portion of the warehouse.

Eduardo distributed safety gear, and, as the men suited up, he went to the front of the lab. The men began pouring chemicals, mixing, firing up burners. White smoke trailed upward as one guy poured his solution into a small metal container. He connected a wire and a small timer box.

"That's what we needed," Nalani said. She pulled her collar up and whispered into an attached mike, "Move in."

Turning from the laptop, I focused down the hill at the warehouse.

A patrolman silently dropped to the ground.

I blinked. What the . . . ?

One of our guys pulled him under a SUV to hide him. Wow, I didn't even see him there.

On the other side of the warehouse, another patrolman quietly dropped, and an agent slid him behind a huge palmetto.

I scanned the area, searching for more agents, unable to locate them.

One by one patrolmen dropped, and our guys slid them from view. I didn't ask if the bad guys were dead or alive. I didn't want to know. They may have been highly trained, but turning bad apparently had taken away their skills.

With all ten patrolmen disabled, the place sat very still. I saw nothing. I heard nothing. No good guys, no bad guys. Just cars, the warehouse, darkness, and an occasional frog croak.

I'd never actually watched a takedown of this magnitude before. We'd discussed it once in one of our PTs. But seeing it live . . . well, it was just plain impressive. These agents were amazing.

On cue, everything happened at once. Piles of sand lifted and agents crawled from beneath them. Palmetto branches stirred and other agents slinked out. Shadowed figures materialized from the darkness, hidden only by the night. A tree rustled to my right, and I jumped as someone emerged.

I glanced at Beaker. Her wide-eyed expression mirrored my thoughts exactly.

Wow.

Some of the agents wore black, others green, and others tan. A few had palm fronds sticking to their clothes. They all wore hoods to hide their faces.

No wonder I hadn't seen any of them.

Stealthily, they crept through the night, weaving around the parked cars until they surrounded the warehouse. Six agents shinnied up the aluminum sides all the way to the roof. How they shinnied, I couldn't tell. I saw no ropes or wires. It reminded me of the Rissala mission and how Wirenut had effortlessly Spider-manned it up the side of a castle with air-lock suction cups.

In the moonlight, I saw the agents make hand signals to one another, from the ones on the roof to those on the ground. Quick flashes of gloved fingers, brushing their shoulders, their faces. Like the signals TL used with us.

An agent on the roof threw back a hatch at the same time the agents on the ground crashed through the front door and busted down the back. Light poured out as our guys rushed in.

Gunshots popped.

I flinched.

Screams.

More shots.

Shouting.

My heart lurched. Where was David? TL? Mr. Share? Adam and Curtis and the rest of Team One?

Nalani grabbed the back of my jumpsuit. I looked over at her. Her whole face tightened, and she nodded once, silently telling me to hang in there.

Me? What about her? She had to be scared to death for TL.

I moved my gaze back to the warehouse.

A man in a lab coat bolted out the back door. An agent followed, tackling him to the ground. He planted his knee in the man's back and cinched his hands to his ankles.

More gunshots went off.

My whole body tensed. Had David gone in with everyone else? With their hoods and camouflaged outfits, everyone looked the same. What had David been wearing? My mind raced to remember. Black. He'd been dressed in all black.

Screams and more shots sounded.

God, what's going on? I can't stand this.

I covered my ears with my hands and squeezed my eyes shut. I couldn't look anymore. I couldn't listen anymore. My heartbeat thundered in my ears. My breath rasped.

My parents had died this way. Violently. Gunshots exploding. That horrible sound was the last thing they'd ever heard.

Suddenly, the place fell completely and utterly silent.

Slowly, I opened my eyes and slid my hands down my face.

Nalani let go of my jumpsuit. "All clear." She signaled Beaker and Ms. Gabrier. "Let's do it."

Beaker grabbed her small suitcase, we pulled our knit caps over our faces, and we left the trees to jog down the sandy hill. My heart thumped in my chest in slow, deep surges. We were about to defuse bombs.

Disheveled people stumbled from the warehouse, men dressed in safety gear and the slinky dressed women, all with their hands secured behind their backs. Blood trickled down their faces, their arms, their legs. Most of the women were crying. The men all looked really pissed off.

Agents shouted orders at them, pointing, kneeling them in the sand. With all the gunshots, I could only imagine what the scene was inside the warehouse.

I followed Beaker and Ms. Gabrier through the back door and caught a quick glimpse of blood and bodies. Someone moaned. My gaze flicked to the person making the painful sound. Dressed in a dark suit, a man gripped his bloody stomach as he sluggishly rolled over. Somewhat hypnotized, I watched him, my mind whirling back years ago to the plane crash. To the bodies that had floated past me . . . My vision blurred as I turned a slow circle, trying to recall what I was supposed to be doing.

Nalani steered me toward the chem lab. "Don't look. Focus on the objective."

I blinked my eyes a few times and swallowed, refocusing.

We wound through stacked wooden crates and pushed through heavy hanging plastic into the lab where Adam and Curtis were already waiting.

"Nobody touch anything," Beaker ordered.

Quickly, yet with the most intense focus I'd ever seen, she began walking around studying the flasks of liquids, bowls of powders, piles of clay, copper wire, magnets, tubes of thick substances, boiling flasks, dishes of crystals. In her chemistry notebook, she jotted down the measurements off scales, weird-looking meters, timers, scopes, syringes, burners, bottles.

Ms. Gabrier gave each of us a heavy lab coat, goggles, and the scenario papers Beaker had drawn up. I swallowed a gurgle of hysteria as I realized a lab coat and goggles would do nothing to protect from a bomb exploding.

Hurry! I wanted to yell at Beaker, but I knew the necessity of intense concentration when everything was on the line. I slipped my black hood off and donned the safety gear.

Beaker cycled back around the room. She pointed to two silver canisters with blue liquid flowing in a glass tube between them. "Curtis. Scenario two hundred and three. You have five minutes."

I blinked. She'd memorized the scenarios? All four hundred and eleven? Oh my God.

Curtis hurried over, flipping through his pages, locating his scenario. Quickly, he silently read it. "What's leum acid?"

"It's that black liquid in the syringe," she answered without glancing up. "It's next to the silver canister."

With a nod he slipped on gloves and carefully took the syringe. I focused back on Beaker.

"Nalani, this one's yours." Beaker indicated a bowl filled with what looked like grape Jell-O. A small copper wire very simply, almost innocently, stuck out the top. "Scenario sixty-eight. Do *not* touch the bowl."

Locating her scenario, Nalani crossed the room. I watched as she picked up tongs, and then I refocused on Beaker. Pick me next, I silently implored. I wanted to get this over with.

Beaker stopped at a flask of boiling pink liquid with yellow smoke puffing up. She inserted a skinny piece of pink paper, brought it out, and studied the end. It turned white. "Adam. Scenario one hundred and twenty-seven."

She moved on as Adam made his way around the table Nalani stood at, reading his scenario as he walked. He stopped, scanned the lab, then went across to where Curtis worked and slid an unused thermometer from the table.

Nervously, I focused in on Curtis and watched as he gingerly unscrewed one of the silver canisters. I glanced back to Beaker. Pick me next, I silently pleaded. My stress was about to explode my brain cells.

She indicated a station with a two-foot-tall silver pot. "Ms. Gabrier. This'll detonate in exactly two minutes."

Two minutes?!

"Scenario four hundred and one," Beaker calmly instructed.

How could she be so calm? And for that matter, how could everybody else? I scanned the room taking in my team's focused, patient movements. I didn't understand. My heart was about to leap from my chest.

"GiGi."

I snapped my attention to Beaker.

She stuck her finger in a gold powder and touched it to her tongue. She waited for a few seconds with her tongue out, then spit on the floor. "Scenario five."

I raced over, my eyes dropping to scenario five. It read vinyl alcohol, odatedrogen, and silver nitrate. Silver nitrate was the only name I recognized. It said to grate metal nap across the top and then stir slowly counterclockwise for ten seconds. My heart gave a relieved beat. Sounded simple enough. Wait a minute, grate? How much. A light scattering or a thick covering? "It doesn't say how much to grate."

"Sprinkle it," Beaker answered. "Like it's salt."

I glanced around my area and located a plastic-wrapped block of what looked like green cheese. Its label read METAL LAP. Carefully, I peeled the plastic off the green block. A grater sat right beside the bowl of gold powder. I picked up the grater and ran the green block across it, watching as it sprinkled the top. I studied the sprinkles, realizing I salted things lightly. Beaker might salt things heavily. I was dying to ask if she would come look, but went on instinct instead.

Taking a stirring rod, I slowly stirred counterclockwise, watching ten seconds tick by on my watch. What if I stirred slower than her? Or what if she stirred slower than me? I pushed the doubtfulness from my mind and kept going counterclockwise. Ten seconds passed, and I glanced up.

Beaker and Ms. Gabrier stood across the room at a very intimidating-looking row of fiercely boiling liquids. Ms. Gabrier handed Beaker a blue balloon.

435

"GiGi," Nalani whispered, dragging my attention behind me. I realized Adam and Curtis were gone and Nalani was already back in her black hood.

She motioned to me. "Let's go. That's the last one. Beaker and Ms. Gabrier will take care of it."

I shuffled over to the side door where she was waiting and took off my safety gear. Slipping my black hood back on, I stepped out into the night and took a deep breath. We headed left toward where all the people still knelt. I checked my watch. Only eight minutes had gone by since I'd disappeared into the lab. Seemed a lot longer.

I surveyed all of our guys, looking for David. But with their hoods and camouflaged outfits, they all seemed alike. One, two, three, four, five . . . I couldn't remember how many TL said we had. Or if he'd even said how many were dressed in black like David. For all I knew, he could've changed into another outfit. I looked at their bodies, unable to distinguish one from the other.

More handcuffed people ushered from the warehouse with our guys behind them.

One of the bad guys strutted out, his head up, all haughty, like he hadn't just been busted. "My father is a very powerful man," he back talked to an agent.

The agent shoved him, and the bad guy went face-first into the sand.

That's the least he deserved.

Nalani and I crossed in front of all the kneeling people. I scanned their angry faces, searching for Eduardo's. I passed by a sobbing woman.

"Shut up," the old man beside her snapped.

These were some of the richest, most powerful people and terrorists in the world. They'd probably never been busted for anything. Most likely they'd always succeeded at getting away with their illegal dealings. They probably thought their money would buy them out of this one.

Sad truth was, for some, it might.

And the women. Boy did they pick a bad time to be a rich guy's decoration.

"I don't see Eduardo," I whispered to Nalani.

She shook her head.

Then it hit me. Maybe he was dead. I wouldn't be able to confront him about my parents. I wouldn't get any answers. And as those thoughts slammed into me, he walked straight out the back door.

I froze.

An agent behind him jabbed a gun in his side, pushing him forward. They strode away from me, past all the kneeling people, and into the night.

Wait. Where were they going?

"No." I sprinted across the sand. Nalani made a move for me, and I brushed her off.

The agent and Eduardo cut the corner of the warehouse, disappearing around the side.

"Wait!" I screamed, bolting after them.

"Stop!" Nalani yelled.

I rounded the corner, eating up the distance between Eduardo and me, and grabbed hold of them both. They stopped and turned.

I shoved Eduardo in the chest. "You killed my parents!"

His lips curved into an evil smile. "Did I now?"

Rage rocketed through my body, vibrating out every pore. I reared back and slammed my fist straight into his jaw.

His head moved slightly with the impact. Blood welled in the corner of his mouth. Staring straight into my eyes, he licked it off and spit it in my face.

I yelled and reared my fist back—

"No."

The female agent's command brought me to a halt, and tears immediately poured out of my eyes.

"Why?" I sobbed. "Why did you kill them?"

"Little girl, I don't know who you are, or your parents." Eduardo shrugged. "If they died, they must have deserved it."

His casual brush-off made more angry tears come. For the first time in my life, I wanted to kill someone. "Y-you took away everything. You made that plane go down. You shot my parents in the head. I-I was only six. You ruined my life."

Blankly, he stared at me. "Ah, yes, the plane crash. Your father was one of my best men. Such a shame to find out he was double-crossing me. Bad things happen to double-crossers. You need to always remember that."

My breath hitched at his admittance to being connected to my father. "What did you do with my mom's body?"

He shrugged again. "Sorry, don't know what you're talking about."

"My mom's body!" I screamed.

Eduardo's brows lifted ever so slightly. "Sure she's dead?"

437

"Okay, that's enough," the female agent spoke.

I switched my gaze to hers, and through her hood in the moonlight, I stared into her blue eyes. I had the unnerving sensation I'd looked into those eyes before.

‹FIFTEEN›

The Female agent broke eye contact with me and manhandled Eduardo along. In the darkness, I turned and stared as they strode down the side of the warehouse toward the front.

I took a step toward them. Wait, I wanted to yell. Where are you taking him? Who are you? Do I know you?

Lightly, Nalani grasped my arm. "Let them go."

"Who is that?" I asked, sniffing.

Nalani shook her head.

I watched as the tall, slender agent led Eduardo away from the warehouse and into the parking area. A black SUV's headlights flicked on.

She opened the back door, illuminating the interior. A person dressed the same as her, in all black with a knit hood, sat behind the wheel.

The female agent shoved Eduardo into the back and climbed in after him. She shut the door, sending the interior into darkness again. The SUV pulled out from the parking lot and onto the dirt road and disappeared into the night.

I turned to Nalani. "What's going on? Who were they? Where are they taking him?"

She shook her head again. "It's out of our hands. The IPNC decides what happens now. I promise you, though, he'll pay for his crimes. He'll pay for what he did to your parents." She gave my hand a tug. "Let's go."

I didn't doubt he would pay. I knew he would. "But who was that agent? That one seemed so familiar. Something about her eyes. Do I know her?" I grabbed Nalani's arm, a thought slamming into me. "They didn't find my mom. She could've swum away. Hidden out. Been pursuing

Eduardo ever since. She could still be working rogue for the government. She could—"

"GiGi." Nalani squeezed my shoulder. "There's no way Eduardo would have let your mom live. You know that, right?"

A couple of long seconds passed, and, reluctantly, I nodded.

"He was playing with you just now. Don't let him mess with your psyche."

I sniffed again, drying up the last remnants of my tears.

"You're an analytical person. You see things in black and white, and you don't like gray areas. The fact that your mom's body was never found is a gray area." Nalani released my shoulder. "Sometimes in this business you don't always get black and white. That's the hard truth. Not everything gets answered, resolved."

Taking a breath, my brain and emotions hesitantly acknowledged her words.

The sound of an engine cut through the night, and I glanced over my shoulder to see a semitruck coming down the dirt road. It rolled to a stop in front of the warehouse.

Handcuffed people shuffled passed me, corralled on both sides by agents. They made their way down the side of the warehouse to the front. The agents opened the semi's back doors, pulled a ramp down, and led the captives up.

Minutes later, the agents filed in behind them, shut the doors, and the semi pulled out.

Nalani took her hood off. "All clear."

I did the same. "What about the dead bodies inside?"

"There'll be another crew here shortly to catalogue evidence and clean things up." She nudged me with her elbow. "By the way, nice punch back there."

I curled my fingers in, noticing for the first time a slight throb. "Thanks."

David rounded the side of the warehouse and nearly smacked right into us. "There you are. You okay?"

Nalani kept going around him toward the back of the building.

Closing the distance between us, I wrapped my arms around his back and pressed our bodies together. I buried my face in his neck, and closing my eyes, I inhaled his familiar scent, took in his warmth, and felt his heartbeat.

David laid his cheek on my head and held me snug against him. I could stand here for eternity wrapped in his arms and die a very content person.

"I couldn't find you," I mumbled. "I was so worried."

"Shh." He tightened his hold. "I'm okay."

He slid his hands up my back, and, cupping the sides of my face, he brought my lips to his. Softly, tenderly, he kissed me, and then pulled back. And still cradling my face, we gazed into each other's eyes. Although neither of us said a word, I knew as I held my eyes to his that our relationship deepened a level.

I didn't know what I would do if anything happened to him.

"As soon as we get home, I'm taking you out." His eyes crinkled. "You and me. Alone. Out. Official date. Yes?"

I smiled. "Yes."

He took a little step back. "Did you talk to Eduardo?"

I nodded. "I hit him."

David lifted his brows. "And?"

"He admitted to being connected with my father. Oh, and that agent that took him. Something seemed familiar about her. Do you know who she is?"

He shook his head. "Sorry."

A throat cleared behind us. "Excuse me, David, I need to speak with you."

We turned to see Mr. Share standing with Beaker.

"How'd it go inside?" I asked her.

She quirked a smile. "Got everything defused. No prob."

"That's great."

From behind them, TL waved me over. "GiGi, over here. Let Mike talk with David and Beaker."

Beaker? Why would Mr. Share want private time with Beaker? I glanced at her in silent question.

She shrugged, as clueless as me.

"Excuse me." I strolled past and headed over to TL.

The three of them wandered away into the shadows of the cars. David and Beaker leaned up against a truck while Mr. Share stood in front of them. The darkness hid their expressions, but I watched them anyway.

TL, Nalani, and Ms. Gabrier headed inside the warehouse, leaving me alone, standing in the sand, staring through the night at David, Beaker, and Mr. Share.

And the more I stared, the more I realized how rude it was *to* stare. So I sat in the sand and made myself look anywhere *but* in their direction.

What the heck was going on?

My mind tried to come up with answers . . . Mr. Share wanted to speak with Beaker about her restoration solution? No, that didn't make sense. He was a computer guy. Why would he care about chemistry? Unless, maybe he wanted to put her solutions in a computer? But then, what did that have to do with David?

No. There was absolutely no reason why Mr. Share would need to talk with David *and* Beaker.

TL emerged from the warehouse. "Let's go."

"What?" I stood. "But what about Nalani and Ms. Gabrier? An-and Beaker, David, and Mr. Share?" We weren't just going to leave them, were we?

TL charged up the hill toward the trees. "Nalani and Gabrier are staying for cleanup. The others will be along shortly."

"But . . ." I followed behind TL. "But I didn't get to say bye to Nalani."

TL entered the woods. "You'll see her again."

I glanced over my shoulder. Mr. Share still stood in the darkness with David and Beaker. None of them had moved. The back door to the warehouse sat open, with bright light shining out. Shadows flicked inside as Nalani and Ms. Gabrier moved about.

"GiGi," TL called, "pick up the pace."

I jogged through the woods and caught up. "For the record, I hate secrets. I'm dying to know what's going on with David and Beaker. And for another record, I *never* want to be in charge of a mission again." Way too much stress.

TL chuckled. "Duly noted. At least you tried, but not everyone's a leader."

This mission had definitely taught me that. "I'm sorry for being an idiot and making bad decisions?"

"Everyone makes mistakes. Always remember that."

I wondered how long it would be before I truly earned back his total trust.

"What about that family?" I asked, stepping over a stump. "The one I overheard Eduardo talking about . . ." Killing. I couldn't quite finish the sentence.

TL nodded. "Everything's fine."

He didn't elaborate, but if he said everything was fine, I believed him.

We didn't talk the rest of the way through the woods. A half mile later we came out the other side. Our van still sat there in between two dunes with a Humvee behind it. Everything else was gone. The jeeps. The other Humvees. The satellite.

A red-haired man helped a little red-haired girl climb up into the Humvee. Inside sat another little girl and boy, also redheads, and a grown woman. The man shut the door, climbed behind the wheel, and cranked the engine.

One of the tiny girls watched me through the window as they pulled away. She sent me a sweet little wave and I returned it. "That's the family, isn't it?"

TL came up beside me. "Yes. Dad's a chemist. Eduardo had kidnapped his kids and wife in order to get him to do what he wanted."

I watched them drive safely across the sand. "They're safe now."

"Yes, they are. Thanks to you. If you hadn't overheard Eduardo's conversation, it's likely we would have never found out about them."

TL's words brought me peace. Thanks to me, a whole family would go on living happily together.

Dialing his cell phone, he stepped away. I stowed my laptop inside the van.

Leaning up against the vehicle, I stared at the woods and waited for David and Beaker to appear.

The ocean swished to shore, TL mumbled softly in the background, an occasional gnat flew past.

And still I waited, my gaze fixed on the trees . . .

Some time later, David stepped from the live oaks first, followed by Beaker. I searched both their faces for signs of anything. But neither of them looked at me, or at each other. They kept their focus down as they approached.

I pushed up from the van. "Hey."

"Hey," David mumbled.

Beaker said nothing.

I took her supplies and put them in the vehicle. "Where's Mr. Share?"

David tossed a backpack in behind her supplies. "He's staying behind to help with cleanup."

"Oh."

And then the three of us lapsed into silence with the two of them staring at their shoes.

Mind telling me what's going on? I wanted to ask, but waited patiently instead for one of them to speak.

"Let's go." TL climbed into the driver's side.

We loaded into the back, and TL pulled out.

Beaker sat beside me and David across. I looked from one to the other and back to the first, waiting for someone to say something. But neither spoke as they stared at their laps.

"Oh good God. Someone tell me what's going on." So much for patience.

David glanced across the van at Beaker.

She shrugged a shoulder. "Go ahead."

He scrubbed his hands down his face, and, leaning forward, he propped his elbows on his knees. He sighed, fixing his attention on the van's flooring.

Seconds passed, and I waited, suspended in suspense.

What? I'm dying here, people.

"The government," David began, "contracted my dad to develop a computerized DNA program. It compares and contrasts the different chains of the double helix. It'll be used in criminal investigations and for medical reasons like organ matching for donors."

David cleared his throat, still focusing on the floor. "My dad's been testing the program, loading up all the DNA currently on file. He pulled up all the DNA that matches his. Of course, my name popped up . . . but so did Beaker's."

I glanced between them. "I don't understand."

David swallowed, and the gurgle echoed in the cargo space. "Did you know my grandfather was a gifted chemist?"

"No. Are you trying to tell me you two are distant cousins or something?"

He rubbed the back of his neck. "Do you remember I told you my mom left when I was a little boy?"

"Yes."

"My dad was on assignment in Jacksonville, Florida, undercover as a fisherman when he met this woman. He was really upset and got drunk one night, and . . . long story short, he had no idea she got pregnant."

My heart slowed to a steady, knowing thump. "Are you saying . . . ?"

444

David brought his eyes up to meet mine. "Beaker and I are half-sister and -brother."

***

We'd been back at the ranch for a week when I stepped from the ranch house into a brisk, sunny, California day.

Off to the right, Parrot galloped his horse across the pasture, with Bruiser holding on tight behind him. Her excited squeals carried on the wind.

Wirenut and Cat came from the side of the house, hands linked, strolling toward the barn.

Mystic and Adam, from Team One, climbed into Adam's car, waving as they pulled down the driveway. Piper, also from Team One, followed them in her car. I'd overheard them say they were going to pick up their friends and head into town to a basketball game.

I heard David's laughter and glanced left. He and Beaker sat on a bench under a sequoia tree. Beaker had transformed back into Goth. She listened while David animatedly described something. They'd been spending a lot of time together over the past week. In fact, he'd spent more time with Beaker than with me.

I didn't care. I was happy they were happy.

Sitting down on the front step, I studied the two of them. Now that I knew they were brother and sister, their similarities popped out at me: their smiles, the shape of their faces, and oddly enough, their legs.

Beaker favored Mr. Share more than David did. I could only imagine what Beaker must be feeling. Meeting a father she never knew she had. Did it make her feel complete? Finished somehow? Did it answer questions she'd always had? Did the pieces of her life puzzle fit together a little better?

I was happy for her, truly I was. But I envied her a little, too, being reunited with lost family. What I would give for that. *Sure she's dead?* Eduardo's question floated through my mind. No, I wasn't sure my mother was dead. How could I be if her body had never been found? Surely, if TL knew something different, he would've told me by now. But TL may not even know one way or the other about my mother. One thing was for sure, if she was still alive, we'd find our way to each other somehow.

My gaze and thoughts drifted back to Beaker. She'd come a long way since first finding out about the Barracuda Key mission. She'd been tested from all sides, emotionally and physically. And I'd learned a lot about her, too. I understood her better now. Underneath all that gruffness beat a sweet heart. It just took a while to find it. It reminded me that all the members of my new family had come from different places, different situations. Our unique backgrounds helped form each of us into who we are now. Beaker had taught me to look beyond a person's appearance to what lay beneath.

Of course, I'd never admit she'd taught me anything.

The door behind me opened. I glanced over my shoulder to see Mr. Share come out. He smiled and touched my head as he stepped around me.

He crossed the yard to the tree David and Beaker sat under. Mr. Share said something, and Beaker nodded. With a slight smile, she stood. He put his arm around her shoulders, and the two of them walked off across the property.

David watched them for a few seconds and then pushed up from the bench and came across the yard toward me.

My stomach flip-flopped as I watched him approach.

He sat down beside me on the step, stretching his legs out in front of him. We sat in companionable silence, our legs barely brushing. After a long minute, he turned and looked at me. I returned his look, curious about what he wanted. But he just continued staring, not saying anything.

I thought back to weeks ago when we'd been in the elevator and he'd done this same deep looking. "What do you see?" I repeated the same question I'd asked him weeks ago.

David's eyes crinkled. I *loved* when they did that. He reached over and trailed his finger along my jaw. "I see beauty that almost makes my heart ache. And not just beauty on the outside." He touched his finger to my heart. "Beauty in here, too."

My heart slammed so hard against my chest wall, I knew he had to feel it, too.

He gave his head a little shake. "When did I become so mushy," he noted with a chuckle.

I smiled at that. I liked him mushy.

Suddenly, I thought of David's first solo mission involving me, before I'd even heard of the Specialists. "How hard was it for you when you came to Iowa to . . ." I didn't want to go into the details. "Well, to get me."

446

David linked his pinky with mine. "It was hard lying to you. TL and I had quite a few heated discussions about it when I would report in."

"You did?" And to think I'd spent all that time in Iowa dealing with my crush on David, and he'd been struggling with his first mission because of me. So it was quite possible even back in Iowa he liked me more than he let on. He'd said he'd been fighting the whole like-me-as-a-friend/like-me-more thing for months. How long, exactly, had the battle gone on?

I wanted, no, I *needed* to know when he knew he liked me. Love at first sight? Or something he had to warm up to? Not that he'd mentioned love, but you know what I mean. "David, can I ask you one question, and then I promise I'll never bring it up again."

He waved me on. "Whatcha got?"

"Way back when you first met me, even though you called me your little sister, did you like me but didn't want to admit it? Or did I slowly grow on you?" I hoped he didn't think my questions were stupid.

Playfully, he groaned. "Why do girls always have to know more?"

I waited.

"Yes. Okay? Yes. I thought you were hot when I first met you."

I grinned. "You thought I was hot?"

"And klutzy."

"Hey!" I bumped my shoulder to his, enjoying the fun. "Did you know I liked you back in Iowa?"

David bumped my shoulder back. "How could I not when you fell all over yourself every time I came around."

My jaw dropped. "I did *not.*" Actually, I had.

He put his arm around me, and I scooted closer as we lapsed into more silence. Idly, we watched Mr. Share and Beaker stroll across the grass, going farther and farther away.

"How's it going with the get-to-know-you-as-a-sister thing?" I asked.

"Good. Beaker said she met some guy CJ in Barracuda Key." He chuckled. "I've only been her brother for a week, but, weirdly enough, I'm feeling protective."

"What'd she say about CJ?"

"Just that she figured out they really didn't have anything in common."

David's and my phone call from last week popped into my mind, and I finally asked the question that had been bugging me. "Why'd we get disconnected last week? Ya know, when you called?"

"Chapling cut in. That's when I first found out my dad was coming to Barracuda Key."

"Oh." That made sense. And to think I'd obsessed over something so simple.

David leaned over and kissed my neck. "What about that date?" he asked.

"What about it?" I flirted back.

bzzzbzzzbzzz.

With a sigh, I glanced down at my cell clipped to my jeans.

***. TL's stat code.

I looked at David. "I can't believe this."

He pushed to his feet and held his hand out to me. "Here we go again."

I took his hand and let him pull me up. "I can't believe I ever threatened to leave. I don't know what I'd do without this place. Without all of you."

David squeezed my hand. "We, *I* don't know what I'd do without you."

My face warmed at his comment.

He gave my hand a quick squeeze and led me inside the door. "I'm glad you're still here."

BOOK FOUR

WHATEVER YOU DO, DON'T LOOK DOWN!

I jerked straight up in the saddle.

"You need to stay awake," Jonathan warned. "Look to your left."

Rubbing my eye, I looked to the left . . . and froze.

We were on a cliff.

And it dropped straight down.

Hundreds, *thousands* of feet down. I couldn't even see the bottom.

Not moving a muscle in my body, I stared at the ledge we were on. Each time one of Diablo's hoofs came down, pebbles skidded over the edge and disappeared.

With my heart galloping, I inched my head to the right . . . and froze.

Another drop-off.

A really, really, *really* big drop-off.

"J-J-Jonathan?"

"Calm down, GiGi. Diablo knows what he's doing. Concentrate on not moving. Don't do anything to set him off balance."

Locking every muscle in my body, I stared hard at the black hairs of Diablo's mane. I concentrated on not moving, not breathing. I heard a short, choppy, shallow intake of air and realized it was me. Squeezing my eyes shut, I forced a swallow, trying to moisten my mouth. I'd rather see darkness than the reality of the minuscule ledge and the vast jungle around me.

I heard another choppy breath come in and out of my mouth and then a deafening roar. "Wh-what was that?!"

‹PROLOGUE›

Darren stared at the door to his grandmother's apartment. He'd been living with her for seven years, ever since his mom left, and every day it was the same thing. He'd come home from school, and she'd be sleeping on the couch.

Maybe today would be different.

Not likely.

Taking a deep breath, he turned the knob on the front door and walked in. Grandmother never locked anything. Nobody on the reservation did. That sense of trust always brought Darren peace.

As he passed through the shadowed living room toward his bedroom, he glanced at the corner where the worn-through couch sat, where his grandmother always was.

Her skinny body lay half on/half off the couch. One leg and arm dangled over the side. Her gray braid trailed across a cushion.

No matter how hard he tried, he couldn't conjure up a good memory of his grandmother. There had to be one somewhere in the recesses of his brain. Perhaps one day he'd recall it and know that she'd loved him, that she'd been happy.

Setting down his backpack, Darren crossed the living room to the couch, and stopped.

He studied her.

Breathing. She wasn't breathing.

Darren tentatively reached forward and placed his hand on her cheek.

Cold.

He slid his fingers to her chest right where her heart should beat.

Silently, he waited, holding his breath, every sense in his body tuned to his palm against her chest.

No beat.

Darren pushed away and stood over her, staring down at her lifeless form. No thoughts occupied his mind.

He waited for his body to react with tears, sickness, sadness . . .

But there was nothing. No emotion at all. Only the familiar emptiness in his heart.

Without a last glance in her direction, he gathered his things, walked from the apartment to the stables down the road, jumped onto his horse—his only friend in the world—and rode bareback across the Arizona desert toward the sun.

***

"Vuv," Talon commanded two days later. Sit.

Darren sat on a low wooden stool across from his tribal chief. Between them a fire flickered in a shallow, stone pit. The smoke trailed upward out of a special opening in the roof.

Darren had never understood Talon's penchant for heat. It could be one hundred degrees outside and he'd still have a fire burning. Although Talon lived in an ordinary one-story home, he spent all his time in this added-on room built to seem like something from a century ago. Animal skulls hung on the walls, and skins covered the floor. A few pieces of roughly made wood furniture sat scattered about.

Talon puffed his pipe and then extended it, keeping his black, heartless eyes level on Darren.

Sharing a smoke with an elder was a great privilege, one any teenage male would jump at. Darren had tried it a few times and ended up coughing for days afterward. So now he preferred not to do it at all.

Talon knew this, yet repeatedly offered Darren the pipe. It was one of the many reasons he had no respect for the tribal chief.

With a grunt, Talon indicated the hand-carved pipe.

Darren shook his head.

Talon's lips sneered, as if he got some twisted amusement from the pipe game.

Darren hated coming to this room. The whole place had a wicked aura. *Talon* had a wicked aura.

Straightening his back, the tribal chief placed his palms on his knees. Barefoot and without a shirt, he wore only a pair of dark jeans.

"Yjoto jixo aae doop?" Where have you been? Talon asked.

"Vjo enuhhu." The cliffs. Darren would still be there if not for his grandmother's funeral ceremony tomorrow.

Someone knocked softly on the door and then quietly opened it, sending in cooler air from the main house. Talon's oldest daughter entered, head bowed, and shuffled across the floor to where Talon and Darren sat.

Darren had never heard any of Talon's daughters speak, or Talon's wife for that matter. They all looked the same, with long skirts, blouses, and braided hair. And they always shuffled around with their heads bowed.

The daughter knelt beside Talon and picked up a tray with the remains of his dinner. As she stood, he grabbed her arm and yanked her to him. The tray thudded to the floor.

"Nov jot ia!" Let her go!

Both Talon and his daughter snapped surprised eyes toward Darren, as if neither could believe someone actually had the nerve to speak up against Talon, to defend a female.

He'd witnessed Talon treat other women harshly, too. And the women never fought back. In one way the subservience annoyed Darren. Why did the women allow themselves to be treated like that? Why wouldn't they just leave? The reservation had no iron gates, anybody could walk off at any time.

Darren's mother had.

In another way the situation irritated him. Actually, it ticked him off. What gave Talon or any man the right to treat women like that? Did it boost his ego? It didn't do that for Darren. It made him physically ill.

With a sardonic chuckle, the chief shoved his daughter away. She quickly picked up the tray and scurried out of the room.

Talon placed a small log on the fire, making the flames grow.

Shadows flickered off his Mohawk and his chest.

Evil and *dark,* two words Darren had always associated with the chief.

Talon rubbed his fingers over the thick, black stripes tattooed down his chin. *"Auet itipfoavjot uu foif."* Your grandmother is dead.

"U mpay." I know.

"Jot eotooapa uu vaoattay." Her ceremony is tomorrow.

Darren wiped a trail of sweat from his cheek. *"Unn do vjoto."* I'll be there.

Silence fell between them as they stared at each other in the dim light.

All he wanted to do was get on his horse and ride, fast and hard. Anywhere. Everywhere. His horse had been and would always be his refuge. But out of respect for his mother, he would attend the ceremony.

Talon cleared his throat and spit into the fire. "You will stay here," he said, switching to English, "in your grandmother's apartment."

No way. Darren had already thought about it. He was leaving as soon as Grandmother's ceremony ended. "I've made other plans."

The chief chuckled low and humorlessly. "What plans? You are seventeen. You have no money."

It didn't matter. Darren would live in the cliffs, the mountains, the woods, any place but here. "I've made other plans."

Talon ran his tongue across his teeth. "You have a unique gift. The gods chose you. You must repay the gods by honoring your blood."

Even in the overheated room, Darren's body chilled. "What do you mean?"

"Your tongue is magic."

Darren had never told anyone about his special ability. His grandmother must have opened her mouth. But not even *she* knew the extent of his gift.

No one did.

You keep this a secret, Darren's mother had made him promise. *Not until you're grown and gone, old enough to have wisdom, do you tell anybody of your talent. People will exploit it if they have the chance.*

He remembered how she'd play a tape in another language, and he'd mimic the speech. They'd laugh. It was a childhood game. One he often thought of fondly.

"My tongue is like anyone else's," Darren lied.

"I have a job for you. It pays well."

"Not interested."

The chief grunted. "You will be."

Not likely.

"The Uopoei Nation does great business. International. Thirty-one countries now. You will translate transactions. Interpret the meetings."

"No thanks."

"It's important business. There's a lot of honor that goes with being involved."

Illegal, I'm sure. "I said no."

Talon smirked as he took a small poker from the fire and touched it to his pipe. "I know where your mother is."

Hope surged through Darren. Talon knew Darren would do anything for that information. "Where?"

The chief puffed his pipe three times. *"Aae fu lad. U vonn aae xjoto aaet oavjot uu."* You work for me, and I'll tell you where your mother is.

***

Squinting against the Venezuelan sun, Darren watched a plane touch down on the deserted runway.

Why did these business transactions always take place in the middle of nowhere?

Two weeks ago he'd been in a Russian forest.

Three weeks ago it'd been the Swedish mountains.

Last week it was a boat in China.

Never once had Darren seen "the cargo." Nor had anybody called it anything other than "the cargo." And Talon never came with Darren on these trips.

Something illegal was definitely going on.

Darren cared, sure he cared.

But he cared more about finding his mother.

Six months, Darren reminded himself. That was what he and Talon had agreed upon. Six months and he'd know where his mother was.

The big guy beside Darren adjusted his dark sunglasses. *"Esta supuesto ser el mejor cargamento."* Supposed to be the best cargo yet.

Darren didn't know the guy's name. Nobody knew anyone else's name. All Darren knew was what languages to speak. Today it'd be Spanish and German.

The plane pulled past them, pushing a warm, fuel-scented gust of wind across the runway. Holding on to his cowboy hat, the South American guy led the way over the packed dirt to where the plane stopped.

The back of it slowly lowered, and a man and a woman walked out, both blond and dressed in white business suits. Behind them in the plane's belly sat a huge silver crate, big enough to hold livestock.

The cargo.

Cowboy-Hat Guy nodded to the man and the woman. *"Bienvenidos."* Welcome. *"¿Todo está listo?"* Is everything ready?

457

"Wilkommen. Ist alles fertig?" Darren translated to the German couple.

The woman glanced beyond him to the semitruck that Cowboy-Hat Guy had driven and the motorcycle Darren rode. *"Haben Sie unser Geld?"* Do you have our money?

As soon as the money and the cargo exchanged hands, everyone would go their separate ways. Darren never knew where "the cargo" ended up.

"¿Tienes nuestro dinero?" He interpreted for Cowboy-Hat Guy.

Cowboy lifted the brown leather duffel bag he held in his left hand.

The woman descended the metal ramp leading from the plane and took the duffel bag.

And then everything happened in a blur.

Cowboy threw the woman to the ground and drew a gun on the blond man. *"¡Policia! No se muevan."* Police! Don't move.

The doors to the semi banged open. Out jumped a squad of guys with machine guns. They raced across the tarmac and up the ramp into the plane.

A squad guy handcuffed the blond man.

Cowboy handcuffed the woman.

Before Darren had time to think, move, or breathe, he was thrown to the ground and handcuffed, too.

Two guys smashed the padlocks on the silver crate, opened the doors, and stepped back.

Nobody said a word.

Darren kept his gaze glued to the crate. From the shadows stumbled a young girl, maybe twelve, dressed in ragged clothes. Then another came out, even younger, dressed the same. And then another.

The cargo.

Darren's stomach rolled on a wave of nausea as girl after girl stepped from the crate. Some crying, others wide-eyed with fear. Some clung to one another while others used their hands and arms to shield the bright sun. There were about thirty in all.

A squad guy ran up the ramp carrying blankets. The girls cowered. *"Dígales que está bien. Somos la policía. Van a regresar a sus padres."* Tell them it's okay. We're the police. They're going home to their parents.

"Es ist O.K.," Darren translated to German. *"Das ist die Polizei. Sie gehen nach Hause zu ihren Eltern."*

458

The girls began sobbing as the police wrapped blankets around their tiny bodies. Darren swallowed as he watched the guys escort the scared girls down the ramp.

Even though he suspected the answer, Darren asked anyway, *"¿Quiénes son?"* Who are they?

"Ahora son niñas inocentes, pero esta noche habrían sido vendidas a la esclavitud." Right now they're innocent little girls, but tonight they'd have been sold into slavery.

Darren's lunch shot a burning path from his stomach. He turned and threw up.

***

The cop unlocked the cell and shoved Darren inside. He'd never been in jail before, never even seen the inside of a police station. For that matter, he'd never been in a squad car before.

Without looking around, he sat on a wooden bench to the left. As long as he kept to himself and didn't seem scared, everyone should leave him alone.

That's what he'd told himself a hundred times since being handcuffed forty-five minutes ago.

"¡ESTÁN AQUÍ!" THEY'RE HERE!

Darren jumped.

A skinny man dressed in red long johns rolled out from under a bench on the other side of the cell. His wispy black hair stuck out in a million directions.

He trotted around the place, waving his arms. *"Estánaquiestánaquiestánaquiestánaquí."*

Another cell occupant shoved the skinny man, and he stumbled across the cement straight into Darren.

His heart slammed his ribs. "Get away from me," Darren ordered in Spanish.

With blurry eyes, the skinny man grinned. "Hee-hee-hee." A rotten stench seeped from the man's mouth.

Darren held his breath.

"Hee-hee-hee." The skinny man slid past, crawled back under his bench, and curled into a tight ball.

Quietly, Darren released his breath.

The guy to his right stood up. Darren chanced a quick look. Over six feet tall, the guy had to weigh more than three hundred pounds. It was amazing the rickety bench had held his weight.

Tattoos covered every spot of his bare upper body and bald head. His black beard hung to the middle of his chest.

Definitely someone Darren did not want messing with him.

The enormous guy lumbered over to the bars. "You looking at me?" he threatened the cop sitting outside the cell.

The cop looked on, bored.

The enormous guy grabbed the bars, gave them a hard rattle, and screamed, "YOU LOOKING AT ME?"

The cop lit a cigarette and checked his watch.

He must see this crazy stuff all the time.

The enormous guy stomped back over to the bench and plopped down. Darren held on so he wouldn't fall off.

Down the hall a door unlocked, probably another crazy on the way. Darren listened intently, but heard nothing.

A few seconds later, a man dressed in a suit stepped into view. He turned and looked straight at Darren through the spookiest light green eyes he had ever seen.

Swallowing, he stared back at the man. What was going on?

The man handed the cop a letter, and the cop slowly perused it. Then he unclipped his keys from his belt and unlocked the cell. *"Vamos."* Let's go. He pointed to Darren.

Darren slowly got up, crossed the floor, and exited the cell.

The man extended his hand. "Thomas Liba. You may call me TL. Follow me, please."

Darren walked beside him down the corridor. *Thomas Liba.* Darren rolled the name around in his brain. Definitely not a Venezuelan. So who was this man? Police? A lawyer? Someone from the U.S. embassy? Whoever he was, Darren vowed to keep his mouth shut. He was only the translator, after all. He definitely wasn't going to tell TL a thing. Not with the whereabouts of his mother at stake.

The man led Darren through a small waiting room and then into a private office. Indicating two black metal chairs, TL took one and Darren sat in the other.

TL leaned down and took a file from beneath his chair. He opened it and sifted through. "Darren Yote. Seventeen years old. Six feet tall. One hundred sixty-five pounds. Black hair, black eyes. Mother's one hundred percent Native American. Father was a mixture of everything. Father died in a car accident before you were born. Mother disappeared when you were seven. Your maternal grandmother was your legal guardian for the past ten years."

Man, this guy knows everything about me.

"You make good grades, but never take a book home from school. The only D you ever got was in Spanish." TL glanced up at Darren. "Interesting."

Darren guiltily swallowed. He'd purposefully made that D so no one would know how good he was.

TL closed the file. "I work for the IPNC. Information Protection National Concern. I head up the Specialists, a group of brilliant, talented young men and women."

What did this man want with him?

"For the past ten years, the IPNC has been following this slave ring. We've made a lot of busts, returned numerous boys and girls back to their homes, but we can't seem to flush out the head of the operation." TL undid a button on his suit jacket and shifted in his chair. "We were all a little surprised when you popped up on the scene. Russia, China, Venezuela, Sweden. You seem to know how to speak pretty much every language."

Darren cleared his throat, but continued to remain silent. This was exactly what his mother had warned him about. All people wanted to do was take advantage of his ability. Talon had.

Quietly, TL studied Darren's face. "Do you know who's in charge of this slave ring?"

"No," Darren lied.

"I think you do. Will you tell me, please?"

"I just told you, I don't know." Darren kept his gaze steady with TL, trying not to show any emotion.

"Perhaps *you're* in charge." TL raised his brows. "Hm?"

This man knew Darren wasn't in charge, so he didn't even bother answering such an outlandish accusation.

Again, TL quietly studied him. Long minutes went by, and Darren kept returning the stare. But . . . this man, TL, wouldn't blink, wouldn't swallow, wouldn't do anything. It was the stillest Darren had ever seen someone be. And it only made him more aware of his own need to blink, to swallow.

More time passed, and with each second, Darren felt, oddly enough, as if he was being pulled into TL's mind. That TL could read Darren's own thoughts.

Swallowing, Darren glanced down at his lap, his heart racing with the uncomfortable yet somehow serene air between them.

"Does this person have something over you?" TL quietly asked.

Thoughts of Darren's mother flooded his memories, and he felt tears press against his eyes. Clenching his jaw, he kept staring at his lap, willing away his urge to cry.

TL reached across and grabbed his shoulder. "Son, I want you to know you can trust me. I'm the good guy."

No one had ever called Darren "son" before. He lifted his gaze and stared into TL's intense eyes and knew, without a doubt, that he could trust this man. "His name's Talon, and he told me if I'd do this for him he'd reunite me with my mother."

TL nodded, taking it in. "Talon's an evil man. And evil people don't keep their word. The reality is that he never intended to reunite you with your mother."

Somewhere in the back of his mind, Darren had known that all along. But holding on to a thread of hope had kept him going, kept him doing what Talon wanted.

"And the truth is," TL continued, "I have the power to find your mother."

Hope surged through Darren at those words. Did this man really have the power to find his mother? He probably did if he worked for the government. They had access to all kinds of things Darren never would. But, what did TL want in return?

"In return for her whereabouts, I want you to testify against Talon," TL said, answering Darren's unspoken question.

Immediately, Darren shook his head. "No. Not until my mother is safe."

With a thoughtful sigh, TL propped his elbows on the chair's armrest. He tapped his fingers together, thinking. "Okay."

"Okay? You'll find my mother?" he asked in disbelief.

TL nodded. "Yes, but on one condition."

"What condition?" Darren asked, his hope slowly slipping away.

"I want you to come work for me."

Darren paused for a split second and then nodded. "Okay, but I have a condition of my own."

"Go ahead."

"I want to bring my horse with me."

‹ONE›

"Gigi," Bruiser yelled. "Get your butt out here. We're dying to see you!"

Ignoring my lovable pest of a friend, I slipped a tiny silver hoop through my left earlobe and took a step back. I scrutinized my appearance in the oversize mirror mounted above the sinks.

I went down the list that Cat had taped to the corner of the mirror.

Blond hair, loose. Check.

Clear lip gloss. Check.

Shine-proof powder. Check.

Black eyeliner on the bottom lid. Check.

Low-rise dark-wash jeans. Check.

Black ballet flats. Check.

Black leather belt. Check.

Light blue, snug, sleeveless sweater, not tucked. Check.

Matching bra and thong, the tan set. Check.

Cat and I had argued about the last item. What did it matter what color underwear I wore? I didn't intend on David seeing it. But Cat insisted it was more of a confidence booster.

Loosening my belt a hole, I took a deep breath. David and I were about to go on our first "official" date. My first date ever.

Was that sad?

Although David did take me to the fair for my sixteenth birthday last year, the night before I got busted by the IPNC. But the fair thing hadn't been a date. I didn't even know he liked me back then. His taking me to the fair had all been a setup leading to my arrest. It truly was hard to believe it had all happened nearly a year ago.

It seemed as if we'd been trying to get to this dating point forever. With school, the Specialists missions, bad guys, training, and any number of other things, David and I barely had time to say hello to each other.

I'm exaggerating, of course, but it sure felt like it sometimes.

Wait a minute. Back up. Lip gloss? I ran my finger over my bottom lip. This stuff would totally come off when we kissed. It'd get all over David. He didn't want slimy lips. No one wanted slimy lips.

I rushed across the tile and wrenched open the door. "Cat, my lip glo—" My kissing issue trailed away as I took in the crowd in our bedroom.

Bruiser rolled off her bed. "It's about time. I was going gray waiting on you." She whistled. "Yowza, babe."

Smiling, I stepped into the room.

Mystic sat on his favorite spot of carpet at the foot of Bruiser's bed. He always sat there when he hung out in the girls' room.

He gave me a quick once-over. "I do believe the moon is in the second house and Jupiter's aligned with Mars."

Huh?

"Don't listen to Psychic Guy. That's from a song. He's being a goof. You're hot." Bruiser bopped Mystic in the back of the head. "Tell her she's hot."

Mystic rubbed his head. "All right, all right. You're hot."

I laughed.

Stretched out across her bed, Beaker brought her nose out from her chemistry book. She stopped chomping her gum and playfully smirked her black lipstick—covered lips. "Yeah, you'll do."

After all the rockiness between Beaker and me, we'd gained an appreciation of each other. Our mission a month ago to Barracuda Key, Florida, had shown me a side of her I never would have guessed existed. Plus, I'd learned to dig her ever-changing hair. Orange was this week's color. It matched the gem in her nose and the ones in her dog collar.

And I still found it amazing that she and David were half brother and sister. Which meant if David and I ever got married, Beaker and I would be . . . sisters?

A month ago I would've gagged at the thought. But now it merely hit me as interesting. Beaker and me sisters. Hmmm. Not that David and I were getting married or anything. I'm jumping ahead. *Way* ahead. We needed to get through our first date.

Parrot reclined on my bed propped up with my pillows. "You look beautiful, GiGi."

My nervous jitters relaxed with his heartfelt compliment. "Thanks, Parrot."

Parrot always said the sweetest, most meaningful things. Whatever girl snagged him would be very, very lucky.

Wirenut winked as he popped a potato chip in his mouth. "Whadaya say you ditch David? You and I'll hit the town. I'll show you how to hot-wire a car."

Lying beside him, Cat elbowed Wirenut in the ribs. "You better be glad I love you. Besides, you know I can hot-wire better than you."

He grinned and planted a hard kiss on her lips. With their olive skin and black hair, they looked like those couples who always dressed alike. They totally belonged together.

She climbed over him and crossed the carpet to me. "Looks like you followed the list. Now what were you going to ask me about lip gloss?"

I glanced over her shoulder to our packed bedroom. Everyone's eyes were silently glued to me. I leaned in and whispered, "Won't the gloss gross David out when we kiss?"

I felt silly asking Cat the question, but it wasn't like I'd kissed a whole heck of a lot of guys. I didn't have any experience to draw on. Every other time David and I had kissed I hadn't been wearing anything on my lips.

Her amber eyes twinkled, and she smiled. "David's really not going to care."

Bruiser loudly cleared her throat. "It's rude to whisper."

Cat squeezed my arm. "Relax. Have fun. And by all means do *not* think about anything back here at the ranch."

"Thanks for all your help getting ready." I hugged her. "There's no telling what I'd look like right now without your list."

It reminded me of my first mission. The modeling instructor had written me list after list so I'd know what to wear every day. So I'd know what made a good outfit. Pathetic, but completely true. I had no sense of style.

Someone knocked on the bedroom door. *David.* My stomach dippity-dipped.

Bruiser boinged onto her bed and flipped off the other side. "Why, whoever could that be?" She swung the door open and checked her watch. "You're one minute late."

David laughed, playfully pushed her out of the way, and came the rest of the way in. He stopped suddenly, his eyes touching each person in the room. "Didn't realize this was a family affair."

"Yep, family affair." Wirenut swung his legs over the bed and got up. "If GiGi had parents, they'd be here to greet you and give you the third degree."

Bruiser went to stand beside Wirenut and put her hands on her hips. "Tonight we're your third degree."

David looked across the room at me. I shrugged. I mean really, what was I supposed to do? Shove past them? Plus, it gave me a moment to slurp up his yumminess.

Disheveled dark hair. Stubble on his face. Perfect, not-too-tight, not-too-loose jeans. Black shoes. Black shirt. I *loved* when he wore black.

Other than our shirts, we matched perfectly.

Wirenut ran his fingers down his trim goatee. "What are your plans for this evening, young man?"

David held a smile back. "Food and the Boardwalk."

Bruiser flipped a red braid over her shoulder. "We don't approve of underage drinking."

"Yes, ma'am."

Wirenut took a chip from his bag and ate it. "Do you smoke?"

"No, sir."

"Her curfew is midnight. One minute past and . . ." Bruiser held her T-shirt out. It read YOU MESS WITH MY FAMILY AND YOU MESS WITH ME.

Bruiser and her silly shirts. And the fact that Bruiser was acting the role of my mother was hilarious—especially since she was the youngest one of us all.

David nodded. "Oh, yes ma'am."

Wirenut tossed yet another chip in his mouth. "What kind of vehicle do you drive?"

"I've got a truck tonight."

"A truck?" Bruiser wagged her finger. "I don't want any of that business of her sitting in the middle getting cozy with you."

Bruiser!

She wagged her finger again. "I want both of you in a seat belt."

"Yes, ma'am."

Another chip for Wirenut. "What about your future, son? You going to be able to support our little girl someday?"

Wirenut! Sheesh.

Bruiser patted Wirenut's shoulder. "Now, honey, it's their first date. Let's see where things go."

"Yes, yes, quite right." Wirenut glanced down at Bruiser. "Anything else, Momma?"

Bruiser shook her head. "I believe that's it, Daddy."

My "father" motioned me on. "All right, this young man seems suitable."

"Oh, thank God. No telling what you would've said next," I said, laughing.

I snatched my purse from my dresser and strode across the girls' room to where David stood. His cologne moseyed through my senses. *Gggrrr.*

"Oh, and one last thing," Bruiser called out. "Don't forget our mother/daughter discussion on birth control. We don't want any more little geniuses running around."

My face caught on fire. Everyone in the room busted out laughing, like they'd all been waiting for that last comment.

The twerps.

David grabbed my hand and tugged me out the door. "Ignore them."

"I can't *believe* she said that." No, actually, I could. Bruiser was ornery that way.

"They wouldn't pick on you if they didn't love you."

True. And I loved them, too.

David led me down the hall past the other bedrooms, TL's office, and the hidden elevator that led to the underground rooms.

My embarrassment faded as I tuned in to the guy beside me. I was going on my first date. And not with some loser either. I had a really hot, funny, sweet, awesome guy.

We passed the cafeteria and stopped in the archway to the common area. TL reclined in an oversize comfy chair, reading the paper.

David knocked on the wall. "Wanted to let you know we're out of here."

TL glanced up. "Be back by midnight."

David and I nodded.

"You two look good." TL went back to his paper. "Be safe."

David opened the front door, letting in the slightly muggy night. "I should have told you that first."

"What?" I slid my purse up my shoulder.

"You look good." David's eyes slowly roamed down my body and back up. "*Real* nice."

I *loved* when he did that eye-roaming thing. It totally turned me on and made me feel sexy.

"Too good you look." I shook my head. "I mean, you look good, too." *Sigh*. Not so sexy after all.

He laughed and gave me a swift kiss. "You're adorable."

"I'm glad someone thinks so." *You're dorky is more like it.*

TL's full-size truck sat parked in the circular driveway. David opened the door for me and then went around to the driver's side.

He climbed in and stretched his arm along the seat back. "Come 'ere."

I unbuckled my seat belt and slid across, more than happy to oblige him. "Bruiser said not to do this."

David smiled. "I'll never tell." He looked at my lips. "I figured we'd better toast."

"Toast?"

"Here's to us not getting a call from TL."

"I'll *definitely* toast to that." My cell had been *way* too active lately.

David leaned in and kissed me. Long and dreamy. Slow. Taking all the time in the world. He tasted minty. Every time we kissed I swore it was the best one yet. But this one topped the rest.

He pulled back. "We could sit here the whole night and keep making out."

Laughing, I glanced at his shiny mouth, and my amusement died. It looked like he'd been eating greasy fried chicken.

"My lip gloss," I realized aloud. Oh no.

"What?" David wiped his hand over his mouth and then checked out his fingers.

I grabbed his slimy hand and rubbed it on my jeans. "I'm so sorry." *I'm an idiot.*

"GiGi," he chuckled, stilling my hand.

Wait. If he looked that greasy I had to look the same or worse. I yanked the rearview mirror over and checked out my face. "I'm sorry." I fumbled with the glove compartment, found a napkin, and scrubbed away the mess. "I *knew* this lip gloss thing was not a good idea," I mumbled.

Cramming the napkin in my jacket pocket, I turned to him.

His eyes crinkled. "You done freaking out?"

"Did that gross you out?"

David softly rubbed my earlobe between his thumb and finger. "Nothing about you grosses me out."

I leaned into his hand. "Thanks."

With another quick kiss, he started the engine. "Seat belt."

"Oh." I scooted to my side and strapped in.

David pulled away from the ranch house, and I reached inside my purse for the lip gloss. Maybe I should have him turn around so I could run back in and borrow Cat's stay-on stuff. It certainly made more sense—if you're going to be kissing a guy, you needed stay-on stuff. Not glossy, glistening stuff.

Surely other girls didn't obsess over whether to reapply or not. I glanced down at the tube, and the spiral swirl of the gloss made me think of the eteus code I'd been working on earlier today. It had the same pattern.

Now if I squared the last number, then multiplied by the root of the one hundred and eighth term, I could quadruple . . . no, that would be countably infini—

"What are you thinking about?" David drove through the ranch's gates. On the visor's remote he typed in his personal code, and the gates closed.

But if I stacked the numerical order and isolated the j—"GiGi?"

"Huh?"

David turned onto the highway. "You're on a date, remember? At least pretend you're having fun."

"I'm sorry. I am having fun." I was on a date with the greatest guy in the world, and he didn't think I was having fun. I sucked at this.

He reached across the cab and took my hand. "Tell me what's bothering you so we can fix it and have a good time tonight."

"Who says something's bothering me?"

David squeezed my fingers. "I'm waiting."

"You know me too well," I grumbled. "Lip gloss or eteus code. Take your pick."

"Let's go for lip gloss."

I held up the tube. "Do you want me to put more on or leave it off?"

"The lip gloss is pretty if you're not going to be kissing someone. But I intend to kiss you at least a billion times tonight. My vote is that you leave it off."

"A billion?"

He caressed his thumb along my hand and smiled. "Possibly a trillion. Good thing you're a genius. Not many girls can count to a trillion."

We both laughed, and the eteus code and lip gloss issues effectively faded away. That was one thing I liked about David. He knew the perfect things to say to lighten a moment.

Twenty fantastic, conversational minutes later, we pulled into the Boardwalk's packed parking lot. The Boardwalk stretched three miles along San Belden, California's coast. Amusement rides, food, dancing, Roller-Blading—you name it, the place had it. It never closed down.

David cut the lights and engine. "Don't you dare open that door."

I held my hands up.

He came around and opened it—very gentleman-like—and I climbed out. Closing the door, he pinned me against the truck and rained kisses over my forehead, my eyes, cheeks, lips, chin, and ears. He moved to my neck and nibbled a path down one side and up the other.

Pressing a kiss to my nose, he stepped back. "I hope you were counting because that covered a big chunk of the trillion."

"Thirty-six," I breathed.

He looked at me. "You *did* count?"

"Yes. Wasn't I supposed to?"

David laughed and took my hand. "Come on."

We wound our way through the sea of vehicles until we stood on the Boardwalk's edge. My stomach grumbled at the smell of fried food.

He gazed right and then left. "Where do you want to start?"

"Food." I hadn't eaten since this morning. "Can we get a hot dog?" Something about the carnival atmosphere made me want one.

"You can have anything you want."

We joined the crowd moving up and down the Boardwalk. Men, women, couples, families, and others our age. Black, white, Hispanic, Asian. Fat, skinny, short, tall. Pierced, tattooed, or plain.

Unique people packed the place. I'd never seen anything like it.

Latin music poured from a flashing nightclub. I glanced in the open doors as we passed. Bodies gyrated to the pulsing sound.

David led me through the crowd over to a hot-dog stand. "How do you want yours?"

"Relish." I normally ordered onions, too. But with the trillion kisses . . .

We took our hot dogs to a vacant bench. With the beach and ocean at our backs, we ate, watching the crowd shuffle by.

There was something meditative about people-watching. Hearing them talk, seeing them laugh, observing their body language. TL taught a whole class on it back at the ranch. It was easy to see who felt happy, who was sad, who had hidden secrets.

"Hiii, Daaavid," two girls flirted, coming toward us.

I recognized them from the university. Their perfection reminded me of all those girls who used to make fun of me back in Iowa, before I joined the Specialists.

They gave me a polite, fake smile. I shoved the last bite of hot dog in my mouth, and relish dripped onto my blue sweater.

I stared at the green clump and oddly enough didn't feel embarrassed. I felt relieved, glad to get it over with. I knew my klutziness would come out at some point.

One of them giggled. That would've intimidated me at one time, made me feel even more awkward. Now it only fueled my self-worth. I mean, really, who cared if I dropped relish? No one was perfect.

Using my napkin, I wiped up the green clump.

"All done?" David asked.

I nodded.

Picking up my garbage, he threw our trash in the can beside the bench. "You ladies have fun tonight." He took my hand. "Let's go."

As we walked through the crowd, I glanced over my shoulder back at the two perfect girls. With matching haughtiness, they stared at our backs.

I smiled, kinda slow and la-dee-da like. *He's my date and not yours.* Rotten of me, but I'd never done that before.

Glancing over to the Ferris wheel, I skidded to a stop as Chapling and the code we'd been tinkering with popped into my brain. "Wait, I have to write this down."

"What is it?" David asked with a grin.

I ripped the notepad and pencil from my back pocket, flipped through pages and pages of code until I found my spot, and began scribbling.

"And that'll circle back around to . . ." I mumbled and continued jotting. "But then if I go this route . . ." Feverishly, I wrote code before I lost any of it. "And then Chapling won't agree so I'll have to do this. . . ." On and on I scripted until I proved every single block.

There. Holding the pad away, I studied what I'd done. Chapling was going to love this.

I jerked my eyes up. David had moved us off the Boardwalk over to the beach. I hadn't even realized we'd moved. "How long have I—"

"Ten minutes."

"Ten minutes? I'm so sorry. I saw the Ferris wheel, and it reminded me . . ." I closed my eyes and groaned. I was *such* a geek.

David tapped my forehead. "I think smart chicks are cool."

He'd said the same thing to me twice before. I opened my eyes. Behind him the Ferris wheel slowly rotated, illuminating the night sky.

A moist breeze blew in from the ocean, and I shivered.

"You're adorable." Wrapping his arms around me, he gave me a tender kiss. "That's thirty-seven."

I smiled. "Wanna ride the Ferris wheel?"

"Definitely."

And we did. We spent hours weaving our way up and down the Boardwalk. We rode rides, played games, ate cotton candy. David won me a tiny stuffed giraffe at a coin toss, and we had our picture taken in a photo booth. It was the best night of my life.

He linked fingers with me as he led me from the Boardwalk through the parking lot back to the truck. In thirty minutes it would be midnight.

"Yo, David," a group of guys called.

He waved. I recognized them from the university.

"A couple of those guys are in my physics study group." David brought our hands to his mouth and kissed the back of mine. "They're so jealous right now."

"Jealous?"

"Because I'm with the tall, hot, smart chick from the ranch."

"Tall, hot, smart chick?"

"That's what they call you."

Nobody had ever called me a tall, hot, smart chick. "What do *you* call me?"

We reached the truck. David leaned back against it and pulled me into his arms. "My girlfriend."

My heart pitter-pattered. He'd never actually called me that before. "Girlfriend?"

He squeezed me. "You don't mind do you?"

I looked into his eyes and smiled. "Umm—"

Bzzzzbzzzzbzzzz.

‹TWO›

Bzzzbzzzbzzz.

David and I pulled apart. We both glanced down at our cell phones clipped to our jeans.

* * *. TL's code to return to home base. ASAP.

David texted TL that we'd be there as quickly as possible.

I smiled a little to hide my disappointment. Sure our date was almost over, but TL's text had cut it a little short. I'd actually been enjoying myself tonight and had almost forgotten my other world. Not that I didn't like working for the Specialists, but I never really got a taste of what it was like to be a normal teenager. I felt like my life was always in mission mode.

David took my hand, obviously picking up on my bummed-out mood. "At least we just about made it through the whole date."

I nodded.

David opened the passenger door. "This is our life, GiGi. I don't know what else to say."

"I know." I climbed inside the truck. There wasn't anything else *to* say. This *was* our life.

Closing my door, David circled around to his side and hopped in. "As much as it sometimes annoys me, I wouldn't swap it for anything in the world. It's a privilege to work for the Specialists. And I'm glad I can share it with you."

I nodded, softening a little at his last statement. David always came across level-headed about this secret life we lived. I didn't know how he did it. He willingly accepted whatever happened. Never once had I seen him not be positive, not be the voice of reason. Never once had I heard him say a negative thing or express discontent.

But then he'd lived on the ranch his whole life. He didn't know anything other than this private world.

He leaned over and kissed me, caressing the back of his fingers down my cheek. "I want you to answer my question before we leave."

"What question?"

His eyes did that sexy crinkle thing. "You don't mind if I call you my girlfriend, do you?"

I didn't even try to hide the huge grin that crept onto my cheeks. "I don't mind at all."

David laughed and started the truck's engine. Any lingering melancholy drifted away as we pulled away from the Boardwalk.

***

Thirty minutes later, we entered the underground conference room and closed the door behind us. I wondered if TL held meetings at such weird hours as part of our training. I'd been to unexpected meetings at five in the morning, three in the afternoon, and midnight.

TL sat at the head of the long metal table with Parrot to his left. Jonathan, our physical-training instructor, sat at the other end. David rolled a leather chair out in his usual spot to the right of TL, and I made myself comfortable beside Parrot.

If history repeated itself, TL was about to take Parrot's monitoring patch. At least that was what happened with me, Wirenut, and Beaker the first time we met TL down here away from the others.

When we first got recruited by the Specialists, TL had required each of us to wear the flesh-toned tracking device. He kept tabs on us everywhere we went. Even the bathroom. I still cringed at that thought.

To my knowledge only Parrot, Mystic, and Bruiser still wore theirs. He'd taken mine, Wirenut's, and Beaker's right before sending us on our first missions.

And since I was in here with Parrot, that meant I was probably going with him.

Inwardly, I sighed, although at this point it really didn't surprise me. So much for working from home base, as TL had originally promised me.

475

TL closed the folder in front of him and looked up. "What can any of you tell me about the Junoesque Jungle?"

Suddenly my mind zinged back to when I was nine years old, the year I tested out of eighth grade. "We had completed a whole unit on the Junoesque Jungle in my science class," I replied. "There are three hundred species per every two acres, more than any other area in the world. Five species of plants that exist there are bougainvillea, curare, coconut tree, kapok tree, and strangler fig. Some of the animals that live there include chimpanzee, tamarin, harpy eagle, kinkajou, silvery gibbon, and toco toucan. Of course I wouldn't know a kinkajou from a gibbon if one walked right up to me and slapped me in the face."

I swept a proud smile over everyone in the conference room, then slowly realized from their perplexed looks that, once again, I'd made a complete nerd of myself.

TL's lips twitched. "Your science teacher would be proud."

Everyone chuckled, and I joined in. Joke's on me. I mean, really, what was the point of getting embarrassed? They expected this stuff from me.

"Yesterday afternoon," TL began, getting everyone back on track, "in Rutina, South America, a sixteen-year-old girl walked out from the Junoesque Jungle and onto an excavation site. She was carrying only one thing."

He pointed a remote to the wall-mounted screen behind Jonathan, and he scooted out of the way. A picture of an old vase flashed into view. "Parrot, do you know what this is?"

Parrot didn't answer at first as he studied the screen. "That can't be the Mother Nature vase." He looked at TL. "I thought that was a Native American myth."

TL nodded. "Not anymore. What do you know about it?"

"I know that it's a centuries-old artifact believed by many native tribes to control Mother Nature."

TL zoomed in on the brown, weathered pottery. "Exactly. This vase is believed to control the elements. It gives the one who holds the vase the power over nature. It is coveted by various Indian tribes." The vase rotated slowly on the screen. Cracked, and missing chunks, the vase was divided into four sections, each engraved with symbols and pictures.

TL froze the screen on one of those sections. "Notice this is a rough depiction of rain. The symbols above and below the rain are a prayer.

Whatever it is a tribe needs, they say the prayer corresponding to the picture."

The vase rotated again, showing us the other roughly chiseled pictures of nature: the sun, a gust of wind, snowflakes, and again the rain.

"How big is it?" David asked.

TL referenced his notes. "It holds approximately a pint of liquid."

A slender Junoesquian girl appeared on the screen, standing with the jungle at her back. She wore a white cotton dress with tiny blue flowers embroidered on it. Her long black hair hung straight down her back. Leather straps attached to the sandals on her feet and crisscrossed up her calves.

As deep blue as my eyes were, hers ran the opposite spectrum. Their icy color contrasted dramatically with her dark skin and hair. Her eyes held uncertainty, and her slight smile spoke hesitance and shyness.

She was beautiful.

Before joining the Specialists, I'd never paid such close attention to a person's physical details. I'd never searched for answers in their eyes and smile. It was incredible how much I could learn about someone by observing them.

"This is Jaaci," TL explained. "She's the only surviving member of the Muemiraa tribe. She's lived in the Junoesque Jungle her entire life."

I leaned back in my chair. "This is the girl who found the vase?"

"Yes." TL folded his hands on top of the table. "Here's where things get tricky. This vase has popped up here and there throughout history. Roughly a century ago it disappeared, seemingly into thin air. It has been a much sought after artifact. And numerous different tribal nations have it documented as being in their possession at one time or another."

TL nodded toward the screen and the picture of Jaaci. "On her father's death bed, he told her about this vase and where it was hidden. He told her to locate it and, once she did, to pay homage to the Muemiraa gods by finding the ocean and throwing it in to reunite the vase with its creator."

"Find the ocean and throw it in?" I couldn't imagine living in the jungle my entire life and my dying father telling me to find the ocean.

Would that be left or right, Dad?

"I suspect her father knew that if the vase got into the wrong hands, it would be used for evil. The vase is intended to work with nature, not control it." TL stood. "But when she walked from the jungle she strolled straight onto an excavation dig. One thing led to the next, and now the whole world knows about this."

He got up and made his way around the table. "As I mentioned before, the vase is centuries old. Documentation shows fifteen different tribal nations have held the artifact at one time. No one can prove they are the rightful owner, but they all want to be. Legend has it that whoever owns the vase prospers beyond imagination and never suffers again. Here's where the Specialists come in, and here's where I hand things over to Jonathan."

Jonathan?

TL gave the remote to Jonathan, and he stood. "I spent a number of years in the jungles of South America, including the Junoesque Jungle, as a warfare specialist with the IPNC. I know most of it like my childhood backyard. A few of the tribes involved are violent rivals. TL and I have discussed things and have decided I'll be point man on this mission."

TL took his seat. "Jonathan will be in charge. I'll provide assistance from home base, which will give me time to wrap up a few other things and attend some meetings with prospective Specialists' clients."

This would be weird. I'd never been on a mission without TL. I wondered what type of leader Jonathan would be.

He'd gone on the Ushbanian mission as my modeling agent. I smiled a little as I recalled our disguises—me as the spoiled model and he as my boisterous agent. He'd worn a different colored eye patch to match every colorful suit and had buffed his bald head every morning. Other than on that mission, I'd never seen him wear anything other than PT clothes.

Looking at him now, all big and bald, with his black eye patch, I found it hard to conjure up his colorful side. And he'd done it so well.

My gaze drifted to his black eye patch, and I wondered, not for the first time, what had happened to his eye.

Jonathan pressed the remote, bringing my wandering thoughts to attention. Three rows of five pictures each appeared on the screen. All head shots of tribal men. "These are the leaders of the fifteen tribes as they appear in their ceremonial garb. In four weeks they will meet in Rutina, South America, to decide who gets the vase. The North and South American Native Alliance has hired us to provide translation services for the talks and to guard the vase. Each chief is allowed to bring one representative with him from his own tribe."

While Jonathan read off the names of each tribe and its chief, I studied the pictures.

Stern and *proud.* Those two words popped into my head first.

Their ages ranged from forty on up. The oldest one looked to be over ninety. None of them smiled.

Some wore their hair in a long braid, others cropped short, a couple were bald, a few wore traditional head pieces, and one had a Mohawk.

None had beards or mustaches, but some displayed facial tattoos, and others nose or ear piercings.

A man along the bottom row drew my attention more than the others. He had a Mohawk and stripes tattooed down his chin.

It wasn't the Mohawk or even the bold stripes that made him stand out, although they did add to his uniqueness. It was the look in his eyes. Stern, like the others, but with menace. Like an I-wouldn't-want-to-be-in-a-dark-place-with-him kind of menace.

"The talks will take place on impartial land occupied by the Huworo tribe. They have no documentation that links them to the vase; therefore, their land is considered neutral territory." Jonathan ran his hand over his bald head. "Parrot, this is your first mission. You will go to this meeting as the official translator. There is no technology allowed. As I've already mentioned, each chief will have a personal representative with him. This person knows both English and their chief's native tongue. You, Parrot, will listen to the chiefs speak in their language, translate to English for the personal assistants, and the assistants will translate into their chief's language. There will be ten different dialects and indigenous languages spoken; you are familiar with six. You have four weeks to learn the remaining four."

I blinked. Four weeks to learn four languages? *Holy crap.* Was that even possible?

Parrot cleared his throat. "Sir, can someone else do this? Another agent?"

Jonathan took his seat. "No one has your linguistic brilliance. No one's of Native American descent. Only a Native American translator is allowed at this meeting."

Parrot nodded but showed no expression.

Why wasn't he excited? He was going on his first mission. And not any old mission, either. One that would take him back to his roots, his people.

TL folded his hands on top the table. "Parrot, I know you have a history with one of those men up there." He paused. "So does Jonathan."

Parrot snapped surprised eyes to Jonathan.

"I was there that day. On that Venezuelan runway. I was the guy in the cowboy hat and dark sunglasses." Jonathan adjusted his eye patch. "I spent a good number of years on that case. Because of you, we made significant headway."

Parrot stared at Jonathan, dumbfounded.

What were they talking about?

"Parrot, you're a different person now," David added. "You can do this."

TL cupped Parrot on the shoulder. "You need to put the past behind you."

With a nod, Parrot dropped his gaze to the table.

I stared at his bowed head and the black shininess of his hair. My mind whirled with questions. Which man on the screen was TL referring to? Had something happened between the chief and Parrot? Or maybe Parrot had lived on one of those chief's reservations. Was whatever happened the event that had led the Specialists to him? And what was this about a Venezuelan runway?

And suddenly it occurred to me that every "bad guy" I'd run into so far had had a personal connection with me or one of my teammates.

Some sort of history, a past, plagued every member of my team. None of us came from pristine childhoods. Some had suffered more than others. Could that be one of the reasons why we'd been recruited?

It made me wonder what things I'd yet to learn, or maybe would never learn, about this group.

"GiGi?"

I snapped my attention to TL. "Yes?"

"Did you hear what Jonathan said?"

"No. I'm sorry. I was thinking about the whole situation." TL had talked to me *many* times about my mind-wandering penchant. I hoped he let this one slide.

He cocked a disciplinary brow.

No, guess this one wasn't sliding.

"What can you tell us about cave drawings?" Jonathan repeated himself.

I quickly got my mind back on track. "They're a system of writing where pictorial symbols represent meanings and sounds."

Actually, Chapling and I had been working with glyphs for a mission in Egypt that Piper and Curtis, from Team One, were currently on. And I was developing a computer program that translated the ancient writings. "They can be found, surprisingly, everywhere. North America, South America, Europe, Australia . . ."

"I know you've been assisting Chapling with the Egypt mission and decoding some drawings. And he tells me you've taken the initiative to create a translation program. According to him, you've made considerable progress."

I nodded, swelling a bit with pride. It really was a cool program.

"Give us a quick rundown."

I took a moment to simplify things in my brain. "Piper found some glyphs, and she and Curtis were poring through research books trying to figure them out. It made sense to me to code it all into a program that'll do the work for them. This way we can scan in the drawings and my program will provide the various translations. But I'm still in the initial stages." And I had a long way to go. It was a good thing the glyphs weren't a key part of the Egypt mission, because I had weeks and weeks of work to do to perfect the program.

With a nod, Jonathan clicked his pen. "Good. The Junoesquian girl, Jaaci, retrieved the artifact from a cave. A cave that has never been documented in history but has always been a legend. According to her deceased father and the legend, the drawings in the cave are an ancient native code revealing a key piece of information about the vase. Obviously, we don't know what that information is, but we are speculating it will reveal who the vase belongs to. So while Parrot's translating the meetings, you'll be in the cave decoding glyphs with your new program."

"But . . ." I detected a whiny note to my tone and concentrated on sounding more collected. "Why can't we just video feed everything back here so Chapling and I can work on it together?"

Jonathan pushed back from the table. "Sorry. It's against Rutina law to photograph or film the caves. Besides that, a good majority of the glyphs are too faded to show up clearly on film."

My shoulders dropped. Of course they were.

The conference door opened and Chapling, my mentor, waddled in. "Sorry. Sorrysorrysorry. Got sidetracked. Sidetracked sidetracked."

I couldn't help but smile. Chapling had a unique way of bringing that out in me.

481

Climbing up into the chair beside David, Chapling plunked a folder down on the table. He looked at TL and then Jonathan. "Am I up?"

They both waved him on.

Chapling rubbed his hands together. "Okay. Preliminary intel has revealed the drawings are a combination of numerous cultural glyphs. It would take a historian years to decipher the pattern." He looked across the table at me. "But with smart girl's new program, it can all come together in a matter of days."

Great. Talk about pressure.

Chapling tapped his fingers together. "Which is a good thing because I just intercepted a message between two unknown parties that they are planning on stealing the vase." He slid his folder down the table to Jonathan.

"Meaning," David spoke, "that you've got to decipher the glyphs as soon as possible and find out what the key piece of information is."

I did say pressure, right?

Jonathan stood. "Do your best to find out who those unknown parties are."

Chapling nodded.

"Anything else?"

Chapling shook his head.

Jonathan nodded to TL, who gathered up the folders in front of him. "Okay, follow us," TL said.

He led us from the conference room and down the hall. When we passed my computer lab, Chapling ducked off inside. We crossed in front of Wirenut's electronic warehouse and Beaker's chemistry lab and came to a stop at one of the mysterious locked doors.

When I first came to the Specialists, these secret doors drove me insane with curiosity. After seeing what was behind three of the six, though, I suspected the remaining doors had something to do with Parrot, Mystic, and Bruiser's specialties.

Then again, in this new life of mine I'd learned not to expect the expected. Just when I thought I'd figured something out, it'd turn out different.

TL pointed to the key pad. "This is coded in Uopoei, your first language. For now your code is simply the address of the last place you lived. I want you to change your code within twelve hours and inform me of the new one."

Parrot nodded. "Yes, sir."

TL stepped aside. "This is your room, your work area. You may come here during any free time you have."

Huh. I had only been allowed one hour an evening in my special room. Granted, now I could go anytime I liked, but in the beginning it'd only been an hour. Come to think of it, Wirenut and Beaker hadn't been limited in their time, either.

Parrot punched in his code. The door slid open to reveal an elevator. This was different. Mine, Wirenut, and Beaker's doors opened directly into our special rooms.

David, TL, Jonathan, Parrot, and I stepped inside the car, and the door slid closed. I glanced around. Nothing unusual. Just a plain old elevator. Except there was no directional panel with numbers and arrows. Instead, a panel of black glass, about one inch wide by six inches long, ran horizontal on the door.

David stepped up and looked into it. A retinal scan. Cool.

"This retinal scan is programmed to read you and me and TL," David explained to Parrot. "You'll stand looking in for three seconds."

The elevator slowly ascended.

Ascended. I *knew* there were floors between the underground conference area and the ranch level. Every day was like a new discovery around this place.

The elevator stopped. David motioned Parrot to do the retinal scan. "This is Subfloor Two."

The door slid open, and I followed the guys out. "If the ranch is ground level and the conference area is Subfloor Four, what's on Sub One and Three?" I asked.

"You'll find out when the time is right," TL answered.

I smiled. I knew TL would say that, but I just had to ask.

We entered a large room approximately fifty by fifty. Flat-screen TVs covered every inch of the four walls. The news silently played on every screen. Countries, dialects, and regions labeled the top of each monitor. Liberia, Australia, the Netherlands, Thailand, and on, and on. Some countries I'd never even heard of.

A control panel, complete with headphones, a keyboard, buttons, and dials, spanned the center of the room. Two white leather chairs sat in front of it.

TL crossed to the center. "Parrot, this is where you'll do your research. Let's say, for example, you're going to Japan." He typed Japan on the keyboard.

All the monitors in front of us tuned in to Japanese television and radio programs.

"This is every single TV and radio station playing in Japan right now. If you want to watch cartoons"—TL picked up a laser remote and pointed the red beam at the cartoon station—"you simply select it."

The flat screens changed channels until Japanese cartoons took up the entire area.

"And for volume"—TL rotated a dial on the control panel—"here's your knob."

Surround-sound Japanese cartoons filled the room.

Neat. Parrot must be ecstatic. I glanced over at him, smiling, excited for him. But his face held no expression as he watched the cartoons.

"You know Japanese." TL muted the cartoons. "Name a language you don't know."

Parrot thought for a second. "There's an island in the South Pacific whose inhabitants speak Loura."

TL keyed in Loura. The screen changed to display different television and radio stations from the South Pacific.

He handed Parrot the remote. "You have five minutes to say this"—he indicated a paper on the control panel—"in Loura." TL turned the volume knob.

Oh my God. Was he kidding?

With a calmness that I certainly didn't feel, Parrot pointed the remote. One by one he flipped through the TV and radio stations.

I watched his concentrated face as he tuned everything out and focused on the new language, listening, learning.

"Fepqu, bee, aor, hikn . . ." Parrot started trying words a minute later.

Words slowly turned to sentences. Sentences took paragraph form. Then Parrot picked up the paper and read it.

My jaw dropped. Granted, it wasn't completely seamless, but certainly better than expected. Unbelievable, in fact. Not even five minutes had passed. Given more time, he would have sounded like a true native of that South Pacific island.

"Good, Parrot." Jonathan slapped him on the back. "Beyond good."

Parrot put the paper down. "Thanks."

I grinned. "Wow."

He spared me a brief smile, and I got the impression he'd rather be anywhere but here.

TL folded his arms. "I'd like you to tell me what you know about North and South Native American languages."

Parrot thought for a minute. "I know there're more than seven hundred Native American languages currently spoken, with about two hundred here in the States and in Canada, about seventy in Meso-America, and five hundred in South America. And none of these languages is primitive. Their structure varies greatly. Probably the most characteristic sounds come from the back of the larynx, and a number of vowels are pronounced as nasal sounds. These languages also tend to use just one word to communicate a complex idea. The word order in a sentence is usually subject-object-verb, but subject-verb-object is also used. And many unrelated tribes have similar consonant systems. Most tribes, depending on their locale, have borrowed words from different countries depending on who they've interacted with over the years."

Parrot stopped. "I could go on, but it's pretty boring."

I blinked. Sheesh, he knew his stuff.

TL picked up an earpiece with a slim mike attached. "This is for one-on-one practice with a native speaker." TL checked his watch. "You're scheduled to converse with a Fino native in a few minutes. It's one of the languages you need to learn for your upcoming trip. After that you need to go to bed and get some sleep and start fresh in the morning. I'll let you all know when you'll begin your series of inoculations. And, of course, horseback-riding lessons, as that will be your main mode of transportation."

My stomach dropped. "Inoculations?" Needles weren't exactly a thrilling thought.

"We're going into the jungle," Jonathan said. "We'll be exposed to malaria, yellow fever, typhoid, diphtheria, and rabies, to name just a few."

I cringed. "Exactly how many shots are we talking about?"

"A lot."

I paused for a second as my brain rewound. "Wait a minute, did you say horseback riding?"

"Yes," TL answered.

I waited, but he said nothing else. Did they really expect me to ride a horse? Hello? *Me?* Queen of incoordination?

TL handed Parrot the earpiece. "I'll leave you to it. Chapling and I will explain the rest of this room to you tomorrow."

"Yes, sir," Parrot responded.

As I followed TL, David, and Jonathan back into the elevator, I glanced back at Parrot. He put the earpiece on and took a seat, looking so sad I wanted to stay and talk or stand silently nearby. Anything to be a friend.

TL stepped up to the retinal scan. "GiGi, Chapling will be expecting you first thing in the morning."

"Yes, sir," I answered, and then it hit me, the things I'd been curious about. Normally I kept my questions in and quietly accepted things. But being with the Specialists had made me more bold.

With a glance at David, I turned to TL. "Sir, I'd like to know the answers to two questions."

He nodded. "Proceed."

"Question number one: Why didn't you take Parrot's monitoring patch? And question number two: How come you gave me only one hour a day in my lab when I first had access to it, yet you put no restrictions on Parrot, Wirenut, or Beaker?" I realized question number two came out like I was accusing TL of picking favorites, but I didn't mean it to. I just wanted to know.

TL folded his arms. "I took Parrot's monitoring patch months ago when we returned from Ushbania."

"Oh." Why hadn't I known? I knew when TL took Wirenut's and Beaker's. Why hadn't TL told me about Parrot?

Because TL doesn't answer to me. I answer to him.

Right.

"Initially," TL continued, "I only gave you one hour because I knew you would become another Chapling if I didn't restrict your time."

I smiled. Chapling lived in the computer lab. He rarely came aboveground. In fact, I'd only seen him up top at the ranch a few times that I could recall.

TL was right. I could *very* easily become another Chapling. TL had seen that tendency in me and made decisions in my best interest. It made me feel all warm and fuzzy that he cared so much.

The elevator opened, and we stepped out. Jonathan headed left toward the front door of the ranch house.

I turned to TL. "Well, thanks for having my back."

"Sure." He chuckled and pointed down the hall. "Now get some sleep. You have a lot of work to do tomorrow. David, come with me."

"Slave driver," I mumbled.

‹THREE›

My watch alarm vibrated at 6:00 the next morning. With a low moan, I fumbled in the dark for it on my nightstand and pressed the button that turned off the alarm.

I swung my legs over the side of the bed and sat for a minute with my eyes closed, debating whether or not I could sneak five more minutes of sleep. I rubbed my eyes and convinced myself I'd gotten more rest than the four hours I really had.

With a resolute sigh, I forced my eyelids open and gazed with envy at my roommates, who all snuggled in, snoring away a lazy Sunday morning.

I pushed up from my bed and padded across the carpet to the bathroom. As I passed Cat's bed, I noticed she'd fallen asleep with her earphones in. A slight *chchch* hissed in the air, telling me music was still playing.

Across the room Beaker smacked her lips and rolled over in bed, rousing me from my sleepy trance, and I continued on to the bathroom.

Twenty minutes later, showered and dressed in jeans and a T-shirt, I made my way from our bedroom down the hall to the cafeteria.

Normally food held no significance in my life. I could take it or leave it. But the cook always served bacon with pecan pancakes on Sunday mornings. The combination rocked my world. As I entered the cafeteria, I inhaled the awesome salty/sweet aroma, and a content smile curved my lips.

With its aluminum tables and chairs, our dining hall resembled a miniature version of a school cafeteria. Except the food was much better.

TL sat alone at a table to my right. An empty plate with syrup remnants sat to his left, and the morning newspaper littered the space in front of him.

Mystic stood at the beverage center making a cup of herbal tea. Beside him stretched the buffet piled with food.

"Morning," I greeted TL, eyeing the mound of bacon on the buffet table.

"Good morning." He folded his paper. "Eat lots. I know it's your favorite."

I smiled. It wasn't often he made casual, nonbusiness conversation.

I crossed the dining hall to the buffet and picked up a plate. Mystic stepped up beside me. Forking up three gorgeous pancakes, I glanced over at him. "You're up early."

He sipped his tea. "I'm going to meditate with the sunrise."

"Mmm." Why anyone would voluntarily get up this early stretched beyond my comprehension.

"The fruit's fresh. I recommend the melon."

I moved down the buffet line, bypassing the fruit, and piled on the bacon.

He *tsked* me, "Bad girl," and snagged a pecan from my top pancake.

"Hey." I slapped his hand with a piece of bacon.

Mystic laughed. "How can somebody so skinny eat all that food?"

I picked up the syrup bottle and drenched my mountain of breakfast. "Not sure. I think this might weigh more than me."

With another laugh, he headed off. "Later, gator."

TL had gone, and so I ate alone, having no problem devouring and sopping up every last bite.

Fifteen minutes later, as I was dumping my garbage, Parrot walked in.

"Hey." I smiled.

"Hey," he replied, a blank expression on his face.

"Food's good," I tried for conversation.

Nodding, Parrot strode over to the buffet, grabbed a pancake, put some bacon on it, and rolled it up. He took a bite and headed right past me.

"You wanna hang out later?" I called to his back, trying so hard to be a friend.

"Thanks, but I've got a lot to do," he answered, not turning back, and disappeared out the cafeteria door.

I didn't take it personally. That was Parrot. Quiet, contemplative, stoic, a guy of few words. And that was when he was feeling fine. Factor in his obvious discontent with this mission, and I knew he'd be locked up tight.

But . . . that wasn't good enough for me. I unclipped my cell from my waistband and texted him. SORRY. CAN U COME BACK, PLEASE? I HAVE A QUESTION.

I sat back down where I'd eaten breakfast and waited.

A few seconds later he reappeared. "What's up?"

I tried to think of a nonpersonal question to ask, something pertaining to the mission, but came up empty. I wanted to *know* Parrot. I motioned to the seat across from me. "Sit. Let's talk."

Parrot sighed, as if it was the worst thing I could have asked him to do. "Please?"

Slowly, he approached the table and slid into a chair across from me.

Conversation wasn't my strong point, and it certainly wasn't his. So I knew this wouldn't be the easiest. "We're going on a mission together. I . . . want to get to know you better. And you need to know me. So what do you want to know?" Good. Not a bad tactic. Have him ask me questions first.

"Playing twenty questions, huh?" he tried for humor.

I smiled. "Whatcha got for me? Ask me anything."

"All right. I'll play." He thought for a second. "Where were you born?"

"Right here."

"You mean in California?"

"Yes, California. Right here in San Belden."

He lifted his brows. "No kidding?"

I told him about living at the ranch as a small kid and how David and I had known each other even back then.

Parrot didn't respond for a few seconds. "That's amazing."

I nodded. "I know. And you? Where were you born?"

"Arizona. On a reservation."

"What was it like to live on a reservation?"

He shrugged. "Same as anywhere, I guess. Most people think we live all basic and old-world. It's understandable ignorance. I lived my whole life in an apartment. Went to school. Did my chores. We had traditional stuff, too, just like any culture has. Ceremonies, holidays . . ."

"Did you get to wear any of those cool clothes I've seen in the movies?"

Parrot laughed. "Yeah, traditional clothes when the occasion called for it."

"Favorite color?" I continued with the questions.

Blue for him. Green for me.

"Favorite food?" He asked.

Tacos for him. Lollipops for me.

"Lollipops aren't food," he teased.

"Sure they are," I defended myself, and we laughed again.

Parrot's cell beeped, and he glanced down. "I got to go. I've got another native speaker who I'm scheduled to converse with in my lab."

I nodded, smiling. "I'm glad we had a chance to talk."

He reached across the table and squeezed my arm. "Me, too. I'll see ya later."

"'Bye." I watched him walk from the cafeteria and then made my way to the elevator and down to Subfloor Four.

Keying in my code to the computer lab, I stepped through, and the door suctioned closed behind me.

Chapling stood in the corner, his arms braced on the table that held the coffee, staring at it as if it were a lifeline.

I smiled at the sight. "Hey."

Around a yawn, he glanced up—"Hey"—and went right back to staring at the brewing coffee. "Just got out of bed. Need caffeine. Major caffeine."

"Where exactly *is* your bed?" I asked, realizing I didn't know such a simple thing.

"Right by TL's room."

"You mean that door that's always closed? I'd assumed it was a closet."

Chapling nodded.

"But I never see you come and go."

Looking up, he smiled broadly. "Yes!" He grabbed the coffee and poured the thick muck into his never-been-washed mug, then took a gurgly sip. "Oh, yes. Yesyesyesyesyes." He held his mug up. "Want some?"

I crinkled my nose. "No." I loved coffee, but not Chapling's brand of "mud."

He waddled across the room and flipped a light switch on, off, and back on again. The cement wall behind the switch shifted back an inch and then slid left, revealing a five-foot-tall compartment wide enough to hold one chubby redheaded little person.

I did a double take. What the . . . ?

491

"It's a tunneling elevator. Goes up and down and side to side. I can go just about anywhere on the ranch in this thing."

"Cool." I crossed the lab to where Chapling stood and crouched down to check out the elevator. "So you go to your room in this?"

He nodded. "Anywhere."

Way back when I first moved into the ranch, I'd been in the barn with TL, Wirenut, David, and Jonathan, prepping for the Ushbanian mission. Chapling had appeared from nowhere, and I'd wondered where he'd come from. "Can you go to the barn in this thing?"

Chapling sipped his coffee. "Yepper."

I stepped back from the tunneling elevator. "I want one." Giggling, he flipped the light switch again, and the door slid from the left to merge seamlessly back with the wall.

Chapling hobbled over to his computer station and climbed up. "So I hear you and David tore up the Boardwalk last night."

Rolling my chair out, I took a seat. "For someone who never leaves this cave, you sure know a lot."

He cut me a sly glance. "Yes, I do, don't I?"

I narrowed my eyes. "What does that mean? What are you up to?"

Chapling's sly glance transformed into pure childish mischievousness. He took his wireless mouse and, *click, click, click,* then turned his monitor so I could see.

Across his flat screen, small black-and-white video boxes flicked on. I ran my gaze over them, realizing they portrayed every room in the ranch as well as the pool, the barn, and all angles of the outside.

In the top right corner I watched as Mystic sat on the hill behind the house meditating. The video box beside it displayed Bruiser stretched out on her bed, still sleeping. In the bottom left corner, Jonathan jumped rope in the barn. I saw Beaker in the bathroom, brushing her teeth. In the cafeteria, Wirenut and Cat served themselves from the buffet line. TL sat at his desk, studying a file. David pulled a T-shirt over his head, giving me a quick glance of his gorgeous bare chest. Behind David, Adam said something and David cracked up. And there in the middle sat me and Chapling staring at his computer.

I waved at myself, and Chapling giggled.

He clicked the mouse a couple more times and the screens flicked to another scene. The date stamp in the lower right corner read yesterday evening. I glanced through all the video boxes on the screen and zeroed in on me and David making out in the truck.

My face caught on fire. I put my hand in front of the screen. "Chapling!"

He giggled again and clicked everything off.

I laughed with him; I couldn't help it. "You're awful. I had no idea you were such a voyeur. Where are all the cameras?"

"The cameras are hidden everywhere. Lamps, light switches, faucets, pictures, furniture. And I'm not a voyeur. I rarely even look at all this. It's just in case something happens."

I folded my arms and gave him my best disciplinary glare. "Then how come you knew about me and David?"

"Because I updated the video software last night. Your smoochy-smoochy scene was kind of hard to ignore."

I felt my face grow warm again. "Well, anyway . . . we've got work to do."

Chapling saluted me. "You're up."

I rolled my chair back over to my computer station. "Let's talk about the Rutina mission. It's illegal to video or to take pictures of the glyphs. Any ideas on what to do about that? Somehow I've got to get them into my computer so I can work with the symbols."

"Yeah, TL, Jonathan, and I discussed that last night. TL's arranged for a hieroglyphic historian and artist to accompany you all on the mission. This guy works for the IPNC. He'll sketch the graphics, and you can scan them into your laptop. The alliance doesn't know about your new program. They just know there're a couple of historians, you and this guy, coming to analyze the cave drawings and provide a translation of them."

I nodded. "Between his expertise and my new program, we should be able to figure out the code."

On the cart beside me, a stack of hieroglyphic books stood waiting. I'd been through about half of them so far, turning their words and pictures into code for my new translation program. I was still in the initial stages, and, although I hadn't said anything, I didn't feel confident I could have it ready in two weeks.

There were so many minute details about cave drawings. And the ones in Rutina were a combination of many different cultures. That was one of the main purposes of my program, though. To take patterned, documented glyphs, break them down, be able to decipher combinations of drawings from different cultures, and come up with a highly probable translation. But even if I worked around the clock, I wasn't sure . . . I just wasn't sure.

And what if I couldn't figure them out? What if my new program didn't come through? What would we do? These cave drawings were a key factor in this mission.

My brain stopped its doubtful tirade as I realized this was all stuff I normally argued to TL. He would then assure me I could do it, and I would force myself to succeed. And sure enough in the end, I'd always come through. Kind of weird I hadn't put up an argument with him this time and, in fact, didn't really want him to know I doubted myself. I wanted him to think I felt confident with my abilities.

Hmmm . . . funny how things had changed. How *I* had changed.

Breathing out a rush of focused breath, I grabbed one of the worn, hard leather books and got down to work.

<FOUR>

My fingers raced over the keys as I input code into my glyph-translation program. A week had gone by, and I wasn't nearly as close to completing it as I thought I'd be.

"Hey."

One week gone, and only three weeks to go before we left for Rutina, South America.

"Hello?"

I concentrated on the recently scanned glyphs and the measurements I'd taken of them. I referenced the meanings from my research books and merged the two. I ran a quick script to assure they understood each other.

"Yo?"

I compared it to yesterday's rendering, hoping, *hoping*, they worked in conjunction . . . I watched as my screen scrolled with garbled language. Aaarrrggghhh . . . What was I doing wrong?

"GiGi!"

I jumped, almost tipping over in my chair.

Chapling stepped into my line of vision. His Brillo-pad hair poofed out into a red Afro as he grinned and waved. "Lunchtime. Go eat."

I narrowed my eyes. "You interrupted me for *that*?"

He showed me a text message on his phone. "Boss man says you have to."

With a groan I rubbed my sore neck. "I have too much work to do to go eat."

Pursing his lips, Chapling leaned forward and checked out my screen. "Want me to take a look?"

"Do you have time?" TL had Chapling working on something that he couldn't tell me about.

He shrugged. "I got time."

"Okay." I'd take any help I could get. Rolling out my chair, I got to my feet.

Chapling took my spot. Climbing up, he studied my screen. Seconds later, he put his chubby fingers on my keys, and they took on a life of their own.

I moved in closer and watched over his shoulder as he wove through my code, quickly making adjustments. He deleted a po-graph formula and added an emblematic cryptogram. He tweaked a cunei theorem and rearranged a subsequence rubric.

Huh, I hadn't thought to do that.

Chapling stopped typing and sat staring at the screen. I waited, my gaze fixed to the monitor, wondering what he'd do next.

He cleared his throat. "You're still here. TL says you have to take at least thirty minutes."

It took a second to realize he was talking to me. "Oh . . . sorry." With a sigh, I turned and set out from the lab, through the underground hallways, and up the elevator to the dining hall.

The place sat empty. A lingering scent of bleach told me everyone had come and gone and the tables had been wiped down. I glanced at my watch, noting it was an hour past the usual lunchtime. On a table to the left sat a few snacks for those who might be hungry in between meals. I grabbed a banana and a granola bar.

As I peeled the skin from the banana, I realized I'd barely seen Parrot in the week since we'd found out about the mission. And most of the times I had seen him, he'd been quiet and had kept to himself.

Taking a bite out of my banana, I left the cafeteria, made my way down the hall to the guys' bedroom, and knocked on the door.

"Yeah?" Wirenut answered. "Come in."

The boys' room looked like a masculine version of the girls' room and always smelled like Mystic's incense. Like ours, their roomy living quarters held enough space for ten more guys. Crème walls and carpet instead of peach-colored. Three twin-size beds with brown comforters in lieu of beige, and a four-drawer, dark wood dresser for each of them replaced the white. A long closet stretched along the left wall where ours spanned the back. A bathroom sat in the back corner with three sinks, showers, and toilets. Posters of skimpily-dressed girls hung from their walls.

Typical.

Wirenut lay sprawled across the carpet writing in a notebook. Green Day played softly in the background. Or at least I assumed it was Green Day because they were Wirenut's favorite. I never knew the names of bands. Other people knew names of bands. I knew names of . . . well, code.

I sat down on his bed. "What are you doing?"

"Calculus." He cursed and erased something he'd written.

This was the focused, don't-bother-me Wirenut. "I know you're busy, but have you seen Parrot?"

Not looking up, Wirenut shook his head.

Mystic came from the bathroom, wiping his hands on his jeans. "Oh, hey, GiGi. Good thing I wasn't naked."

I smiled. "Good thing."

He pointed to Wirenut. "Unless you want your head bitten off, I highly recommend you go nowhere near him." Mystic went to his dresser and pulled out a pair of socks. "I gave him a citrine crystal, but he refuses to use it."

"A citrine crystal?"

Mystic sat down on his bed and put on his socks. "It unites personal power. Endurance. Helps you mentally focus and control your emotions."

"That sounds handy." I glanced down at Wirenut. "Why won't you use it?"

Wirenut rolled onto his back. "Because it's mumbo jumbo." He scrubbed his hands over his face. "Listen, if you're going to be in here, then I'm leaving. Otherwise, you all need to get out of here. I've got hours of homework ahead of me."

"Come on." Mystic grabbed his wallet and headed from the room. "Leave the grouch to his books."

I followed Mystic into the hall. "Where ya going?"

He shoved his wallet down his back pocket. "Please. It's Sunday. Our one and only free day. Where have I gone every Sunday for the past six months?"

I rolled my eyes. "To the Boardwalk to watch the girls Roller-Blade."

Mystic crossed the hall to David's room and knocked. Adam, David's teammate and roommate, opened the door. At six feet five, with blond hair and blue eyes, he and I could easily pass for brother and sister.

"Ready?" asked Mystic.

Adam switched please-tell-me-you're-not-going eyes to me.

I held up my hands. "Boys only."

Bruiser came out of our room and bounded up beside me. "You two going girl watching? Won't be near as much fun today. Have you been outside? It's drizzling. I bet there won't be any bikinis. They'll all be in rain gear."

Adam leaned down nose to nose with Bruiser's five-foot height. She had to love that. She liked him. Big-time.

He waggled his brows. "You'd be surprised what girls wear when they're out and about on a Sunday afternoon in front of a couple hot, eligible men."

Bruiser busted out laughing. "Hot, eligible men? Oh, that's funny."

Smiling, Adam picked her up and set her aside. "Let's go, Mystic."

They made it to the end of the hall. "Hey," I called over Bruiser's gasps for air. "Have either of you seen Parrot?"

Adam and Mystic shook their heads.

"Didn't even sleep in the room last night," Mystic said.

Waving them off, I looked down at Bruiser. "How about you?"

She sniffed and wiped her eyes. "Nope."

I made my way down the hall to TL's office. I peeked inside his open door. "Excuse me. Is Parrot in his language room?"

At his computer, TL didn't stop clicking keys. "No."

"Do you know where he is?"

"Yes."

I waited, but TL didn't expound on his answer. "Can you tell me where?"

TL continued typing. "He's in the barn."

"Okay, thanks."

"GiGi?" TL stopped typing and looked up as I turned around. "This is a hard time for Parrot."

"I know, sir. That's why I'm trying to find him."

I left the ranch house, crossed the wet, grassy yard to the barn, and entered the wide-open doors. The front half served as our physical training area, complete with weights, mats, hanging bags, and other various gymlike stuff.

The back half of the barn served as a . . . well, a barn. Complete with stalls, horses, hay, and gear.

The place always sat deserted on Sundays with everyone enjoying their day off.

A muffled sneeze filtered through the air. Parrot had the worst hay allergies. It always made me smile at the fact that he loved horses yet was allergic to hay.

I strode through the musty training area back to the stalls and peeked over each door. Parrot stood in the second to the last, leaning against the wood wall, idly petting a horse's nose.

"Hey." I propped my arms along the top of the half door.

Parrot glanced over, looking so emotionally and physically tired that I just wanted to rock him to sleep.

He brushed his fingers across the horse's muzzle. "I brought Carrot with me when I came to the Specialists."

By Carrot, I assumed he meant the horse. Sad to say, I didn't know any of the animal's names. "Let me guess, you named him Carrot because he likes carrots."

"No, I named him Carrot because he was orange when I found him."

"Orange?"

He gave the horse a sugar cube. "Some kids had spray painted him as a joke."

"That's not funny."

"No, it wasn't." Parrot stroked the length of Carrot's head. "He's been my best friend for ten years."

How sad.

But then I never even had a best friend, animal or human, until I joined the Specialists.

I picked a piece of hay from the feed bin. "I know you're not looking forward to the trip. Want to talk about it?"

"No, not really." Parrot paused, stroking the horse's ear. "But I want to warn you about somebody."

"Okay."

"There's a chief who'll be there. His name's Talon. He's not a nice man, especially to women." Parrot stopped petting the horse and looked me dead in the eyes. "Be careful. Don't go anywhere near him. I mean it, GiGi."

Parrot's serious tone brought goose bumps to my arms. "What does he look like?"

"Mohawk, stripes tattooed down his chin."

499

Another chill zinged my skin. "I noticed him out of all the others when we saw the photos of each chief. He looked menacing."

"He's more than menacing. Talon is evil. His soul is dark."

I thought about all the bad guys I'd run into since joining the Specialists. I thought about the different degrees of "darkness" to their personalities and wondered aloud, "What do you think makes a person go bad? Are they born that way? Do they voluntarily become bad? Is it the way they're raised?"

Parrot shrugged. "Talon had a great father. I remember him interacting with us kids on the reservation, playing games or just talking with us. He was a very warm man. Powerful, too. He never made me feel any less for being half Native American. I'll never forget him."

"What happened to him?"

"He died from old age, natural causes. And our customs say that the oldest son steps up and takes over."

"And that was Talon?"

Parrot shook his head. "No, Talon had an older brother. I remember him well. He was just as wonderful as his father. He would have made a great chief."

"*Would* have?"

"After their father died. Talon and his brother went up into the cliffs for prayer." Parrot looked at me. "Talon was the only one who returned."

My eyes widened. "Did Talon kill his brother so he could become chief?"

"That's what everyone on my reservation speculated, but it could never be proven. Talon said his brother slipped and fell off one of the cliffs."

"Oh my God."

"I remember my grandmother told me once that, even as a boy, something was off in Talon. That he always had an evil spirit." Parrot rubbed his horse's ear. "Just listen to me and don't go near him."

"Okay."

Questions spiraled through my brain about Talon and Parrot and their history together. Was Talon the reason Parrot got recruited by the Specialists? What had happened to Parrot's family? Had he been abandoned, orphaned? Was he a runaway?

I studied the side of Parrot's face, wanting to ask him all those questions, but something about his expression told me he wouldn't answer them. Not yet, at least. "Do all those languages stay in your head?" I asked instead.

Parrot grabbed a brush hanging from a nail on the wall, clearly more at ease with the direction of our conversation. "Yeah, sort of. They all hang out in the back of my head waiting for me to call them up."

"Don't you ever get confused? I can barely keep English straight."

"No." He shrugged. "I don't know how to explain it. It's just natural for me, always has been."

"Do you ever forget a language?"

"Sometimes." Parrot stroked the brush down the horse's side. "But all I have to do is hear someone speak it, and I'm good."

"Huh." I twirled the hay I held between my fingers. This language thing fascinated me. "And the new languages? How do you learn them so quickly?"

It took me a whole week to learn five words in Ushbanian. Talk about slow.

He mulled my question around for a few seconds. "I listen for the rhythm, the clicks, the guttural thumps." He chuckled. "That doesn't make any sense to you, does it?"

I laughed with him, pleased to hear his lightened mood. "You're right, it doesn't."

A quiet minute passed as I watched him brush the horse and listened to its heavy breaths.

"Dreams?" I asked. "What language do you dream in?"

"They're silent and black and white, like an old movie."

"That's your brain's way of telling you it needs quiet for a while." I put the hay in my mouth and chewed on the end. "Think about it. You've got a whole world living in your head. It has to wear out your poor brain."

Parrot smiled. "That's a good way to put it."

"Excuse me, GiGi?"

I glanced over my shoulder. David, my *boyfriend*, stood across the barn in the doorway backlit by a ray of sun that filtered through the cloudy sky. My stomach fluttered. With my preoccupation with my translation program, I'd barely seen him in the past week. And I certainly hadn't gotten any more of his yummy kisses.

"Be right back," I said to Parrot, who smiled and nodded. I jogged across the barn to my *boyfriend*, David.

His dark eyes crinkled. "Hey, gorgeous. Long time no see."

"Hey."

David took my hand. "TL's sending me to Egypt to help Piper and Curtis with a few things."

My joy at seeing him drained away. "What?"

"I'm leaving tomorrow morning. I don't know how long I'll be gone. Do you want to go for a walk or something? Just the two of us?"

But I'd be leaving for South America in a few weeks. What if David didn't get back before I left? It'd be forever before we saw each other again. "What are you helping them with?"

He squeezed my hand. "I'm not allowed to say. I'm sorry." Nodding, I looked down at our joined hands. "It sucks having secrets."

David moved closer. "Yes, it does. But one day we'll both have the clearance to talk freely with each other about our work."

He had more clearance than any of us.

A breeze flowed in, messing my hair. He smoothed the stray strands from my cheek. "So what do you say? Want to go for a walk?"

I glanced back through the barn to the stalls. I didn't want Parrot to be alone. He needed somebody other than his horse, and I wanted him to know he could count on me as a friend.

With a soft smile, I turned to David. "I would *love* to spend time with you. *Believe* me. But Parrot's back there all alone, and I think he needs a friend right now. I'm sorry. Please understand."

Making the right decision, picking Parrot over David, a friend over my boyfriend, brought me peace and a sense of maturity I'd never experienced before.

David kissed my cheek. "Don't apologize. Your dedication to your friends is one of the many reasons I adore you. We'll find each other later."

He slipped something from his back pocket and brought it around. A lollipop! I grinned. He was the greatest guy on the entire planet. He handed it to me and gave me another quick kiss.

"That's forty-one," I said as he stepped away.

He looked at me, clearly not understanding, then it dawned on him, and he smiled. "No, it's thirty-nine."

I watched him stroll away, scrolling my mind through every kiss. I never miscalculated anything. Surely, he'd made a mistake.

Then it hit me, and I giggled silently to myself. I'd included the kisses in my dreams last night.

I'm such a goof.

I made my way back to the stall and peeked over the door again. With his eyes closed, Parrot sat propped against the wall, his legs outstretched in the hay. His horse stood beside him with her head hung low, resting her muzzle on his shoulder.

The tender scene brought a small smile to my face.

"Thanks for staying," Parrot whispered, not opening his eyes.

His heartfelt words flowed through me, settling a content warmth in my soul. I was so glad I'd made the decision I'd made. "You're welcome," I whispered back.

I unlatched the stall door, stepped inside, and relatched. Shuffling across the hay-covered floor, I slid down beside Parrot, linked fingers with him, and laid my head on his shoulder.

Closing my eyes, I listened to his horse breathing. I inhaled the scent of clean hay and absorbed the slight lifting of his shoulder as he breathed.

Time passed, and the three of us stayed like that—Parrot and I quietly bonding and his horse breathing softly on his shoulder.

A few minutes later, Parrot rested his cheek on my head. "I never met my dad."

My heart gave a slow thump, realizing Parrot was about to open up a bit. "No?"

"He died before I was born."

How sad. At least I had *some* memories of mine. "Do you have any pictures of him?"

"Some. I don't look anything like him."

"You look like your mom?"

He lifted his cheek from my head. "My grandmother, actually. Or, at least, what she looked like before she got sick."

"Sick? Is she . . . gone?" Death was never an easy topic to discuss. Most people dodged it altogether. Only someone who had experienced it could truly understand the depth the pain ran.

Parrot nodded. "She was sick a long time. I have no idea what she died of. She refused to go to the doctors."

"Did she raise you?"

Silence.

"I guess that's what you could call it," he cryptically answered.

I imagined if she was sick, Parrot probably raised himself while taking care of her. "And your mom?" I asked.

"I had her until I was seven, and then my grandmother took over, but she was already sick at that point."

"What happened to your mom?"

Seconds ticked by quietly, and, from his silence, I knew the subject of his mom was closest to his heart and most likely off limits.

He laid his cheek back on my head. "I don't know," he said so quietly I almost didn't hear him. "I don't know where she is."

"Is TL trying to find her?"

"Yes."

I squeezed his hand. "Then he will."

With a quiet sigh, Parrot got to his feet. He paced the stall, not looking at me, obviously in deep thought. With each turn of his pace, I detected agitation growing in him. Finally, he shook his head. "I don't know, GiGi, I don't know. He should have found her by now."

"Parrot . . ." Even I knew the difficulties in finding someone.

"With all the technology and the resources around this place. With all the people he knows. He should have found her."

"Parrot . . ." He was getting agitated, a side of him I'd never seen before.

He pointed his finger at me. "And you know what just occurred to me? TL's manipulating me just like Talon did. All everybody wants from me is my language ability, and no one gives me anything in return."

I got to my feet. "That's not true."

"TL's used me for exactly what he wanted, and he hasn't come through with his end of the bargain yet in finding my mother."

"Parrot . . ." I didn't know what to say. I knew exactly how he felt. I'd felt the same way a couple of times.

Parrot kicked some hay across the stall. "I should give him an ultimatum, just like you did. Find my mother or I'm leaving the Specialists."

"You don't want to do that. I made a *huge* mistake when I did that. There are other ways to handle your frustration. And I realize that now because of all the mess I got in with bulldogging my way to Barracuda Key and getting Eduardo." I took a step toward him. "Please listen to me—"

Parrot spun toward me. "I'm *tired* of listening. I'm *tired* of doing what people want. I'm *tired* of not getting what I want."

I put my hand over my heart, feeling his frustration all the way to the core of my soul. "I know what it's like to lose a parent and to do anything for retribution or to get that parent back. Not many people can say they understand what you're feeling, but you *know* I do. All of us here are like you in one way or another. None of us have homes, have families. You don't want to leave. Please, please, *please,* listen to me and believe what TL has told you. He *will* find your mother."

Parrot closed his eyes and dropped his head back. "I just want my life to make sense. I want things, for once, to come together for me."

I closed the small distance between us. "I want the same thing. I want my life to make sense, too. I want to feel settled. I want to feel completed. Being here with all of you is the first time I've felt a smidgen of wholeness." I grabbed his arm. "And I know you feel the same way. Trust that feeling. It's a good thing. It's right. You're meant to be here."

He opened his eyes and looked straight into mine.

"Don't let personal emotions cloud your judgment. It's okay to trust us, your team. We love you." I smiled. "I love you. I won't let anything happen to you. Just like I know you won't let anything happen to me."

Parrot stared deep into my eyes, then reached out and pulled me into his arms.

I hugged him hard, hoping he felt my raw honesty. Hoping he made the right decision.

He pulled out of our hug a good solid minute later. "Who knew you'd turn out to be the resident psychologist?" he said, smiling.

We both chuckled at that.

Parrot nodded. "I'm going to do this mission. And afterward, if TL still hasn't found my mother, well, we'll see."

It wasn't exactly what I had hoped to hear, but it was something. And I understood where Parrot was coming from. Now all I could do was hope that he decided to stay, and I wondered if I could somehow help find his mom.

***

Later that night, I went for a walk. With all the talk about Parrot's family, I was missing my parents a lot. I needed to clear my head. As I made my way out of the ranch into the yard, I found David near the pool. With a three-quarters moon and a clear sky full of stars, it cast a romantic aura over the quiet night.

He lay on a lounge chair staring up at the stars, and as I approached, he lifted his head and smiled.

Holding out his hand, David nodded me toward him, and I crawled onto his lounge chair. Neither one of us spoke a word as we lay side by side, holding hands, staring up at the sky.

Some time later, he pulled me close, and I rested my cheek on his chest.

He let out a long sigh. "I'll miss you," he whispered, and minutes later began breathing heavy.

I listened to him sleep, smiling. I'd miss him, too.

***

One week later, I met TL and Parrot at the elevator hidden behind the mural. We were scheduled to begin our inoculations.

Nothing like a good needle to start your day out right.

Jonathan walked up. "Everybody ready to get stuck?"

We all smiled.

The elevator opened, and we boarded at the ranch level. TL pulled what looked like a quarter from his pocket and pointed it to the bottom left corner of the car.

Parrot and I exchanged a curious glance. What was going on?

He pressed the center of the quarter, and a yellow laser shot out. "We're going to Subfloor Three."

I perked up. "Subfloor Three?" How cool. "What's on it?"

TL pointed the quarter to the bottom right corner of the car, and a yellow laser shot out again. "Brand-new medical clinic. We just finished it two weeks ago."

How in the world? "You mean people have been down there building a clinic, and none of us knew it?"

"Yes." TL did the quarter-laser thing to the bottom right corner.

I hadn't seen anybody come and go from the ranch. "How did they get down there?" Maybe another secret passageway like Chapling's?

TL did the quarter-laser thing to the final corner and the elevator slowly descended. I waited for him to answer my question, but he didn't.

"TL, did you hear my question?"

TL put the quarter back in his pocket. "Yes. And I'm not answering it."

And there you had it. Yet another secret.

The elevator opened, and we all stepped out into what looked like an empty hospital emergency room. I scanned the area and estimated it to be roughly fifty by fifty feet.

To the right sat three rooms with their doors standing open. I peeked inside and saw, basically, a hospital room with a bed, TV, bathroom, and a couple of chairs. To the left sat three rooms as well. One appeared to be an operating room, the other had equipment in it, and the last mirrored a dentist's exam room.

Along the back wall sat cabinets with medicines, gauze, needles, rubber gloves, and other miscellaneous medical supplies. Beside the cabinets sat a couple of wheelchairs, IV stands, and a crash cart.

"You are looking at a fully functional hospital," TL said. "From now on, for anything we need medically, we go here. And this"—he pointed toward one of the exam rooms—"is Dr. Gretchen."

Parrot and I turned . . . and simultaneously flinched.

Dressed in a white lab coat and taking up the entire doorway stood the biggest woman I had ever seen. She towered at least six feet four inches and probably weighed two hundred and fifty pounds of solid muscle.

With her salt-and-pepper hair pulled back in a tight bun, hands fisted on her hips, and legs spread wide, she scowled back at us.

I swallowed.

She moved her scowl from me, to Parrot, and landed on Jonathan. "Jonathan," she growled in a voice deeper than Jonathan's.

I turned and looked at Jonathan. I swore I saw him swallow uneasily, too. "Been a long time, Gretchen."

She snorted. "I see you're still wearing that eye patch."

Jonathan didn't respond.

Parrot and I exchanged a quick, inquisitive glance.

"Dr. Gretchen has worked for the IPNC for twenty years," TL began the introduction. "She's one of the best doctors I've ever worked with. She and I have been talking over the past several weeks, and I'm incredibly pleased to announce that she's accepted my offer to work for the Specialists as the head of our medical clinic."

I smiled, deciding this was a woman I definitely needed to like me. With my klutziness, there was no telling how often I might be down here. "Nice to meet you, Dr. Gretchen."

She took her eyes off Jonathan and narrowed them in on me. I kept my smile in place.

With a brusque nod in my direction, she tromped across the clinic and over to the cabinets.

In my peripheral vision I saw Jonathan wipe sweat off his forehead. Interesting. These two obviously knew each other. I wondered what the history was, exactly. Had they been on missions together? Had they trained together? Had they dated?

The last thought almost made me laugh. I couldn't see the two of them together.

Dr. Gretchen pulled out a series of needles and vials. I tried real hard not to look at the size of the needles.

"I'll do the guys," she rasped, "in Exam Room One. And the girl in Exam Room Two."

I didn't bother telling her my name was GiGi, not "girl." I figured that'd come in time.

Carrying a tray with the supplies, she stomped into Exam Room Two, and I followed. "You can do the guys first, if you want." I knew my suggestion wouldn't fly, but I threw it out there anyway.

Dr. Gretchen shut the door. "Drop your pants. Lean over the table. This one's going in the butt."

"Okay." So much for my suggestion.

I dropped my pants and leaned over the table. I saw her reach for a needle and squeezed my eyes shut. I heard her unwrapping something. Then she pulled down my underwear a little, and I felt something wet, presumably alcohol.

I cringed, knowing what came next. I waited, and waited . . .

She smoothed something in place and snapped my underwear up. "All done. See you tomorrow for the next one."

"All done? But . . ." I twisted around and pulled my underwear down, and sure enough there was a bandage. "I didn't feel anything."

Dr. Gretchen got this cocky look. "Of course you didn't. TL said I was the best."

I pulled my pants up. "How big was the needle you used?"

She picked up a clean one from the tray and held it up.

My eyes widened. "That's huge!"

She smirked. "And Jonathan's going to feel every inch of it."

Spinning on her heel, she swung open the door and trudged out. I hurried behind her and watched as she flung open the guys' door. "Drop your pants," she grunted. "This one's going in the butt."

The door closed.

TL stood nearby, leaning against the wall. With a quick glance in his direction, I pressed my ear to the door, wishing beyond wishes that I could be in there to watch.

"You first, little guy," Dr. Gretchen said.

I knew she was referring to Parrot, because Jonathan was in no way little.

A couple of seconds ticked by. "All done," she rasped.

"And now you, Jonathan." I could visualize her getting an evil smirk on her face.

A couple more seconds ticked by . . .

"Ahhh! Ooowww!" Jonathan yelled. "Dammit, Gretchen!"

I put my hand over my mouth to hold in my laugh.

A couple seconds later, the door opened, and Dr. Gretchen nearly floated out with a huge grin on her face. She winked at me and whistled her way across the clinic, then disappeared into another room.

Parrot came out first, obviously trying to hold in a laugh, then Jonathan, holding his butt. Without a look in any of our directions he wiped his eye, stomped over to the elevator, and pressed the button. As soon as the door opened, he stepped inside and jammed his finger on the button. The door closed, and TL broke out in a laugh.

It was the first time I'd ever seen TL do such a thing, and Parrot and I joined in with him.

***

PT, Physical Training, rolled around a few days later. I entered the barn and saw Parrot warming up and headed straight for him. "Hey, you. How's it going in your language lab?"

He smiled a little. "It's a pretty cool setup."

I pulled my hair back in a ponytail. "You going to be ready?"

"Not a problem."

"I wanted to ask you something." I slid a folded piece of paper from my pocket. "I'm inputting some cave drawings from Argentina into my program, and I keep seeing this pattern of words." I handed him the paper. "Does it mean anything to you?"

Parrot studied the rows of letters. A couple of seconds ticked by. "How weird. This is written in both French and Spanish." He pointed to this first word. "First word French, second is Spanish, alternating across the line in that pattern. Drop down to the second line and it switches out. Third line switches again." He handed back the paper. "But that's from the seventeen hundreds. They don't use words like that now."

I folded the paper and slipped it back into my pocket. "I should have come to you days ago." I'd wasted *way* too much time on that one aspect. Sometimes I forgot how valuable my team was. "Thanks."

"No problem."

"All right," Jonathan graveled. "Spread out. Arm's length between you." Jonathan raised his arms to demonstrate, and winced, touching his upper arm where he, Parrot, and I had gotten another vaccine.

I looked at Parrot, and we silently laughed.

Used to the routine, my teammates and I took our spots in the barn/training area and went through our usual stretching drill. It seemed so empty with David, Piper, and Curtis gone to Egypt. And Tina and Adam were meeting with TL about something.

"Okay," Jonathan said about ten minutes later. "Balancing act today." He pointed across the barn to where he'd set up what looked like an obstacle course with balance beams, square tiles suspended by ropes hooked to the roof, and a platform with wheels. "Parrot and GiGi will encounter all types of terrain in the jungle: rivers, trees, bridges, waterfalls, boulders. So we're going to work out the kinks and fine-tune our equilibrium, while I give you some general information about the jungle. Very simply, you are going to traverse these obstacles without falling off. There are mats below you, so don't worry about it if you do fall."

Ugh. Equilibrium was definitely *not* my specialty. Thank God for mats.

"I want the lineup to be," Jonathan continued, "Wirenut, Bruiser, Beaker, Cat, Mystic, Parrot, and GiGi."

I breathed a sigh of relief at being last as we all shuffled across the barn.

Wirenut climbed right up on the balance beam. "Do we get bonus points for theatrics?"

Ignoring Wirenut's humor, Jonathan nodded to the beam. "Anytime you're ready."

Being so agile, I knew Wirenut would do well at this. Bruiser and Cat would, too. It'd be interesting to see how the rest of us would do.

Wirenut danced effortlessly across the balance beam, throwing in a couple of spins for show. He threw his foot out and touched the first floating tile, then the next, and then the next. Ten in all, pretty much sailing across them. He plopped down on the platform supported by wheels, faked like he was going to fall, and, with a silly snort, skipped across it. He did a flip in the air off the end, and then bowed.

We all dutifully laughed and applauded.

"When you're in the jungle, or any other situation for that matter, you have to understand your strengths and weaknesses," Jonathan said. "You can't assume your team member will pick up your slack. You are the only person you can rely on." He nodded to Bruiser. "Go ahead."

She stepped up onto the balance beam and shot Wirenut a dude-I'm-so-going-to-outdo-you look. Turning around, she did a series of backflips all the way down the beam and off, landing hands down on the first floating tile. She walked across the tile with her hands, keeping her toes pointed in the air, then landed on the wheeled platform in a split. She bounced up, caught air, and sailed off the other end.

I'd seen her in action plenty of times, but her skill level still amazed me.

With a cocky wink to Wirenut, she strutted past him, blowing her nails and buffing them on her shirt.

"The jungle," Jonathan spoke. "There is no other landscape like it in the world. Dense vegetation. Heat, humidity. Steep, mountainous terrain. Rivers. All of these things hinder movement. Restrict visibility." He nodded to Beaker.

She climbed up with no showmanship to her at all. Holding her arms out for balance, she carefully made her way across the beam. Reaching out, she grabbed the ropes supporting the floating tiles and used them to wobble across. She jumped down onto the wheeled platform and stood for a second balancing herself, then crossed it and jumped off.

Not bad. No doubt our cheerleading training for our last mission had helped her.

"If you're in a situation you're not comfortable with," Jonathan said, "stop and think. Ask yourself: What is my objective? What is my terrain? Is there an enemy nearby? Is there a team member nearby? How much time do I have to meet my objective? What resources do I have at my disposal?" He nodded to Cat.

She climbed up and traversed the obstacle course, doing just as well as Wirenut.

Then Mystic, who, of course, had to meditate to channel the balance gods before gracefully completing the course.

Then Parrot, who seemed to perform a little better than Beaker, but not as well as Cat. I was sure his years of horseback riding gave him a natural balancing ability.

"Lastly"—Jonathan looked right at me—"be confident with your movements. The jungle is no place to question yourself." He nodded me to the balance beam.

I walked over, going over everything Jonathan had just said . . . and felt a bit overwhelmed.

With all eyes on me, I stepped up onto the balance beam. So far no one had fallen off. Mystic almost had at the floating tiles and Beaker nearly lost it on the platform, but they'd both managed to recover.

Everyone knew I had exactly zero coordinated bones/muscles/organs/ligaments and whatever else in my body. And I knew, just knew, that they knew I was about to really entertain them.

I glanced over at them all lined up, trying to hide their smiles.

"Whenever you're ready," Jonathan encouraged me.

Taking a deep breath, I pulled my shoulders back, stretched my arms out for balance, and fastened my gaze to the end of the beam. Carefully, I put one foot in front of the other and made it all the way to the end. I turned to my friends with a "take-that" smirk.

"Save that look until *after* the floating tiles," Wirenut teased.

Bruiser snorted.

If I didn't love them so much, I might have had to hate them.

Grasping the ropes supporting the floating tiles, I placed my right foot on the first tile . . . and swung forward . . . then backward . . . and forward . . . then backward . . . The swaying motion made me dizzy, and I squeezed my eyes shut. Both my legs and arms began uncontrollably shaking.

My teammates busted out laughing, and I fell flat on my face on the mat below.

Sigh. At least we had a full-service hospital now. I suspected that Dr. Gretchen and I were going to be fast buddies.

***

A couple of days later I met Jonathan, Parrot, and TL outside the barn. Parrot stood with his horse, Carrot, beside him. And TL had a pretty brown one beside him.

Off to the side was Dr. Gretchen, holding a doctor's bag.

I gave her an inquisitive glance.

With a wink to me, she held up her bag. "Just in case, GiGi."

I smiled weakly. Great. She'd been here only a week and already knew I pretty much needed her on call. Well, at least she addressed me by my name now.

TL held up the reins. "This will be your mode of transportation in the jungle."

"Right," I replied, clearly not looking forward to this.

"Have you ever ridden a horse?" Jonathan asked, turning toward me.

I shook my head. I mean, really, did they even need to ask?

Parrot reached up and stroked his hand down Carrot's muzzle. "Give her a pat."

Cautiously, I approached and reached my hand out to touch her muzzle. Carrot snorted and jerked her head away.

I took a quick step back. "This isn't going to work." Clearly they were going to have to think of another way to transport me through the jungle.

"It's obvious you're scared," Parrot said. "She's picking up on it. Don't let her see that you're intimidated. Take charge. Be confident. Be sure of your movements. You're the boss."

"Easier said than done." I took a fortifying breath and stepped toward her again. Quickly, with what I thought was confidence, I gave her a pat. Carrot just stood there and let me do it.

Cool.

Parrot walked around her, trailing his hand over her body. "Now this. Let her get used to your movements."

Following Parrot, I strolled around her, gliding my hand over her back and sides. Again, she just stood there and let me do it.

Not bad.

"Now mounting." TL grabbed hold of the saddle. "Watch." Standing on his horse's left side, he grabbed the saddle horn, placed his left boot in the stirrup, and effortlessly jumped up and swung his right leg over. "Now you try." He nodded to Carrot.

Parrot stepped back to give me room. I circled around her again, letting her feel my touch. I figured that would be the smart thing to do. Grabbing on to the saddle horn, I hoisted my left tennis shoe into the stirrup. With a grunt I pulled myself up . . . and slid right back down.

Carrot sidestepped away, and I one-foot hopped to keep up. "Whoa, girl, whoa." I glanced up at her, and she slanted me a haughty look.

"Did you all see that?" I jabbed my finger at the horse. "She gave me a look."

Parrot laughed. "She did not give you a look. She's picking up on your body language. Don't hesitate at all. Walk up, put your foot in the stirrup, and go right up into the saddle."

Walk up, put my foot in the stirrup, and go right up into the saddle? I almost snorted. That takes coordination, and coordination definitely did not exist in my repertoire of gifts.

"Don't just pull up either," Jonathan advised. "Use your leg muscle to push at the same time you're pulling."

"Shouldn't one of you be helping me?" Especially since they all sounded like such experts.

"You need to do this on your own," Jonathan commented.

I looked at Parrot, and he nodded his agreement.

I didn't know why I had to do this on my own. Probably had something to do with me and Carrot bonding. My new BFF. Blah, blah, blah.

Taking another fortifying breath, I stepped up to her side. I grabbed the saddle, wedged my foot in the stirrup, and pushed/ pulled myself up.

My leg swung over, and I found myself sitting astride Carrot.

She turned her head and winked at me, and I blinked. Now that definitely had to have been my imagination. Horses couldn't wink, could they?

"She's proud of you," Parrot said.

"She is?"

Parrot nodded. "Definitely."

I swelled a bit with pride.

"Okay, now use the reins to tell her what you expect." TL walked his horse forward. Gently, he tugged the reins to the right, and his horse followed his lead. Then he demonstrated the same technique going left.

Looked easy enough. Wedging my right tennis shoe in the stirrup, I took hold of the reins. Carrot didn't move.

"Um, go?"

"Give her a gentle tap with your heels," Parrot instructed.

I did, and she moved.

Grinning like a goof, I carefully tugged the reins to the right, and she followed my lead. I went left next, and she followed.

Quite pleased with this, I stroked my hand down Carrot's neck. "*You are the most beautiful, bestest horsey in the world.*"

SHANNON GREENLAND

Parrot chuckled.

Who would've thought riding a horse would bring me so much joy. No wonder Parrot loved it so much.

TL swung off his horse. "Now let's have you try this horse."

"What? Why can't I stay on her?" I nearly whined.

"Because you need to be exposed to different horses."

"TL's right," Parrot agreed. "Just because Carrot likes you doesn't mean all horses will. You have to get used to different personalities and learn to adjust your body language to fit each horse."

Reluctantly, I dismounted and made my way over to the other horse. I reached my hand out for a pet, and he snorted and reared up.

With a sigh, I stepped back. This was not going to go well.

***

A week later I walked into the conference room for our last meeting before the mission. We left for South America in one day, and I still had a few tweaks here and there to make on my translation program.

Jonathan sat at one end of the long metal conference table, and TL sat at the other. Parrot had already taken the seat to the left of TL, so I rolled the one out to his right, David's usual spot. I smiled to myself as I sat and swore I detected a hint of David's cologne.

Pushing back from the table, Jonathan stood. At our first mission briefing, I'd wondered what kind of leader he'd be. So far he'd proven to be just as confident and organized as TL.

"Parrot," Jonathan began. "How are things on your end? TL tells me you've been in your language lab working hard. We leave tomorrow. Are you prepared?"

Parrot nodded. "Yes, sir."

"Parrot's been ready since last week," TL chimed in. "He's more than prepared. He's going to do fine."

Since last week? That meant he learned four languages in three weeks. Jeez. Talk about amazing.

"Tell us what you've been doing in your language lab," Jonathan prompted.

"Well, every day I start out by watching an hour's worth of programming from the different regions that will be represented at the talks. I follow that up with one-on-one conversations over the telephone with the actual assistants who will be attending the talks with the chiefs, not only to get to know them personally, but for a real flavor of their dialect. I've been listening to recordings of the tribes themselves, the women, the children, the everyday activities. And I've been meeting via video conferencing with different historians, learning about the customs of the indigenous people I'll be dealing with." Parrot smiled a little. "I have to say, it's a pretty darn cool lab."

I smiled.

Jonathan turned to me. "And your program, GiGi? All set?"

"Yes," I lied, then immediately felt guilty. "Well, I have a few tweaks, and then, yes, it'll be ready. I need to cross-reference the cave drawings in Rutina with known, documented glyphs and come up with a translation."

I didn't mention the fact that I really didn't feel confident about my program. They wouldn't understand. And if they did, they'd just tell me everything would be fine.

TL clicked his pen. "She'll do fine."

See?

Jonathan referenced his folder. "As you know, we've been hired by the North and South American Native Alliance to provide translation services with both language and the cave drawings. We've also been hired to guard the vase. So in other words, they know we're the Specialists, former government employees who now work privately providing highly skilled services. But they don't know our real identities."

Parrot raised his hand. "But you know I know one of the chiefs. *He* knows my true identity."

"We realize that," TL answered. "Which is why you'll go in disguise. You'll be meeting with a makeup artist tonight to be outfitted."

"Parrot," Jonathan continued, "will go under the name Flint Dunham. GiGi will be Hannah Flowers, and I'll be going as Shane Young."

Oooh, I liked Hannah Flowers. It had a sort of country girl quality to it.

Jonathan looked first at me and then Parrot. "The talks are scheduled to go for one week. As you all know, Chapling intercepted a message that two unknown parties are planning to steal the vase. More intel has revealed that these two unknown parties are chiefs who will be attending the talks. At this point we do not know which two chiefs they are, but Chapling is continuing to research that.

"This mission is going to be a bit different from others in the past in that we're stepping back in time. This is a ceremonial tribal gathering, free of modern-day conveniences. The men sleep in one area and the women in another. The cave is approximately one mile from the village. The talks will take place in a ceremonial hut located in the center of the village. We'll arrive and depart via horseback. The glyph historian has been there for a week getting a jump-start on things. Our contact will meet us at the airport to take us into the jungle. We'll sleep, eat, and wash outside."

Bathe outside? Wait a minute. . . .

"GiGi"—Jonathan nodded to me—"cultural differences between men and women are very strict. Our contact in Rutina has informed us that Jaaci will be your hostess. It's important that you do exactly what she does."

"But wouldn't it make sense that one of the Huworo women would be my hostess since they're hosting the talks?"

He shook his head. "Only married women in the Huworo tribe are allowed to host. And they're only allowed to host Native Americans. Since you're nonnative, Jaaci has been taken in by the Huworo and given the job."

I didn't know if I liked the fact I'd been deemed a "job."

"Chapling," Jonathan continued, "has installed updated satellite chips in our phones. However, being so deep in the jungle, there will probably be noncommunicative spots. We'll have to figure that out when we get there. Other than our cells and GiGi's laptop, which have been pre-approved by the Alliance, we're taking no technologies with us."

I nearly pouted. No technology? That meant no cool gadgets or neat gizmos. What a bummer. At least I'd have my laptop, my own private version of the Swiss army knife. Only Chapling and I knew the cool things it was capable of.

"The alliance," Jonathan went on, looking at me, "does not know about your new program. Please remember that it's top secret. They think you're there as an assistant to the glyph historian, who will be joining us from the IPNC."

I nodded my understanding.

"Let me stress a few things. The Mother Nature vase is, like TL originally said, a highly coveted item. You are to trust no one. A lot of people want this vase, and I'm sure, if properly motivated, they would stop at nothing to get it. Let me remind you that a few of these tribes are long-standing rivals. I'm fully expecting some sort of altercation. Should anything happen to me, you both know how to get ahold of TL. Like he said, he'll be here at home base handling meetings and wrapping up important details."

Should anything happen to me. That statement brought goose bumps to my skin and reminded me of the dangerous, life-threatening situations we were in while on missions.

"Questions?" Jonathan asked.

Parrot and I shook our heads.

"We pull out at oh-seven-hundred hours." Jonathan closed his file. "Dismissed."

<FIVE>

Early the next morning we boarded our plane. I tucked my laptop under the seat in front of me, and about five minutes later, my cell vibrated. I checked the display.

BREATHE. I'M THINKING OF U.

I smiled at my *boyfriend's* message. David was on a top secret mission and yet risked a security breach just to reassure me.

I had been in a plane crash when I was six, the same one that killed my parents. It didn't take a genius to figure out why I hated flying so much.

I'd learned to tolerate it, though. I had no choice. It came with being a Specialist. Travel was inevitable, and this flight marked my seventh one. Not bad for a girl who was inconsolable the first time around. David had been there that first time, telling me to breathe. Somehow just thinking of him always made the trip go smoother.

I texted him back. I'M BREATHING AND THINKING OF U 2.

I put my cell phone away and turned to Parrot. "How are you?"

He yawned. "Tired. After the farewell party, I wasn't able to sleep."

I lowered our shade and handed him the pillow wedged between my seat and the wall. "Try to sleep now. We have a long week ahead of us."

Through another yawn, he nodded, put the pillow behind his head, and closed his eyes. Just as our plane took off, I heard him inhale a soft snore. It made me smile.

Hours later, in the late afternoon, our plane touched down in Maires, the capital city of Rutina.

Jonathan, Parrot, and I departed the plane into muggy brightness.

"¡Hola!" A small man with a bushy kinky beard called from the other side of the security fence. I assumed he was our local contact.

Jonathan hitched his chin. *"Hola, Guillermo. ¿Cómo estás?"*

"Bien. Bien."

Jonathan hadn't said if Guillermo was an IPNC agent or not. Since the Specialists used to be a division of the IPNC, and because we were so small, TL still used IPNC agents for freelance work, like this.

We grabbed our duffels and backpacks from the luggage trolley and made our way across the steamy tarmac.

Couples, families, and singles bustled along with us, finding their luggage, talking on cell phones, heading toward the security gate.

The airport stood off to the left. Jonathan had explained that only certain airlines accessed the terminals and everyone else used the outdoors.

Too bad we weren't one of the "lucky airlines."

We joined the long line to security check, and, while the sun baked us, we waited our turn.

Men in military fatigues wandered the crowd, holding machine guns in front of them. Dark shades hid their eyes, and their faces wore matching scowls.

All around us everyone spoke Spanish. The more I listened to the rapid-fire rolling *r*s, the more I wanted to know what they said.

The woman in front of me laughed at something her friend said, and they both glanced back at me.

"What did they say?" I whispered to Parrot.

He smiled. "Tell you later."

It couldn't be that bad if he was smiling . . . through his mustache. His disguise was too cool. The makeup artist had lightened his hair to brown and woven in extensions, making it fall straight to his shoulders. He wore blue contacts that seemed so real, even if you looked close, you couldn't see the rims of them. He had a mustache and beard trimmed neatly to his face. And randomly placed moles on his forehead, neck, chest, and arms. The moles wouldn't come off unless a specific solution was used to take them off.

Shifting, I peered over everyone's heads (being tall had its advantages) to the security gate, and sighed. We still had at least sixty people in front of us.

Sheesh, you'd think they'd have more than one security check.

Using my shoulder, I wiped sweat from my cheek and fantasized about an icy soda. I repositioned the strap on my laptop case to crisscross over my body and tried to ignore the heat. Maybe if I ran code, my brain would be too sidetracked to think about it.

<c&8#2x02 6l4s6o01 |+2!9)3@8|>

<2&09x#2 #8(3$7*4 =i18n>

<%</p> (rfc2616) :w3.gro>

Raised voices brought me from my temporary reprise. I focused on the military men pushing through the crowd, not caring if they shoved a woman, child, or man aside.

I turned to Jonathan. "What's going on?"

He barely shook his head in response.

They yanked a blond woman from the line, and my gut clenched. I watched wide-eyed as they dragged her kicking, clawing, and screaming to an awaiting van.

Her echoing wails brought cold prickles to my skin.

Was this actually happening? Out here in the open? And why wasn't anybody doing anything?

I glanced around. Nobody even looked in the frantic woman's direction. I turned to Jonathan.

He death-gripped my arm a split second before a military man yanked me in the opposite direction.

Jonathan held tight to me as the guard barked something in Spanish.

Jonathan calmly responded.

The guard gripped my other arm and barked the order again.

Jonathan calmly responded.

The guard gave another yank on my arm, and I grimaced and tried to move closer to Jonathan.

He didn't move, but he seemed to grow in size as he pulled back his shoulders, accentuating his already straight posture, solid muscles, and towering height.

The guard didn't let go of me, but it occurred to me then how small he was next to Jonathan. I'd say the guard stood about five foot eight. Shorter than me even.

Jonathan slowly and deliberately enunciated his Spanish, not so calmly now, more threatening and serious.

The guard switched his narrowed dark eyes to me and then beyond me to Parrot.

I swallowed.

Letting go of my arm, the guard stepped to the side. He jabbed his machine gun in the direction of the security shack and snapped out an order in Spanish.

Still holding on to me, Jonathan gave a little tug. "Get your backpack. Let's go." He glanced over his shoulder and motioned with his head for Parrot to follow.

Leaning down, I swung my oversize backpack over my shoulder. "What's going on?" I whispered.

"Not sure. Be quiet and let me do all the talking."

Not a problem, seeing as how I didn't know the language.

The heat from the asphalt seeped up through my flip-flops as we crossed the tarmac.

Jonathan eased his hold on my bicep, and my muscles immediately pulsed with the release of pressure.

I glanced down at my forearm, where the guard had yanked, and saw deep red stripes. I'd probably bruise.

Another man stood guard at the security shack's door. He shifted his gun and gave the metal door two hard whacks. The sound of his fist connecting with metal vibrated in the air around me.

The door opened and a guard dressed just like the others appeared. Both men nonchalantly pointed their machine guns in our direction, telling us in their silent, threatening terms not to try anything.

Jonathan's hold on my bicep tightened again as he led me through the door. Cigarette smoke and air-conditioning overpowered the small, dim interior, bringing goose bumps to my sweaty body.

To the right, a small window let sunshine filter in. In the back left corner a metal desk sat catty-cornered. A man in a suit sat behind that desk, with another guard standing to his side. Newspaper clippings and wanted posters littered the walls.

The guard who had let us in closed the door and moved into position to block the exit. With his feet spread wide, he held the gun diagonally across his body. He grunted something in Spanish, and Parrot looked at Jonathan. Jonathan nodded once, and Parrot moved away from us to stand by the window.

The guard beside the man in the suit stepped out from behind the desk and came straight at me. I resisted the urge to back up as he approached.

Before I had time to blink, he yanked my backpack off my shoulder, and I sucked in a breath. He grabbed hold of my laptop strap, and I ducked before he yanked that and dislocated my shoulder. Luckily, my ducking at the same time he yanked slid the laptop right over my head without injury.

He tossed my stuff against the wall, and I watched in horror as my laptop bounced against the cement.

"Don't say anything," Jonathan ordered, handing over his duffel bag and indicating Parrot to do the same.

The guard tossed their stuff on top of mine. Briskly he patted down Parrot, Jonathan, and me. Then he shoved Jonathan and me toward the desk. Behind me, I heard a zipper as the guard began rifling through our things.

The man in the suit slowly rose to his feet. His serious brown eyes surveyed me from top to bottom and back up. He picked a cigarette from an ashtray and took a long drag and exhaled, squinting at me through the smoke.

Holding back a cough, I quietly cleared my throat as the man continued to scrutinize me.

What was going on? I wanted more than anything to look at Jonathan, but kept my gaze steady with the man in the suit.

He stubbed his cigarette out and continued studying me as he slowly ran his fingers back and forth across his bristled chin.

He said something to me in Spanish.

"I'm sorry. I don't speak your language."

He let out an annoyed sigh and switched his attention to Jonathan. The two of them began a rapid-fire discussion. Back and forth they spoke, and the more they spoke the more agitated the suited man became.

He slammed his fist down, and I jumped. Jonathan didn't even move. The man jabbed his finger at scattered papers, bringing my attention to his desk and upside-down color sketches of a woman.

I tilted my head slightly, trying to make out the drawings.

Jonathan and the suited man continued their argument as I studied the sketches. Something about the woman seemed familiar.

The phone rattled, and the suited man yanked the receiver from its cradle. As he talked, he turned one of the drawings around so we could see it.

The woman had blond hair and light either blue or green eyes. The large shape of the eyes, the thick upper lashes, and the defiant, alert look flashed my brain back to Barracuda Key. My last mission.

A female agent had interceded when I'd confronted Eduardo Villanueva, the man who killed my parents. The female agent's face had been hidden behind a hood, but those eyes . . . something had seemed familiar.

I stared at the picture, itching to pick it up. This woman had the same eyes. My focus switched as I took in her whole face and my gaze touched each of her features.

These policemen thought I was this woman, probably because of the blond hair and eye color. But to me it was obvious I was not.

I glanced over at Jonathan to find him staring at the picture as well. I wanted more than anything to ask him if he knew that woman, but doubted he'd tell me if he did.

Fastening my attention back on the sketch, I decided the woman was probably in her late twenties or early thirties. Was it a recent drawing, I wondered, or an old one?

A list of aliases headlined the sketch and beneath it her crimes. The crimes were written in Spanish, though, so I focused in on the alias names.

Yetta Blomqvist, Wandella Dacey, Fabiene Uarov, Sabine Hiordano . . . on and on I read the names, all from different nationalities. I almost laughed when I got to the last one, Oki Li Ming. The woman in the sketch was most definitely not Asian. I scanned the names again, but none of them rang a bell.

The man in the suit slammed the phone down, jolting me back to attention.

He snapped a hand out and barked an order to Jonathan.

Jonathan glanced over his shoulder to Parrot and nodded, reached inside his back pocket, then said to me, "Give them your passport."

Unsnapping the side pocket on my cargo pants, I slid my passport out and handed it over.

Behind me, the guard who'd been searching our luggage said something. I glanced over my shoulder to see my backpack wide open, with extra computer batteries, bras, underwear, clothes, and toiletries scattered. I nearly groaned at the sight, not only because my box of tampons was on display, but because it had taken me *forever* to get everything packed.

524

Then I saw my laptop opened and powered up, and my jaw clenched. No one touched my laptop without asking. *No one.*

The guard repeated what he'd said, and I just looked at him.

"Give him your password," Jonathan translated.

"What?!"

"Do it," Jonathan emphasized.

For a couple of seconds I didn't say anything. *Calm down, GiGi, calm down.* Other than Chapling, no one knew how to infiltrate my computer. Different passwords led to different levels of my computer. To any regular person they would find only standard software packages.

"BBCGMPW," I gave him my first-level password, the first initials of my teammates and me. Beaker, Bruiser, Cat, GiGi, Mystic, Parrot, and Wirenut. Just thinking of them helped to calm me down.

Jonathan repeated the letters in Spanish, and the guard typed them in. While he waited for my screen to appear, he pulled a folder from Jonathan's backpack and brought it to the suited man.

I watched as the man rifled through the file. It contained documentation that we had been hired by the North and South Native American Alliance. Proof that we were who we said we were.

Shoving the folder closed, the suited man yanked a piece of paper from a desk drawer. He slammed the blank paper down in front of me and put a pen on top. *"Escribe tu nombre cinco veces."*

"Write your name five times," Jonathan translated.

Normally I wrote with my right hand. But TL taught all of us to use the opposite hand when on a mission. I had to admit, I'd gotten quite good at writing with my left hand.

Hannah Flowers, I scrawled my fake name five times.

The man in the suit tore the paper away and with a hard jaw he studied the signatures, comparing them to my passport.

I felt a smile tug at my mouth, suddenly amused by his mannerisms. Snapping, yanking, banging, and barking. I wanted to tell him that if he were more in control, like Jonathan or TL always were, his point would come across more effectively. The suited man was angry, we all got it. And I bet he was really upset none of us was acting intimidated.

He looked up at me then, and his eyes narrowed. *"¿De qué te estás sonriendo?"* he shouted.

"He wants to know what you're smiling at," Jonathan repeated, and I swore I heard a hint of amusement in his voice.

I flattened my mouth and dropped my head. "*Lo siento.* I'm sorry." I did know how to say that in their language. Plus, I figured the whole dropped-head, submissive thing would make him feel authoritative and not press the issue.

He grunted and walked from behind the desk across the room to the door. I heard him open it and start speaking to the guard posted outside.

With my head still dropped, I looked at the sketch of the woman again. I quietly but quickly reached out, snagged it, and slid it from the desk. I didn't know who this woman was, but I wanted to know. Especially with the similarities to the agent in Barracuda Key who had taken Eduardo.

Carefully, and very rapidly, I folded the drawing into a small square.

"Front of pants," Jonathan barely whispered.

Head still bowed and body held very still, I tucked the sketch down the front of my cargos, wedging it in the elastic of my underwear.

Seconds later the door closed, and the suited man came to stand back behind the desk.

I turned my head a fraction to the right, and moving only my eyes, I peeked at the guard who'd been searching our things.

He was busy clicking through my laptop looking at random files. Many of them fake, serving as decoys in case something like this ever happened.

The man in the suit took his seat behind the desk. I smelled more than heard him light up another cigarette.

Lifting my head, I brought my eyes up to meet his.

He leaned back in his creaky chair and propped his heels on the edge of the desk. Closing his eyes he took a long drag, and then blew it out through his nose.

What a nasty habit.

At least thirty minutes ticked by as Jonathan, Parrot, and I stood there in silence and the suited man continued smoking. I wanted to remind him that secondhand smoke was just as harmful as if we were smoking ourselves. But, of course, I kept my opinion to myself.

The guard finally finished searching our things and came back to his original position standing next to the suited man.

The phone rattled, and everyone in the room except Jonathan jolted.

The man in the suit picked it up, said a few things, and then listened. "Gracias." He hung up the phone. "You are free to leave." He dismissed us using perfect English.

I was astonished. He could speak English? I should've suspected. One of the main things I'd learned in the Specialists was that people were never what they seemed.

Following Jonathan's lead, Parrot and I quickly crammed our belongings into our backpacks and duffels and quietly shuffled from the shack.

Bright heat hit us in a wave as we stepped outside. I took a deep, clean breath, welcoming the muggy warm reprieve from the smoky air-conditioned room.

Beside me Parrot did the same.

I glanced at my watch. We'd been in there for over an hour. *Time flies when you're having fun*. I rolled my eyes at my own stupid humor.

"Don't say anything," Jonathan instructed, quickly leading us toward the gate.

Guillermo, the man who'd greeted us when we first arrived, still stood on the other side of the fence.

A guard with a machine gun opened the chain-link gate and motioned us through.

Silently we filed past. And continuing not to speak, we followed Guillermo through a gravel parking lot, zigzagging around vehicles.

We came to a stop at an old green Land Rover with a rusted white top. It had a tire mounted on its hood, a steel rack on top, and a ladder climbing up the back. A shovel, pick, and hatchet were strapped to the white top. The vehicle looked well used, uncomfortable, and in dire need of a bath.

Guillermo turned the knob on the back window, and it popped up. Jonathan tossed his duffel in, grabbed my backpack and did the same, then signaled for Parrot.

"Climb in," Jonathan told us.

Taking my laptop off, I handed it to Jonathan and climbed up through the window. Jonathan gave me my computer, and I crawled across our stuff he'd tossed in. Two padded benches sat facing each other. I took the one on the left. Parrot climbed in and took the bench across from me. Jonathan closed and latched the back window, cutting off our meager fresh air.

Through the muddy side glass I watched as he and Guillermo came down the side of the vehicle to the front. Guillermo climbed behind the wheel while Jonathan hopped into the passenger side. Guillermo cranked the diesel engine, grinded it into gear, and drove off.

Jonathan slid open the rectangular window that connected the front to the back. "If you guys need air, open the sides."

Parrot and I moved at once, winding open the side windows to let in a stream of humid air. Guillermo and Jonathan opened their windows and began a conversation in Spanish.

I looked at Parrot.

"They're talking about what happened in the guard shack," he translated.

"So Guillermo's one of us?" I whispered to Parrot.

"I'm with the IPNC," Guillermo answered.

"Oh. Sorry." I didn't know why I'd apologized. But it embarrassed me Guillermo had heard my whisper. I should've just asked him straight on.

Guillermo drove us from the airport and onto a two-lane highway.

Parrot pushed out what sounded like a stressed breath.

"You okay?" I asked.

"GiGi, I was really scared back there."

I smiled a little at his admission. "I know—me, too."

"You've been on a lot of missions. Does that kind of stuff happen all the time?"

I thought back to being kidnapped in Ushbania, thrown in a dungeon in Rissala, and coming face-to-face with my parents' killer. "Yes." And strangely enough, I didn't feel nearly as shaken up as usual.

I mean, I'd actually been amused at the gruff manner of the man in the suit. If that would have happened on my first mission, I would have been a nervous wreck. It made me feel a bit evolved, for lack of a better word. Like I was finally getting the hang of this new life of mine.

Parrot didn't say anything else, and so I turned to the world outside. I tried to take in some scenery, but the muddy windows made it nearly impossible.

Sometime later we exited the highway onto a dirt road. Parrot and I gripped our benches as the Land Rover bumped down the road.

"You doing okay?" Parrot asked.

I smiled at the sweet question. "Yeah, I'm okay. You?"

Parrot shrugged. "I'll survive."

I reached across the small distance and squeezed his knee. "Remember I'm here for you. I'm a great listener. And I'm excellent at keeping secrets. If you ever want to talk . . ."

"Thanks." He looked away, and I took that as my cue he was done with the topic.

The Land Rover hit a pothole, jolting me, and I felt the sketch scratch my bare skin. "Oh!" I reached inside the front of my cargos and pulled it out. Gingerly, I unfolded the sweaty drawing, praying the wetness wouldn't tear it. I needed to get it scanned and into my laptop before it was damaged.

I blew on it, trying to dry it a bit.

Using his T-shirt, Parrot dried his sweaty face. "Hey, pretty slick. I didn't know you took that."

I smiled at his surprise.

"Can I see it?" Parrot asked.

I handed it over. "Careful, it's wet."

Gingerly, he took it, cradling it in his hands.

Pulling the rubber band from my limp ponytail, I smoothed my damp hair and redid it. "What does it say below the picture?"

He studied it, balancing it in his hands as the Land Rover bumped down the road. "She's wanted for arson, wire fraud, assault, larceny, burglary, stalking, conspiracy, robbery, drug manufacturing, embezzlement, perjury, extortion, murder, forgery, money laundering, manslaughter, kidnapping . . ."

On and on he read, and when he finally finished, I simply blinked. "Is that even possible? For one person to commit all those crimes?"

With a shrug, he handed the paper back. "I don't know what to tell you."

"Just because it says it on paper doesn't mean it's true," Jonathan commented through the window. He nodded to the sketch. "Get that scanned into your computer as soon as you can. I want to know who that woman is."

"Yes, sir." He'd read my mind.

Then the Land Rover jerked to a stop, and the drawing tore in half.

‹SIX›

I stared at the moist, frayed edges of the torn picture, and my heart sank. The tear zigzagged through one eye, down the nose, and slashed across the mouth. Key features that any identification program would need to make a match to this sketch.

I should've never gotten it out and opened it up. Especially in a bumpy vehicle. For a genius I could be real stupid sometimes. Now I may never know who this woman was.

Parrot reached across and touched my shoulder. "We'll fix it, GiGi. We'll fix it. I'll help you."

Giving Parrot a tiny smile I really didn't feel, I pulled a folder from my laptop case and opened it up. I slid two pieces of paper out, carefully laid the sketch between them, and tucked the papers back inside the folder. With a sigh, I put it back inside my laptop case and zipped it up. Why did I always make such stupid mistakes?

Guillermo rolled up his window and shoved open his door. "Okay, this is it," he said, interrupting my disappointment. "We go the rest of the way on horseback."

Jonathan rolled up his window, too. "Close up back there."

Parrot and I wound the side glass shut while Guillermo popped open the back hatch and began unloading our things.

I climbed out first and came to an abrupt stop.

I looked around and saw green. Everywhere. In every shade imaginable. Huge, gigantic leaves, some as big as me. Weird plants like nothing I'd ever seen. And trees—my head dropped back as I followed one all the way up—trees as big as skyscrapers.

I turned a slow circle—I couldn't see anything but green. I couldn't even tell where the Land Rover had come from. It appeared as if the foliage had immediately covered our tracks.

And—I straightened a bit—the jungle seemed to pulse and grow right in front of me as it closed us in.

I shut my eyes and gave my head a quick shake.

"I'd recommend you change your shoes," Guillermo suggested, nodding down at my flip-flops.

I completely agreed. Flip-flops and trekking through a jungle were two things that obviously did not go together.

Kneeling beside my backpack, I dug through the disorderliness the guard had left and found a pair of socks and what I affectionately referred to as my kick-butt boots. TL had given each of us a pair.

Very military, with steel toes and thick heels, the black boots laced halfway up my calves. Parrot already wore his, so I sat on the Land Rover's bumper and tied mine on.

"This way," Guillermo said as he stepped through a humongous bush.

"Be back in a minute." Jonathan threw his bag over his shoulder before disappearing into the same pumped-up greenery.

I finished with my boots and zipped my backpack closed.

Jonathan reappeared first, with Guillermo close behind, each with two horses in tow.

Parrot caught sight of the animals and breathed a sigh, as if just looking at them brought him comfort. With a slight smile, he stepped right up.

"Hey, beautiful," he cooed, stroking the muzzle. "I bet you're about five years old." He ran his hand across the horse's neck and down the length of its body.

The brown horse huffed and twitched as Parrot crossed in front of it and trailed his hands along its other side. "You like that, do you?" He laughed.

The brown horse huffed and twitched some more, and I smiled. "I think she has a crush on you."

"The feeling's mutual." Parrot grabbed hold of the horse's mane and effortlessly swung himself up, like he was climbing onto a tricycle instead of a huge animal.

He looked up at Guillermo. "Sorry, I didn't ask. May I ride her? What's her name?"

"Her name's Abrienda. And, yes, you can ride her. I don't think she'd like it too much if I separated you anyway."

Parrot leaned down and nuzzled her ear. "Did you hear that? It's you and me, Abrienda."

My smile got bigger. I couldn't help it. This was the happiest, most content I'd seen Parrot in a long time.

Jonathan handed Parrot his backpack, and Parrot strapped it to the horse's saddle. Guillermo and Jonathan fastened the rest of the duffels and backpacks to the saddles, shoved their feet into the stirrups, and swung themselves up. Leaving me still sitting on the Land Rover's bumper.

All three guys looked down at me.

I checked out Guillermo's pretty white horse, Jonathan's friendly speckled one, Parrot's gentle brown one, and then I looked at mine . . . and swallowed.

Shiny and black, mine stood large and fierce. It might have been my imagination, but he seemed *a lot* bigger than the other horses. Like leader-of-the-pack kind of big.

The horse didn't move as he proudly stared back at me. And I swore his eyes narrowed with dark mischievousness. It was as if he was thinking, *Ah, Blondie's scared of me. That's good. That's reeaally good.*

Nice horsey.

"He's friendly," Guillermo unconvincingly reassured me.

Uh-huh. Sure. "Maybe if I knew his name."

"Diablo," Guillermo answered.

I eyed the horse. "Diablo. Does that mean something?"

"Satan," Parrot said, trying to hide his amusement.

Great. Shouldn't that tell everybody something? Hello? The horse's name is Satan. That couldn't be good. "Can't I ride double with one of you?"

Guillermo shook his head. "Sorry, the trail's too treacherous for double. Diablo's used to strangers. And he's used to the jungle. He knows where he's going. You'll hardly have to do anything at all."

Jonathan's saddle squeaked as he repositioned himself. "Take your laptop off and strap it to the carabiners on the saddle. It'll give you more balance when you mount."

Recalling my brief horse-riding training, I pretended to be confident as I walked around Diablo, running my hand over his body, letting him feel my touch. I took my laptop case and hooked it to the saddle. I wedged my left

532

boot into his stirrup, grabbed hold of the saddle, and swung right on up. I couldn't help but sigh with relief.

Diablo growled, making his lips vibrate with the rush of air.

I stiffened a little with the sound.

Guillermo walked his horse past the Land Rover. "It'll take us two hours to get there. It'll be dark by then. Everybody stay close. You do *not* want to get lost in the jungle at night."

Jonathan nodded for Parrot and me to follow Guillermo. "I'm bringing up the rear," he said.

We left the small clearing, and our Land Rover, behind and disappeared into the jungle.

In silence we rode in single file, spending most of our time tucked close to our horses to avoid the low-lying branches and vines.

Ducked down on Diablo, I tried to take in some scenery, but my crouched position made it impossible. I ended up resting my hands and cheek on the saddle horn, and for a span of time I stared off to the right watching green Goliath-like leaves, plants, and trees go by.

At some point along the way, I yawned and closed my eyes and melted into the rocking motion of Diablo's steady gait. . . .

I dreamed of David smiling, his eyes doing that sexy crinkling thing as he looked back at me. Of his linking pinkies with me, warmly whispering something into my ear. I dreamed of burying my nose in his neck and slowly breathing in his unique David scent. Of—

"GiGi."

—kissing me, nuzzling my neck—

"GiGi."

I jerked straight up in the saddle.

"You need to stay awake," Jonathan warned. "Look to your left."

Rubbing my eye, I looked to the left . . . and froze.

We were on a cliff.

And it dropped straight down.

Hundreds, *thousands* of feet down. I couldn't even see the bottom.

Not moving a muscle in my body, I stared at the ledge we were on. Each time one of Diablo's hoofs came down, pebbles skidded over the edge and disappeared into God knows where.

With my heart galloping, I inched my head to the right . . . and froze.

Another drop-off.

A really, really, *really* big drop-off.

"J-J-Jonathan?"

"Calm down, GiGi. Diablo knows what he's doing. Concentrate on not moving. Don't do anything to set him off balance."

Locking every muscle in my body, I stared hard at the black hairs of Diablo's mane. I concentrated on not moving, not breathing. I heard a short, choppy, shallow intake of air and realized it was me. In my peripheral vision, the ledge inched by as Diablo *clop-clopped* along, following Guillermo's horse.

Squeezing my eyes shut, I forced a swallow, trying to moisten my mouth. I kept my eyes squeezed shut. I'd rather see darkness than the reality of the minuscule ledge and the vast jungle around me.

I heard another choppy breath come in and out of my mouth and then a deafening roar. "Wh-what was that?!"

‹SEVEN›

"It's a waterfall, GiGi," Jonathan calmly responded. "Relax. You don't want to spook Diablo with your tenseness. Concentrate on unlocking your muscles. You're stiff as a board."

"That's because there is a HUGE dropoff on both sides and a TINY ledge supporting us and a NIAGARA-like waterfall."

"But it's easier on the horse if you move with him. Just relax."

With my eyes still closed, I drew a long breath in through my nose and blew it out slowly through my mouth. *Calm down, GiGi. Jonathan's right. You need to relax. For Diablo's sake and everyone's safety.*

Again, in through my nose and out through my mouth.

But . . . IT WASN'T WORKING!

With a gust of air, Diablo shook his head and took a few steps back.

"Calm. Down," Jonathan gritted through clenched teeth.

"I'm trying!" I hissed back.

My horse took more steps back, forcing Parrot's horse to back up, too.

"GiGi," Parrot snapped. "Please. Calm. Down."

And then I did the only thing I could think of. I recited code, this time out loud.

"<A ferh= 78hic>

"<!TNEMELE (led|sni)>

"<(%owofl)>"*

Somewhere in my subconscious, I registered Diablo calming down a little.

"<%oi1 7m %oxl 6n>"

Continuing to mumble code, I concentrated on my muscles, flexing, releasing, leaving them loose. I straightened my back and said another string of code, focusing on Diablo's movements and allowing my body to feel them.

"*<deru [DK] gasi {LP}>*"

"Good, GiGi, good," I heard Jonathan say.

I opened my eyes and looked somewhat casually at Guillermo's back as he rode in front of me. I glanced at the ledge stretched in front of him. It was definitely as small as my imagination had made it out to be. We had only about twenty feet to go before we were back on an expanse of jungle ground.

"*<MNB / asd / POI />*"

To my left a waterfall poured from the side of a cliff, gushing through holes in the rock. It roared like an animal as water shot out and dropped into the eternal bliss.

As comfortable as I now felt, I didn't look down. I didn't kid myself that I'd be indifferent to the drop-off. Instead, I concentrated on watching the waterfall, moving with my horse's stride, and reciting more code.

Moments later Diablo left the ledge and stepped onto a cleared area of the jungle. I peeked over my shoulder to see Parrot and Jonathan leave the ledge as well. I glanced beyond Jonathan, and my jaw dropped. The skinny ledge stretched a good solid mile between the two jungles. I couldn't believe I'd just come across that.

Parrot moved his horse up beside mine. "You okay?"

I nodded. "Wow."

He swiped sweat from his face. "No kidding."

"Were you nervous?"

Parrot gave me an incredulous look, and I laughed.

"Seems Diablo is just as much of a nerd as you are," Parrot teased. "Who would have thought code would calm him?"

I gave Diablo's neck a pat. "Nerds unite."

Parrot pointed over his shoulder through the thick overgrowth to where the sun was setting. "It'll be dark soon."

I nodded.

We rode in silence side by side across a clearing that, as soon as we passed through it, closed in to surround us with foliage. My thoughts drifted to what had gone on today: the sketch of the woman, the plane ride, security . . . "Hey, Parrot, what did those girls say in front of us at the security checkpoint?"

Parrot shrugged. "It's nothing. Don't worry about it."

Yeah, right. "Tell me."

"Really, it's nothing."

"*Tell* me."

Parrot sighed. "They thought you and Jonathan were, ya know, together."

"*What?*" I laughed. "But he's *old*."

"They . . . thought he was your sugar daddy."

I coughed. "My *what?*"

"Your sugar daddy. Ya know, one of those men who—"

"I know what a sugar daddy is. Oh my *God*. That's gross."

We both laughed, and I realized how nice it was to have a momentary reprieve from the tension of this mission to just enjoy each other's humor.

"Single it up," Guillermo directed us as the foliage closed in tighter around us. "We have only about five miles left. And we're not outfitted for camping, so keep up."

Parrot took his spot behind me, and we continued our safari through the Junoesque. The sun soon disappeared, and darkness settled in around us. The farther into the jungle's thick overgrowth we trekked, the blacker it became.

I'd never known darkness like this. I couldn't see Guillermo in front of me or even my horse, Diablo, for that matter. I felt, not saw, the foliage around me, brushing my arms and legs and occasionally slapping my face.

If not for Guillermo, Parrot, Jonathan, and, of course, Diablo, I would've been out of my mind in fear of what might have been out there in the inky night.

As if on cue, the jungle suddenly became alive with sound. Click clacks. Snaps. Croaks. High-pitched wails. A deafening hiss and hum. It came in stereo from all directions. A symphony of bugs, an orchestra of nocturnal animals. It was the craziest, most all-encompassing sound I'd ever experienced.

Overwhelmed with the energy and overpowering sounds, I hunched down close to Diablo and pressed my fingers to my ears. "Is this normal?" I nearly shouted.

"Yes," Guillermo shouted back.

And then suddenly I felt them, biting my neck, my forearms, my ears, and any exposed skin they could get to. "They're attacking me!" I yelled.

In the darkness I fumbled for my backpack and unzipped the front. I dug out my bug repellant and started spraying it on me, in the air, on Diablo. It helped. A little.

I shoveled blindly through my backpack and found the one and only jacket I'd packed. Frantically, I shoved my arms into it and zipped it up. I'd roast in this heat and humidity, but at least my arms would be covered from the bugs.

Ahead of me Guillermo lit a lamp, and immediately it cast light around us. I sucked in a breath at the sight.

Bugs. Everywhere.

Big ones. Small ones. All colors.

Like something out of a sci-fi movie.

Again I began spraying the air with bug repellant. The insects merely flew through the fog as if it gave them a renewed strength.

Guillermo stopped his horse.

"What are you doing?" I sprayed a red one coming right at me. "We need to gallop through this stuff."

"It'll be like this the whole rest of the way," Guillermo called over the sound.

"What?!" Was he kidding?

Guillermo dismounted from his horse, slid a machete from his saddle, walked over to a tree, and sliced a tumorlike growth from the side of the trunk. He scooped up a handful of tiny squirming bugs, rubbed them together in his hands, then smeared brown liquid guts on his neck, arms, face, and through his hair and bushy beard.

Ew! "What is that?"

"Termites." He scooped a handful and brought it to me.

I shook my head. "No, no, no, no, no." Termite guts were going nowhere near my skin.

With a shrug, he continued on to Parrot, who immediately took the bugs, squished them, and began rubbing the goo on himself. Jonathan did the same. I cringed as I watched them, feeling a little sick to my stomach.

Something sharp sank into my exposed neck. I swatted it and felt the same sharpness on my cheek, then my thumb, then my wrist. Screw this. Bring on the termite guts. "Okay, I'll take some!" I yelled almost desperately.

Guillermo brought me a handful of squirming termites, and I didn't stop to think. I took them, rubbed them between my hands, and began spreading the gut liquid on my exposed skin. I didn't even want to *think* of what I must look like.

Within seconds, the bugs flew right past me. Like I had an invisible force field around me. "What about the horses?"

Guillermo climbed back up in his saddle. "They'll be fine. These bugs don't like their blood."

I surveyed Diablo's body, and sure enough he stood bug-free.

"And the village we're going to?" I asked. "Are we going to have to wear termite goop there, too?"

"They burn special spices that ward off the bugs," Guillermo answered.

Oh, thank God.

Guillermo gave his horse a gentle nudge, and we were on our way again. The small lamp he carried gave us a dim yellow glow to navigate by. And as the minutes ticked by, I became used to the jungle's nighttime opera.

No one spoke as we rode along. No one *could* speak with the noise. The darkness seemed to get even darker, if that were possible. Seconds ticked into minutes and at least another hour went by. When *would* we be there? Hadn't Guillermo said it would be only a couple of hours way back at the Land Rover?

"How much longer?" Parrot called through the night.

I smiled as that question brought a sudden memory of my parents to my mind. I'd been five, and my parents and I were in a car. Dad was driving, and Mom was in the passenger seat. I didn't remember where we were going, but I was restless and couldn't wait to get there.

"How much longer?" I'd whined with excitement.

"'Bout another fifteen minutes," my dad replied.

Fifteen minutes went by.

"How much longer?" I asked again, fidgeting with my seat belt.

"'Bout another fifteen minutes," my dad replied.

And on it went, fifteen minutes going by, me asking my dad, and my dad answering the same way. We probably drove for hours having that exact conversation. My dad had either been incredibly patient or truly enjoying my excited misery.

I sighed through my smile, enjoying the bone-deep warmth that came with a memory of my parents. I reached down and rubbed Diablo, just needing some contact and touch.

A flashing flame in the distance brought my attention back to the present. I squinted and made out a few lights scattered through the thick foliage. I kept my eyes peeled to the flickering glow as we drew closer. I saw some sort of hut come into view, and then another, and another.

Diablo followed Guillermo and his horse through a maze of enormous plants, and then we stepped into a clearing. And it was like stepping back into another century.

Fires surrounded by stone barriers flickered throughout the village in no particular order. A large circular-shaped thatched-roof hut occupied the center of the clearing. So large I estimated it could hold approximately fifty people. Tall, flaming torches marked the north, south, east, and west corners of the hut. Smaller, triangular-shaped huts dotted the landscape around the larger one, and a few square ones scattered the area as well.

Although I couldn't see well through the dim light put off by the fires and torches, it appeared as if each hut had a small garden in the back.

An opening on each of those triangular dwellings signified its entrance. Other than that, there were no openings in the straw structures. The square ones, however, had no walls at all, only thatched roofs. At such a late hour, it stood to reason the place sat quiet and still. Everyone was probably asleep.

A movement off to the left drew my attention, and I watched as a dark-haired man walked straight across the clearing without a glance in our direction. With his neatly combed hair, khaki pants, white shirt, and boots, he looked to be in his early twenties. Maybe a college student? An open book in hand, completely oblivious to his surroundings, he pushed his metal-rimmed glasses up as he read and continued marching across the village.

I almost laughed. I hadn't expected to see a studious little nerd reading a book in the middle of a jungle.

Guillermo urged his horse forward, and we followed. Silently, the four of us filed into the nighttime clearing. Diablo did his vibrating-lip, gush-of-air-out-of-his-mouth thing, and the sound ricocheted through the night.

The nerd jerked at the intrusion and whipped around. His book went one way and his glasses the other. He stood there for a second in shock, staring at us coming toward him. I realized then what we must look like, soaked through from sweat and the humidity, with dried brown termite guts all over our skin and hair I'd probably run screaming in the opposite direction if I saw us.

The nerd gave his head a quick shake, and I watched with amusement as he scrambled to pick up his book and glasses. He blew the dust from his lenses and slipped them on, then went back to staring at us.

His mannerisms reminded me . . . of me.

Huh.

Guillermo brought his horse to a stop right in front of the nerd and said something in Spanish.

"I'm sorry. I don't speak Spanish," the nerd responded.

Yep, definitely reminded me of me.

"My name is Guillermo. This is Hannah," he introduced, nodding to me, "Flint, and Shane. We're here for the talks."

The nerd's face brightened. "Oh! Right! Right!" He pushed his glasses up his nose. "I'm Professor Quirk. I'm the resident expert on the cave drawings."

I blinked. "*You're* the professor?" I'd imagined him a *lot* older. "But you're so young."

Professor Quirk looked right at me. "And your purpose here is . . . ?" he asked with a bit of playfulness to his tone.

"I'm here as your quote/unquote assistant. I'm the computer specialist."

"*You're* the computer specialist?" He blinked. "But you're so young."

I narrowed my eyes. "Touché."

Behind his wire-rimmed glasses, he imitated my narrowed eyes.

So this was the guy I'd be holed up with in a cave for the next week. I wonder how *that's* going to go.

Professor Quirk pointed to the other side of the clearing. "You can corral your horses over there." He directed our attention to the triangular-shaped huts bordering the left side of the clearing. "Those first two are for single men." Then he indicated the ones bordering the right of the clearing. "First two over here are for single women. All the other huts are for the families. This big one in the middle is the ceremonial one. It's where the talks will take place."

Guillermo nodded. "Thanks."

"No problem. See you all tomorrow." With that, Professor Quirk turned and continued on his path.

Guillermo led the way through the clearing toward the other side where some horses stood corralled. As we passed the huts, I peeked into the openings but saw only darkness inside. I wished there was another girl with me so I wouldn't have to go into the "single-women" hut by myself. At least Parrot had Jonathan and Guillermo.

We came to a stop at the corral, and all three guys swung their legs over the saddle and effortlessly slid from their horses. I pulled my boots from the stirrups, lifted my right leg to swing it over the saddle, and instantaneously felt a cramp. "Ohhh."

Grimacing, I dragged my leg the rest of the way over the saddle and plunked down to the dirt. My legs immediately began to spasm. "Oh, my God." I grabbed my thigh and massaged it.

The guys unhooked our bags from the horses. They took the saddles and harnesses off. They lined up all the gear along the corral and led the horses inside the gate. They did all this while I continued crouching, massaging my legs. How they could move, I had no idea. One of them might have to carry me to my hut.

Parrot grabbed my stuff and came over to me. "Walk it off. You'll feel a lot better in a minute."

As Guillermo led my horse away, I took my first steps, gritting my teeth at the ache.

A few seconds into my hobbling, Parrot came to an abrupt stop. I glanced up at him first, and then followed his line of sight across the clearing.

There in the doorway of the huge center hut, lit by one of the torches, stood a beefy man with a Mohawk and a tattooed chin. His face held hardness, his eyes stoic darkness.

"Talon," Parrot whispered.

‹EIGHT›

Through the darkness I stared at Talon as he looked back at us. In the past year I'd been with the Specialists I'd seen some real scary bad guys. Talon stood short and squatty, and even from the distance I saw the evil in him. This was one man not to mess with.

Standing beside me, Parrot made no move. I could almost feel the fear vibrating off him.

Jonathan stepped up behind us. "You're in disguise," he reminded Parrot. "Talon has no idea who you are."

Parrot barely nodded his comprehension.

Guillermo strode past us. "Come on. Let's call it a night."

Carrying our duffel bags and backpacks, we made our way through the village, crossing to the side of Talon, who still stood in the entryway to the big circular hut. In my peripheral vision, I saw Parrot keep his vision glued to the ground. I chanced a glance at Talon and saw him staring right at Parrot.

Was it possible he recognized him?

No way. I barely even recognized him.

We came to a stop at the first triangular-shaped hut, one of the two that Professor Quirk designated as the "single-men" hut. Guillermo crouched to step inside.

"Wait." I stopped him. "What about me?" Weren't they going to walk me to my hut? Granted, it sat right on the other side of the clearing, but still.

Guillermo glanced up. "Sorry. Single men aren't allowed to go near the single-women huts after nightfall. You'll be fine." With that, he disappeared into the straw structure.

Single men couldn't go near single women? What was this, the 1800s?

I turned to Jonathan, hoping he'd have something better to say.

He merely nodded. "Guillermo's right. You'll be fine."

"B-but how do I know which hut?" Were they kidding me? This was ridiculous.

"Professor Quirk said the first two are designated for single women," Jonathan said.

"Yes. Still, what do I do? Do I look inside of one and if it's packed go to the next one? Do I find an empty spot on the ground inside? Is there a cot? A hammock? My God, am I going to get a blanket? *A sheet?* What if there's nothing nowhere? Do I sleep outside? What about wild animals? Should I find some more of that termite stuff? What if—"

Jonathan put his hand on my shoulder, much like TL did when I slipped into one of my hysterical, neurotic moments. "Calm. Down. You. Will. Be. Fine." Carefully Jonathan enunciated each word, probably so they could sink into my overloaded brain. "Peek your head inside the first hut. If you don't see a place to sleep, then go to the second hut. There will be a bed for you in one or the other, I promise. It may be a hammock. It may be a blanket on the floor. I don't know, but there will be something. I promise."

He gave my shoulder a little shake. "Did you understand everything I said?"

I blew out a shaky breath, knowing I was acting ridiculous. "Yes."

"Good. We'll see you in the morning." Jonathan ducked into the single-men hut, leaving me alone with Parrot.

He had to be tied up in knots, yet I was the one freaking over a stupid hut. "How are you?" I asked, reaching for him.

Parrot didn't respond to my touch. With a face void of emotion, he nodded across the clearing. "Go ahead. I'll stand here and make sure you're okay."

"Do you want to tal—"

"Go ahead," he interrupted me, making it more than obvious he didn't want to talk.

With a sigh, I turned and made my way through the darkness across the clearing to the single-women huts. Halfway there, I glanced over my shoulder to make sure Parrot still stood there. Sure enough, he did. As much as I absolutely adored him, this moment made me appreciate him even more. This was all I needed. Someone to watch me and make sure I would be okay. He'd recognized that.

David would've recognized that, too.

I reached the first hut and ducked inside. It took a few seconds for my pupils to adjust to the dark. In the dimness I made out hammocks hanging randomly throughout the space. Squinting my eyes, I ran my gaze over each sleeping hammock occupant and located an empty one in the back.

I peeked my head back out the opening, exchanged an "I'm okay" wave with Parrot, and then meandered through the sleeping bodies to the back.

I didn't bother changing or cleaning up at all—I was thoroughly exhausted. I just dropped my things, climbed into the hammock, and stretched out. I lay there, staring up at the thatched roof, idly listening to the heavy breaths and soft snores of the other women.

I inhaled deeply and picked up a woodsy-spicy smell. I willed myself to sleep, but thoughts of the day occupied my mind. The jungle, horseback riding, bugs, Guillermo, the Land Rover, security, the sketch . . . Who was that woman? I felt confident she and the agent I had spoken to on my last mission were one and the same. But who was that agent?

I rolled over in my hammock, closed my eyes, and my mind drifted to David. . . . I wished so much he was here.

***

A gentle touch to my shoulder made my eyes flutter open. A girl about my age stood above me, softly smiling down. I blinked a few times before focusing in on her olive skin, shiny straight black hair, and unique light blue eyes.

"You're Jaaci," I said, realizing she was the Junoesquean girl who had walked from the jungle carrying the Mother Nature vase. She was the whole reason we were here.

Nodding, she took a step back, and I swung my legs over the side of the hammock. I took a second to look around the hut now that daylight had come.

Bamboo poles had been tied together and used as supports for the thatch walls and ceiling. Bushels of fruit and vegetables hung on ropes from the bamboo poles. Seeing the bananas made my stomach growl.

Rough, splintery boards lined the walls. Personal items had been placed on them, things like clothes, small boxes, bowls with jewelry, blankets, baskets with beads, and strips of cloth.

As I watched, a half dozen tribal women busied themselves unhooking hammocks, rolling them, and storing them on the boards next to the other personal items. The women all dressed the same, in colorful, lightweight, knee-length dresses with leather sandals. They all had black hair worn in a long braid. Some wore jewelry, some had bright tattoos on their ankles or wrists, and most looked to be in their teens or early twenties.

"Axw xaqu xe foxlu," Jaaci said.

I scrunched my face. "Do you speak English, by any chance?"

Jaaci shook her head and shrugged, obviously having no idea what I'd asked.

She held out a small a box containing a bar of soap, a rag, and a comb. *"Foxlu."*

"Bath," I understood. "Yes, definitely." I touched my crusty termite-gut hair, then ran my tongue over my unbrushed teeth. *Ugh.* Definitely time to bathe.

Like I'd seen the other women do, I unclipped and rolled my hammock and stowed it on one of the rough wood planks.

I rifled around in my backpack and found soap, a toothbrush, a comb, and a change of clothes. At the bottom of my backpack lay my little stuffed giraffe, the one David had won for me on our date. Just seeing it brought a smile to my face.

I followed all the other girls out into the early morning. Awesome-smelling food assaulted my senses, and I inhaled deeply. I realized that I hadn't eaten since lunch yesterday.

In the daylight, I took in the village. No one was up and around but us girls. All the other huts sat quiet. I checked my watch, calculated the time change, and suddenly felt groggy. Five in the morning? Were they kidding me? It was inhumane to be up at this hour. No wonder nobody else was up and around.

With a sweet smile, Jaaci nodded me in the direction the other girls were walking. We left the clearing and entered the jungle.

Minutes later we stepped onto the bank of a wide, softly rolling river. The girls began taking off their dresses and stepping naked into the water. I stood for a second, stunned, unable to completely wrap my brain around the fact that a bunch of girls were getting naked, out in the open, and stepping into a river. To bathe, nonetheless. And absolutely unselfconsciously, at that.

None of them paid me one single mind as they took their rags and soap and washed. They didn't even look at each other. Obviously, this was something they did together every day.

This must be the single women's time to bathe, I realized, noticing no one else around.

"Axw enob," Jaaci called, waving me into the water.

Well, I could stand here and remain clothed and filthy or get over my hangups, strip, and be clean. I ran my tongue over my teeth again, remembered the crusty termite guts, and opted to get clean.

I fought the urge to cover myself with my hands and tried to act as if I did this every day. Stark white next to their brown bodies, I stepped into the slightly chilly river, my foot slipped on a mossy rock, and I slapped down on my butt.

Inwardly, I groaned. Of all the times for my klutziness to come out, it had to be when I was stepping naked into a river. Leave it to me to make the grand entrance.

A few of the girls glanced quizzically in my direction and then went right back to bathing. A few others let out harmless, good-natured laughs. And a few others just stared at me. *What? Haven't you seen a blond-haired naked white girl sprawled across the rocks before?*

No. Come to think of it, they most likely hadn't.

As soon as I could, I slipped into the water to hide myself and sort of swished my arms and legs around. I glanced down into the water and could make out everything to my knees. Below that, though, my legs disappeared into murkiness. "There aren't any weird fish in here, are there? Piranhas?"

A few of the girls gave me that same quizzical look, and I sighed. I wished someone around here spoke English.

"Weos?" Jaaci held out a brown bar of soap and a rag.

I sighed through a smile, realizing I'd left my soap onshore, and took hers. "Thanks. My name's Hannah, by the way." I pointed to my chest. "Hannah."

"Ha-na," Jaaci tried.

I nodded.

Seeing as how most of the girls had finished and were getting dressed, I began scrubbing my body as quickly as I could. I didn't want to be the only girl left in the water.

A whistling in the distance had me glancing around. That couldn't be a wild animal.

The whistling got a little closer. The pitched vibrations sounded like something from an opera. If that was a wild animal, it certainly had talent.

The sound came closer, and I narrowed in on a spot of jungle about twenty feet in front of me. From the overgrown foliage stepped Professor Quirk.

He wore the same clothes as last night, only wrinkled and untucked. His hair stood on end, his glasses were foggy, and he hadn't shaved. He'd either been up all night or fallen asleep in his clothes and hadn't bothered to clean up yet.

Segueing into a new song, he flipped a page in the book he held and continued reading. As he neared the river he briefly glanced up, then stepped onto a rock that protruded from the water. He stepped on another rock and then another, slowly making his way across the river, still reading his book.

Halfway across he stopped and slowly turned in our direction, obviously realizing there were a bunch of naked girls bathing and dressing. Through his foggy glasses, he stood very still and stared at us.

I crouched real low in the water to the point where only my head stuck out. Even then, I knew I had to be a beacon next to all the other girls. None of them seemed to even notice Professor Quirk standing on a river rock in the distance, staring at us.

I opened my mouth to shout for him to leave, but something made me stop. I studied his dazed stance and realized . . . he didn't even see us. Chapling looked exactly like that when he got lost in thought. And I knew from experience that when I got wrapped up into code, the entire world disappeared into nothing.

Professor Quirk reached behind his glasses and rubbed his eyes before turning back to his book and continuing on across the river.

I finished scrubbing away the termite guts and stood thigh deep scrubbing my hair.

"Jyyzf," Jaaci said.

I opened my eyes and turned around. "What?"

She pointed to my backside. *"Jyyzf."*

Twisting, I looked behind me. Something black and slimy was attached to my right butt cheek.

What the . . . ?

I twisted and looked a little closer . . . "Oh my God, a leech!" I reached for it—

"*Le!*" Jaaci yelled, shooting through the water at me. She grabbed my hands and shoved them away.

I jostled in place. "Get it! Oh my God, get it!"

Jaaci held her hands up in a universal sign for hold still. She got down on her hands and knees and felt around on the river bottom.

I jostled some more, blinking soap from my stinging eyes. "Get it!"

She brought a small flat rock from the river and turned me around. Using the sharpest edge, she slowly scraped it between my butt cheek and the leech. I tried real hard to hold still, but OH MY GOD I HAD A LEECH ATTACHED TO MY BUTT!

It stung a little as I felt a tiny suction release. She took the flat rock, sliced the leech in half, and threw both halves across the river and into a bush. I watched the pieces fly through the air, hoping beyond hope that thing was dead.

I looked back at my butt cheek and saw a bloody trail. "What do I do?" Stitches? A shot? Antibacterial ointment?

Jaaci took her soap and rag and motioned for me to clean the area. I scrubbed and rubbed so hard, I nearly took my skin off.

With a laugh, Jaaci signaled for me to stop.

As quick as I could, I rinsed my hair and beelined it out of there. So much for bathing in a river. From this point on, I think I'd rather be dirty and stinky.

I dried off, dressed, and combed my hair, then followed all the girls into the jungle.

About halfway through, we passed a bunch of guys as they made their way down to the river. Carrying soap, I assumed they were going to bathe as well. I caught sight of Parrot and waved. He gave me a small smile in return. I searched the line for Jonathan or Guillermo, but didn't see them. Maybe the older guys bathed separately from the younger ones.

I realized as I stared at the line that none of the guys or girls were looking at each other. With their gazes focused down, they silently filed past not speaking, touching, or looking.

What the . . . ? How weird. I'd have to remember to ask someone about that. Someone who spoke English, that is.

We girls exited the jungle back into the clearing. It was 6:30 now, and people were up and milling around. Children laughed and played with sticks, hitting a rock around. Behind the triangular-shaped huts, women knelt in the gardens, tending to the crops. Men gathered around the big ceremonial hut, discussing matters. Underneath the square open structures, elderly women busied themselves cooking over open flames.

When did they all bathe? I found myself oddly wondering.

It occurred to me as I watched everyone how historical this event was. At no other time in history had representatives from both North and South American tribes gathered in one place. I felt truly honored to watch history in the making. In fact, it gave me goose bumps. . . . Silly, I know. But it did.

I followed the girls back inside our hut, where we deposited our things. Some of them filtered off to the gardens, others went to help the elderly women cook, and yet others disappeared inside the big ceremonial hut. I found myself standing outside, glancing around, wondering where I was supposed to go.

I still didn't see Jonathan or Guillermo. And Parrot would still be down at the river bathing. Professor Quirk was nowhere to be seen either, and I didn't know how to get to the cave and the glyphs without him. Rather than stand here idly, I made my way across the clearing over to the corral where the horses were.

Smiling at Diablo, I held out my hand. "Good morning. Did you sleep well?"

In response, he did that cute horsey growl and slowly lumbered toward me. He nuzzled my hand while I rubbed his head.

"I wish I had an apple," I cooed. "I promise to steal one from one of these gardens. That is, if they grow them in this country."

"They do." Professor Quirk stepped up beside me. "After breakfast we'll head to the cave. Sound good?"

I nodded and took a quick second to check him out now that we stood close. He'd cleaned up since I'd seen him at the river. He'd shaved and changed clothes. His freshly washed hair lay dark and smooth against his head. Through his clean glasses, I made out brilliant green eyes. He stood a little taller than me, lanky, but in okay shape. The kind of shape that came with being active, not so much from working out.

"I saw you this morning," I told him.

He furrowed his brow. "You did? Where?"

I kept my smile in check. "The river."

"When I was bathing?" he nearly squeaked.

"No." My lips curved. "When *I* was bathing. Or rather, when all of us girls were bathing."

"What?"

I laughed. "I knew you didn't see us. You were completely zoned out."

Shaking his head, he blushed. "I don't even want to think about the scene I missed out on."

I couldn't recall ever having seen a guy blush before. Well, except for Chapling.

Taking some hay from a bin, I fed a thatch to Diablo. "So, how long have you worked for the IPNC?"

"Five years. How long have you worked for the Specialists?"

"Only a year." I glanced over at him. "Quirk isn't your real name, is it?"

"No." He smiled. "Is Hannah yours?"

I stared at his smile and, oddly enough, thought he had the best teeth I'd ever seen. "No."

Quirk chuckled. "Some secret life we live, huh?"

Pulling my stare away from his gorgeous smile, I gave Diablo another thatch. "Guillermo works for the IPNC, too. But you two acted like you didn't know each other."

"We don't. IPNC's a big organization. Guillermo works solely in South America. I travel all over." Professor Quirk turned to me. "Mind if I ask you a personal question?"

Personal. I shook my head, feeling a hint of nervousness.

"How old are you?"

"Why?" I teased. "How old are you?"

One half of his mouth curved up. "I asked you first."

I smiled. "Seventeen." I didn't bother telling him I was *almost* seventeen. "And you?"

"I'm twenty-three."

"So the IPNC recruited you at eighteen?" Almost the same age as me.

"Good job, genius."

Playfully, I nudged his shoulder.

"Yep, they recruited me the day I graduated from high school," he continued. "They funded my undergraduate, masters, and doctoral studies." He returned my playful nudge. "To be recruited so young, you must have a high IQ like me. So . . . what's your IQ?"

"What?" I laughed. "What difference does that make?"

Quirk shrugged. "Mine's one sixty-one."

"Feeling competitive, are we?"

He managed to cringe a bit guiltily. "A little. So, what's yours?"

I didn't answer him right away and almost decided to lie, but told the truth instead. "One ninety-one."

Professor Quirk got really quiet, and as the seconds ticked by, he silently stared at me through unblinking green eyes.

I knew it. I shouldn't have said anything. People always thought of me as a freak of nature when they found out my true intelligence.

He swallowed. "My God, that's hot."

‹NINE›

I took a step back. "Wh-what?"

Professor Quirk took a step back, too. "I'm sorry. I'm so sorry. Believe I just said that I can't." He shook his head. "I mean—"

"It's okay." I laughed when it occurred to me I should probably be embarrassed or offended or something. But how could I be when this guy reminded me so much of me that it was purely laughable? Klutzy, glasses, tall, lanky, way too intelligent, and even the talking-backward-when-nervous thing. Now if he pulled out a lollipop, that'd be way too weird.

He smiled sheepishly. "You sure?"

"Believe me, I'm more than sure."

Parrot stepped up between us. "Morning," he mumbled, reaching a hand out to Abrienda, his horse, and she came over to take the berries he held.

"How'd your group bath go?" I asked Parrot.

"Fine." He shrugged, obviously still not in a talking mood.

I sighed, starting to get annoyed with his quiet demeanor. If Quirk wasn't here, I'd definitely say those exact words to Parrot. I mean, I know seeing Talon had brought back old memories, but didn't Parrot trust me? Why wouldn't he confide in me? That's what family was for. I thought we had bonded back at the ranch.

Turning, I propped my back up against the wooden corral and idly surveyed the goings-on around the village. A good solid minute went by as I watched everyone work, and my mind became curious. "I'm very interested in finding out how things work around here."

Professor Quirk hoisted himself up onto the corral, propping his boots on a low wooden barricade. "I've been here a week, and I'm just now figuring it all out. We're on Huworo land, so everything that occurs here is based on their customs."

I plucked a piece of hay from the bin and chewed on it. "Even though there are fifteen different tribal nations represented?"

Quirk nodded. "Out of respect they have to go by Huworo traditions."

Parrot turned, too, joining us in looking at the village.

"When girls and boys turn fifteen, they are moved into one of the single-men or-women huts. They stay there until they're married. Couples and families take up all the other huts. When a boy and girl get married, the whole village works together to build them their own private dwelling with a garden out back. The gardens"—Quirk motioned to them—"are maintained by wives and daughters. Meals, meetings, and festivities take place in the big circular hut in the middle."

The professor pointed to the open-square structures where older women busied themselves cooking. "The women cooking are those who have reached the age of forty and never married or women whose husbands have died. After they get done cooking, you'll see them sewing, scaling fish, doing artwork."

"What do the men do around here?" I asked. It didn't sound like they did much of anything.

"Hunt, make tools, build structures, attend meetings," Quirk answered.

"This morning when we went to bathe, none of the girls and guys looked at each other." I glanced up at him. "Why is that?"

"They're considered unclean until after morning baths," Quirk answered. "Huworo customs say unclean singles can't lay eyes on each other."

"Huh. Interesting. Where are the tribal chiefs staying?"

"Each chief was allowed to bring one representative with him." Quirk hopped down from the corral. "They're all staying in the ceremonial hut."

Jaaci stepped from the big circular structure, caught sight of me, and smiled.

I returned her smile and waved. "That's Jaaci," I told Parrot and Professor Quirk.

Sidestepping the playing children, she laughed and made her way across the dirt to where the guys and I hung out at the corral. Coming to a stop right in front of me, she rubbed her belly. *"Lirjvc?"*

"Hungry?" I nodded. "Definitely." I turned to Parrot. "This is Flint," I introduced him, using his alias. I pointed to Professor Quirk. "And Quirk."

"F-lint," she tried the name. "Ka-wirk." Smiling softly, she bowed her head to each one.

Professor Quirk stepped forward to shake her hand. "Nice to meet you."

Jaaci came out of her bow, looked at his hand, and then glanced at me, obviously at a loss. Guess they didn't shake hands in her tribe. I stepped forward and shook his hand, showing her what he wanted. Understanding, she repeated my gesture.

She switched her attention to Parrot then. "F-lint," she tried his name again, holding out her hand.

He managed a small smile as he returned her handshake.

Taking her hand back, Jaaci gestured over her shoulder. We followed her across the dirt and into the ceremonial hut.

A large circular table took up the center. On top of the table sat big steaming bowls and platters of fruit. Stacks of smaller pottery bowls and plates occupied the middle of the tabletop.

It smelled heavenly.

Situated in a U shape around the circular table sat all the tribal chiefs. I scanned their faces and zeroed in on Talon's. Sitting on a short stool, he carried on a conversation with the chief beside him and didn't even glance up at the entrance where we stood.

Behind the chiefs in the same U shape sat a row of men and behind them a row of younger boys. Children and women sat on straw cushions along the perimeter of the ceremonial hut. I caught sight of Jonathan and Guillermo in the row of men and smiled. Jonathan smiled back.

I noticed that a thick leather strap crossed Jonathan's chest, with a pouch on the end. Since we were in charge of guarding the vase, I presumed the pouch held the vase.

Jaaci showed Parrot and Professor Quirk two empty stools in the row with the younger boys, and then led me to the back to sit with the women.

A few more families filtered into the hut, taking their places depending on their age and sex.

Quietly, I sat taking in the scene. This hut had been built the same way as the one I slept in last night, only a lot bigger. Openings high up in the thatched roof let in morning light and provided ventilation. I imagined they would close those somehow if it began raining. A long table stretched the

555

length of one wall and held hammocks and personal items that I assumed belonged to the chiefs, since Professor Quirk said they slept in here.

For the most part, everyone spoke in a low tone with their neighbor. It put a sort of hum in the air. I estimated nearly fifty people filled the area. I caught another whiff of breakfast, and my stomach growled.

Jaaci looked over at me and laughed. And it occurred to me then that she wasn't a part of this tribe either. Her people had died, she'd found the Mother Nature vase, and here we all were. I wished she spoke English so I could ask her what her customs were. Or, for that matter, I wished I spoke her language. But that would never happen. I had not one lingual bone in my body.

I was brought abruptly from my thoughts when the oldest chief shot to his feet and began yelling something, and the whole place fell silent. He stomped over to where the food was, scooped his hand into the steaming stew, and brought out a clumpy, dripping handful. With a very angry face, he shouted something in his language.

I looked around the hut, trying to figure out what was going on.

Another chief got to his feet and, with his hands behind his back, bowed to the angry chief. He said something in a very calm voice.

The angry chief slung the stew back into the bowl and stomped across the hut and straight out the door. His assistant got up and hurried after him.

I could not *wait* to ask Parrot what was going on.

The calm chief began chanting. Two teenage boys stood, and a woman along the back did, too. Together the four of them continued chanting. It put a calm aura throughout the hut.

I glanced at Parrot and saw him bow his head in reverence.

Once they finished and took their seats, everyone began talking again. In unison, all the women stood. Following their lead, I got to my feet, too. Some of them went to the big table in the center and began ladling stew from the big steaming bowls. They placed fruit onto the small plates and served various chiefs, men, younger guys, and children. Then they went back and got more stew and fruit, brought it back to where we women stood, and began eating.

For a minute there, I thought maybe they were going to serve me.

More women left our line and repeated what the others had done. I could only assume maybe they were serving their families.

Jaaci left our line on round three, motioning for me to follow. Copying what I'd seen the other women do, I ladled stew into bowls and piled fruit on plates. With a bowl in each hand I turned to the crowd and realized I'd caught the attention of quite a few people.

Not like everyone fell quiet to stare or anything, but definitely a dozen or more men and women were looking at me. Suddenly self-conscious, I glanced at Jonathan, and he motioned me over.

He took the food from me. "They're staring at your blond hair," he whispered. "Don't worry about it, you're doing fine." Guillermo took his food, too. "Some of the older men believe blond hair means you've been touched by the gods."

I rolled my eyes. "Did you tell them in America most people think blond hair means you're stupid?"

Guillermo laughed at that.

"What happened with that older chief?" I whispered.

"Now's not the time," Jonathan answered. "I'll tell you later." With a nod, I headed back to the food and caught sight of Jaaci serving Parrot and the professor. I ladled stew into a bowl, piled fruit on a plate, and balancing both, I turned to take my seat and ran smack into Jaaci.

My stew went down the front of her dress and my fruit went flying through the air.

"Oh, my God!" I reached for Jaaci. "I'm so sorry."

Someone shouted something, and I whipped my head to the left to see Talon standing. With a clenched jaw, he grabbed a couple pieces of my fruit off him and, staring at me, slung them to the floor.

I sucked in a breath.

Shouting something else, he took a step toward me, and simultaneously every one of my team members got to their feet.

Talon dragged his dark, menacing gaze off me and looked at each of my team members. Jonathan, Guillermo, Quirk, and finally Parrot.

A couple of quiet seconds ticked by.

Switching his gaze back to me, Talon slowly sat down, and in my peripheral vision I saw my team members take their seats, too.

Gradually, the entire hut began eating again.

Swallowing, my heart pounding, I glanced at Jonathan. He nodded for me to get some food.

Jaaci touched my arm and I turned to her. "I'm so sorry," I said.

Smiling as if she understood me, she shook her head and waved me off. But I couldn't help but stare at her beautiful dress that was messed up because of me.

She indicated the food, and we served ourselves. It could have been my imagination, but I swore I felt Talon's glare boring a hole into my back.

I didn't chance a look in his direction as I followed Jaaci back to our straw mats. We sat down and dug into the food.

I scooped a hunk of meat out of the stew and chomped down, loving the mild spicy, oniony taste. "What is this?" I motioned to my bowl.

Jaaci shook her head, clearly not understanding my question.

I tried again, scooping up some of the meat. "What?"

She nodded, *"Kafferw,"* and pointed to the other side of the hut where an elderly woman sat with a rather ugly-looking monkey on her shoulder.

I paused, then I froze as I realized, *"Monkey?* This is monkey stew?"

Jaaci smiled.

Suddenly, my stomach didn't feel so well. Swallowing back rising bile, I slowly put the bowl down and pushed it out of my way. I covered my face with my hands and told myself to not get sick.

My whole body warmed, and each voice in the room seem to amplify as I willed my stomach to settle.

People talked.

Metal spoons scraped against pottery bowls.

Someone laughed.

With my hands still covering my face, I concentrated on breathing in and out through my mouth so I wouldn't smell the oniony stew.

Jaaci put her hand on my back. *"Cei enoc?"*

Still breathing through my mouth, I shook my head. I had no idea what she'd asked me. Without looking at her, I spoke. "I need some fresh air."

I got up and didn't look at a single soul as I left the ceremonial hut. It was probably rude to leave in the middle of a meal, but frankly, I didn't care. It was either that, or the whole tribe would have seen my breakfast coming back up. And after spilling food on Jaaci, I didn't need any more humiliation.

Standing outside, I closed my eyes and drew in a long breath of air. "You will not get sick," I told myself on exhale. I inhaled again. "You will not get sick," on exhale. I repeated that over and over, and, when I felt steady enough, I opened my eyes.

"Better?"

I jerked around. "Professor Quirk? How long have you been there?"

"Long enough. I take it you found out we were eating mo—"

"Don't." I held my hand up. "Don't say it."

He smiled and paused. "I'm glad someone else is as klutzy as me," he said, changing the subject.

I rolled my eyes. "You have no idea."

He laughed at that.

Out of the corner of my eye, I saw the old chief who had stomped out of breakfast. I nodded toward him politely. He returned my nod, and when he was out of sight, I turned to Quirk. "Any idea what that yelling and stew flinging was all about?"

Quirk nodded. "Yeah. Their tribe considers the monkey a sacred animal."

"Yikes. No wonder he was so mad."

"It was a pretty big insult to serve monkey. This faux pas can affect the relationship between these two tribes for years. But that's not our problem. We have glyphs to decode. You ready to see the cave and the drawings?"

Eagerly, I nodded. "Definitely."

I jogged over to the hut I'd slept in and retrieved my laptop.

Quirk met me outside. "Here," he said, handing me a cloth pouch hanging from the end of a thin rope. "It's for the bugs." He held up the one he wore around his neck. "One of the Huworo people gave it to me the first day I got here. I don't know what's in it—some herbs, I think—but whatever it is, it works great."

"Thanks." I put it around my neck. "Too bad I didn't have this last night. Termite guts are about as disgusting as I want to get."

He laughed at that and motioned me into the jungle.

"So you've been here a week," I struck up a conversation.

He stepped over a downed tree. "Yes. I've been holed up in the cave sketching the glyphs. It will make your job a lot easier since I already have half the cave sketched. You can scan my drawings into your computer and plug them into your translation program. Which"—he glanced over at me—"I've been extremely eager to see. There's no other program like it, I hear."

I nodded a little, feeling a swell of pride at my creation. Too bad it had to remain top secret.

"Too bad it has to remain top secret." Professor Quirk ducked under a low branch. "That would be an amazing thing to introduce into the world of historians."

I blinked. "I was just thinking that." How weird.

He smiled a little. "What made you create the program? Are you interested in cave drawings?"

"A couple of our agents are on a mission where cave drawings are involved. I thought the program would make things go smoother for them." Unsure of how much I could say, I stopped there.

Quirk nodded, but didn't ask any more questions.

We continued on, and out of the corner of my eye, I noticed he was staring at me. Suddenly, he ran straight into a bush and caught himself as he stumbled over it.

I smiled and reached for him. "You okay?"

Quirk sighed. "Yes."

I smiled again at his exasperated tone. He *did* say he was as klutzy as me.

Trying to regain his composure, he cleared his throat. "It's amazing that the whereabouts of this cave has never been documented. If Jaaci's dying father hadn't told her about it and the Mother Nature vase, it'd still be a historical mystery. I studied all about it in my course work. Most of my professors felt it was a legend." Quirk looked back at me. "Have you seen the vase yet?"

I shook my head.

"The Huworo chief gave it to your leader to guard, the guy with the eye patch. What's his name again?"

"Shane," I answered, using Jonathan's alias.

The professor nodded. "I've analyzed the inscriptions and have estimated that the glyphs date back to AD 1100."

"Wow."

"You can say that again."

"Wow."

Professor Quirk laughed.

I followed him around a huge tree trunk. "The drawings are supposed to reveal a key piece of information about the vase. Any ideas yet?"

He shook his head. "This is my specialty. But to be honest, I've never seen anything like it—the pattern, that is. I've seen the symbols before, but they don't seem to follow a pattern, or at least one that I know of."

"Hopefully, that's where my program will come in."

"Hopefully," he agreed.

We emerged from the jungle and came to an abrupt stop. In front of us stretched a very *long* swinging rope bridge, connecting the ledge we stood on to a ledge *way* across a *huge* gap in land.

Swallowing, I took in the void between the two ledges and estimated it to be about half a mile. "Wh-where's the cave?"

Professor Quirk pointed across the gap. "Over there."

I closed my eyes. *Figures.* Nothing's ever easy in this business. "H-how far down?"

"C—"

"Wait." I held up my hand. "I don't want to know."

He stepped onto the swinging bridge. "Come on."

Holding on to the ropes that encased the bridge, Quirk began making his way across. As he did, I studied the engineering of the clearly unstable structure. Wood planks served as stepping pieces, positioned about an inch apart. Rope wound the ends of the wood and knotted into the thick twine of the netted walls and handrails. The bridge appeared wide enough for only one person at a time.

I'd feel a lot better if something on the swinging structure resembled steel. Or concrete. Or something else equally stable. No wonder we'd had balancing lessons in PT.

Roughly halfway across, Quirk glanced back at me. "Come on," he yelled.

"I'm going to wait until you get across." One person's weight was enough for this spindly thing.

I heard him mumble, "Chicken," and narrowed my eyes. I'd show him chicken.

Feeling a surge of courage, I grabbed on to the handholds and stepped onto the first wood plank. My confidence quickly dwindled as the bridge swung slightly. I swallowed again, closed my eyes, and told myself not to look down.

That was like trying to tell me not to peek at Chapling's new subelesup code.

I knew I *would* look down, so I opened my eyes to go ahead and get it over with, and my heart stopped.

This canyon, or whatever it was called, disappeared into nothingness, just like before when I'd been on Diablo crossing the ledge. Tightening my grip on the ropes, I felt my body make the bridge shake again and tried to loosen my muscles, but couldn't.

I stared as daylight filtered down into the canyon, becoming darker and darker with the depth, until only blackness colored the area.

"Stop holding your breath," the professor yelled.

I realized then I wasn't breathing and gulped in some air. With stiff, unbending muscles, I commanded my legs to move and dragged first my right boot and then my left back off the wood and onto the ground. I glanced up to see that Quirk had made it all the way across. I thought he was supposed to be klutzy.

"Are you kidding me?" the professor yelled.

I lifted my right fist, and for the first time in my life, I flipped somebody off.

He barked a laugh in response.

It made me want to flip him off again, double time.

Taking a breath, I stared hard at the bridge and a ghost of a memory floated through my mind. I saw four-year-old me holding my mom's hand. We stood on a rope-and-wood bridge that stretched about twenty feet between two pieces of land. A river bubbled ten feet below us.

My mother and I wore coats, gloves, and scarves, and my dad stood on the bridge, too, facing us. Laughing, he shifted his body weight and made the bridge swing. My mom laughed, too, and tried to tell him to stop but couldn't get the words out between her giggles. I squealed and squeezed my mom's hand and squealed some more.

"You coming or what?" Professor Quirk yelled, snapping me from the memory.

I felt a smile curving my lips and breathed a content sigh. Holding on to that memory, I stepped back onto the swinging bridge and walked all the way across. I didn't look down once and instead recalled the rest of that afternoon with my parents. My family had hiked through the woods, picnicked on a big flat rock, drove the winding mountainous road to the top, and stood looking out over a valley with colorful autumn trees.

"Wasn't so bad, was it?" Quirk asked, as I stepped off the other side of the bridge. "I saw you smiling."

I narrowed my eyes. "Optical illusion."

"Truth is, first time I did it I was scared out of mind."

"Thanks for telling me that *after* I made it across."

Quirk shot me a not-so-innocent smile. "We're almost there." He led me back into the jungle and around the biggest rock I'd ever seen.

Stopping around the back side of this boulder, he pointed to a dark opening in a hill covered by a thick green vine. "The cave." Leaning down, Quirk stepped into the darkness of the opening. "Let's do this."

Ducking down, I followed the professor into the dark cave.

Quirk flipped on a flashlight. He swept the beam along the walls and ceiling, illuminating a tunnel that stretched in front of us. "This goes for fifty feet and then it opens up into the room we'll be working from."

"*Fifty feet?* Now's probably not a good time to tell you I'm a little bit claustrophobic."

"No. Not really. However," he sighed, "I am as well. More than a little."

"Well, you've been here a week," I tried to reason. "Surely you've gotten used to it."

"Yeah. Not so much."

It occurred to me then. "What the heck did you specialize in glyphs for if you're claustrophobic? Hello? Cave drawings are generally found in caves."

Quirk turned to me. "You can stop talking any time now."

I motioned him forward. "Lead the way."

In our crouched stance, we hobbled down the tunnel. I flicked my gaze from wall, to ceiling, to floor, keeping an eye out for bugs, bats, or anything else suspicious. "I thought caves were supposed to be dirty. I don't see any bugs or slimy things."

"This is a dry cave. There's been no water intrusion. If my research holds true, this is the first time that this cave has seen climate since it was sealed shut a century ago. Plus, I swept it out."

"You swept it out?"

"I don't like an unclean working environment."

"A little OCD, are we?"

Quirk shrugged. "A little." He got down on his hands and knees. "What are you doing?"

He swept the flashlight down the length of the ceiling showing where it dropped dramatically toward the floor. "We crawl the rest of the way."

Great. I slid my laptop around my body to rest on my back and became one with the floor. We crawled down the clean, freshly swept tunnel on our bellies. I found myself appreciating Professor Quirk's obsessive cleaning habits.

"It's amazing that Jaaci fearlessly entered this cave to live out her father's dying wish to retrieve the Mother Nature vase. Can you imagine?"

Quirk didn't respond to my comment. "Professor Quirk?"

His shaky breathing echoed back to me. I lifted my head and stared at his boots as he belly-crawled in front of me. "Professor Quirk?"

"K-keep talking."

Oh boy, the last thing I needed was a wigged-out professor. I racked my brain for something to talk about and came up empty. Of all the times for me to come up empty. And then it occurred to me, "Uh-huh, look who's scared now, Mr. I-Made-It-Across-the-Bridge."

He stopped moving. "Are you making fun of me?"

I smiled. "Yes, I am."

Quirk started moving again. "I've decided I don't like you anymore."

His teasing tone made me smile even bigger. "So I was thinking, it's kind of weird to call you 'Professor,' don't ya think? Professor sounds like a title someone older should have. Someone bald and pudgy. How about I just call you Quirk? Although, whoever came up with Quirk for your cover could have done a better job. I mean, really, Quirk? Come on."

"Quirk's fine."

"Good. Quirk, it is."

A few seconds went by, and I heard his breathing pick up and thought he might be getting a little nervous again. "Um, tell me where you're from."

"S-Seattle."

"Seattle, huh? I hear there's lots of rain there."

He didn't answer.

"So, um, you said the IPNC recruited you and paid for your college. How'd they find you?"

"High school test scores."

"Ah, yes, the ole test scores. Do you think you'll stay with the IPNC or transfer to another branch?"

"Don't know."

I searched my brain for another question and all I came up with was, "What's your favorite color?"

On and on I talked, asking him ridiculous questions, while we slowly crawled our way down the tunnel. It seemed like it took forever. And I had to admit, I did quite the bang-up job of mindlessly chattering and keeping Quirk's brain preoccupied. Well, to me it wasn't mindless chatter. I very thoroughly explained the filament of a nonsuffixion NFD syntagma.

Sometime later Quirk slid from the tunnel. "We're here," he breathed.

I crawled out after him. feeling just as relieved as he sounded.

"Listen," he said as he turned around and touched my arm. "Thanks for your help back there."

I shrugged. "No biggie."

"And I now know more about NFD syn-whatever than I ever thought possible."

I smiled. "Glad to help."

He returned my smile, but didn't make another comment. Quiet seconds ticked by as we stared into each other's shadowed faces. Slowly, his smile faded, and his eyes dropped to my lips. In that moment I knew things had shifted between us, and my stomach started uncontrollably whirling.

I looked away.

"Do you, um, have a boyfriend?"

Still not looking at him, I slowly nodded as my heart raced around in my chest. I didn't think my voice would come out even if I tried.

"Lucky guy."

I smiled, an image of David coming to my mind.

Clearing his throat, Quirk shifted onto his feet and away from me, and I glanced up. I couldn't help but compare him to David.

Quirk was the kind of guy who would understand my brain, kind of like Chapling did. My mentor and I connected on a whole other level. It would be that way with Quirk. I adored David, but that was the one thing missing. Sometimes I felt like he really just didn't "get" me. He thought I was more cute, adorable. He thought smart chicks were cool.

I closed my eyes to clear my head. Why was I even comparing Quirk to David? David was great.

"This room is fifteen feet in diameter," Quirk said, interrupting my thoughts.

Using the flashlight, he walked away from me. I watched as he paced the perimeter of the circular room, leaning down to turn on battery-operated lanterns. Section by section the room began to glow, and simultaneously my jaw dropped.

Cave drawings covered every inch of the walls, ceiling, and floor. Row after row of engraved symbols. Column after column of etched images. Every intricate carving looked to be about the same size. There wasn't an untouched part of the room. It was breathtaking. "No wonder you love this so much," I said in awe.

With the room glowing now, Quirk stood in the center, making a slow circle as he took everything in. "I've been here a week, and I still get the shivers every time I look at it."

I rubbed my hands up and down my arms, sort of feeling those shivers, too. Like we were on sacred ground or something.

Laughing, Quirk looked at me. "It's amazing to think someone stood here in AD 1100 and did this." He pointed to the ceiling. "Look at the intricacy of the animals there." He pointed to the floor. "And this row . . . I can't get over it." He turned another circle. "This room is ancient code, and you and I are going to break it. We're going to make history!"

I smiled at his excitement, even though I really didn't feel it. Whoever created and hid this room obviously never wanted it to be found. I felt like I might be messing with the gods or something.

"Know where the vase was?" Quirk asked.

"No."

He crossed the room to where a small rock ledge protruded from the wall. "It was sitting right here, as peaceful as you please."

"Hmmm . . ." Quirk continued studying the circular room, and I realized he was zoning out.

Ready to try my new program, I unzipped my laptop case. "Well, let's get busy."

"Did you know that many carvings are considered sacred?" Quirk asked, clearly not having heard what I'd said.

"Yes, actually, I do." I pulled my laptop out. "I'm ready when you are."

"The writings began about five thousand years ago. The first ones were written in three languages: Greek, demotic, and hieroglyphic. A French Egyptologist recognized the word *Ptolemy*, which was encased in a cartouche, and was able to match it up to the Greek spelling." Quirk put a finger in the air. "Ptolemy, by the way, was a ruler of Egypt."

"Mmm-hmmm." I plugged a battery into the power jack, and turned on my laptop. "Now just show me where your drawings are and—"

"Some hieroglyphs stand for words, others sounds, and yet others syllables. Depending on which way the graphics point determines how you read them. Left to right or right to left. They can also be read up and down." He tapped his fingers together. "Just remember when you're deciphering, the hieroglyphs match up to sounds, not letters."

I resisted the urge to tell him that I already knew all this. I had to know it in order to create my translation program. "Um, can we just—"

"Egyptians focused on consonant sounds, not vowels." He tapped his forehead. "Although there were determinatives that you could tack onto the end to give a hint to its meaning."

"Quirk?"

"Oh." He put that finger in the air again. "There're all different kinds of symbols. You can use birds, arms, legs, leaves, worms, squiggly lines, bowls, lions, squares . . . but I've been rattling on about Egypt. Now, Mayan drawings are even more exciting . . ."

My eyes glassed over. I imagined this was what other people felt like when I got off on one of my computer tangents. "Quirk?"

" . . . the pictorial intricacy and calligraphic style of Mayan glyphs are, in my opinion, like no other . . ."

With a sigh, I dug out two lollipops from my laptop case. I unwrapped both, put one in my mouth, crossed the room to Quirk, and stuck the other in his mouth. He fell quiet. Like a baby, he sucked the lollipop, still studying the room.

"Now if you would please give me your drawings, I can get them scanned and start deciphering this code."

Pulling the lollipop from his mouth, he looked at me. "This is really good. What is this, raspberry?"

I nodded. "The sketches?"

"Oh, yes. I left my portfolio in here yesterday." It sat propped against the wall. He opened it and handed me a stack of wax paper. "Be careful. Those are originals."

Propping myself up against the wall, I laid the stack beside me and took my ultra-thin, extremely cool, portable wand scanner from my laptop case. Page by page I input the images into my program while Quirk stood with his back to me, sketching parts of the room he hadn't gotten to yet.

We worked for hours, stopping only once to change batteries in the lanterns and eat meat jerky he'd brought. I didn't ask what kind of meat. I didn't want to know.

By my estimation, he'd managed to sketch half the room in the week he'd been here. Which meant it would take him another whole week to sketch the rest, right in time with the length of the mission. Hopefully, my program wouldn't need all the glyphs to decode the message.

A few hours later, he put his portfolio back together. "I need fresh air and real food. And it's going to be dark soon. I don't want to go back through the jungle at nighttime." Quirk came over and sat down beside me. "What's your program got so far?"

After a few clicks, I studied the screen . . . and my whole body sank. "Nothing."

"It's okay." Quirk shrugged. "Maybe tomorrow."

"Maybe."

We extinguished the lanterns, crawled back through the tunnel entrance, and traversed the swinging bridge. As we made our way through the jungle, we ran into Jonathan.

"I tried to get over to the cave," Jonathan began, "but Guillermo and I had to go into town for an emergency conference call with the IPNC and our top guy at the Specialists."

By "top guy" I knew he meant TL, but because of Quirk, Jonathan didn't say his name.

"Intel told us weeks ago that two chiefs were planning to steal the vase. Last night another message was intercepted. Unfortunately, we still don't have the identity of the chiefs, but the message indicated a hit man has been hired. For whom, we're unsure."

"Hit man?" I asked. "You mean someone from one of the tribes?"

"Yes. For all we know, he or she could be part of the talks, a Huworo native . . . no telling. But all the chiefs know you're in the cave decoding the glyphs for a key piece of information about the vase, presumably its rightful owner. We do not believe one of our team members is in immediate danger, but watch each other's backs."

Quirk and I nodded our understanding.

"And do your best to decipher the code as soon as possible."

I didn't think now was a good time to tell Jonathan my program had given me nothing today.

"How's your program doing?" he asked.

"So far so good," I sort of lied.

"Do you have anything yet?"

"Hopefully, by tomorrow." I dodged a direct answer to his question, not wanting to admit I had doubts, *serious* doubts, that my software would come through. I glanced down at the pouch he wore. "Can we see the vase?"

Carefully he removed the leather pouch from his body and handed it to me. I undid the tied strap and pulled out the vase wrapped heavily in thick layers of protective cloth. One by one I unfolded the layers, and as I got closer and closer to revealing the artifact, it occurred to me I probably shouldn't be doing this. I might break it. And then where would that leave everything?

GiGi ruins history.

I handed the wad back to Jonathan. "You do it. I don't trust myself."

With big, confident fingers, he unfolded the wrapping and held it out for us to see. Quirk and I both moved closer, neither one of us touching it. Usually things appeared different in person, but to my surprise, the vase looked just like it had up on the screen back at the ranch.

I glanced up at Jonathan. "Aren't you worried you might break it or lose it or someone might steal it?"

He arched an incredulous brow, as if that was the silliest thing to worry about.

Okay, it probably was for someone like Jonathan or TL. But me? It was definitely something to worry about. I couldn't imagine being given this priceless artifact to guard.

Jonathan wrapped it back up. "Let's call it a day. I want to touch base with Flint," he said, using Parrot's alias.

We followed Jonathan back to the Huworo village.

Quirk walked toward the single-men hut, and, when he was out of hearing range, Jonathan turned to me. "When I was in town, I told TL about what happened back in the airport security shack yesterday. He wants you to get that drawing of that woman to Chapling as soon as possible."

"Sure. No problem."

"And"—Jonathan cleared his throat—"I have a message for you from David."

My stomach swirled. "David?"

"He was on the conference call earlier. He said he tried texting you, but it didn't go through."

Huh. I checked my cell and saw I had no signal. Even with our new satellite chips, the jungle still made it difficult. I looked up at Jonathan in expectation of David's message.

He managed to look a bit embarrassed. "David says hi."

I waited for the rest of the message, but Jonathan said nothing. "Hi?" I asked. "That's it?"

Jonathan gave a terse nod. "I told him I was not a telegram service and to limit his message to one word."

I narrowed my eyes. "How generous of you."

With another nod, Jonathan headed off in the opposite direction. "I'll be back in a few minutes to head over to the talks. Remember the drawing. Try to find a signal for your computer so you can send the scan to Chapling."

"Yeah. No problem," I said, preoccupied.

Hi. One word. David was on the other side of the world and yet he still, in one word, managed to make me feel like he was right here.

With a sigh, I took my laptop and cell phone in the hopes of finding a nearby signal. Someplace high up. I looked up into the thick foliage and turned a slow circle. Maybe I could climb a tree? "What are you doing?" Quirk asked.

I jumped. "I thought you went back to your hut."

He smiled. "I did. But I wanted to go for a walk. Need to clear my head of all those cave drawings. So what are you doing? Looking for monkeys?"

"Ha-ha." I held up my laptop. "I need a signal."

Quirk nodded. "I know the perfect place." He started walking, and I followed. We went across the village and past the corral and then came to a stop. He pointed up. "Watchtower."

I craned my neck all the way back and sure enough at the top of a very *tall* tree sat a watchtower. I squinted my eyes and made out a man, presumably the watch person. I swallowed. "That's really far up."

Quirk shrugged. "You said you wanted a signal."

"What are you two doing?" Jonathan asked, coming up behind us.

Quirk pointed up. "She said she needed a signal."

Jonathan looked up and whistled. "That should do it." He motioned toward the ceremonial hut. "However, I think you should come with me to

571

the talks instead. It'll be interesting for you to witness your teammate in action."

I held up my laptop. "Do the other thing later then?"

Jonathan nodded.

"I didn't realize I was allowed in the talks. I thought only natives could attend."

"Only the chiefs and the translators are allowed to speak. Anyone else can witness it." Jonathan started walking slowly toward the big circular structure, and Quirk and I stepped in line beside him.

"How are the talks going?" I asked.

"Every chief has valid documentation to prove the Mother Nature vase belonged to his tribe at one time in history. None of the chiefs is willing to give up his rights to the artifact." Jonathan shook his head. "It's wearing Flint out."

I sighed. "I hate hearing that."

Jonathan stopped at the entrance to the ceremonial hut. "They are very interested in finding out what those glyphs say exactly."

"We're trying our best," Quirk commented, motioning to the opening in the hut. "Shall we?"

Jonathan and I followed Quirk inside. Like breakfast this morning, everyone sat in designated areas, depending on their gender and age. Parrot, however, sat right dead center with the chiefs. The personal translators sat behind them.

Jonathan took his spot beside Guillermo, and I found an empty straw mat beside Jaaci along the back wall. She smiled at me as I situated myself beside her. I located Talon among the chiefs. He sat directly across the U shape from Parrot, right in Parrot's line of sight. And although Talon's back was to me, it appeared as if he was staring straight at Parrot.

I switched my gaze to Parrot and found him looking everywhere *but* in Talon's direction.

A chief wearing a nose ring lifted an old parchment rolled and secured with a black leather strap. *"Lu ymbarsiqr misysac va gyc sga tyra em ioq nirrarreim em dedsaam svamsu sgqaa . . ."*

He continued in his native tongue, and my brain went numb trying to keep up. A minute later the chief finished, and everyone turned their attention to Parrot.

Parrot took a second or two, probably trying to translate what was said in his own brain, and then spoke, "My ancestors noted that we had the vase in our possession in fifteen twenty-three. Mother Nature relieved the great drought of that year. We had the best crops ever. And then the Bidum warriors raided our village and stole the vase."

The chiefs' personal translators leaned forward and whispered into their ears, converting Parrot's English into their chief's language.

"Xjisit auys qsuug na qiuqmf seofif auys wommehf?" shouted a chief with black dots tattooed over his face, chest, and arms.

Everyone turned to Parrot. He took a second . . . "Where's your proof that my people raided your village?"

The translators simultaneously whispered into their chiefs' ears.

"Sgys tyra qefgsdokka zakimfr . . ." The chief with the nose ring spoke again.

Everyone turned to Parrot. He took a second . . . "That vase rightfully belongs to my people. Stealing it doesn't legally make it yours."

The translators simultaneously whispered into their chiefs' ears.

"Oyq," a chief wearing a colorful robe grunted. *"Xir xycepy oeip . . ."*

Everyone turned to Parrot. "Yes, but before your people had it, we had it. Where's your proof that your people didn't steal it from us?"

On and on the talks went, with no hope of resolution in sight.

And after a while, I found myself studying Parrot. To any person who really didn't know him, they would think he was fine by looking at him. Calm, controlled, patient. But I'd known Parrot nearly a year, and although he hid it well, I detected the exhaustion and stress in him. Little things like reaching up to rub his temple, blinking slow from dry eyes, the fatigue in his voice, and the way he kept forcing himself to sit up straight.

I couldn't imagine so many voices circling around in my head, bumping into each other, pushing and shoving for space. I'd probably go insane with the overload.

I wished I had the power to call an end to things and give him a break.

Suddenly, a deep grunt vibrated through the hut, and I snapped to attention.

A chief with very long hair shot angrily to his feet. He yelled across the U shape at the chief with the black-dot tattoos, and that chief got to his feet, too.

Back and forth they yelled, and it sounded as if they were using some of the same words. Parrot got to his feet and tried to keep up, but with their fast exchange and loud voices, Parrot's voice was overpowered.

Then the two chiefs charged at each other, and I sucked in a breath.

Other chiefs and assistants rushed the two who were about to fight and pulled them apart. They were all shouting over one another. The chief with the long hair shoved others out of his way and stormed from the hut. The chief with the tattoo plopped back down on his stool. And then slowly everyone trickled back to their seats.

I looked at each of my team members, and they seemed as caught off guard as me.

Things quieted and, just as I thought the talks would begin again, Talon stood. Up to this point he'd been quiet. For the first time since I'd come in, Parrot gazed straight across the U and into Talon's eyes.

And then Talon lifted a finger and pointed it right at Parrot.

‹ELEVEN›

To Parrot's credit, he kept his gaze passively fastened on Talon as if he were any other chief standing there pointing his finger. Parrot showed no signs of recognition, no signs of fear, only a hint of question floated in his eyes.

All the chiefs stared at Talon waiting for him to speak.

"Baet pawkot yaeng doe yote ratag," he finally said, before turning and walking straight out of the ceremonial hut.

The chiefs silently looked at one another, clearly wondering what was going on. I switched my attention to Parrot and found him looking straight at me.

The same chief who had chanted at this morning's breakfast stood and said something in his language.

Everyone looked at Parrot. "Today's events are over," he translated.

The chiefs' assistants whispered the translation into their ears, and then everyone started getting up and filing out of the hut. With my laptop in tow, I made a beeline for Parrot.

"Let's talk," I said, grabbing his arm, not giving him a chance to say no.

We wove our way through the departing crowd, across the village, and stopped at the corral. Our horses Diablo and Abrienda came right over.

"Tell me what's going on," I demanded, not giving him the time to decide if he wanted to talk to me or not. I'd been more than patient with Parrot's silence, but it was evident I'd have to pull information from him.

And I thought *I* was hard to talk to.

I planted my hand on my hip. "I want to know the story of you and Talon." I wasn't being nosy, or a bully. I knew if Parrot didn't talk to someone, he was going to explode from the stress. "What did he just say to you?"

He turned and stalked off.

What the . . . ?

I stalked after him. "Stop."

Blatantly ignoring me, Parrot marched right into the jungle.

"Parrot! Stop!"

He threw his hand up, telling me to bug off.

It only fueled my fire. I ran to catch up, dug my fingers in his arm, and spun him around. I jabbed my finger in his face. "Now listen. I'm sick of you keeping everything secret. This is starting to affect the mission. If I have to be concerned about Talon, that maybe he is the hit man, then I need to know. I want you to talk. Now."

Parrot jabbed his finger right back in my face. "And I'm sick of you bugging me. This has nothing to do with the mission. Just leave me alone!"

"No."

His face hardened. "Get. Out. Of. My. Face," he gritted.

"No," I ground out through clenched teeth, fully aware I was pushing *both* of us beyond the limit.

Parrot growled, a very out-of-character reaction. He turned away from me and, with fisted hands, let out a loud yell. It echoed through the jungle, and my stomach clenched with the primal sound of it. Like all the frustration and anger over his entire life had just erupted from his body.

With another yell, he spun and kicked a tree. And kicked it again.

I reached for him. "Parrot, stop. You're going to break your toes."

He turned away from me and put his hands over his face. "Please. Just leave me alone."

Putting my laptop down, I stepped up behind him and wrapped my arms tight around him. He tried to pull away, and I squeezed him harder.

Parrot inhaled a choppy breath. "Oh, God." Another choppy breath and then a quiet sob. The painful sound broke my heart.

Laying my cheek on his shoulder, I held on tight, while his body shook with sadness. I wondered if this was the first time he'd ever had a good cry.

Minutes passed, and I continued holding him.

He took some deep breaths, trying to get control of his emotions.

Finally, he sniffed. "Do you remember the day we all first met?" he mumbled into his hands.

I nodded against his shoulder, not wanting to let him go yet.

Parrot pulled away, and I reluctantly released him. With his back to me, he used his T-shirt to wipe his face. A few seconds passed as he gained more control. "I said I was taken in by the police for flying in a restricted airspace." He turned around and looked me right in the eyes. "I lied."

My heart paused a beat. "What do you mean you lied?"

He studied my face, as if trying to figure out exactly how much he could or would say to me.

I reached out and gripped his hand and looked him deep in the eyes. "Listen to me. Nothing you tell me will change who you are. Be truthful. Don't worry. None of us have had a past worth bragging about."

Parrot dropped his gaze to our clasped hands and quietly contemplated them. "I used to work for Talon," he said a few seconds later. "I interpreted deals for him. Slave trade. Mostly young girls." His voice broke.

I put my hand over my mouth.

He brought his pain-filled eyes up to meet mine. "It's not something I'm proud of. I was so ashamed. I never wanted any of you guys to know."

I rubbed my thumb over his knuckles. "It's okay."

Parrot sniffed and used his free hand to wipe his eyes. "Talon told me he knew where my mother was. And if I worked for him for six months, he'd reunite me with her."

"Oh, Parrot." I would do anything, too, to bring back my parents, if only for a few special moments with them.

"I didn't know it was slave trade. I never knew what the 'cargo' was."

I saw regret in his face, along with a hint of disgust at what he'd been involved in.

He looked up into my eyes. "I need you to believe that."

"I do." Closing the small space between us, I gave him a hug. "You know I do." I stepped away. "Do you have any news about your mom?" I asked, hopeful.

Parrot shook his head, his eyes welling up again. "No."

"Why isn't Talon in jail?"

"Because I refused to testify. Talon's the only one who knows where my mom is. When she's found, I'll testify and put him away."

"Why not just go ahead and testify?"

Adamantly, he shook his head. "No. I won't do anything until she's found. I'm not going to take any chances. TL knows that." Parrot grasped my upper arm. "Promise me you'll be careful and stay away from Talon." He gave my arm a little shake. "Promise."

The conviction in his voice gave me a chill. "I promise."

Nodding, he stepped away.

"What did he say to you back there at the hut?"

"That my mom would be so proud."

"Oh, no."

Parrot sighed. "I know. He knows who I am. Why else would he say that?"

I nodded my agreement. "We have to tell Jonathan."

Together we turned, and at the exact same second caught sight of Talon standing behind a tree watching us. Parrot and I froze as we stared back.

Talon made no expression, made no attempt to hide. He headed off diagonal to us, disappearing farther into the jungle.

We watched him go until we couldn't see him anymore.

"Do you think he heard us?"

Parrot closed his eyes and rubbed his forehead. "He may have."

"Where do you think he's going?" I asked.

"I have no idea."

Cautiously, we made our way back toward the village as darkness settled in around us. It was no wonder Parrot didn't want to come on this mission. His specialty, his gift, had been abused and used against him. And now here he had to face the same man who'd maltreated his talents. The man who knew where his mother was.

"Thanks for being honest and talking with me," I said.

Parrot smiled a little in response.

As we exited the jungle, Jonathan came right toward us. "Where have you been? I don't want you two going off alone. With the new intel, I'm not taking any chances."

"Yes, sir," we answered.

"Parrot needed some time to think, and I followed him," I explained. "But as we were heading back, we saw Talon. He must have followed us into the jungle."

"What happened?" Jonathan asked.

"Nothing," Parrot answered. "He watched us silently and then headed off in the opposite direction. We left immediately and were coming to tell you when you met us."

"Where'd he go?" Jonathan asked.

We shrugged.

Jonathan nodded. "Okay, I'll get Guillermo on that. He knows this jungle better than anyone. What did Talon say to you back at the hut?"

Parrot pressed his fingers to his temples. "That my mother would be so proud."

Jonathan furrowed his brow. "Not good. It's a little too coincidental. You both need to be on alert. Be very careful. If Talon *does* know it's Parrot, there's no telling what he may do." Jonathan turned to me. "You must keep an eye on your laptop at all times. And it's set with the highest security settings, correct?"

"Yes, sir."

With a nod, Jonathan glanced up at the watchtower. "You still have to send Chapling the scan, but I don't want you going up there. That's too far up without safety gear. We'll find a signal somewhere else."

Behind Jonathan, something moved, and I peeked around him to see the Huworo chief striding toward us across the clearing. Two men walked with him, staying one step behind. With stern faces, bald heads, and yellow painted chests, they carried spears in front of them.

"Um, Jonathan," I said, and he turned around.

The Huworo chief came to a stop right in front of us. He nodded first to me, then Parrot, and then to Jonathan. *"Ruf Lepre olb Qerif Okupazol Ojjazolu . . ."* he spoke in his language.

"The North and South American Alliance," Parrot translated, "has decided the vase will be more secure under the watchful eyes of my trained guards."

Jonathan didn't respond for a second. "I assure you, I am highly skilled in the job you have hired me for."

Parrot translated.

The Huworo chief repeated himself, motioning for the guards to take the pouch and the vase from Jonathan.

Jonathan held up his hands to let the guards know he would cooperate and then slipped the pouch over his head and gave it to the Huworo chief.

The chief nodded, turned, and headed back across the clearing.

I looked at Jonathan and knew without him saying one single word that he was really PO'ed. "What's going on?"

Jonathan shook his head. "Don't know. But I don't like it at all."

"Couldn't you do anything?" Parrot asked as we walked back to the village.

"No. The alliance hired us. If they want someone else to guard the vase, I've got nothing to say about it." He strode off. "I'm going to find out why they've taken it back and where they're going to keep the vase."

I took a breath. "Something's not right."

We entered the village, and Parrot nodded toward the ceremonial hut, where Jaaci stood in the entryway, waving us over. "Dinnertime," Parrot said. "Let's go."

"*Great.* Wonder what's on the menu tonight? Roasted armadillo? Sautéed rat? Grilled bobcat?" Feeling a bit whiny about the whole food issue, I followed Parrot across the village.

Someone had lit the outside torches, casting the area in a campsite glow. We stepped into the ceremonial hut, and I immediately noticed that Talon's stool was empty, as well as that of a chief who occupied the seat two down from him and the Huworo chief. Parrot and Jonathan noticed, too.

The guys went their way, and with dread I took my spot beside Jaaci along the back wall. I sighed, feeling like this had been one of the longest days of my life. Actually, yesterday had been long, too.

Quietly, I sat watching women bring food in and set it on the big round table in the middle. I eyed the platters, trying to make out the food. Unlike the monkey stew, tonight's dinner had no smell.

Like before, everyone took their spots according to gender and age. The Huworo chief entered just in time to do the chanting prayer with his family. Then the women began leaving our area to serve their families. I tried to see what they served and made out something green and something else white. I waited for my turn, and following Jaaci, I went up to the center table.

A variety of vegetables had been spread across huge serving platters. I breathed a sigh of relief when I saw them. Something short and gray filled the serving bowls. I watched as Jaaci scooped the objects out and onto small plates.

It was probably bad manners, but I picked up one of the objects and inspected the ridged stubbiness of it.

What the . . . ? I blinked.

A grub?

***

The next morning I woke up starving because, *hello*, I didn't eat the grubs, and vegetables hold your stomach off for only so long. I did the morning bath ritual with the other single women. Breakfast consisted of fruit and fish, thank God, something I recognized.

I put my cloth bug pouch around my neck, got my laptop, and found Quirk outside the big ceremonial hut. Together we made our way through the jungle toward the cave. As we walked, I filled him in on what had happened the night before with Talon and the Huworo chief taking the vase.

When we got to the swinging bridge, my phone beeped, alerting me I had a signal.

"You go on ahead," I told Quirk. "My phone gets a signal here, so my laptop would, too. And I need to send something back to home base."

"Sure. Be careful, though. You really shouldn't be out here alone."

"I'll be fine."

With a nod, he continued on and I sat down beneath a tree. I powered up my computer and scanned the drawing of the mysterious woman. Although the sketch was in two pieces—thanks to my klutziness—I still managed to get a decent scan. I hooked up my foldable satellite dish and keyed in the scrambler code.

HI! Chapling typed.

I smiled, HI! SENDING U A PIC. I watched as my computer transferred the file to Chapling back at the ranch.

WOW! SHES HOT! he typed.

I laughed, CAN U FIGURE OUT WHO SHE IS?

I'LL GIVE IT A WHIIIRRRL. PEACE OUT.

I laughed again, PEACE OUT.

I logged off and closed my laptop, eager to get to the cave and Quirk. He was right, I really shouldn't be here alone.

"I could make good money off you."

I jerked my head up and froze, and my heart picked up its pace. "T-Talon," I stuttered, and then immediately realized I'd just shown my fear.

An evil smile crept into his face. "You know my name. I'm honored."

I swallowed and concentrated on slowing down my heartbeat, on not showing fear.

Dressed in a traditional breechcloth with no shirt, he folded his arms over his thick chest. Even though he stood five feet seven, his stance made him seem an intimidating seven feet tall. He leveled his dark eyes on me, and they reminded me of all the other bad guys I'd faced—soulless, evil, lacking a conscience. They made my skin crawl.

I swallowed again and focused on forming a complete sentence. "What are you doing here?"

"It is to your benefit that you translate those cave drawings to my benefit."

I glanced across the swinging bridge to where Quirk had gone, but didn't see him. I brought my gaze back to Talon's. Putting my laptop aside, I stood. At least then I would be taller than him.

Talon's face didn't change expression. "It is to *your* benefit that you translate these drawings to my benefit," he repeated.

"Are you threatening me?" I tried to come across calm, but even I detected the uneasiness in my voice.

He took a step toward me, and I lost my small sense of confidence. "Your distance keep." I shook my head. "I mean, keep your distance."

Talon's lip curled up with my show of nervousness. He took another step closer, knowing full well he had the advantage. "Do you value your friends' lives? Do you value your life?"

Swallowing, I nodded, wishing Quirk or Guillermo or Jonathan or *someone* would appear out of the jungle.

Talon took another step toward me. "Then you *will* falsify your findings. I want the vase."

I didn't answer. I didn't trust myself to speak.

He took another step, and I gave in and moved back, coming up against the tree. One more step for him and he stood mere inches from me. I looked down into his face trying so hard not to show my fear.

Talon ran his creepy gaze down my body and back up. "Yes, I could make some money off you."

My body began to tremble. "M-m-move away."

He leaned forward. "Good money."

I turned my face away, shaking so hard my entire body vibrated. Way back in the recesses of my mind, I knew I could overpower him. I'd been trained to. But I also knew that at this point overcoming my fear was pretty much hopeless.

Talon touched his finger to my windpipe. "You *will* do as I've asked." He applied pressure, and I coughed. "Women are useless. And smart women, even more." He applied slightly more pressure, and I gagged.

He could do anything to me right now, and no one would know. The realization hit me hard at the exact second he stepped back.

I kept my face turned away, and in my peripheral vision I saw him disappear back into the jungle.

With shaky relief that I was still alive, my body slumped at the base of the tree. I sat for a few minutes, taking deep breaths, fighting tears, getting my heart back in rhythm, going over everything that had just happened, and how I'd reacted so weakly.

All my training, all the confidence I'd gained during my time with the Specialists—gone in a moment. I hated myself.

I heard a rustle of leaves, and my heart jumped. Guillermo stepped from the jungle, and I let out a breath.

He held up his hands. "It's okay. It's just me. I saw everything that happened. I've been following Talon since last night."

Relief and then anger sparked in me. "Why didn't you help me?" God, I'd been so scared.

"I needed to see what would happen. What he'd say. What he'd do. I wouldn't have let him hurt you." Guillermo nodded to the swinging bridge. "I'm going to stand here and watch you until you get to the cave. Get Quirk and get back to the village. We need to have a meeting."

Grabbing up my stuff, I made my way as fast and safely as I could across the bridge. At the cave's entrance, I turned and waved to Guillermo, and he disappeared back into the jungle.

I checked my phone for a signal, hoping to have a quick call with David. I just needed to hear his voice. But I'd lost the temporary satellite transmission. With a sigh, I clipped my phone on my belt. I'd have to be strong and handle things on my own.

I crawled into the cave and told Quirk what happened. Together, we went back to the village, found the talks on a break, and saw our team waiting for us at the corral.

"He's violated every rule of the alliance," Guillermo spoke, obviously having already told Jonathan and Parrot what had happened. "This is enough to get him kicked out of the talks. But in doing that we won't know who he's working with to steal the vase. We know there is someone else, but we need proof."

Jonathan looked first at me and then Parrot. "Do *not* go anywhere unless you have someone with you."

We both nodded. "Yes, sir."

"Hannah, you need to get working on those cave-drawing translations. The faster we can know what those drawings say, the quicker we can end these talks. Have you found anything yet?"

"I'm working on it," I replied. "My program hasn't revealed anything, but once I input more drawings, I should have some preliminary results."

"Good," Jonathan replied. "As for the vase, I've spoken to the Huworo chief. It is being kept at the lookout tower."

I craned my neck all the way up and saw the two bald guards standing post on the watchtower. Not a bad place to keep the vase.

"The chief had heard from one of his people that there have been more whispers about the vase being stolen. He felt that the vase would be safer up in the tower. While I disagree, I have no power to argue with him."

Quirk cleared his throat and, with a slight nod, indicated the ceremonial hut. My team turned to see Talon standing in the entryway watching us.

"Let's break up," Guillermo said, and he and Quirk strolled off.

"Jonathan," Parrot began, "it's very likely Talon knows who I am. If he does, that means he has the upper hand."

Talon knew Parrot would do anything for the truth about his mother. The question was, *would* Parrot really do anything?

"Yes," Jonathan agreed. "But he doesn't know what *we're* capable of."

‹TWELVE›

Quirk and I spent the next day in the cave—he was drawing the glyphs and I was scanning them into my translation software. We worked for hours, and at the end of the day I *click-click-clicked*. But again, my program gave me nothing.

Quirk was beginning to doubt my software.

I was frustrated. I had hoped to have something by now, but some of the glyphs just weren't matching up. According to my program, there were at least a dozen possible translations, but I didn't want a dozen *possible* ones, I needed one real one. It made me feel a bit stupid, to tell you the truth. I'd failed at a lot of things, but never computers. I knew them better than I knew myself.

It was dark when Quirk and I finally exited the cave and headed back.

As we stepped from the jungle, we saw a frenzied village. The single women and girls were running around, talking fast, giggling, obviously excited about something.

I noticed they'd changed from their traditional clothes into more ceremonial-looking garments. They wore small skirts and short tops, with beads around their wrists, necks, and bare stomachs. Considering I'd seen them dressed primarily in knee-length, sleeveless dresses, the traditional bikini-looking clothing came as a total shock.

Eager to see what was going on, I hightailed it toward the ceremonial hut and ran straight into Guillermo.

"What's going on?" I asked.

"Some of the chiefs have bowed out," he said as a greeting.

"What happened?"

"Through the course of the talks they've realized their tribes have no claim to the Mother Nature vase. They headed home earlier today."

"Is Talon one of them?" I hoped beyond hope.

"No, and he's been very 'well behaved' today. He's done nothing out of the ordinary. He didn't go anywhere or do anything he wasn't supposed to." Guillermo narrowed his eyes. "He's up to something."

Out of the corner of my eye, I caught sight of some girls hurrying into the ceremonial hut. I nodded toward them. "What's going on?"

"Full moon harvest dance."

I blinked. "Full moon what?"

"It's to ensure a prosperous harvest. It's the Huworo custom." Guillermo nodded to the ceremonial hut. "Let's go. It's an honor to attend this ceremony."

Torches had been lit to illuminate the night village. I followed Guillermo across and into the ceremonial hut. Things had been rearranged. Instead of the women sitting along the back, the men and chiefs occupied that area. The women sat right in front of the men. Everything had been cleared from the middle.

The teen girls stood in a large circle facing inward, and the teen guys surrounded them facing outward. In the middle of them all, a fire flickered. Like the girls, the guys had changed for the event into a small bikini bottom. They wore identical red-and-yellow stripes painted down their faces and bare chests.

Guillermo gave my arm a slight pull and led me over to Jonathan, Parrot, Jaaci, and Quirk, who were standing in an empty space along the back wall.

The same chief who had chanted at each meal stood, and the entire hut fell silent. Carrying a thick piece of wood with feathers tied on both ends, he strode to the center of the hut and came to a stop in front of one of the guys.

Bowing his head, the guy went down on both knees in front of the chief. The chief touched his feathered staff to the guy's right shoulder, then left, then his head, and then ran the staff down both of his arms. The chief closed his eyes and chanted something in his language.

"What's he saying?" I whispered to Parrot.

"That guy is the oldest single male," Parrot translated. "He'll lead the dance. The chief is praying for a good harvest."

Jonathan cleared his throat, his way of telling us to be quiet.

The chief finished the prayer, reared back with the staff, and slammed it right into the guy's chest.

I cringed.

The guy didn't even flinch. He jumped to his feet with an adrenaline-filled yell.

An old man whom I hadn't seen before entered the hut, banging his palm against a drum propped under his arm.

Immediately the girls and guys moved, circling in opposite directions with their backs to each other. Linking fingers, the girls closed their eyes, lifted their faces upward, and began singing a high-pitched song.

At that second the moon beamed in through the opening in the top of the ceremonial hut, illuminating the girls' faces.

The old man with the drum wove his way around the hut, taking oversize slow steps as he beat out a rhythm. *Ba. Ba. Badadaba. Ba. Ba. Badadaba* . . .

The chief shouted something, and, keeping their eyes closed and faces lifted, all the girls turned to face the guys' backs. The girls linked fingers again and continued circling, singing their high-pitched song.

Ba. Ba. Badadaba. Ba. Ba. Badadaba . . .

The guys linked arms at their elbows and began a deep guttural chant. Unlike the girls, their eyes stayed open, but they kept their gazes fixed to the ground.

Ba. Ba. Badadaba. Ba. Ba. Badadaba . . .

Everyone in the hut started chanting as the girls and guys circled faster and faster. The whole ceremony was powerful and gave me chills as I watched it unfold.

The chief raised the staff above his head, and slowly circling it in the air, he chanted something in the Huworo language. The girls and guys broke apart from their circles and all the older men and women sitting along the hut's perimeter got up. The old man continued banging the drum, and everyone, except the visiting chiefs, started dancing.

A couple minutes ticked by, and as I watched, I realized each person's awkward dancing maintained a unique rhythm.

The old man drummer crossed in front of us, and the Huworo chief danced toward us. He came to a stop right in front of Jonathan and said something. We all looked at Parrot.

"It's his wish that we join the dance," Parrot translated.

"No, thank you," I immediately replied.

"It would be considered a slap in his face," Guillermo put in, "if we don't participate." He looked at Jonathan. "We don't want to offend him."

"I'll do it." Quirk shot away from us as if he'd been dying for the invitation and joined the mass of dancing bodies, gyrating in his own unusual version of the dance.

Jonathan nodded to the chief. "It's our honor to participate."

Parrot translated, and with a satisfied smile, the chief writhed his way back into the group. Guillermo followed, and Jonathan looked at Parrot and me.

"Consider it part of your training," Jonathan rationalized.

Parrot and I gave each other matching looks of dread with an underlying hint of *how do we get out of this*?

Jonathan probably saw our wheels turning because he arched a disciplinary brow. "Do it." With that, he left our side and joined the seizuring bodies.

Jaaci stepped in front of both of us. With a sweet smile, she took my hand and then Parrot's and led us into the throng.

Dropping our hands, she spun away and into the crowd.

I turned to Parrot to say, "Well, here goes nothing," but found him standing with his eyes closed. His face appeared meditative as his body began to sway, absorbing the beat of the drum.

Without opening his eyes, he stepped forward into the group and began his dance.

I'd never seen Parrot so lost in his own personal moment. It made me wonder if he'd performed a ritual dance similar to this one in his pre-Specialist life

Someone bumped into me, and I realized I was the only one *not* moving. All around me people gyrated to the old man's drum, and without another thought, I joined in. Throwing my arms up I did what I labeled "whatever" moves. The dance was perfect for someone uncoordinated like me. It took on no style.

As I was getting into the rhythmic beat of the drum, I heard a voice rise above the music.

"Kipbup!"

A few people stopped dancing.

"Kipbup!"

More people stopped.

Someone screamed.

I spun around and saw one of the guards standing in the entrance covered in blood.

‹THIRTEEN›

Chaos broke out. Women screamed, men ran from the hut, and I frantically looked around for my team.

Parrot and Quirk quickly came up right beside me.

"What going on?"

"*Kipbup* means murder," Parrot said. "Someone's been murdered."

"*What?!*" I looked around and saw Jonathan running toward us.

"Stay here," he ordered as he and Guillermo raced past us.

I glanced around the hut, trying to recall who I had seen, who'd been missing from the harvest dance, who could possibly be dead. I caught sight of Jaaci and breathed a sigh of relief. She could very easily be a target.

Outside I heard a woman's wail, and it brought cold prickles to my skin. "Who died?"

Parrot shook his head. "I don't know yet. But it looks like the guard tried to save the person."

More people hurried from the hut as others came back in. Then Jonathan reappeared, motioning us out.

Quirk, Parrot, and I followed Jonathan out of the hut. Many of the Huworo people had gathered at the base of the tree where the watchtower was. I looked all the way up . . .

And sucked in a breath.

Covered in blood, one of the guards dangled by a rope around his neck. His body swayed in the air as a couple of Huworo men slowly pulled him up onto the watchtower's platform.

I put my hands over my mouth. "Oh, my God."

"Come on," Jonathan said, directing us into the jungle. We walked in silence and about a quarter of a mile in, came to a stop. From his backpack he pulled three pieces of wood that had been shaped into knives. He gave one to each of us. "Keep this on you at all times. Don't be afraid to use it. And do *not* trust anyone."

I took my knife and knew without a doubt in my mind I would use it if I had to.

"Listen to me," Jonathan emphasized. "These hand-carved knives are *extremely* sharp and dangerous. Only use them if absolutely necessary." He looked at me and Quirk. "You two, I don't want you coming out of that cave until you know what those glyphs say."

We nodded. "Yes, sir."

Jonathan turned to Parrot. "Don't leave the village."

Parrot nodded his understanding.

Back to the village we went. Quirk and I packed up enough food and water to get us through the next twenty-four hours. With renewed determination, I knew, without a doubt in my mind, that I would figure out the ancient code.

One person had died. There was no telling what would happen next. That dangling guard could have been any one of my team members.

In the dark, Jonathan escorted us to the cave. "I'll check on you when I can. Guillermo will try to keep a watch on the cave entrance as well. I wish I had more people. Someone to post outside the entrance at all times."

"We'll be fine," I reassured him.

With a nod, he headed off.

Inside the cave we illuminated the lanterns. I plugged a new battery into my laptop and powered up. While Quirk began working, I analyzed every line of code in my program. . . .

<kso=^9# +lqy-#0!>
<\alt ~7s, nqk=.?"@>
<'bamo {77%%} [1]>

"Here," Quirk threw something at me, jarring me from my concentration.

I looked at the foil-wrapped rectangular object. "A PowerBar? Where did you get a PowerBar in the jungle?"

"I packed it in my luggage. But clearly you need it more than me." Quirk handed me a sketch.

591

How sweet of him to bring me a PowerBar. It reminded me of David, when he brought me lollipops.

Unwrapping the PowerBar, I took a bite, and Quirk and I dove back into our work. He sketched, I scanned, and hours ticked by. Vaguely, I registered Jonathan checking in on us.

Click, click, click . . . I stared blurry-eyed at the screen. . . . Seconds rolled by in sync with the script scrolling my monitor.

"Well?" Quirk leaned over my shoulder. "Anything?"

My heart gave a happy little pitter-patter. "We've gone from a dozen possible translations down to four. That's progress." *Major* progress.

Quirk nodded. "Definitely." He held his hand out to me and pulled me to my feet. "Let's take a one-minute stretch break and get back to work."

One minute later we were back at it again. He sketched faster than I'd ever seen him. I scanned, reorganized the data, and more hours ticked by. Again, I vaguely registered Jonathan checking in.

Click, click, click . . . I kept my eyes fastened to the screen. . . . "We've gone from four down to two." I glanced up at Quirk. "Almost there."

With a nod, he continued sketching. "You doing okay? Tired?"

I should have been, but pure adrenaline surged through my veins. "I'm fine. You?"

"Peachy."

I laughed a little at that.

Sometime later Quirk handed me a sketch. "That's the last one. It's all up to you now."

I scanned it and, tuning everything out, focused on my program. I changed the results of the docket, redefined the prequibble, and corresponded the conspecti with the raciocinata.

Hours later I *click, click, clicked* . . . and took what felt like my first breath since starting. "We've got it."

***

We packed up and headed back to the village. Sixteen hours had taken us into the early afternoon of the next day.

I found Parrot at the corral and stepped up beside him. My horse, Diablo, came right over. I gave his nose a pet.

"Well?" Parrot asked me.

"I've deciphered it."

He smiled. "I knew you would. I don't suppose you're going to tell me."

"I have to tell Jonathan first—by the way, where is he?"

"He'll be back in a few. He and Guillermo are having a meeting." Parrot pointed up to the watchtower. "New guard."

I glanced up. "What has happened since I've been gone?"

He let out an exhausted sigh. "Couple of chiefs got in an all-out fistfight. A few others have bowed out. There are still eight left, and none of them are budging on the quote/unquote proof the Mother Nature vase belongs to their tribe." Parrot shook his head. "And there was another attempt at stealing the vase."

"Oh, my God. Please tell me no one died this time."

"No. Jonathan was there to intercede."

"They should have just left him as the official guard to begin with." I glanced up at the watchtower again and experienced a quick image of that dangling body. "Who tried to steal it?"

"Believe it or not, one of the young girls."

"What?!"

Parrot shrugged. "I'll be glad when all this mess is over."

"You and me both. I can't wait to go home." Where lollipops, my bed, food, friends, and David were waiting.

"You can say that again." Parrot took a sip from a brown pottery mug.

"What are you drinking?"

"Cinnamon coffee. Jaaci gave it to me." He handed me the mug. "Try some. It's good."

I did. And it was.

We stood there in companionable silence, Parrot and I both petting the horses. Something moved behind us, and we both turned to see Talon approach.

Beside me Parrot visibly stiffened, and I whispered, "Relax. Don't let him see you're nervous."

Coming up right beside Parrot, Talon leaned his back against the corral. With a thin sliver of wood, he picked his teeth, all relaxed, like he was hanging out with his pals in the barnyard. "With your blue eyes, long hair, and beard, I almost didn't recognize you. Almost, Darren with the magic tongue."

Darren. I'd forgotten that was Parrot's real name.

Slowly, Parrot turned to face Talon. "What do you want?"

Talon sneered. "That's right. I still have information about your mother." He let out a pleasant sigh, making a sarcastic show of enjoying this. "What a pretty young girl she was. You two favor each other. Let's see"—he made a show of pondering—"her name was . . . Sarah. That's right, Sarah."

Parrot took a step forward, and I knew he was about to blow.

Talon made a *tsk*ing noise. "Poor little Sarah. Or should I call her by her new name, Sparrow. What a sad life she led. Sold into slavery. Little Sparrow was quite popular among the slave trade."

"What?!" Parrot shouted. "Where is she?"

Talon smirked. "Well, I'm going to need something if you want that kind of information."

I stepped up. "I'm not falsifying my findings."

Talon shrugged. "That's nice, but I still want the vase, and that's what I'll have." Talon flicked his toothpick aside. "Meet me back here tonight. Midnight. You don't have the vase, I'll give the order that your mother be killed."

"How are we supposed to get the vase?"

Talon sneered. "Sounds like your problem, not mine." He glanced up at the watchtower and sighed. "Too bad one of the guards had to die. If he would've just handed over the vase like I'd asked—"

"Did you kill him?" Oh, my God.

"I didn't say that, now, did I?" Talon looked straight at me. "I do have many loyal people who work for me. People willing to do anything."

Hit men, but I didn't say it. I grabbed Parrot's arm. "Let's go." With all my strength I pulled him away.

"I always thought she left," he said when we were out of earshot from Talon. "I didn't know Talon sold her into slavery."

I rubbed Parrot's back. "And you still don't know. He could be lying. It's no wonder TL's had problems finding her. If her name has been changed, and she is in some sort of slave ring, there's no telling how many times she's been sold and resold. How many times her name has been changed."

With a moan, Parrot covered his face with his hands, and I realized I'd probably been too graphic with the possible details of his mom's situation.

Jonathan emerged from the jungle as we passed by the single-men hut. "What's wrong?" he asked.

I looked at Parrot and his clenched jaw, and I knew he wasn't opening it to explain. I turned to Jonathan. "Talon alluded to the fact he killed the guard or possibly hired a hit man to do it. And he told us to steal the vase and meet him at the corral at midnight."

"Or?" Jonathan asked.

I put my arm around Parrot. "Or he'd give the order for Parrot's mom to be killed."

Jonathan looked right at Parrot. "Your mom is not going to die. We'll play Talon's game, but our way. We're meeting him at midnight."

***

I lay wide awake in my hammock, incessantly checking my watch.

11:11 P.M.

I went over everything in my head that Jonathan had planned. We'd have a pouch with a fake vase. Parrot and I would use it as leverage in obtaining his mother's location. We'd give Talon the false artifact, and Jonathan and Guillermo would move in.

11:23 P.M.

I listened to the night sounds. A symphony of bugs, frogs, and a million other jungle night crawlers filled the air. Jonathan, Guillermo, and Quirk would be watching from the woods the whole time. Nothing would go wrong.

11:39 P.M.

An occasional soft snore, heavy breath, or the sound of a body shifting filtered past me in the single-women hut.

11:51 P.M.

I swung my legs over the side of the hammock and, with a deep breath, left the hut. I crossed the village, squinting toward the corral. Through the night I made out the shadows of the horses as they restlessly moved around.

I saw a person standing inside the corral holding a long object. And then another person beside him.

As I passed the ceremonial hut, something moved in my peripheral vision, and I turned to see Parrot coming toward me, holding the pouch with the fake vase.

I waited for him to catch up. "There's someone with Talon."

Parrot's gaze flicked to the corral. "That's the leader from Southern Mexico. Looks like we know who the other bad chief is."

I nodded toward the corral, absolutely determined Talon would not intimidate me this time. "Let's do this."

We approached the corral fence. The horses shifted with agitation at having Talon and the other chief inside the area.

Diablo and Abrienda tried to come over and say hi to us, but Parrot held his hand up and shook his head, and, surprisingly, the horses kept their distance.

Talon nodded to the pouch. "I'm not even going to ask how you got that away from the guards." He smirked. "Aren't you just sly these days?"

My gaze switched to a long spear Talon held in his hand. "What did you bring that for?" I asked, proud of my gutsy voice.

Talon shrugged. "Never know when you might need a good spear."

I didn't like that answer.

"I'm not into dramatics." Talon held out his hand. "Toss the pouch here, and I'll tell you where your mother is."

I put my hand on Parrot's arm. "Doesn't work that way. You tell us where his mom is, and we'll give you the pouch."

Talon narrowed his eyes.

"And," I continued with my bold ultimatum, "you lie to us about his mom, and you suffer. I think you've figured out by now that we have the ability to make you do just that. We have access to top secret things. Things you could only dream of." I pinned him with the stealthiest gaze I'd seen TL do. "You will be hunted down, both of you, and made to suffer.

"And, you lay one finger on my friend, and the same applies." Because once the location of Parrot's mom was revealed, he'd be free to testify against Talon. Talon knew that. Maybe that's why he'd brought the spear. To end Parrot's life.

Silence fell over us as my threat lingered in the air. I concentrated on not swallowing, blinking, or moving. I kept my icy eyes on Talon, letting him see every ounce of the truth in what I'd said. Somewhere in the back of my mind, I knew I'd gone too far, but I also knew I'd carry out the threat if need be.

The chief beside Talon swallowed, and the sound gurgled in the air. The nervous reaction pleased me.

Talon grunted. "Darren will not testify against me."

"Done," Parrot immediately agreed. "Tell me where my mother is."

"Poland. The city of Racpap. On Nublin Street. Number Twenty-three." Talon held his hand out for the vase, and Parrot tossed it to him.

Like two greedy boys, the chiefs eagerly untied the pouch and began unwrapping the thick layers of protective cloth.

Parrot and I turned away and started back across the village.

"Racpap. Nublin Street. Twenty-three," he recited. "Racpap. Nublin Street. Twenty-three."

"Pick up your pace," I whispered. "Talon's about to discover the vase is fake."

"WHAT IS THIS?!" Talon yelled through the night.

Parrot and I took off running. We wove through the village, dodging behind huts, jumping gardens, and disappeared into the jungle. Hearts pounding, we ran as fast as we could through the dark to the river. Plants slapped us, thorns stabbed us, limbs tripped us, but we kept going.

Minutes later we emerged at the river, our predetermined meeting place.

Gasping for air, I braced my hands on my knees. "Jonathan"—I took a breath—"and Guillermo"—I took another breath—"should have got him by now."

Sucking in air, Parrot nodded.

Out of the comer of my eye, a shadowed figure emerged from the jungle. I jerked up.

The Huworo chief stepped onto the river's bank. He said something in his language and nodded to the right.

"He says," Parrot translated, "he saw everything that happened. And this is not a safe place. Talon is heading right toward us."

"But what about Jonathan?"

Parrot turned to the Huworo chief, asked him that question, and the chief responded.

Parrot didn't say anything at first. He didn't even look at me.

"What?" I nearly shouted.

Parrot rubbed his hands down his face. "Oh, my God."

"WHAT?!"

"The chief says Jonathan has been killed and Guillermo's been seriously injured."

My whole body went numb. "Wh-what?" I shook my head. "That can't be."

Jonathan's words echoed in my brain. *If anything happens to me . . .*

The Huworo chief said something.

"He says," Parrot translated, "that we have to hurry. Talon's very close."

I shook my head again. *Something's not right.* "I want to see his body. I don't believe he's dead."

Something rustled in the jungle, and the chief took off running.

Parrot grabbed my arm and raced after the chief down the bank of the river. Tugging my arm free, I kept up the pace, glancing back every now and then to where we'd come from. The river cut around a corner, and I lost track of where we were.

The clouds parted, and the nearly full moon lit up the area.

More of Jonathan's words echoed through my brain. *Don't trust anybody. . . .*

My breath hitched with the overwhelming emotion. Jonathan was dead. TL was on another continent. David, too. Guillermo was seriously injured. And I had no idea where Quirk was.

Breathe, GiGi, breathe.

I still had Parrot, I reminded myself.

The chief darted off into the jungle, and we followed. The foliage surrounded us, blocking out any meager rays of moonlight. I tripped over something and felt Parrot pulling me up. He ran into a tree, and I was there to catch him. We both rolled down a bank and helped each other up. I tasted blood. With the amount of things scraping my face, there was no telling where it was coming from.

An animal roared through the night, and my already pounding heart leapt.

Oh, my God. We're going to die.

Right as that thought went through my brain, we emerged at the swinging bridge that spanned the canyon and led to the cave.

Sucking in air, Parrot and I looked around.

The chief said something. I turned in his direction and stumbled backward mere inches from the canyon's edge.

Holding a gun at me and Parrot, the chief repeated what he'd said.

"He says," Parrot gulped a breath, "that we either end our lives in the canyon or he's going to shoot."

"What?" I caught my sob. *Don't trust anybody. . . .* "Oh, my God." And then I started crying.

Parrot wrapped his arm around my shoulders.

"Lower the gun," a voice spoke to my left, and I jerked around.

Quirk stood at the border of the jungle with a rifle pointed straight at the Huworo chief. A shadow emerged behind him. I recognized the figure a split second before I screamed, "Quirk!"

And then everything happened lightning quick. Raising a rock high above his head, Talon slammed it down on Quirk's skull, and he fell flat on his face. Talon brought his spear back and slung it through the air, and with a squish, it pierced the Huworo chief's chest, sending him sailing through the dark into the canyon. Then Talon swung Quirk's rifle up into his hands and pointed it right at me and Parrot.

Neither one of us moved.

He cocked the rifle, making it more than apparent he wasn't talking, just shooting. I shoved Parrot away from me and dove in the opposite direction at the exact second Talon fired.

The booming sound echoed through the canyon and vibrated my body. Immediately, I recalled what Jonathan had said during PT.

What is my objective? To disable Talon.

What is my terrain? A canyon behind me, jungle in front.

Is there an enemy nearby? Yes.

Is there a team member nearby? Yes. One alive, one now unconscious.

How much time do I have to meet my objective? ASAP.

What resources do I have at my disposal? Dirt, rocks, my knife, canyon, swinging bridge.

With that thought, I grabbed a handful of rocks and dirt and slung it at Talon.

With a string of curses, he wiped his eyes, and I used that opportunity to move. I pulled my knife from the back of my pants and threw it in his direction.

He roared out in pain, and his face slowly morphed into an evil I didn't think I'd ever seen before. Like something else had taken over his body. With a deep, guttural scream, he pulled my knife from his thigh, nailed me with his possessed eyes, and raised the knife high above his head. Blood dripped from the tip down his face. With an inhuman grunt, he charged me.

I dodged to the right a split second too late. The knife grazed my side, and I hissed in a breath.

Talon laughed.

"Leave her alone!" Parrot yelled. "It's me you want."

Talon laughed again right as the moonlight disappeared, plunging us into darkness. I heard his evil chuckle as he scurried away from me.

I stayed very still and quiet as my eyes adjusted to the night, and I searched every shadow, trying to see where Talon had gone. I made out a figure to my right and narrowed my gaze. I watched as Parrot stealthily climbed a tree, lifted his knife above his head, and then leapt. I heard two bodies collide, and Talon's grunt echoed through the night.

I couldn't figure out where Parrot's knife had gone. If he'd injured Talon. If Talon had knocked the knife away.

I raced toward them as they rolled across the ground, coming up against the swinging bridge. Talon got on top, and I saw a jagged cut crisscross his back. He brought his fist up and slammed it into Parrot's jaw.

Parrot kneed him in the side, gaining top ground. He brought his fist back and nailed Talon in the mouth. A chunk of white flew through the air, and I hoped it was Talon's tooth.

I searched the ground, looking for a rock or any sort of weapon. I caught sight of Parrot's knife, grabbed the wooden handle, and lunged toward them. Parrot shifted, and I brought the knife down, jamming its jagged edge into Talon's shoulder.

He growled as he yanked my hair and slung me over him, and I smacked onto the bridge. With a scream I jumped to my feet, spun, and rammed the heel of my boot into Talon's head. At the same time Parrot jabbed his elbow into Talon's throat. Parrot lifted his forehead, ready for a head butt—

"Stop," I told him.

Parrot froze.

"He's out."

Neither one of us moved for a second.

Then slowly Parrot lifted off, and the two of us stood looking down at Talon. His thick body lay sprawled half on the bridge, half on the ground. Blood trickled from his eye, his mouth, and a gash in his forehead. Dirt and mud smeared his chest, arms, and legs.

I stepped over him. "We need to find something to tie him up with."

Parrot slid the knife from his shoulder. "I'll watch him. You go."

I hurried over to the jungle's edge and got down on my hands and knees, searching for long weeds, big leaves, anything to tie Talon up until we dragged him back to the village. My fingers connected with a thick vine. "Got something!"

With all my strength I dragged it from the thick overgrowth, turned, saw Parrot glance over his shoulder at me, and at the same time Talon lifted up. "PAAARRROOOTTT!"

Talon grabbed Parrot's ankle and yanked, sending him off balance, toppling over the canyon's edge.

"NOOO!" I screamed.

Parrot's horse, Abrienda, shot out from the jungle, and I stumbled away. I caught a glimpse of Jonathan on her back and nearly passed out.

Jonathan leaped off Abrienda and took off in the direction Parrot had gone. The horse reared up on her hind legs right over Talon, coming down only inches from his face.

He screamed and punched and kicked, grabbed fistfuls of dirt and rock, and threw it at her.

Baring her teeth, Abrienda let out a crying whinny, kicked out her front hooves, and came right down on top of him.

The sounds of bones crunching echoed through the night, and I cringed.

My horse, Diablo, flew right past me, and I caught a glimpse of Guillermo on his back.

I scrambled over to Jonathan, Guillermo, and the spot where I'd seen Parrot last. Guillermo was directing my horse, Diablo, back. Gripping a rope in his teeth, my horse slowly inched back, pulling with all his might at the rope. On his belly, Jonathan reached over the ledge and latched on to Parrot's forearm.

I stretched out right beside Jonathan and grabbed whatever I could on Parrot as Jonathan and Diablo pulled him up.

When I saw Parrot's bloody face, I burst into happy tears. As soon as his body was clear, I grabbed on. And somewhere in the recesses of my subconscious I registered Jonathan hugging us both.

‹FOURTEEN›

Turned out the Huworo chief was the hit man, hired by Talon to kill anyone who stood in the way of his getting the Mother Nature vase.

Talon's coconspirator, the Southern Mexican chief, was taken away. He would stand trial with the alliance for sabotaging the talks. Apparently, he was involved in Talon's slave trade, too, and would stand trial in six different countries for his crimes.

Jonathan had given the information concerning Parrot's mom to TL. And that was all we knew at this point.

The Huworo chief had told us Jonathan died and Guillermo was seriously injured. Obviously, that was a lie. Apparently, the Huworo chief had shot them with sleeping darts, and they'd been unconscious for a while.

And now here Quirk and I stood the next afternoon in front of all the other chiefs. A white, gauzy bandage covered the back of Quirk's head where ten stitches had been put in.

We had the final glyph translation of the ancient code and were about to reveal it.

And I suspected *no one* was going to be happy.

Since we would be speaking English, Parrot wasn't needed for the chiefs. He sat in the back near Jaaci to translate for her. Besides my team members, she was the only non-chief allowed in this meeting.

"Good afternoon, gentlemen," Quirk greeted them.

All the chiefs' personal assistants leaned in and whispered the translation in their leader's ear.

"As you all know, I and my assistant"—Quirk indicated me—"have been working in the cave for the past days sketching the drawings, researching, and coming up with a translation. We were hired to give you the translation. What you do with it is up to the alliance." Quirk smiled. "And we are very pleased to have broken the ancient code."

He paused for the translators. . . .

"The code was supposed to reveal a key piece of information about the vase, and, as suspected, that key piece of information deals with the ownership of the Mother Nature vase."

The translators whispered. It may have been my imagination, but it seemed as if every chief in the hut leaned forward, waiting for the answer.

"The owner of the Mother Nature vase is"—Quirk paused—"the Muemiraa tribe."

Translation occurred, and everyone began speaking at once. Clearly, no one was happy.

He held his hand up to let them know he had more to say. Slowly, the hut quieted.

"As we all know, Jaaci is the only remaining member of the Muemiraa tribe." Quirk looked at Jaaci. "So she is the owner of the vase."

Parrot translated to Jaaci, and her eyes widened in complete disbelief.

Quirk nodded to me, and I took that as my cue to finish.

"The code also revealed that the person granted ownership of the Mother Nature vase will be deemed a prince or princess." I looked at Jaaci again. "In this case, a princess."

Parrot gave Jaaci the translation, and she looked across the hut at me in stunned amazement.

I could only imagine what I'd feel like if I'd just found out I was a princess. And the owner of a centuries-old artifact.

"Lastly," I continued, "based on documented proof, a century ago the Muemiraa tribe split, forming the Iokojoja people. That makes Jaaci, through her blood connections, a member of the Iokojoja people. She is a princess of the Iokojoja people."

Translation occurred, and my gaze went straight to Jaaci. I was happy for her. She had a family again. A real family. With bloodlines that traced back centuries.

I'd give anything for that.

***

The chiefs met after we left the ceremonial hut, deciding if they would accept our translation of the ancient code. Roughly thirty minutes later they had.

That afternoon, all the chiefs, along with my team, Quirk, and Guillermo, escorted Jaaci to the river. The same river we had bathed in every morning.

Quirk served as the official recorder, sketching the scenes and detailing in words the historical events taking place.

All the chiefs and Jaaci were dressed in beautiful ceremonial garb. Some wore enormous headdresses, others intricate breastplates, and still others had their entire bodies decorated with paint.

And Jaaci . . . she wore her hair long and loose, and her white leather dress hung all the way to the ground with a slight train, as if she was getting married.

Parrot couldn't take his eyes off her. Heck, I couldn't either.

I'd heard the words *ethereal* and *celestial* before, but I'd never truly understood their meaning until now. Until looking at Jaaci.

In sequence, old to young, all the chiefs said a prayer in their language. I supposed they were blessing the vase as they passed it around, handing it finally to Jaaci.

Closing her eyes, she raised it above her head, saying her own prayer.

Goose bumps popped on my skin as I listened to her.

In a handwoven cloth, Jaaci wrapped the vase and carried it down to the river, where a canoe waited with the Iokojoja chief and his family. Turning, she bowed to all of us, and we silently watched as the canoe backed away from the shore. Parrot had told me their tribe lived a day's trip away on the river.

After they disappeared from sight, we all trekked through the jungle back to the village, and hours later, the chiefs and their assistants packed up and left. My team packed as well.

"Hannah," Quirk called me over as Jonathan and Guillermo were double-checking everything packed on the horses.

I followed him behind one of the huts.

"I wasn't sure if we'd get any privacy, so I just wanted to tell you I really enjoyed working with you."

I smiled. "Me, too. Who knows, maybe we'll be on another mission sometime."

He smiled back. "Maybe."

And then before I knew what was happening, he leaned in and gave me a kiss. "Thanks for 'getting' me."

Dumbfounded, I stood there, staring into his green eyes. He'd just kissed me.

"Um." He took a step back. "I—I can't believe I just kissed you." He let out a shaky laugh. "Oh, boy."

He'd just kissed me.

"Oh, boy. Are you okay?"

I gave my head a little shake and managed a wobbly smile. "Yes." And then I did something totally unexpected. I told him my real name. "My name's Kelly."

"Kelly," he said my name. "I'm Randy."

We both smiled.

He held out his hands. "Okay." And with a nod, Quirk/Randy walked right past me back toward the village.

I turned and watched him walk away, and David popped into my mind. Oh, my God. What would he think?

Quirk/Randy had kissed me. He'd really kissed me. I touched my fingers to my lips, and my stomach butterflied. His lips had felt soft and warm. David's lips were soft and warm, too . . . yet different. What did the kiss mean exactly? It had felt nice. Different. And Randy was right. I did "get" him. Just like he got me.

Should I tell David? My great *boyfriend*?

Yes, I probably should. I couldn't keep something like that from him. He'd tell me if some other girl had kissed him, right?

"Hannah," Jonathan yelled, interrupting my thoughts. "Let's go."

Suddenly, the urgency to get home doubled. I longed to see David.

***

It took us three days to horseback our way from the jungle and hop a couple of different planes from the country of Rutina back to America. A canceled flight, an extended layover in Dallas, and finally we arrived back in San Belden, California. Home. Guillermo had stayed in South America, and Randy had gone his own way in Dallas.

It was 1:00 in the morning when we arrived at the ranch. I couldn't wait to fall in the bed and sleep for eternity.

Jonathan nodded to the elevator. "TL wants to see us."

Parrot and I exchanged a tired glance.

With a yawn, I stepped onto the elevator. The door closed and we began descending. Four floors down we stepped off and followed Jonathan to the conference room, where TL stood waiting. He gave us a both a hug as we entered, and I sighed. I was home.

Parrot and I sat right beside each other, our chairs touching, our bodies as close as possible. We'd bonded in a way deeper than I'd connected with any of my other team members. Maybe it was because it had been just Parrot and me out there on the ledge, mere inches away from falling to our death. I'd been in dangerous situations before, but I'd always known TL or David or someone was nearby. Not this time, though. I'd truly believed that Jonathan was dead and that Parrot and I were on our own.

Parrot had almost died.

With that thought, a chill went through my body, and I reached under the table and clasped his hand. He grabbed on to mine tight as if he'd been thinking and feeling the same things.

Closing the door, TL came to sit in his seat at the table's head. For a few seconds all he did was survey our faces, taking in our bruises and cuts.

"I know the shaman of the Huworo tribe doctored you up, but I want both of you to see Dr. Gretchen first thing in the morning. I've instructed her to give you a complete physcial."

"Yes, sir," we responded.

"I want both of you to know how very proud I am of the job you've done. You've each far exceeded my expectations." TL turned to Parrot, his expression softening a bit. "I have news on your mother."

Parrot straightened in his chair.

"The address information Talon gave you was inaccurate. No surprise there. But her slave name, Sparrow, was correct. We confiscated the personal files of Talon's partner, the Southern Mexican chief. Using the information we found there, we were able to locate your mother. She will be here in the States in a few days."

Parrot let out a breath, like he couldn't quite believe what TL had just said. "Is she okay?"

"She's extremely malnourished. So when you see her, you need to be prepared. It's been ten years. A lot changes in a person in that time."

Nodding, Parrot dropped his gaze, trying to hide the tears welling in his eyes. Under the table I squeezed his hand again, so pleased for him.

TL turned to me. "How's your side?"

I put my hand over the gash that had been stitched and bandaged. "Fine." I wanted to ask him when David was due back, but figured this wasn't the appropriate time.

"Get some rest." TL gave us both a small smile. "You both need it." He glanced over his shoulder at Jonathan, who still stood at the door. "If you don't mind staying for a few minutes . . ."

Jonathan nodded.

Parrot and I made our way back up to the ranch level and split apart when we got to our rooms. Quietly, I opened the door to the girl's dormitory room and tiptoed in. Cat, Beaker, and Bruiser were fast asleep. I dropped my stuff on the floor next to my bed, changed clothes, did my thing in the bathroom, and dropped onto my mattress. I lay there for a few minutes with my eyes closed, listening . . . to the *quiet*. No bug noises. No frogs. No night crawlers. It was amazing how loud the jungle really was . . . and how quiet the non jungle really was . . . and how, believe it or not, I'd gotten so used to the jungle noises. I sort of missed them.

Maybe I'd download a few of those nature songs to listen to at night. With a content smile and sigh, I felt my whole body relax and fell right to sleep. . . .

"GiGi."

Somewhere far away in the jungle my name echoed. A big bug fluttered past my arm, and I brushed it away.

"GiGi."

I grumbled. "I don't want to bathe."

"GiGi."

"Whaaat?"

Something closed over my mouth, and my eyes shot open at the same time I executed a wonka-jonk, Bruiser's term for her version of the karate chop.

The person above me blocked my wonka-jonk and quietly pinned me to the hammock—er, um, bed. That's right, I was in a bed. In my home. Back at the ranch.

Through the dark I blinked my eyes real hard and focused in on the face above me . . . David!

His eyes crinkled when he realized I realized who he was.

"Oo ot pose to bee een ere," I mumbled into his hand.

David uncovered my mouth.

"You're not supposed to be in here," I whispered. He could get in major trouble if TL found him in here after curfew. But . . . who cared. David was here!

Putting his finger over his lips, he threw my covers back, took my hand, and led me from the room. Together we tiptoed down the dimly lit hall, past TL's door, through the cafeteria, and into the kitchen. With each step we took my heart banged harder and harder. Where were we going?

We crossed the kitchen, and David pulled open the door to the pantry. He led me inside and shut the door, plummeting us into darkness. This was the first place we'd ever kissed. And with that thought, I felt him move close.

"I heard a leech ate your butt." I could hear the humor in his voice, and I laughed.

He flicked a switch, and dim light illuminated the area. Like TL had done, David's gaze touched each of my bruises and cuts. I followed his eyes as they roamed over my cheeks, forehead, and chin. He reached out and carefully touched the spot on my side where'd I'd been knifed. And leaning forward, he gently pressed his lips to each mark on my face.

I closed my eyes and melted into his warmth, his strength, his familiarity.

He took a small step away, and from behind his back he brought out a lollipop. "Will this make things better?" he asked softly.

I smiled. "Always."

"Turn around," he said.

"What?"

He twirled his finger. "You heard me. Turn around."

With a quizzical look, I turned my back to him. I heard a slight rustling, and then David brought a necklace down in front of me and fastened it around my neck.

"What did you do?" I held out the silver emblem etched with odd writing.

He turned me back around. "It's a cartouche from Egypt. It's your name."

"David!" I hugged him. "It's beautiful. Thank you."

He smiled. "You're very welcome. It's your graduation gift."

"My what?"

"TL told me you graduated college. Congratulations."

"Oh. Thanks. Truthfully, I didn't graduate. I tested out of the last semester."

"Why didn't you tell me?"

"Don't know." I shrugged. "No big deal, really. Just another test."

"No big deal?" David raised his brows. "You're sixteen, and you graduated college."

"Almost seventeen."

"And you graduated college."

"Yeah? So?"

He stared at me with a perplexed look while I stared back.

Shaking his head, he chuckled and closed the minuscule space between us. "My God, I missed you." He backed me up against the door and covered my body with his. He started kissing me, and kissing me, and kissing me . . .

. . . I'm so glad I'm wearing my cute pajamas . . .

. . . and kissing me . . .

. . . Thank God I brushed my teeth . . .

. . . and kissing me . . .

. . . and I'm not even thinking about Quirk/Randy . . .

"You're thinking," he grumbled, leaving my mouth to nibble my neck.

He pressed soft kisses all over my face and neck and then picked up my hands and did them and my arms.

"How many kisses was that?" he asked.

"Hmmm . . . ?"

"You're supposed to be counting kisses, remember?"

How in the world did he expect me to remember that when I highly doubted I could conjure up the SAQ code right now? Oh, wait. I focused. No, I probably could.

"My bad. I made you think." He went straight for that part of my neck again, and my whole world spun.

"There." David chuckled. "Objective met."

***

Two days later, I was in the garden pulling weeds, my chore for the day.

David stepped from the barn, caught sight of me, and came over. Kneeling beside me, he began helping.

"You don't have to do that," I told him.

He shrugged. "I know."

Together, we worked in silence and my thoughts drifted to Randy. They'd been doing that a lot since I'd gotten back.

"David?"

"Hm?"

"Would you tell me if another girl kissed you?"

David stopped working and looked up at me. "Why?"

I kept working, focusing so hard on the weeds, my eyes nearly crossed. "Because . . . because someone else kissed me." There. It was out. Finally.

My heart boinged around in my chest while I waited for his response.

"Who? Who kissed you?"

I kept working. "The glyph professor."

"Did he ask or did he just kiss you?" he asked, not sounding too happy.

"He just kissed me. But . . ." I didn't want him to think Randy had mistreated me or anything.

"But what?"

I kept working. "But nothing. It's just I didn't want you to think he'd forced me to kiss him or anything."

"So what are you saying?"

I didn't know how to answer that.

"Would you stop working, please?" he snapped.

I looked over at him. He did *not* look happy.

"What are you trying to say to me?" he repeated himself.

I took in his irritated face, thought of his wonderful heart, and felt like a complete idiot for bringing it up. "David," I sighed. "It didn't mean anything. You trust me, right?"

He jerked a nod.

And I decided to be completely honest with him. He deserved that. "The professor was cute and just a few years older and we . . . clicked, on an intellectual level. But I told him about you and how wonderful you are, and he completely respected that. And then when we said good-bye to each other, he gave me a quick kiss. I think the kiss surprised him as much as it did me, but that's all there was to it. He went his way, and I went my way, and that's that. And it's been bugging the heck out of me because I don't like keeping things from you. That's one of the good things about us. At the base of it all, we're friends."

I reached out and touched his arm. "I wouldn't do anything to hurt you."

"You don't think we click on an intellectual level?" His voice sounded so hurt, it made me feel horrible.

"Not like Chapling and I do."

"This professor guy was like Chapling?"

"Well, no, not exactly." God, I didn't know what to say to make things better.

David got up. "Let me just have some time to think."

"David," I said to his back as he walked away, but he didn't turn.

I tried to imagine how I would respond if the situation was reversed, and, truthfully, I'd probably be walking away right now, too.

A limo pulled through our security gate, drawing my attention away from David. It circled our driveway and came to a stop in front of the house. The driver got out and walked around to open the door for the passenger.

A tall, extremely skinny, dark-haired woman stepped out, wearing jeans and a long-sleeved blouse.

"Oh, my God," I realized out loud, "that's Parrot's mom."

The door to the house opened, and out came Parrot. He and his mom stood very still, staring at each other with only ten feet or so of space separating them.

My heart ached as I watched them.

They moved at once, running toward each other and colliding together. Even though I stood in the side yard, I could hear them crying.

Gripping each other tightly, they rocked each other and cried out the ten years they'd been apart.

The overwhelming emotion seemed to ripple through the air as all my teammates slowly, quietly trickled out from wherever they were to witness the reunion.

I wondered how they all felt, having to watch this, feeling happy for Parrot, but wishing it for themselves, too.

I knew I wished it for myself.

And I wondered what this meant, if anything, for Parrot and his future with the Specialists.

TL approached them a few minutes later and said something. The two of them nodded, climbed in the limo, and pulled away.

Everyone slowly began trickling back to where they'd come from, and TL turned in my direction. With two fingers he waved me over.

I jogged from the side yard across the driveway to the front. "Yes, sir?"

"Conference room. Now."

With a nod, I followed him into the house and down to Subfloor Four. We walked into the conference room, and I'd hoped David would be there.

"Hihihi!" Chapling greeted me instead.

I grinned. "Hi! I missed you." He'd been gone since I returned.

He giggled and leaned in. "Guess what," he whispered.

"What?"

"My mom got married again."

"Again?"

"Her eighth one." Chapling shrugged. "It shouldn't take long for her to move on to the ninth."

"*Eighth* marriage?" Holy sheesh. I realized then that I knew very little about Chapling's personal life. Mother, father, brothers, sisters, where he grew up . . . did he have a *girlfriend?*

Nah, somehow I couldn't see Chapling with a girlfriend.

"Chapling, do you realize I don't know anything about you?"

He fluttered his pudgy hand. "We'll purge our souls later."

TL shook his head. "You two get sidetracked so easily."

We both laughed at that.

TL looked at Chapling. "Why don't you tell her why we're really in here."

"Oh rightright." Chapling held up the sketch of the woman I'd stolen in South America. "I know who this is!"

I waited, but he didn't expound on the information. "Who?" I prompted.

"This is your sister."

"My *WHAT?*"

"Before your father joined the IPNC, he was married to another woman, and they had a daughter," TL responded. "Truthfully, I never even knew your father had had another wife. The daughter is fifteen years older than you."

I shook my head. "My father was married before my mother?" I hadn't known. *Obviously.* Or I wouldn't be so dumbfounded right now. "I have a-a-a *sister?*"

TL nodded. "Yes, you do."

"Wh-where?" I stammered.

TL shook his head. "We're not sure. But we're going to find her."

Don't forget to check out the next book in
The Specialists series.

When someone close to TL disappears, The Specialists pull out all the stops. GiGi is brought into another mission along with Bruiser and Mystic. This time, it's a fight to the end, and someone doesn't make it out alive.

BOOK FIVE

‹PROLOGUE›

HOW THE SPECIALISTS RECRUITED MYSTIC AND BRUISER

"Now you listen to me, young man." Joe's foster father jabbed his finger in Joe's face. "I am *sick* and *tired* of your lax attitude."

Joe stared blankly at his foster father, the man he'd lived with for the past six months. He wanted to react, but what was the point?

Joe's foster father took a step closer to him. He began ticking items off on his fingers. "You will rise from bed promptly at five a.m. You have exactly twenty minutes to prepare yourself for the day." He ticked off another finger. "Breakfast is served at 5:20. And even if you are done before the rest of us, you will remain seated at the table."

Another finger got ticked off. "Morning chores and prayers are from 5:45 until 6:45. Your mother—"

"She's not my mother," Joe quietly interrupted.

His foster father narrowed his eyes. "Your *mother* will have the living room set up for school by seven a.m. You are to be seated with notebook and pencil in hand prior to her starting." He ticked another finger off. "We do not tolerate tardiness." He leaned down right in Joe's face. "Are you getting all of this?"

No, I'm not, Joe wanted to say. What did the man think he was, stupid? "Yes," Joe answered instead.

His foster father straightened and ticked another finger. "Homework is due . . ." He continued to outline the day, down to every precise second. The same day Joe had been living over and over again since coming here.

It was driving him slowly to the point of insanity.

His foster father leaned down again, hovering over Joe where he sat in the dining room chair. "If your parents," he jabbed that stupid finger in Joe's face again, "had raised you with more structure and stability, you wouldn't have any problems following orders."

Digging his fingers into the wooden armrests, Joe got slowly, purposefully to his feet. He stood only five foot ten, but he still had height over the man. "Don't. You. *Ever* bad mouth my parents. They were two hundred percent more kind and decent then you will ever be."

It wasn't often someone could get a rise out of Joe. But his foster father could. Anybody who spoke badly of Joe's parents would *definitely* get a rise out of him.

The man pulled his shoulders back. "You know what? I'm done with you. I'm calling your social worker and sending you back to the state. I've got better things to do then put up with your disrespect and obvious lack of manners."

"Back to the state?" Joe smirked. "Fine by me. I'd rather live in a thousand boys' homes then under your roof."

His foster father turned red all the way up to his military crew cut. He jabbed his finger toward the door. "Get out!" he yelled.

Calmly, Joe nodded, when what he really wanted to do was punch the man in the face.

Turning, Joe strode across the living room, snagged his backpack from beside the couch, and went straight out the front door. He cut across the creek in the back yard and disappeared into the hills of Tennessee. What little Joe had was in his backpack. He'd left a few things back at his foster family's house. He didn't care. Everything and everyone Joe had ever loved was gone. Whatever he'd accumulated in the past six months . . . well, it just didn't matter.

Joe walked for hours through the Tennessee woods and hills he'd grown up in. He knew how to survive. He wasn't worried. His parents had raised him in nature. Joe could live for months, *years* on what God's earth provided.

Subconsciously, he headed in the direction of where his whole world had come apart six months ago. As he neared the spot, his heart picked up pace, and he nearly buckled with the overwhelming presence of his family's souls, still drifting, still not settled, searching, searching for peace.

Joe emerged from a forest of pine trees and crossed a meadow of dandelions. The same meadow he had played in nearly every day with the commune's other children.

He sucked in a breath with the rush of wind carrying the screams of those who were gone. Sometimes he wished he didn't hear, he didn't feel, he didn't see the pain others had gone through or were currently experiencing. Joe wished his gifts would let him see laughter and happiness, like his mother's had. Why had he inherited the sorrow of the world?

Joe sucked in another breath as the memory of his little sister's wail pierced his heart. Why couldn't he have saved them?

Squeezing his eyes shut, he willed away the sounds, the touch, the images.

It's okay, baby. Joe heard his mom's voice in the wind. *You're home. Go forward. Don't be afraid.*

He opened his eyes and watched the dandelions white seeds float on another rush of August wind. Joe lifted his face to the heavens and absorbed the sun's heat.

Slowly, he moved forward toward the edge of the meadow where the woods began again, marking the border of his home. He stepped into the woods and stood in the shadows, staring at the burnt ground where his home used to be. Why anyone would have done this, he'd never know.

Sixty one people, his family, had died that day. And he was the only survivor.

With a deep breath, Joe turned and left the Tennessee ridge he'd always known as home. He made his way through the woods down the hill to the valley. Just like it had been six months ago, the old town had only one grocery store, one post office, a hardware store, and no stop lights. Population: two hundred and fifty.

He walked into the grocery store and over to the fruit and vegetable section. He loaded up on bananas, tomatoes, and cucumbers, and then grabbed a bag of shelled pecans and a box of powdered milk. Combined with what nature always provided, he'd be able to live for months in the hills.

With a nod to a woman with a baby on her hip, Joe rounded the corner and headed to the cash register.

"In national news, Janie Spieth, seven year old daughter to Wisconsin governor, William Spieth, has gone missing. Experts expect foul play, although no ransom note has been issued. . ."

Joe stared at the black and white television, into the eyes of little Janie Spieth, and felt the familiar tug of her soul. She was alive. Her energy told him that.

He closed his eyes as a chill ran through his body, giving him goose bumps. Little Janie was freezing.

Her sob echoed in Joe's ears, followed by a boat's horn.

An image of a freight liner floated past, and Joe focused on the name painted on its steel side. STOCK AND ROLL LINER he made out.

Little Janie's tear streaked face flashed in his brain as she cuddled a baby doll in the dark.

"'cuse me, you gonna go or what?"

Joe's eyes snapped open, and he turned to see the young woman with her baby. He motioned them ahead to check out and focused back on the television.

"If you have any information," the reporter continued, "pertaining to the whereabouts of Janie Spieth, please call this number. . ."

Joe memorized the number, quickly paid for his groceries, and went to the nearest pay phone. Disguising his voice, he called it in, just like he had done two hundred and twenty three times before. Two hundred and twenty three children and adults had been located because of him.

That thought brought a smile to his face.

He hung up the phone and turned to grab his groceries from the ground.

"Interesting information you have there. Want to tell me how you got it?"

Joe whipped around to see a dark-haired man staring at him through peculiar light green eyes. Taking a step back, Joe regained his composure. "I don't know what you're talking about."

The man slipped his hands into the front pockets of his camouflaged pants. "I've been following you."

Joe took another step away. "What do you mean you've been following me?"

"My people and I have been watching you for the past six months. You've placed quite a few similar phone calls from a pay phone near your foster family's home. We had your voice analyzed and realized you were the same person who'd been calling in leads for a few years now. I saw you leave your foster family's home this morning. I followed you into the woods, up into the mountains, back to your home, and now down to here."

"Who are you?" Joe asked.

The man slipped his hand from his pocket and held it out. "Thomas Liba. I work for the government."

"The government?" Joe took another step away, not shaking his hand. His parents had warned him about the government.

Mr. Liba put his hand back in his pocket. "Two hundred and twenty three people you've helped save. That's some track record."

Joe's eyes widened. This man *did* know a lot.

Mr. Liba nodded to the grocery bag in Joe's hand. "Can't survive in the woods on just that. You need other supplies."

"I was heading to the hardware store," Joe told him before he realized what he was saying.

"Planning on disappearing?"

Joe didn't answer him.

"Joe Green," Mr. Liba said his name. "Seventeen years old. Five foot ten. One hundred and eighty five pounds. Blonde hair. Blue eyes. Grew up in a commune in the Tennessee hills. Home schooled. Your father was the commune's teacher, your mother, the healer. Your little sister lived to be ten year's old. And you, my boy, inherited your mother's gift of sight. Your world was perfect until earlier this year when your home was targeted in a hate crime by people who only understand one way of life. They brutally—"

Joe squeezed his eyes shut. "Don't. Please."

"You had gone to gather herbs," Mr. Liba continued. "There was nothing you could have done. By the time you returned—"

"Please. Stop." Joe had seen enough of it already. Had relived it many times. He didn't need any reminders.

Mr. Liba didn't say anything else, and after a few seconds Joe opened his eyes, looked straight into Mr. Liba's, and saw all the way to his soul.

Flashes of his life reeled passed. Him as a little boy being horribly beaten, locked in a closet, starved . . . as a young teenager being ganged up on by older guys . . . as a young man in training alongside other men, learning how to fight . . . later in life rescuing people from terrible situations . . .

This man, Mr. Liba, had a stern, but gentle soul. A soul that was a little lost. A soul to be trusted. One full of kindness. Yet one not to be messed with.

This is your destiny. Joe heard his mother's voice.

Mr. Liba swallowed, and Joe sensed this man had lost a little bit of control and didn't like it. Mr. Liba knew Joe had just seen his childhood.

Mr. Liba cleared his throat, clearly uncomfortable. "I would appreciate it," he said, "if you would not share with people what you just saw in me."

Joe nodded. "We all have our secrets. And I now know I'm supposed to come with you. I also know you've got to get to Chicago ASAP. That someone very important needs your help."

Mr. Liba just looked at Joe. "You're something else."

They climbed into the black van parked in the grocery store lot. As they pulled away, Joe's mind drifted to last year. . . "Jimmy Williams was from Chicago."

"Twelve years old," Mr. Liba picked up on the conversation. "Taken from the ball field. Missing one month. You called in the lead that got him rescued."

Joe nodded. "Barely in time. The follow up news stories reported Jimmy was near starvation when he was finally found."

"Yes," Mr. Liba agreed. "But thanks to you he made it."

Joe breathed a soft sigh. Yes, Jimmy had made it.

They drove in silence for a while, and Joe closed his eyes, allowing his thoughts to drift with Mr. Liba's. He was personally connected to someone in Chicago. A man who had an integral part of Mr. Liba's past. A man Mr. Liba thought very highly of. A man who had secrets of his own.

Joe opened his eyes, feeling intrusive into Mr. Liba's emotions, and purposefully cut the connection between them. "Tell me about the Specialists," he prompted.

A hint of a smile curved Mr. Liba's lips as he began speaking. That conversation led to another and then another. . .

They only stopped once and eight hours later arrived in Chicago. Mr. Liba pulled up in front of a condemned firehouse. Through the windshield and the dark, Joe studied the deserted building. Something red flashed in his peripheral vision and he turned to see a petite red-headed girl running down the alley toward them.

"That's her," TL said.

Sprinting down the dark Chicago alleyway, Molly jumped a huge puddle, rounded the backside of a dumpster, and shimmied up a six foot tall concrete wall.

She needed to get to Red.

Dodging the chunks of glass lining the top of the wall, she swung over and down and landed on her feet.

He had not sounded good when she left.

She ducked under a CONDEMNED sign, slipped through a hole in the chain linked fence, and trotted up a flight of rickety stairs. Pulling back heavy plastic, Molly climbed through the window of the deserted firehouse she had called home, along with twelve other kids, for the past ten years.

A small battery operated lamp put a dim yellow glow in their bedroom. Mattresses, foam, and old cushions piled with blankets and sheets lined the walls. She'd done everyone's laundry yesterday in the tub downstairs, so it smelled better than usual in here.

Molly turned to the corner where she knew Red, the man who had raised her, would be. He lay bundled up under his own blankets as well as others that kids had laid on him. It was a muggy August night outside, but as usual, Red was freezing cold.

He opened his eyes and looked at Molly.

She grinned. "Hey, Red."

Through his bushy gray beard, Molly made out a few teeth, and knew he was smiling back. He coughed, filling the air with a gurgled lung sound.

Molly looked around at all the empty beds and tried not to show her irritation. "Everybody leave you, huh?" She tried to make a joke.

She'd made it clear many times there was to always be someone, *anyone*, here watching Red. If it weren't for him they'd all still be on the streets.

Ten years ago when she was five years old, Red had found her under a bridge about a mile from where they were now. She'd been in a fight with a boy a few years older. Red had broken the fight up, sent the boy home, and when he found out Molly had no home, Red had taken her "under his wing". He'd brought her here to this firehouse and had been the only family she'd ever known. He'd brought her into the world of fighting.

Molly crossed the floor to where he lay and knelt down beside him. She reached out and put her hand on his clammy forehead. As usual it felt hot. *Too* hot.

Slipping her backpack off her shoulders, she rummaged around inside for the things Red had sent her to get: Ibuprofen, Gatorade, and cough medicine.

"Red," Molly whispered. "Please let me take you to the emergency room."

He'd been like this for three straight weeks and wasn't getting any better.

"No," he rasped and coughed again. "I told you, I've been like this before. I'll be fine."

Molly sighed. She'd known him ten years and that was what he always said when he got this way. That it was just side effects of things that had happened when he was in the military. To her it seemed more serious than 'just side effects'.

He didn't want to go the hospital because he was afraid.

Afraid they'd find out who he was. Afraid they'd find all of the street kids. Afraid he'd die. Afraid this warehouse would be raided. Afraid of everything and everyone.

And although he'd never admitted it, Molly suspected he was hiding from something, from someone.

Red brought his arm out from under the covers and with a shaky hand opened the cough medicine. Molly handed him four Ibuprofen, and he swallowed them dry, then gurgled down some of the cough stuff and set the bottle aside.

He gave a slight nod for her to go on. "Skedaddle, little one. The fight starts soon." He pointed a finger at her. "And you promised me you wouldn't fight tonight. You need a break."

Molly nodded slightly as she slipped her hand into his. She studied his dirty fingernails and large rough hands. *Please don't die*, she wanted to say, but knew he'd bop her upside the head if she did.

Red squeezed her fingers. "Go on. I'll be here when you get back."

"Bobby can handle the fights," Molly suggested, referring to one of the other street kids. "I'd rather stay here with you."

"Jonesy will be back any second." Red let go of Molly's hand. "I won't be alone for long."

Jonesy. Molly almost snorted. Jonesy was *the* most irresponsible of the kids that lived here. In fact, Jonesy was the one who was supposed to be watching Red right now.

Slowly, Molly got to her feet, knowing Red would engage in an all out argument with her if she didn't leave.

"Who's fighting tonight?" he rasped.

"Larry the Louse and Charlie big man Cheeseburger." Molly shoved her hands in her back pockets. "Cheeseburger's gonna win."

Red chuckled. "Yeah, he's got Larry two to one in weight."

Molly snorted. "What's that got to do with anything? Everybody's got me in weight."

Red smiled. "True. And you manage to submit 'em every time."

Molly shrugged. "What can I say? I was taught by the best." The best being Red.

She'd never seen another fighter more skilled than him. And although he didn't talk much about his past, he had said he'd been trained in Asia. He'd taught all the other kids that lived here to fight, too. Mostly to defend themselves on the streets. None of the others loved the art as much as Molly, though.

"I knew the moment I met your scrappy little five-year-old self, you had a gift. You had that boy twice your size bloodied up and in a heap on the ground. Fighting comes naturally for you, Molly. It was easy to teach you. You've got it flowing in your blood." He huffed out a breath. "Yep, you're something else." Red chuckled and it rolled right into a coughing fit.

Cringing at the sound, Molly went to her bed, got a roll of toilet paper, and brought it back to him. She unrolled a wad and handed it to him and watched him spit up blood.

"Red," she whispered.

"Go on now, Molly."

"Red . . ."

"When's your next fight?" he changed the subject.

"Not 'til tomorrow."

He nodded toward the door. "Go on now."

Nodding, she backed away, staring at his body as he rolled to his side and put his back to her.

She slipped through the heavy clear plastic covering the doorway and out onto the steel landing. Pulling a slim flashlight from her front pocket, she twisted the head and shined the light down the spiral staircase that led from one floor to the next, five stories down to the bottom.

On floor four, Red and her and some of the other homeless kids had set up a make shift kitchen with stuff they'd found on the streets: a two burner propane camping stove, couple of aluminum bowls for sinks, dishes someone had thrown out right after Christmas, and even an ice box that kept things cool for a week.

On floor three they had running water. Red said someone at city hall forgot to turn it off when they condemned the firehouse some twenty years ago. It wasn't hot water, but at least it was water. There had already been a tub on floor three when Molly came to live here. Red had insisted if she was going to stay she had to bathe every two days, hot water or not.

Molly smiled at the memory. She'd been so filthy when he'd found her fighting that kid in the dirt.

Floor two of the firehouse was nothing. Just steel beams. No floor even.

Floor one was dirty and nasty, but safe. They purposefully stayed clear of it, though, so if anyone on the street happened to look in a window they'd see only a condemned building in dire need of a cleanup.

The fight club was in the basement below floor one.

With the fight club on her mind now, Molly put the flashlight in her mouth, stepped from the landing, snaked her body around the steel pole, and whooshed all the way down five stories to the bottom. She crossed the floor to the corner where Red had installed a trap door.

Pulling the rug aside, she used the rope handle and lifted open the hidden door. Sounds of the fight club shot out the opening. Yells, chants, grunts, and a thumping bass from the room's stereo.

A stairwell led from the trap door down to a landing. The landing led to nowhere, just the ceiling rafters of the firehouse's basement. If Molly or one of the other kids that lived with her wanted to get down to the fight club, they simply slid down a rope that had been attached to the rafters.

Tonight, though, Molly would stay in the rafters. She was in charge of emceeing the fights.

Jogging down the stairwell, she hopped onto the landing, grabbed the bullhorn she'd left there last night, and walked out onto the rafters. From her high up view point she surveyed the crowd.

About thirty of the usual customers. Mostly men. She did recognize a few new people. That was good. That meant the club was growing. All of them entered through a secret passageway in the nearby train station. That was part of the allure. The secretiveness, exclusiveness, the betting, hoping for a gruesome fight. It fulfilled some dark side of them.

Molly didn't care as long as they threw around their money. Money her and Red put aside for all the kids. To one day make a better life. She felt a bit of pride at that. Thanks to her, this fight club existed. She'd begged and begged Red to let her turn the basement into a fight club. Last year, he'd finally given in. And they'd seen nothing but profit since.

A whistle pierced the air above the sound of the crowd. Molly looked down and straight into Bobby's eyes. He winked at her, indicating he'd gotten all the bets and it was time to start.

Hanging onto the steel rafters, Molly held the bullhorn up to her mouth. "Ladies and gentlemen," she yelled. "Welcome to tonight's fiiiggghhhttt!"

Everyone screamed.

"Tonight," she continued, "we have two of the best street fighters in Chicago. We have Larry the Louse and Charlie big man Cheeseburger."

The crowed roared.

Molly's hand tightened around the bullhorn. "There are no rules in this fight club. Be clean, be dirty. Fight good, fight nasty. Knock 'em out, leave 'em standing. No rules, except . . ." She purposefully paused, just like Red had suggested, knowing it was what the crowd expected, knowing it would get a rise out of them.

"Blood, blood, blood," they chanted.

Molly rolled her eyes. "No rules except BLOOOD. We have to see BLOOOD."

The crowd roared.

And then everything happened lightning quick. Some of the patrons pulled guns out and yelled, "Freeze!"

Someone else threw a canister and the underground club erupted in smoke.

Molly didn't spare a second. She sprinted across the dark rafters onto the landing and up the stairs. She shoved open the trap door, climbed through, shut it behind her, and covered it with the rug.

Red. She had to get to Red.

Taking the spiral stairs two at a time, she hoofed it up five stories. And barely winded, she threw the plastic aside and ran into the bedroom. A tall man stood beside where Red lay.

Without a second of thought, Molly flew across the room, caught air, and executed a round house, landing the heel of her left foot in the man's sternum, right at his lung meridian point.

627

He stumbled back and gasped for air.

"Stop." Red commanded.

Molly came down on both feet, hands up, ready for anything that came next. "Who are you?" she asked the man.

The man held his hands up, palms out. "My God, Red, you're right."

Red chuckled. "I told you she was something else. This girl's got a gift."

Molly didn't take her gaze off the unknown man.

"Thomas Liba," Red said, "I'd like you to meet Molly. We have no idea what her last name is or when she was born. But she said she was five when I found her, which would make her almost fifteen now. She's four foot eleven. Ninety five pounds. Red hair. Green eyes. She is, hands down, the best fighter I've ever trained."

"Molly," Red continued, "this man is here for you. I want you to go with him."

Molly still didn't take her gaze off the man, Thomas Liba. "What are you talking about? I'm not leaving you."

"Do you remember Tommy, that fourteen year old kid I told you about?" Red asked.

Molly nodded. "Yeah, you said he pulled a knife on you and asked for all your money."

Thomas Liba chuckled at that. "And my life has never been the same."

"He was a street kid," Red put in. "Just like you. I took him in and trained him. This is him, Molly. This is Tommy."

Molly eyed the man.

Red coughed. "You and I both know I'm sick. I need help. But I can't go to a hospital. Tommy can help me. He can help you. There's a lot about my past you don't know. One day I want to share it with you. But I have to get better." He paused. "Molly, look at me."

Slowly, she took her eyes off Thomas Liba and focused down into the face of the only family she'd ever known.

"Go with Tommy," Red said. "You can trust him. I promise I'll get better, and we'll see each other again."

"When?" she asked.

Red shook his head. "I don't know. But I've never broken a promise to you. If I say we'll see each other again, then we will. If you don't go with him, I can't get help. I *won't* get help. And don't worry about the other kids. Tommy's got lots of connections. He's going to make sure they get treated well."

For a long minute, Molly stared into Red's eyes. She would do anything for him. And she knew he would do anything for her. If this was what Red wanted, this was what she would do.

Molly nodded to Thomas Liba. "I'm yours."

He nodded back. "Call me TL."

<ONE>

Wirenut pulled the ranch's van into the Boardwalk's packed parking lot. The Boardwalk stretched three miles along San Belden, California's coast. Amusement rides, food, dancing, roller blading—you name it, and the place had it. It never closed down.

He turned around in his seat to face all of us. "Now kids," he jokingly began, lowering his voice to an authoritative tone. "I want you to remember we represent the San Belden Ranch for Boys and Girls."

Wirenut looked at me. "Okay, Miss tall Blondie. You will behave yourself. No hacking into anyone's computers. You hear me, GiGi?"

I saluted him, hiding my smile. "Yes, sir."

"And you." Wirenut looked at Beaker. "No mixing of strange chemicals. And absolutely no more body piercings."

Snapping her gum, Beaker nodded her pink dyed head. "You got it."

"And you." Wirenut narrowed his eyes at Bruiser. "Youngest member of our clan and today's birthday girl. No beating anyone up."

Flipping a red braid over her shoulder, Bruiser batted her lashes. "I'm only here to celebrate my sweet sixteen."

"And you." Wirenut switched his attention to Parrot. "No speaking any foreign languages. English only tonight."

Parrot smiled.

"You." Wirenut nodded to Mystic. "Mr. Thick Neck. No reading of fortunes."

Mystic put his hand over his heart. "Never."

Wirenut turned to the van's passenger seat where Cat sat. "You," he softened his tone, "my gorgeous, Mediterranean, goddess are allowed to break into *anything* you want to."

"Hey!" we all objected.

Cat reached across the space between them and tugged on Wirenut's dark goatee. "And you are absolutely *not* allowed to tinker with anyone's electronics."

Wirenut pulled her over for a swift kiss. "Deal."

I smiled, a little sad despite the happiness around me. They're cuteness together made me miss David.

"Okay, enough already," Bruiser said, pulling open the van's side door. "Let's paaarrrty!" She jumped out. "It's my birthday. Yo, yo it's my birthday. Everybody say woot-woot, it's my birthday." She danced across the parking lot. "It's my birthday. Yo, yo it's my birthday. Everybody say woot-woot, it's my birthday."

We laughed at her silliness as we piled out of the van.

As we walked through the parking lot, memories of David flooded back. We'd gone on our first date here at The Boardwalk. We'd ridden the Ferris wheel and explored all the eclectic shops. We'd eaten too much junk food and shared beautiful kisses. He'd won me a stuffed giraffe.

Inwardly, I sighed. I had really messed things up with him when I told him about kissing Professor Quirk on my last mission. David had said he needed space and time to think. And then TL had sent him on a pre-op assignment that had turned into a month long trip. I'd heard from David exactly twice a week via text messages. Unfortunately, they were the kind of texts he'd send a friend, not a girlfriend.

HEY. JUST WANTED U TO KNOW I'M HERE SAFE.

HEY. THINGS R GOING WELL.

HEY. I'LL BE COMING BACK SOON.

No *I miss you. I'm thinking of you.* Or even *sweet dreams.*

He came back yesterday, gave me a hug hello, and told me we would talk. We hadn't had that talk yet, and I hoped beyond hope that when we did, things would be back to normal between us. Fun, romantic, light hearted.

Parrot looped his arm through mine, and I turned and smiled into his dark eyes. Our friendship had gone to another level since our mission together. We'd bonded in a way I hadn't bonded with my other teammates. We'd almost died in the jungle on that cliff.

I still shuddered every time I thought of it.

Actually, I'd experienced one too many close calls since joining The Specialists over a year ago. Being kidnapped in Ushbania, thrown in a dungeon in Rissala, and coming face-to-face with my parents' killer in Barracuda Key.

"What'd you get Bruiser for her birthday?" Parrot asked, bringing me from my thoughts.

"A gift certificate to that T-shirt shop she loves." Bruiser lived in T-shirts, each with their own unique saying. She wore one today that read, KISS ME. IT'S MY BIRTHDAY & I'M AWESOME. "What'd you get her?"

"Well, my mom has recently begun making Native American jewelry. I bought Bruiser a pair of turquoise earrings." Parrot glanced over at me. "You think she'll like them?"

"Oh, Parrot." I smiled at his sweet question. "Yes, I'm sure she'll like them." I squeezed his arm, so glad he'd decided to stay. After being reunited with his mom, none of us were sure if he'd stay on the ranch or leave. *I can't imagine life without you all*, he'd said very simply.

Mystic and Beaker came up beside us. "I made her my own personal blend of herbal tea," Mystic said. "She should drink it once a day for tranquility, relaxation, and sedation. Lord knows she could use it twice a day."

Beaker snorted. "You know as well as we all do that she's not going to drink that."

True. Mystic and Bruiser were always messing with each other. Him trying to calm her down and her trying to toughen him up.

Mystic smiled. "I meditated about it. She'll drink it."

"What did you get her?" I asked Beaker.

"Six hours of argument-free chemistry tutoring." She waved her blue nail-polished fingers through the air. "No more. No less."

"Very generous of you." Beaker had tried on numerous occasions to tutor Bruiser, but they always ended up in a fight.

I glanced over my shoulder to see Wirenut and Cat holding hands, meandering across the parking lot toward us. I knew Cat had gotten Bruiser a makeup kit in an effort to bring out her feminine side. That kit would go in a bathroom drawer and gather dust. Bruiser had no girly-girl side; she was a tomboy through and through.

And Wirenut? Funny enough, Bruiser had begged him to show her how to hot wire a car. So after today's outing, that was the first thing on Bruiser's list. Hot wire a car.

We stepped from the parking lot onto the sidewalk that began The Boardwalk, and I stopped. Slowly, I turned around, feeling that creepy sensation that someone was watching me. I'd felt it a lot since returning from my last mission. I searched the full parking lot, looking for anything, anyone that may seem odd. I'd never been the paranoid type, but since I'd found out I had a sister, subconsciously I'd convinced myself she was looking for me, too.

Parrot tugged on my wrist. "You okay?"

Nodding I turned back around. "Thought I heard something, that's all." Maybe I was just being paranoid.

Up ahead I saw Bruiser talking to David. He'd driven separately with Adam. David's yum factor was pretty much off the scales today. With that dark, five o'clock shadow and form fitted long sleeve T . . . sometimes he was so hot I could barely stand it. He said something and Bruiser laughed. David laughed, too, and the sound made my stomach flutter.

They were the only two that had come from Team One. The rest of them, Piper, Curtis, and Tina, were gone on missions.

Leaning down from his towering height, Adam gave Bruiser a birthday kiss on the cheek. Her freckly face turned bright red to match her hair as she playfully pushed him away. I smiled. That was probably the best gift ever for her. Bruiser had a big time crush on Adam.

We all approached and David glanced up at me before giving me a slight smile. I wanted to ask him when we would talk, but now wasn't the time. This was Bruiser's day.

Wirenut came around and put Bruiser in a head lock. "Okay, birthday girl." He knuckle rubbed her head. "What do you want to do first? Sky's the limit."

She flashed this innocent, dimpled grin. "Sky's the limit?"

Everyone nodded, but me. I knew that innocent grin. She was up to no good.

Her grin got bigger. "Anything I say goes?"

Everyone nodded, but me. I didn't like this one bit.

Bruiser batted her lashes. "I want one of those old timey pictures. Ya know, black and white, where we all have on a costume."

I narrowed my eyes. Something wasn't right. An old timey picture sounded a little *too* easy.

She looked at each of us through wide, childlike eyes. "Everybody in?"

They all nodded.

"And it's my birthday, so I get to choose what you wear, 'kay?"

No one nodded that time, probably because they'd finally realized she was up to no good.

Cat stepped forward. "Come on everybody. It's her birthday. Let's all be good sports."

Reluctantly, let me repeat that, *reluctantly* we followed her down The Boardwalk to the old timey photo shop. She'd made a reservation, the little twerp, and so we got right in. She'd even pre-arranged our outfits.

And I had to admit they weren't that bad . . . for the girls.

There we all stood, we girls dressed in old western gunfighter outfits, complete with duster coats, suspenders, six shooters and holsters, leather pants, black boots with spurs, and cowboy hats.

And the guys? Our barmaids. Complete with fish net stockings and garter belts, high heels, form-fitted dresses, hand fans, and feathers in their hats.

Leave it to Bruiser.

Outside the photo shop, Bruiser handed me the picture. "Look at the guys." She busted out laughing. "Oh, yowza, that's funny. That's going right on top of my dresser when we get back."

Cat and Beaker crowded in beside me as we looked at the black and white photo, all of us girls smiling and all the guys frowning. I glanced at David's legs in the fish net stockings and couldn't help but grin.

I studied Beaker and David's faces, like I frequently found myself doing, looking for similarities. They'd found out during the Barracuda Key mission that they were half brother and sister. It made me think of my own sister, the one I'd just found out about. I knew exactly what she looked like from the wanted picture of her that we'd obtained on my last mission.

There was a lot about us in common, like our eyes and the shape of our faces. I wondered what kind of person she was. Funny? Serious? Quiet? Loud? And I wondered where she was. Even with my computer expertise, I had yet to nail down her current identity and location. Her aliases were too numerous, and she seemed to move around every few days. And it appeared that she'd recently become an independent agent, working for whoever hired her.

She was a puzzle, that was for sure, but I hadn't given up. I'd been leaving bread crumbs through cyberspace in hopes she'd find them and follow them back to me. She was my only family, and I *would* find her. Or she'd find me first.

"You and David have the same nose," Cat told Beaker, bringing me from my thoughts.

"Food," Wirenut announced. "I need food."

Cat rolled her eyes. "You're always hungry," she laughed, playfully tapping his belly.

Bruiser picked an outdoor Mexican place, we all ordered, and right as our food arrived, Mystic's cell went off.

Every one of us turned and looked. *My* cell was always the one going off, not my team members.

I unclipped my phone from my pants and checked the display. Huh. No text messages.

David's went off next, which was usual. Being TL's, our team leader's, right hand guy, David's cell stayed more active than the rest of us.

He checked the display, then looked at Mystic. "That's TL's stat code. We're out of here."

I checked my phone again and gave it a little tap. Maybe I just hadn't gotten my text yet. I glanced up at David, and he shook his head. "Only me and Mystic," he said in answer to my unspoken question.

I looked at Mystic, and he shrugged, clearly as perplexed as me.

The two guys took off running, and all my team members dug in to their food. I sat at the outdoor table, idly watching them eat, listening to the ocean, completely sidetracked by what had just happened.

What was going on? I mean, I knew that one day we would all be going off on missions at different times, but up until now, it had always been me and one of the others. I wondered why I wasn't involved this time and more than a little curious to find out the details.

We finished eating and spent the rest of the time doing exactly what Bruiser wanted. We rode every single ride, including the tilta whirl (barf). We ate way too much ice cream. We played nearly every video game in the arcade.

At seven that night we pulled through the ranch's gate and up the long driveway to our house. Wirenut and Bruiser stayed with the van for the hot wiring lesson, and the rest of us filed inside.

The guys went off to their room and me and the girls went to ours.

I plopped down across my bed, and Mystic strolled straight in our room.

I sat up. "So?"

Mystic sounded as stunned as he looked. "I'm going on my first mission."

"You are?"

Cat came out of the bathroom. "Congratulations."

"Thanks," Mystic responded, still not moving from his stunned spot.

Beaker kicked her black flip flops off and shoved them under her bed. "Where you going?"

Mystic shook his head. "I can't tell you yet."

The secretiveness was the worst part of being a member of The Specialists.

"When are you leaving?" I asked.

Mystic blinked. "Tonight."

Beaker and I looked at each other. "*Tonight?*"

Cat sat down on her bed. "That's weird. No training? No preparation?"

"TL said there wasn't any time. He and David are going with me."

I was dying to ask Mystic if he'd seen his special room. All of my team members who had been on a mission had been introduced to their room, complete with training items specific to their specialty. Beaker had a state of the art chemistry lab. Wirenut, an electronic warehouse. Parrot a language facility. And I, of course, had a kick butt computer lab.

David peeked his head in the door. "Mystic, come with me. We need to talk about a few things."

Without a glance in my direction, David headed off and Mystic followed.

Cat lay back on her bed. "GiGi, is there something wrong with you and David? I know he's been gone a month, but I figured you two would be connected at the hip since he returned. What gives?"

I glanced across the room to Beaker, who looked right back at me, obviously curious what my response would be, too. I hadn't told any of my team members about the Professor Quirk episode. And normally I didn't just go around sharing my personal business. But something made me want to share and possibly get some advice.

"I . . ." I began and then stopped. How did I say this exactly? "I," I tried again, and then sighed. "Another guy kissed me, and David's upset. But I don't think it's so much the kiss as it is that I told David this other guy 'got me'."

Neither Cat nor Beaker uttered a word.

"Oh, yeah!" Bruiser rushed into the room. "That was awesome! I can't believe I just hot wired a car. I'm totally going out on the town tomorrow night and becoming a criminal." She stopped and looked at each of us. "What's wrong? Looks like someone ate your last lollipop."

Laughing, Wirenut came in behind her. "That was too cool. She actually got it the first time around." He looked at each of us. "What's wrong?"

Parrot stuck his head in the door. "Heard the commotion. I take it you hot wired?" He looked at each of us. "Something wrong?"

"GiGi," Beaker and Cat said in unison, "kissed another guy."

Everyone turned and looked at me, and I felt about as big as my pinky toe.

"I didn't say *I* kissed another guy." Pushing off my bed, I stood and gave Cat and Beaker a dirty look. "So glad everybody knows my personal business now."

Beaker shrugged. "David *is* my brother. I'm naturally going to take his side."

"Beaker," Cat got onto her and then turned to me. "GiGi," she softened her tone.

I waved them off. "Never mind." I didn't need their disapproval on top of my already confusion over the situation. "I'll see you guys later." Snagging a lollipop from my dresser, I walked past Wirenut and Parrot and out the door.

"GiGi," Bruiser called. "Come back. Let's talk. We were all just shocked, that's all. And everyone knows Beaker's an idiot."

Ignoring her, I strode down the hallway, past TL's office, and came to a stop at the mural that hid our elevator. Placing my hand on the globe light fixture, I waited while it scanned my prints and the mural opened to reveal the secret elevator.

I stepped inside, punched in my personal code, and the elevator descended. I unwrapped my lollipop and plunked it in my mouth. *Mmm, pina colada.* I realized then that this was one of the lollipops from the candy bouquet David had given me when I returned from my mission with Wirenut.

David was always doing sweet things like that. Somehow that thought made me feel even worse.

The elevator stopped at Sub Floor Four, the doors opened, and I stepped out. I chunked the wrapper in the garbage and told myself I was not going to think of David anymore.

I headed off to the right and down the hall to where my lab was, along with all the other secret rooms. When I first arrived here at the ranch, these undisclosed doors had driven me absolutely insane. But now I knew what lay behind nearly every one.

I came to a stop at my lab door and as I began punching in the code to enter the room, I heard voices coming down the hallway.

"Oh, GiGi. Goodgood, you're here." Chapling, my mentor, said. "I want you to meet someone."

I punched in the last few code segments on the key pad and with a smile turned . . . and gasped. I stumbled back, straight through the lab door, missed the step down, and landed on my butt.

"Ooohhh," I groaned.

"Kelly?" The guy used my real name.

I looked up and straight into the eyes of, "Professor Quirk?"

Neither one of us said a word as we stared into each other's eyes. I was sure his brain was circling the same thought as mine.

What the . . . ?

Quirk's brows lifted. "Kelly? Wh—" He glanced over his shoulder at Chapling and then back to me. "I don't—"

Chapling hobbled up beside him. "GiGi?" He looked between the two of us. "You two know each other?"

Slowly, we nodded, still staring at each other.

What would Quirk be doing here?

I realized my mouth was open and closed it. And then I realized I was still on the floor where I'd stumbled and fell. Quirk must have realized it, too, because he reached forward to help me up.

I took his hand and let him pull me to my feet. "Randy," I said, using his real name.

He smiled, and it shot butterflies right through my stomach.

"You're GiGi?" Randy realized. "Chapling's told me all about you."

Chapling stepped up beside us. "I didn't realize you knew Randy."

I looked down at him. "How do *you* know Randy?"

Chapling bobbed his bushy brows. "Couple of years ago we worked on something together for the IPNC."

"Oh."

"Yeah, he's my bro," Randy commented, elbowing Chapling.

Chapling giggled. "Yeahyeah, that's right. Everybody joked we were brothers."

Smiling, I looked between the two of them, finding that absurdly funny. They looked nothing like brothers. Chapling was a little person with frizzy red hair, freckles, and lots of chub. Randy stood six feet of in shape leanness with dark hair, adorable green eyes, and way too cute wire rimmed glasses.

Wait a minute. Why was I thinking of him as adorable and cute? He was a klutzy nerd.

Well, so was I.

Chapling waddled off and over to his coffee station in the corner of the computer lab. "How funny. Funnyfunny. You two know each other."

Randy and I smiled at each other.

Chapling dumped old coffee into the sink. "Where'd you all meet?"

"Junoesque Jungle," we answered in unison, referring to my last mission.

"The Junoesque?" Chapling poured water into the coffee maker. "Hm." He glanced across the lab at Randy. "What were you doing in the jungle?"

"He was the glyph expert," I answered for him.

"Well, what do you know?" Chapling dumped the old grounds and piled in new ones.

"You didn't know?" I asked.

Chapling shook his head. "Nope."

This organization continued to amaze me. Chapling was fairly high up in The Specialists and yet he hadn't had clearance to know his friend Randy was on my last mission.

TL walked in the open door, pressed the button to close it, and it made a suction noise as it slid together. He looked up at me and Randy, and I got the distinct impression he was in a bad mood.

"Did you show Randy around?" TL asked Chapling, and he nodded. "You two know each other, of course, from the Junoesque mission," TL continued. "I was very impressed with Randy's work. I've asked him to come on board for a few weeks as a historian consult on a few things I have going on."

"What?"

Chapling and Randy jumped, and TL just looked at me.

I cleared my throat. "I mean, what?" Holy crap. Joining The Specialists? This wasn't good. This *so* wasn't good. I know it was only for a few weeks, but this *so* wasn't good.

The lab door opened and in walked David.

I swallowed.

TL gave him a brusque nod, and my thoughts went back to wondering why TL seemed so upset. "David meet Randy. He'll be here for a few weeks as a historian consult. He comes to us from the IPNC."

David stepped forward and shook Randy's hand.

I watched it all in a sort of slow motion. My boyfriend meeting the guy that kissed me.

Chapling grabbed the still brewing coffee and poured himself a mug. "Isn't it weird that GiGi and Randy already know each other?"

David glanced between the two of us. "You two know each other?"

I tried to swallow, but the *huge* lump in my throat prohibited me.

"Yep," Chapling went on. "From GiGi's last mission. Randy was the glyph expert."

David didn't respond for a second, and I watched as it slowly dawned on him. He turned and stared right into Randy's eyes. "*You're* the professor?" *You're the guy that 'gets' my girlfriend?* I imagined him saying.

Randy nodded, clearly not picking up on things.

"David," TL said, "Randy will be staying in the guest room. Take care of getting him settled." With that, TL walked from the room.

Everyone stood in silence. David staring at Randy. Me looking between the two of them. And Randy looking between me and David.

"Yes!" Chapling smacked his lips. "Nothing like caffeine straight to the veins." Carrying his coffee mug, he waddled over and climbed up into his computer chair and started clicking away, completely oblivious to the three of us.

"Um," Randy pushed his glasses up his nose. "Wanna show me to my room?"

Without a glance in my direction, David turned and strode from the computer lab. "Yeah, let's go."

Randy gave me a *what's-going-on?* look to which I sort of smiled and shrugged.

In silence I watched the two of them leave the computer lab. I was in trouble. *Big* trouble.

***

Later that night, TL, Mystic, and David left for the mission. No one had a clue where they were going, but all of us were dying to know. Never, in the time I'd been here, had a mission occurred so quickly. Usually there were weeks of preparation before someone left.

Whatever it was, it had to be really important.

David hadn't even had a chance to said goodbye.

And Mystic hadn't even received his going away party, tradition for all first missions.

"Did you meet the new guy?" Cat asked.

I glanced up from where I sat in the corner of the rec room, idly watching Bruiser and Parrot across the room playing air hockey while Wirenut cheered.

I nodded. "Yes." And went back to watching Bruiser and Parrot.

Cat sat down in the oversized, leather chair beside me. "Cute, huh?"

I nodded. "Yes."

Beaker plopped down in the other leather chair. "Wonder how old he is."

"Twenty three," I answered.

Cat snuggled further down in her chair. "Wonder where he came from."

"IPNC." The same organization we used to belong to before going private.

Beaker kicked her legs up on the table in front of us. "I heard he's a historian."

I nodded, still watching the air hockey. "Yes."

"Suppose he has a girlfriend?" Beaker asked.

I shook my head. "He doesn't."

No one said anything for a few minutes, and then Cat looked over at me. "You sure know a lot about him."

"Yes," I agreed.

They didn't reply, obviously waiting for me to continue.

I sighed, resigned to the inevitable. "He's the guy that kissed me."

Beaker coughed. "*What?*"

I finally took my eyes off of the air hockey match and drug them over to Beaker and Cat. "He was on the mission with Parrot and I."

Cat sat up in her chair. "Does David know?"

I nodded. "Yes."

"What did he say?" Beaker asked.

I shook my head. "Nothing."

Cat blinked. "What are you going to do?"

"I don't know." It wasn't like I had a lot of experience with this sort of thing. "I don't suppose either of you have any words of wisdom."

Beaker shrugged. "Sorry. I've never had a boyfriend. Can't help you."

Cat shrugged, too. "I've never cheated on a boyfriend."

"I didn't cheat," I defended myself.

Beaker narrowed her eyes. "You *kissed* another guy."

"No. *He* kissed me."

They just looked at me.

I rolled my eyes. "I guess this is the time when an older sister or mom would come in handy, huh?"

They both nodded.

"Oh and what I said earlier about David being my brother . . ." Beaker waved her hand in the air. "Whatever. You know I'm here for both of you and all that crap."

I let out a humorless laugh. "Gee, thanks." Leave it to Beaker to be reluctantly supportive. Which, actually, was *tons* better than what she was before.

Randy appeared in the doorway. "Kelly? Can I see you?"

Beaker and Cat exchanged a look. *Kelly?* They mouthed in unison.

The truth was I sort of liked that he called me Kelly instead of GiGi. It had been a long time since my real name had been used.

Slowly, I got to my feet and crossed the rec room to where he stood in the door. I followed him across the hall and into the cafeteria that sat empty at the late hour. He slid into one of the aluminum, picnic type tables, and I sat down across from him.

Quietly, we looked over the table at each other, and the more staring seconds that passed, the more anxious I became.

"You all settled in?" I struck up a conversation.

He nodded.

And then we fell back into the silently-staring-at-each-other thing.

Honestly, conversation was *so* not my strong point.

"I can't . . ." he let out a nervous chuckle. "I can't believe you're here. I'm here. I didn't think I'd ever see you again."

I smiled a little, really not knowing what to say, and thanking God David wasn't here to walk in on us.

"Um, I kind of got the hint that David's your boyfriend. And, I, um, also got the hint that he knows about you and me."

"Did he say anything?" I immediately asked.

Randy didn't answer me at first, and then his face slowly curved into a sad smile. "He means a lot to you."

Swallowing, I nodded, feeling like in some way I was hurting Randy's feelings.

He lowered his gaze to his hands clasped on top the table. "Kelly, the last thing I want to do is come between you and your friends, you and your boyfriend." He brought his gaze up to mine. "It matters to me what people think. I don't want to come in and mess things up. And I'm not going to lie to you. I think you're great. But you and David are together, and there you go."

Randy got up from the table. "And even if you and David weren't together, it's not a good idea for people who work together to date. So," he held his hand out to me, "friends?"

I didn't know what to say. David and I weren't together. Or at least we'd never really broken up. And why did it feel like Randy was breaking up with me when we weren't even dating?

Inwardly, I sighed. Life was a lot easier when only computers rocked my world.

I reached out and did the only thing I could. I smiled and took his hand. "Friends."

***

Two days later we had just finished up a PT session and were walking out of the barn. Mystic, TL, and David pulled up. The car doors opened, they climbed out, and walked straight into the house without a glance in our direction.

TL and David disappeared into TL's office and shut the door, making it more than obvious that no one was to disturb them. Mystic went straight to his bedroom, and we all followed.

"What's going on?" Wirenut asked him.

Mystic didn't look at any of us, just shook his head.

Bruiser and I exchanged a glance.

"Are you okay?" she asked. "Did you get hurt?"

"I'm fine," Mystic mumbled.

Beaker stepped into the room. "Is everything done? Is the mission over?"

644

Mystic grabbed a purple bag off his dresser. "I really need to be alone." With that, he slipped past all of us and out the door.

Cat turned to Wirenut. "What's in that purple bag?"

"His mojo stuff," Wirenut answered. "Ya know, crystals and herbs and whatever else he needs to become one with the universe."

None of us spoke for a few seconds.

Beaker heaved a sigh. "Well, I guess I'm going to go," she shrugged, "do whatever."

Bruiser looked at Parrot. "Wanna go for a ride?" she asked, referring to the horses, and Parrot nodded.

Wirenut grabbed his iPod and he and Cat stretched out on his bed to listen to music, which left me standing in the boy's room with nothing to do.

"Well," I headed toward the door, "guess I'll see you guys later."

Wirenut and Cat waved bye. I headed down the hall to the hidden elevator and descended to Sub Floor Four. I punched in my code to the computer lab and went on in. As usual, Chapling sat bent over his station clicking away.

I walked up behind him and saw that he was updating our video monitoring software. I glanced at all the black and white images stacked on his screen. They showed where everyone was and what everyone was doing. I saw Jonathan, our PT instructor, go into TL's office.

I saw an image of TL's office with him on the phone, David looking through a file, and Jonathan listening to TL's conversation. All three of them looked incredibly concentrated and definitely stressed.

I was dying, *dying*, to know what was going on.

Then I saw an image of Mystic up on the hill meditating. He'd placed some different colored crystals in front of him, and I found myself curious what each crystal was for.

I touched Chapling on the shoulder, and he jumped.

"Ohmygod. Ohmygodohmygod." He grabbed the sides of his fuzzy head. "Don't scare me like that."

I smiled. "You didn't hear me come in?" Stupid question, of course he didn't hear me. I was completely oblivious, too, when I was working.

"Nooo, I didn't hear you." Chapling clicked a few keys. "What's up?"

I pointed to the image of TL's office. "Any idea what's going on?"

Chapling shook his head. "Not yet." He pointed to my station. "I sent you code. We've been hired to review it for infections."

With a nod, I stepped over to my station and sat down. Taped to the side of my flat screen was a picture of me and David as little kids, taken right here at the ranch. I smiled as I looked at the image of him and I holding hands, grinning for the camera.

I missed him.

With a sigh, I keyed in my password, brought up the code, and got down to work. Hours zoomed by as I lost myself in thousands of lines of data. I tagged the deprecations, ascribed the client agents to depiction, and formatted the cipher for essentials. I repeated that process over and over again with each subsection of records and then partitioned the intervals.

"GiGi?"

I focused on the elements and continued—

"*GIGI?*"

I jerked my head up. "What?"

Chapling stood at the door. "Let's go. TL wants us."

"Oh." I blinked my eyes a few times. As quick as I could, I secured my station and followed Chapling out the lab and down the hall to the conference room.

Around the table sat TL, David, Jonathan, Mystic, Bruiser, and . . . Nalani? What was TL's wife doing here? I looked straight at her and gave her a huge smile that she did not return.

Something was wrong. Something was *really* wrong.

I pulled a leather chair out beside Bruiser and sat down. "What are you doing here?" I whispered to Bruiser, and she shrugged.

Chapling closed the door and sat beside David.

No one said a word as we stared at TL, waiting.

Seconds later, he closed a file he'd been studying and stood. "For those of you who do not know, this is Nalani Kai, my wife."

I blinked, taken aback that he'd just said that. Nalani being his wife was a big time secret I had accidentally found out and TL had sworn me to secrecy.

TL didn't say anything for a few seconds, and I got the distinct impression he was trying extremely hard to control his emotions. "Someone . . ." he inhaled and released a quick breath. "Someone has kidnapped our daughter."

‹THREE›

What?

Oh.

My.

God.

What? TL had a daughter?

I looked at Nalani. TL and Nalani had a daughter?

I put my hands over my mouth. *Oh, no.*

TL pointed his remote at the wall mounted flat screen, and an image of a little girl flashed into view. With huge brown eyes, tiny glasses, and curly black hair, she stared back into the camera with a big toothless grin.

Happy was the first word to pop into my mind.

"This is Zandra," TL monotoned, completely void of any emotion. "She's seven years old."

Zandra was beautiful. Absolutely gorgeous. An incredible mix of Nalani and TL's best physical qualities.

"She was taken three days ago," TL continued, "from the back yard of her maternal grandmother's home. No one saw anything. A note was attached to the ball she was playing with." TL clicked the remote and a piece of yellow paper flashed onto the screen.

I squinted and made out the one and only typed sentence.

TRY TO FIND HER OR SHE DIES.

My heart paused a beat as I read the last word. DIES.

"Try to find her or she dies," TL read. "That is all we have received. No ransom, no phone calls, just this one-sentence note. We have no idea who the kidnappers are or what they want in exchange. Through our work with the IPNC, Nalani and I have made a lot of enemies over the years. The kidnapper could be anybody from anywhere in the world."

I looked between the two of them, puzzling at their stoic, blank expressions. Their daughter had been kidnapped and yet they maintained that ever present control. How? How was that even possible?

I glanced over to Nalani, hoping to send her an encouraging look, but she didn't return my glance. As I stared at her, I saw her jaw flex and realized she was doing everything possible to keep it in control.

"Of course," TL continued, "we have no intentions of standing peacefully by waiting to be contacted by the kidnappers." TL put the remote down on the table. "This is where all of you come in." TL nodded to Mystic. "Unbeknownst to everyone here at the ranch, Mystic is considered a very precious asset to the government."

Bruiser and I exchanged a curious glance.

"Before Mystic came to us," TL continued, "he anonymously submitted information to Lost America, our nation's missing person's foundation. When I recruited him, he had successfully helped find two hundred and twenty three people. Since he's been living here at the ranch, he's been working behind the scenes, providing information that has led to the rescue of sixteen more missing people."

What?

Bruiser and I exchanged another surprised look. From her perplexed expression, I gathered she didn't know about this either.

Mystic had been working for TL this whole time? Behind the scenes? I hadn't known. Why hadn't Mystic said anything?

Stupid question. Mystic hadn't said anything because TL didn't want any of us to know.

And—a thought occurred to me—when I'd first met Mystic, he'd said he was taken in for operating a 1-900 psychic scam. It was probably a cover TL had given him.

TL rolled his chair out and took his seat. "Needless to say, we have kept Mystic's identity closely guarded."

I smiled to myself as he answered my unspoken question.

"Only myself, David, Chapling, and a few high up people in the government know of Mystic's ability." TL turned to Mystic. "Tell everyone how your specialty works."

"I need to see into a person's eyes to understand what they're feeling," Mystic explained. "Unfortunately I see mostly their pain, not their happiness. It can be a picture of them or an image on T.V. Normally that's all I need to feel them, hear them, to see them."

No one responded as those words floated in the air. I could only imagine the things Mystic must see on a daily basis just by looking into someone's eyes.

That thought sent a chill racing up my arms. I didn't think I could handle looking into a person's eyes and seeing only pain.

What a burdening ability to have. I wondered if Mystic could block it somehow. And—I suddenly realized—what had he seen in me?

"Tell them," TL prompted Mystic, "what you saw with Zandra?"

"I saw fighting. But fighting like I've never seen before. It was organized, but not like boxing. There was an octagon, but no cage, and no gloves. Just raw fighting. I heard different languages being spoken. There was a medium sized crowd of people sitting around the octagon. I'd say about fifty people. And the men, the fighters, they were very bloody. I heard the snap of a bone . . ." Mystic closed his eyes. "That's a sound I never want to hear again."

He took a breath and opened his eyes. "I also got the sense that this fighting is rooted in one place here in the States and has been for years. That people come from all around for this gruesome fighting where money is exchanged."

Mystic looked across the table at Bruiser. "I also got the distinct feeling that many men have died during these fights. That it's almost *preferred* for a man to perish. It's why people bet such big money. In hopes that someone will die . . ." Mystic's voice trailed off as he slowly shook his head.

"I don't have anything else," he continued a few seconds later. "But I know without a doubt in my mind that I need to be around these fights if I'm going to locate Zandra."

"Okay, Bruiser," David cut in. "Tell us what your thoughts are after hearing this description."

For the first time ever, I saw Bruiser in a serious mode. Gone was her perpetual grin and silliness. She was focused as she began speaking. "The type of fighting that Mystic is describing is found more commonly overseas in less regulated countries. You can, however, find underground clubs throughout America. But death of a fighter most certainly is *not* part of the equation, unless, of course, an accident occurs."

She scooted up in her seat. "But here in America there is one very exclusive, underground club where fighters get paid bonuses if they kill their competition. I've never been to this club, but I've heard all about it. The club is called Demise Chain, and it's located in the Pacific Northwest in the little town of Teacup, Washington."

Teacup? What an innocent sounding city for such a horrible thing going on.

"The worst part of this," Bruiser continued, "is that less skilled fighters are brought over from other countries with a promise of American citizenship if they compete in Demise Chain. Little do they know that they are the ones that will die during the match."

"Die?" I gasped, and Bruiser nodded.

It was amazing to me how just a year and a half ago I was in my own little world, completely oblivious to this world. Since joining The Specialists I'd found out way too many disturbing things about the human race.

Bruiser nodded. "Like I said, I've never seen one of these fights. But the man who raised me competed in one. He barely made it out alive." She paused for a second. "We're talking MMA, here. Everything goes."

"MMA?" Mystic asked.

Good question. I had no clue either.

"Mixed martial arts," she answered. "It was made popular by UFC in the early nineties. But it's been going on a lot longer than that."

I raised my hand. "UFC?"

"Ultimate Fighting Championship," Bruiser answered. "You can see it on T.V. now, it's so popular. MMA. A combination of karate, judo, Wing Chun, and whatever else, all in one fight. Striking, grappling. Basically whatever it takes to win."

"You all should know," TL inputted, "that Bruiser was raised and trained by one of the world's elite fighters. She knows more about martial arts than anybody I've ever met, and I've been in this business a long time. She is, hands down, the most talented fighter I have ever seen. Her input into this mission is imperative."

I glanced over at Bruiser to see her shyly look down. Her embarrassment was very out of character for her. TL's kudos had brought a side out in her I'd never seen.

"It is our goal," David carried on the conversation, "to get Mystic in the room where these fights are going on and—"

Bruiser huffed out a humorless laugh, cutting David off. "Good luck on that one. Demise Chain is closely monitored. It's like the mafia, or for that matter, the White House. You don't just walk in the front door. You have to earn your way in."

"Precisely," TL agreed.

Bruiser frowned. "And so how is Mystic going to get in?"

I smiled to myself. I didn't bother informing her that TL could do just about anything. Bruiser would figure that out soon enough.

"As David said," TL continued, "we need to get Mystic in that room. We've looked at it from all angles, and hands down our best bet is to have him be a competitive fighter. That is our objective. From there and what he discovers, we will move onto the next phase of things—finding Zandra."

"Did you say I'm going to be a competitive fighter?" Mystic asked.

"Him, a competitive fighter?" Bruiser balked.

I listened closely, wondering how I factored into all of this.

Ignoring Mystic and Bruiser's outbursts, TL pointed the remote at the screen. A gray haired gentleman popped up. Wearing a coat and tie, he grinned for the camera, coming across adorable and sweet. He looked like what I imagined everyone's grandpa should look like.

"This is Harry Noor." TL announced. "He is the owner of the Demise Chain."

"Him?" Bruiser laughed.

"Harry Noor," TL went on, "has his own set of fighters called Warriors. Recently, he put the word out he's looking for some new Warriors. He also put the word out he's looking for a computer specialist. He wants a program designed exclusively for him that can identify top notch fighters. A program than can also advise competitors during a fight what they should and should not be doing differently."

"Um, that's called a coach," Bruiser identified the obvious. "And how in the world does he expect a program to advise a fighter?"

TL glanced at me. "That's for the computer specialist to figure out."

"Harry Noor," David explained, "is quite the gadget man. He's got to have the latest and greatest of everything—the first of a kind. He's also tight with his money and doesn't want to dish out the dollars needed to hire top notch trainers. And he's all about having things computerized. He wants a program that will identify his new Warriors. And that is what we're going to give him."

"David and Mystic," TL picked up on the conversation, "are going to be those new Warriors."

"Wait a minute. I'm not fighting?" Bruiser asked.

"Warrior?" Mystic shook his head. "I'm not fighting."

I didn't like the idea of *anybody* fighting, not after the way Bruiser had described it. Wait a minute; did TL just say David's fighting, too? My heart skipped a beat as I glanced over at David. *No.*

"As of right now," TL continued, not answering Bruiser or Mystic, "Harry Noor allows each of his Warriors to have a trainer. Jonathan will be David's trainer, and I will be Mystic's." TL looked at his wife. "Nalani has already secured a job as the new hostess of the Demise Chain. She's in charge, basically, of greeting people when they come in." TL turned his attention to Bruiser. "And you will be Mystic's girlfriend."

"His *girlfriend?*" she nearly squeaked.

"I can't fight," Mystic repeated himself. "It's against everything I believe in."

TL's jaw hardened and I could tell he was not in the mood to deal with any objections or questions.

David must have picked up on it, too, because he quickly took over the conversation. "Women aren't allowed to compete in the fights," he answered Bruiser. "But we definitely need you there as our fighting consultant. Mystic's girlfriend is the only cover we can give you that will put you close enough to the fights."

Bruiser and Mystic eyed each other across the table. They did not look happy.

"The fighters are kept separate from each other," David went on. "Mystic needs to interact with everyone until he sees what he needs to see regarding Zandra. This makes it imperative that Mystic fight as many competitors as possible."

I raised my finger. "And me and Chapling?"

TL nodded to Chapling. "Chapling, of course, will work from home base."

Of course. I remembered a time when *I* was promised *I* would work from home base. But, truth be told, I'd gotten to the point where I sort of liked the traveling, the missions. *Sort of.* Of course, I'd never admit that out loud.

TL looked between me and Chapling. "You two are going to design that state-of-the-art, one-of-a-kind program to identify Harry Noor's new Warriors. And when David and Mystic show up for Warrior tryouts, you need to figure out how your program will identify them as top notch fighters and get them hired on with the Demise Chain. After that, you'll be on hand working for Harry Noor, advising his fighters. Obviously, if it's anybody other than Mystic, you'll give bad advice. Anything to advance Mystic in the competition."

"Um," *Hello?* Did they not see the fact that I knew absolutely nothing about fighting? For that matter, I'd never even played a fighting video game. Heck, I couldn't even remember the last time I'd played a video game, period. Not that we were talking about video games, but it was all I could think of that related.

Chapling clapped his hands. "No problem. Noprobnoprob. This'll be fun. A little Physics, electricity, throw in some magnetism—Oooh! And we can get those absorption pads from storage and switch out the acceleration wires for recording force faction. Oooh!" He rapid fire clapped. "We should totally get Dr. Gretchen involved. Have you seen what she's got in her cabinets?" He scratched his head, making his brillo pad hair poof out. "Yeahyeahyeahyeahyeah."

He pushed back from the table and jumped down from his seat. "She's got that really cool," he snapped his fingers, "what do you call it . . . oh I can't remember right now." Chapling waddled over to the conference door, opened it, and walked right on out.

Everyone just looked at each other.

David turned to me. "Back on track. Harry Noor is meeting with prospective computer designers in one week. He'll pick the person he wants to work with after seeing their presentation. He *will* pick you."

I lifted my brows and asked the obvious. "And if he doesn't pick me?"

"That's not an option," David responded.

Great. Talk about pressure.

"A couple days after that," David continued, "the Warrior try outs will occur, and the following evening will be the night of fighting that Mystic and I will compete in."

TL clicked his pen. "There are a lot of unknown facts here. Who is the person who kidnapped Zandra? What does he or she want? What do the fights have to do with it?" TL clicked his pen again. "We're working with a lot of indefinite details. And that doesn't make me comfortable in the least."

Not to mention the fact his, *their*, daughter's life was at stake. With that thought I glanced at Nalani again and found her sitting there staring blankly at the table in front of her. Slowly, her eyes closed, and although it was slight, her brows drew together with the stress and sadness of the situation.

"Switching modes." TL pushed back from the table and stood. "Each of you has a specialty. In order to expand on that talent and further your knowledge, you need materials. You need your own special place to go for privacy, research, and practice."

I knew he was talking about our special rooms. Only Mystic and Bruiser had not been introduced to their rooms. TL had introduced the rest of us to our rooms right before we went on our first missions.

TL looked at Bruiser. "Bruiser, you are the only member of your team who has not seen your training room." He nodded. "Time to take a look."

What? I looked across the table at Mystic. *You've seen your room?* I mouthed.

He nodded.

Huh. I'd been there every other time my team members had been shown their special area. Why not Mystic?

TL opened the conference room door. "David's going to take over from here. It's late. Please do eat. Get some rest. Training starts first thing in the morning. Bruiser, I want you and David to meet me in my office in one hour. We need to discuss the MMA training needed for this mission."

Bruiser nodded.

Jonathan and Nalani followed TL out of the conference room, leaving me, Mystic, and Bruiser alone with David.

"When did you all remove your monitoring patches?" I asked, referring to a device we all had to wear when we first moved in.

"About a month into living here," Bruiser answered.

Mystic shrugged. "About the same time."

"Same time as me then," I realized.

"Bruiser," David cut in, "ready to see your room?"

"Definitely!" She pushed back from the table.

"Can we come?" I asked. "And what about Mystic's room? Can we see his?"

David nodded. "I don't have a problem with that."

He led us from the conference room and down the hall of secret rooms, past all the doors I knew of, and came to a stop at tall, beige, double wide filing cabinet.

This file cabinet had been here up against the wall from pretty much day one of me arriving to the ranch. I hadn't given it much attention. I did open it once and found it unlocked, with every drawer empty. I'd figured it was extra storage, and TL would move it somewhere when he was ready.

Stepping to the side, David motioned Mystic forward, and Bruiser and I exchanged a puzzled glance.

Mystic slowly ran his fingers along the top of the cabinet, almost as if he was a magician silently telling it abracadabra. The cabinet shifted out from the wall and slid to the side, revealing a tunnel glowing in a soft blue light. My nostrils flared a little as they picked up a waft of incense.

I stood there for a second, staring at the tunnel, smelling the incense, trying to work through what had just happened.

"There are identity stamp sensors painted into the perimeter of the cabinet," David explained. "They are rigged to read mine, Mystic's, Chapling's, and TL's prints."

"Oh." That made sense.

Mystic stepped into the blue glowing tunnel, and we followed. About six feet in, the tunnel opened into a large circular room I estimated to be fifty feet in diameter.

The walls had been painted light purple, and on the walls scripted with the color teal were the words love, peace, joy, breathe, and harmony. A wooden table stood in the center of the room with a yellow pottery vase. Smoke trailed up from the vase, and I assumed it contained the incense. Oversized, vibrant pillows and cushions piled the area around that table. I guessed that was where Mystic meditated.

Soft music trickled through the air, settling the sound of hollow wind chimes through me. Around the circumference of the room, about every few feet, stood wooden tables with bowls of brightly colored stones.

To our immediate right, there were three glass cabinets with see-through doors. Crystals lined the shelves. Big ones, small ones. Round, jagged, lumpy. Clear, green, red, yellow, and purple. Bowls, too, with various herbs in them. My gaze trailed over the top shelf where a row of pendants lay. I smiled at one shaped like a fairy.

Across the circular room I saw a bookshelf with about fifty books. I could only assume they dealt with mystical themes.

Diagonal to where I stood sat a desk with a computer on top. It seemed so out of place in this gypsy world atmosphere. Surrounding the desk and hanging from the ceiling were long beads that acted as the desk's walls. Diagonal in the opposite direction sat another desk surrounded by hanging beads as well. Decks of cards sat on top that desk, and I gathered they were Tarot or something of that nature.

There was so much to look at I couldn't possibly take it all in. But I did notice a telescope off to my left with an extension leading up and through the ceiling. I didn't know a lot about telescopes, but from what I did know that one looked top of the line. And keeping in mind we were on Sub Floor Four, that was one high powered star gazer.

Peaceful. That word definitely described this room.

"Ya know," Bruiser whispered. "This room makes me want to take a nap or meditate or something."

I smiled. Napping and meditating were two words *definitely* not in Bruiser's vocabulary.

She wandered over to one of the tables with the bowls of stones. "What do these do?" She reached out.

"Stop." Mystic commanded. "Don't. They're not ready for the human touch yet."

Bruiser lifted her hands away and glanced over at me. "Ready for the human touch?"

I shrugged.

"Okay," David said, stepping back into the tunnel. "Let's go see Bruiser's room.

‹FOUR›

We walked down the blue glowing tunnel that led out from Mystic's room and stepped back into the hallway. Mystic abracadabra his fingers over the filing cabinet, and it slid back into place.

Mystic, Bruiser, and I followed David through the underground corridors back to the elevator that we all had used when coming down here. David punched in his personal code, and we stepped inside.

Bruiser and I exchanged a questioning glance. "But what about her room?"

"Your room," David answered, "is on Sub Floor Two."

"Sub Floor Two?" I perked up. Cool. I'd wondered what else was on that floor.

One, of course, was our ranch level. Sub Two contained Parrot's room. Sub Three, I'd discovered while prepping for my last mission, was the clinic where Dr. Gretchen worked. And we'd all known what was on Sub Four since day one—our conference room and the other secret rooms.

David pointed to the elevator's control panel. In the center of it was a small black box which looked like a camera. "This is an exhalation analyzer. It is programmed to read your DNA via your breath. Step forward and breathe into it."

An exhalation analyzer? And here I'd always thought it was a camera.

"Freakin' A, that's cool." Bruiser stepped up to the analyzer and breathed a quick, fast breath.

The elevator ascended, stopped at Sub Two, the door opened, and Bruiser's mouth simultaneously dropped.

I peered over her head—being tall always had its advantages—and into, well, a gymnasium was how I supposed it would be described. Then again, the only physical training room I'd ever been in was our barn where we had daily PT. So I wasn't exactly an expert when it came to identifying work out rooms.

"Where's Parrot's room in relation to this?" I asked.

"On the other side of the wall." David motioned his head across the room. "Separated by five feet of concrete."

Mouth still open, Bruiser slowly stepped into the enormous room.

This place was bigger than all the other secret rooms. An octagon in shape, I estimated it covered over one hundred square feet. A fighting rink sprawled the center of the room, bordered by thick wire mesh. It had a red floor with some sort of Asian symbol painted on it.

Bruiser wandered off to the left, and I watched her as she found her way around the room in a sort of daze. She passed by a wall with an assortment of weapons: swords, knives, throwing stars, numb chucks.

She reached up for a sword, and taking it from the wall, turned to David. "Sparring?"

He nodded. "They're dull."

With a nod, she continued around the room, idly swishing the sword through the air. She passed by punching bags, a collection of body pads, hanging rings, a rack of dumbbells, and came to a stop at the edge of a section of bamboo flooring.

Kicking her running shoes off, she stepped onto the bamboo and gave a slight bounce. A slow smile curved her face as she turned to all of us. "Oh, yeah."

And then she launched into a series of spins that looked like a cross between martial arts and gymnastics. I'd seen her in action many times, but her speed and agility always left me speechless.

She came to a stop just as quickly as she had begun and wandered off the bamboo and over to a book shelf. She stood for a second perusing, and then reached up and slid one free. She opened it and flipped through. "Sa-weet. The latest meridian book."

I turned to David and Mystic. "Meridian?"

"Pressure points in your body," Mystic answered. "Used in holistic healing and martial arts among other things."

"Hmmm." It sounded like Mystic and Bruiser's specialties shared similarities. Of course, I wouldn't point that out to them. They were the antithesis of each other.

While Bruiser continued looking through her books, I took in the rest of the room. A shower in the corner, a climbing wall, dangling ropes, thick poles I assumed were for some workout reason, and like Mystic's place, Bruiser had a desk and computer.

Like I said, I knew next to nothing about gyms, but this seemed pretty darn cool.

Bruiser closed the book and with it tucked under her arm, turned to David. "Unbelievable. There's not one thing I can think of that I don't have."

David smiled a little. "Well, if you do think of something, just let me or TL know, and we'll get it for you."

Bruiser grinned. "Can I have an endless supply of chocolate?"

David gave her a playfully disciplinary look. "Within reason."

She laughed and started bouncing in place. "Can I stay?"

David nodded. "Not long. Remember we have a meeting with TL. Dinner and rest and we start first thing in the morning."

She gave another bounce. "Is this where we're training for the Demise Chain mission."

David nodded again.

Bruiser headed over to a punching bag. "Oh, goodie,"

David stepped back into the elevator, and Mystic and I followed.

Mystic pressed the Sub Four button and the doors closed. "I'm heading to my room."

David started to say something and Mystic held up his hand. "I know dinner and rest and we start first thing in the morning."

David smiled his acknowledgment. The elevator descended, Mystic got off, and the door closed, shutting David and I alone in the elevator.

Immediately my stomach kicked in with nervousness.

Neither one of us moved to punch in our code, and I detected uneasiness in him, too.

"Do you realize," I softly said, "this is the first time we've been alone in a month?"

Smiling a little, he turned to me. "And this will probably be the last time we have an alone moment until after this mission."

659

I nodded, understanding if we were going to finally talk about things, now was it. "Can we talk?"

Folding his gorgeous, muscular arms over his beautiful chest, he leaned back against the wall. "Yes, let's."

"I thought—" he started at the same time I said, "You know—"

We both laughed a little, and he motioned me to go ahead.

"You know," I began again, "the last real conversation we had was over a month ago. And we both know how that played out. I told you about Professor Quirk, and you told me you needed time to think. And then you got sent away on a mission, we exchanged a few text messages, no phone calls, and here we are."

David nodded. "Being a Specialist doesn't give much time for other things, does it?"

I chuckled a breath. "That's putting it lightly."

He smiled at that. "And so?" he prompted me.

I sighed. "David, I guess at this point I just want to know what's on your mind. I know you're not happy about Professor Quirk, but let me remind you *he* kissed *me*."

David nodded. "I know that, GiGi. You're a beautiful, intelligent woman. Guys are going to hit on you. That's just a fact of life."

I tried not to get flattered at the beautiful part, but I *was* a girl after all. "Then why do I feel like we're going to break up over this?"

He didn't respond, just kept looking at me.

"David?" And then it dawned on me, and my heart paused a beat. "*Are we breaking up?*"

"GiGi," he quietly sighed. "It wasn't the kiss. It was never the kiss."

"Then what?" I asked, surprised that I could talk with a huge lump forming in my throat.

"It was the 'we clicked on an intellectual level' part. That really hurt."

I swallowed. "Oh, David. I'm so sorry. I didn't mean—"

With a shake of his head, he held up his hand. "Tell me what you want."

For you to touch me, to hug me, to tell me we're okay. But instead, I shook my head, unable to collect my suddenly spinning thoughts. *What can I say to save this? What can I do?*

"That's just it," he softly responded. "I don't think you know what you want."

I want you, I wanted to say, but instead responded, "What do *you* want?"

He gave me a sad smile. "You shouldn't have to ask me that."

"But . . ." hadn't he just asked me that exact same question?

"And now," David continued, "with Randy temporarily here, I don't know. I just don't know."

I swallowed.

"I don't know what else to do." He closed his eyes. "I thought we were fine, great in fact. Then this thing with Randy comes up. Now he's here, and obviously there's something between you."

"What? No," I denied. "We're friends, that's all."

David's expression softened as he gazed at me, not saying anything.

Finally, he nodded. "Truth be told, GiGi, somewhere deep inside I knew this wouldn't work. Dating, living under the same roof, working for the same organization. It's too much. It's too close."

Pushing off the wall, he ran his hands down his face and sighed. "Yes, we're breaking up. I've been thinking and rethinking the whole problem for the past month. Usually, I don't take so long to make decisions. But I find myself acting out-of-character when I'm around you."

I didn't like him labeling me as a problem. But, weird enough, I experienced a spark of hope that he acted 'out-of-character' around me. Surely, that had to be a good sign that he thought of me special enough to act so differently when he was around me.

David reached around me, punched in his code, and the elevator began ascending. "Yes, it's definitely not a good idea for people who work together to date."

"That's what Randy said," I mumbled and then immediately realized I shouldn't have.

David shook his head. "Nice, GiGi."

"I'm sorry."

"Listen, we work to close together for there to be any awkwardness between us. So," he held out his hand, "friends?"

I felt like I was back in the cafeteria with Randy.

David lifted his brows, waiting.

And so I did the only I could. I reached out and took his hand. "Friends."

***

Dinner and a good night's sleep did not happen to me. All I could think of was David. I played and replayed every moment we'd spent together. Every word we'd spoken. Every kiss, every touch. Come five in the morning, I'd had about enough of my wildly running thoughts. I got up, dressed, and made my way down to the lab. I did the only thing I could to forget about David, I dove into my Demise Chain assignment.

I had exactly six days before I went in front of Harry Noor with my state-of-the-art program. Mystic and David had exactly eight days until tryouts, eight days to learn how to be world class fighters. *Plenty of time*, I tried to convince myself.

I spent hours researching something I never thought in a million years I would. Fighting. I watched countless videos that had been filmed all over the world, some legal, some not so much.

I poured through archived files of the library, the internet, and, believe it or not, the History channel. I played a few fighting video games. I analyzed programs that were currently on the market. I hacked into servers to find out which software developers Harry Noor, the owner of Demise Chain, was meeting with. And then I hacked into those developer's computers to see what they'd come up with.

I knew TL didn't like me hacking things without prior approval, but this was for him and his family. He wouldn't mind.

Back to my research . . . I took notes. I cross referenced those notes with other notes. And then I found myself with a whole list of questions for Bruiser.

List tucked in my pocket, I walked into our bedroom and found her lying on her bed with her head buried in her pillow.

"Hey," I said, plopping down beside her on her bed. "Why aren't you training?"

"We're on a ten minute break," she mumbled into the pillow.

"What's up with you?" She rarely, if ever, looked down and out.

She let out a long, loud sigh. "GiiiGiii," she whined, "I don't want to do this."

"Do what?" And then it dawned on me. "The mission? But why? It's fighting. It's what your specialty is."

"I'm not going to be fighting. I'm going to be Mystic's stupid girlfriend." She rolled over. "I'll be standing on the sidelines looking all dumb and air heady."

I laughed. "Who says you have to be dumb and air heady?"

Bruiser heaved another sigh. "TL. Just a few minutes ago before he told us to take a break."

"What?" That didn't make any sense.

"He says Harry Noor likes his girls sweet and innocent and a tidbit dumb."

I laughed again. "What? But you're not going to be Harry's girl, you're Mystic's."

Bruiser wiggled up on the bed. "I know. But TL wants to do everything possible to be in Harry Noor's good graces. He doesn't want to do anything to raise flags, piss anybody off, etcetera."

I nodded. "Well, that does make sense. Mr. Noor *is* the owner of the Demise Chain, and we want to get into the fights. And we definitely need to play all of our cards right. And if TL thinks you're being sweet, innocent, and a little dumb will contribute to that, then he knows what he's talking about."

With a groan, Bruiser dropped her head back. "Why do girls always have to play the sidelines? I can fight better than David and Mystic. *I* should be competing, not them." She slammed her fist into her hand. "I'd bust some people up."

"Bruiser, you're not on the sidelines. You're part of a top secret mission to save TL's daughter." Hello? Did she not see this? "I've been on four missions now, and you'd be amazed what roles people play and how they all fit together into a sort of puzzle to solve the greater problem."

"I mean, my God," I continued, "Jonathan was my modeling agent in Ushbania. Do you think he really liked that? And me? Ug. I was a model? And Nalani in Rissala was a greasy, toothless boat captain. And Beaker in Barracuda Key a cheerleader? Can anybody say snort? And then down in the Junoesque Jungle, I had no control. I was just another female, serving the guys, sitting in the back. My point is, it all comes together in the end, and every role is just as important as the next."

"I hear what you're saying." Bruiser scrunched up her face. "It's just . . . well, fighting is my one true talent. I'm not as smart as the rest of you guys."

"What? What are you talking about? That's absolutely ridiculous," I argued. Bruiser was one of the smartest girls I knew. And funny. And great to be around.

"Hey." Mystic stuck his head in. "Can I come in?"

We both waved him in.

He lowered himself to his usual spot at the foot of Bruiser's bed. And folding his legs up, he took what I referred to as his meditative position.

We both stared at him, waiting . . .

"This mission is against everything I believe in. Everything my parents taught me." He looked up at us. "And I'm trying to figure out a way to tell TL I can't fight. There's got to be a way to get me in that room without requiring me to fight."

I almost rolled my eyes. Why did it seem like it was my job to convince my team members to go on missions? When had I become the ranch's Psychologist?

"I know," Bruiser agreed. "I'm not happy about this either. I say we both go and talk to TL. There's got to be some other way. And, dude," Bruiser reached over me and bopped Mystic in the head, "I can't believe you don't want to fight. I'd give anything to be in your shoes."

"Guys." I held up my hands. "TL would not design a mission and put you into a role unless he felt you were fully capable. And he's certainly not going to redesign a mission based on your comfortableness. Believe me, I know." I felt like a broken record. Hadn't I said similar things to all my other team members?

"It's an honor," I continued, "to be chosen."

The both just looked at me.

"Listen," I said, none so gently. "This is part of our new life. It comes with it. God knows I've done things I didn't want to." I got up off the bed. "That's the bottom line. So you just have to suck it up."

They both scowled at me.

I walked from the room, feeling like a crabby butt for my harshness, and not quite understanding why I had gotten so irritable with them. I guess I just didn't have the patience right now. Maybe it was the whole thing with David and Randy. I didn't know.

"Jeez, Kelly, can you be any less understanding?"

I turned to see Randy leaning against the hallway wall.

"Everybody gets scared when they're prepping for their first mission, especially when it's out of their realm of comfortable zone. Everybody experiences second thoughts." Randy pushed up from the wall.

David came out of his bedroom. "I agree with Randy."

Great, now I felt even worse.

David knocked on my open bedroom door. "Hey, guys, can we talk?"

Mystic and Bruiser waved him in and Randy followed.

With a sigh, I turned and walked off, feeling more and more horrible about myself with each step. I needed to apologize. Next time I saw them I would.

***

That evening I found myself in my lab pounding my head. Give me something to hack or a code to break and no problem. Design a state-of-the-art, not-like-anything-else fighting program from scratch? Sheesh. What did they want from me?

I had a ton of questions and knew Bruiser had the answers, but after what had happened earlier, I didn't feel comfortable approaching her. Or Mystic for that matter.

Chapling sat over in the corner behind some patch panels. I couldn't see him, but I knew he was testing (on himself) the Influence-Sway Skins (his creation, his term) that he'd taken from Dr. Gretchen and tweaked to fit our needs. The Skins would not only record muscle aptitude, they would give us a multi-dimensional image of the skeletal. If they worked, we'd use them in conjunction with the Combat-Thrash program (my creation/my term) that I had yet to fully develop. The program that would coach any fighter to greatness.

"OW!" he yelped.

Guess the testing wasn't going so well.

My cell buzzed and I looked at the display.

* * * TL's stat code.

Chapling waddled out from behind the patch panel, rubbing his chest through his T-shirt. "I need to find someone else to test things on." He squint his eyes at me.

I held my hands up. "No. Nonononono."

He smiled. "Let's go. Did you get the stat code?"

I nodded and followed him out the computer lab and down the hall to the conference room.

665

<FIVE>

Chapling rapped softly on the closed conference room door, and TL opened it.

Around the table sat everyone going on the mission: Nalani, Jonathan, David, Mystic, and Bruiser.

Chapling and I took seats beside each other to TL's left.

TL ran his gaze over everyone in the room, taking a second to make eye contact with each of us. "I'd like to start out by saying this is an incredible place we live. Regardless of your backgrounds, I hope each of you realize what an honor it is to have been picked for this program. You are an elite, talented, intelligent group, and I'm proud to say you are on my team."

No one uttered a sound as we stared at him. I was sure they were picking up on the same thing as me. While his words were complimentary, his tone came across disappointed.

Pushing back from the table, TL stood, and rolling his chair in, he rested his hands on top of the leather seat back.

My eyes wandered down to his ring finger where he wore no wedding band. I looked across the table to Nalani's finger and saw the same. What kind of relationship did they have that not even in the safety of the ranch did they wear rings? I didn't understand the two of them.

TL took a breath. "David, go ahead."

David hit the remote, and the wall inserted screen flickered. An image of Zandra popped up with a rag tied around her eyes and tears streaking her face.

I sucked in a breath as I stared at the curls matted to her little cheeks.

"This picture arrived today," David explained. "We traced it and have found out it was mailed a block away from where Zandra was taken. This picture was probably snapped moments after she was kidnapped." He pressed the remote, and another image came into view.

It was a note, just like the first. FIND HER OR SHE DIES.

David put the remote down. "That message came with the picture."

"What about prints?" Chapling asked.

David shook his head. "Nothing." He turned to Mystic. "Do you get anything looking at that?"

Mystic shook his head. "No, I'm sorry. I need to see her eyes."

"Again," TL spoke up. "The kidnappers could be anybody. Nalani and I have so many enemies." TL stopped for a second and rubbed his hand across his forehead. "What do they want? It doesn't make sense. Do they want me? Nalani? Money? To free someone from prison? I don't know." He rubbed his forehead even harder. "At this point, I'm beginning to doubt if they want anything at all. Maybe they're just playing a game. I'm beginning to doubt their intentions . . . and what exactly their plans are with," TL swallowed, "with our daughter," his voice cracked a little.

I swallowed, too, at the raw emotion in his tone. At the horrible things that *could* happen to their daughter.

Dropping his head, TL pressed his fingers into the sides of his temple.

"Please . . ." Nalani squeezed her fingers together so tight her knuckles turned white. "Please, you all in this room, you're our only hope."

My stomach clenched at the desperation in her voice. And I realized this was the first time I'd heard Nalani speak since first seeing her.

She looked first at Mystic and then Bruiser. "TL told me you two are hesitant to do this mission."

I glanced over at my team members to find them both dropping their heads. I couldn't believe it. I couldn't believe they'd actually gone to TL. I loved my teammates, but at this point I felt incredibly disappointed in them, too. I didn't care what hesitancy I might have, it was TL and Nalani's daughter, for God's sake. Did Mystic and Bruiser not see this?

"I can't make you do this," TL softly spoke, taking his fingers from his temple and dragging his gaze to both Mystic and Bruiser. "I could have gone to anybody. I know people on all levels of the government. But I brought this to you because I know you're the best, *we're* the best."

Mystic and Bruiser kept their heads down. I didn't know about them, but I would feel very guilty and definitely a little "in trouble" if TL were putting me on the spot right now.

"Look at me," Nalani requested.

Mystic and Bruiser raised their eyes.

Nalani released her white knuckled fingers and laid them flat on her chest. "I'm here asking you as a mother to find my daughter, *our* daughter."

That hit home. Although I had very few memories of my mother, I knew she would spare no resource to find me if I'd been kidnapped. Heck, if the roles were reversed, I'd go to the ends of the earth to find *any* missing family member. And I knew my team members would do the same.

Inhaling a long, soft breath, Mystic closed his eyes. It might have been my imagination but I swore he was listening to something.

A few seconds ticked by and no one said a word as Mystic sat there meditating. I looked around the room to see what everyone thought, and they were all staring at him.

After a few more seconds, he gave a slight nod, opened his eyes and gazed straight into Nalani's. "You may definitely count me in."

With a shaky smile, she nodded. "Thank you." And then she turned to Bruiser.

"I'm sorry," Bruiser immediately apologized, looking from TL to Nalani, and back to TL. "I'm so, so sorry. I can't believe I acted so immature in thinking of myself, when people I love are in need of my talents. Sir, you may unequivocally count on me in any way."

Closing his eyes in what looked like pure relief, TL slowly turned his back to us. "Thank you." Then he opened the door and walked straight from the room with out dismissing us.

I couldn't recall a time I'd seen him struggle so hard to maintain composure.

He'd always been there for us. We would most certainly be there for him.

***

I worked the whole next day along side Chapling writing and rewriting code. I just wasn't happy, and neither was Chapling. We had to create one bang up Combat-Thrash (fighting analysis) program and all we had as of

668

now was mediocre at best. Five days was all we had left. Seven was all Mystic and David had.

"Maybe we need to see the training stages of a superior fighter," I suggested. "All we've watched and researched is the end product. I think we need to see exactly, in person, how a fighter becomes a fighter."

Chapling snapped his finger and pointed at me. "Smartgirl. Let's go."

Camera in hand, we made our way up to Sub Floor Two where we knew Bruiser and the guys were training. We texted Bruiser to let her know we were in the elevator, and she let us in.

Chapling and I found an empty corner, set our camera up, and settled ourselves on a pile of mats. Laptops in front of each of us, we tuned into Bruiser and the guys.

And I tried very hard not to stare at David's sweaty, clingy T-shirt. "Can you recap what you've done so far and what the training schedule will be like until competition day?"

"Conditioning, sparring, specific technique," Bruiser ticked off her fingers. "Conditioning, sparring, specific technique. We cycle through those three things, spending two hours on each and then starting back over, making for a packed twelve hours. We eat a high protein, high fiber diet to repair muscle tears. And each day I introduce a new technique. A new art. David and Mystic have to be as well rounded as possible. They have to do in seven days what others spend years perfecting."

Bruiser crossed the floor and grabbed up a handful of four-foot bamboo poles. "Kumite is one of the three sections of karate. It's training against an adversary. Balance is a key here and learning the basics by feel. If you get your lights knocked out, you're going to be disorientated. You need to have a mental scope for a guide, a clock in your head to orient you until your senses come back. *If* they come back."

She handed TL, David, Mystic, and Jonathan each a pole. "Karate involves modification. It's about your senses, muscle memory, and imagery. You have to be able to use your wits with strategy. You have to be unpredictable. One of the key factors in winning or at least holding your own in a fight is the ability to anticipate your opponent's movements."

"Allow me to demonstrate." She pulled a black scarf from the elastic waist band of her shorts and tied it around her eyes. She lifted her hands and waved them on with her fingers. "Hit me."

Mystic and Jonathan exchanged a glance. TL and David exchanged a glance. Chapling and I exchanged a glance.

Was she serious?

Bruiser waggled her fingers again. "Come on. What are you waiting for?"

"B—" Mystic almost looked pained. "But you're so small."

She smirked and waved them on again. "Let's go. No holding back."

TL lunged first, bringing the pole back and swinging it at her. I knew TL's power, and clearly, he was holding back.

Bruiser dodged the swing, grabbed his pole from behind, twisted it free, and tossed it across the gym. "I. Said. Don't. Hold. Back."

All the guys smiled at her irritable tone. All the guys, but TL.

In fact, I hadn't seen any expression on his face over the last couple of days but that of focus and concentration.

He looked stressed to the max.

David went next, stealthily slipping to the left and coming at her from below. She slammed her foot down on the pole, flipped it up with the toe of her running shoe, and jabbed the end into David's side.

With a grunt, he fell to his knees and grabbed his side. "Man, Bruiser."

Jonathan attacked next, not giving her a chance to respond to David, and whipped his pole toward the back of her knees. She leapt straight up and flipped backwards over Jonathan, snatched the pole from his grasp, and swept him off his feet.

With a thud, he landed on his butt. "Lord, girl," he chuckled. "You're something else."

Blindfold still on, she turned to Mystic. "Come on, dude, be a man"

Mystic swallowed. "I think I'm afraid of you."

Bruiser smiled. "As you should be." And then she sprinted toward him.

His eyes widened as he held up the pole and backed away. She came to a stop right in front of him, reached out, and bopped him in the side of the head.

Mystic jerked. "Hey!"

She bopped him in the other side of the head. "You're a sissy. How do you expect to compete in less than two weeks? I'm just a little girl, and I'm about to beat you up." She shoved him in the chest. "You're going to be up against guys twice your size. And they're going to laugh in your face if you back away from them."

Standing on her tiptoes, Bruiser leaned in closer until their faces were mere inches away from each other. "They're going to laugh, and then they'll beat you to a bloody pulp. Now," she butted her forehead into his face, "hit me, you girl."

Mystic narrowed his eyes, and I swore it was the first time I ever saw him look irritated. He slid his pole up between them and shoved her away.

She took a few steps back. "Good. Come on."

He lifted the pole, holding it like a spear, and slung it at her.

Bruiser didn't move, just lifted her hand and caught it. "Didn't expect you to do that. Not bad." She tossed the pole back to him.

Looking a little proud of himself, Mystic caught the pole.

Very quietly TL signaled the guys, and they all moved at once, coming at her from opposite directions.

They swatted and jabbed and rushed at her. She dodged and kicked and flipped.

They swung and struck. She punched and blocked.

They lunged and poked. She disarmed and tossed their weapons.

They reached for her, and Bruiser, looking a bit 'done with it', whirled and touched Jonathan in the back of the neck. Spun and flicked David in the hip. Whipped around and poked the tip of her elbow to Mystic's shoulder. And shot straight up in a split and tapped TL in the chest with her toes.

All four guys fell to the floor, moaning and heaving for breaths.

Bruiser took her blindfold off. "I think I broke a nail." And then she giggled at her own silly humor.

Chapling and I just sat there, staring at the remnants of the Jackie Chan scene we'd just seen.

I realized then he and I were gripping each other's hands, and I let go. "Sorry."

"Wow." Chapling blinked. "I think Bruiser's my new idol."

"I think we need Bruiser on *all* our missions." I turned to Chapling. "She barely even touched them that last time around."

He nodded. "Like I said, my idol."

Bruiser went over and helped each of the guys up, tapping them at different places on their backs.

"What's she doing?" I asked.

"Resetting our meridian points," Mystic moaned as Bruiser did him.

I slipped my notepad from my pocket and took a second to jot down everything I'd just seen. In my peripheral I saw Chapling's fingers begin racing over his laptop keys. This was exactly what both of us needed.

I looked up at the injured guys and they seemed, amazing enough, to be recovering. "What did it feel like before you guys dropped to the floor?"

TL straightened his shoulders. "Compression."

Compression?

I pondered that for a second and realized to really comprehend that word I would need to feel it. And then—the obligatory light bulb went off in my head—that was what my Combat-Thrash program needed. To incorporate all five senses.

My heart kicked in with that awesome rhythm that comes with solving a problem. I turned to Chapling and he was typing away, the light bulb having gone off in him, too.

"Chap?"

He held up his finger for me to wait, keyed a few more things, and then looked over.

I smiled. "We're going to make history. First program of its kind. We need—"

"The senses!" Chapling answered for me.

"Oh my God, that's exactly what I was thinking."

He clapped his hands. "Of course it was. We're smart that way."

I put my laptop aside and stood.

Chapling looked up at me. "What are you doing?"

I straightened my T-shirt. "Feeling compression."

His bushy red brows lifted an inch. "For real?"

I gave one definitive nod, more to convince me than to assure him. "I'm going in."

"I changed my mind. *You're* my idol."

I took a deep breath. Here went nothing. "Bruiser, do that to me."

All the guys and Bruiser turned to look at me.

Pulling my shoulders back, I took a few steps toward them. "I'm serious. I really need to be involved in all aspects of training for this mission if I'm going to create a program that will blow Harry Noor out of this world."

I waved my hand through the air. "This is all so foreign to me, this fighting thing. I've spent much of my time swimming through research videos and books and it's really getting me nowhere. Fighting is a full body sport, and it just occurred to Chapling and I that we need to incorporate all five senses into our Combat-Thrash program. Compression. That's what TL said. And that's what I need to feel."

672

"She's taking one for the team," Chapling said from behind me. "Because *I'm* definitely not volunteering my little self for a compression experiment."

"Combat-Thrash program?" Bruiser asked.

I shrugged. "That's what I've decided to call it."

She snorted. "It's a stupid name."

I narrowed my eyes. "Are you going to show me compression or what?"

Bruiser glanced over at TL, and he nodded her ahead.

She smirked, looking at little *too* happy if you asked me.

Perhaps I should have apologized to her *before* I asked her to compress me.

Bruiser waved me over, and I crossed the mat to her, getting this odd feeling I was walking the plank or something.

I came to a stop right in front of her and looked down. "I'm sorry for not being a very good friend to you and Mystic and getting cranky and all that."

One side of her lip curled up. "Apology accepted."

And then she reached out and touched my neck and my whole world went black.

***

Sounds of classical music drifted through my brain and my eyelids fluttered open. A blurry image of Dr. Gretchen with her salt and pepper hair stepped into view.

She smiled. "Welcome back."

I tried to sit up, and she patted my shoulder.

"I suggest you lay right there for a minute or two. You're in the infirmary. It's eleven at night. You've been out," she peeked at her watch, "for nearly two hours."

She brought a cup to me and held a straw to my lips. I took a long sip.

"What happened," I asked a few seconds later.

"You don't remember?"

I thought for a second . . . "Oh, compression. That's right." Bruiser's fingers had felt like rocks. "Wait a minute . . ." my brain trailed off as I recalled everything. "Why didn't she 'reset my meridian points'?" I asked, using Mystic's term.

Dr. Gretchen chuckled. "She did. You didn't respond."

I closed my eyes. Of course I didn't respond. Leave it to me to be the dork that doesn't respond right to something.

Dr. Gretchen sat down in the chair beside my bed. "GiGi," she sighed. "You've got to be more careful. Some of us are made for combat, and some of us are, well, like you."

I opened my eyes. "What does that mean?"

She gave me a tolerant look. "You know exactly what that means."

Sadly, I did.

"You've been here more than anyone else," she reminded me.

I held my hand up. "Point taken." I swung my legs over the side of the bed to get up and closed my eyes on a wave of nausea. "Maybe I'll just," I scooted back on the bed and stretched out, "lay down a little while longer."

Dr. Gretchen smiled a little. "Brilliant idea." She settled back in her chair. "You know, David came to see you while you were out."

I perked up. "He did?"

She nodded.

My stomach flippity-flopped at the thought of him looking in on me. What did that mean exactly? Was he looking in on me as a friend? Or as an I-might-want-to-get-back-together-with-you sort of thing? And then it occurred to me . . . had I been *drooling*? I had been in a coma after all.

"Why don't we visit for a while?" Dr. Gretchen suggested.

I nodded, completely sidetracked by the fact David had been here, and waited for her to start the conversation.

She didn't.

"Um," I searched my brain for something to say . . . my thoughts drifted through the time I'd known Dr. Gretchen . . . and suddenly it hit me. "Hey, I've been dying to ask you a question."

She waved me on. "Shoot."

"Why do you and Jonathan hate each other so much?"

‹SIX›

Dr. Gretchen half-snorted/half laughed. "Jonathan and I don't hate each other."

I gave her an incredulous look. "Right."

She heaved a heavy sigh. "Really, we don't."

"That's not what Jonathan said." It was low ball of me, seeing as how Jonathan hadn't said anything one way or another.

Dr. Gretchen's eyes narrowed to two tiny beads. "What did he say?"

I shrugged and glanced away. "This and that."

"Listen." She shoved out of her chair. "It wasn't *my* fault the spear went through his eye."

A spear? I concentrated on not showing that I really had no idea what she was talking about. "Not according to him."

Her entire face clenched. "*I* wasn't the one who wanted to go spear fishing. That was *his* brilliant idea."

"Hmmm." I looked up at her with an expression that I hoped said Jonathan had said otherwise.

Dr. Gretchen jabbed her finger in my direction. "He's just embarrassed because the shark scared *him* and not me."

Shark? I waited for her to keep going with the story, but she didn't. And so I fed her another line. "He said the shark didn't even faze him."

"*What?!*" she shouted, and I jumped.

"Of all the nerve!" She turned and took a stomping pace around the room. "I thought he was man enough to own up to things by now." Dr. Gretchen whipped around and jabbed her finger in my direction again. "Is he still saying when the shark swam by I was the one who got scared and pulled the trigger on the spear gun?"

I nodded, hoping God didn't strike me down for all this.

She let out a grunt. "I can't *stand* him."

I watched her pace away from me, fists clenched, breathing heavy, more angry than I'd ever seen her. But I still didn't hesitate from asking, "So what really happened?"

Dr. Gretchen shook her head, and I could visualize her mind reeling back the years. "It happened five years ago. We used to work together in the IPNC. Ten years we worked out of the same division and finally he asked me out. Australia is where we happened to be at the time. Went spear fishing on the Great Barrier Reef. A shark swam by, he freaked in the water, and ran straight into my spear."

I couldn't help it, I laughed. "*That's* how he lost his eye?" And here we'd all thought he'd gotten injured on some top secret mission.

"Yes, that's how he lost his eye." She turned to me. "But you want to know the real kicker?"

I nodded. Oh, this was too juicy and good.

"He never asked me out again. He's too embarrassed."

A knock sounded on the open door and we both glanced over to see Jonathan standing there.

I swallowed. Oops, bad timing.

Dr. Gretchen grabbed a bed pan and slung it across the room. It sailed through the air to thunk Jonathan smack in the nose.

"Ow!" He grabbed his nose. "What are you doing, you crazy woman?"

"How dare you tell everybody I was the one who," she quoted the air with her fingers, "'accidentally' speared your eye."

"I didn't tell anybody anything," he loudly defended himself.

Dr. Gretchen pointed to me. "Not according to GiGi."

They both fell silent, and slowly, they turned to look at me.

I gulped a swallow and tried my best for innocence. "Um, I was practicing my getting-information-out-of-someone-when-I-really-don't-know-anything skill."

They narrowed their eyes, or, I should say, Jonathan narrowed one eye.

"TL taught a whole class on it just a few weeks ago. How to lead someone in a conversation to get information out of him or her." I looked between them. "My homework was to practice the lesson on someone." I gave Dr. Gretchen a big fake smile. "Hope you don't mind you were that someone."

It was true. TL *had* taught a whole class, and all of us *had* been given that assignment. I just didn't realize I was going to do my homework until now.

Jonathan busted out laughing. "How do you like that, Gretch?"

She shook her head, and I got the distinct impression she was growing reluctantly amused with the whole situation.

I swung my legs over the bed, got up, and made my way toward the door. "Well, if you don't mind telling TL I did my homework assignment, that'd be great." And then I bee lined it out of there before I got into trouble.

"Just remember," Dr. Gretchen yelled after me, "I can make your medical needs pain*ful* or pain *free*."

I immediately recalled the inoculations me, Parrot, and Jonathan had received prior to leaving for the jungle. Parrot and I hadn't felt a thing. Jonathan, on the other hand, had screamed through every single needle.

As I pressed the elevator button, I gave her a sweet wave that I hoped would smooth things over.

In response, she let out an evil giggle.

Great. Juuust great.

***

Even though it was eleven at night, I wasn't tired in the least. Probably because of my two-hour nap slash coma I'd been in. So I headed to my lab, punched in my code, and the door swished open.

Chapling and Randy both glanced up from the corner where the coffee pot sat. Seeing Randy made my stomach flip flop. My reaction to him both confused and bothered me. How was it possible both David *and* Randy could make me feel this way? I never wanted to be *that* girl that bopped from one guy to the next, but this little love triangle made me feel that way.

Randy smiled a little. "Hey."

"Hey," I greeted him back.

It seemed like it'd been a week instead of a day since I'd seen him last.

I pulled out my computer station's chair and took a seat. "What are you doing in here?"

"Having a late night cup of coffee," Randy answered, purposefully rolling his eyes down to Chapling so I would look.

"Chapling?" I noticed his sick expression. "You okay?"

He shook his head, but didn't speak.

"He found out," Randy spoke for him, "that he's going on the mission with you."

"What?!" I broke into a smile. "That's awesome!"

Chapling shook his head.

"He's never been on a mission," Randy spoke for him again.

"*What?!*"

My surprised outburst made Chapling look sicker. Randy gave me a you're-not-helping-him look.

"Oh, Chapling." I stepped forward. "You'll be fine. I'll be there, and TL, and David, and everybody." I walked over to him, leaned down, and gave him a hug. "I promise. You'll be fine. I've got your back."

Chapling nodded, still not speaking.

"That's what I keep telling him." Randy looked me up and down. "How are you feeling? I heard about what happened."

I waved him off. "Fine. Chapling gets to be the guinea pig next time."

Chapling half-heartedly chuckled at my joke. At least he'd come out of zombie mode. Actually, he was handling it fairly well. I remembered the first time I was told I was going on a mission. I'd nearly passed out.

"We need to get baseline data on everybody," I told Chapling, knowing talking work was definitely the way to get his mind off things.

"Already did," he responded.

"Oh, yeah, when'd you do that?"

Chapling reached for his coffee. "When you were, ya know, passed out."

I smiled. "Thanks."

He returned my smile, looking a bit better then when I first walked in.

"So, Chap, I did have a few questions about the project I'm working on for TL." Randy nodded to one of the open computer stations. "Mind helping me real quick with some research?"

"Oh sure. Suresuresure." Chapling waddled across the lab to his station and climbed up in his chair.

"Thanks," I whispered to Randy, knowing he was trying to keep Chapling sidetracked.

"You're welcome."

678

While the guys logged in and started talking, I situated myself at my station and got down to work.

I lost myself in my own little world, analyzing the baseline data Chapling had recorded. I took the film footage of Bruiser and the guys and turned it into 3-D animation. I applied basic principles of Geometry and physics in analyzing each movement and what could have been done differently for the guys to succeed in their fight with Bruiser.

I tweaked the 3-D animation, redoing the fight, and observed the new results. I watched as an animated figure of Mystic forced Bruiser into a compromising situation. It wasn't likely that anyone would ever defeat Bruiser in real life, but watching it in animation was really darn cool.

Actually, the whole thing reminded me of a complicated board game. Fighting was definitely a thinking man's game that used a combination of mathematics and fighting skill to win.

I factored more options and measured the outcomes and angles. I definitely needed more data, both internal and external. I needed to observe more training to visualize their muscle movement from the inside out.

I turned to Chapling and with a glance around the room, noted Randy had left. "Hey, are those Influence Sway Skins ready?"

Oblivious to me, Chapling fiddled with a new hologram machine we'd gotten a few weeks ago. It portrayed some sort of military game. I wondered why he was fiddling with that when we had a mission to pull together.

"Chap?"

Eyes glued to the hologram image in front of him, he waved his finger incased in a virtual reality wrap and made one warrior stab another.

"CHAPLING?"

He jerked back. "What?"

"Are those Influence Sway Skins ready? I want to get some internal muscular data."

"Oh yeah. Yeahyeahyeah. They're ready."

I nodded. "Good." And then my gaze wandered to the hologram game as he went back to playing it. Again, I wondered why he was wasting his time when . . .

My thoughts died off as I got drawn in watching one warrior battle another. Once again that obligatory light bulb went off in my head.

Hologram. We needed to make the Combat-Thrash program a hologram. Nobody else presenting for Harry Noor was doing a hologram.

My heart kicked in with my idea I couldn't wait to share. "Chap?"

He didn't glance away from his game. "Yeah?"

"Are you thinking the same thing I'm thinking?"

"Probably. Incorporate holograms into the Combat Thrash Program?"

"Yep, we're thinking the same thing." No wonder he was playing the game.

Chapling spun on his stool in my direction. He pointed his wrapped finger back and forth between the two of us. "We rock the house."

I laughed. "That we do."

***

Four days left until Chapling and I went in front of Harry Noor. Six days until Mystic and David did. That's all I could think of as I strolled into the cafeteria the next morning for a quick breakfast. I ran straight into Mystic and Bruiser. They both gave me a 'look'. It took me a second to remember that the last words between us weren't exactly pleasant.

Granted, I *had* apologized to Bruiser, but even I knew that had been a last minute, don't-hurt-me-too-bad apology. Right before she, of course, had put my lights out.

Without a second thought, I went straight over and sat down across from them. "Listen, I know I lost my patience and was mean. I know it. You know it. Everyone screws up at sometime or another. So can we please just make up and be friends again?"

They both just stared at me.

"Please?" I prompted.

Mystic shrugged as he shoved a chunk of watermelon in his mouth. "I suppose."

"Oh, gee, thanks."

Bruiser folded her arms. "I guess I owe you an apology, too."

I raised my brows. "Oh?"

"You know," she waved her fingers through the air, "for putting you in a coma and all that."

"Yeah, well, Dr. Gretchen said my body just didn't respond to the • resetting-the-meridian-point thing."

Mystic and Bruiser exchanged a sly glance.

I frowned. "What?" And then it dawned at me. "You didn't reset my meridian points, did you?"

She smirked. "Not really."

My jaw dropped. "Bruiser!"

She lifted her hands. "Hey, you want to be all irritated with me and Mystic, it's the least you deserved."

My jaw dropped even further. And then, I couldn't help it, I laughed. After all, it wasn't literally a coma, more like a very long nap.

Mystic and Bruiser exchanged a knuckle tap.

Ha ha. Jokes on me.

Parrot sat down beside me, sliding a small plate of bacon in front of me. "It's the peppered kind. I know you love it."

I gave him a smile. "Thanks."

Parrot took a sip of his cinnamon coffee. Since being introduced to it on our last mission, it seemed to be the only thing he drank nowadays. "What's so funny?" he asked.

I shook my head. "Nothing. Just Bruiser and her silliness."

Wirenut sat down on the other side of me. "Hey, no fair having fun without me."

We all smiled.

"Where's Beaker and Cat?" Bruiser asked.

Wirenut shrugged. "Something about girl talk."

"What do you do when you do that?" Bruiser asked, bringing my attention to who she was staring at—Mystic.

With his eyes closed, he sat peacefully, seemingly lost in some other world. He'd looked like that in the conference room, too.

Mystic didn't respond at first and right when I thought he *wouldn't* answer, his lips curled into a soft smile. "I'm listening to my mother."

None of us had a response to that, and in fact, didn't even exchange a glance. Our gazes were fixed on Mystic.

His eyelids fluttered open, and I saw peace there. I could only imagine how it would feel to hear my mother's voice.

And then he told us about his mother, his father, his baby sister. And how he'd been raised in a commune in the hills of TN. How people fueled by hate had viciously killed his family, not only blood, but those he had grown up with.

Wirenut spoke next. He shared his horrid past and how he'd watched his parents and older brothers be slaughtered by his evil uncle. He described growing up in boys' homes and the criminal path he'd taken that had finally gotten him recruited by TL.

Bruiser went next, describing abandonment as a small girl and being found by a wonderful man who raised her and other street kids. She told us about learning to fight by this man, Red, and how she hoped to one day see him again.

Parrot picked up the conversation, sharing his past. His mother being sold into slavery, his father dying, his grandmother sick and raising him. He described being manipulated by his Indian chief to translate deals involving children and women being sold into slavery.

Somewhere in the conversation Beaker and Cat sat down. Cat had been raised by the same man who slaughtered Wirenut's family. She'd been lied to her whole life and found her first truth and freedom when joining the Specialists.

Beaker described her abusive, neglectful mother. How she'd been pegged a drug user in school and no one liked her. How she'd lived out of the locker rooms in the high school and because of a fluke explosion she'd caused, found her way to the Specialists.

And then I shared my story, losing my parents in a plane crash. Moving from foster family to foster family. Being pegged a freak because my IQ made people scared of me. And how David had been my very first friend. David had recruited me into this new lifestyle.

When we finished, none of us uttered a word. But the feeling of family and unity was so strong between all of us, I was sure they felt it, too.

The conversation picked up again as Beaker told us about the very unexpected news that her and David were siblings.

Bruiser dropped a bomb, revealing her and TL were raised by the same man.

Parrot shared stories of being reunited with his mother.

Mystic revealed he'd known all along about our pasts.

Wirenut pulled his shirt up and showed the horrid scar he always hid.

I told them I'd just found out after my last mission that I had a sister.

I didn't know, we didn't know, if we were saying stuff we weren't supposed to say. Things TL might not want us sharing. But we didn't care. It flowed from us. None of us held back.

We shared our fears, our hopes, our desires. We put ourselves out there, raw and impure.

682

It was amazing, truly amazing, the level our bond deepened. It was like we'd been waiting for this moment for over a year. Secrets revealed. Souls bare. Each of us knew without a doubt that we would be connected forever.

Under the table, Parrot took my hand. I grasped Wirenut's, and he clasped Cat's. She reached across the table and took Beaker's, and her and Bruiser linked fingers. On it went to Mystic and back to Parrot, all of us quietly holding hands, and for the first time truly becoming one.

***

That afternoon Bruiser wanted everybody to meet outside for the day's training. So carrying my video cam and tripod, I pulled my laptop strap further up my shoulder and crossed the yard to the barn.

That weird sensation hit me again.

Someone's watching me.

Maybe I *was* being paranoid. Stopping in my tracks, I turned a slow circle, searching the ranch's property: the house, pool, the hills, trees, and the fence in the distance that ran the ranch's perimeter. Nothing seemed out of the ordinary, but still, that sensation hit me strong.

Mystic came up beside me. "What's wrong?"

I shook my head. "Nothing."

He nodded to the barn. "Let's go."

We entered the barn to see Bruiser in the corner shadow boxing. Before this mission, I, of course, had never used the term shadow boxing, but now I felt comfortable throwing it around.

While she continued doing her thing, I set my cam and tripod up and pressed record.

Bruiser stopped boxing the air and dropped to her fists for a rapid round of pushups. She boinged to her feet and turned around. "Good you're here."

David, TL, and Jonathan walked in behind us.

Bruiser bounced from foot to foot, like I'd seen athletes do when they were trying to keep their bodies warm. "Okay." She clapped her hands. "Six days left to make Mystic and David competitive fighters. Today we're doing a little bit of everything. Striking, take down, submission. Like I said, MMA."

"And right when you're the most tired," Bruiser continued, "we're taking it outside in the fashion of the Greeks. We're going to throw rocks, run piggy backed with one another, bench press each other, military press wood beams, and squats until you drop. No modern day equipment. We're going to condition our bodies like the warriors used to."

I got exhausted just listening to the rundown.

A shadow flicked in my peripheral vision, and I turned to see an average sized man with a bushy gray beard step into the barn.

"Sounds like the Molly I know," the man said.

"Red!" Molly squealed and sprinted across the barn.

‹SEVEN›

With a smile, I watched Bruiser and Red embrace.

"How's my spunky Molly?" Red asked, squeezing her tight.

She returned the squeeze. "Oh, Red, I missed you so much."

Ever since I had known her, Bruiser had always been happy go lucky, fun, never took anything serious. And she pretty much wore a perpetual grin on her face. But seeing her here with Red brought out a glow in her that I had never seen before. She seemed to beam with excitement and for the first time since I'd known her, her body came across relaxed, content.

Which was funny, seeing as how I had never noticed that she seemed *un*content in any way until now. It was amazing how much body language showed a person's emotions.

"How do you feel?" Bruiser asked as she stepped back from Red. "You look great."

Smiling down at her, he tweaked her chin. "I'm fine. Perfect in fact."

"How long are you here for?" she asked.

Red glanced over her head to TL. "We'll find out in a second."

TL crossed the barn to where Red stood and went straight into his arms. No handshake. No greeting. Just a heartfelt, long hug. Red turned his head and whispered something into TL's ear, and he nodded his head.

Although TL's back was to me, I imagined his eyes squeezed tight as he received the warm embrace. I probably didn't, but I thought I heard TL sniff back tears. That sound, that small sniffle, brought tears to my own eyes, and at that moment, I truly felt TL's pain.

And for the first time ever, I saw TL in a different light. I saw him vulnerable, just a man fighting for his family. I saw him human, as weird as that sounds, and not as some sort of super hero immune to pain and able to accomplish anything.

Red whispered something else to TL and gave him a pat on the back. TL discreetly rubbed his face on Red's shirt, took a deep breath, and turned to us.

"Team," TL addressed us. "I'd like you to meet the man who raised both me and Bruiser, our father, Mr. Red Cartlynn."

By 'father' I knew he didn't mean blood related, but it made no difference. Here stood the man who raised both TL and Bruiser. How crazy was that? Every day around this place revealed something new—that was for sure.

"Please feel free to call him Red," TL continued. "You are standing in the presence of one of the most highly decorated veterans in our nation. An Army Ranger, sniper, with four combat tours in Vietnam. Later recruited into the CIA. Went MIA in southeast Asia. Crossed the border into Thailand. Studied under the world's best fighters. He is one of the elite. However, he still suffers from the lingering affects of hepatitis and malaria while he was a POW." TL glanced over to Red. "So he's going to take it easy."

Red chuckled. "Complete burnout and being double crossed by a few unnamed people sent me into hiding. Glad that I did. I would have never met Tommy and Molly."

Tommy? That cute nickname for TL made me smile.

TL pointed to each of us, introducing us. "That's GiGi, our computer specialist. And Mystic, our clairvoyant. David, my right hand. And Jonathan in charge of physical training. You'll the meet the rest tonight at dinner."

We all smiled and nodded hello.

"Red," TL continued, "has agreed to join us here at the ranch as our warfare specialist."

"Really?" Bruiser nearly squealed.

Red nodded. "Really. And I'm also going to be assisting in training you all for this mission."

Her excitement was so evident it nearly vibrated off of her.

Red waved his hand in the air. "Okay, I've interrupted you enough. Carry on."

Straightening her tank top, Bruiser turned to us. "Alrighty, before we move into Greek conditioning, I want to feel the anger. It doesn't matter what your personality is, when you are competing, you have to maintain a level, thinking head and at the same time channel fury. You want power behind your muscles, and fury, mixed with concentration, is the way to obtain it."

She turned to Mystic and her face transitioned into obvious doubt. "Are you going to be able to channel fury?"

Mystic shrugged, not looking too convinced. "Sure."

"Just think of what really pisses you off, and use *that*," Bruiser slammed her right fist into her other hand, "to put power behind your punch."

I turned to Mystic, doubting anything ever pissed him off. "Well?"

His jaw clenched. "My foster father."

His foster father? Hmmm . . . I wondered at the type of man who could get this reaction out of peaceful, in-touch-with-the-world Mystic. His foster father must have been a real jerk.

Bruiser pointed her finger at Mystic. "You're really irritated. I can see it on your face. That's good. And sometimes that's not so good. Depending on your opponent, it'll work to your advantage to either show that fury or mask it." She walked straight up to him. "Hit me with your fist."

Jaw still clenched, Mystic shook his head.

She got right in his face. "I'm not doing this again with you. When I tell you to do something, you do it. We have a little over a week to train for this fight. So enough already. Think of your foster father and hit me."

Mystic reared back and slammed his fist into Bruiser's gut.

I sucked in a breath.

Mystic sucked in a breath.

And Bruiser smiled. "Not bad."

Not bad? I'd be bent over moaning from that. Mystic wasn't exactly a small dude.

He reached for her. "I'm sorry. Oh my God, Bruiser, I'm so sorry."

She smiled even bigger. "Felt good, didn't it?"

Mystic frowned. "No."

Bruiser wagged her finger in his face. "Liar. You know that felt good. Come on, admit it."

Mystic just looked at her.

"Come on," she egged him on, "admit it."

He shrugged. "Okay, a little."

She jabbed her finger in the air. "Ah-hah! It would've felt superb if it would have been your foster father, huh?"

Mystic reluctantly nodded, clearly not liking this violent side of him. He reached for her again. "Seriously, you okay?"

She waved him off. "Didn't even feel it. Okay," she turned to all of us. "Originally, I wanted to do some striking and MMA work first, but I've changed my mind. Let's do a little Greek style conditioning." Bruiser pointed to me. "You *sure* you want to do this?"

I nodded. "Experiencing the training and the world of a fighter first hand will give me a 'one up' on those designers who will be presenting to Harry Noor. And afterward I'll take statistics on everybody. Using Chapling's Influence Sway Skins, I'll trace pulse velocity, strapping adroitness, fortitude, faction, lactic acerbic dissolve, and a few others. I'll amalgamate that with my Combat Thrash Program and come up with at least three variations to arrangements that will outrival a unit feat."

Everyone just looked at me.

I sighed. "Never mind. Just trust I know what I'm doing." Where was Chapling when I needed someone to understand me?

Bruiser pointed to the barn doors. "Let's take it outside."

Everyone filed out as I grabbed the video cam, tripod, and my laptop. I followed the group outside and behind the barn.

Bruiser had turned the side yard into an old fashioned training ground. There were a pile of mid-sized boulders off to the left. Between two trees about six feet from each other she'd tied thick rope—two strands up high and two down low. I studied the get up as I set the cam back up, trying to figure out exactly what those ropes would be used for.

Bruiser beckoned Red over with a nod of her head. "Flexibility is a key factor in conditioning your body for a fight. I expect you two," she pointed to David and Mystic, "to do what I'm about to show you ten times a day."

Mystic and David nodded their understanding.

Bruiser positioned herself between the trees and held her arms up and out to her sides. Red tied her right wrist to a rope high up on one tree and her left wrist to the other tree, leaving her upper body sprawled and stretched.

He took her left ankle next, lifting it, pulling it, and tying it to the left tree. With the tiptoes of her right foot only, she stood supported.

"Ready?" Red asked her.

She nodded.

Grasping her right ankle, he took it out from under her and stretched it over to the other tree, tying that leg off as well.

Sprawled to the max, her legs stretched and strained sideways to form a perfect split. I cringed as my own legs ached just watching her.

Bruiser smiled. "This, my friends, is awesome for flexibility. And obviously it takes a partner to tie you up. David and Mystic, you two are competing. Like I said, this is most certainly an exercise I want you to do every day. You'll start off with five minutes and build your time from there. I, personally, love to hang for thirty or more minutes."

Thirty or more minutes? Ug. That hurt just thinking about it.

"And no worries," she continued. "The rope won't take you any further than you're ready for."

With that, she nodded to Red. He adjusted the rope around the tree, and her body dropped, hyper extending her stretch by pulling her legs straight up to form a V.

Ow! That couldn't be good for her body.

Bruiser nodded to Red again, and he loosened her ties one-by-one, letting her body drop back into a standing position.

Once free, she waved David and Mystic over. "David, you're first."

He stepped up between the trees, and she tied off his wrists first, showing Mystic how the ropes worked. She did David's legs next, first his left, and then his right, leaving him stretched, dangling between the two trees, shaking, cringing, and sweating more and more by the second.

I almost closed my eyes. I couldn't stand to watch him. He seemed like he was in so much pain. And he wasn't even doing a split. In fact, he was fairly far away from accomplishing the split portion of the training.

"You're doing great," I felt compelled to tell him.

He barely nodded.

"Three minutes," Bruiser informed him, adjusting the ropes so that he dropped slightly more into the split position.

Closing his eyes, he breathed deeply, working through the pain. It was a physical and mental strategy that TL had taught all of us.

Inhale through the nose.

Exhale through the mouth.

Inhale through the nose.

Exhale through the mouth.

Three minutes passed, and Bruiser showed Mystic how to release the ropes, softly dropping David back into a standing position. He stood for a few seconds, shaking his legs and arms, probably trying to get sensation back into them.

Mystic went next, doing phenomenally well. I didn't know why it surprised me, really. I'd seen him in all sorts of contortion, meditative positions. I guess it always took me off guard because of the size of his 'football' like body, very thick and stout.

He did his five minutes amazingly fast, definitely accomplishing a split, but not the hyperextension.

After he'd been loosened and lowered to the ground, Bruiser turned to the rest of us. "This is a fighter's stretch, and something I'd like you all to experience at least once. But it's certainly not something you need to do every day." She looked at me. "Who's first?"

I took a step back. What was she looking at me for?

"You said," she reminded me, "that you wanted to experience all aspects of training to be a fighter."

I narrowed my eyes. She just *had* to remind me of that, didn't she?

Bruiser raised her brows, a little too sweetly if you asked me. "Well?"

"Fine." I put my laptop down and walked over to the tree-torture area.

Bruiser and Red tied my wrists. Mystic did my left ankle, and I stood supported only by my other foot. I looked down at David who had his fingers wrapped around my right ankle.

"You ready?" he asked.

I nodded.

Gently, David slid my foot from under me, and I dropped into a forced split. *Ow!*

I clenched my jaw and sucked in a breath through my teeth. *Ow!*

"Breathe," TL instructed.

I sucked in another breath.

Oh my God! How had David and Mystic done this?

"Are you ready to be lowered into a split?" Bruiser asked.

"*What?!*" Wasn't I already in a split? "No! Don't touch me."

Bruiser chuckled. "GiGi, really. You're hardly even stretched."

"*What?!* You've got to be kidding me." I felt like I was about to crack in half. "Let me down."

Bruiser glanced at TL, and he shook his head.

Fighting the urge to glare at him, I squeezed my eyes shut and tried not to focus on my screaming, shaking muscles.

"It's just a few minutes," David quietly spoke. "You can do this. Breathe and think of code."

690

I listened to his mellow, deep voice and inhaled a breath. On exhale, I conjured code for the Combat-Thrash program:

*<!Phrase % element "Em" (	)>*
<!Entity (%ostyfon;~%ophse;)- -()(%oline:)>
<(%oline:)-(𠀋)>

I continued to code, my eyes closed, inhaling and exhaling in a subconscious deep rhythm. I went over every axiom, matching it to its component, and uniting it with all the rudiments. And, strange enough, I solved a fissure in the data that had perplexed me.

"That's five minutes," Bruiser announced, bringing me from my concentration. "You didn't even flinch when I lowered you a few more inches."

I looked down my body and saw that I was suspended in the air mere inches away from doing a complete split. "Wow."

Mystic and David went through the motions of letting me free, and much like David, I had to stand for a second and shake out the kinks.

TL went next, doing, of course, fabulously well.

Red stepped up, doing just as great as Bruiser.

And Jonathan followed, not doing as good as I thought he would have.

We moved onto bench pressing each other next.

"It's all about balance and strength," Bruiser explained. "In an actual fight, you're manipulating a person's body weight. Lifting a person is completely different than lifting weights. Bench pressing each other is a guaranteed way to accelerate your strength training."

She paired Mystic with Jonathan, TL with Red, and me with David.

"What about you?" I asked.

Bruiser shrugged. "I'm too little. It won't be a challenge to anybody."

I wasn't sure what she meant by that until she gave instructions, David was lying on his back, and I found myself on top of him.

With our faces definitely within kissing distance, I gave him a little smile. "Hey."

"Hey." He smiled back.

We locked our fingers palm to palm, he pushed me straight up, and I found myself above him looking down into his too sexy face.

"Give me a set of twelve," Bruiser instructed.

In my peripheral, I saw TL and Jonathan in the same position as David, bench pressing their partners up. All of us on top were lowered down by our partners, paused for a second, and then they pushed us back up.

THE SPECIALISTS

I tried really hard to ignore David's scrumptious cologne. And bicep bulges. And chest striations. And every other straining flexed muscle as he pushed me up and lowered me back down. Pushed me up. And lowered me back down.

I just kept smiling. I mean, really, how great was this?

If I'd been a self conscious girl, I would've been offended by his red, exerted face. But let's face it, at five foot ten I wasn't exactly the smallest girl ever created.

The set of twelve ended, and we switched positions with me on bottom and him on top. We linked hands palm to palm, Bruiser gave the go ahead, and I pushed with all my might.

Nothing happened.

I pushed again, every muscle shaking, my arms literally vibrating from the effort.

Still nothing happened.

"Stop holding your breath," David said.

"I." Quick breath. "Can't" Quick breath. "Lift you."

"And down," Bruiser told everyone, and through the sides of my eyes I watched as Mystic lowered Jonathan and Red lowered TL.

One of them grunted, and it pleased me beyond words that someone else was having difficulties, too.

Up and down we went, or I should say they all went, going through the motions of the exercise. I just sort of pushed with all my might, held my breath, and waited for Bruiser to say 'down'.

We finished that and moved onto throwing rocks, or I should say heaving small boulders.

We finished that and ran each other piggy backed across the yard.

We finished that and military pressed wood beams over our heads.

We finished that and did umpteen rounds of squats holding the same small boulders.

We finished that right as the sun was going down, and I literally dropped to my shaking knees. I couldn't tell you how happy I was to see everyone else gasping for air, too. Why I ever thought I needed to be involved with the actual training stretched beyond my comprehension. Frankly, I never wanted to see Bruiser again in my life.

Not really, but you know what I mean.

"And that, my friends," Bruiser proclaimed, "is a mere smidgen of the way Greek warriors trained before going into battle. Now we need a good

692

high protein, high fiber meal, and then we'll meet back here for striking and take down."

News flash. I had no intention of participating in tonight's 'striking and take down'. I needed a nap.

"GiGi?" Bruiser prompted. "Didn't you want to take data or something?"

I got up—*ow*—and hobbled over to my laptop case—*ow*. I got out the Influence Sway Skins, powered up my laptop, and turned to everyone. "If you could please take your shirts off, I want to get a reading on your muscle adroitness and compare it to data Chapling already took on you." I looked at all of them. "Who's first?"

David took his shirt off. "I am."

‹EIGHT›

I stared at David's bare, sweaty, muscular, tanned chest.

I stared.

And I stared some more.

I only slightly registered everyone else taking off their shirts, and Bruiser tucking her tank top in the elastic of her shorts, leaving her standing in a black sports bra.

I think I must have forgotten how scrumptious David's body was. How I could have forgotten, I had no idea. This body of his was most definitely *not* one a person should or could forget.

"GiGi?" David said.

I blinked—*oh!*—and snapped to attention. "Sorry." Idiot. I was *such* an idiot. "Okay." I held up the Influence Sway Skins. "I'm going to attach these square pads to various spots on each of your bodies and take muscular recordings. I'll compare the results to the base line reading Chapling took of each of you. The range of the data will help us put the finishing touches on the Combat Thrash Program. I'll organize the program's code to recognize David and Mystic's output, tweak it, and identify them as superior fighters, resulting in Harry Noor picking them for Demise Chain."

I ran my gaze over the whole group. "Got it?"

They all nodded.

I brought the Combat Thrash Program up on my laptop. It took a second for the program to boot and detect the wireless skins. It beeped, signaling me it was ready for muscular readings.

Here went nothing.

I walked across the grass to David and stopped right in front of him. Up close and personal with his bare chest was almost more than I could handle. Purposefully focusing all my attention on the Influence Sway Skins, I peeled the protective, hygienic back off of each square pad and began placing them at key points on David's body.

His stomach. His chest. His biceps and triceps. His thighs. His hamstrings. And ended with his calves.

I walked back over to my laptop, *click, click, clicked,* and it began recording his body. I watched my screen as the Influence Sway Skins x-rayed through his epidermis and brought up a 3-D image of his muscular skeletal. I smiled as I watched electrical pulses run up and down his body, recording his inner workings.

A box popped up in the bottom left corner comparing the current recordings to his base line data. Another box popped up in the upper right hand corner showing a video image of David doing the Greek style conditioning. Another box popped up in the upper left hand corner displaying a 3-D image of what David was capable of in a fictitious fight. I, of course, would tweak that part to make David and Mystic stand out above all the others. And the only thing missing was the hologram image, which I knew would be our slam dunk in securing this job.

I finished with David and used new pads each time I did the others: Mystic, Bruiser, TL, and then Red. I'd get a baseline reading on Red later to round out the data. I'd lie and tell Harry Noor I'd traveled around the world to obtain data on the best fighters. It'd give me a one up on the other programmers.

And it wasn't a total lie. Red and Bruiser *were* some of the world's best fighters. I just hadn't traveled for the information. It'd been conveniently right here at my disposal.

Plus Chapling had been working hard hacking into the computers of the most renowned competitors, obtaining their medical records, training schedules, eating diaries . . . anything to give more validity to our program and make us stand out above the other designers.

We were definitely going to kick butt.

***

The next afternoon I strode toward the barn with some last minute questions for Bruiser. Chapling and I had a mere three days left until we went in front of Harry Noor. Mystic and David had only five.

I pulled the barn door open and stepped inside. Sounds of classic rock surrounded me, and I stood for a second letting my eyes adjust to the dim interior.

I realized then that someone had covered the windows with dark cloth, and candles flickered in the corner on a table. Bruiser and Mystic sat across from each other having . . . a romantic lunch?

What the . . .?

"Um," I took a step back. "Sorry. Sorry to interrupt."

Bruiser glanced up, looking so put out that I almost laughed.

I looked between them. "What are you two doing?" This definitely wasn't right. Mystic and Bruiser didn't like each other *that* way.

Bruiser rolled her eyes. "Wasting valuable training time playing boyfriend and girlfriend."

I laughed. "You're doing what?"

Mystic swatted at a fly. "TL said if we were going to be boyfriend and girlfriend on the mission, then we had to have a few lovey dovey moments."

I laughed again. "Oh, this is too good."

Bruiser scowled.

Mystic picked up a piece of paper from the table. "Okay, it says we have to make polite conversation while eating a meal."

I nodded to the paper. "What is that? And who set up all this candlelight and fancy stuff?"

Mystic swatted at the fly again. "This is a list of things TL wants us to do on this quote-unquote date. And the candlelight stuff was here when we got here." He swatted the fly again.

Bruiser leaned forward and snatched the fly from midair. "Would you leave the poor thing alone?"

Mystic and I exchanged a surprised glance.

"TL's list of things." Bruiser snorted as she walked over to the window and let the fly go. "Who's going to know anyway? I say we tell TL we did it and move on with our lives."

"I'll know," Adam announced as he stepped into the barn carrying a tray.

Bruiser turned from the window. "What are you doing here?"

"TL sent me." Adam held up the tray. "I'm your waiter."

"Our *what?*" Bruiser almost shouted.

Oh, yeah, this was too good. Bruiser's crush, Adam, serving her and Mystic while they played lovey-dovey. This—I sat down on the floor—I had to watch.

Mystic looked at me. "What are you doing?"

I smiled. "Watching."

Bruiser scowled again. "Is that allowed?"

We all looked at Adam, and he shrugged. "Sure, why not."

I batted my lashes at Bruiser, and she narrowed her eyes.

Hey, it was the least I deserved after all the stuff she'd seen me be put through. Model training, cheerleading prep, endless horrible PT's . . .

All in waiter role, Adam crossed the floor. He put the tray down on a smaller, linen covered table that sat off to the side. Then he pulled Bruiser's chair out. "Madam."

She plopped down in it, and ignoring Adam's help, scooted her own self up.

Adam took Bruiser's folded napkin from the table, snapped it open, and laid it across her lap. He did Mystic's next. "According to that list," Adam began all proper, "you are to have polite conversation. You are to eat a meal together. You are to hold hands. You are to exchange one kiss. You are," he glanced between them, "going to act like you adore each other. And I will determine when that goal is met." He looked at Bruiser. "And *you* are to act girlie and sweet and innocent." Adam smiled. "Got it?"

Mystic nodded, and Bruiser scowled again.

"You look like Beaker," I told her, and she stuck her tongue out at me.

I laughed. Bruiser was a tomboy through and through, a girl that would rather punch out her problems than talk through them. This 'date' had to be mild torture for her.

Adam pointed to a blue disc clipped to his shirt. "I'll press this," he pressed it and a buzzer went off, "when you're not doing things correctly."

Straightening his back, Adam walked over to the tray and picked up a carafe of what looked like apple juice. He took each of their wine glasses and filled them up. "Polite conversation," he reminded them.

"What lovely," Mystic started, "green eyes you have, my dear Bruiser."

She scoffed.

Buzz.

"Your hair," Mystic tried again, "glows vibrant in the light."

She rolled her eyes.

Buzz.

Adam put plates down in front of each of them. "We'll stay here all day," he sweetly reminded Bruiser, "if need be."

Bruiser looked down at her plate. "Peanut butter and jelly?"

Adam waved his hand through the air. "We pull out all the stops her at restaurant de Adam."

Using his fork and knife, Mystic cut a chunk of his sandwich, very much in proper role. "What beautiful weather we're having today."

Bruiser grabbed her sandwich and took a purposefully huge bite.

Buzz.

I put my hand over my mouth. This was too funny.

Mystic took a sip of his apple juice. "Did you sleep well last night, my sweets?"

Bruiser just looked at him.

Buzz.

Mystic delicately wiped the sides of his mouth. "I heard you downloaded some new music. Tell me about it."

Bruiser glanced at her watch, shoved back from her chair, and tossed her wadded napkin on top of her sandwich.

Buzz.

She planted a sweet, dimpled smile on her face, and both guys watched in suspicious curiosity.

I watched, too. What was she up to?

Gently, very ladylike, she pushed her chair in. She took her wadded napkin, folded it nice and neat, and placed it beside her plate. "Silly napkin. I'm not sure how it got so wadded."

I chuckled silently. I knew Bruiser, and I think I knew what she was up to.

Batting her lashes, holding her innocent grin, she rounded the table to where Mystic sat. She ran her fingers through his short, sandy blonde hair. "I'm so fortunate you're in my life." Cupping his cheek, she tilted his face up to hers. "You are the best boyfriend in the whole world, and I'm so silly to have ignored your pleasant conversation."

She placed a kiss to his forehead. "Thank you for telling me I have lovely green eyes and vibrant red hair." She traced her finger down his nose. "Yes, it is beautiful weather we're having today." She pressed a feathery kiss on his cheek. "And, my *sweets*, I slept very well last night. Thank you for asking."

Trailing her hand down his arm, she linked fingers with him and brought his hand to her lips. She put a soft kiss on each knuckle. "You're right. I did download some music. Just some nature sounds to meditate by."

Bruiser meditate? Not likely.

"So let's see," Bruiser delicately traced her finger over the top of his hand, "the list said polite conversation. Check. Act girlie and sweet. Check. Hold hands. Check. And exchange one kiss." She let go of his hand, gently cupped his face, and placed a tender kiss to his lips. "Check."

"And you," she turned to Adam, closing the small distance between them. "You should expand your menu at restaurant de Adam." She traced her finger down his chest, poked his belly, and then pressed the blue button.

Buzz.

Bruiser spun on her heel, strutted straight past me, across the barn, and out the door. I watched her go, her small hips swaying in exaggeration, and then turned back to the guys.

Neither one of them had moved from their spots, Mystic sitting and Adam standing, staring at the path Bruiser had just taken.

I studied Adam's face and got the distinct impression he'd just seen Bruiser in a new light. A definitely feminine, attractive light.

I pushed myself up, remembering why I came here to begin with, and told the guys, "See ya later." I needed to track Bruiser down for a few quick questions.

I left the barn, saw Bruiser in the distance stepping inside the house, and took off after her.

I heard a rustling noise to my left and whipped around. I searched the pool and the yard beyond all the way to the tree line and the fence that bordered our property. It might have been my imagination, but I thought I saw a shadow move. "Who's out there?" I yelled, feeling a bit silly, wishing instead I would have yelled, *is it you, sister?*

Mystic stepped from the barn. "Did you say something?"

I shook my head. "No. I keep feeling like someone's watching me. Weird, huh?"

"Nah, it's not weird. It's called the theory of shadow scrutiny. It's your psyche, body, and spirit all speaking with your outer organization."

"Huh?"

Mystic arched his arm through the air. "Basically, if you feel someone's watching you, then someone probably is."

I glanced around. "My sister?"

He shrugged. "Couldn't tell you."

"Can't you use your psychic ability to figure it out?"

Mystic laughed. "It doesn't work that way, GiGi."

With a sigh, I turned and started back across the yard. Mystic fell into step beside me, and seconds later we entered the house.

A giggle had me glancing right into the rec room where Beaker and Randy sat playing cards. Wait a minute, Beaker and Randy?

She giggled. He laughed. And I narrowed my eyes. *What* was going on?

Smiling, they both glanced up at me and Mystic.

"Hey," Beaker greeted us.

"Hey," we both responded.

Randy held his cards up. "Uno. Anyone up for a game?"

We both shook our heads, and Randy and Beaker went back to playing.

Mystic and I continued on down the hall, past the cafeteria, rounded the corner and saw Bruiser standing with her ear to TL's door.

"What are you doing?" I whispered.

She put her finger to her lips and shook her head.

I heard it then, TL and Nalani arguing behind his door.

"You told me," Nalani said, "when I got pregnant that we'd leave this life."

"Keep your voice down," TL responded.

"You told me," Nalani repeated, her voice cracking.

"Neither one of us," TL pointed out, "expected you to get pregnant."

"And what exactly does that mean? God, Thomas, we both know you only married me because of Zandra."

"I was trying to do the right thing," TL defended himself.

"Why?" Nalani asked. "Why did you even bother marrying me?"

Because I love you, I hoped TL would say.

"Why?" Nalani repeated.

He paused. "Because I wasn't about to bring a bastard child into this world."

Nalani scoffed. "What, like you were? Get over it, Thomas. So you had a crappy childhood. Every one of these kids here did. *I* did. That's how we met. Or have you forgotten that?"

"Keep. Your. Voice. Down," TL gritted.

"I don't want to keep my voice down," Nalani fired back. "I'm *tired* of 'keeping my voice down.' I'm *tired* of hiding. I'm *tired* of slinking around trying to keep things secret. I want a real life now. I want to live with my husband and my daughter."

"We decided together," TL came back, "that your mother should raise Zandra."

"And that's a decision I've regretted nearly every day of Zandra's life."

"Oh, yeah?" TL's voice finally pitched loud. "How many enemies do you have? How many enemies do I have? We chose this life early on and with that comes consequences. We couldn't chance Zandra's life, your life, my life. Do you think I like keeping it hidden that you're my wife and that I have a daughter? I have to. I can't chance that someone will take their anger for me out on you."

Silence.

"Do you realize," Nalani softly replied, "that's the first semi-loving thing you've said to me in a long while."

More silence.

Go to her, I willed TL. Hug her. Tell her you love her.

"I wasn't the one who left," TL finally responded, his voice back low.

Nalani sucked in a breath. "How dare you. How dare you bring that up. You know why I left. I *had* to."

"You didn't *have* to do anything. I would have helped you. Between the two of us, we had the connections needed."

Me and Mystic and Bruiser all exchanged a curious glance. What were they talking about?

"It's your fault," TL spoke, every syllable riddled with emotion. "Your fault our daughter's gone. And I'll never forgive you."

I put my hand over my mouth. Oh my God. How horrible. They loved each other. They did. I'd seen them together on missions. I'd witnessed the love. This awful thing that had happened to them was making them nasty to one another. Couldn't they see that? They should be united over this, not driven apart.

"My fault?" Nalani's voice broke, and my heart hurt for her, for him, for them both. "You son of a bitch," she cried. "How dare you blame this on me?"

"Zandra was in *your* care," TL shouted, "when she was taken."

"I know!" Nalani yelled back. "Don't you think that's killing me?"

Her footsteps echoed across the room, and we realized too late she was heading toward the door. She wrenched it open with tears streaking her face and caught sight of all of us.

Immediately, I felt guilty for having intruded.

Firming her jaw, Nalani walked right past us, down the hall, and out the front door.

Me, Mystic, and Bruiser exchanged a pained look before turning to TL.

He stood with his back to us, staring at the wall. "Get me David," he quietly spoke.

<NINE>

The next afternoon Chapling and I walked into the conference room for our last meeting before leaving for Harry Noor. We would trial our program today.

Around the table sat everyone involved with the mission. TL, Nalani, David, Jonathan, Mystic, Bruiser, and Red.

Chapling and I took seats to TL's left.

TL closed the door and remained standing. "I am too close to this mission emotionally to run it successfully and efficiently. I've had an in depth discussion with David and have decided effective immediately that he is in charge. However, I'm still going on this mission. As previously outlined, I will be playing the role of trainer. I'll also be acting as mission advisor to David, but all decisions will come from him, not me."

Whoa. I was totally not expecting that. I looked across the table at David's focused expression and thought what a stressful mission to be in charge of. I mean, my God, we're talking about TL's daughter here.

With a nod to David, TL sat, and David stood. "Okay, team, I am going to outline the mission and then give the floor to Chapling and GiGi." David began walking around the table, placing green folders in front of each of us.

I opened my folder to see a giant picture of Zandra right on top. I began leafing through the other papers—standard things we should know for the trip. Information on location, parties involved, aliases, mission details, equipment list, etcetera . . .

David set the last folder in front of Bruiser. "First, let's briefly recap things. Last Monday, TL and Nalani's seven-year-old daughter, Zandra, was taken from her maternal grandmother's home. We still have no idea what they want. TL and Nalani both have many enemies. So the kidnapper could be anybody."

"Myself, Mystic, and TL traveled to the abduction site," David continued. "It was there that Mystic saw images of the Demise Chain fight club. Unfortunately, he saw no images of Zandra, but he knows without a doubt that he needs to be involved in the Demise Chain if he is going to find Zandra." David looked at Mystic, and he nodded his agreement.

"TL and I immediately dove into researching the Demise Chain," David went on. "Between Red's input and our own research, we've discovered a few things. First, it's a closed club. You have to be invited in. Harry Noor is the owner of the club and the owner of a handful of fighters labeled Warriors. Recently, he put the word out that he's looking for some new Warriors. He also put the word out he's looking for a computer specialist to design a program that will identify top notch fighters that can be his Warriors."

"Obviously, the better his Warriors are, the more money Demise Chain makes." David glanced at me and Chapling. "Additionally, this computer specialist will be able to advise his Warriors during a fight what to do differently, all based on technological physics. And that sets the ground work for the mission. GiGi and Chapling will be leaving tomorrow to interview with Harry Noor, show him their new program, and get hired on. Two days after that, Harry and his new computer specialist will be meeting and testing prospective fighters."

David nodded to Mystic. "Mystic and I will show up with our personal trainers, Jonathan and TL. GiGi and Chapling will have their program rigged to identify Mystic and I as top notch fighters. Harry Noor will bring us in as Warriors, and we will officially become Demise Chain competitors."

David turned his attention to Nalani and Bruiser. "Now for the ladies. There are no women fighters allowed. And the only way ladies are allowed in the audience is if they are on the arm of an invited guest. However, fighters are allowed to have wives and girlfriends at their sides. Bruiser will be traveling as Mystic's girlfriend, but clearly, her role is our fighting consultant. All of us will be wearing hidden communicative devices. Mystic and I will be counting on her to coach us through our actual fights, along with the input from the Combat Thrash Program."

"Nalani has already secured a job within Demise Chain as the hostess. She will be our one inside person, serving as back up, on guard for anything that might happen. Because of their personal connection to this mission, Nalani and TL are the only two who will be in disguise." David rolled his chair out and took a seat. "Once Mystic starts interacting with the fighters, he'll know what our next move is, who has Zandra, and where she is. Obviously, we'll regroup and go from there."

"The format of Demise Chain," David continued, "is that fighters go up against each other, the winners move on to the next round, and so forth. By the end of the night there is a grand winner who is awarded the purse. Currently there are six Warriors. They all fight each other as well as the visiting competitors. Harry Noor could care less who wins, just as long as it is one of his Warriors."

"Red is going to be here at home base ready to give input as needed." David opened his folder. "Now for aliases. Jonathan will be Trainer Jones. TL, Trainer Tim. Nalani, hostess Nan. Bruiser, girlfriend Bee-bee. I'll be Warrior Daniel. Mystic, Warrior Michael. Chapling, computer specialist Charlie. And GiGi, computer specialist Gertrude."

Gertrude? I nearly rolled my eyes. What a horrible name.

David looked around the room. "Before I turn things over to our computer team, are there any questions?"

Chapling raised a pudgy finger. "Um . . . what if something goes wrong? I mean, there're not a lot of definitive details here. Who's to say GiGi and I are going to sufficiently wow Harry Noor with our brilliance? I mean, well, of course we're brilliant, but do you all not see this whole mission hinges on us?"

"And," he continued rattling, "if we don't secure that job, the whole thing is down the drain. What do we do then? Huh? Huh? Okay, and if we do, by some act of God, get the job, our program might have a glitch in it and not identify Mystic and David as top notch fighters."

Chapling glanced at me. "Not to say our program will have a glitch."

"It won't," I assured him.

"Oh!" He threw his hands up, completely ignoring my reassurance. "And once Mystic gets his next image, what are we all going to do? Just walk out of there? And what about our trainers, TL and Jonathan? What if Harry Noor doesn't allow them?"

"And—"

"Chapling," I interrupted, "everything's going to be okay." Sheesh, he reminded me of me. This was what I must look like in one of my frantic states. "I know the mission isn't cemented and certain things hinge on other things, but that's just the way it goes. You can't know for sure what's going to happen every second. You just sort of roll with it and have the confidence it'll succeed."

"But . . ." Chapling's voice trailed off, and then a few seconds later he blew out a shaky breath and nodded. "Okay. Okayokay." He gave everybody a guilty shrug. "It's my first mission."

"You'll be fine," TL spoke.

I reached over and rubbed Chapling's back. "You'll be fine," I whispered.

"Plus, Chap, we'll have several more briefings. One when you get done meeting with Harry Noor, another one after Warriors tryouts, another one when Mystic sees what he needs to see. There'll be plenty of communication throughout the different stages of this mission." David closed his folder. "At this time I'd like to turn things over to our computer team."

Chapling and I both pushed back from the table and made our way over to the wall inserted flat screen.

"Daisy," Chapling addressed our ranch's main computer. "Show time."

GREETINGS, she typed in big bold letters across the center of the wall screen.

I turned to our team. "Tomorrow we're meeting with Harry Noor. Some of the world's best program designers will be there, too. The competition will be tough."

"But," Chapling interrupted. "Smart girl here hacked into all their computers and knows what fighting program they've all designed."

I smiled. "We've, basically, taken the key components of their program and coded it into one I've affectionately deemed the Combat Thrash Program. Okay." I stepped to the side of the screen. "Without further ado, I'd like to introduce the Combat Thrash Program. Daisy, do your thing."

Daisy cranked on the speakers, and out poured hard rock. On the screen, shooting in as if someone was throwing a ball of video, were flashes of actual fights timed to the music thumping the room. Clip after clip ending with one man hitting another, and his blood spraying out to transform into animated 3-D.

Then the screen divided into a dozen small boxes, each displaying two animated men fighting. The screen flashed, much like a camera does, x-raying through the animated men to show their muscular skeletal.

The music trailed away as the animation continued, and Chapling and I turned to our team.

"We'd like to ask Mystic to come up," I said, nodding to him.

"Daisy," Chapling prompted, "may I have the Influence Sway Skins?"

A tray slid out from below the wall mounted screen, and on the tray sat a slim, rectangular box.

Chapling took the box and opened it. "These are one-of-a-kind devices, made exclusively for this mission. They will provide us with an image of Mystic's muscular make up, record and measure his strapping intensity and breadth, and in layman's terms give us a thumbs up or down if he'd be a good fighter."

I nodded. "Clearly, Mystic simply standing here while we measure him doesn't give us an indication of his reasoning skills. Which is why we'll also be recording his cognitive thought processes as he engages in a two minute mock fight with Bruiser."

"Mystic," Chapling addressed him, "if you could take off your shirt and roll up your jeans."

While he did that, I waved Bruiser up. "When Mystic and David actually go in front of Harry Noor, they'll be expected to engage in the same sort of mock fight with one of the Warriors. This will give Harry a visual of them actually in action and us the data we need to inform Harry Noor if Mystic and David are good fighters. Which, of course, the answer will be yes."

I watched as Chapling placed wireless Skins all over Mystic's body. "Nice color," I complimented him. He'd changed the Skins from white to skin color.

"Thanks." When Chapling finished, he stepped back. "Daisy, record adroitness aptitude now." And then he nodded for Mystic and Bruiser to begin.

In the corner of the conference room Bruiser and Mystic threw some phony punches, kicks, and elbow strikes, each taking turns with offensive moves and defense blocking. At the two minute mark Chapling stopped them.

A large 3-D image of Mystic's muscular structure appeared on the screen. "This," I pointed to the screen, "is Mystic's image. Daisy," I commanded our computer, "show us excellence."

Patches of translucent yellow slowly filled his image, from his toes all the way up to his brain.

"The yellow represents a match between excellence and Mystic's body composition, including his brain patterns." I turned to the screen. "Daisy, give percentage."

99.9 PERCENT.

I smiled. "As you can see, Mystic matches the best fighters in the world at a ninety-nine point nine percent."

"Which," Chapling put in, "is a fib."

"A fib," I agreed, "that will get Mystic a slot as a Warrior."

Chapling clapped. "Okay, now for the best part."

I turned to our team. "Like we said, everything we've showed you thus far is basically a combination of what all the other program designers will be doing. But we've got something they don't."

"Daisy," Chapling spoke, "finale please."

A life size hologram of Mystic appeared on top of the center of the conference table. Every one of my team members simultaneously pushed away, their eyes wide in amazement.

Another image popped up of a *huge* man. "This is—"

"Utotiz." Bruiser interrupted. "He holds the world title in MMA."

"Based on the data we just took of Mystic, and all known information on Utotiz, we're going to see these guys in action. Daisy," I told the computer, "fight."

Both holograms moved at once, coming toward each other.

Utotiz jabbed his knuckle between Mystic's nose and mouth.

Mystic unleashed an upward kick at Utotiz's head.

Utotiz feinted a kick, then rammed his heel into Mystic's shin.

Mystic executed a double punch to Utotiz's chest.

Utotiz grabbed Mystic's arm and wrenched it behind his back. He took the waist band of his jeans, lifted Mystic high above his head, and threw him to the ground.

Blood went flying through the air, and I took that as my cue to stop the hologram.

Mystic swallowed. "Was that my blood?"

Chapling cringed. "Utotiz *does* hold the world title."

"Obviously, when we get in front of Harry Noor," I addressed the team, "Mystic and David's hologram will succeed in submitting whomever they have a hologram fight with."

David put his finger in the air. "Now what about the other portion of this? Actually advising the Warriors during a fight."

I nodded. "Well, of course our program has thousands and thousands of combat data. Very simply, we'll be recording the fights as they occur and advising the Warriors on what to do when. Watch." I turned to the wall inserted screen.

"Daisy, phase two of Combat Thrash Program," I requested.

Two fighters appeared on the screen.

"This is a film taken from an underground fight club in Russia," I told my team. "These fighters are approximately two minutes into a fight."

While the fighters continued grappling, a smaller screen split off and to the left, turning the men into an animated image.

I pointed to the man with red hair. "Any coach can tell that man what to do differently, but we can tell him *exactly*. Notice the dark haired man has the red haired man in a shoulder lock. Any coach would tell red hair to front roll out of it as an escape, but based on both men's physiological make up, in this instance red hair should front roll out to the right at a thirty degree angle."

"Daisy," Chapling commanded, "show thirty degree escape versus normal."

Another animated box moved off and to the right. The one on the right showed the normal response with red hair front rolling and dark hair twisting his wrist to keep him in place.

The animated box on the left showed the revised response with red hair front rolling at a thirty degree angle, successfully escaping the shoulder lock, and gaining top ground.

"Wow," Bruiser exclaimed. "That is too cool."

Chapling and I shared a smile. Getting kudos from Bruiser was the slam dunk.

Around the room everyone gave their approval and congratulations, and Chapling and I exchanged a pleased look.

"Obviously," I pointed out, "when Mystic and David are fighting, Chapling and I will be there with our program to advise them what to do and what not to do. Our advice combined with Bruiser's will give them the knowledge needed to succeed." I looked around the room. "Questions?"

Everyone shook their heads

David nodded. "It goes without saying, you two have done a superb job." He stood. "You'll fly out at 0900. Dismissed."

<TEN>

At 0900 the next morning, Chapling and I boarded our plane to Washington State.

And he was not okay.

Chapling swallowed. "Gi-GiGi?"

"It's Gertrude," I reminded him in a whisper.

"G-Gertrude?"

"Yeah, Charlie?"

"I-I think I'm going to be sick."

I yanked my attention up from the magazine I held. "*What?* No." I waved my finger at him. "You're not going to be sick."

He swallowed again. "I'm not?"

I shook my head. "No." *God*, no. Because if he got sick, then I would sure get sick. "What are you nervous about? You've flown before. *I'm* the one who hates flying." Or at least I used to.

Actually, *hate* flying would have been the operative word. I loathed it. Dreaded it. Wanted to hurl every time I thought of it. And, in fact, had passed out the first time I found out I would be getting on a plane.

My parents died in a plane crash, so it didn't take a genius to figure out my phobia.

But since joining the Specialists I had flown eight times, and this flight marked my ninth one. I was getting to be a bit of an expert at this flying thing. It wasn't so bad anymore. Or, at least, that's what I had convinced myself of.

My cell buzzed, and I looked at the display. David's usual preflight message to me. BREATHE.

Chapling's cell buzzed and he looked at his display. BREATHE, C, BREATHE. Smiling, Chapling held it up for me to see. "David."

I held mine up. "Me, too."

And then we both sat there for a second, grinning like goofs.

Chapling tucked his cell away and a few seconds later he began fidgeting again.

"What's wrong now?"

"It's not the flying. It's the," he looked around before leaning in, "the mission. It's my first, and I'm really," he waved his hands, "nervous."

I gave him what I hoped was a comforting smile, and recalled how TL always talked to me when I felt uneasy—in a sort of talking-me-off-the-ledge way.

I put my magazine aside. "I know its nerve racking. *Believe me*, I know. Not only the travel and the assignment, but the fact this whole thing hinges on us. *And* we're on our own. There is no TL for guidance."

Chapling leveled with me a 'look'. "You call that helping?"

I laughed. "Sorry. Serious, though. Think of everybody back at home base. They've got our backs. If anything goes wrong, we simply contact them, and the Army rolls in. Not really, but you know what I mean. TL has more resources than the President, it seems. He won't let anything happen to us. I couldn't think of a better person to have on my side. Well, except maybe genius, Adara Hamalitz."

Chapling's eyes widened. "Oh, no kidding. Wouldn't that be cool? Man, I've got a whole list of people I'd love to break bread with, and Adara Hamalitz definitely makes my top three."

"Break bread with?"

"Lunch. Have lunch." Chapling snapped his fingers. "You know the first thing I'd ask him?"

I shook my head.

"To explain that experiment he did back in 1899 with movement of molecules."

My jaw dropped. "I've always wondered about that to."

And so the conversation went, discussing the great minds of the world, both past and present. Their theories, their experiments, their discoveries. We were so into the conversation we never even realized the plane took off, flew through choppy skies, and landed two hours and fifty-three minutes later.

We exited the airport and took a taxi to Harry Noor's mansion in Tea Cup, Washington. Because this would be a day trip, we brought only our laptops. Roughly forty-five minutes later we pulled into one side of the town and right out the other.

Seriously, we did. It was that small.

I counted a few one story homes, a grocery, a post office, a hardware store, oh, and a lingerie parlor, strange enough.

No red light. Not even a stop sign.

Okay, small would be the operative word.

I did spot a sign that said Harry Noor, Mayor.

The taxi drove down a dirt road lined by huge trees.

"Those are Douglas Firs," Chapling informed me.

I looked over at him. "I didn't know you knew about trees."

He shrugged. "I'm from Washington."

"Really?" I'd been working with Chapling over a year and hadn't even known that small, personal part about him. Frankly, there was a lot we didn't know about each other. "How long did you live in Washington?"

"'til I got married and moved away."

"You've been married?!" Oh my God. I would have never guessed.

He nodded. "Yeah, but me and Sophia, we were so young."

"Was Sophia your childhood sweetheart?"

"Nah. She was doing a photo shoot in my home town. That's how I met her."

I raised my brows. "Photo shoot?"

"Yeah, Sophia Packard? You ever heard of her?"

My jaw dropped. "Sophia Packard? *The* Sophia Packard? As in the cover model?"

Chapling nodded and glanced out the window. "Oh good." He clapped his hands. "Looks like we're here."

The Sophia Packard. Holy cow. I laughed. "We *really* need to have lunch sometime and just talk."

Smiling, he nodded. "That sounds great."

The taxi pulled up in front of a mansion, or palace I would think better described it. It sat so out of place in little Tea Cup, Washington that it was purely laughable.

Sprawling a good half acre and towering at three extended height stories, the stone structure probably could have housed the entire population of little Tea Cup *and* the surrounding towns. Why one man needed this monstrosity stretched beyond my comprehension.

As the taxi pulled through the gates, the driver let out a whistle. "What does this person do for a living?"

"Investments," Chapling and I answered in unison.

And actually, according to our records, that was exactly what Harry Noor filed on his taxes every year. Investment Broker. I supposed there wasn't a category labeled Underground Fight Club Owner and General Abuse of Mankind.

The taxi pulled to a stop and an *enormous* tattooed man opened the door.

Chapling got out first, dropping his head back to look up at the man. "You're big. Reallyreally big. How big are you?"

"Six five," he answered in an unusually high pitched voice.

Chapling must have thought it, too, because he shot me a humored look.

I paid the driver and slid out next. I was a tall girl, and this guy was huge. But next to Chapling, he looked like a giant.

Chapling held his arms out to his sides. "You're wide, too. You probably shop at one of those big and tall places don't you? Or is it big and wide?"

I elbowed Chapling to the side. "Ignore him. He doesn't get out much."

Huge-tattoo man laughed, and it took me off guard. First, because he had all his teeth (for some reason I thought he wouldn't), and second, because I hadn't expected him to laugh. I'd expected a serious, stern nod or a blank look at least.

I mean, weren't guards supposed to be perpetually angry?

But then, who's to say he was a guard. He could be a visiting relative. The lawn man. The pool man. The—

I gave my head a little shake. I was getting *way* off track.

I held out my hand. "I'm Gertrude and this is Charlie. We're here for the program design demonstration."

Huge, tattooed man nodded. "I figured with the laptops and all." He turned toward the mansion-slash-palace. "Follow me."

Up the stone entryway we went on steps so wide Chapling had to take two foot steps for every one stone step. Huge-tattoo man opened a wooden front door, and we stepped in behind him right into a narrow hallway.

For some reason I had imagined large open spaces, but as we walked down the long narrow hallway, small rooms opened off the right and the left. Cramped rooms, but incredibly tidy, like no one had ever stepped foot in them: bedrooms, living rooms, kitchens, bathrooms. It was the oddest design I think I'd ever seen. Surely, the small rooms connected somehow to make bigger suites.

And, weird enough, the rooms sat empty. Not that I'd expected anyone, but with such a large house it sure seemed like there should be someone.

We continued on down the eternally long hallway and finally came to another wooden door, much like the front door to this mansion. Huge-tattoo man opened it to reveal a stairwell.

He stepped to the side. "Take those stairs down and you'll find everybody."

I smiled at him. "Thanks."

He grinned back. "You're very welcome."

His response made me chuckle. This man just didn't seem like the type to grin and laugh and be polite.

The door closed behind us, and we descended the steps.

"Nice guy," Chapling commented, and I nodded.

Fifty two steps later (not kidding, there were a lot, and yes, I really did count), we came to another wooden door.

"Going to be a chore going back up those," Chapling mumbled as he turned the door's knob.

It swung open, and we found ourselves in a room I estimated to be about half the size of a football field.

Chapling stepped in. "Good grief this is big." He looked around. "And dirty."

I nodded as I stood, taking everything in. The entire place looked like it was in dire need of a good scrubbing. Dingy concrete spanned the entire floor with suspicious stains all over. A non-caged octagon that looked about twenty years old occupied the center of the room with rows of metal chairs surrounding it. Equipment, like Bruiser had back at the ranch, but in much poorer quality, sprawled the back left corner.

"You'd think with all his money," Chapling mumbled, "he'd clean this place up."

"You'd think," I agreed. Honestly, I was afraid to touch anything.

Off to the side was an arched open doorway with PRIVATE posted above it.

Chapling motioned to the back right corner, and I saw Harry Noor there with the other computer programmers. "Looks like we might be the last to have arrived." Blowing out a nervous breath, Chapling nodded. "Here goes nothing."

As we made our way around the octagon toward the group, I glanced around, taking everything in. Surely there had to be another way in or out of this place besides those stairs we'd just come down.

We approached the group, and I counted seven program designers plus Mr. Harry Noor.

"I'm giving each of you," he was saying, "fifteen minutes. No more, no less. At the end of everyone's presentations, I will immediately make my decision." He looked straight at me and Chapling. "You're late."

I smiled. "I'm sorry, our—"

Harry Noor flicked his hand through the air. "I don't care. I hate explanations."

O-kay. For such a sweet-looking-little-old grandpa, he was sure rude.

Off to my left, one of the computer nerds snorted his immature amusement. What was this, competitive elementary school?

Harry Noor looked me up and down first, then Chapling, and then came back to me. "You don't look like a program designer."

I glanced behind him at the myriad of stereotypical geeks, and then with a shrug said, "You'd be surprised what's in this brain of mine."

He barked an overly loud laugh, and everyone jumped a little.

Well, at least I'd amused the guy.

Harry Noor motioned for me and Chapling to sit with the others on the floor. "We'll start with the first to arrive and end with blonde-brainy and her little friend."

Chapling and I exchanged a glance. We were the last to go—exactly what we had hoped for. We'd sit back, watch all the others, and then make last second adjustments if need be.

Geek #1 went first. Tall, skinny, bald, glasses. He nervously stuttered his way through his presentation, and five quick minutes later, took a bow.

Chapling looked at me. *A bow?* he mouthed, and I held back a smile.

Harry Noor shook his head. "You can go."

As if he'd been expecting the dismissal, Geek #1 hurriedly mumbled his thank you, packed up his stuff, and scurried off.

I wanted to tell him he'd done an okay job, the poor, insecure, nervous guy. But I figured I'd better just keep my mouth shut.

Geek #2 went next. Medium height, heavy, long hair, glasses. A little nervous, too, his presentation lasted ten minutes. A presentation I'd grade about a C. Okay, maybe C+

When he was done, Harry Noor flicked his hand through the air. "You can go."

"B-but—"

Harry narrowed his eyes. "Go."

Geek #3 went next. Short, scrawny, shaggy hair, glasses. He took the full fifteen minutes, doing, in my opinion, a bang up job.

But, of course, we knew what kind of job he would do, as well as all the others. I *had* hacked into their computers after all. I knew more about them then they probably did. I even knew their eye glass prescriptions.

Harry Noor motioned for Geek #3 to sit back down. "Stay for now."

Chapling and I exchanged a slightly worried glance.

Geek #4 and 5 did their thing, and Harry Noor sent them home.

Geek #6 stayed—the one who had snorted when we first came in. The dweeb.

Geek #7 went home.

And then it was our turn. We stood, and knowing we only had fifteen minutes, we plunged right in.

"We've traveled all around the world," I fibbed, "obtaining data for our Combat Thrash Program."

"She came up with that name," Chapling happily supplied, and Harry merely looked at him.

Clearing his throat, Chapling gave me a boy-isn't-he-a-fun-one? look to which I launched right back into weaving my excellent introductory tale to Mr. Harry Noor.

Chapling busied himself setting up the laptops, and when he was ready, he gave me the signal.

We did everything exactly as we had in the conference room yesterday. Using Daisy (that for security purposes we temporarily renamed Darlene), we commanded our laptops to begin the music, video, and animated introduction.

When it finished I asked Geek #6 (the snorter), "Would you mind coming up?"

Geek #6 shook his head. "No thank you."

"Do it," Harry Noor commanded, and I couldn't help but smirk.

We stripped him down to his boney chest and attached the Influence Sway Skins. A 3-D image of his muscular skeletal appeared.

"We'll measure strapping intensity and cognitive thought processes," I told Harry Noor, "as he engages in a two minute mock fight with me."

"*What?*" Geek #6 squeaked.

With a nod, Harry sat forward in his chair.

Geek #6 and I began our mock fight. Or more like I threw punches and kicks and he yelped and dodged. When we finished, I commanded, "Darlene, percentage of match to excellence, please."

0.25 PERCENT.

Chapling and I both laughed, we couldn't help ourselves.

Geek #6 tore the Skins off and threw them to the ground. "Not funny."

I turned to Harry Noor. "As you can see, he clearly is not suited for fighting."

Harry smiled. "Clearly."

"During the creation of the Combat Thrash Program," I explained to Harry Noor, "my data was entered into the system. We'll use that for the finale."

Chapling and I exchanged an excited look.

He pointed his laptop toward the octagon in the center of the room. "Darlene, finale please."

A hologram of me and Geek #6 appeared in the octagon. We approached each other, or rather I approached him, and basically beat him into the ground while he scrambled his weenie little self out of the way. I had to admit, I looked pretty darn good up there.

The hologram fight ended. I turned to Geek #6 and batted my lashes. He sneered back.

Chapling glanced at his watch. "Sorry, we went over our fifteen minutes."

Harry Noor waved him on. "No problem. Finish up."

That had to be a good sign.

Quickly, we explained the rest of the program pertaining to the advisement of fighters during an actual competition. Using the same footage from Russia that we'd used yesterday in the conference room, we showed the dark haired man fighting the red haired one. We illustrated the shoulder lock and demonstrated the success of rolling out at a thirty degree angle versus normal.

When we finished I powered down and turned to Harry Noor. "It's all based on a person's unique geometrics and the intermolecular attraction of all elements involved." I smiled. "And that concludes our demonstration."

Harry didn't say anything. The two remaining geeks didn't say anything. I didn't say anything. Chapling didn't say anything. Everyone just sort of looked at each other.

More quiet seconds went by and still nobody said anything.

Finally, Chapling bowed.

And I held back a smile. Leave it to Chapling. I looked down at him, and he gave me an I-thought-maybe-that's-what-I-was-supposed-to-do shrug.

Harry turned to the Geek #3 and #6. "You can go." He turned to me and Chapling. "Congratulations. You're hired."

‹ELEVEN›

We flew back to San Belden, California late that night and got off the plane. As Chapling and I waited for our taxi, I got that weird sensation, *again*, that someone was watching me.

I turned to Chapling. "Do you feel strange or weird in any way?"

"I always feel weird," he answered.

I laughed a little. "I mean, right now, do you feel as if someone's watching you?"

Chapling looked around. "No. Do you?"

"Yeah, I've been feeling this way on and off pretty much since I got back from my last mission. And I keep thinking about . . . well, my sister."

He shrugged. "Yeah, it could be her."

I smiled.

"Before this mission you and I both were doing a lot of research, trying to find her, purposefully leaving identity stamps through cyberspace." Chapling shrugged again. "If she's half-way computer savvy, she found them."

I turned a full circle, my heart jumping a little bit. Hearing someone agree with me made it even more real.

Through the dimly lit area, I searched the airport, the people standing, and the parking garage in front of us. *My sister.* It was almost too much to comprehend.

I smiled into the night, hoping she really *was* watching. *Hi sis*, I mouthed.

Our taxi pulled up and forty five minutes later we found ourselves in the conference room surrounded by our team.

We told them everything that had happened. We described the layout of the mansion, the things we'd seen, the people we'd interacted with.

David nodded. "Everything's right on track. Warrior try outs are in two days. TL and I are going to do some last minute checks with the mission, and everyone else maintain training schedule. Dismissed."

My team filed out and I purposefully lingered, taking my time packing my things. I wanted to talk to David. Just to say hi, exchange a few sentences, and tell him about my sister—it seemed crazy that I hadn't had time to do even that. But more importantly I wanted to find out if he was okay. He had to be stressed to the max over this very personal mission to TL.

David didn't notice me lingering, his focus was so intent on a file.

"Hi," I softly said, and he glanced up.

I noticed then how blood shot his eyes were and it melted my heart. Poor guy.

I didn't care we were 'just friends'. I walked right up to him and wrapped my arms around him. "You okay?" I whispered.

He didn't hesitate in returning the hug. Squeezing me tight, he buried his face in my neck and just stood breathing me in.

I closed my eyes and inhaled his scent and warmth, too. God, I'd missed this. Him. Us.

Neither one of us said anything for a good long while and sometime later he pulled back. "Thanks," he said, smiling a little.

I traced my finger across his brow and down his stubbly cheek, drinking in his handsome, caring face.

He stared into my eyes, and I got the distinct impression he really wanted to say something but couldn't bring himself to say it.

Instead, he reached up and caressed his thumb around the curve of my ear.

I swallowed, wanting to say so much, but not knowing if it was the right time. If he would accept my words. If he would reciprocate.

"Thank you," I said instead, "for the text on the plane. Chapling and I both appreciated them."

David's eyes did that sexy crinkling thing. "You're welcome."

"Do you know how wonderful you are?"

He took a step back, glancing away in what seemed like embarrassment.

Lightly, I grasped his upper arm. "David, seriously, do you know how wonderful you are?"

720

He shrugged. "Just doing my job."

"No, you're not. You're doing what's you. What's David. You're thinking of everyone else always, making sure everyone's fine. You're amazing. Here you are with this huge stress on your shoulders. My God, TL and Nalani's daughter, and you're in charge. And yet you still think to text me and Chapling to make sure we're okay."

I tugged his arm a little so he'd look at me. And when he did, I repeated, "You're amazing."

David shrugged his embarrassment, and he was so cute I couldn't help myself, I leaned forward and kissed his cheek.

"David," TL interrupted, sticking his head in the open doorway. "My office, now."

David gave me a tender smile, "Thanks," and then gathered up his things and headed out.

I watched him go, happy I'd lingered and talked with him, and knowing I'd given him a margin of comfort he'd needed.

David *did* spend a lot of his time emotionally supporting others when he desperately needed that support himself. Sure he got it from TL, but David needed it from me. I'd been so used to him being the strong one, the one in charge, the one with all the answers that I hadn't fully comprehended the importance of him being able to lean on me. He wasn't invincible, although he easily seemed that way.

I walked from the conference room, smiling to myself, feeling a boost to my confidence as a person and a woman. I was an equal partner to David, and it had taken me this long to figure that out. And I knew without a doubt in my mind that this 'friend' business wasn't going to cut it.

I wanted him back.

***

Early in the morning two days later, Chapling and I boarded a plane back to Washington. A taxi picked us up, drove us to Teacup, and dropped us at the mansion. The same huge, high-voiced, tattooed man led us through the house and down that interminably long stairwell to the gym.

Everything looked the same.

"Mr. Noor said you should set up," the tattooed man instructed. "Warrior tryouts will commence at precisely one p.m."

Again, I thought how this guy's proper demeanor seemed so out of place in the situation.

With that, he left us, and Chapling and I made ourselves at home. We were the only ones in the whole place throughout the entire morning. I didn't know what I had expected, but complete solitary was not it.

I guess I'd expected fighters to be training or people to be coming in or out. And where were the prospective Warriors? Shouldn't they be here by now? Where was my team?

At precisely 1:00 p.m. Harry Noor walked through the PRIVATE archway and into the gym.

"Charlie, Gertrude," he said, "greetings."

Chapling and I smiled. "Mr. Noor."

"All set?" he asked, and we nodded.

He blew a whistle, and from the same archway filed a whole group of men. I would say some big, some small, but even the small ones were big. Halfway down the line I spotted Mystic, and at the end I saw David.

I surveyed the guys, counting twenty in all, and then each fighter had his trainer.

Shirtless, the fighters lined up in a row with their trainers standing behind them—of course, TL with Mystic and Jonathan with David.

I didn't think I'd ever been greeted by so many shirtless men. So many *muscular*, shirtless men. And to my surprise, most of them had no hair on their heads or their bodies. Maybe they thought being bald made them look more mean? Not to my surprise, the majority of them had tattoos.

I glanced down the line, noting Mystic, at five-foot-ten, stood the shortest. And then I looked straight at David. Stone-faced, completely in role, he stared straight ahead. TL had shaved his head for his disguise and wore a fake bushy beard. Even though some distance spanned between us, I could tell he'd put in dark contacts. Honestly, if I hadn't known the man behind Mystic was TL, I wouldn't have recognized him.

I glanced around for Bruiser, before remembering girlfriends weren't allowed in tryouts, only in the actual fights.

No introductions were made. Harry Noor simply nodded for us to begin. So much for a warm and cozy start.

Chapling and I busied ourselves pasting the wireless Influence Sway Skins on each of the fighters for the baseline reading. I headed straight for David.

Not even glancing at me, he maintained his rigid posture and stoic expression. I took my time putting each Skin on him, slowly smoothing them into place. I wasn't flirting or teasing, don't get me wrong, this was *so* not the time to flirt. I just wanted him to feel my touch, to know I was here.

It worked, because as I smoothed the last Skin into place, he brought his eyes down to my face. His expression remained blank, but his eyes spoke volumes. Appreciation, warmth, affection, longing . . . *love?*

I tried hard to show him those same things before turning away and getting down to work.

When we finished taking baseline readings of each man, I turned to Harry Noor. "We're ready for the mock fights."

Harry blew his whistle again, and from the PRIVATE archway came six *gigantic* men. No, gigantic didn't fully describe them. Enormous. Massive. Gargantuan. Colossal. None of them under six feet five, and every one of them solid, beefy muscle, bone, and skin.

I blinked a few times, trying to make sure I was seeing what I was actually seeing, and noticed our greeter, the high voiced guy. To my surprise, in the line up, he stood the smallest. And that guy was *huge.*

I chanced a quick look in Mystic's direction, and he swallowed as he took in the site of the current Warriors.

It hit me then. Oh my God, Mystic and David had to go up against these guys? That was so not good. Not good on too many levels. I didn't want Mystic and David to go up against these guys. Not even with the Combat Thrash Program and Bruiser's coaching did I feel confident Mystic and David would succeed.

Heck, succeed? Survive was more like it.

Harry Noor gave instructions that each fighter would go up against a current Warrior in a two minute round. During that time, Chapling and I would continue taking data, and after the two minute mark, would have a percentage of excellence. After all tryouts were complete, we would commence with the hologram portion of the afternoon, and Harry Noor would make his decision.

"What are you looking at, you freak?" someone yelled, and Chapling and I whipped around.

The fighter standing beside Mystic towered over him, his face stuck right in Mystic's. "Get your eyes off me," the fighter growled.

To Mystic's credit, he took a step *toward* the fighter, not away, inching his face even closer. "You got a problem?"

The two just stared at each other, and I knew what Mystic really wanted to do was apologize, discuss peace, and turn the other way.

And then it dawned on me as I watched them face-to-face, that Mystic was searching the fighter's eyes, looking for a possible Zandra clue.

"Men," Harry Noor grunted. "Save it for the octagon."

Mystic and the fighter slowly turned away from each other, giving that whole I'm-meaner-than-you-I'm-top-dog look.

Warrior #1 stepped up onto the raised octagon and motioned fighter #1 to join him. With his Skins still on, fighter #1 cockily strutted over and up. The two men went at it, while we recorded data. They threw punches and kicks, jabs and strikes, and within thirty seconds fighter #1 had been knocked out.

"I doubt he's going to be chosen," Chapling mumbled through the side of his mouth, and I held back a smile.

On and on it went, each Warrior going up against a fighter. Some of the fighters held their own, some not so much. So far only fighter #1 had been knocked out.

Halfway down the line, it was Mystic's turn. He stepped up onto the octagon to face a Warrior just as horribly huge as the others. I crossed my fingers and toes and said a prayer to the fighting gods on behalf of nonviolent Mystic.

Mystic closed his eyes, probably channeling the same gods, and to my surprise pulled a Bruiser. His eyes shot open as he simultaneously lunged forward, feinted left, dodged right, leapt up, and jabbed his elbow in a meridian pressure point on the Warrior's shoulder.

Mr. Warrior dropped to his knees.

Chapling and I exchanged an impressed glance. Bruiser would be so proud.

Without making an arrogant show, Mystic simply reached down, reset Mr. Warrior's meridian point, and helped him up. A little disoriented, the Warrior shook his head to regain his equilibrium, then stood for a second just staring at Mystic.

Mystic stared back and I knew, once again, he was searching for Zandra clues. With a respectful nod, Mystic reached his hand out, and the Warrior took it. They exchanged manly compliments and left the octagon side-by-side, slapping each other on the back.

Leave it to Mystic to make friends with a giant.

I glanced over to see if Harry Noor showed any sides of being impressed. With slightly narrowed eyes, he watched Mystic's every move as he walked beside the Warrior. That had to be a good sign. So far he hadn't watched any fighter that closely.

The rest of the fighters standing in line went. A couple did really well and most held their own up against the Warriors. Only one got knocked out. So far, hands down, Mystic had done the best.

Finally, it was the last person's turn—David. I glanced at the octagon to see which Warrior he'd be up against and found the high-pitched guy standing there waiting. It was weird, I know, but I kinda liked Mr. high-pitch guy. He'd been so gentlemanly to me and Chapling.

My gaze traveled down his body to his ankles and the supportive, half-sock he wore on each one. I studied each ankle, noticing the right one looked a bit thicker, and then I saw a hint of an ace bandage peeking out the top.

David strode down the line right past Mystic. Completely in role, he and Mystic showed no signs of recognition to each other.

I stepped forward. "Excuse me; I need to check your Skins." Pointing to my laptop, I turned to Harry Noor. "According to the Combat Thrash Program," I lied, "one has come unattached."

Harry nodded for David to approach me.

I smoothed my finger across a Skin attached to his stomach, leaning close to inspect it. Beside me, Chapling faked being busy with the laptop.

"Right ankle," I whispered, not moving my lips.

"Oh, goodgood," Chapling mumbled.

David barely nodded his understanding.

I stepped back. "All good."

Harry motioned for David to continue on, and he stepped up onto the octagon. Harry blew his whistle, and lightening quick, David dropped to the matt and swept his foot right into Mr. high-pitch's bad ankle.

A snap echoed through the gym, and I watched wide-eyed as Mr. high-pitch fell to the matt, grabbing his ankle. He didn't make a sound, but the agony on his face told me something bad had happened.

I glanced at David, wanting to tell him he didn't have to go and break the guy's ankle. But, I reminded myself, it would be a lot worse than this during the actual competition. Mystic and David both would not only inflict some major pain, but take it themselves. Neither one of them would walk out of this mission unscathed.

And, I reminded myself, these fighters came here expecting this. They were kidding themselves if they thought this would be a friendly encounter.

"Was that a bone?" Chapling asked, looking a little sick.

I shook my head. "I think it was a tendon or ligament or something." Since joining the Specialists, I'd heard bones break, and that was most definitely not a bone.

A couple of the Warriors stepped up onto the octagon to help Mr. High-Pitch down. He couldn't walk. David had seriously injured him.

"Let's move on," Harry instructed, clearly feeling no concern for his injured Warrior.

While Chapling went down the line of fighters taking their Influence Sway Skins off, I dove into the Combat Thrash Program, checking and double checking that David and Mystic were set to go.

Harry came over to me. "I'd like to see holograms first."

"Which titled fighter would you like to see these prospective Warriors go up against?" I smiled a little. "I have Utotiz's data," I proudly said, referring to the world MMA title holder.

Harry Noor's brows lifted. "Utotiz?" He turned his back to everyone so only I could see his face. "He happens to be a guest fighter in tomorrow's fights," he whispered.

I held my smile in check, when what I really wanted to do was freak out. "Utotiz?" Holy crap. David and Mystic would be going up against the world title holder?

Harry looked a bit smug. "The purse is ten million dollars. Most ever. Why do you think I hired you? One of my Warriors *must* win that fight." He stepped to the side. "Now let's see holograms."

I glanced across the room to TL, but he didn't return my glance.

"Gertrude?" Harry prompted me.

"Sorry." I gave my program the go ahead, and in the center of the octagon appeared an image of Utotiz.

My God he looked mean.

While everyone watched, the hologram of Utotiz went up against each fighter in quick thirty second rounds. Just long enough to show Harry how each prospective Warrior would do. Of course, my program showed real data on everyone but Mystic and David. Some of the fighters did horrible, some okay. Mystic and David definitely held their own.

When all holograms were complete, Harry turned to me. "Now let's see percentage of excellence."

I did some *click, click, clicks,* and a list appeared on my screen. Beside each fighter's name was a percentage. David and Mystic were 99.9.

Harry studied the list, before turning to the line of fighters. "I'm going to call six names. If your name is not called, you and your trainer are to leave immediately. If your name is called, you are to be here tomorrow night promptly at six p.m."

‹TWELVE›

With the fights being tomorrow night, we checked into a hotel. After we dropped our things, we met in TL and Mystic's room. Bruiser and Nalani had already checked into the hotel and were sitting on one of the beds waiting. I noticed TL seemed even more tense than usual.

With a slight smile to everybody, Chapling and I busied ourselves setting up our laptops with a LCD projector that turned our screens into a large image for everyone. Right as we finished, Mystic and Jonathan came in.

"The kidnappers have made contact," TL announced as soon as everyone was seated. "Not more than ten minutes ago."

No one said a word.

"Why didn't you tell me?" Nalani whispered.

With a pained look, TL shook his head and handed Chapling his phone. "It's on there. Project it up for everybody."

Chapling connected TL's phone to our laptop, and few seconds later an image flickered into view up on the wall. I stared at the long brown object, trying to figure out what it was and then realized . . . "Oh my God."

A long, curly lock of Zandra's hair had been placed around a note different than the others. SHE MIGHT ALREADY BE DEAD.

"Nooo," Nalani moaned, putting her hands over her face.

TL sat down beside her and pulled her into his arms. I watched as they clung to each other, neither one looking at the image on the wall. I was so relieved to finally see them pull together, to comfort each other, instead of pushing the other away.

David motioned for Chapling to cut the picture. "Get a trace on that," he said, and Chapling got down to work.

"Okay," David said, nodding to me. "Bring up the club's layout."

I clicked a few keys, and a diagram of the fight club popped up, complete with the octagon and all.

"All this is new." Using a laser pointer, David circled the locker room area. "As you can see from the dozens of small rooms, the fighters are kept completely separate until they actually walk onto the octagon. To reiterate, it is imperative for Mystic to make it to the end. That is the only way he will be able to interact with as many fighters as possible and see what he needs to see regarding Zandra."

David highlighted two stairwells before drawing our attention to the one Chapling and I had used. "This one is where the patrons enter and exit." He highlighted the other one. "This entrance is located inside the locker room area and is used by the fighters and their trainers. From the outside of the mansion, this would be a side entrance."

I glanced over to Nalani and TL to see them still hugging, yet giving David their undivided attention.

"And this is used by Harry Noor." David put an X over an elevator. "It drops him in a private room in the locker area. All three entrances are highly guarded. Once Mystic knows where we're going next, TL will make contact with officials on the outside. They will be ready to raid and bring Demise Chain down."

"Mystic," David went on, "had an opportunity to interact with a couple different fighters. Unfortunately, he did not secure the next clue to Zandra's whereabouts."

David continued speaking, debriefing Nalani and Bruiser on the events of the day, how the tryouts went, and other miscellaneous things.

When he was finished, I raised my hand. "Harry gave us a list of all the fighters that will be there tomorrow night. We uploaded the list and have been compiling data." I clicked a few keys. "Let's see competitors and stats."

Numerous video boxes popped up on the screen, showing individual footage of tomorrow's competitors including the visiting fighters and the Warriors. A list of their stats appeared beside each video box: height, weight, reach, age. And in the middle of them all towered Utotiz.

"We'll be merging this information with our Combat Thrash Program," I told the group. "We'll have a best guess of what that fighter is going to do before he does it."

"Great." David glanced around the room. "Questions?"

Everyone shook their heads.

David turned to Chapling. "Anything yet?"

Staring at the screen, Chapling shook his head. "Whoever the kidnappers are, they've got computer knowledge. I can't trace the origin of the picture. It's set to relay through hundreds of internet protocol addresses. By the time I trace it to one, its programmed to echo to another."

I let out a frustrated breath and heard someone do the same.

"Okay," David redirected us a few seconds later. "Let's review this fighting footage. These are the people we're going up against tomorrow. We need to be as familiar with them as possible." With that, David nodded to me to bring up the first fighter.

***

The next afternoon Chapling and I arrived back at Harry Noor's mansion. To my surprise the huge, high-pitched guy met us as our taxi pulled in.

Supported by crutches with his ankle in a cast, he opened the door for us. "Welcome."

"How are you?" I asked as I climbed out.

Smiling, he nodded. "I'll survive."

I couldn't imagine him doing anything mean to anybody. I couldn't imagine him as a 'bad guy'. But then I'd encountered quite a few 'nice' people since joining the Specialists that had turned out to be bad.

Minutes later, we entered the fight club area. And throughout the next few hours a couple of workers showed up. One guy began sweeping the dingy floor and another walked around the octagon, squirting stains, unsuccessfully wiping them up. A third guy busied himself setting up more metal chairs. I found myself wondering, and more than curious, how this whole night would play out.

And what if Mystic never did secure our next clue?

My God, what then?

At some point Harry emerged from the locker room area and came straight to me and Chapling. "Here," he said, handing us small boxes.

Chapling and I opened them.

"An earpiece?" Chapling asked.

"To communicate with the Warriors during their fights," Harry responded.

Chapling looked at the earpiece. "But . . . that's illegal. That's cheating."

Harry didn't respond to that, and instead inched closer. "Why do you think I hired you, you idiot? I want you telling my fighters what to do and what not to do. That Combat Thrash Program better come through for me tonight. There's ten million dollars at stake."

He inched closer, purposefully intimidating Chapling. "Let's put it this way. You make me happy. I make you happy. I profit. You profit. Got it?"

Chapling swallowed. "Got it."

Harry turned his glare on me.

I put my earpiece in. "Got it."

Jerk. I wanted to tell him these bulky devices were *so* last year.

"I've already met with the Warriors," Harry informed us, "and they know to listen to whatever you tell them."

He'd met with the Warriors? That meant David was here. And Mystic, and the rest of my team. Just that thought made my insides do a little happy dance.

Harry tapped his ear. "I'll be listening, too." He pointed across the club where a table had been set up with cameras and other computers. "I want you over there. No one is to know what you're doing. If they ask, you're filming the fights." With that, he walked away.

Chapling looked up at me. "I don't like him," he whispered.

"Me neither," I whispered back.

Across the club, the door we'd come through opened, and a woman stepped through.

Wearing fish net stockings, a tight mini jean skirt, and revealing silver tank top, the blond haired woman sashayed through the door. She had a snake tattooed on her right arm and a motorcycle on her left. In red high heels and matching nail polish and lipstick, she swung her kinky hair out of the way.

White trash popped into my mind first as she popped her gum and looked around the place.

"Oh, she looks too great," Chapling commented.

"Who? *Her?*" He needed his eyes checked. This woman definitely did not look great. Cheap, sure, but great? Not so much.

"Her and TL both did a great job with their disguises."

"*That's* Nalani?"

Chapling looked up at me. "You didn't know?"

I shook my head and glanced back across the club to where she stood. Oh my God, she *definitely* was unrecognizable.

Harry caught sight of Nalani then and waved her over. They'd met, of course, when she'd been hired on as the hostess. With her rough-around-the-edges look, she fit right in with this underground, seedy place. She was the perfect woman to greet people later on when they showed up.

Chomping her gum, Nalani strolled across the club straight toward Harry Noor. From my distance I couldn't hear what they were saying, but they exchanged handshakes.

A few more words and Harry disappeared back into the locker room area. Probably to threaten and verbally bash his fighters.

Nalani spun on her heel toward us and crossed the distance between us. Completely in role, she held her hand out to us. "I hear you guys are the computer nerds." She pumped each of our hands. "I'm Nan, the new hostess."

Blowing a bubble, she rubbed her ear lobe between her thumb and forefinger indicating it was time for us to activate everyone's earpieces for communication. Each of us already wore the transceivers, which were tiny moles on the inside of our ears. Dr. Gretchen had implanted them yesterday before we left the ranch to board our planes.

Through wireless connection, they communicated with a microphone embedded in our back molars. And as a backup, a microphone had also been injected into the lymphoid tissue between the mouth and the pharynx (Dr. Gretchen's terminology).

At the last second, Dr. Gretchen had advised two transceivers and two microphones because of the nature of the mission. With fighting, there was no telling what would get knocked out or disabled.

Everyone had agreed. Hence a transceiver in both ears, and a microphone in a molar and a tonsil.

As Nalani headed away, Chapling squatted down in front of his laptop sitting on the floor and programmed our team to begin transmission. Looking over his shoulder, I saw that he also hacked into Harry's frequency, assuring his ear pieces would not cross with ours.

"Brilliant," I mumbled.

"Thanks, smartgirl." He did a few more clicks. "It looks like the Warriors are wearing receivers. They can listen, but they can't speak to each other. Harry's voice and our voices are the only ones they can hear." *Click, click, click.* "I'll create a toggle feature to mute our voices when we want to talk without Harry listening."

"Charlie, check," Chapling began routine assurance all technology was working.

"Gertrude, check," I parroted.

"Nan, check."

"Tim, check."

"Jones, check."

"Bee Bee, check."

"Michael, check."

"Daniel, check," David finished, and I couldn't help but feel reassured at hearing his voice.

Chapling and I grabbed our things and headed over to the table Harry had designated us to be at.

Through my ear mole, I heard a door open.

"Michael," Harry Noor grunted. "Do you have your earpiece in?"

"Yes I do," Mystic answered.

"You will stay in this room until someone comes to get you. You will not leave until then. And let me remind you, you *will* listen to the advice my computer specialist gives you. Do you understand?"

"Yes," Mystic responded. "I understand."

Then there was a pause, and I listened hard, trying to figure out what was going on.

"I watched you closely," Harry finally continued, "in the tryouts. And I can say I'm duly impressed. Michael, I do believe you're going to win me ten million dollars."

Okay, that was good. Harry needed to be impressed with Mystic.

"I will," Mystic confirmed.

"And you," Harry spoke, "you are not to give Michael advice unless I tell you. After tonight, I doubt I'll need any of the trainers. That Combat Thrash Program is going to take us to the top."

TL didn't verbally respond, but I imagined he was nodding or something.

"Now, who is this?" Harry asked all gentlemanly.

"This is my girlfriend, my good luck charm, Bee Bee."

"Hi," Bruiser greeted Harry in that fake sweet voice she did so well. "It's so very, very nice to meet you."

"Likewise," Harry returned the greeting. "Come with me, dear, and I'll escort you out."

I heard the door open and then close, signaling Harry had left Mystic's room.

"That guy's something else," Mystic said.

"Hm." TL agreed.

A few seconds later, Bruiser appeared from the PRIVATE archway. Wearing an innocent, flowery sundress, sandals, and her red hair in a long braid, she grinned up at Harry as he escorted her to a seat.

She looked all of her sixteen years, and definitely not any older. And yet Harry seemed entranced by her, hanging on her every word. Hypnotized, mesmerized, spellbound.

Then it occurred to me . . . *ick*. What a pervert, all in to a sixteen-year-old.

Harry touched the tip of her nose. "You sit right here. I'll get you a virgin daiquiri," he told her, almost as if he was relishing the fact she *was* so young and sweet and innocent.

"Gag," Bruiser mumbled after Harry had walked off. "What a pedophile."

More time went by and Harry escorted other fighters' girlfriends and wives out. None of them looked as innocent as Bruiser, and none of them garnered the attention Bruiser received. Harry, literally, was waiting on her hand and foot.

A few minutes later someone turned on music, filling the club with hard rock.

More time ticked by and the room slowly filled up. Nalani greeted the men and their dates as they entered through the stairwell. I imagined the patrons probably enjoyed entering that way. It added to the underground, secretive, fight club aura.

As I sat beside Chapling at our table, I surveyed the people milling about. They ranged in age from twenties to eighties. Strange enough, some of the men wore suits and others dressed as if they were going clubbing, yet others wore jeans. The women, too. Pants, skirts, dresses, high heels. Some wore their hair up, others loose and down. From what I could tell, all nationalities were represented, everyone from African American to Hispanic to Caucasian to Asian.

And everyone came across like they were on their best behavior. I didn't know what I had expected in an underground fight club, but manners weren't it.

Harry appeared some time later dressed in jeans with holes and a fashionable shirt. I glanced at my watch. 9:00 p.m. The fights would start promptly at 10:00 p.m.

Harry Noor had no date on his arm as he worked the crowd. He shook hands with the men, politely pecked the women on the cheek, laughed, and talked. Unfortunately, our Warriors mikes hadn't been activated, so I had no idea what he was saying.

He gave every appearance of the perfect gentleman. Just watching him, one would never guess he ran Demise Chain.

Through our mole earpieces, Nalani made sure she repeated back everyone's names. And when people weren't looking, she'd describe what was going on. I knew she was doing the narration for the benefit of our team back in the locker rooms.

9:45 p.m. Almost show time.

Harry and Nalani led certain patrons to reserved seating, and the rest remained standing around the octagon.

"Oh, hi, Mr. Noor," I heard Bruiser greet through our earpieces.

I leaned to the left to see through the crowd. Harry had come to stand behind her.

He put his hand on her shoulder. "Are you doing okay, my sweet dear?"

With a big dimpled grin, she held up her half empty, daiquiri glass. "Just swell."

I almost laughed.

Harry tapped her shoulder. "It's about to get gruesome. Should you want to hide your eyes, you come find me."

Bruiser batted her lashes. "'kay."

"She does that too well," Chapling mumbled.

Harry climbed the few steps to the octagon. The hard rock music slowly muted in time with the club's lights dimming.

Everyone quieted.

I glanced around the club and up the walls to the ceiling, curious where the sound and light technician was hidden.

"What are you looking for?" Chapling asked.

"The sound and light person."

"Harry's a techy guy. I'd say there isn't one. I'd say it's all controlled by a remote in his pocket."

I looked up to see Harry's hand in his pocket as he fiddled with something, and a spotlight gradually grew to illuminate him.

I glanced over at Chapling. "You're too good."

Smiling, he shrugged. "I try."

"Welcome," Harry greeted the crowd through a mike attached to his shirt. "Welcome to Demise Chain."

A scurry of excited conversation floated across the crowd.

"Many of you are return spectators, and others are first timers. No matter your seniority, everyone is treated the same at Demise Chain. As you know, there are no rules, there are no rounds. The fighters compete until one goes down."

Someone in the crowd grunted a yell.

"You will see every competitor tonight. There will be time to place bets before each battle. And the last remaining fighter will go up against . . ." Harry paused, I was sure to build suspense. "Utotiz, the world MMA title holder."

A whispered, eager bustle danced through the crowd.

"The winning purse is the biggest one we've had yet . . ." Harry paused again. "Ten. Million. Dollars."

Someone sucked in a breath. And then someone else. Then the whole crowd erupted in buzzy chatter. I imagined all the high rollers cha-chinging money in their brains.

Harry Noor held his hands up to quiet the crowd. "Without further ado, I bring you a Warrior up against a visiting fighter from Yugoslavia."

The crowd erupted in a roaring cheer as the spotlight turned to the PRIVATE archway.

The mike in my ear that Harry had given me crackled, signifying it had been turned on. Chapling rechecked our frequency, assuring the adjustments he'd made were still there.

I turned my attention to the archway, hoping beyond hopes it wouldn't be David or Mystic first.

‹THIRTEEN›

A tall, lanky competitor jogged through the archway. I recognized him from the footage we'd compiled as a visiting fighter from Yugoslavia. A short, pudgy man followed behind and I assumed he was the Yugoslavian's trainer.

In my peripheral vision, I saw Chapling's fingers race across the keyboard as he pulled up all information on the Yugoslavian fighter.

The spotlight followed the Yugoslavian as he jogged through the crowd, weaving his way to the octagon. He trotted up onto the octagon, and the spotlight left him to illuminate the archway again. One of the Warriors walked through. With a hard expression, and an even harder body, he strode with purpose through the crowd. Not once did he take his gaze off the Yugoslavian in the octagon.

People parted, slapping his back as he passed them. This Warrior must be a popular one.

He stepped up onto the octagon, the spotlight faded, and the entire fighting area became illuminated.

I looked from the Warrior's lethal expression over to the Yugoslavian. Although he hid it well, I definitely picked up on a hint of oh-my-God-this-guy's-huge.

In the middle of the octagon stood Harry Noor. He pointed to the Yugoslavian. "Patrons of Demise Chain, I'd like to introduce you to our Yugoslavian competitor."

The Yugoslavian raised his arms, but no one cheered.

I kind of felt bad for him.

Harry Noor pointed to the Warrior. "And one of our Warriors, fighter Sean."

The crowd erupted in yells and screams, and Harry made his way off the octagon. The crowd continued yelling, and the club filled with hard rock music. The two fighters stood on opposite sides, glaring at each other. As soon as Harry gave the go ahead they would charge.

Chapling tugged my shirt, bringing my attention down to the computer screen. The Combat Thrash Program had picked up a medical file from last week on the Yugoslavian. He'd been to a surgeon regarding a bulging disc in C4 and C5. Quickly, I scanned the file before reviewing the program's suggestion. It recommended the Yugoslavian's neck as the target area to begin.

Chapling and I exchanged a look. I didn't want to tell the Warrior to go after the Yugoslavian's neck. He could permanently paralyze the guy.

"Why aren't you giving fighter Sean that information?" Harry said from behind us, and we jumped.

"B-b-because . . ." Chapling's voice nervously trailed off.

With an agitated sigh, Harry said into his earpiece. "Sean, go after the neck." And then he turned to us, and his whole face morphed into an evil that seemed rooted in his soul. "*Don't* screw me over. You will regret it if you do."

Quickly, we both nodded. "Yes, sir."

One more threatening look and Harry walked off.

Chapling and I didn't say anything to each other, just turned our attention back to the octagon. I had this sick feeling deep in my gut that something bad was about to happen.

The hard rock music continued screaming while the fighters glared at each other. The buildup made the crowd go wild. Exactly what Harry wanted, I was sure.

Then the music stopped. A loud horn went off. And the fighters charged.

The Warrior grabbed the Yugoslavian's head on both sides, gave it a yanking twist, and the Yugoslavian fell limply to the ground.

I sucked in a breath. "Oh my God."

"D-d-did he just break his neck?" Chapling stuttered.

The crowd jumped to their feet, roaring, possessed by the graphic show they'd just seen.

"Good job," I heard Harry congratulate Warrior Sean.

Wide eyed, heart thundering, I stared at the Yugoslavian's lifeless body. And the realization struck me hard. That could have been David or Mystic.

Shaking my head, I turned to Chapling. *No*, I mouthed, aware of our earpieces. *David and Mystic can't do this.*

Someone grabbed my arm and turned me around, and I found myself staring into Nalani's calm, focused eyes. *Yes. They. Can.* She mouthed back.

"Report in," I heard David request.

Nalani turned her back to us and the crowd and calmly recounted everything that had just happened. While I listened to her speak in monotone, I searched for Bruiser through the still cheering crowd.

Completely in role, she stood by her chair clapping right along with everyone else. I drug my gaze off of her and over to the Yugoslavian who was being dragged away by two club workers. I looked back at Bruiser to find she had stopped clapping and was staring through the crowd right at me.

"Everything's going to be okay," she softly mumbled.

Slowly, I nodded, although I didn't mean it. How *could* everything be okay? I'd just watched a man uselessly die, and it was highly probable I would see more. And Chapling and I were here to help that happen.

Glancing behind me, I noticed Nalani had walked off. I *click, click, clicked* on the laptop, disengaging our earpieces, and turned to Chapling.

"I'm not doing this," I told him. "I'm not giving advice that will lead to someone else dying. The Combat Thrash Program isn't about that. This mission isn't about that. This is about finding Zandra."

Chapling nodded, looking more serious than I could recall him ever looking. "We're in control back here. No one knows what our computers are churning out. We give whatever advice we want to give and leave it up to the fighters to battle it out. That's the way it should be anyway. Unless it's Mystic or David, of course. We'll give them whatever they need to survive this ridiculous show."

"And if Harry comes back here again?" I asked, already knowing what I would do.

"We'll have two versions of the program." Chapling *click, click, clicked,* creating another version. "The real one for us, and the fake one should Harry come back. There's no way he's going to be privy to the real data."

"And our team? We're making this decision without them."

Chapling continued clicking. "I've known TL a long time. This is what he would want. And I'm going to tell him right now." Chapling reengaged our earpieces, leaving Harry's frequency turned off.

I listened as he told our team what he and I were going to do. He sounded more authoritative than he had since I'd known him, leaving no room for discussion or questions. He'd made up his mind and no one was going to tell him otherwise.

I was proud of Chapling.

"Affirmative," David agreed after Chapling had finished.

"Affirmative," TL backed him up.

I breathed a sigh of relief.

The hard rock music cranked up again, and we reengaged Harry's frequency. The Yugoslavian had been taken away, and the spotlight shown bright on the archway. I held my breath, hoping it would not be David or Mystic.

"I'm up," David said into our earpieces, and my heart paused a beat.

A guy the height and weight of David stepped through. I recognized him as a competitor from England and immediately brought up his data. He made very little show as he trotted up to the octagon.

The spotlight switched over to pick up David as he came through with his trainer, Jonathan, close behind. Shirtless and dressed only in kickboxing shorts, David jogged across the floor and up to the fighting area. His face looked hard and mean. Definitely a face *I* wouldn't want to see staring back at me at the start of a fight.

"This guy likes to stand up," I told David, repeating back what the Combat Thrash Program was giving me. "His ground skills are poor. So take him down quick. He's also never gotten out of a leg lock. If you can get him in that, you'll submit him. He always starts out with a kick. And he's never thrown the first offensive move. He's a defensive guy. He waits for you to come to him."

"Turn it around on him," Bruiser added. "Wait for him to go first. He'll throw that kick. Take him down with that, and dislocate his hip."

I looked at my computer screen, and sure enough, that was exactly what the Combat Thrash Program had recommended. But dislocate his hip? Was that really necessary? Yes, I reminded myself. This was a battle to the end. We had to get rid of as many fighters as possible. Dislocating a hip paled in comparison to death.

I repeated the things Bruiser had said for the benefit of Harry listening. He'd thrive on the dislocated hip thing.

The hard rock music faded away. Harry Noor did the introductions as both fighters lightly bounced from foot-to-foot. Harry left the octagon, the horn sounded, and neither fighter moved.

My gaze bounced between the two of them as they continued volleying from foot-to-foot, staring at each other across the octagon. The crowd yelled, cursed, wanted them to move, but neither one of them did anything.

Finally, the English fighter moved forward, slowly making his way across the matt to David. David continued bouncing, watching the guy approach. I looked at the guy's face and picked up on a hint of hesitancy and confusion. Probably because no one had ever waited for him to do the approaching.

As expected he threw a kick. David grabbed his lower leg in mid air, leapt up, snaked both his legs around the English guy's one, and fell straight back, bringing them both to the ground. With the English guy's foot tucked under David's armpit, he used his hands and legs to twist the English guy's leg.

He squirmed and clenched his jaw, trying his hardest to wiggle out.

I brought my concentration down to my laptop and read off what the Combat Thrash Program was recommending. "Yank his leg and twist back the other way, and you'll dislocate his hip."

David gave a hard yank, followed by an immediate jerk in the other direction, and the English guy let out a yell. David released him and boinged to his feet, completely unharmed from the match.

The crowd cheered, and I breathed a sigh of relief.

"Good job" Harry complimented into our earpieces.

Still in role, David threw his arms up in victory and then turned away from the injured man and jogged off the octagon. A couple of club workers helped the guy down and the hard rock music cranked up again.

Two more fighters came out, bloodied each other up, and one got knocked unconscious. The night continued with the same routine. Fighter after fighter. Hard rock music. Harry. Loud horn. For the competitors that were Warriors, Chapling and I gave them a cleaned up version of Combat Thrash Program strategy. Enough to allow them to win, but not enough to do real damage to other fighters.

In between it all, Nalani was giving up-to-date verbal reports for the benefit of our team members back in the locker room.

David didn't make another appearance. And Mystic hadn't come out yet. But with over twenty competitors, this night would definitely be a long one as fighters were dwindled down to the remaining two. There seemed to be no set schedule as Harry picked and chose who would fight who.

Chapling and I continued updating the Combat Thrash Program as it collected information from all the fights going on. When it finally was time for Mystic or David, we'd have even more data to assist them with.

"I'm coming out," Mystic said into our earpieces.

I watched the archway, and into the spotlight stepped a Warrior. The same Warrior that Mystic had gone up against during tryouts. The one he'd made 'friends' with. In fact, this was the first time all night that two Warriors were fighting each other.

Chapling muted our mikes. "Not good. This guy knows Mystic's technique."

I nodded. "I know."

"I want Michael to win," Harry said into our earpieces. "I've turned off the other Warrior's communication. As of seconds ago, he'll hear nothing from us."

What a double crosser. "And I bet he didn't tell the other Warrior of his plans."

Chapling shook his head. "I can't stand this guy."

"Let's hope all the Warriors gang up on him afterwards."

Chapling turned our mikes back on while I studied the Combat Thrash Program. It pulled up medical records, past fights, preliminary strategies. This guy had a wife and five kids. Sheesh. What the heck was he doing involved in all this?

The money, I reminded myself. Bad pays good.

The spotlight illuminated Mystic as he stepped through the archway. Unlike the other fighters, his expression held peace, confidence, and a hint of secretiveness, like he knew something no one else did. Strange enough, his calm facade came across more menacing than the others.

He seemed to float across the floor as he made his way to the octagon. I glanced beyond him to see his trainer, TL, following close behind. Mystic stopped right beside Bruiser and gave her a big boyfriend-girlfriend kiss to which Bruiser shyly smiled. I bet Harry just *loved* that one.

Mystic stepped up onto the octagon and both fighters stared at each other across the space. At this point the other Warrior had to know he'd been cut from communication. He had to know he was going to lose this fight. I felt bad for him, with the five kids and all. Plus, he'd sort of made friends with Mystic.

I would make this as painless as possible for the guy.

"Okay," I began, studying my laptop screen. "Michael, do not use meridian points. This guy knows that strategy. He likes to grapple, so keep him up on his feet. He's a weak kicker, strong puncher. He's got a long reach. He's also had more head injuries than any other fighter tonight."

"Hence the cauliflower ears," Bruiser added.

I continued, "The Combat Thrash Program says a right elbow strike to the left ear is your preliminary best bet. Knock him unconscious."

"If you feel the strike from your shoulder all the way to your hip," Bruiser put in, "you know you've got it. If not, you better follow through with another one."

I glanced through the crowd to Bruiser who had her hands over her mouth, pretending worry, using it as a cover to continue speaking. "Start slow, fists up. Since you've used pressure points on him, he's going to be focused on blocking you from touching his body. Confuse him with some easy punches. Allow him to get one in, make him feel like he's winning. Then feint left, elbow strike like GiGi said, and be done with it."

The hard rock music faded, Harry introduced them, and the horn sounded.

Cautiously, fists up, they both moved toward each other. Mystic did exactly what Bruiser coached. He threw an easy combination: left jab, followed by a straight right, then a left hook. The Warrior expertly blocked with counterpunches. He landed one to Mystic's eye, breaking skin, causing a gush of blood.

"No big deal," Bruiser commented. "A little blood. Some Vaseline and tape and you'll be all good."

Then Mystic feinted left and landed a right elbow strike to the Warrior's left ear.

Muscles rippled down Mystic's side in a ricochet affect and I knew he'd landed a solid one. The Warrior stumbled back, right off the octagon, and landed on the front row. A woman squealed as she jumped to get out of the way and the Warrior passed out.

Mystic raised his arms in victory and the crowd cheered.

"I wish someone else would die," I heard a guy comment.

I wanted to punch his lights out.

With a bloody eye, Mystic left the octagon, and I breathed another sigh of relief.

The fights continued as more competitors got disqualified.

"It's almost to the end," Chapling commented, and I nodded my agreement.

I wondered when David or Mystic would come back out, and who they'd be up against next.

"I'm coming out," Mystic said into our earpieces.

"Me, too," David commented.

Chapling and I exchanged a glance. *They're going up against each other?*

‹FOURTEEN›

"I've disengaged Daniel's earpiece," Harry said. "I want Michael to win."
Good thing, seeing as how it was our mission to make sure Mystic won.

"Let's make this look good," David commented as he came through the archway.

I didn't bother looking at the Combat Thrash Program. There really was no point. They both knew who had to win. But Chapling and I pretended to be doing our jobs in case Harry was watching.

Mystic came out next with a couple of butterfly bandages on his swollen eye. Strolling across the floor, he stopped here and there to shake hands with people and exchange slaps on the back—anything to give him a glance into their eyes.

"This is what I recommend," Bruiser began. "Take no more than a minute. We don't want to wear Mystic out. Give the audience a little show with some shadow moves, pulling the force before complete execution. David needs an injury, something to the face. And do a throw or two to make things look authentic."

"And *don't* tell each other what you're going to do," Bruiser warned. "Whether you'd mean to or not, you'll react before you should and give yourselves away."

Good advice.

"Oh, and break open Mystic's cut again," she commented on a side thought.

Now, that's not very good advice.

Harry introduced David first, then Mystic. The hard rock music faded, the horn sounded, and both guys cautiously came toward each other.

Slowly, they circled, fists up, sizing the other one. They threw a few sparring punches, like Bruiser had suggested.

Then David grabbed both sides of Mystic's head and brought it down as he rammed his knee up.

Chapling and I both sucked in a breath.

"Nice," I heard Bruiser say.

Blood trickled down Mystic's face, and I realized David had broken Mystic's cut back open. Again, just like Bruiser had instructed.

Mystic swung his leg forward up between David's legs and swept to the left, knocking David to the ground. Before David had time to react, Mystic scrambled on top and pressed his forearm into David's throat.

With strained faces the two guys glared at each other as Mystic continued choking David. I watched David's face grow more and more red and thought maybe Mystic was doing a little *too* good of a job at the choking thing.

"O-kay," David wheezed.

"Sorry," Mystic mumbled.

Wedging his hands between their bodies, David dug his fingers into Mystic's sides and shoved him up, following with his knee. Mystic went flying over David's head and thunked onto his back.

Both guys quickly shot to their feet.

"Go ahead," David encouraged. "Make it look good."

Mystic came at David, throwing a series of punches to his face, succeeding at bloodying
him up.

Cringing, I watched yuck gush from David's nose and hoped Mystic hadn't accidentally broken it.

"Okay, let's end this thing," Bruiser instructed. "Harry liked when you did pressure points. Do David and reset him without Harry knowing. David, you stay down. Let the club workers drag you off."

Mystic whipped behind David and poked his finger into his lower back, sending David crashing face first to the matt.

I gritted my teeth praying *that* didn't do even more damage to poor David's face.

The crowd roared in excitement, and I kept my gaze glued to David's lifeless form. Mystic made a show of walking around David in victory, jabbing him with his bare toes. I knew he was resetting his meridian points. And in just a few minutes David would be back to normal.

Mystic jogged from the octagon, and the club workers climbed up for David. They drug his body across the floor and back through the PRIVATE archway.

I listened closely, waiting for David to speak, but heard only silence. What if something had gone wrong? What if Mystic had hit the incorrect pressure point? What if he hadn't reset things properly?

Harry went through the motion of introducing more fighters. But I didn't hear a single word as I ducked my head and pressed my mole ear piece, listening for signs of David.

Thank God for Chapling who expertly handled things because my focus was shot.

More minutes ticked by, and I couldn't take it anymore. I muted our Harry communication and asked, "David?"

"He's okay," Jonathan reported in.

I breathed out and looked over at Chapling. "He's okay."

Chapling smiled. "I heard."

The fight started and ended within thirty seconds with a knock out.

"I'm good," David finally notified all of us as the unconscious fighter was being dragged away.

"This is it," Chapling told me. "Mystic versus Utotiz."

"Ladies and gentlemen," Harry announced into his mike, "the fight you have been waiting for. If you haven't placed your bets, now is the time. Ten. Million. Dollars. The biggest purse yet."

I scanned the crowd to see men signaling the club workers. I assumed they were placing and taking bets.

Harry pointed at Mystic still standing on the fighting area. "You've seen Michael in action tonight. You know what he's capable of. This is a fight to the finish. A fight to the death. Someone will not make it out alive."

The crowd roared with a rush of primal adrenaline, and Chapling and I exchanged a glance.

Mystic will *make it out alive*, Chapling mouthed.

I gave one affirmative nod. Mystic would indeed make it out alive. Utotiz was going down.

Harry directed everyone's attention to the archway. "And now let me introduce Utotiz, the world title holder in mixed martial arts."

The spotlight illuminated the archway and out stepped Utotiz. Seven foot one. Three hundred and thirty one pounds. Like many of the other competitors, he had a bald head. Unlike the other ones, he had no tattoos. I knew from my research that he'd never lost a fight. He looked different from the last film footage I'd seen of him. He seemed heavier, like he'd put a layer of fat on over his muscular frame.

With the hard rock music blaring, Utotiz slowly made his way to the fighting area. No one slapped his back or tried to shake his hand. In fact, they gave him quite the wide berth. Truth be known, I would've, too. This guy did not look like someone to be messed with.

A hard expression on his face, he stepped up onto the octagon, and I swore I saw it vibrate.

Mystic knew everything there was to know about Utotiz, but I repeated anyway, "Utotiz has no known method. He'll get you standing up. He'll get you down. He's skilled in all areas of MMA."

"Hence the reason why he's the title holder," Bruiser added.

"Combat Thrash Program," I continued, "is recommending he make the first move and then predictions will be made from there."

"I agree," Bruiser added. "If he starts out with a strike, he'll likely try to take you down. If he starts with a kick, he'll try to fool you by keeping you up. He's a python. He'll snake his way around you and squeeze the life out of you. Be careful. And with his adrenaline pumping, he may be immune to meridian point strategy."

The horn sounded and both guys cautiously approached. They got within six feet of each other, and Mystic suddenly stopped. Utotiz took another step closer, and Mystic just stood there. Another step for Utotiz, and Mystic simply stared into his eyes.

"Mystic?" Bruiser hesitantly spoke.

Another step for Utotiz, and Mystic's face glazed over.

"Michael," Harry hissed. "What is your problem?"

Utotiz took another step, and Mystic's arms fell to his sides.

I watched in horror—what was Mystic doing?—and suddenly I realized . . .

I muted Harry's mikes. "He's got an image of Zandra," I told my team.

With an evil smirk now, Utotiz closed the miniscule gap between them. Mystic's eyes slowly lowered, and I immediately recognized that expression. He was hearing something. His mother? Zandra?

Utotiz reared back and slammed his fist into Mystic's jaw, sending him spinning to the ground.

"Michael!" Harry yelled. "Get up!"

Mystic just laid there, completely in a trance.

The crowd screamed and yelled for Utotiz to finish him.

"Mystic!" I hollered.

"Mystic," TL encouraged, "get up."

"What's going on?" David asked from back in the locker room.

Utotiz slowly, cockily climbed on top of Mystic. In a dominating stance, Utotiz straddled Mystic's thighs, reared back again, and slammed his fist into Mystic's jaw. Blood went flying through the air.

The crowd cheered.

Utotiz slammed his other fist down. Mystic's head flew to the left.

The crowd grew louder.

"Son of a—" Harry growled.

Another fist from Utotiz, and Mystic's head flew back the other way.

Frantically, I searched through the crowd for TL and saw him shoving his way through the people trying to get to the octagon.

Again and again Utotiz brought his fists down, slowly pulverizing Mystic.

"Someone do something!" I screamed.

In my peripheral vision I caught sight of Bruiser's red braid as she slipped through the front row and leapt onto the octagon. She flew across the matt, caught air, and landed a spinning kick to Utotiz's head.

He went sailing off Mystic and landed a few feet away.

The entire club quieted.

Letting out an inhumane grunt, Utotiz got to his feet and slowly turned to face Bruiser.

She stood in her sweet little sundress with her long red braid down her back. Surprise flicked across Utotiz's face at the sight of her. Her expression held focus, concentration, and a hint of cockiness that she knew exactly what she was capable of.

Seeing their size difference made me think back to the first couple of days we'd lived on the ranch. She'd gone up against Jonathan in a brief sparring match and had effectively kicked his butt. It had reminded me of David and Goliath.

Same thing applied here. Utotiz outweighed her by more than two hundred pounds. And he stood over two feet taller.

I'd seen Bruiser in action. I knew what she was capable of. But I had my doubts. She'd never gone up against someone of this caliber.

She reached back, unzipped her sundress, and stepped out of it. Pulling her shoulders back, she stood in a blue sports bra and tight-fitting, blue, cut shorts. She kicked her sundress to the side, making it more than obvious she wanted a fight with Utotiz.

I'd seen her body many times, but her incredible lean definition always amazed me. Every muscle on her tiny body stood out visible.

Someone in the crowd yelled, showing his approval. He wanted to see David and Goliath, too. Then someone else, and someone else, until the entire club filled with cheering.

I searched through the crowd for Harry and found him standing off to the side, closely studying them.

TL stepped onto the octagon and went over to Mystic. He leaned down and grabbed him up in a fireman's hold. As TL carried Mystic off, he passed Bruiser and gave her a nod of approval for her to go ahead and fight. TL wouldn't have done that if he wasn't completely sure of her capabilities.

My gaze followed them as they disappeared through the archway. A trail of blood dripped from Mystic's face and it sent a pang straight to my heart. I hoped Bruiser annihilated this guy.

"Do you want to see these two fight?!" Harry yelled into his mike.

The crowd cheered even louder.

The horn went off, and Bruiser shot across the matt. She dove between Utotiz's legs, hooking her feet on his ankles, and sent him face first into the floor. She whipped around, grabbed his right ankle, and snaked her body around his lower leg. With every muscle standing out in striation, she twisted his ankle.

If it weren't for the earpieces we wore, I wouldn't have heard the ligament pop because the crowd was cheering so loud.

Arching his back, Utotiz swung his left arm and knocked Bruiser off of him. She rolled across the floor and boinged to her feet, using her hand to wipe a spot of blood from her mouth.

Wasting no time, she rushed him right as he was getting to his feet. She flipped up, wrapped her ankles around his neck, and corkscrewed her body down the front of him and around the back. Digging her fingers into his hips, she twisted hers and his body in opposite directions until another pop echoed through our earpieces.

Chapling cringed. "His neck?"

I kept my attention glued to the fight. "I think so."

Utotiz sucker punched her in the kidney, and she released him and rolled away. I got the impression it wasn't the kidney punch that made her release—I'd seen her take a lot worse. She was simply ready to move onto another maneuver.

Utotiz moved, favoring his good ankle, trying to hold his neck in place. Although he hid it well, I definitely saw traces of pain trail across his face.

Bruiser ran toward him. Utotiz threw a punch. Bruiser dodged it, grabbed his wrist, and swung her body behind him, taking his arm with her. She wove her legs around his bad ankle, bracing herself behind him, and twisted his lower arm. Utotiz stumbled forward, his arm and leg locked by her little body, and tried to shake her off.

Through my earpiece she grunted with exertion, and I glanced down at my laptop screen. According to the Combat Thrash Program she was trying to dislocate his shoulder, using his bad ankle for leverage.

"Raise his arm up twenty degrees," I read the program's recommendation, "and twist again."

She did exactly what I said, and another pop echoed through my earpiece.

Bruiser released him and took a few steps away. "Thanks, girl."

I smiled.

Utotiz turned to face her. His nostrils flared, and I saw anger, frustration, embarrassment, and irritation cross his expression. Favoring his good leg with his dislocated arm hanging at his side, he stood fuming at her. Bruiser walked a slow, wide circle around him, sizing him up. He tried to follow with his neck and body, but ended up just standing there while she strolled around him.

She's dislocating all of his major joints, I realized as I stared at Utotiz's disjointed limbs. What a brilliant strategy.

The longer Bruiser stood there looking at him, the louder the crowd cheered.

Bruiser walked straight up to Utotiz, stopping a foot away. She stared up into his eyes with a somewhat pleasant, yet curious, you're-so-going-down expression.

Utotiz held her stare for a good solid minute. Then with a sneer, he cleared his throat and spit right in her face.

Bruiser reached up, wiped the spit from her cheek, and flicked it back at him.

Quicker than I'd seen him move so far, Utotiz brought his good arm back and punched her in the face, sending her spinning away through the

... wasting not a second to recuperate, Bruiser spun right back, landing the heel of her right foot square with the knee of his good leg.

Letting out a deep growl, Utotiz fell to the matt. I looked down at my computer and zoomed in on the image of them. She'd completely knocked his kneecap loose, leaving it floating on the side of his leg.

I swallowed.

With an ankle gone on one leg, knee on the other, dislocated shoulder, and a popped neck, Utotiz laid on his back with only a good arm left.

Bruiser walked over to him and braced one foot on each side of his hips. She stood there, looking down at him, while he struggled to sit up. Slowly, she lowered herself until she straddled him, copying the dominating position he'd done to Mystic.

Using his good arm, Utotiz latched onto her neck and squeezed.

With a clenched jaw she looked at him. "This is what you get for beating up one of my best friends."

She flailed into him, punching his face right, left, right, left, right, left . .

The crowd roared and screamed and yelled.

Right, left, right, left . . .

And Utotiz slowly lost consciousness.

‹FIFTEEN›

The doors to the underground club flew open, and cops rushed in. "Freeze!" They yelled, pulling guns, chasing people who had begun to run.

I looked up at the octagon to see Bruiser climbing off Utotiz. Our little dynamo had just defeated the world title holder in mixed martial arts.

"Team," David spoke, "come back to the locker rooms."

Nalani joined me and Chapling, and together we made our way around the club toward the PRIVATE archway. None of the cops bothered us, probably because they had our pictures and knew we were one of the good guys.

People screamed and ran, but really, how stupid was that? This was an underground club. There *was* no place to run.

Off to the side, a cop had Harry pinned against the wall as he searched him. That was the least he deserved. This night of Demise Chain events was probably the cleanest ever. Only one person had died.

We rallied back in the locker room area and from there exited to an awaiting van that Red drove. Mystic had regained consciousness, but his face was badly beaten. All of my team members had gotten their share of nicks and bruises from missions, but Mystic looked the worse. It hurt my heart to see his lumpy eyes, gashed cheeks, and split lip.

My poor, peaceful, non-violent Mystic.

I moved to sit beside him as the van bumped along, and I reached out and took his hand. He smiled through his swollen face to assure me all was okay.

No one spoke as the van continued moving along. A while later we pulled off the main road and wound our way through a heavily wooded

The van pushed through a blanket of dark greenery and came to a stop in front of a one story log cabin.

I peeked at my watch. 5:00 a.m.

Red jumped out and came around to open the back of the van. My team filed out and into the log cabin.

"This is a safe house," TL informed us as he turned on a few lamps.

We all took seats around the living room of the log cabin.

Chapling got his laptop out and I followed his lead.

"You're up," TL told Mystic.

"I saw it in Utotiz's eyes," Mystic spoke from my right. "He's the brother of the kidnapper. His sister took Zandra as retribution to something that happened to her in the past. I don't know what that event was, but it was incredibly significant in her life. Utotiz only just found out about the kidnapping, which explains why I didn't see anything in him while I was studying film footage of his fights."

"Zandra's unharmed," Mystic assured TL and Nalani. "She's scared. But she's unharmed. She's right here in Washington State. Utotiz has a cabin on Mount Mission. That is where his sister is holding Zandra."

David turned to me and Chapling. "Get us a satellite image of the cabin. And get us everything you know about this sister. I want a picture ASAP."

With a nod, Chapling and I dove into cyberspace. While we clicked away, our team continued discussing the situation. I blocked out their voices and concentrated on my work . . .

"Okay," Chapling announced. "Satellite image secured."

He depressed a button on the side of his laptop, and out slid a slim three-by-one inch projector. He pointed the projector to the wall above the fireplace and an image appeared. He manipulated the picture, rotating it, zooming in, until a small cabin came into view.

Supported by stilts and tucked into the side of the mountain, the cabin sat surrounded by thick Washington trees. A wall of glass spanned the front of the cabin, looking out over the mountain, the trees, and the valley below.

Chapling manipulated the satellite and zoomed through the early morning shadows to view through that wall of glass. Darkness filled the interior of the cabin, and Chapling switched to infrared.

An image of a woman came into view as she slept on the couch. Beside her was a shotgun.

Chapling scanned the loft of the cabin, zooming in on a double bed. An image of a little girl came into view as she slept with her arms wrapped around a stuffed doll. Her foot stuck out the bottom of the blanket displaying a rope tied around her ankle and secured to the bed.

Nalani gasped, and I glanced over at her. With her hands over her mouth, she stared at the image of her daughter, and her eyes welled with tears.

"She's okay," Nalani whispered, looking over to TL.

Nodding, he didn't return Nalani's glance, just kept staring at the image of his daughter.

My laptop dinged, and I checked it. "I have the background. Her name is Kimberly Tanner, and she is Utotiz's older sister." I emailed Chapling her image, and he projected it up onto the wall as well.

"Kimberly is thirty-eight years old," I continued. "Five foot three inches. One hundred and thirty pounds. Brown hair. Hazel eyes. She has been in and out of mental institutions since the age of twenty-one when a freak accident took her baby girl. She's recently been released from a private facility in Georgia. She was released just days before Zandra was taken. She received a computer science degree from the University of Georgia. And it says here, she's married to an IPNC agent." I looked up at my team. "That's weird."

TL pushed out a heavy breath. "I know her."

Every person in the room gave TL their full attention.

"Kimberly Tanner?" Nalani closed her eyes. "Oh my God."

Rubbing his head, TL slowly lowered himself to the corner of the couch. Slumping forward, he braced his elbows on his knees and stared at the wood floor beneath his boots. "I was twenty-one years old. Brand new to the IPNC. We were on a mission right here in the states. Kimberly Tanner was in the wrong place at the wrong time. With her baby in her arms, She stepped right into the line of fire. *My* line of fire."

"And you killed her baby?" Bruiser whispered.

TL nodded, still not looking at any of us. "Yes, I killed her baby. She was only four months old."

No one said a word as it all sank in. I thought about the missions I'd been on and the situations I'd been in. Accidents could happen at any time. Accidents *had* happened. But killing a baby? Oh my God. How had TL dealt with that tragedy?

"The IPNC paid her money. *I* paid her money. I've checked in on her throughout the years. Made sure she had the best treatment." TL shook his head. "It wasn't enough. I didn't do enough. I thought she'd come through everything okay."

"Well, her computer degree and her marriage to an IPNC agent explain how she knows about Zandra." David motioned for Chapling to turn off the projector. "How in the world did she end up marrying an IPNC agent?"

TL pressed his fingers into his temples. "It happened shortly after the accident. One of the agents got emotionally caught up in the situation, visited her at the hospital, ended up marrying her."

Out of pity? I wondered. Or out of love?

"That IPNC agent isn't involved in this," Mystic spoke up from beside me. I turned to see him staring at Kimberly's picture on my laptop.

"How do you want to handle this?" David asked.

Finally, TL looked up. "I'm going in alone."

***

It took us four hours to cross the state and weave our way up Mount Mission to where Kimberly Tanner was holding Zandra. A half mile away we stopped the van on a dirt lane that led to the cabin. I imagined in the winter these switch-back roads would be impassable.

Me, Chapling, Mystic, and Bruiser stayed in the van. Jonathan, Red, David, and Nalani got out and quietly made their way through the trees to surround the small house.

We still wore our mole earpieces for communication. No one carried a weapon. TL had insisted. He was going in alone.

In the van we brought up satellite imagining and zoomed in on the house. Kimberly Tanner was up now and sitting in the kitchen drinking coffee. Up in the loft, I didn't see Zandra on the bed. The rope that had been tied around her ankle dangled free. The bathroom door was closed, so I assumed she was in there.

Chapling detailed everything we were seeing for the benefit of our team.

On our laptop screen, we watched as TL stepped from the woods, approached the front door, and knocked.

Kimberly jumped up, grabbed the shotgun from the couch, and ran over to the door.

"She's got her shotgun," Chapling reported.

Kimberly peeked through the side window to see who it was, caught sight of TL, and ducked down. Cradling the shotgun, she crouched below the window, wide eyed, trying to be very quiet.

TL knocked again. "Kimberly," he spoke softly, "I know you're in there. I've come unarmed. Put the shotgun down. Let's talk."

Kimberly blinked a few times, swallowed. Then in one quick movement, she stood up, cocked the gun, swung the door open, and pointed it right at TL's head.

He didn't move. I knew TL. He could have easily disarmed her and gotten this whole thing over with. But he cared for Kimberly. It mattered to him what he had done to her. It still haunted both of them. That one horrible event had changed their lives forever.

"Where's Zandra?" he asked in that same calm tone.

"In the bathroom."

"Is she okay?"

"Yes."

TL moved forward, and Kimberly backed up, still holding the gun to his forehead. Once inside, he closed the door.

"Where're all your people?" She nodded toward the bank of windows that looked out over the mountain. "I thought for sure you'd railroad in here with your entourage."

"They're out there," he spoke truthfully. "They can hear everything we're saying. But no one is armed. I assure you."

Kimberly snorted. "So you're here to talk me off the ledge, so to speak?"

TL didn't answer that question. "Kimberly, I want my daughter back. I know why you took her. You wanted me to feel the pain that you felt when I killed your daughter."

Kimberly squeezed her eyes closed. "Shut up."

"I did kill your daughter, Kimberly, and I'm so sorry. You and I both have lived with that tragedy for seventeen years. If I could rewind the time, that is the absolute one thing I would change. But I can't rewind the time. And taking my daughter won't make you feel better."

"YES IT WILL!" she screamed, startling everybody in the van.

TL didn't even blink at the outburst.

Kimberly's eyes shot open, and she pressed the gun firmer to TL's forehead.

down on his knees and looked up at her. "You want to kill —one. Kill me. Let my daughter go. My wife is here. She wants our daughter back, too. Take me. Let Zandra go."

Shaking, Kimberly stared down at TL. Her finger twitched on the trigger as she gazed into his eyes.

"No," she whispered. "No. No. No." Tears began streaming down her face. "N-n-no."

Shaking violently now, Kimberly continued pressing the gun to his head, holding his stare. "NO! NO! NO! NO!" She let out a gut wrenching scream and swung the gun away.

A shot boomed and glass shattered. Everyone in the van flinched. I immediately brought my attention back to the satellite image on the laptop screen.

The cabin's wall of glass had a huge gaping hole in it. Kimberly stood with her back to TL, gripping the shot gun.

Still on his knees, TL reached a hand out. "Kimberly, give me the gun."

She didn't respond.

"Kimberly."

With calmness she hadn't had seconds ago, she turned around, pointed the shot gun at TL, and pulled the trigger.

I gasped. Then immediately I realized nothing had happened.

TL remained on his knees, silently gazing up at her.

She reached in her pocket and pulled out a shot gun shell. Keeping her eyes leveled on TL's, she reloaded the gun.

"Kimberly," TL softly requested, "don't do this."

I got the impression TL had seen something in her eyes that we couldn't see.

Kimberly turned her back to him, swung the barrel up and into her mouth, and squeezed the trigger.

Bruiser sucked in a breath.

"No," TL whispered.

I squeezed my eyes shut.

"Daddy?" Zandra cried.

‹SIXTEEN›

A month had gone by since that tragic day on Mount Mission. Kimberly Tanner had died. I'd thought a lot about it over the weeks. Thought a lot about that final tragic scene. Could things have been done differently? Yes. Would it have made a difference in the outcome? Who knew? But I had come to the conclusion if Kimberly Tanner hadn't taken her life on that mountain, she probably would have committed suicide someplace else.

I think she went to that cabin knowing how it would all end.

I'd watched TL closely over the past month. He'd seemed distant, for sure. I hadn't talked to him about what had happened. No one had. I could only imagine what demons he was battling over the whole thing. He'd probably relived and questioned those last few moments constantly since it had happened.

And now as I sat here outside with everyone, I watched TL and Nalani with Zandra. I wondered what all had factored into his decision to leave The Specialists. That's right, I did say leave.

TL resigned. Effective tomorrow he would no longer be living here at the ranch, which was the purpose of today's picnic—a goodbye party for TL. Was it solely Kimberly Tanner that had made him resign? No, probably not. I was sure it was many things. Kimberly, Nalani, Zandra, past experiences. He'd had enough. He was ready to move on. Understandably.

So who would be in charge? Red. It seemed fitting as he had helped raise lost kids just like us. I suspected he needed it, this lifestyle, the change, the activity, the focus. He'd been out of things for too long.

And Red's right hand person? David, of course.

"Kelly?"

..ay spot on the ranch's front steps, I glanced up. "Hey, Randy."

..e smiled. "I'm leaving. Just wanted to say bye."

I stood up and gave him a hug and felt . . . friendship. Nothing more. It made me smile. "You take care, you. I'm sure we'll see each other again."

"I'm sure."

"Randy." David approached. "Heard you're leaving. Wanted to tell you good luck."

The two guys exchanged a hand shake.

"Take care of this girl," Randy said, nodding to me. "She's a bit of a klutz."

"Hey!" I defended myself.

Laughing, Randy saluted us and headed off to his awaiting cab.

With a wave, I watched the taxi pull away before sitting back down on the steps. David took the spot beside me and together we lapsed back into quietly taking in the picnic fun.

Off to the left, Beaker sat under a tree visiting with Parrot and his mother. His mother had moved into a small house in town, and they saw each other a couple times a week. She'd gained weight since her return from slavery. Her hair had grown out. She looked happy and healthy. So did Parrot.

To the right sat a long table piled with sandwiches, salads, fruit, chips, drinks. As usual, Wirenut stood nearby grazing on the food. Beside him, Cat said something and he poked her in the ribs. They both laughed and then Cat took off running and Wirenut chased her. He threw a carrot stick at her back, and she sped up. Their goofiness made me smile.

All the members of Team One, Adam, Piper, Curtis, and Tina were playing a two on two badminton game beside the barn. Although Adam hid it well, he kept cutting sideways glances toward Bruiser. Hmmm . . . I was curious to see how that little romance would evolve.

Jonathan came out of the barn with Dr. Gretchen on his heels. Although I couldn't hear them, their body language spoke volumes. Dr. Gretchen planted her hands on her hips and barked something to his back. He waved his hand through the air in a bug-off answer. She barked something else, and he spun around and got right in her face. Neither one of them said a word as they snarled at each other. And then Dr. Gretchen grabbed his T-shirt and yanked him back inside the shadows of the barn.

I laughed to myself. Wonder what *they're* doing?

A splash had me glancing right to the pool where Mystic had been giving Chapling swimming lessons for the past hour. In that patient way of his Mystic explained to Chapling *again* how to tread water, and Chapling flailed his arms. It was hard to believe Chapling had made it all the way to his mid thirties and never learned to swim.

Beyond the pool TL and Nalani bounced a volleyball with Zandra, Bruiser, and Red. Nalani looked the happiest I think I'd ever seen her. And although there was clearly a lot on TL's mind, he came across happy, too.

"You're going to miss TL." I stated the obvious to David.

"Very much. He's made the right decision. It's time to focus on his family."

"Will you stay in touch with him?" I asked.

David shrugged. "Doubt it. They'll have new identities. Live in a new country."

"I'm sure TL will find some way to keep up communication. Encrypted emails. Secret messages."

David smiled. "I hope so." He looked over at me. "Guess who I saw meditating yesterday?"

I shrugged.

"Bruiser."

"You did not!"

David chuckled. "I did. And guess who was shadow boxing in the barn the other day?"

"Mystic?" I guessed.

David laughed again. "Unbelievable."

I laughed with him. "Amazing is what it is."

Mike Share, David's dad, came out of the house and caught sight of us. "Hey kids."

We both smiled.

He scooted past us. "Sissy and I are going to the movies later. Wanna join us?" he asked David. "A little family bonding?"

David smiled. "Sure."

Mr. Share continued on, crossing over to the tree to join Beaker, Parrot, and his mom.

"How long's your dad in town?"

"Just for the week. IPNC's sending him to Alaska on Sunday."

..d for you." I was glad for all my teammates. We'd arrived here a ..nd a half ago quite the hodge-podge group. And look, just look, at ..ie interesting twists and turns our lives had taken.

We'd grown, we'd developed . . . coming here, joining The Specialists, was hands down the best decision I'd ever made. I finally had a family.

"GiGi?"

"Hm?"

David turned to me. "I've been trying to figure out how to say what I want to say and . . ." he sighed. "I'm just going to be blunt." He took a deep breath. "I want you back. I don't want to be just friends. I miss you."

My heart paused a beat, and my insides went to liquid mush. "Oh, David."

He reached out and took my hand. "You've got me all twisted up inside. I don't quite know what to think of you, Miss GiGi."

I smiled. "I never wanted to be just friends to begin with."

Closing his eyes, David brought my hand to his lips. Slowly, he pressed a kiss to each knuckle and then rubbed his cheek across the back of my hand.

I stared at the side of his face, drinking in his slight stubble, his handsome dark features, his delicious scent. My stomach whirled as he opened his eyes and stared deeply into mine. They did that sexy crinkly thing and I fell a little more.

"Whadaya say," he whispered, "when I get home tonight from the movies, you and I go on a late night picnic in the moonlight."

I swallowed. "Sounds great." Sounded heavenly, actually.

The sound of an engine had us glancing away from each other and down the driveway to the gate. It swung open and a banged up beetle bug drove through. It putt-putted up the driveway and came to a stop in front of the ranch house.

I tried to see who was inside, but the windows were unusually dark tinted. The door opened, and a tall blonde woman climbed out.

She propped her sunglasses on top her head and gazed at me across the top of the beetle bug. "Hello, Kelly. I'm your sister."

I didn't move from my spot on the front step. I couldn't move. Numb with shock, disbelief, and joy, I stared across the driveway at my older sister. *My older sister.*

David nudged me out of my staring trance, and slowly, I got to my feet.

I didn't remember crossing the gravel. I didn't remember rounding the front of her Beetle Bug. I didn't remember anything as I stood in front of her staring up into her familiar eyes.

She shut the door of her car and turned to me. One corner of her mouth tilted up in a half smile as she returned my stare. She stood taller than me with a slender, athletic build. Her blonde hair was darker and her skin tan. Her face was similar, yet different. She wore no makeup, only a slight sun burn.

Swallowing I held out my hand. "Hi."

She took my hand. "I'm Sandy."

"Sandy," I repeated, and then we both moved at once, pulling each other into a warm, snug embrace.

A good solid minute later, we pulled apart, and I gazed back up into her face. "You look like dad."

She smiled. "So do you." Shaking her head, she huffed out a laugh. "Unbelievable. I have a baby sister."

"You didn't know?" For some reason I thought she had and because of top secret reasons chose not to have a relationship with me all these years.

"I didn't even know I had a dad until a few years ago."

I furrowed my brow. "What are you talking about?"

"Our dad and my mom were married. They got divorced and she moved to Europe. She never told him she was pregnant. She had me and raised me in Germany. From day one she told me my dad was dead. That'd he'd died in a car accident."

"That was a lie."

Sandy nodded. "She didn't want me to go looking for him, I guess. When I was eighteen she broke the news to me that she was a secret agent for the German government. She recruited me into the life."

Sandy took the shades off her head and slipped them on over her eyes. "Years later I figured out I could make more money working independently, so I broke from the German government."

"How did you find out about dad?" I asked.

"I decided one day to research who he was, his death. And that's where it all unfolded. I found out about his connection with the IPNC, Eduardo Villanueva, and I discovered he had a wife. I also found out they'd died in a plane crash. I never knew about you, though." She smiled. "Good job leaving clues in cyberspace so I'd find you."

I grinned. "Thanks."

ᴧook her head. "And to think of all the years we could've had
ᴧr."

"Well, just think of all the years to come."

We both smiled at that.

"So you never knew dad?" I asked.

"No, I'm sorry to say." She reached out and took my hand. "But I'm looking forward to knowing you."

I squeezed her hand. "Me, too." In my peripheral, I saw everyone standing around staring at us. With a big smile, I turned to them "Hey, everybody! Come meet my sister!"

THE END

Thank you to all my fabulous readers who made this series such a success. I hope this installment brought you what you were hoping for in this final book. I'm sad to say goodbye to GiGi and all her friends. Who knows maybe one day I'll resurrect them!

~Shannon Greenland

ABOUT THE AUTHOR

Shannon Greenland was born and raised in Tennessee. She's traveled the world extensively, and currently lives on an island off the coast of Florida. *THE SPECIALISTS : MODEL SPY* was her first novel for young adults. Visit her on the Web at www.shannongreenland.com.

TO BE THE FIRST TO HEAR THE LATEST NEWS ABOUT SHANNON AND HER BOOKS, SIGN UP TO HER NEWSLETTER

Made in the USA
Columbia, SC
16 April 2020

2R00462